K. Baedeker

Handbook for Travellers on The Rhine, from Holland to Switzerland

SALZWASSER VERLAG

K. Baedeker

Handbook for Travellers on The Rhine, from Holland to Switzerland

1st Edition | ISBN: 978-3-75258-393-9

Place of Publication: Frankfurt am Main, Germany

Year of Publication: 2022

Salzwasser Verlag GmbH, Germany.

Reprint of the original, first published in 1864.

THE RHINE.

HANDBOOK FOR TRAVELLERS

ON

THE RHINE,

FROM HOLLAND TO SWITZERLAND.

BY

K. BAEDEKER.

With 15 Maps and 13 Plans of towns.

SECOND EDITION, REVISED AND AUGMENTED.

COBLENZ:

1864.

PREFACE.

The principal object of the following volume is to render the traveller as independent as possible of landlords, coachmen and guides, and thus enable him the more thoroughly to enjoy and appreciate the objects of interest he meets with on his tour.

The entire contents of the book have been compiled from the personal experience of the editor, and the country described has within the last few years been repeatedly visited by him solely with the view of gathering fresh information.

The Maps and Plans, the result of much care and research, will be of essential service to the traveller, and enable him at a glance to select the best routes &c.

Railway, Steamboat and diligence time-tables, as well as information respecting telegraphic communication, are contained in "*Hendschel's Telegraph*" (10 Sgr.), published at Frankfurt on the Main, and issued monthly during the summer season. Implicit reliance, however, cannot be placed on such publications, notwithstanding the care with which they are compiled, and the traveller is recommended to obtain the necessary information from the local time-tables as he proceeds on his journey.

Careful attention has been devoted to the subject of Hotels, on which so much of the tourist's comfort depends. In addition to the more splendid establishments, the names of houses of less pretension have been introduced, to meet the convenience of a large portion of the travelling public. Those hotels which the editor and his friends have found particularly comfortable and moderate are indicated by asterisks (*), which must however be received with caution. Exactitude is impossible where changes of management are frequent and where the treatment the traveller meets with is very often contingent upon circumstances which can be neither altogether controlled nor foreseen.

The fairness of the charges in the different hotels enumerated has been invariably tested by the personal experience of the editor, or from an inspection of numberless bills with which he has been furnished from numerous quarters; but it is hardly necessary to remark that the constant fluctuations in the price of provisions cannot fail to influence Hotel charges generally. Carriage fares and fees to guides are also liable to similar variations; but these items of expenditure, if given approximately, will prove of service to the tourist, in enabling him to form a fair estimate of the demands which can justly be made upon him.

CONTENTS.

Maps.

I. Skeleton Tour.

The following plan for a 6 weeks' tour of the Rhine will be found to be the most convenient and expeditious; it begins with Frankfurt and ends with Dortmund: —

	Days.
Frankfurt (R. 39)	1
On foot: *Taunus* (Königstein, Soden, Homburg, R. 40)	1
Darmstadt (R. 41)	½
On foot: *Melibocus* and *Odenwald* (R.R. 41 and 42) .	1
Heidelberg and environs (R. 43)	1
Carlsruhe (R. 50)	½
Baden and environs (R. 52)	1
On foot: *The Black Forest*, Murgthal, Allerheiligen, Renchthal, Kniebisbäder, Tryberg falls, Kinzigthal (R. 63 a. and b.)	3
From *Offenburg* to *Freiburg* (R. 59)	1
On foot: *Höllenthal*, *Feldberg*, *Wiesenthal*, *Wehrathal* (R. 23 c.)	2
Bâle (R. 65)	½
On foot: *Badenweiler* and environs (R. 62)	2
From Freiburg to *Breisach* (R. 60), *Colmar* and *St. Hippolyte* (R. 58)	1
On foot: The *Vosges* (R.R. 57 and 58)	3
Strasburg (R. 54)	1
To *Saarburg* and back by railway (R. 57)	1
From Strasburg to *Landau* (R. 55)	½
On foot: *Haardt Mountains*, Madenburg, Trifels, Maxburg, Neustadt (R. 45)	2
From Neustadt to *Speyer* (R.R. 46 and 48)	½
Worms (R. 47), *Mayence* (R. 35), *Wiesbaden* (R. 37). .	2
On foot: *The Rheingau* from Eltville to Rüdesheim (R. 34) and *Bingen*. Rochus-Chapel and Scharlachkopf (R. 26)	1
Excursion to *Kreuznach*, Münster am Stein, Oberstein and back to Bingen (R.R. 28 and 29)	1
From Bingen by steamboat to *Bacharach*, on foot to *Caub*, *Oberwesel*, *St. Goar* and environs (R. 25). . .	1
By steamboat to *Stolzenfels*, *Coblenz* and *Ehrenbreitstein* (R.R. 20, 21 and 24)	1

Ems and *Nassau* (R. 22) by railway 1
By Moselle-steamboat to *Alf,* on foot through the volcanic *Eifel* (R.R. 32 and 33) 3
Treves and environs (R. 31) 1
By steamboat from Treves to *Coblenz* (R. 32) 1
By steamboat to *Andernach* (R. 18), on foot to *Niedermendig*, the *Laacher See*, the *Brohlthal* (R. 19). From Brohl by steamboat to *Remagen*, Apollinarisberg (R. 18) 1
The *Valley of the Ahr* to Altenahr (R. 17) (on foot 2 days) by carriage 1
By steamboat to *Königswinter* (R. 15), on foot through the *Seven Mountains* (R. 16) 1
Bonn and *Cologne* (R.R. 10 and 14) 2
By Railway to *Aix-la-Chapelle* (R.R. 2 and 4), in the evening by Railway to *Düsseldorf* (R. 3) 1
Düsseldorf and *Elberfeld* (R.R. 6 and 7) 1
On foot from Elberfeld to *Hagen* (Wupper valley, Ennep road) Railway to *Dortmund* (R. 7) 1
From Dortmund by railway (R.R. 8 and 9) in 4 hrs. back to *Cologne.*

The rapidity of railway communication is taken into account in these calculations. The pedestrian excursions are all within the reach of any tolerable walker.

It may strike some that six weeks is an unreasonable period to devote to a journey which, with the modern accessories to speed, it is possible to perform in a single day, but it need hardly be stated that a very imperfect acquaintance with the beauties of Rhenish scenery is to be obtained by those whose impressions are formed from the window of a railway carriage, or even from the deck of a steamer. Such cursory glances may satisfy those who are making the Rhine simply the highway to the more gigantic, but scarcely more impressive and instructive scenery of Switzerland; it is hoped, however, this volume may find favour with those who desire an intimate acquaintance with this beautiful country and its countless and unrivalled attractions, too many of which have been unexplored, and must ever remain sealed to those who will not be tempted to diverge from the oft-trod track. Whilst the editor of this work hopes to be the means of opening fresh sources of pleasure and instruction to the traveller, each individual, being the best judge of his own resources, must avail himself of the time, means, strength and inclination he has at his own disposal.

The railways by which in different directions the Rhineland is intersected, and the numerous steamboats which navigate its rivers, afford so many opportunities for travelling, that the enterprising tourist need ever pass an unprofitable day. Much discernment is of course necessary to determine where the public conveyances should be employed and where abandoned, as in many instances the best objects and points of observation are only accessible to the pedestrian or by private conveyance. Much valuable information on these points will, it is hoped, be afforded in this work. Those who are in delicate health, or would desire to escape from the bustle of high roads and public conveyances, are recommended to the following places, which are particularly well adapted for repose after the fatigue and excitement of travelling: Schloss *Bürgeln* (p. 247), especially for single gentlemen; *Freiburg* (p. 238); *Achern* (p. 217), *Oppenau*, *Allerheiligen* (p. 216), the latter for gentlemen; *Carlsruhe* (p. 206), *Weinheim* (p. 174), *Zwingenberg* (p. 172); *Neustadt* in the Haardt (p. 196); the baths of *Cronthal* in the Taunus (p. 170); *Niederwalluff* (p. 137) and *Geisenheim* (p. 134) in the Rheingau; *Lorch* (p. 174), *Oberwesel* (p. 99), *St. Goarshausen* (p. 97), *Camp* (p. 95), the latter for gentlemen, on the Middle-Rhine; *Honnef* (p. 56), at the foot of the Seven Mountains.

The traveller need hardly be reminded that a superfluity of luggage is a sad hindrance to the complete success of a tour. It is a source of expense, anxiety and trouble, and he who would spare his pocket many an inroad, and his temper many a trial, will provide himself with as small a quantity as possible of those articles which are always more or less the "impedimenta" to travelling. For a tour of two or three weeks the editor's entire equipment consists of an umbrella sufficiently stout to serve the purpose of a walking stick, a Mackintosh, and a small travelling bag slung over the shoulder, containing a couple of flannel shirts, a pair of worsted stockings, slippers, and the necessary articles of the toilette. Opportunities for having linen washed and shoes mended (always to be accomplished in a single night) occur constantly during the traveller's progress, rendering a large supply of clothing totally unnecessary. More extended tours entail of course the necessity of a somewhat longer catalogue of requisites, but under all circumstances the tourist is strongly recommended to avoid being encumbered with more than he can conveniently carry himself. The comfort of being able to quit a steamboat or railway station without detention need only be experienced to be appreciated. Travellers may often advantageously and at a trifling expense send on their luggage through the agency of the post.

II. Steamboat Navigation.

The Rhine is navigated by more than 100 steamboats, from the local vessels of fifteen or twenty horse power to the powerful tug-steamers of upwards of four hundred. During the last few years the average number of travellers availing themselves of this mode of transit has been upwards of one million annually. Since the completion of the Rhenish railway a considerable saving of time is effected by only employing the steamers on those portions of the river which are remarkable for the striking beauty of the scenery upon its banks. The following vessels of the united (since 1853) Cologne and Düsseldorf Company are recommended for their speed: "Hohenzoller," "Merkens," "Loreley," "Prinz von Preussen," "Prinzessin von Preussen." Those to be avoided as "slow coaches" are the "Elisabeth," "Königin," "Mannheim," "Victoria" and "Germania." These boats ply during the summer months to the number of six or seven a day. The vessels of the Netherlands Company are too uncertain to be depended upon for short distances, and are principally employed for the transmission of merchandise.

Tariff of Fares.	Single ticket.				Return ticket (valid for 1 year).			
	Cabin.		Steerage.		Cabin.		Steerage.	
From **Mannheim** to	*Thlr.*	*Sgr.*	*Thlr.*	*Sgr.*	*Thlr.*	*Sgr.*	*Thlr.*	*Sgr.*
Worms	—	6	—	4	—	9	—	6
Mainz	—	18	—	12	—	24	—	15
Bingen	—	27	—	18	1	5	—	23
Coblenz	1	24	1	6	2	9	1	15
Cologne	3	—	2	—	3	24	2	15
Düsseldorf	3	14	2	19	4	10	2	27
Rotterdam	6	—	4	10	7	15	5	—
From { **Mainz** or **Biebrich** } to								
Bingen	—	9	—	6	—	12	—	8
St. Goar	—	23	—	15	1	—	—	19
Boppard	—	27	—	18	1	5	—	23
Coblenz	1	6	—	24	1	16	1	—
Cologne	2	12	1	18	3	—	2	—
Düsseldorf	2	26	1	27	3	10	2	12
Rotterdam	5	12	3	18	6	24	4	8
From **Bingen** to								
St. Goar	—	14	—	9	—	18	—	12
Boppard	—	18	—	12	—	24	—	15
Coblenz	—	27	—	18	1	5	—	23
Cologne	2	3	1	12	2	20	1	23
Düsseldorf	2	17	1	21	3	6	2	4
Rotterdam	5	3	3	12	6	12	4	8

Tariff of Fares.	Single ticket.				Return ticket (valid for 1 year).			
	Cabin.		Steerage.		Cabin.		Steerage.	
	Thlr.	*Sgr.*	*Thlr.*	*Sgr.*	*Thlr.*	*Sgr.*	*Thlr.*	*Sgr.*
From **Coblenz** to								
Neuwied	—	6	—	4	—	9	—	5
Remagen	—	18	—	12	—	24	—	15
Bonn	—	27	—	18	1	5	—	23
Cologne	1	6	—	24	1	15	1	—
Düsseldorf	1	20	1	3	2	3	1	12
Rotterdam	4	6	2	24	5	9	3	15
Boppard	—	8	—	5	—	12	—	8
St. Goar	—	12	—	8	—	18	—	12
Bingen	—	23	—	15	1	5	—	23
Mainz	1	—	—	20	1	15	1	—
Mannheim	1	15	1	—	2	9	1	15
From **Bonn** to								
Cologne	—	9	—	6	—	12	—	8
Düsseldorf	—	23	—	15	1	—	—	19
Rotterdam	3	9	2	6	4	5	2	23
Rolandseck	—	6	—	4	—	9	—	6
Remagen	—	8	—	5	—	12	—	8
Coblenz	—	23	—	15	1	5	—	23
Mainz	1	23	1	5	2	20	1	23
Mannheim	2	8	1	15	3	12	2	8
From **Cologne** to								
Düsseldorf	—	14	—	9	—	18	—	12
Rotterdam	3	—	2	—	3	24	2	15
Bonn	—	8	—	5	—	12	—	8
Rolandseck	—	12	—	8	—	18	—	12
Remagen	—	15	—	10	—	24	—	15
Coblenz	1	—	—	20	1	15	1	—
Mainz	2	—	1	10	3	—	2	—
Mannheim	2	15	1	20	3	24	2	15
From **Düsseldorf** to								
Rotterdam	2	17	1	21	3	6	2	4
Coblenz	1	12	—	28	2	3	1	12
Mainz	2	12	1	18	3	18	2	12
Mannheim	2	27	1	28	4	10	2	27
From **Rotterdam** to								
Cologne	2	15	1	20	3	24	2	15
Mannheim	5	—	3	10	7	15	5	—

The first-class, or state cabin, situated in the stern of the vessel and connected by folding doors with the public cabin, is of limited dimensions and rarely occupied except by invalids and persons of the highest distinction. It may be engaged for a sum equal to sixteen times the cabin-fare. The second-class cabin is frequented by the ordinary travelling community, and the passengers are of course free to any part of the deck. Third-class, or steerage passengers, are limited to the fore part of the vessel as far as the funnel. The portion of the deck appropriated to cabin passengers is protected from the sun by an awning.

2 children under 12 years of age are charged one fare.
1 child in the cabin pays steerage fare.
1 adult with a child in the steerage pays cabin-fare; children in arms are free.

Tickets must if possible be taken before embarking. Passengers failing to do this should obtain them from the conductor immediately on going on board, otherwise they are liable to be called upon to pay the fare from the steamer's first point of departure, a custom not unknown on English railroads.

Each passenger is allowed 100 pounds of luggage free, for which he must either be responsible himself, or have its safe custody ensured on board, the charges for which are as follows:

From Mannheim to Cologne:	3 Sgr.	for each trunk,
	2 „	for a travelling bag,
	1 „	for a hat box;

from shorter distances, as from Mannheim to Coblenz, or from Coblenz to Cologne, half the above charges are made. This precaution saves much trouble and prevents occasional loss. Where articles are missing the following compensation is given: for a trunk 30 Thlr., for a travelling bag 10 Thlr., for a hat box 5 Thlr.

Single travellers unencumbered with luggage are recommended not to take their tickets till the steamer is in sight, as in case of detention the alternative of the railroad is open to them.

Passengers provided with tickets of not less than 20 Sgr. in value are at liberty to break their journey, provided they signify their intention to the conductor before he collects the tickets. Should the journey be resumed at a station nearer the traveller's destination than that at which he disembarked, the ticket ceases to be valid for the intervening stations.

Towards the end of summer or the beginning of autumn Rhine fogs begin to prevail, in consequence of which the punctuality of the steamers it not to be relied on, and travellers are frequently subjected to a very vexatious detention. Should the steamer be more than three hours behind the time specified in the time-tables, the fare may be reclaimed.

Refreshments are provided on board the steamers in the style of the hotels and at similar charges. Although it is a rule of the Company that a tariff of charges shall be conspicuously exhibited, it is not always to be seen, and the following items are therefore given:

Coffee with bread and butter		8	Sgr.
Table d'hôte at 1 o'clock		20	„
— at a later hour	1 Thlr.	—	„
½ bottle of good table wine		6	„
Cup of coffee		2	„

Dinners "a la carte" are not recommended.

Travellers starting at an early hour in the morning will find the breakfast furnished on board more enjoyable than a hurried meal before leaving the hotel. Passengers are strongly recommended to pay for what they order "on delivery." If left to his own discretion, the waiter will defer tendering his account until the point of the traveller's disembarkation is in sight, when the hurry and bustle of the moment too readily favour imposition.

Travellers should be on their guard against the importunities of waiters who offer spurious books, maps &c. for sale at exorbitant prices.

III. Hotels &c.

It is found that little variation occurs in the accommodation and charges of first-class hotels in the principal towns and watering-places throughout the whole of Germany, but it not unfrequently happens that in old-fashioned hotels of unassuming exterior, as much real comfort combined with more moderate charges is found as in the modern establishments, where magnificence of decoration sometimes usurps the place of comfort. The editor has therefore endeavoured to the best of his ability to direct the attention of the discerning traveller to houses of this description, premising at the same time that few hotels are deserving of unqualified praise or blame. As has been already remarked, the treatment of a guest varies greatly according to circumstances; a change of waiters sometimes disorganizes the entire system of an establishment; but the attention a traveller meets with depends mainly upon his own demeanour. Those who travel with a superabundance of luggage, who are difficult to please, who find indiscriminate fault, and who impose unnecessary trouble, must not be surprised if they find their bills swell into proportions for which they are not prepared. To such a class of travellers the charges mentioned in this volume will scarcely ever apply. The editor here hazards a few observations on two vexed questions in connection with hotel management: the payment of servants, and the highly obnoxious charge for "bougies." As regards "service," the editor entertains a strong conviction that the majority of travellers prefer a fixed and moderate eharge being appended to the bill, but which shall insure them against importunities for private donations. This desirable practice is observed in the majority of respectable hotels; where it is not, the following fees may suffice: 5 Sgr. or 18 kr. for the head waiter and half that sum for the porter per diem.

On the subject of the charge for bougies two opinions cannot exist; the cost of lights should be included in the eharge for apartments, a small percentage being added if necessary. It constantly occurs that the merits of a really good and otherwise respectable hotel are overlooked in the irritation created by this paltry eharge. Not only is the ordinary demand of 5 Sgr. exorbitant in itself, but the candles placed in a room are frequently charged for, even when not used; and although upon remonstranee the demand cannot be maintained, altercation and dissatisfaetion inevitably result. If hotel-keepers combined to discontinue this vexatious practice, they would be conferring a boon upon their customers and essentially contributing to their own respectability and interest.

Where the traveller remains for a week or longer at an hotel, it is advisable to pay, or at all events to eall for, his aecount every two or three days, by which means erroneous insertions are more easily avoided. Verbal reckonings are also highly objectionable. A waiter's arithmetic is faulty, and the faults are seldom found to be in favour of the traveller. A habit too often prevails of presenting the bill at the last moment, when mistakes or wilful impositions must be submitted to, for want of time to investigate them. Those who purpose starting early in the morning will do well to ask for their bills on the previous evening.

The habit of putting clothes and boots outside the bed-room door to be brushed is sometimes attended with inconvenience. The editor was once unfortunate enough to be despoiled of a great portion of his wardrobe through this incautious act.

English travellers too often impose considerable trouble by ordering things almost unknown in German usage; and if ignoranee of the language is combined with unaequaintance with the customs, misunderstandings and disputes too often ensue. They are therefore strongly recommended to aequire if possible such a proficieney in the language as shall render them intelligible to the servants, and above all to eonform in their orders and requirements to the manners and habits of the eountry. For this purpose *Baedeker's* "Travellers' Manual of Conversation" will prove a useful companion.

Valets de plaee generally charge 1 florin or 20 Sgr. for half a day, and 1—1⅓ Thlr. for an entire day. This sum is slightly in excess of the tariff fixed by the police, but cannot be regarded as exorbitant.

IV. Remarks on the Geology of the Rhine.

For Geologists the maps of the Rhine-province and Westphalia by *von Dechen* (Berlin, pubd. by Schropp) are of particular value. They are admirably executed according to the Prussian Ordnance maps, in the proportion of 1 : 80,000. The following sections have been published (price 1 Thlr. each): *Ochtrup, Tecklenburg, Lübbecke, Cleve, Coesfeld, Münster, Bielefeld, Höxter, Geldern, Wesel, Dortmund, Soest, Warburg, Crefeld, Düsseldorf, Lüdenscheid, Berleburg, Aachen, Cöln, Siegen, Minden, Malmedy, Mayen, Berncastel, Trier.*

From Bâle to Bingen the valley of the Rhine is lake-like and filled with more recent deposits, but at the latter place it suddenly changes its character and becomes so narrow, that barely room is afforded for the high-roads and railways which skirt it on either side. The river rushes impetuously between almost perpendicular rocks of considerable height, intersected here and there by narrow gullies. Towards Coblenz the valley gradually expands, the hills become less abrupt, and the rocks disappear. From Coblenz to Andernach a broad basin extends itself on both sides of the stream, which at the last-named place again assumes the character of a narrow rocky defile. Near Bonn the river again gradually widens, and the "Seven Mountains" appear, forming the grand closing scene of the picturesque portion of the Rhine. This chain of mountains, in diminished proportions, accompanies the Rhine on its right bank as far as Cologne, Düsseldorf, and nearly to Duisburg; below the mouth of the Ruhr the country presents a uniformly flat appearance.

Thus the Rhine valley between Bingen and Bonn intersects a widely extended range of high land, stretching W. as far as the Schelde above Valenciennes, and E. to the Diemel near Stadtberge, and consisting of upheaved and much contorted strata of *slatey-grauwacke* and *quartzose-rock*, one of the oldest formations in which fossils are found. Formerly geologists reckoned these slate and grauwacke formations among the so-called *transition rocks*, but since the fossiliferous strata have been more accurately classified, the Rhenish slate mountains are believed to hold the second place according to age among the fossiliferous formations. The oldest of these is, according to the eminent geologist Sir Roderic Murchison, called the *Silurian system,* and that to which the Rhenish slate Mountains belong, the *Devonian system.* All other fossiliferous formations are more recent.

From Bingen to the confluence of the Sieg below Bonn all the strata intersected by the Rhine belong to one and the same epoch, as they contain the same organic remains. These strata consist of many different kinds of *clay-slate,* the purest modification of which is the *roofing-slate.* The latter is yielded in great abundance by various quarries on the banks of the Rhine, the most important of which are those of Caub (p. 100), whence it is sent in all directions and even as far as Switzerland. The clay-slate forms transitions to the kind of sandstone called *grauwacke;* it is here mostly fine-grained, and, in combination with a quartzose cementing matter, passes into *quartzose-rock,* which, on account of its great hardness and indestructibility, assumes the most grotesque shapes, and between Bingen and St. Goar greatly enhances the beauty of the Rhine valley.

The S. limit of the range of mountains intersected by the Rbine is formed by the *Taunus*, of which the *Great Feldberg* rises to tbe height of 2708 ft., and the W. limit by the *Soonwald*, *Idarwald*, and *Hochwald*, the highest point of which is the *Walderbeskopf* (2518 ft.). So great a height is not attained by the *Westerwald*, *Eifel*, *Hohe Venn*, or any of the other slate mountains in the range.

In proportion to these beights are also the bills which bound the valley of the Rhine; they are highest where the river intersects the Taunus and the Soonwald, but decrease in height farther down.

Between the periods when the Rhine first began to cut a passage for itself through the above mentioned higblands, and when tbe strata forming these highlands were deposited at the bottom of what was then an ocean, a vast interval of time must have elapsed. In this enormous interval all the fossiliferous systems in the world must have been formed. The formation of the Rhine valley from Bingen down to the sea is *more recent* than tbe deposits of the middle section of the Tertiary system, called by Sir Charles Lyell *Meiocene*, in which the clays of Vallendar and the brown coals of the Westerwald, the Seven Mountains, and the neigbbourhood of Brübl are found. Of an equal age with these tertiary formations are the *basalts* of the Rhine (p. 73), which occur in the most grotesque shapes on the slopes near Linz, Kaisersberg and Ockenfels, on the Erpeler Ley, in the Unkeler Bruch (where in 1846 a considerable landslip took place, see p. 52), at Rolandseck (at the foot of which the railway has laid bare some remarkably situated columns), at Petersberg, Nonnenstromberg, and many other peaks of the Seven Mountains.

The Rhine valley, ancient as it is in the ordinary sense of the word, is tben, geologically considered, of very recent formation; and the extinct *volcanoes*, numerous cones of which may be seen from the Rhine at Neuwied, such as the Camillenberg and the peaks of the Hummerich at Plaidt and Kruft, are still more recent. From the peak at Fornich a stream of lava descends into the valley of the Rhine, the large perpendicular columns of which may be seen from the river (p. 187). The valley had nearly attained its present depth when the eruption which produced this stream of lava took place. This is proved by the fact, that all the other lava streams in the vicinity of the Laacher See and the Eifel have been poured into valleys already formed. The pumice-stone, which extends over the whole basin of Neuwied, the only place in Germany where this volcanic product is found, must have been discharged at a still more recent date than most of the lava-streams.

In the flat parts of the valley, through which the Rhine flows, at first narrow, and then gradually widening, are found beds of *loam* and *rubble* which the stream has deposited. Similar masses are also met with on the terraces parallel with the river, at a height of 400—800 ft. above the level of the water. The strata could only have been deposited by the agency of flowing water, and must have been deposited long before the valley attained its present depth. These terraces are distinguishable from the peaks formed by the uncovered slate by their long horizontal ridges; they prove that the Rhine valley has been gradually hollowed out by the action of water, though its rugged aspect might give rise to the conjecture that it had been the scene of some mighty convulsion of nature.

V. Wine.[1]

Wine is a subject which the traveller who visits the land of the grape will naturally expect to be treated of. It is far too comprehensive to receive justice in a work necessarily so limited as a guide-book, but as a highly important article of commerce, as a peculiar feature of the country, the object of the unwearying industry of a large population, as forming an article of luxury by which the most homely taste and the most refined palate may alike be gratified, and lastly as a poetic theme from the days of Anacreon to the present time, no work of this character could be considered complete, which did not make some brief mention of the grape, its culture and produce.

---

[1] For fuller information on this subject, the traveller is referred to "Some Words on Rhine Wines," an interesting pamphlet which may be, procured of the principal booksellers in the Rhineland.

The recent liberal modification of English duties upon foreign wines has of course given an increased impetus to the traffic in this article between Great Britain and other countries. Possibly one of the earliest and least satisfactory results of this relaxation has been that an immense quantity of inferior wine of fictitious body and sweetness has been thrown upon the English market, by which the public taste for the Rhenish vineyards can hardly be improved; but, when that shock is recovered from, there can be little doubt that the Rhine wines of the second and third class will, from their moderate price and wholesome and agreeable qualities, take their proper place at the English table, from which they have been hitherto partially excluded by oppressive fiscal regulations, now happily removed. Smith in his "Wealth of Nations," alluding to the duties and prohibitions with which the English and French have mutually oppressed each other's industry, observes that "the spirit of hostility, which has subsisted between the two nations ever since 1667, has hitherto hindered them from being moderated on either side;" but a happier era is now inaugurated, ignorance and prejudice have veiled their faces before modern enlightenment, and the recent commercial treaty between Great Britain and France, the benefits of which England has extended to other countries, forms an epoch in liberal legislation, the importance of which it is impossible to over-estimate.

We do not believe with the over-sanguine that the wines of Germany, or any other country, will ever supplant what may be termed the national beverages of Great Britain. A bottle of Hock, albeit the bouquet emitted from its graceful neck be ever so fragrant, will stand a poor chance by the side of a foaming "pewter," when a thirsty mechanic is the arbitrator of their respective merits; nor do we believe that the stalwart young athletæ of England, after their exertions in the "outrigger" or the cricket-field, will ever be proof against the blandishments of the exhilarating and strength-supporting production of the "immortal Bass;" but we decidedly anticipate that with increased facilities there will be a growing partiality for the sound and wholesome produce of the Rhenish vineyards, before which many prejudices will fade away. No error has been more prevalent than that the Rhenish and Moselle wines possess an injurious acidity. The celebrated chemist Liebig on the contrary affirms, that not only is the exquisite bouquet of the Rhine wines owing to the free acid, but that some of their *most salutary properties* arise from the tartar present in them. To this he attributes the immunity enjoyed by the inhabitants of the banks of the Rhine and

Moselle, indeed of all who use the German wines, from the uric acid diathesis; and if Liebig should be considered under the influence of national partiality, Dr. Prout, and many others who have investigated the subject without prejudice or favor, may be mentioned as entertaining the same opinion. There cannot be a greater error than indiscriminately to denounce the acidity of wine—the *kind* of acid present is, however, an important point, and tartaric acid is the best; but there is another advantage possessed by Rhenish wines, which stands out in prominent relief, namely the total absence of brandy, with which the wines of Spain, Portugal and Sicily are invariably saturated, to the utter destruction of their natural flavour and injury to the health of the consumer. Dr. McCulloch has forcibly pointed out the evils of adding brandy to wine. The pure light wines of Germany produce an agreeable exhilaration of mind, very unlike the mere physical excitement, almost amounting to ferocity, which results from the immoderate use of the largely brandied wines so much in vogue in England; the diseases which attend spirit-drinkers, chiefly disorders of the liver, are commonly met with amongst consumers of wine to which brandy has been adventitiously added, though such maladies rarely, if ever, follow even the intemperate use of pure wine. It is evident that the addition of alcohol to wine is unnecessary for its preservation, for it is notorious that Rhine wines sometimes retain their excellence for a century; yet in these the quantity of alcohol is seldom more than eight or nine per cent, that is, in professional terms, 17—21° of proof, according to Syke's Hydrometer, used in the Test-office of the London custom-house—indeed the very property of keeping is mainly attributable to the fact that the fermentation is more perfect in Rhenish wines than in those of Spain and Portugal, in which latter countries fermentation is checked by the addition of brandy, while with the white wines of France, the same object is effected by sulphuration—processes by which the richness and sweetness of new wine are artificially retained.

The connoisseur is generally in the habit of giving the preference to France as a wine-growing country, and calls it in his enthusiasm, par excellence "the vineyard of the earth," and doubtless the wonderful fertility of her soil, and her delicious temperature, varied though it be, give her a proud pre-eminence over the rest of the globe; within her sunny regions every description of wine is produced, Champagne of different degrees of excellence, Burgundy, as a red wine unrivalled in its perfection, the exquisite produce of the Gironde and la Drôme, and the luscious wines of Herault. But yielding, as one in candour must, the palm to France for her red wines, Germans may view with just pride their noble river, perhaps the most beautiful stream in the world, on the banks of which from Mayence to Bonn, a distance of 90 M., the cultivation of the vine may be seen in the greatest possible perfection, the result of which is the production of a variety of white wines with which no other country can compete.

In Germany the wine-culture may almost be said to assume the form of a passion, which pervades all classes from the prince to the peasant. The reigning potentate has his vineyards, and might almost be called a wine-merchant on an extensive scale, and his Kellermeister is an official, the importance of whose office it would be difficult to overrate. The peasant, too, owns his little patch of vineyard, which he cultivates with assiduous care and affection.

It must be admitted that the traveller meets with no inconsiderable difficulty in procuring that which in his imagination must be of very easy attainment, namely a bottle of good wine. As in a sea-port town in England it is often difficult to obtain good fish, the voracious maw of the great metropolis absorbing all that comes within its reach, so, in the very garden of the vine, unanticipated obstacles to the hoped-for enjoyment present themselves. If the frugal traveller, fresh from England with the taste of Port and Sherry hardly out of his mouth, contents himself with ordering a bottle of the ordinary table-wine, which he sees is very palatable to the unvitiated taste of the natives, he is likely to be little captivated by his first impressions of the highly-extolled produce of the Rhenish grape, and if his eye wanders over the "Weinkarte" in search of the rarer productions of the Rheingau — to say nothing of the bewilderment generally attendant upon such a search — he will find that he can only gratify his longings at a cost equal to, if not exceeding, his whole day's expenditure, for a bottle of Johannisberger or Steinberger cannot be obtained at an hotel at less than four thalers a bottle. It is a well-known fact that the prices charged by the inn-keepers for the table d'hôte dinners with their endless variety of dishes, frequently followed by ice and fruit, are wholly unremunerative, and they are consequently compelled to put a profit upon their wines of about one hundred per cent. This is a difficulty not easily overcome, and the readiest solution we can offer the traveller, between the Scylla of the very cheap, and the Charybdis of the expensive wines, is to recommend him, should the table-wine not prove sufficiently palatable, to order a bottle of Rhine or Moselle at a thaler, or a thaler and five groschen (about 2 fl.), at which price the most fastidious taste ought to be gratified. In the wine-gardens and other places of public resort, it is the custom among the natives to order simply white or red wine at six, eight, or ten groschen (20—36 kreuzers) a bottle, by adopting which course a fair estimate may be made of the ordinary wine of the country.

The Rheingau, a district of about 15 M. in length, produces the finest wines of the Rhine. Here is situated *Schloss Johannisberg*, a most favoured spot, yielding a wine, up to a recent period considered without a rival. When it is stated that these celebrated vineyards are confined to a space of about 40 acres, it may be easily seen how little of this rare product falls to the share of the ordinary public. The first quality can only be obtained in the most favourable seasons; the grapes are selected with the utmost care from the ripest bunches — not a drop of the precious juice is allowed to escape — the yield, under the most auspicious circumstances, is therefore very limited. This may be considered as the veritable nectar, which the vulgar lip seldom profanes. It was, until recently, the custom to sell these wines only in bottle, but this practice is now abandoned, and they are now sold in the cask at Schloss Johannisberg by public auction. This celebrated wine is less remarkable for its strength than for its raciness, the delicacy of its flavour and its bouquet. The other wines of the immediate vicinity are distinguished by the name of *Johannisberg-Klaus;* the vineyards belonging to Count Schönborn also yield a wine highly esteemed. There is also "Johannisberger" produced from the vineyards at the side of the Schloss and the village of that name, but these are inferior to many of the other productions of the Rheingau. In this neighbourhood are the districts of *Rüdesheim* and *Geisenheim*, the first of these producing a fine and generous wine, the principal characteristics of which are mellowness and body. Bingen, on the left side of the river, is a favourable district for strong wines; the hill in the rear yields *Scharlachberger*. Below Bingen, on the opposite side of the Rhine, is *Assmannshausen*, the red wine of which holds a high rank in the estimation of the connoisseur, and in good vintages bears no mean comparison with Burgundy of the best class, being made from the same species of grape, but unfortunately, like the latter, is often seriously impaired by travelling. The "*Marcobrunn*" vineyard, situated between *Hattenheim* and *Erbach*, produces a wine of exquisite flavour and bouquet, but the wine which competes most successfully with Johannisberger, and indeed trenches closely upon its celebrity, is the *Steinberger*, produced from an estate belonging to the Duke of Nassau on the hill at the back of Hattenheim, and cultivated with the utmost care. Many circumstances contribute to the increasing reputation of the Steinberg wine. The Duke of Nassau, it is well known, spares no expense in the cultivation of his vineyards, upon which the utmost care is bestowed under the personal supervision of the Duke's Kellermeister and his subordinates. The estate of Johannisberg is held by the head of the Metternich family as a fief of the crown of Austria. In the hottest seasons the lightness of the soil of the Johannisberg vineyard is occasionally detrimental to the perfection of the yield, the grapes being apt to ripen before they attain their proper size and maturity. This was the case in 1857, which, with 1858 and 1859, are the three best years in succession on record, when the Steinberger reached a marked pre-eminence over its rival, a circumstance owing principally to the heavier nature of the soil. *Hochheim*, though situated on the Main, is considered to yield a Rhenish wine of a very superior quality.

It may not be out of place here to name a respectable house from which the above-mentioned first-class wines can be procured. To connoisseurs and purchases of Hock and Moselle we can highly recommend among others Messrs. *H. & J. Espenschied*, of Coblenz, their cellars being well known on the Rhine as containing a choice variety of wines of the first growths, such as Steinberg, Johannisberg, Marcobrunn, Gräfenberg, Rüdesheim, &c.

The valley of the *Ahr* may be regarded as the most N. point at which the culture of the grape is brought to any perfection; its light and wholesome red wines are chiefly consumed in the neighbourhood of their growth. *Walporzheimer* and *Ahr-Bleicherte*, when procured from respectable sources, without the "improvements" introduced by the chemist Chaptal, and subsequently "improved upon" by Dr. Gall, are of a ruby colour, strenghtening and astringent in their properties, and bear a resemblance to Burgundy of an inferior class.

Whilst thus briefly dwelling upon Rhenish wines in general, mention must be made of the effervescing wines which were first manufactured 40 years ago at Esslingen, Würzburg and Treves, but with indifferent success, and subsequently in Mayence, Hochheim and Coblenz, in which latter place there are now six thriving manufactories. These wines are known generally in England under the denomination of sparkling Hock and Moselle, and are distinguished from the French wines by the predominance of the flavour of the grape, a quality they owe to the comparatively small quantity of cognac used in their preparation. It is well known that in the inferior qualities of genuine champagne the flavour of cognac, or some other spirit, conceals the want of flavour of the wine. In England the consumption of these wines is considerably on the increase. It must, however, be confessed, that, in their unsophisticated state, they do not find the same favour among the Germans; and to show the extent to which prejudice can be carried, it may be mentioned that at Hochheim not only are the bottles labelled with the names of the first French growers, but the brands on the corks, the metallic covering of the bottles, and peculiarities in packing are so closely imitated that the most practised eye does not detect the deception, and in this disguise are these wines freely consumed in the country of their manufacture. The process is exactly similar to that of Champagne, for which it often does duty in England. When obtained in unexceptionable quarters, it is a light and most agreeable beverage, but unscrupulous individuals too often employ the process as a vehicle for getting rid of wine of very inferior quality, sweetness and effervescence concealing for the moment the real nature of the article.

In bringing these few remarks to a conclusion, it may not be out of place to caution the traveller against employing any other than the most respectable wine-merchants. The art of adulteration is unhappily widely known, and, what is worse, the label and cork are not always guarantees that the wine is what it professes to be. It may also be stated that excellence of quality is wholly incompatible with lowness of price. Good wine bears a high price even on the spot where it is grown. What is a light and agreeable beverage in Germany will hardly pass muster in the English climate, especially where the palate is often cloyed with the strong wines of Spain and Portugal. As a light, agreeable, and wholesome summer beverage the Rhenish wines of the 2nd and 3rd class may of course be imported at a very moderate price, the duty upon such in bottle being now reduced to 2*s.* 5*d.* per gallon; but the highest class of Rhine wine, of which Marcobrunner may be taken as a good sample, cannot be drunk in England under six or seven shillings a bottle.

For the convenience of the traveller a list of some of the best known Rhine and Moselle wines is appended; it might be extended considerably, but it would be found impossible to discriminate between the numberless wines of third and fourth-class growth.

Wines.	Where grown.	Class.	Properties.
Johannisberg . . .	Rheingau.	I.	Raciness, delicacy, bouquet.
Steinberg	do.	,,	The above properties combined with strength.
Rüdesheimer-Berg	do.	,,	Mellowness and body; the first from the Orleans, the latter from the Riessling grape.
— Hinterhaus .	do.	,,	
Marcobrunn	do.	,,	Fine flavour and bouquet.
Hochheim-Dom-Dechaney	do.	,,	Mellowness combined with peculiar and excelleut flavour.
Gräfenberg	do.	,,	Of almost equal standing to Marcobrunn.
Geisenheim-Rothenberg	do.	,,	Great delicacy and flavour.
Johannisberg-Klaus	do.	II.	Generally characterised more by bouquet than mellowness.
Rauenthaler-Berg .	do.	,,	Mellowness.
Hochheim	do.	,,	
Hattenheim	do.	III.	
Geisenheim	do.	,,	
Winkel	do.	,,	
Rüdesheim	do.	,,	Mellowness.
Bodenthal	do.	,,	
Assmannshausen .	do.	I.	Fine red wine resembling Burgundy.
Rupertsberg	Rhenish Bavaria.	III.	Possess more mellowness and body than bouquet and flavour.
Deidesheim	do.	,,	
Forst	do.	,,	
Ungstein	do.	IV.	
Königsbach	do.	,,	
Scharlachberg . . .	Rhenish Hessen.	II.	Possess body and flavour, but less delicacy and raciness than the wines of the Rheingau.
Nierstein	do.	,,	
Liebfrauenmilch .	do.	III.	
Laubenheim	do.	,,	
Engehöll	Rhenish Prussia.	III.	Agreeable light wines.
Steeg	do.	,,	
Kreutzberg	Ehrenbreitstein.	IV.	A good full-bodied red wine.
Walporzheim . . .	Valley of the Ahr.	III.	Good aud wholesome red wines; astringent.
Ahr-Bleichert . . .		,,	
Scharzhofberg . . .	Moselle.	I.	Light, wholesome aud agreeable wines of peculiar fragrance, recommended to persons of sedentary habits.
Scharzberg	do.	,,	
Brauneberg	do.	II.	
Pisport	do.	III.	
Graach	do.	,,	
Zeltingen	do.	,,	

Fall of the Rhine.

Height above the level of the sea of

	Feet.		Feet.
The Toma-See, source of the Vorder-Rhein	7240	The Rhine at Bacharach	211
The Rheinwald Glacier, source of the Hinter-Rhein	6822	" " " the Lurlei	205
Reichenau, at the confluence of the Vorder- and Hinter-Rhein	1804	" " " St. Goar	197
The Lake of Constance	1089	" " " Boppard	192
The Rhine at Bâle	752	" " " Coblenz	179
" " " Strasburg	448	" " " Neuwied	165
" " " Speyer	304	" " " Andernach	161
" " " Mannheim	284	" " " Brohl	156
" " " Mayence	256	" " " Bonn	134
" " " Bingen	232	" " " Cologne	115
		" " " Düsseldorf	82
		" " " Wesel	48
		" " " Emmerich	31

Average breadth of the Rhine.

	Feet.		Feet.
At Bâle	528	At Neuwied	1260
" Strasburg	744	" Unkel	840
" Mannheim	1200	" Bonn	1488
" Mayence	1380	" Cologne	1212
" Bingen	1608	" Worringen	1992
Between Bingen and Coblenz	1200	" Düsseldorf	1140
At Coblenz	1116	" Schenkenschanz (Dutch front.)	2544

Depth of the Rhine.

	Feet.
Between Bâle and Strasburg	3—12
" Strasburg and Mayence	5—24
" Mayence and Bonn	9—72
At the Lurlei	72
Between Bonn and Cologne	10—30
At Cologne	18
" Mülheim	25
Between Mülheim and Düsseldorf	12—31
At Düsseldorf above the town	62
" " below the town	23

Length of the Rhine.

		Engl. Miles.
From	Bâle to Strasburg	$83^1/_6$
„	Strasburg to Lauterburg	$28^1/_6$
„	Lauterburg to Mayence	$33^1/_3$
„	Mayence to Biugen	$17^2/_3$
„	Bingen to Coblenz	$38^1/_3$
„	Coblenz to Cologne	$58^2/_3$
„	Cologne to Düsseldorf	34
„	Düsseldorf to Emmerich	$65^3/_4$
„	Emmerich to Briel (North Sea)	$97^2/_3$
From	Bâle to the North Sea	$456^3/_4$

An auuual sum of 125,000*l.* is expended on the construction of dams and other river-works. Of this the government of Baden pays upwards of 40,000*l.*, that of Prussia almost as much.

Abbreviations used in the Handbook.

R. = room	N. = north
L. = light	S. = south
B. = breakfast	E. = east
D. = dinner	W. = west
S. = supper	r. = right
exc. W. = exclusive of wine	l. = left
inc. W. = inclusive of wine	min. = minute
A. = attendance	hr. = hour.

M. = English mile.

NB. The best hotels aud everythiug particularly worthy of uote are indicated by an asterisk.

1. From Brussels to Aix-la-Chapelle.

By express train in 5 hrs.; fares 18 fr. 37, 13 fr. 2 c. Custom-house formalities on arriving at the station of Aix-la-Chapelle or Cologne. The finest views between Louvain and Liège are to the right. The entire district between Liège and Aix-la-Chapelle is replete with interest.

Brussels (Hôtel de Bellevue, *de Flandre, de l'Europe, de la Grande Bretagne, de France, de la Règence, Windsor, all in the upper part of the town, near the park; *Hôtel de Suède, de l'Univers, de Saxe, de l'Angleterre, des Etrangers, de Hollande, in the lower part of the town; of the second class: *Hôtel de Brabant, Grand-Monarque, Bélier; more moderate: *Hôtel Callo, *des Brasseurs, for travellers of moderate requirements), see *Baedeker's Belgique et Hollande.*

Shortly after the train has left the handsome *Station du Nord*, the royal palace of *Laeken* is seen rising above the fertile meadow-land on an eminence to the l. The stream which winds through the pastures is the *Senne.* To the r. stands the Château of the Marquis *van Assche.* In 10 min. stat. **Vilvorde** is passed. Near this little town, the most ancient in Brabant, to the l. of the line, is an extensive *Penitentiary,* with numerous windows resembling loop-holes, capable of receiving 2000 convicts. In 25 min. the train stops at the station of

Malines, Flem. *Mechelen,* Ger. *Mecheln.* (*Hôtel de la Grue, Hôtel de Brabant,* both in the market-place, near the cathedral: *St. Antoine*, rue d'Egmont; *St. Jacques*, in the Corn-market; table d'hôte in all at 1 o'clock. Near the station, *Cour Impériale*, unpretending and reasonable. "*Déjeuner de Malines,*" a dish regarded as a triumph of Belgian culinary skill, may be ordered by the curious). Malines is the central point of all the Belgian railways, which here diverge in four different directions; travellers should therefore be careful to avoid mistakes in case of a change of carriage. Malines is equidistant (15 M.) from Brussels, Antwerp and Louvain.

The town, situated on the *Dyle*, with a pop. of 33,855, is reached by the rue d'Egmont. It contains handsome squares, broad and regular streets and palatial edifices, but is entirely destitute of animation. Malines labours under the imputation of being a century behind other Belgian towns in commercial prosperity — a circumstance mainly attributable to the supineness and want of enterprise of its corporation. In 1551, when the Brussels and Antwerp canal was constructed, this intelligent body exerted their influence to prevent its approach to the town. Two centuries later, on the construction of the canal from Louvain to Antwerp, a similar infatuation pervaded its councils, and at a more recent date they declined to permit the railway to traverse the precincts of the town, which is in consequence visited by a very small proportion of the vast concourse of travellers which annually passes through its station. As an archiepiscopal residence it is a place of some importance. By a bull of Pius VII. in 1802 the cardinals of Malines were authorized to exercise ecclesiastical jurisdiction over the bishoprics of Mayence, Treves and Aix-la-Chapelle, a privilege they enjoyed till 1821.

The *Cathedral of St. Rumbold (*St. Rombaud*), commenced in the 12th and completed in the 15th cent., is a structure of no great architectural merit; the clumsy, unfinished tower is visible for miles round. The construction of the latter (340 ft.; proposed height 480 ft.) was commenced in 1452, with the aid of the contributions of the pilgrims who in that year resorted to the cathedral to purchase the indulgences granted by Pope Nicholas V. on the occasion of the Turkish war. A stone in the wall of the platform bears the name of "Louis XV.," who ascended to this point in 1746. The dial of the tower-clock is 48 ft. in diameter.

The interior of the church (nave 90 ft. high, 39 ft. broad) is imposing, and contains several fine pictures which merit inspection, especially the *Altarpieee by *Van Dyck*, in the S. transept, representing the Crucifixion, painted in 1627, judiciously cleaned in 1848. This is considered one of this great master's finest works, and is remarkable for the admirable disposition of the figures and the profound grief and resignation expressed by the Virgin (sacristan's fee 1 fr.). In the N. transept: Adoration of the shepherds, by *Quellyn;* on the same side two altarpieces in chapels: Circumcision, by *Michel Coxcie*, a native of Malines and pupil of Raphael, painted in 1587, and the Last Supper by *Wouters*. Adjacent to the latter, in the last N. chapel, is a marble monument by the Liége sculptor *Jehotte* to the archbishop Count Méan (d. 1831), who is represented kneeling before the angel of death. The passage round the choir contains a number of pictures by *Herreyns* and others, dating from the commencement of the present century, as well as 25 smaller paintings of the *van Eyck* school, all representing scenes from the life of St. Rumbold. The *Pulpit* is of carved wood, of the kind frequently seen in Belgian churches; below is represented the Conversion of St. Paul, above it John and the women at the Cross, and Adam and Eve with the serpent. The Choir contains several episcopal monuments of the 17th cent. and modern stained glass. A sum of 400*l.* is annually expended on the restoration of the edifice.

The Grande Place contains several ancient buildings, among others Les Halles, dating from 1340, now the guard-house, and the *Beyard,* or *Town-hall,* of the 15th cent.

The *Statue of Margaret of Austria (d. 1530), daughter of Maximilian I. and Mary of Burgundy, celebrated as a diplomatist, regent of the Netherlands and tutoress of Charles V., was erected in 1849, as the inscription records. The epitaph she jestingly composed on herself after her second betrothal (with the Infante John), during a storm whilst on her way to Spain, is well known: *"Ci-gît Margot, la gente demoiselle, qu'eut deux maris et si mourut pucelle"*; and her motto: *"Fortune infortune fort une."*

In the vicinity of the cathedral is the Church of St. John, an insignificant edifice, but remarkable for its *High-altar-piece with wings, representing the Adoration of the Magi, by *Rubens*, which he himself considered one of his best works. On the inner side of the wings: the Beheading of John the Baptist, and the Martyrdom of St. John the Evangelist; on the outer side: the Baptism of Christ, and St. John in the Island of Patmos, both in Rubens' best style. The carved pulpit represents the Good Shepherd.

The Church of Notre Dame, the first to the l. on approaching the town from the station, contains (in a chapel behind the high-altar) *Rubens*' celebrated Miraculous Draught of fishes, an admirably coloured picture with wings, painted in 1618 for the Guild of Fish-mongers for the sum of 1000 florins. The *Botanical Garden* contains a bust of the eminent botanist Dodonæus, a native of Malines.

The *Dyle*, which intersects the town, and 6 M. below it falls into the Nethe, forming the *Rupel,* is subject to the rise and fall of the tide, whence the erroneous conjecture that Malines derives its name from *maris linea*, the boundary of the sea.

As the train approaches Louvain, stat. *Wespelaer* is passed, to the r. of which are seen the estate and park of the family of Marnef, a favourite resort of the townspeople of Louvain. The park contains a profusion of grottoes, Chinese bridges, Greek temples, and a motley array of statues and busts of the Greek mythological deities, literary and other celebrities, Rousseau, Voltaire, the Prince of Orange etc. According to the partial judgment of the vicinity, this is the most attractive property in Belgium; those who have leisure may test the accuracy of this opinion.

Louvain, Flem. *Leuven*, Ger. *Löwen* (**Hôtel de la Suède; Cour de Mons; Sauvage*), comp. *Baedeker*'s *Belgique et Hollande.* —

The traveller who is detained at Louvain should not fail to visit the **Hôtel de Ville, a magnificent edifice in the later Gothic style, erected in 1448-63, and the Gothic *Church of St. Peter, dating from the 15th cent., and remarkable for the symmetry of its proportions. The carved wooden stalls in the Church of St. Gertrude also well merit inspection.

Tirlemont, or *Thienen* (*Hôtel des quatre saisons*, at the station; *Plat d'Etain*, *Hôtel de Flandre*, both in the market-place; at the station, "*Buffet-restaurant tarifé*"), occupies an extensive area, the town-walls being nearly 6 M. in circumf., but is thinly populated (12,178 inhab.). The *Church of St. Germain, believed to date from the 9th cent., is one of the most ancient Christian edifices in existence; the well-preserved tower is incontestibly of Roman origin. Tirlemont was the birth-place of the celebrated Jesuit Bollandus, the author of the *Acta Sanctorum*. Those who continued the work after his death termed themselves Bollandists.

On leaving Tirlemont the train traverses a lofty embankment, affording an extensive view. In clear weather the Lion and the Prussian monument on the field of Waterloo may be distinguished in the distance to the r.

Between the stations of *Esemael* and *Landen* the line intersects the plain of *Neerwinden*, the scene of two important battles. In the first the allies under William III. of England were defeated in the Spanish war of succession by the French under the Marshal of Luxembourg, July 29th, 1693; in the second the French under Dumouriez and Louis Philippe, at that time "Général Égalité," were defeated by the Austrians under the command of the Duke of Coburg, and driven out of Belgium.

Landen was the birthplace of Pepin of Landen, ancestor of Pepin the Little and Charlemagne, and "major-domo" of the French King Clotaire II. He died here in 640 and was interred on the hill which still bears his name. With him commenced the ascendancy of the Carlovingian line.

From Landen a branch-line diverges to Aix-la-Chapelle, pursuing a somewhat shorter but less interesting route. The principal stations are *St. Trond*, *Hasselt* (capital of the province of Limburg, the scene of a victory gained by the Dutch over the Belgians, Aug. 6th, 1831) and *Mastricht*.

Beyond stat. *Waremme*, the line intersects the well-preserved Roman road, termed by the people of the country the *Road of Brunhilde*, from Bavay (*Bavacum Nerviorum*) near Mons to Tongues, 9 M. to the S. E. of Waremme. The *Hesbaye*, a district of which Waremme was formerly the capital, was noted for the strength and bravery of its inhabitants, as the old proverb testifies: "*Qui passe dans le Hesbain est combattu le lendemain.*"

The undulating, agricultural district of Brabant, with its somewhat phlegmatic Germanic inhabitants, is quitted near stat. **Ans** (450 ft. higher than Liége) for a mining tract of country with a Walloon population of Celtic origin, distinguished by the activity and vivacity of their disposition.

As the train descends the rapid (1 : 30) incline to Liége, a fine view of the populous city and the animated valley of the Meuse is obtained.

Liége, Flem. *Luik*, Ger. *Lüttich* (**Hôtel de Suède*; **Bellevue*; **Hôtel d'Angleterre*; *Hôtel de l'Europe*; *Hôtel Schiller*, etc.), pop. 97,544; comp. *Baedeker's Belgique et Hollande*. — The traveller whose time is limited should visit the Palais de Justice, the Church of St. Jacques, the Cathedral (*St. Paul*), and, for the sake of the view, the Citadel.

On quitting Liége the Meuse is crossed by the handsome *Pont du Val Benoît*. Numerous lofty chimneys afford indication of the industrial prosperity of the district. The extensive zinc foundry of the Vieille-Montagne company is next passed, and the *Ourthe*, which is here joined by its affluent the *Vesdre*, crossed. **Chênée**, the first station beyond Liége, is another manufacturing town.

Chaudfontaine (*Grand Hôtel des Bains*; *Hôtel d'Angleterre*) is a small, but picturesquely situated watering-place, a favourite resort of the inhabitants of Liége. The warm spring (104° Fahr.), which rises on an island in the Vesdre, is pumped up and conveyed to the bath-estab. by means of a large water-wheel. Since 1862 Chaudfontaine has enjoyed the amenities of a "Cursaal."

Before entering the tunnel, the picturesque castle of *La Rochette* is seen on an eminence to the l. As **Le Trooz** is approached, the traveller perceives the ancient castle of that name, perched on the rocks to the r. of the line. For upwards of a century a manufactory of gun-barrels has been established in the building. Farther on, to the r., the castle of *Fraipont*.

Between stat. **Nessonvaux** and *Pepinster*, to the r. of the line, stands the Château de Masures (*masure* = ruined house), erected by the late Vicomte Biolley, a wealthy manufacturer of Verviers, and said to occupy the site of a hunting-seat of King Pepin. At **Pepinster** (*Pepin's terre*) a branch line diverges to **Spa** (*Hôtel d'Orange*; *Hôtel Britannique*; *Hôtel de Flandre*, *de York*, *de Bellevue*, etc.; *Cour de Londres*, moderate), 7½ M. distant; see *Baedeker's Belgique et Hollande*. The next stat. **Ensival**, to the l. of the line, is almost contiguous to Verviers.

Verviers (*Hôtel du Chemin de fer*, at the stat.; *Hôtel des Pays-Bas*, in the town), with 28,691 inhab., is a busy, commercial town of recent origin, and consists almost exclusively of manufactories, the residences of their owners and the habitations of the operatives. In Verviers and its environs upwards of 350,000 pieces of cloth, worth 3,020,000*l*., are annually manufactured. The town itself contains nothing worthy of note.

As stat. **Dolhain**, a modern town, picturesquely situated in the valley of the Vesdre, is approached, the ancient fortress of **Limburg** is seen on an eminence. This is almost the sole remnant of Limburg, the once flourishing capital of the duchy of that name, destroyed by Louis XIV. in 1675. The castle was the family seat of the powerful ducal family of Limburg, to which the emperors Henry VII., Charles IV., Wenceslaus, and Sigismund of Germany belonged. The view obtained from this eminence is fine, but scarcely sufficiently so to arrest the passing traveller. Pedestrians, however, will be well repaid by a walk (8—10 hrs.) from Dolhain by Verviers to Liége.

Herbesthal, the first Prussian village, is the frontier-station (luggage examined at Aix or Cologne). Beyond stat. *Assenet*, the village of *Lontzen* and the castle of *Welkenhausen* lie to the l. of the line. The train crosses the valley of the Geul by a handsome viaduct of 17 arches, 120 ft. in height. To the l. lies the village of *Hergenrad*, and in the distance beyond, the *Eineburg* or *Emmaburg*, situated on the brow of the wooded mountains, a country residence of Charlemagne, where, according to tradition, the intimacy between the emperor's daughter Emma and his secretary Eginhard was formed.

The train next passes through two tunnels of 540 ft. and 2350 ft. respectively, reaches stat. *Ronheide*, and finally descends by a considerable incline to *Aix-la-Chapelle*.

2. Aix-la-Chapelle.

Hotels. *Hôtel Dremel (Grand Monarque, R. 20, L. 6, B. 12, A. 8 Sgr.) and *Hôtel Nuellens, opposite to the Elisenbrunnen, both 1st class hotels with corresponding charges. Hôtel Frank or Bellevue. Dragon d'Or. *Hôtel Hoyer (Imperial Crown Hotel) very good (R. and B. 18, D. inc. W. 22½, A. 5 Sgr.) Hôtel de l'Empereur, with baths. Grand Hôtel, more a boarding house. — Of the 2nd class: *Hôtel Schlemmer (Elephant); *König von Spanien, *Hôtel Royal, Hôtel du chemin de fer, all three near the Rhenish railway station.

Bavarian beer in the rock-cellars at the foot of the Lousberg (p. 9).

Restaurant in the *Klüppel to the E. of the Elisenbrunnen; *Bernarts in the Adalbertstrasse.

Carriage (*Vigilante*) for 1 pers. 5 Sgr. from the station to the town.

Porcelain and Glass at Gerdes-Neuber's, not far from the Elisenbrunnen, opp. to the Klüppel.

Railway to *Cologne* see R. 4, to *Düsseldorf*, *Crefeld*, *Ruhrort* R. 3, to *Mastricht* 5 trains daily in 1 hr., to *Landen* expr.-tr. in $2^3/_4$ hrs., to *Antwerp*

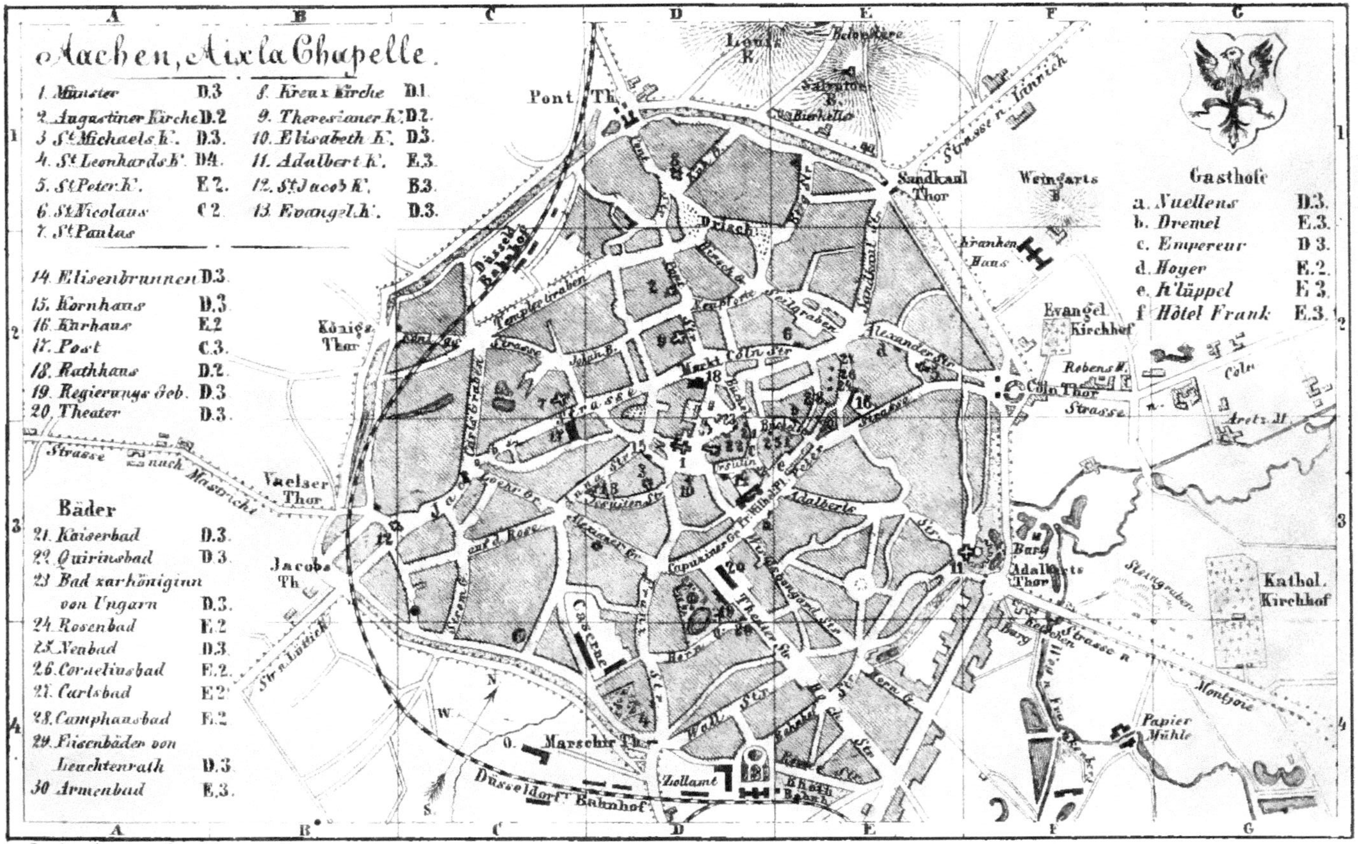
Aachen, Aix la Chapelle.
1. Münster D.3
2. Augustiner Kirche D.2
3. St. Michaels K. D.3.
4. St. Leonhards K. D.4.
5. St. Peter K. E.2.
6. St. Nicolaus C.2.
7. St. Paulus
8. Kreuz Kirche D.1.
9. Theresianer K. D.2.
10. Elisabeth K. D.3.
11. Adalbert K. E.3.
12. St. Jacob K. B.3.
13. Evangel. K. D.3.
14. Elisenbrunnen D.3.
15. Kornhaus D.3.
16. Kurhaus E.2.
17. Post C.3.
18. Rathhaus D.2.
19. Regierungs Geb. D.3.
20. Theater D.3.
Bäder
21. Kaiserbad D.3.
22. Quirinsbad D.3.
23. Bad zur Königinn von Ungarn D.3.
24. Rosenbad E.2.
25. Neubad D.3.
26. Corneliusbad E.2.
27. Carlsbad E.2.
28. Camphausbad E.2.
29. Eisenbäder von Leuchtenrath D.3.
30. Armenbad E.3.
Gasthöfe
a. Nuellens D.3.
b. Dremel E.3.
c. Empereur D.3.
d. Hoyer E.2.
e. Klüppel E.3.
f. Hôtel Frank E.3.
Pont Th.
Sandkaul Thor
Weingarts
Kranken Haus
Evangel. Kirchhof
Rebens W.
Cöln Thor
Cöln Strasse
Königs Thor
Vaelser Thor
Strasse nach Mastricht
Jacobs Th.
Str. n. Lüttich
Marschir Thor
Zollamt
Düsseldorf Bahnhof
Rhein. Bahnh.
Düsseld. Bahnhof
Templergraben
Drisch
Markt
Adalberts Thor
Burg
Kathol. Kirchhof
Steingraben
Strasse n. Montjoie
Papier Mühle
Strasse n. Jülich
Caserne
Theater Str.
Louis B.
Salvator B.
Belvedere
Arets M.

5 trains in 4½–6, to *Ostend* 3 trains in 7–9 hrs., *to Paris* (pr. Erquelines) 2 expr.-trs. in 11¼ hrs.

Telegraph Office at the station of the Rhenish railway.

English Church in the Anna Strasse. Resident chaplain.

Aix-la-Chapelle, or *Aachen*, contains but few reminiscences of its ancient grandeur as an imperial city. Almost the only buildings of a remote date which still exist are the cathedral, the corn exchange, townhall, and some of the gates. It now presents the appearance of a prosperous modern town with its numerous manufactories, handsome streets and well-stocked shops. Of the *Aquisgranum* or *Civitas Aquensis* of the Romans, the station of the *Legio prima*, no trace is visible. Even the reminiscences of Charlemagne, the founder of Aix-la-Chapelle, which was his birthplace and favorite residence, and the second city in his empire, are but scanty. From his death (814) to 1531 Aix-la-Chapelle was the scene of the coronation of all the German emperors (37), and was called *par excellence* the free city of the holy Roman empire. The insignia of empire were here preserved till 1793, when they were taken to Vienna and deposited in the Imperial treasury. A large proportion of the population (54,000, 2000 Prot.) is engaged in manufactures of various kinds (cloth, needles, machinery, looking-glasses).

Aix-la-Chapelle has frequently been the scene of Imperial diets, ecclesiastical convocations, and congresses, the last of which was that of 1818, at which three monarchs (Prussia, Austria, Russia) were present, and in which it was determined to recal the German troops still in France. In May, 1668, the peace between Louis XIV. and Spain was here concluded, and the second peace of Aix-la-Chapelle, of October, 1748, terminated the Austrian war of succession.

The **Town-hall** (*Rathhaus*), erected in 1358, contains a hall restored in the ancient style, and decorated with *frescoes by *Rethel* and *Kehren*, and small statues of 36 German emperors.

Frescoes in the Kaisersaal. 1. The emperor Frederick Redbeard at the grave of Charlemagne; 2. Fall of the "Irmensäule"; 3. Battle with the Saracens at Corduba; 4. Conquest of Pavia in 774; all by *Rethel*. 5. Baptism of Wittekind and Alboin; 6. Coronation of Charlemagne in St. Peter's at Rome; 7. Construction of the Cathedral of Aix-la-Chapelle; 8. Abdication of Charlemagne and Coronation of his son Louis; all by *Kehren*. — The town-council hall contains portraits of Fred. William III., Napoleon, Josephine, the emperors Leopold II, Charles VI. and VII., the empress Maria Theresa, and lastly the oldest and most celebrated portrait of Charlemagne by an unknown master.

Towards the W. stands the *Granusthurm*, an ancient semicircular tower, which formerly belonged to the Imperial palace and connected it with the cathedral. The square tower on the E. side dates from the commencement of the 13th cent. The fountain in front of the Rathhaus is decorated with a statue of Charlemagne, of little value as a work of art, erected in 1620.

The **Cathedral**, or *Münsterkirche*, consists of two distinct parts in different styles of architecture. That portion erected by Charlemagne in 796—804 and consecrated by Leo III., improperly called the nave of the church, is an octagon of 50 ft. in diameter, surrounded by a sixteen-sided gallery and terminating in a cupola; it is one of the most remarkable monuments of early Christian architecture, but its effect is unfortunately much marred by modern disfigurements. The marble and granite columns which support the octagon were brought from Rome and the palace of Ravenna. They were wantonly broken by the French in 1794 and taken to Paris, but were brought back in 1815 and restored to their places in 1845 at the expense of the late king Fred. William IV. Under the gilt chandelier, presented by Frederick Barbarossa, is the tomb of Charlemagne, indicated by the inscription "*Carolo Magno.*" This tomb was opened in the year 1000 by Otto III. and the body of the great emperor found, seated on a marble throne, used afterwards for the coronation ceremonies, and still to be seen in the gallery, or "*Hochmünster*". The ancient sarcophagus of Parian marble, in which the remains of Charlemagne reposed for 50 years after the opening of his tomb, has also been placed here; on the front is represented the Rape of Proserpine.

The lofty and elegant **Choir*, added to the original part of the edifice in 1353—1413, but in a totally different style, contains good modern stained-glass windows, representing scenes from the life of the Virgin. The *Pulpit*, richly adorned with gold, precious stones, and carved ivory, was presented by Henry II. (The sacristan uncovers the pulpit and sarcophagus, 1—3 pers. 15 Sgr.)

The **Sacristy** contains the so-called "Great Relics," which are held in the highest veneration by the superstitious; they consist of a robe of the virgin, the swaddling clothes in which the infant Saviour was wrapped, the bloody cloth with which the body of John the Baptist was covered after his execution, and the cloth with which Christ was girded when on the Cross. These are publicly exhibited only once in seven years, and attract vast crowds of religious devotees. Among the numerous *Smaller relics* are the leathern girdle of Christ, a part of the true Cross, the girdle of the Virgin, &c., all of which are preserved in curious and richly ornamented caskets and monstrances. Among the treasures are exhibited the skull, gigantic arm- (really leg) bone, and hunting-horn of Charlemagne. The smaller relics are shown for a fee of 1 Thlr. for 1—8 pers.

The church-doors, as well as the brass gates of the archways of the upper gallery, date from the time of Charlemagne, the peculiar *Cloisters* with their short pillars belong to the 12th and 13th centuries.

On the r. and l. sides of the principal entrance are a brazen wolf and pine-apple of Roman origin, supported by modern pillars. They formerly belonged to a fountain in the fish-market; the water flowed from small apertures among the hair of the wolf, or, when these were closed, from holes in the pine-apple which crowned the summit of the fountain.

The other churches of Aix-la-Chapelle contain few objects of sufficient interest to detain the traveller. — Near the cathedral is situated the ***Corn-Exchange** (Pl. 15), decorated with statues of the 7 electors, probably of the 12th cent.

The celebrated warm *Sulphur-springs*, known as early as the Roman period, rise partly in the town and partly in the neighbouring village of Burtscheid. The principal is the *Kaisers-quelle* (on the slope of the market-hill, in the Hôtel de l'Empereur), which supplies the Kaiserbad, the Neubad, the "Queen of Hungary," and the Elisenbrunnen. The Quirinusbad and the three lower springs in the *Comphausbad* are somewhat less powerful in their effects.

In the gardens near the pump-room of the **Elisenbrunnen** (Pl. 14) a band plays from 7 to 8 a.m. during the season. Near it is the handsome *Theatre* (Pl. 20), in the broad street leading from the railway station into the town.

The old **Curhaus** (Pl. 16) in the Comphausbadstrasse, erected in 1782, on the E. side of the town, contains ball, reading, refreshment and other rooms (adm. 5 Sgr.), open from 10 a.m. (reading-room from 8) to 10 p.m.; adjoining it is the new **Cursaal**, opened in 1863. Music in the garden from 3 to $4\frac{1}{2}$ o'clock.

Burtscheid, or *Borcette* (*St. Charles; Rosenbad; Schwertbad*), now connected with Aix-la-Chapelle by a series of new buildings, is also celebrated for its baths. The *Kochbrunnen* (156° Fahr.) with the other warm springs, unite their waters and form the so-called *Warm brook*, separated by a footpath from the *Cold brook;* both of which unite in the *Warm pond*, $\frac{1}{2}$ M. from Burtscheid.

The ***Lousberg,** a wooded eminence 200 ft. in height, 2 M. distant from the Rhenish station, and $\frac{3}{4}$ M. from the Pont-Thor, is intersected with walks and pleasure grounds; at its base is the *Felsenbierkeller* (rock beer-cellar, p. 6). The summit commands a fine survey of the busy town and environs of Aix-la-Chapelle and the undulating country in the vicinity; to the E. is the rich, grassy *Soersthal*, with numerous country residences and coal-mines. The white *Wallfahrtskirche* (pilgrims' church), on the adjacent *Salvatorberg*, is a conspicuous object in the landscape.

The **Frankenburg** (p. 12) which is situated 1 M. to the E. of the station, was once a hunting seat of Charlemagne. The ancient ivy-grown tower belongs to the original building, but the principal part dates from 1642. The pond which surrounds the castle was once a large lake, in which, according to an ancient tradition, the magic ring of *Fastrada* (R. 35), the last wife of Charlemagne, was sunk, and attracted the monarch to this spot, where he sat for whole days gazing pensively on the lake, and mourning for his lost consort.

About $^3/_4$ M. farther in the same direction is **Trimborn,** a grove where a Roman legion-stone and a gigantic sarcophagus were discovered. The artificial ruin at the entrance is constructed of the fragments of a chapel of the time of Charlemagne.

A marble monument, erected on the Treves road, a few minutes' walk to the S. of the town, marks the spot where the three monarchs met in 1818 to express their gratitude for the victory of Leipsic.

The grounds and promenades of the **Carlshöhe,** $^3/_4$ M. from *Ronheide* (station on the line towards Belgium), afford the finest view of Aix-la-Chapelle.

In the vicinity of the *Geul-viaduct* (on the line towards Belgium, $3^3/_4$ M. to the S.W. of Aix-la-Chapelle) stands the ancient castle of **Emmaburg,** from which Eginhard, the private secretary of Charlemagne, is said to have abducted the princess Emma. Near it are the extensive cadmia mines and zinc foundries of the society *Vieille Montagne,* in the parish of *Moresnet,* neutral ground belonging to Prussia and Belgium in common.

3. From Aix-la-Chapelle to Düsseldorf, Crefeld, and Ruhrort.

By Railway to Düsseldorf in $2^1/_2$ hrs.; fares: 2 Thlr. 9, 1 Thlr. 22. or 21 Sgr.; to Ruhrort in $3^3/_4$ hrs.: fares: 2 Thlr. 25, 2 Thlr. 4, or 26 Sgr.

This line forms the N.W. side of the triangle described by it in conjunction with the Cologne and Aix-la-Chapelle, and the Cologne and Crefeld lines. Travellers proceeding by this route from Aix-la-Chapelle to Düsseldorf effect a saving of 1 hr., and, on the journey to Oberhausen and Berlin, of 2 hrs. The second-class carriages are not inferior to those of the first class on the Rhenish-Belgian line. The country which is traversed presents little to interest the tourist in search of the picturesque, but is, in a commercial point of view, a district of great importance, and one of the most industrial and densely populated (720 inhab. to 1 sq. M.) in Prussia.

The line has two stations at Aix-la-Chapelle, one at the *Marschierthor,* near the Rhenish station, another at the *Templerbend,* near the *Pont-Thor.* It intersects the walls of the

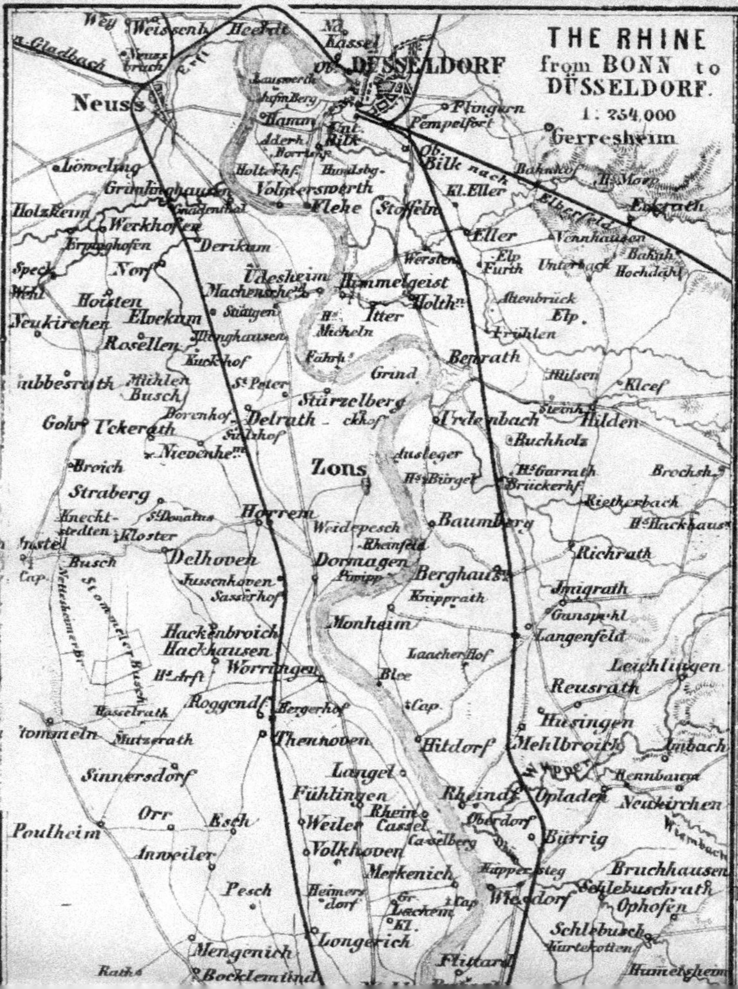
THE RHINE
from BONN to
DÜSSELDORF.
1 : 254,000
DÜSSELDORF
Neuss
Gerresheim
Flingern
Pempelfort
Bilk
Hamm
Kl. Eller
Eller
Volmerswerth
Grimlinghausen
Holzheim
Werkhofen
Derikum
Norf
Üdesheim
Himmelgeist
Itter
Benrath
Hilden
Stürzelberg
Delrath
Zons
Baumberg
Horrem
Dormagen
Berghausen
Richrath
Immigrath
Langenfeld
Monheim
Hackenbroich
Hackhausen
Worringen
Roggendorf
Reusrath
Leichlingen
Hüsingen
Mehlbroich
Thenhoven
Hitdorf
Opladen
Neukirchen
Langel
Fühlingen
Rheindorf
Bürrig
Sinnersdorf
Orr
Esch
Poulheim
Weiler
Volkhoven
Merkenich
Bruchhausen
Schlebuschrath
Ophofen
Wiesdorf
Pesch
Longerich
Schlebusch
Mengenich
Flittard
Bocklemünd
Straberg
Delhoven
Broich
Gohr
Uckerath
Rosellen
Elvekum
Hoisten
Neukirchen
Löveling

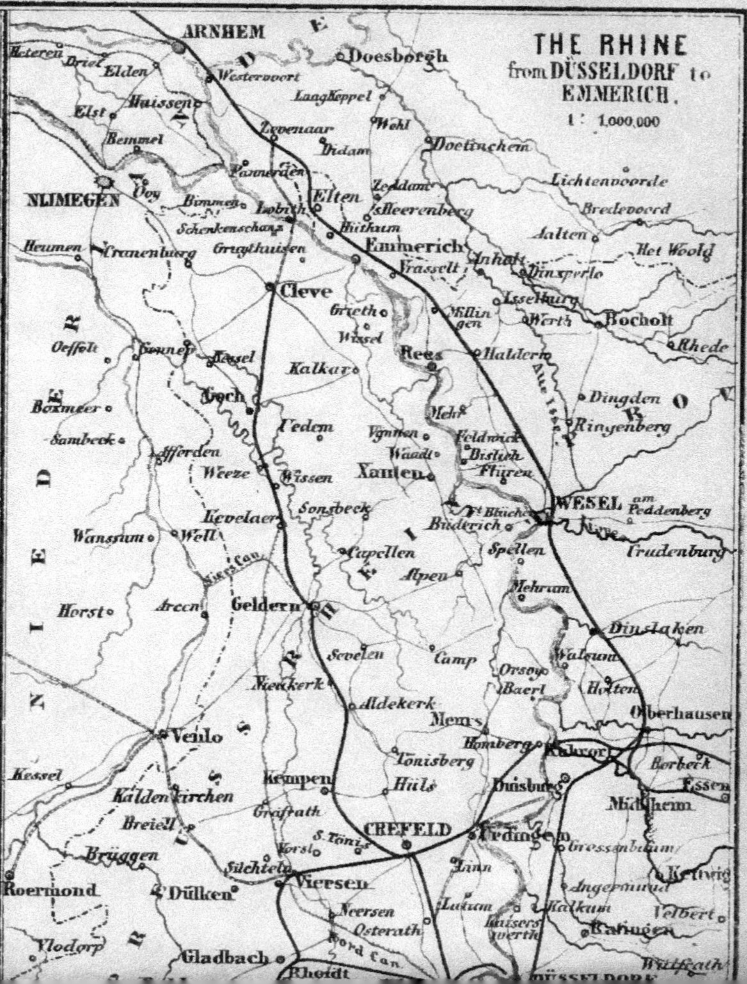
THE RHINE
from DÜSSELDORF to
EMMERICH.
1 : 1,000,000
ARNHEM
Doesborgh
NIMEGEN
Elst
Bemmel
Doetinchem
Lichtenvoorde
Bredevoord
Aalten
Het Woold
Elten
Emmerich
Cleve
Bocholt
Rhede
Rees
Kalkar
Goch
Kessel
Uedem
Dingden
Ringenberg
Xanten
Weeze
Wissen
WESEL
Büderich
Kevelaer
Sonsbeck
Capellen
Alpen
Wansum
Well
Horst
Arcen
Geldern
Dinslaken
Sevelen
Camp
Nieukerk
Aldekerk
Orsoy
Baerl
Oberhausen
Mörs
Homberg
Ruhrort
Venlo
Kempen
Tönisberg
Hüls
Duisburg
Essen
Mülheim
Kaldenkirchen
Kessel
CREFELD
Uerdingen
Grefrath
Brüggen
Süchteln
Viersen
Roermond
Dülken
Neersen
Osterrath
Lank
Kaiserswerth
Ratingen
Velbert
Kettwig
Gladbach
Rheidt
Vlodorp

WESTPHÄLISCHE EISENBAHNEN.
Mafsst 1: 1000 000
CÖLN-
DÜSSELDORF-
AACHENER EISENBAHN.
Mafsstab 1: 1000 000
2 Meilen
English miles
Kilometres
CÖLN
BONN
Brühl
Mülheim
Deutz
Siegburg
DÜSSELDORF
ELBERFELD
Barmen
Essen
Dortmund
Duisburg
Neuss
AACHEN
Düren
Jülich
Erkelenz
Gladbach

town and passes by the foot of the Lousberg (p. 9). At **Richterich** the *Mastricht line* diverges to the l. and joins the Liége and Löwen line at *Landen.* (From Aix-la-Chapelle to Mastrieht in 1 hr.)

At **Kohlscheid**, opposite to **Bardenberg**, both mining villages, the line begins to descend the pretty and animated *Wurmthal*, at the extremity of which **Herzogenrath** (French *Rolduc*) with its old castle, situated 200 ft. lower than the last-mentioned stations, is reached. On the heights to the l. is seen the ancient abbey of *Klosterrath.*

Near **Geilenkirchen** are seen the castles of *Rimburg*, *Zweibrüggen*, and beyond it, *Trips.* The train now leaves the Wurm, traverses the fertile and undulating Duchy of Jülich, crosses the grassy plain of the *Roer* between **Lindern** and **Baal**, passes **Erkelenz**, an ancient town with fine church of the 14th cent., and a ruined castle, **Wickrath**, and **Rheydt** (*Krüsemann*).

Schloss Dyck, seat of the Prince of Salm-Reifferscheid-Dyck, with beautiful park and grounds, contains one of the finest collections of cacti in Europe, (*Inn opp. to the gate of the château). *Schloss Liedberg*, on an eminence 3 M. N. from the latter, commands an extensive view.

Gladbach, or *München-Gladbach* (*Herfs*), **Viersen** (*Hilgers*), the next stations, as well as the neighbouring towns of **Odenkirchen** (*Krosch*), **Dülken** (*Siemes*), and **Süchteln** (*Horst*), lie in one of the richest manufacturing districts in Germany, which previous to the American war annually imported upwards of 4 million pounds of cotton-yarn from England, and can boast of one of the most considerable silk and velvet manufactories (at Viersen) on the continent, as well as numerous other branches of industry. The workmen employed in these establishments are an industrious and thriving race, and generally own the cottages and gardens they occupy.

At *Gladbach* the line to **Kleinenbruch**, **Neuss** (p. 39), **Obercassel**, and **Düsseldorf**, diverges off to the r.

The Crefeld train continues in a N. direction, crosses the *North Canal*, commenced by Napoleon as a means of communication between the Rhine at Neuss and the Meuse, and reaches **Crefeld** (**Oberheim*, R. and B. 18 Sgr., D. inc. W. 20 Sgr.; **Wilder Mann*), seat of the principal silk and velvet manufactories in Prussia. The quantity of raw silk imported in 1853, principally from Turin and Milan, exceeded 750,000 lbs. The Crefeld fabrics, worth 1,500,000*l.* annually, vie with those of Lyons in quality and finish, and are largely exported to America.

The population (14,000 in 1835) now amounts to 51,000, of whom 13,000 are Protestants, and 1000 Anabaptists; the latter settled here, where they found protection under the Princes of Orange (1600—1702), when they were banished from the

Duchies of Jülich and Berg. In 1702 Crefeld and the adjacent County of Meurs became Prussian. In June 1758 Prince Ferdinand of Brunswick gained a victory over the French under the Prince of Bourbon-Condé in the vicinity of Crefeld. The battle field is marked by a monument. (Railway to Cologne see R. 11).

The train next passes **Uerdingen**, a manufacturing town on the Rhine, and reaches **Homberg**, the terminus of the line. Passengers are conveyed by steamboats from here to **Ruhrort** (* *Cleve Hotel*), to the station of the Cologne and Minden railway, on the opposite bank of the river.

The *Ruhr*, which unites with the Rhine at Ruhrort, forms an excellent harbour, capable of accommodating 400 vessels, the best river-haven in Germany. The productive coal-mines of the Ruhr yield 1¼ million tons annually, about half of which is exported to Holland and the remainder conveyed in barges, towed by tug-steamers, of which Ruhrort alone possesses 16, to the Upper Rhine. Opposite to the station are the extensive iron-works (6 blast, and 108 puddling furnaces) of the Phœnix Company. From Ruhrort by a branch line to **Oberhausen** (p. 24), a station on the main line, in 20 min.

4. From Aix-la-Chapelle to Cologne.

By the Rhenish Railway in 1½—2 hrs.; fares: 2 Thlr. 15, 1 Thlr. 25, and 1 Thlr. 8 Sgr. Return-tickets valid only for day of issue and day following.

Few lines in Germany exhibit such varied forms of railway engineering in so short a distance as that between the Belgian frontier and Cologne. The viaducts near Aix-la-Chapelle and over the Geul and the tunnel of Königsdorf are among the most remarkable structures of the kind in Germany.

On leaving the station the train crosses the valley of the Wurm and passes close by the *Frankenburg* (on the l.), once the favourite residence of Charlemagne; it then passes through the *Nirmer Tunnel* (½ M.), traverses the *Reichsbusch* wood, and stops at the *Kambacher Mühle*, the stat. for the flourishing and rapidly increasing town of **Stolberg** (*Hissel; Welter*).

The mines of Stollberg and its environs were first worked in the 17th cent. by the Protestants who were banished from France and Aix-la-Chapelle, and to them the town is indebted for its present prosperity. The principal products of the district are zinc, lead, and silver; there are also numerous manufactories of various descriptions, the coal for the supply of which is found in abundance in the neighbourhood. Scarcely another locality in the whole of Germany exhibits so many branches of industry within so small a space. The number of workmen employed in these different establishments amounts to upwards of 12,000, and the annual value of the zinc, lead, silver and coals yielded by the mines exceeds 450.000*l*.

The train now traverses a most picturesque district, with numerous coal-mines and iron-foundries, crosses the *Inde* and enters a tunnel, on emerging from which, it stops at

Stat. **Eschweiler** (*Raisin*), a manufacturing town. Farther on, to the l., near the village of *Nothberg*, lies the *Röttgen Schloss*, an old castle with four towers. The pottery village of **Langerwehe**, on the hillside, now comes in sight. To the r., on the hills, are several villages, among which is *Werth*, said to have been the birthplace of the celebrated imperial general Johann von Werth, who gained many victories over the French and Swedes in the 30 years' war, and in July, 1636, even penetrated as far as Paris itself. The blue mountains in the distance to the r. are the spurs of the *Eifel*.

To the r. the view is now bounded by the *Hochwald*, a long ridge of hills, from which in the distance rises the variegated sandstone peak of *Burgberg*. At the base of the wooded heights lies the village of *Merode* with a handsome old turreted castle of the same name, seat of a wealthy Belgian family. The *Roer* is next crossed, and the train stops at

Stat. **Düren** (*Bellevue*), the *Marcodurum* of Tacitus, a busy, manufacturing town, situated in a fertile plain. Beyond stat. **Buir**, the church-spire of *Kerpen* is seen to the r. Stat. **Horrem** is situated in the luxuriant vale of the *Erft*. On the l. stand the castles of *Frenz* and *Hemmersbach* or *Horrem*. This valley abounds with castles of the Rhenish nobility, who have founded an institution for the education of their sons at *Bedburg*, 6 M. to the N.W. of Horrem. The valley of the Erft is soon quitted by the Königsdorf tunnel, 1 M. in length, on emerging from which

Stat. **Königsdorf** is reached. Farther on, to the r. in the distance, is seen the village of *Brauweiler*, with its ancient Benedictine Abbey, now a reformatory and workhouse. The old *Abbey Church*, erected at the commencement of the 13th cent., in the late Romanesque style, contains an engraved tombstone of the 15th cent., and some ancient frescoes on the vaulted ceiling of the chapter-house, both valuable in the history of art.

As Cologne is approached the line traverses a rich and fertile plain, studded with detached houses and factories. The hills to the r. are the spurs of the Vorgebirge, a low range of hills which commence on the l. bank of the Rhine between Cologne and Bonn. Cologne s. R. 10.

5. From Rotterdam to Düsseldorf.

By Steamboat daily (Düsseldorf Co. dep. at 6, Netherlands Co. at 8 a.m.; the former in connection with the Gen. Steam Nav. Co. three times a week, the latter with the "Batavia" once a week, in 24 hrs.; less fatiguing and expensive than by railway; fares: 2 Thlr. 4, 1 Thlr. 13 Sgr.; 100 lbs. of luggage free.

By railway in $6^3/_4$ hrs.; fares: 6 Thlr. 16, 4 Thlr. 22, and 3 Thlr. $9^1/_2$ Sgr. The principal stations are Gonda, Arnheim, Emmerich (Prussian custom-house), Wesel and Oberhausen.

Rotterdam (*New Bath Hotel; *St. Lucas; Arend; Adler's Engl. and American Hotel; Weimer; Verhaaren; the last two for travellers of moderate requirements), see *Baedeker's Belgique et Hollande.*

Soon after the steamer has quitted the "*Boompjes*" or quay, with its handsome rows of houses and animated traffic, the machine-factory and wharf of

r. *Fijenoord* is reached. It belongs to the Netherlands Steamboat Co. and employs upwards of 700 hands. Permission to inspect this interesting estab. may be obtained from the director M. van Oord at Rotterdam. Ferry-boat to Rotterdam every quarter of an hour, fare 5 cents.

l. *Kralingen*, with extensive salmon-fishery; the utmost care is here employed to ensure the security of the dykes which confine the river.

r. *Ysselmonde*, opp. to the influx of the *Yssel* (not to be confounded with the river of that name in Guelders) into the Meuse (Maas). The turreted château in the vicinity belonged to a former burgomaster of Rotterdam.

r. *'t Huis ten Donk*, a handsome country residence, surrounded by trees which extend to the water's edge.

l. *Krimpen*, near the confluence of the Leck (as the Rhine is here termed) and the Meuse.

r. *Kinderdijk*, a long row of neat houses, with numerous windmills, derives its name (= children's dyke) from a tradition that some children in a cradle were here landed in safety during an inundation.

l. *Lekkerkerk*, protected by long dykes from the inundations of the Leck.

r. *Streefkerk*, with a picturesque church.

l. *Schoonhoven;* r. *Nieuwpoort.*

r. *Ameyde*, where the *Zederick* Canal intersects the entire island of *Betuwe;* l. *Jaarsveld.*

l. *Vreeswyk*, whence on the arrival of the steamboats a diligence runs to Utrecht, and also a passenger-boat on the canal which here connects Utrecht with the Rhine. Vreeswyk is the limit of the rise and fall of the tide.

r. *Vianen* (Brederode). Between this and Culenborg are water-gates or sluices, by means of which the entire district may be laid under water in case of a hostile invasion. To the r., and farther on, to the l., are situated two fortified block-houses, constructed for the defence of the river.

r. *Culenborg*, with its low tower, surrounded by wood, was once the seat of the powerful counts of that name, who acted a prominent part in the struggles of the Dutch in 1566 to liberate themselves from the Spanish yoke.

l. *Wyk by Duurstede,* now a fortress, the *Batavodurum* of the Romans, was in the time of Charlemagne a flourishing commercial town. The steamboat here enters the Rhine, properly so called. The narrow river which diverges to the l. retains the name of Rhine, and passing by Utrecht and Leyden, empties itself into the North Sea.

l. The tower of *Amerongen;* then *Elst,* a long straggling village.

l. *Rhenen* (König von Böhmen) possesses a Gothic church, the tower of which, erected between 1492 and 1531, is the finest in Holland.

Halfway between Rhenen and Wageningen rises the *Heimenberg* (*Ridder), a slight eminence commanding an extensive view. The *Königssitz,* a bench on the summit, derives its name from Frederick, Count Palatine and king of Bohemia, who having been expelled from his territory after a battle near Prague in 1620, repaired to Rhenen, where he lived in retirement under the protection of his uncle Prince Maurice of Orange.

r. *Opheusden,* with a flying bridge.

l. *Wageningen,* a small but ancient town of some importance, connected with the Rhine by a canal, and situated 4½ M. from the railway stat. *Ede.*

r. The villages of *Renkum* and *Heteren.*

The banks now become more elevated and picturesque; the district to the l. is termed the *Veluwe,* to the r. the *Betuwe,* signifying respectively the barren and the fruitful tract. To the l. the castle of *Doorenwaard* with its two towers; beyond it *Duinhoog;* then *Oosterbeek,* with several villas, birthplace of the Emp. Henry III. (1017). To the r. the spire of the village of *Elsen;* then the small castle of *Meinerswijk.* The wooded chain of hills to the l., as Arnheim is approached, is sprinkled with country residences.

l. **Arnheim.** (**Zon*, outside the N.W. gate, the nearest to the railway stat. and the pier of the Netherlands Co.; **Zwynshoofd* [*Schweinskopf*, boar's head, a sign frequently seen in Holland] in the town; **Hôtel de Bellevue; *Hôtel des Pays-Bas*, near the pier of the Düsseldorf Co.; *de Pauuw*, not far from the stat. good 2nd cl. house.) — Arnheim with a pop. of 20,904 (½ Rom. Cath.), was long the seat of the Dukes of Guelders, and is still the capital of the province of that name. An ancient proverb describes the inhabitants as: "*Hoog van moed, klein van goed, een zwaard in de hand, is 't wapen van Gelderland*" (High of mood, little of good, sword in hand, is the coat of arms of Guelderland). The town, situated on the S. slopes of the chain of hills of the Veluwe, was newly fortified after its capture by the French in 1672. In 1813 the French, who again occupied the town and possessed a strongly fortified camp in the vicinity, were expelled by the Prussians.

Although a good specimen of a clean Dutch town, it offers little to detain the traveller. The *Groote Kerk* (large church) contains several monuments of Dukes of Guelders. The *Town Hall* derives its local appellation of *Duivelshuis* (devil's house) from the grotesque figures with which it is adorned.

The environs far surpass those of any other Dutch town. The estate of * *Hartjesberg*, the property of a wealthy Dutch gentleman, deserves a visit (entrance near the railway stat., $\frac{1}{2}$ M. to the N. of the town). The park and grounds are open to the public; the traveller, however, is recommended to apply to the custodian (at the lodge), for the sake of gaining access to the Belvedere, or tower, the prospect from which will amply repay the ascent.

Immediately below the town is situated the *Rehberg*, a slight eminence laid out as pleasure-grounds. Higher up is the country-seat *Heidenoord* (or "*de Koepel,*" = cupola); in the adjoining wood are walks and benches in all directions. In the opp. direction, 3 M. to the E. of Arnheim, lies the flourishing village of *Velp*, the hills near which are studded with elegant country residences and pleasure-grounds.

To the l. the *Yssel* diverges to the N. and flows into the Zuider Zee. To the r. *Huissen.*

l. *Haus Loo,* or *Candia,* an old castle; then the village of *Pannerden.*

Near the village of *Millingen* a small gun-boat, moored in the middle of the stream, indicates the vicinity of the frontier.

l. *Lobith,* the last Dutch village; opp. to it lies the ancient frontier of *Schenkenschanz,* formerly considered the key of the Netherlands, and once situated at the bifurcation (now lower down) of the Waal and the Rhine. Near this spot Louis XIV. crossed the river, at that time nearly dry in consequence of the unusual heat, June 12th, 1672, with a large army, for the purpose of conquering Holland. On this occasion the Prince of Condé was wounded. As *Emmerich* is approached, the wooded heights on which the town of *Cleve* (p. 17 and 39) is situated, are perceived to the r.

l. **Emmerich** *(Holländischer Hof)*, the frontier town of Prussia, clean, and possessing as many Dutch as German features. The *Münster* church, at the lower extremity of the town, is in the transition style of the 11th—12th cent.

(Railway by *Arnheim* and *Utrecht* to *Amsterdam* in 4 hrs.; fares 3 Thlr. 16½, 2 Thlr. 20, or 1 Thlr. 23¼ Sgr.)

r. *Grieth.*

l. *Rees,* once strongly fortified.

r. **Xanten** (*Ingenlath*), 2¼ M. from the Rhine, is a town of great antiquity, and was the *Castra vetera* and *Colonia Ulpia* of the Romans, the head-quarters of the 30th (*Ulpia victrix*), the 18th, and 19th Legions, which were destroyed in the battle of the Teutoburgian wood. Here too stood the castle of the Nibelungen, and here Siegfried the dragon-slayer (p. 49) was born. On the *Fürstenberg*, an eminence in the vicinity, was situated the Prætorium of Quintilius Varus. The **Collegiate church of St. Victor*, erected in 1213—1522, is a masterpiece of Gothic architecture. The choir, locked by a fine copper gate, is worthy of attention; the cloisters contain several tombstones valuable in the history of art.

The traveller descending the river who wishes to proceed direct to Cleve should here leave the steamboat and take a carriage (1½ Thlr.) to **Calcar**, the Gothic church of which contains a remarkably fine altar-piece by Johann of Calcar, and below it some admirably carved wood-work. Calcar was the birth-place of the celebrated Prussian General von Seydlitz (d. 1773), the conqueror at the battle of Rossbach. A handsome monument to this hero stands in the market-place.

l. **Wesel** (**Dornbusch*), a strongly fortified town, with a population of 13,000 (7000 Rom. Cath.), is situated at the confluence of the Rhine and Lippe. The Rathhaus, or Town-hall, is a handsome building, and dates from 1396. St. Willibrord's church contains a marble tablet which records that Peregrine Bertie, son of Willoughby d'Eresby and Catharine, Duchess of Suffolk, was born here in 1555. The exiles, who were Protestants, and had fled from the persecutions of Queen Mary, were permitted by the magistrates of Wesel, as no other residence could be found, to take up their quarters in the church, which was then unoccupied. — The boat then passes through the bridge which connects the *Island of Büderich* with Fort Blücher, the tête-de-pont of Wesel on the r.

r. *Orsoy,* formerly fortified and frequently besieged.

l. *Ruhrort* (p. 12), at the influx of the Ruhr, where the boats of the Netherlands Co. only touch.

r. *Homberg* (p. 12), terminus of the Aix-la-Chapelle line, where the Düsseldorf Co.'s boats touch.

r. *Uerdingen* (p. 12), whence the church-tower of Duisburg (p. 20) is visible rising from the plain.

l. *Kaiserswerth* (p. 19). The walls and bow-windows of an old castle of the Hohenstaufen are visible from the river.

l. *Düsseldorf.*

6. Düsseldorf.

Hotels. Prince of Prussia, Prince Frederick and European Hotel, near the station. *Breidenbacher Hof, Drei Reichskronen and Hôtel Domhardt, in the town; charges: R. 15, B. 8, D. 20 Sgr. — *Kölner Hof; *Römischer Kaiser, a good second-class house (R. and B. 20, good table d'hôte 17 Sgr.)

Cafés. Geisler, in the Mittelstrasse and on the Ananasberg in the Hofgarten; Jungius, Burgplatz 11, good supply of newspapers. The summer-theatre and the Harmonie Hall, where the musical festivals are held once a year, as well as "Geisler's Garden" (refreshments), now belong to the town.

Restaurants. Railway refreshment room at the Cologne-Minden station; *Stelzmann, opp. to the station; *Seulen, *Drevermann and Germer in the Carlsplatz. Railway refreshment room at the Elberfeld station.

Exhibition of art in the Alleestrasse, 781; admission 5 Sgr.

Carriages. For a drive in the down 5 Sgr., 1/2 hr. 10, 1 hr. 15 Sgr.

English Church Service performed by a resident chaplain in the smaller Protestant Church, Bergerstrasse.

Düsseldorf (46,849 inhab., of whom 8604 are Prot., and 600 Jews) is a handsome and regularly-built town of comparatively modern origin. It was chosen at the commencement of the 15th cent. as a residence by the Dukes of Berg, and on their becoming extinct in 1609, it continued to be the residence of the princes of the Palatinate till 1716, when they transferred their seat to Mannheim and afterwards to Munich. Under Joachim Murat (1806—8), and Napoleon (1808—13), Düsseldorf continued to be the capital town of the Duchy of Berg; in 1815 it became subject to the crown of Prussia.

Düsseldorf may be called the Rhenish cradle of art; its **Academy of Art** (Pl. 2) conducted (1822—26) by Cornelius, up to 1860 by Schadow (d. 1861) and subsequently by Bendemann, enjoys a widely extended celebrity. It is situated in one of the wings of the Electoral palace, rebuilt since its almost total destruction by the French in 1794.

All the valuable pictures of the once so celebrated Düsseldorf *Gallery*, founded at the beginning of the 18th cent. were, during the unsettled times of 1805, taken to Munich by Max. Joseph, king of Bavaria, under the pretext of ensuring their safety. The town has since then been unable to recover them, and they form to this day the most valuable part of the collection in the old Pinakothek.

The Gallery now contains a valuable collection of upwards of 14,000 original sketches and drawings by the most celebrated artists of all schools, and 248 water-colour copies of Italian masters by *Ramboux*, affording a good survey of Italian art from the 14th to the 16th cent. It also contains a few good pictures.

The *Town-Collection (admission 5 Sgr., open from 9 to 6 o' clock) in the r. wing of the Academy, recently commenced, contains some fine modern pictures.

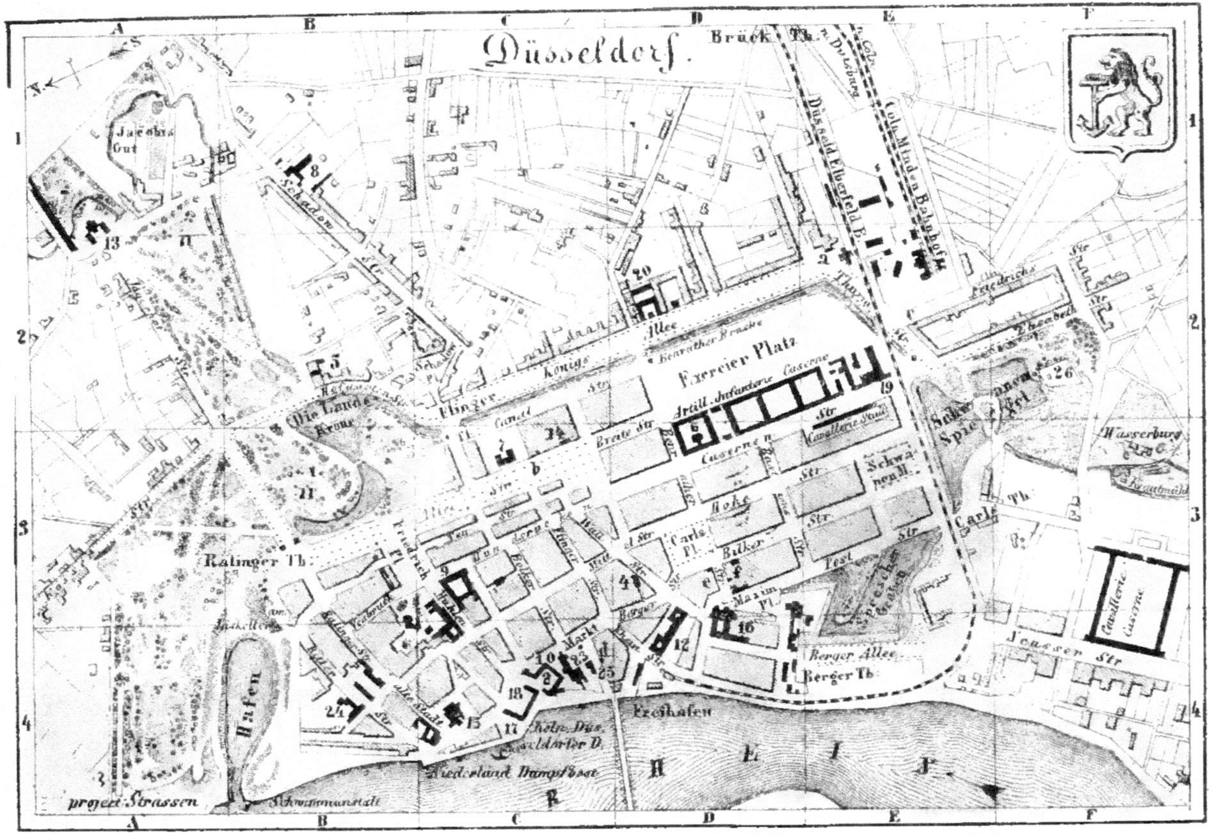

d. drei Reichskron C.4. e. Domhard D.3. f. Röm. Kaiser D.3.

Zahlen Erklärung

1. Ananas Berg (Restaur.)	B.3.
2. Altes Schloss	C.4.
3. Botan. Garten	B.2.
4. Evangel. Kirche	D.3.
5. Friedrichsbad	B.2.
6. Garnisons Kirche	D.3.
7. Gymnasium	C.3.
8. Geisler's Garten	B.1.
9. Hof Kirche	C.3.
10. Hauptwache	C.4.
11. Hofgarten	B.3.
12. Justizgebäude u. Arresthaus	D.4.
13. Jägerhof	A.1.
14. Kunstausstellung (permanente)	C.3.
15. Lamb. Pfarr Kirche	C.4.
16. Maxim. Pfarrk.	D.4.
17. Malerschule	C.4.
18. Mauth	C.4.
19. Postamt	E.2.
20. Posthalterei	D.2.
21. Präsid. d. k. Regierung	C.3.
22. Regierungs Geb.	C.3.
23. Rathhaus	C.4.
24. Ursuliner Kirche u. Kloster	B.4.
25. Theater	C.4.
26. Neue Anlagen	F.2.

Gasthöfe

a. Prinz v. Preussen	E.2.
b. Breidenbacher Hof	C.3.
c. Europ. Hof	E.2.

The palace contains a **Library**, of some value; in the court is a marble statue of the Elector Johann Wilhelm, who was born in Düsseldorf (d. 1716). An * **Equestrian statue** of the same elector stands in the market-place.

The churches of Düsseldorf present few features of architectural interest. That of **St. Andreas** (Pl. 9) contains several good modern pictures, and in a separate hall of the choir the embalmed remains of several electors, princes, and princesses of the place. **St. Lambertus** (Pl. 15) belongs to the transition style of the 14th cent., and contains a marble monument to the last two dukes of Cleves and Berg, erected in 1629. On one of the N. pillars is the tombstone of the celebrated chancellor *Melchior Voetz* (*Voetius*) (d. 1675).

The handsome new **Post-office** buildings, near the railway stations, are erected in the Florentine palatial style; the black marble pillars which support the steps were brought from the Neanderthal (p. 20).

The * **Hofgarten** (Pl. 11) is tastefully laid out, and affords most delightful walks. Near the entrance is situated a large hot-house for tropical plants (*Victoria-Regia-Haus*); near it a black marble pillar with bust of Queen *Stephanie of Portugal*, a princess of Hohenzollern (d. 1860). — The **Jägerhof** is fitted up as a princely residence, and was till 1848 seat of Prince Frederick of Prussia; since 1850 it has been occupied by the Prince of Hohenzollern-Sigmaringen. — The adjoining **Jacobi's Garden** was once the property of the eminent philosopher Fred. Henry Jacobi (d. 1819), and a favourite resort of many of the greatest men of the day, of Goethe and Herder among others. It now belongs to a society of artists, and is the central point of their social life.

In the vicinity of Düsseldorf there are several excellent Protestant institutions of various kinds. **Düsselthal,** formerly a Trappist monastery, situated near the Cologne and Minden line, a little to the N. of the town, is now converted into a Protestant establishment for homeless children, 180—200 of whom are here educated. Connected with the institution is a seminary for teachers of the poor.

The ancient town of **Kaiserswerth** (*Pfälzer Hof*), 1½ M. W. from the **Calcum** station, which the train from Düsseldorf reaches in 20 min., is the seat of similar charitable institutions on a much greater scale than those above mentioned. They were founded by the Protestant pastor *Fliedner* in 1836, and comprise a hospital (500—600 patients), a training school for Protestant Sisters of Charity, Governesses' institution, orphan asylum, female Reformatory, and establishment for the cure of female lunatics.

The old *Church* of Kaiserswerth, in the Romanesque style, erected in the 12th—13th cent., contains an admirably executed *Shrine* of the 13th cent., in which the relics of *St. Suitbertus*, who first preached the Gospel here in 710, are preserved. Of the ancient palace in which the Emperor Henry IV. once resided nothing is now left but a few fragments, called the "Königsburg".

In the wood to the l. of the station of **Grossenbaum** is the *Castle of Heltorf*, property of Count Spee, which contains various treasures of art, among which may be mentioned some **frescoes* of the older Düsseldorf school.

Duisburg (*Rheinischer Hof*), the next station, is also a very ancient town, fortified by Charlemagne, from 1145—1201 Imperial town, then a member of the Hanseatic league, and till 1818 seat of a university founded in 1655. The *Salvatorkirche* is a handsome Gothic edifice of the 15th century. Population 14,000 (Rom. Cath. 5000). The *Rhenish-Westphalian Institution for Deacons*, whose duty is to assist the clergy in attendance on the sick, convicts, &c., connected with a hospital, school for homeless boys, and Reformatory (the latter at *Lintorf*, 6 M. distant), is a Protestant establishment, and has a widely-extended sphere of utility.

7. From Düsseldorf to Dortmund by Elberfeld.

Comp. Map R. 4.

By Railway in 3—4 hrs.; fares: 72, 53, or 35 Sgr. (comp, p. 23). The district traversed is picturesque and industrial; the grand construction of the line itself is an object of interest. Views to the l.

The station is by the "Prince of Prussia" hotel (p. 18). From the convent of **Gerresheim** (first station, fine church of the 12th cent.), the Archbishop Gebhard of Cologne (d. 1601) abducted the beautiful Countess Agnes of Mansfeld. After passing **Erkrath** (hydropathic estab.), the train ascends a steep acclivity to **Hochdahl** (large iron-foundry of *Eintracht*), which lies 480 ft. higher than Düsseldorf.

One mile to the l. of Hochdahl is situated the romantic **Neanderthal** (**Steineshof; Holthöfer*), a narrow wooded ravine through which the *Düssel* flows. The valley contains several limestone caverns, the largest of which, 90 ft. long, 40 ft. broad, and 16 ft. high, was a favorite resort of the eminent Protestant preacher and poet *Joachim Neander*, who lived at Düsseldorf from 1640 to 1660, and from whom the valley derives its name. This cavern is best visited from the Steineshof, from which it is $^3/_4$ M. distant. The quarries of the valley yield black and grey marble, which is cut into monuments, vases, &c.

At **Vohwinkel** (stat. for *Gräfrath* and *Solingen*) is the junction of the *Prince William* line (Steele-Vohwinkel), principally used for the coal-traffic of the Ruhr.

The *Prince William Railway traverses the mountains which form the boundary between the Wupper and the Ruhr, then continues along the narrow winding valley of the *Deile,* and at Dilldorf enters the broad and picturesque valley of the Ruhr, which affords a most striking contrast to the ravine of the Deile. At the small town of Steele (*Badenberg*) the Prince William line unites with the "Bergisch-Märkisch", which now affords direct communication between *Dortmund*, *Bochum*, *Steele*, *Essen*, *Mühlheim* and *Duisburg.*

At **Sonnborn** the train suddenly enters the valley of the *Wupper*, which it traverses, and then skirts the hillside, commanding a view of Elberfeld in the valley below.

Elberfeld (**Curpfälzer Hof*; **Weidenhof*, near the Döppersberg stat.; *Mainzer Hof; Post*), with a pop. of 54,000 (12,000 Rom. Cath.), and the adjoining town of **Barmen** (*Clever Hof*), with 45,000, form together a series of streets of nearly 6. M. in length, intersected by the road, the railway, and the Wupper, which is the principal source of the industry of this flourishing manufacturing district. With the exception of some English towns, there is probably no spot in the world which is so densely populated. Its principal manufactures are cotton, silk, ribbon, and turkey-red dyed goods. Some of the churches are handsome structures, but are all, like the towns themselves, of very modern date.

One point in Elberfeld well deserves to be visited by the lovers of the picturesque — the *Elisenhöhe, situated in the *Haardt*, or so called "English Grounds," which contain a statue of *St. Suitbertus*, an Englishman who first propagated Christianity in this district (d. at Kaiserswerth in 713). The summit of the tower commands a most magnificent and peculiar view of the whole valley of the Wupper, crowded with its numerous factories, handsome private residences, and other buildings.

The train next stops at the station of **Barmen** (see above), and **Rittershausen.** At the latter the line crosses the *Wupper*, leaves the Duchy of Berg, and enters the Grafschaft Mark. The next station is **Schwelm** (*Hôtel Rosenkranz; Prinz von Preussen*), $1/2$ hr. distant from Elberfeld by railway.

Not far from the **Schwelmer Brunnen,** a mineral spring now seldom resorted to by invalids, begins a long and deep railway cutting, where numerous fossils are found; on emerging from it at **Milspe** a most striking view is obtained of the valley of the *Ennepe.* (About 1 M. up the valley from the station is situated the *Klutert*, a large stalactite cavern.)

At **Gevelsberg**, a long straggling village on the Schwelm road, Count Frederick of Isenburg slew his cousin Engelbert, Archbishop of Cologne, on his return from the Diet of knights at Soest, before which he had summoned the Count to answer for his misconduct with regard to the Abbeys of Essen aud Werden. The Count was condemned to death, and, when he was apprehended a year later, broken on the wheel at Cologne,

The valley of the *Ennepe* is also noted as a manufacturing district, and contains numerous iron-hammers and foundries, especially at the station of **Haspe.**

Hagen (*Deutsches Haus; Lünenschloss*), another manufacturing town, lies $3/4$ M. from the station. (Railway from

Hagen to Siegen, or *Ruhr-Sieg* line, see p. 41). Soon after passing it, the train crosses the *Volme*, and a second time at **Herdecke.** The view to the N. W. is here bounded by the *Ardey mountains* which descend precipitously into the valley of the Ruhr.

On one of these mountains, 4½ M. from Herdecke, rise the ruins of ***Hohen-Syburg**, once the fortress of Wittekind, the last Duke of Saxony, who for 32 years fought against Christianity and the Franconian power, till he was conquered and compelled to submit to the rite of baptism by Charlemagne in 775. The ceremony, so says the tradition, was performed by Pope Leo himself in the presence of the emperor, who became godfather to the heathen duke. The font still exists and the effigies of the emperor and Pope are still distinguishable above the door. The small church is incontestibly one of the oldest in Germany. View very fine. *Inn near the ruin. At the foot of the hill the *Lenne* falls into the Ruhr.

The train now skirts the *Kaiserberg*, where Charlemagne is said once to have had a camp. On an eminence of the r. bank of the Ruhr the picturesque village of **Wetter,** with a ruined castle, comes in view. On the opposite (l.) side, lies the picturesque village of *Volmarstein* (* *Wehberg*), with an old castle commanding a magnificent prospect, a spot much frequented by visitors from the neighbourhood. The train now crosses and follows the course of the Ruhr, and soon reaches the long straggling manufacturing and colliery-town of **Witten** (*Hotel Gräfe; * Glitz*, on the l. bank, opp. to the town). The background of the picturesque landscape is formed by the castle of *Steinhausen*, situated on a wooded eminence. Farther down the valley are the ruins of the castle of *Hardenstein*, in ancient times a seat of Wittekind (see above).

The finest point of the valley of the Ruhr is at the small town of **Blankenstein** (*Forstmann*), 6 M. from Witten. *Gethmann's Garten, situated here, commands a noble prospect of the valley, and is much resorted to by lovers of the picturesque from the neighbouring towns. From Blankenstein the traveller may proceed on foot by **Hattingen** to **Nierenhof** (4½ M.), a station on the Steele and Vohwinkel line.

The tract of country from this point to the mouth of the Ruhr at Ruhrort (p. 12) is one of the principal colliery districts in Prussia, and yields considerably more than one third of the coal consumed in the kingdom.

Dortmund (*Römischer Kaiser*, in the town; *Bellevue*, at the station; pop. 22,093, ⅓ Rom. Cath.), which is reached in 25 min. more, one of the most important stations on the Cologne and Minden line, was once an imperial town and member of the Hanseatic league, and was governed by its own counts. Some of the churches are the only buildings which still bear testimony to the antiquity of the place. The choir (1421—50) of the church of *St. Reinoldi* contains old stained-glass windows, on some of the panes of which is represented the Imperial eagle in the Westphalian colours (green, black, and white). The altar is decorated with an old carved-wood Crucifixion, with the 12 Apostles; choir-stalls in the late Gothic style of the 15th cent., pulpit, rich "renaissance" style. The lofty and elegant **Marienkirche*, nave Romanesque, choir Gothic, contains a picture, representing the Adoration of the Magi, painted at the commencement of the 15th cent. by a master of the Westphalian school, a branch of that of Cologne. The Gothic *Dominican Church* (choir 1353) also contains an altar-piece by a master of the same school, painted in 1508. The carved stone shrine near the high-altar also deserves inspection.

In the history of the middle ages Dortmund is a place of great importance. When, on the fall of Henry the Lion (1182), a complete state of anarchy and lawlessness prevailed throughout the whole of Germany, the celebrated Vehmgericht, or Secret Tribunal, was formed in Westphalia, and, in the 14th and 15th centuries, had extended its sway over the whole empire. The number of the initiated, who were bound by the most fearful oaths to execute the decrees of the tribunal, is said to have exceeded 100,000. In Westphalia alone was the *Freigraf*, or president of the society, privileged to hold meetings for the purpose of receiving new members. Dortmund was the seat of the highest court, and here, in the "*Königshof under the linden-trees*", the Emperor Sigismund was himself initiated in the year 1429. Latterly, however, the tribunal degenerated to little more than a common police-court, before which the inhabitants of Dortmund and the vicinity carried their grievances. The last session held by this society here took place in 1803.

One of the lime-trees in the Königshof at Dortmund still exists, and is believed to be upwards of 400 years old. It stands on a slight eminence to the W. of the station.

8. From Dortmund to Düsseldorf by Oberhausen.

Comp. Map R. 4.

By the Cologne and Minden line in $2^3/_4$ hrs.; fares: 64, 43, or 32 Sgr.

The journey from *Dortmund* to *Düsseldorf* by this route is less interesting than that above described. The country traversed is one of those flat agricultural tracts so characteristic of many parts of Germany, and described by Tacitus, *Germania 16.*

The principal place of interest on this line is **Essen** (*Schmidt; Sauer; Berghaus;* pop. 17,054, Prot. 6000), $1^1/_2$ M. from the station, one of the most ancient towns in the district, and till 1802 a free Imperial town. The **Münsterkirche* (with octagonal choir of the 10th cent.), founded by the Emperor Otto III., contains a curious old brazen chandelier, presented in 998 by the Abbess Mechtildis, sister of Otto III., and, among other treasures, four golden crosses, richly decorated with precious stones, presented in 974 by the Abbess Alhaidis, daughter of Otto I., and a MS. of the Gospels, with a covering of gold and carved ivory, a gift of the Abbess Theophanu (d. 1060). The *Cloisters*, as well as a fine altar-piece of 1522 by *de Bruyn*, were restored in 1850. Essen is the central point of this extensive colliery district, and is surrounded by innumerable foundries and manufactories. Of these *Krupp's Cast Steel Works* deserve especial mention; the products of this vast estab. (portions of machinery, steel cannons, etc.) have acquired a European reputation. To the S. of the town, at the Kettwiger Thor, is situated the station of the Witten-Duisburg-Oberhausen railway.

The small and picturesquely situated town of **Werden** on the Ruhr was once the seat of a very ancient Benedictine Abbey, where the "Codex argenteus," a translation of the Gospels made in the 4th cent. by order of the Gothic Bishop Ulfilas, a most valuable specimen of the ancient German language, was formerly preserved. It fell into the hands of the Swedes in the 30 years' war, and is now deposited at the university of Upsala. The * *Church* deserves particular inspection, especially the beautiful portal on the N. side. The crypt (1059) contains the stone sarcophagus of St. Ludgerus (d. 809), the first bishop of Münster.

Near **Oberhausen** (*Railway refreshment-room) is one of the most extensive foundries in this district, which employs 1600 men and contains 8 different steam-engines. The land is poor and sterile, but its richness in coal renders it in many places worth 700—800*l.* per acre.

Oberhausen is the most animated station on the line, and is daily passed by about 80 trains.

9. From Düsseldorf to Cologne.

Comp. Map R. 4.

By the Cologne and Minden Railway in $1^1/_4$ hr.; fares: 30, 20, and 15 Sgr. The express trains stop at the Central station at Cologne, the ordinary at Deutz (p. 38). — By steamboat in 5 hrs. (down in $2^1/_2$ hrs.). Conveyances see p. 18.

Beyond stat. **Benrath** stands a handsome royal *Palace* among the trees to the l., erected in 1756—60 by the Elector Palatine Charles as a residence for his widow. Beyond stat. **Langenfeld** the line crosses the *Wupper* (p. 21), passes close by the castle of *Reuschenberg* (to the l.), and at stat. **Küppersteg** crosses the *Dühn*. The river is approached at **Mülheim**, a wealthy, manufacturing town, which owes its prosperity to the Prot. citizens who emigrated from Cologne at the beginning of the 17th cent. Below the town, on the Rhine, lies *Schloss Stammheim*, a seat of Count Fürstenberg, containing an extensive collection of engravings and portraits.

The steamboat-journey from Düsseldorf to Cologne in somewhat tedious; the Rhine here presents no features of natural beauty, though some of the places on its banks possess an historical interest.

Köln.
1 Allerheiligen Capelle H.5.
2 Bank E.4.
3 Bahnhof (Central Pers.) G.5.
4 Bürger Hospital E.4.
5 Casino E.5.
6 Casernen C3. F3. E3. H4.5.6.
7 Civil Arresthaus H.3.
8 Diorama F.3.
9 Dom G.5.
10 Elend (de Grootesche FK.) C.6.
11 Evangelische Kirche E.4.
12 Erzbischöfl. Palais G.3.
13 Festungs Bauhof C.3.
14 Garnisons Lazareth A.5.
15 Gürzenich (Kaufhaus) E.5.
16 Gymnasium (Fr. Wilhelm) C.5.
17 Gymnasium (Jesuiten) G.4.
18 Hauptwache F.6.
19 Jabach'sches Haus E.5
20 Jesuiten Kirche G.5.
21 Justiz Pal. (Appellh) G.4.
22 Museum F.4.
23 Polizei Direction F.4.
24 Postamt F.3.
25 Priester Seminar H.5.
26 Rathhaus F.5.
27 Regierungs Pal. G.3.
28 St. Alban E.5.
29 St. Andreas G.4.
30 St. Aposteln E.2.
31 St. Cäcilien E.4.
32 St. Columba F.4.
33 St. Cunibert I.6.
Gasthöfe
a Hôtel Disch F.4.
b Mainzer Hof F.4.
c Wiener Hof F.4.
d Holländ. Hof E.6.
e Köln. Hof E.6.
f Königl. Hof E.6.
g Hôtel de Russie E.6.
h Hôtel du Nord G.6.
s Hôtel du Dôme G.5.
t Hôtel Victoria E.6.
Hahnen Thor
Weyer Thor
nach Bonn
Schützengraben
Promenaden
Neu Markt
Heu Markt
Holzmarkt
Neues Th.
Severin Thor
Bayen Th.
Bayenthurm
Bayenhaus
Sicherheits Hafen
Rhein Au
Bayen Strasse
Badeschiffe
RHEIN
Köln Düsseldorfer Dampfboote
Siegburger Thor
Hafen
Lith. Anst. v. Ed. Wagner Darmstadt
Maassstab
100 50 0 100

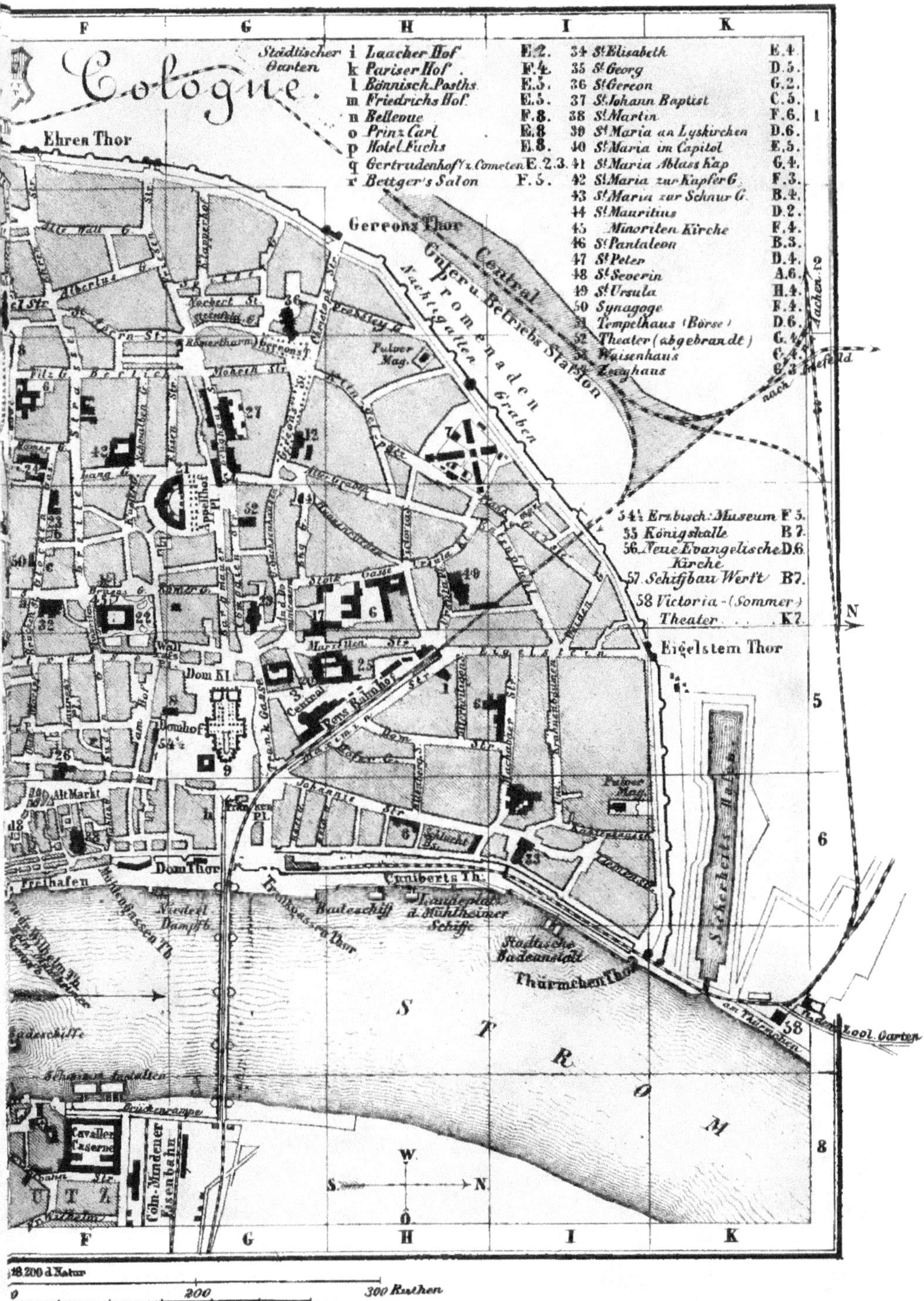

Cologne.
Städtischer Garten
i Laacher Hof E.2.
k Pariser Hof F.4.
l Bönnisch.Posths. E.5.
m Friedrichs Hof E.5.
n Bellevue F.8.
o Prinz Carl E.8.
p Hotel Fuchs E.8.
q Gertrudenhof (z.Cometen E.2.3.
r Bettger's Salon F.5.
34 St.Elisabeth E.4.
35 St.Georg D.5.
36 St.Gereon G.2.
37 St.Johann Baptist C.5.
38 St.Martin F.6.
39 St.Maria an Lyskirchen D.6.
40 St.Maria im Capitol E.5.
41 St.Maria Ablass Kap G.4.
42 St.Maria zur Kupfer G. F.3.
43 St.Maria zur Schnur G. B.4.
44 St.Mauritius D.2.
45 Minoriten Kirche F.4.
46 St.Pantaleon B.3.
47 St.Peter D.4.
48 St.Severin A.6.
49 St.Ursula H.4.
50 Synagoge F.4.
51 Tempelhaus (Börse) D.6.
52 Theater (abgebrandt) G.4.
53 Waisenhaus G.4.
54 Zeughaus G.3.
54½ Erzbisch: Museum F.5.
55 Königshalle B.7.
56 Neue Evangelische Kirche D.6.
57 Schiffbau Werft B.7.
58 Victoria-(Sommer-) Theater K.7.
Ehren Thor
Gereons Thor
Central Güter u. Betriebs Station
Promenaden
Nachtigallen Graben
Pulver Mag.
Eigelstein Thor
Sicherheits Hafen
Dom Kl.
Domhof
Central Pers. Bahnhof
Alt Markt
Dom Thor
Freihafen
Cuniberts Th.
Thürmchen Thor
Städtische Badeanstalt
Landeplatz d. Mühlheimer Schiffe
Badeschiff
Trankgassen Thor
Mühlengassen Th.
Niederl. Dampfb.
STROM
Brückenrampe
Cavallerie Caserne
Cöln-Mindener Eisenbahn
nach Crefeld
nach Aachen
nach dem Zool. Garten
am Thürmchen
W.
S.
N.
O.
F G H I K
1 2 5 6 8
1:8200 d. Natur
0 200 300 Ruthen
7 8 9 10 11 1200 mètres

10. Cologne.

Hotels. *On the Rhine:* *Hôtel de Hollande (Pl. d.), R. 16, L. 6, B. 10, D. 20, A. 6 Sgr.; Royal Hotel (Pl. f); *Hôtel de Cologne (Pl. e), R. and B. 23, D. 17, A. 7½ Sgr. — *Near the Rhine:* *Hôtel de Russie (Pl. g), No. 4. Fried. Wilhelm Strasse; Victoria Hotel, in the Heumarkt. — *In the town:* Hôtel Disch (Pl. a); *Hôtel de Mayence (Pl. b); *Hôtel de Vienne (Pl. c), all three near the post-office; in the two latter excellent tables d'hôte (20 Sgr.); *Hôtel du Nord (Pl. h), near the railway bridge. — *Second-class houses:* *Hôtel Ernst and *Hôtel Kleff, R. and B. 20, D. inc. W. 18 Sgr., both near to the central station; *Hôtel de Paris (Pl. k) Drususgasse 3, R. and B. 20, D. inc. W. 19 Sgr.; *Laacher Hof (Pl. i), Near the Neumarkt, in the W. part of the town; *Hôtel du Dôme, Domhof 7, D. 17 Sgr. — *In Deutz* (1st Cl.) *Bellevue (Pl. n), and *Prinz Carl (Pl. o), R. 15, L. 5, B. 8, A. 6 Sgr.; Hôtel Fuchs.

Restaurants. Hôtel de Cologne; Gertrudenhof; *Lenz, Sandbahn No. 1; *Wanscheidt, in the Salomonsgasse; at the two latter beer may be procured, viands moderate; *Gürzenich Restaurant (entrance from the Martinsstrasse); "Kölner Banket-Haus" in the Schildergasse. *Refreshment-room at the central station.

Cafés and **Confectioners.** *Café du Dôme; St. Paul, nearest to the central-station; Kobell, in the Schildergasse. — Mosler (best confectioner), Oben-Marspforten; Reichard (good ices), Hochstrasse; Börse, in the Heumarkt, well supplied with newspapers.

Oysters and **Delicacies.** Bettger and Co., kleine Budengasse 6 (Pl. r); room fitted up in the Moorish style.

Public Resorts. The gardens of the hotels at Deutz, which command a fine view of Cologne, and where a military band plays on summer evenings. The bridge of boats is a favorite promenade. The Bayenhaus on the Rhine, at the S. extrem. of the town. Zoological Garden (p. 37), Brühl (see R. 36).

Theatre in the Comödienstrasse, representations daily. Summer-theatre (Victoria-theatre), 5—8 p.m., at the Thürmchen (see above); another at the Königshalle (see above).

Concerts once a fortnight in winter in the Gürzenich. Cologne is the seat of the Rhenish School of Music.

***Diorama** (Pl. 8), Wolfsgasse 5, near the Neumarkt (p. 34). Admission 15 or 10 Sgr. The second places are scarcely inferior to the first.

Zoological Garden, ¾ M. below the town nearly opposite to Mülheim; grounds tastefully laid out, valuable collection of animals; adm. 10 Sgr. Adjacent to it is the *Botanical Garden* of the "Flora" company.

Military music daily at 11½ (Sundays at 12) in the Neumarkt.

Baths. *Warm* at Siegen's, in the Schildergasse; in the floating bath-establishment, entrance from the bridge. *Cold* in the Rhine, below the Trankgasse, to the rear of the Rheinau, and at the Bayenthurm; on the r. bank below the garden of the "Bellevue" in Deutz, near which is also the Swimming-bath, 5 Sgr.

Railway Stations. The trains to *Bingen*, *Aix-la-Chapelle* and *Crefeld*, and the express trains of the Cologne and Minden line (R. 8), start from the Centralstation (N. from the Cathedral), ordinary trains on the Cologne and Minden, or Giessen line (R. 52) start from Deutz.

Steamboats, see Introd. Small steamers ply continually to Mülheim (2 Sgr.), starting from the bridge of boats.

Carriages. 1—2 pers. 5, 3 pers. 7½, 4 pers. 10 Sgr. for each drive within the town or to the stations. To Deutz at the same charges, with the addition of 6 Sgr. for bridge-toll. By time. For ½ hr. 1—2 pers. 7½, 3—4 pers. 10 Sgr. For waiting, 2½ Sgr. for every ten min. Before 7 a.m. and after 10 p.m. 5 Sgr. more than the above fares is charged.

Porterage from the steamboat to the carriage for 1—2 packages 1 Sgr., for each additional package 6 Pf. For a hand-cart into the town, with luggage not exceeding 3 cwt., 7 Sgr.

Eau de Cologne. The best may be procured at one of the firms *Farina*, opp. to the Jülichsplatz, Hochstrasse 129, &c., and at *Zanoli's*, in the same street.

Painted porcelain vases, fruit-baskets, &c., in the Drususgasse, opposite the new Museum.

English Church Service performed by a resident chaplain at No. 8 Rheingasse.

Plan where time is limited: *Cathedral*, interior, and walk round the external choir-gallery (p. 28); *St. Gereon* (exterior and interior, p. 33, Pl. 36); *Church of the Apostles* (exterior, p. 33, Pl. 30); *St. Maria im Capitol* (interior, p. 34, Pl. 40); *Gürzenich* (p. 35, Pl. 15); *Façade of the Town-hall* (p. 35, Pl. 26); *Museum* (p. 36, Pl. 45), *iron bridge* (p. 37).

Two days. The above-mentioned churches from 7 to 10 a.m. The **Museum* (p. 36), and *Diorama* (p. 25, Pl. 8). In the afternoon the **Cathedral*, the *Archiepiscopal Museum*, walk along the Rhine and on the bridge, evening in the hotel-gardens at Deutz (p. 38). The principal churches &c. may be most conveniently visited in the following order: cursory glance at the *Cathedral* (p. 28, Pl. 9); *St. Cunibert* (p. 32, Pl. 33); **St. Ursula* (p. 32, Pl. 49); *Jesuits'* (p. 32, Pl. 20); *St. Andreas* (p. 32, Pl. 29); through the Comödienstrasse (l. *Courts of law*, Pl. 21; l. *Arsenal*, Pl. 54; r. *Government buildings*, Pl. 27; l. *Romans' tower*, p. 33); **St. Gereon* (p. 33, Pl. 36); **Apostles'* p. 33, Pl. 30), the new *Mauritius Church* (Pl. 44); cross the Neumarkt (l. the horses' heads, p. 34), past the *Hospital* (p. 34, Pl. 4), to *St. Peter's* (p. 34, Pl. 47); leaving the latter by the S. door in the Sternengasse, past *Rubens' house* (p. 34, Pl. 19), to **St. Marien* (p. 34, Pl. 40); leave the latter by the N. door in the Lichhof, proceed to the **Gürzenich* (p. 35, Pl. 15); *Town-hall* (p. 35, Pl. 26); **St. Martin* (p. 36, Pl. 38); *Minoritenkirche* and the adjacent **Museum* (p. 36).

The names of the streets leading to the Rhine (W. to E.) are painted red, of those parallel to the Rhine (N. to S.) black.

[*Police-station* (Pl. 23), Glockengasse 30. — *Royal bank* (Pl. 2). Cäcilienstrasse 4. — *General post-office* (Pl. 24), Glockengasse 25—27. — *Telegraph-office*, at the Central station.]

Cologne owes its foundation to the Ubii, who when hard pressed by the Suevi, removed their capital town from the r. bank of the Rhine to the l., to the spot which the present city of Cologne occupies. Here, A.D. 50, Agrippina, the daughter of Germanicus, and mother of Nero, founded a colony of Roman veterans, which was called *Colonia Agrippinensis,* and afterwards *Colonia Claudia Agrippina.* The new settlement soon became the capital town of Lower Germany. In 308 Constantine the Great commenced to construct a stone bridge over the Rhine, which connected Marspforten with what was then the island of St. Martin, and thence crossed to Deutz; the remnants of the pillars may still be seen when the river is very low. The present Rathhaus, or Town-hall, is believed to occupy the site of the *Prætorium* of the Roman colony; from here the old Roman wall extended towards the Gürzenich (Merchants' Hall), and beyond it to the church of St. Maria im Capitol, past which the Rhine is said formerly to have flowed, and to have surrounded the present Altenmarkt, at that time an island. The above-mentioned bridge formed a continuation of the present streets "auf der Brücke" and "oben Marspforten"; it was, however, destroyed at the time of the Norman invasion, and in 960 taken to pieces by order of the Archbishop Bruno, who also caused the l. arm of the Rhine to be filled up.

In the middle ages (12th—15th cent.) Cologne was a most flourishing commercial town. In 1201 it became incorporated in the Hanseatic league, and as such had its principal depôt at the Guildhall of London. In 1212 it became a free town of the empire. Subsequently the archbishops, who were continually at variance with the citizens, endeavoured to assert their authority over them, but were repeatedly thwarted: the city maintained its freedom, so that the archbishop Engelbert was compelled in 1262 to transfer his residence to Brühl, and afterwards to Bonn. Feuds between the nobles and the burghers, which occasioned the expulsion of a whole corporation of weavers in 1370, who migrated to Aix-la-Chapelle and Eupen, and of the Protestants in 1608, who settled at Crefeld, Elberfeld, Düsseldorf, and Mülheim, proved very prejudicial to the prosperity of the city. Cologne, however, still held its rank as the first Rhenish town, and was moreover celebrated as a cradle of the fine arts. Some of the pictures of the Cologne school are to be seen at the Cathedral (p. 29) and the Museum (p. 36), whilst others are preserved at the old Pinakothek at Munich, to which they were taken by the well known picture-collectors Boisserée at the time of the French Revolution. The only names of celebrity which have come down to our time are those of *Meister Wilhelm* (1380) and *Meister Stephan* (1410). The town likewise boasted of a university, founded in 1388, and celebrated as a philosophical and theological school. In later ages, however, it lost its importance, and was finally abolished about the close of the last century.

Until the occupation of the town by the French in 1794, Cologne had maintained its privileges as a free Imperial city, but had lost much of its ancient splendour and prosperity. By the peace of Campo Formio in 1797 it became subject to France, and was a town of the Roer Department, the capital of which was Aix-la-Chapelle. In 1802 its monasteries and other ecclesiastical establishments were secularized, and declared national property. On Jan. 14th, 1814, the Russians took possession of the place, and when, shortly afterwards, the town became Prussian, it began to recover its former importance. Since then it has rapidly increased in size and affluence, and the energy and and public spirit of its citizens have rendered it one of the most considerable commercial cities in Germany. The completion of the railway bridge in 1859, one of the most massive structures by which the Rhine is crossed, has given an additional importance to the place.

The population of Cologne is 113,081 (12,338 Prot., 2990 Jews), and the garrison consists of 4813 soldiers; Deutz has 5739 inhabitants and a garrison of 1719. The majority of the streets are narrow and gloomy, and the 34 public squares are planted with trees. The kitchen-gardens and vineyards, which formerly occupied more than one quarter of the area of the town, are rapidly giving place to new streets and buildings. Before the first revolution Cologne, once dignified with the name of "holy", contained upwards of 200 places of worship and ecclesiastical establishments; the number of churches is now 25, two of which are Protestant.

The ****Cathedral** [1], or *Dom*, the grand point of attraction, justly excites the admiration and wonder of every beholder, whilst its still unfinished condition is suggestive of the abortiveness of human designs. The master-mind which planned this noble pile is unknown, and the original designs, the offsprings of his fertile brain, are for ever lost; could his dreams have been realized, there is no doubt, that, as now it is the most beautiful fragment in existence, so it would have been in its completion the most magnificent and stupendous edifice ever raised by human hands to the service of the Creator. The foundation-stone was laid by the Archbishop Conrad of Hochsteden (p. 60), Aug. 14th, 1248, in presence of the Emperor William, the opponent of Frederick II.

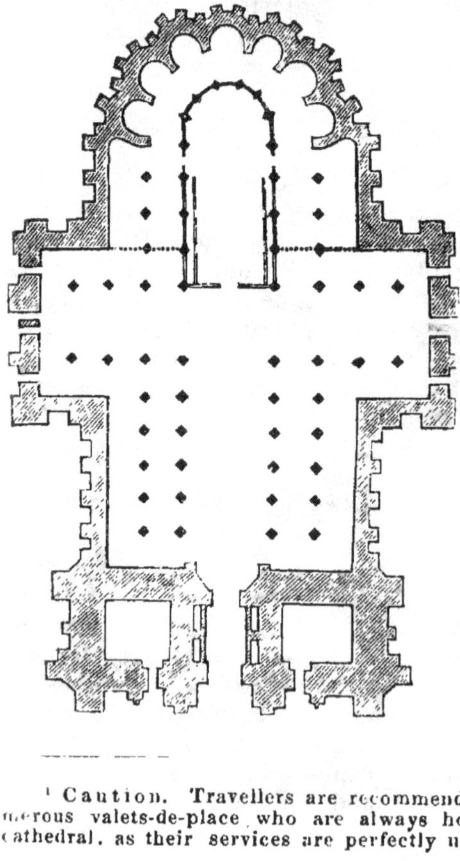

[1] Caution. Travellers are recommended not to engage any of the numerous valets-de-place who are always hovering about, in and near the cathedral, as their services are perfectly unnecessary. The Nave with the

The first projector of a plan for the erection of a cathedral was the Archbishop Engelbert I., surnamed "the holy", who was murdered on the Gevelsberg at Schwelm by Frederick of Isenburg in 1225, and whose bones are preserved in a silver casket in the treasury of the cathedral. The first architect is believed to have been *Meister Gerard* of Riehl, a village near Cologne, to whom the Chapter made a grant in 1257 in recognition of his valuable services.

The construction of the sacred edifice progressed but slowly, chiefly owing to the continual differences between the archbishops and the townspeople, and the choir was not consecrated till 1322, under Archbishop Henry (Count of Virneburg). The building was subsequently proceeded with, but at last completely abandoned at the commencement of the 16th cent. Since then it fell more and more to decay, and was in 1796 converted by the French into a hay-magazine, its ruin being rendered more complete by the abstraction of the lead from the roof.

The late enlightened king of Prussia, Frederick William IV., and his predecessor rescued the sacred edifice from total destruction. The latter caused it to be examined by the eminent architect Schinkel in 1816, and from that time up to his death in 1840, he expended upwards of 200,000 Thlr. (30,000*l.*) upon its restoration. In addition to the above sum, donations and subscriptions amounting to 120,000 Thlr. (18,000*l.*) were devoted to the same object. During the reign of Fred. William IV. a sum of 1,500,000 Thlr. (225,000*l.*), more than half of which was contributed from the royal purse, was laid out on the building. The entire sum expended between 1842 and 1864 has exceeded 300,000*l.* The interior of the cathedral has been completed since 1863. The partition which separated the choir from the central nave is now removed, so that the impression produced by the majestic proportions of the whole is most profound. The magnificent *Southern Portal*, 220 ft. in height, which alone cost 700,000 Thlr. (105,000*l.*) was finished in 1859, as well as the less elabo-

---

stained-glass windows is open to the public the whole day, the choir, when divine service is not being performed. The following are the only authorized fees (1—5 pers.): 1. For opening the high-choir, the choir chapels, and the Dombild (cathedral picture), 15 Sgr.; 2. For the attendant who conducts the visitors along the upper choir-gallery, round the exterior of the cathedral, and to the summit of the tower, 15 Sgr.; 3. For opening the treasury, the shrine containing the relics of the Magi, and the Dombild, $1^1/_2$ Thlr. Cards to be procured from the Suisse, who is generally to be found in or near the transept. Any payment in addition to the above fees is entirely gratuitous. The treasury and shrine of the Magi possess interest for judges of art only.

rate *Northern Portal*, both of which were exclusively designed by Zwirner (d. 1861), the talented architect who conducted the work since 1833. Upon the *Southern Tower* the crane with its long projecting arm (55 ft.), the landmark of Cologne, is exactly in the same position as it was 400 years ago, as may be seen from a painting in the Hospital of St. John at Bruges. The entire structure, exclusive of the towers, is now nearly completed. The central tower (of iron) and the iron frame-work of the roof of the body of the church and transept were completed in 1861.

The Cathedral stands on a slight eminence (55 ft. above the Rhine) which in the time of the Romans formed the S. E. corner of their camp. The interior is 421 ft. long and 140 ft. broad; the transept is 234 ft. long, and the choir 140 ft. high. The portion appropriated to divine service occupies an area of 70,000 sq. ft. The S. tower exhibits the most complete harmony of design, but has attained little more than $^1/_3$rd (189 ft.) of the projected height (476 ft.).

Stained-glass windows. The five windows in the N. aisle, executed in 1508—9, are considered among the finest existing specimens of the art. The new * windows in the S. aisle were presented in 1848 by King Ludwig of Bavaria, and prove that the almost obsolete art has in some respects re-attained, if it does not surpass, its ancient glory.

Choir. Pedestals, which project from the 14 pillars of the central part, bear statues, of value as specimens of the sculpture of the beginning of the 14th cent. They represent Christ, the Virgin, and the 12 Apostles. The 9 frescoes by Steinle, and the tapestry, representing the Nicene creed, recently worked by ladies of Cologne, on the wall behind the choir-stalls, are worth inspection. The carved stalls themselves belong to the 14th cent. Above the inner gallery of the high-choir is a series of admirable old stained-glass windows, representing the kings of Judah &c.

Chapels. 1st (Maternus) on l. (to the N.): Tombstone of Archbishop *Philipp v. Heinsberg* (d. 1191), in the form of a town-wall with towers, gates, and turrets, an allusion to the fact of his having been the founder of the fortifications of Cologne. Fine old carved altar-piece, representing the Passion.

2nd. (Johannis) Tombstone of Archbishop *Conrad of Hochsteden* (d. 1261), the founder of the cathedral. The altar of *St. Clara*, with paintings by the celebrated Cologne master Wilhelm, is also worthy of note.

3d. (Engelbertus) in which the bones of Archbishop *Engelbert von der Mark*, now preserved in a silver casket in the treasury, reposed till 1633.

4th. (Chapel of the three kings or Magi). Here are preserved the bones of the Magi. which were brought from Constantinople by the Empress Helena, afterwards taken to the cathedral of Milan, and finally, after the destruction of Milan in 1164, presented by the Emperor Frederick Barbarossa to Archbishop Reinold of Cologne. The gorgeous shrine which contains the relics was constructed towards the close of the 12th cent., and was once richly adorned with gold, pearls, and precious stones, the greater number of which disappeared during the French dominion. Near this chapel repose the remains of the Electors of the house of Bavaria, and in front of it, under a stone without incription, is interred the heart of Marie de Medicis (p. 34). Opposite, at the back of the high-altar, is the tombstone of *St. Engelbert.*

5th. (Agnes Chapel). Contains the celebrated **Dombild,* termed by Goethe "the axis on which the history of art on the Lower Rhine turns," a picture in compartments, representing the Adoration of the Magi, St. Gereon and St. Ursula, and the Annunciation. It bears the date 1410, and is probably a work of the Master *Stephan* (p. 27).

6th. (Michael's Chapel). Tombstone of Archbishop *Walram of Jülich* (d. 1349) Carved altar-piece of the 15th cent.

7th. (Stephen's Chapel). Tombstone of the imperial *General von Hochkirchen* (fell in 1703 at Landau in the Spanish war of succession). Near it is the *tombstone of Archbishop *Frederick of Saarwerden* (d. 1414), admirably decorated with figures of saints. The chapel itself contains an altar-piece by *Overbeck*, representing the Ascension of the Virgin. The stained-glass windows were presented in 1857 by a society at Bonn und Münster, formed for the purpose of furthering the construction of the cathedral.

The Schatzkammer or Treasury (entrance from the passage of the N. choir), contains a silver shrine with the remains of St. Engelbert, valuable ecclesiastical vessels, especially one presented by Pope Pius IX. in 1848, the sword of office worn by the Elector of Cologne at the coronation procession at Frankfurt (R. 39), priestly robes, 10 carved ivory tablets, &c.

The visitor should by no means omit to walk round the *inner gallery of the choir and those on the exterior of the choir, or to ascend the now completed central tower (admission by card, see p. 29, by the S. Portal), as thus a better idea may be formed of the grandeur of the whole structure. The external gallery commands a magnificent *prospect over the sea of houses, the plain intersected by the Rhine and the Seven Mountains in the distance.

The **Archiepiscopal Museum** (*Erzbischöfliche Museum*), opposite to the S. side of the cathedral, containing a collection of ecclesiastical and other objects of art of the middle ages, occupies the site of the archiepiscopal palace of the middle ages.

In the immediate vicinity of the W. Portal, at the end of the Unter-Fettenhennen Strasse, an old Roman inscription on the wall of the N. W. corner house of the Domkloster (cathedral convent) marks the place where the *Pfaffenpforte*, one of the ancient town gates, formerly stood.

The remaining objects of interest in Cologne are enumerated in the order recommended at p. 26.

St. Cunibert (Pl. 33), on the Rhine, in the N. part of the town, was consecrated by Archbishop Conrad in 1248, the same year in which he laid the foundation stone of the cathedral. It contains some fine old stained glass in the choir, and several small pictures of saints on gold ground, probably of the old Cologne school.

* **St. Ursula** (Pl. 49) is said to have been erected at the beginning of the 12th cent. by the Emperor Henry II. The choir to the l. contains a monument, erected in 1658, to *St. Ursula,* an English princess, who, according to one of the many legends extant, on her return from a pilgrimage to Rome was, with her 11,000 virgin attendants, barbarously murdered at Cologne. The bones of these virgin martyrs are kept in cases, placed round the church. Ten old pictures of the Apostles, to the l. of the S. entrance, are painted on slate, and bear the date 1224. Under the organ a Crucifixion in stone is well executed.

The **Jesuits' Church** (Pl. 20), erected about 1636 in the style peculiar to this order, is overloaded with decorations. The bells were cast out of the metal of the cannons taken by Tilly at Magdeburg, and by him presented to the church. The entrance hall of the *Priests' Seminary*, adjoining the church on the N., contains a handsome marble monument of the Master of the Teutonic order *von Reuschenberg* (d. 1603).

The **Church of St. Andreas** (Pl. 29), with Romanesque nave and raised Gothic choir, contains a richly-adorned modern side-altar, where the shrine (15th cent.) with the relics of *Albertus Magnus*, who lived and died in the contiguous Dominican convent, is preserved. In the adjoining street "*Unter-Sachsenhausen*", are situated two palatial edifices, one the property of the *Schaaffhausen Banking Co.*, the other of the *Cologne Fire Insurance* and the *Hail Insurance* companies.

In the Comödienstrasse on the r. is the *Theatre* (Pl. 52), re-erected since its destruction by fire in 1859; on the l. the *Courts* of *Justice* (Pl. 21), the *Arsenal* (Pl. 54), erected in 1601;

on the r. the palatial *Government buildings* (Pl. 27). Farther W. in the same direction, at the corner of the Apernstrasse, is the *Roman tower*, inlaid with stones of different colours, which is believed to have formed one of the corners of the Roman town. The interior is undoubtedly of Roman origin, the exterior belongs to the middle ages, and the upper part is modern. After traversing the Steinfeldergasse the Church of

* **St. Gereon** (Pl. 36) is reached. This church, dedicated to the memory of the 408 martyrs of the Theban legion, with their captains Gereon and Gregory (afterwards the patron saints of Cologne), who perished here in the persecution of the Christians under Diocletian, occupies the site of an ancient church, said to have been founded by the empress Helena. It was formerly known by the appellation of the church *ad aureos sanctos,* from the circumstanee of its being roofed with gilded metal plates. The nave is probably as ancient as the 7th eent.; the choir belongs to the 13th, and is constructed in the transition style from the round to the pointed, the latter predominating.

The entrance hall contains old tombstones of crusaders. The nave consists of a decagonal vaulted cupola, from the sides of which project the sarcophagi of the martyrs. Upwards of 200 of their skulls, some of them enveloped with velvet, are arranged round the choir under gilded arabesques. Traces of ancient frescoes have recently been discovered. (Attendant's fee for 1—3 pers. 10 Sgr.)

About 100 yds. to the E. of the church, in the street planted with trees, is situated the *Archiepiscopal Palace* (Pl. 12), in front of which stands the **Mariensäule*, a handsome monument erected in 1858 in commemoration of the promulgation of the doctrine of the immaculate conception. The statues are from drawings by Steinle.

Farther to the N., in the Klingelpütz, is the *Arresthaus* (Pl. 7), a prison constructed in a radiating form.

The * **Apostles' Church** (Pl. 30) in the Neumarkt, a remarkably handsome structure with its towers, pinnacles, and cupola, was commenced in 1200, when the Romanesque style had attained its highest perfection.

When the plague raged in Cologne in 1357, Richmodis von Lyskirchen, wife of the knight Mengis von Adocht, was attacked by the malady, and having fallen into a deathlike swoon, was interred in the Apostles' church. Being awakened from her trance by a thievish gravedigger in his attempts to possess himself of her ring, she returned to the house of her husband, who, imagining he beheld an apparition, declared he would sooner believe that his horses could ascend to the loft of his house than his departed spouse return *in propriâ personâ.* Scarcely had the words escaped his lips, says the legend, than horses' hoofs were heard mounting the stairs, and their heads were speedily seen looking out of a window in the upper story of the house. (Two horses' heads are still to be seen, affixed to the upper story of the house with the tower on the N. side of the Neumarkt, where they were placed in commemoration of the miraculous event.) The lady recovered and lived for many years afterwards.

[Near the Neumarkt is the Diorama (p. 25); the *Roman Tower* (p. 33) is on the way from St. Gereon's to the Apostles' church.]

The new **Mauritius Church** (Pl. 44) (Mauritius Steinweg) is an edifice in the Gothic style.

The **Hospital** (Pl. 4) is a large and handsome edifice; the patients are waited on by sisters of Charity. It may be inspected in the afternoon; the visitor is expected on entering his name in the book to give a donation towards the funds of the establishment. Attendant's fee 5 Sgr.

St. Cecilia (Pl. 31), erected about 1200, is contiguous to the hospital and serves as its chapel. The crypt, which contains remnants of Roman masonry, deserves inspection.

St. Peter's Church (Pl. 47), adjacent to the latter, was built in 1524, and contains an altar-piece (the crucifixion of Peter) by *Rubens*, brought back in 1814 from Paris, whither it had been taken by the French. It is concealed by another picture of little value which the sexton removes for the somewhat exorbitant fee of 15 Sgr. A copy of the picture hangs over the N. side-entrance. The inspection of the old carved altar with paintings ascribed to Lucas of Leyden costs 5 Sgr. more.

The S. entrance of St. Peter's is in the Sternengasse where (No. 10) Rubens was born (1577) (comp. p. 41). In the same house Marie de Medicis, widow of Henry IV. of France, died in exile (1642).

***St. Maria im Capitol** (Pl. 40), so-called from its occupying the site of the Roman Capitol, is said to have been founded at the close of the 7th cent. by Plectrudis, consort of Pepin of Héristal and mother of Charles Martel. The present edifice was commenced in the 11th cent. The S. (Hardenrath's) chapel contains frescoes by *Israel of Mekenem*, the finest of which represents a group of choristers. The N. chapel (baptistery) contains an altar-piece of 1521, ascribed to Albert Dürer, representing the dying Mary, surrounded by the Apostles. The old *stained-glass* windows and the rich sculpturing under the organ (executed in 1523) deserve mention. On the door of the N. entrance are carved wooden reliefs of the 11th cent., and on the external wall of the choir a stone effigy of Plectrudis (probably the lid of a sarcophagus). Adjacent to it is a small pointed archway, adorned with stone carving, lately restored, which forms the entrance gateway from the Königsstrasse.

Farther to the E., in the same line of streets, is situated the **Templars' Lodge** (*Tempelhaus*, Pl. 51) in the Rheingasse, No. 8. It dates from the 12th or 13th cent., and is frequently alluded to in the annals of the city as a corporation or guild-hall. It is now used as an *Exchange*, and contains collections of the Chamber of Commerce, Navigation Society, &c. The walls of the three apartments on the ground-floor are covered with paintings in the taste of the middle ages, emblematical of priesthood, knighthood, and citizenship, the three elements of the state in those times.

The **Gürzenich** (Pl. 15) (named after the citizen by whom it was founded) erected in 1441—74, improved and enlarged in 1856, is the most considerable of the non-ecclesiastical edifices of Cologne. The new painted statues above the E. gateway represent *Agrippa* and *Marsilius*, respectively the founder and defender of the town during the Roman period. The large **Hall* on the first floor was employed in the middle ages on festive occasions, and served as a banquet-room when the emperors visited the city. In 1857 it was entirely remodelled, and contains stained-glass windows representing the arms of the once allied towns of Cologne, Jülich, Cleve, Berg, and Mark, St. Peter as patron saint, two imperial eagles, the arms of the city, those of the 22 different corporations &c. The two large, richly carved chimney-pieces, with allusions to the former history of Cologne, are worth inspection.

The ***Rathhaus** or Town-hall (Pl. 26), facing the Stadthausplatz to the W. and the old market to the E., was founded in the 13th cent., and attained its present form in 1549. The **Portal*, added in 1571, is in the new Romanesque style. It rests upon 16 marble pillars with open arches, and bears six long Latin inscriptions recording the gratitude of the citizens to *Julius Caesar*, *Augustus*, *Agrippa*, *Constantine*, *Justinian*, and the German Emperor *Maximilian*. The *Reliefs* contain an allusion to an ancient tradition.

The Archbishop Engelbert (p. 27) sought the life of the Burgomaster Gryn. He invited his intended victim to a banquet and caused him to be conducted to a room where a hungry lion had been placed to devour the obnoxious citizen. The latter, however, contrived to thrust his l. arm down the animal's throat, while he stabbed it with the r. hand.

The *Chapel* of the Rathhaus which formerly contained the Dombild (p. 31), was, before the banishment of the Jews, (1349), a synagogue. The Gothic tower of the Rathhaus at present contains the *Wallraf Library* and *Archives*, open daily from 10 to 12.

***Gross-St. Martin** (Pl. 38), near the Rhine, consecrated in 1172, is a bold and elegant Romanesque fabric. The massive tower, one pinnacle of which is yet incomplete, rests upon four arches, nearly 100 ft. in height and 40 ft. in width, the only counterpoise of which consists of the handsome half-rotundas. The lower part of the church was erected more than a century later and exhibits the transition to the pointed style. The antique font, decorated with lions' heads and foliage, a present from Pope Leo III., is a rare specimen of the stone carving of the 8th cent. On the upper side-altars are placed 6 new stone statues by Hoffmann of Rome, to the l. St. Martin, St. Eliphius, and St. Brigitta, to the r. the Virgin with angels. The N. aisle contains a fine Descent from the Cross, by *du Bois*, and Christ before Annas, by *Honthorst*. The pulpit rests on a recumbent dragon.

The **Minoritenkirche** (Pl. 45) is of the 13th cent., and is said to have been built in their leisure hours by the same workmen who were engaged in the construction of the cathedral. It contains the tombstone of the celebrated theological disputant *Duns Scotus* (d. 1309), the inscription on which records: *Scotia me genuit, Anglia me suscepit, Gallia me docuit, Colonia me tenet.* The beautiful cloisters on the N. side are in the late Gothic style. The church is now undergoing a thorough repair, the expenses of which were borne by Herr Richartz (d. 1861), a wealthy and public-spirited citizen of Cologne. At his expense likewise (30,000*l.*) the new

***Museum** (*Wallraf-Richartz*) (Pl. 22) has been constructed. The statues at the principal portal (N. side) as well as those on the E. side, represent characters of distinction in the annals of the city. The building contains the late Professor Wallraf's valuable collection of antiquities of Rome and the middle ages, and pictures by ancient and modern masters (adm. gratis on Sundays, holidays and Wed. afternoons, at other times for a fee of 7½ Sgr.)

Ground-floor. On the *right* the *Roman Antiquities*, on the *left* ancient weapons and armour. The *lower* cloister contains several *Mosaic pavements*, the *upper* is occupied by a collection of vases, stained-glass etc. — In three saloons to the l. is situated the *Permanent Exhibition* of the Cologne Art-Union. The staircase is adorned with *frescoes* representing the different epochs in the history of art at Cologne.

The Upper Story contains pictures of the Dutch, Italian and French schools, as well as the works of several eminent modern artists. The principal attraction of the gallery, however, consists in the collection of paintings of the old Cologne school by *Meister Wilhelm* and his followers (12—84), *Meister Stephan* and his school (85—112), and painters of the *Van Eyck* school (113—372).

St. Severin (Pl. 48), at the S. extremity of the town, was founded at the commencement of the 11th cent., but the greater part of the edifice is in the Gothic style and therefore belongs to a later date. The tall pointed spire was added about the close of the 15th cent. The "Last Supper"

by *de Bruyn*, a winged altar-piece to the r., is one of the finest works of this master. The sacristy contains a fresco by the Master *Wilhelm* (p. 27), which is unfortunately in a bad state of preservation.

St. Pantaleon (Pl. 46) is mentioned in ancient documents as early as 670. Archbishop Bruno (d. 965), brother of Otto the Great, is said to have employed the remnants of the bridge of Constantine (p. 26) in building the abbey and enlarging the church. To the r. by the High-altar is the tombstone of the *Empress Theophania* (d. 999), consort of Otto II., and to the l. that of *Count Hermann von Zütphen*, abbot of the monastery, and brother of St. Irmgard, both of them erected in the last century. The fine old Gothic sculpturing under the organ has been lately restored. The church is one of the most ancient buildings of Cologne of the Christian period, and is fitted up as a garrison church.

The new Prot. **Trinity Church** (Pl. 56) in the "basilica" style, is situated in the Filzengraben, not far from the harbour, and the **Synagogue** (Pl. 50) in the Moorish style, with its handsome cupola, in the Glockengasse.

One of the most remarkable works of its age is the well-preserved **Town-wall**, with its broad, deep fosses and fine gate-towers. Begun at the close of the 12th cent. under Archbishop Philipp, and completed in the 15th, it describes a semi-circle of 3800 yds., the chord of which is formed by the bank of the Rhine.

The wharves, from the N. extremity of the town to the **Bayenthurm**, exhibit an animated and interesting scene. Near the tower is the *Sicherheitshafen*, or Safety-harbour (where vessels take refuge in winter from the dangers of the floating ice), with its ship-building establishment, and beyond it an extensive cotton-factory. The warehouses of the *Freihafen*, or Free harbour, were erected in 1838 in the same style as the Gürzenich. The town may now be entered by the Mühlengassenthor; following a N. direction the new Domthor is soon reached, through which the traveller arrives at the **Iron Bridge**, 1312 ft. in length. Part of it, 24 ft. in breadth, is used as a railway-bridge, the remaining part, 27 ft. broad, serves for the ordinary traffic.

The Trankgassen-Thor by the bridge, to the N., leads to the extensive *Rhine-wharf*, following which and passing St. Cunibert (p. 32), whence the steamboats to the Zoolog. Garden and Mülheim start, the traveller crosses the entrance to the old *Sicherheitshafen*, and reaches the *Victoria-Theatre* (p. 25), and farther down, the **Zoological Garden** (open daily in summer from 6 a.m., in winter from 8 a.m., till sunset; admission see p. 25). There is usually a military concert here on Wed. afternoons. The grounds are well laid out and the collection of animals meritorious. Good refreshment-room. — In the immediate vicinity is situated the *Botanical Garden* of the "Flora" company. — Carriages see (p. 25). — The steamboats between Cologne and Mülheim have a station near these gardens, where a bell is rung to apprise visitors of the approach of the boats returning to Cologne.

At the harbour, the glacis of the town-fortifications is entered; it is planted with trees and laid out with walks, and affords an agreeable promenade round the town. To the l., between Gereon's and the Ehren-Thor, lies the **Town-Garden**, with horticultural school. Parallel with the town, and about 100 yds. from its walls, is a long series of **Forts**, connected with the fortifications. Beyond the last of these lie the grounds of the Cologne machine manufactory, forming a sort of suburb.

The extensive **Cemetery** is situated on the road to Aix-la-Chapelle, but contains no monuments worthy of note.

On the r. bank of the Rhine, opposite to Cologne, lies **Deutz** (Hotels see p. 25), the tête-de-pont of Cologne, the *Castrum Divitensium* of the Romans, founded probably in the 1st century, and afterwards strengthened by Constantine. It was undoubtedly a Roman fortress, and existed up to 1114, was repeatedly restored and again destroyed in later ages, but never attained any importance as a town, as a settlement here would have been inconsistent with the privileges of the town of Cologne. Subsequently to 1816 Deutz was fortified in connection with Cologne by the Prussians. The buildings of the former Benedictine abbey now serve as an extensive artillery workshop. The *Cologne and Minden Railway Station* (p. 25) is situated near the new *Cavalry Barracks*.

One of the finest existing edifices in the Gothic style, similar in plan and style to the Cathedral, is the church of the Cistercian abbey of ***Altenberg**, founded in 1255 and consecrated in 1379. This magnificent fabric, situated in the Dhünthal, 12 M. N. E. from Deutz, was most judiciously restored by the late king of Prussia, by whose ancestors, the Counts Adolf and Eberhard vom Berge, the abbey was founded in 1133. Several members of the same family are here interred. A single traveller may avail himself of the Lennep diligence from Cologne early in the morning as far as *Strasserhof*, through which it again passes on its way back to Cologne at 8 p.m. Altenberg is about $1^1/_4$ M. distant; good halting-place at *Schmitz's* inn, in *Engelrath*, near Strasserhof. Those who are unwilling to devote an entire day to this excursion, may take the steamboat or railway to *Mülheim*, and walk thence by *Odenthal* to *Altenberg* (9 M.); in the evening back by the diligence from Strasserhof. It is less expensive for a party of 3—4 persons to take a carriage from Deutz to Altenberg in 2 hrs., fare about 4 Thlr.

11. From Cologne to Crefeld and Cleve.

Comp. Map R. 4.

By Railway to Crefeld in $1^1/_2$ hr.; fares: 1 Thlr. 13 Sgr., 1 Thlr. or 21 Sgr.; to Cleve in $3^1/_4$ hr.; fares: 3 Thlr. 5, 2 Thlr. 10 or 1 Thlr. $17^1/_2$ Sgr. Return tickets for day of issue and following day only. Trains start from the Central station (p. 25).

The district traversed by this line is flat, but possesses some places to which an historical interest attaches.

Worringen, the *Buruncum* of the Romans, was in June, 1288, the scene of a battle fought by the troops of Cologne and Brabant and the Duke of Berg against the Archbishop of Cologne and the Duke of Guelders, by which the Duchy of Limburg became annexed to that of Brabant. *Horrem* is the station for **Dormagen,** the *Durnomagus* of the Romans, and station of the 22nd Legion (*Transrhenana*). M. Delhoven has a fine collection of Roman antiquities.

Neuss (*Drei Könige; *Rheinischer Hof*), at the same time a station on the Aix-la-Chapelle and Düsseldorf line (p. 11), is one of the oldest towns in Germany, founded by the Ubii in 35 B. C., and often mentioned as a Roman fortress by Tacitus, under the Name of *Novesium*, the station of the 6th and 16th Legions. In 1474 Neuss was in vain besieged by Charles the Bold of Burgundy during 48 weeks, and in 1586 was conquered and treated with great severity by Alexander Farnese. It once lay on the Rhine, which is now $1^1/_2$ M. distant. The handsome **Quirinuskirche*, founded in 1209, belongs to the transition period from the Romanesque to the Gothic. St. Quirinus, to whom the church is dedicated, is believed to have been a Roman soldier who perished in the persecution of the Christians. The grammar-school contains a considerable collection of Roman antiquities.

The train then proceeds by stat. *Osterath* to *Crefeld* (p. 11). The next stat. *Kempen*, an ancient town with a well-preserved church in the Romanesque style, is believed to have been the birthplace of Thomas a Kempis (d. at Zwolle, 1471). The fertile district now begins to assume the Dutch character. *Geldern*, the next station of importance, formerly the capital of the Duchy of Guelders, has belonged to the Prussian dominions since 1713. The train here crosses the *Niers*, and passes the stations of *Kevelaer* (much frequented by pilgrims), *Weeze* and *Goch* (a place of some importance in the middle ages). The sand-hills which form the culminating point between the Rhine and the Meuse are now approached and gradually ascended, and to the l. the town of *Cleve* shortly comes in sight.

Cleve (**Maiwald*, on the S. side, **Robbers*, to the W. of the town; **Hôtel Laferrière*, contiguous to the palace, moderate;

Kaiserlicher Hof), once the capital of the Duchy of the same name, is a clean town, delightfully situated on the brow of a wooded eminence, 4½ M. to the W. of Emmerich. The *Stiftskirche*, erected in 1345, contains several monuments of the Counts and Dukes of Cleve (the finest is that of Adolf VI., d. 1394), and one of Margaretha von Berg (d. 1425).

On an eminence in the centre of the town rises the *Palace* of the former dukes, with the lofty **Schwanenthurm* erected by Adolf I. in 1439, on the site of an ancient tower, believed to have been built by Cæsar. The Schwanenthurm, as well as the *Clever-Berg*, ¾ M. distant, commands the most charming prospect on the Lower Rhine. To the S. extends a range of hills on which lies the *Prinzenhof*, property of the Princess of Waldeck and Pyrmont, once the seat of Prince Moritz of Nassau, the governor of the Duchy appointed by the Elector of Brandenburg. To the N. lies the series of hills, known by the name of the *Thiergarten*, laid out with park-like grounds, which adjoin the road to Nymegen. Diligence from Cleve to *Nymegen* in 2¼ hrs. Railway in construction.

From Cleve to Hanten on the Rhine (see p. 17).

12. From Cologne to Frankfurt by Giessen.

By Railway to Giessen in 5¼ hrs.; fares: 4 Thlr. 12½, 2 Thlr. 28½, or 2 Thlr. 6½ Sgr. From Giessen to Frankfurt by express in 1 hr. 33 min., by ordinary trains in 1¾—2½ hrs.; fares: 1 Thlr. 23, 1 Thlr. 6, or 22 Sgr.

The train starts from Deutz and traverses a flat country at some distance from the Rhine. The first station of any importance is **Siegburg** (**Stern*), which communicates with Bonn by diligence several times a day (9 Sgr.; omnibus 4 Sgr.). The buildings of what was formerly a Benedictine Abbey on the hill are now employed as a *Lunatic Asylum*.

After crossing the *Sieg*, a view of the Seven Mts. to the r. is obtained, and the station *Hennef* is reached. The castle of *Allner*, situated on the skirts of the wood to the l., stands at the entrance to the narrower part of the valley of the Sieg, which the line now ascends. Farther on, the convent of *Bödingen* is seen to the l., surrounded by vineyards, and on the opposite side the village and ruined castle of *Blankenberg*. Beyond stat. *Eitorf* the convent of *Merten* is seen on an eminence to the r., and here the wooded hills which enclose the valley increase in height. **Schladern**, with the ruined castle of *Windeck*, is one of the finest points on the line. Beyond the station of *Wissen*, on the l. bank of the Sieg, stands the handsome castle of *Schönstein*, property of the Prince of Hatzfeld-Wildenburg.

At **Betzdorf** the line leaves the valley of the Sieg and enters that of the *Heller*.

The first portion of the line to Siegen was opened in Jan. 1861; stations: *Kirchen*, *Niederschelden*, then

Siegen (*Goldener Löwe; near the stat. a restaurant, beer) (7100 inhab.), an ancient town with two castles of the Princes of Nassau-Siegen, who became extinct in 1743. The lower castle contains a monument to the celebrated Prince Maurice of Orange (d. 1625). Siegen, as has lately been discovered, was the birthplace of *Rubens*. The town is the central point of the iron-traffic of this district.

The Railway from Siegen to Hagen (*Ruhr-Sieg* line) (in $3^1/_2$ hrs.; fares: 2 Thlr. 25, 2 Thlr. 4, 1 Thlr. 13 Sgr.) continues to follow the course of the Sieg from Betzdorf, and beyond *Creuzthal* enters the valley of the *Hundem*, from which it emerges at *Altenhundem*, and proceeds in the valley of the *Lenne* to *Altena* (Queimann). The old castle in the vicinity of the last-named place was the family residence of the Counts von der Mark, and commands a fine view. At *Hagen* (Deutsches Haus; Hôtel Lünenschloss) is the junction of this line with the railway to Elberfeld and Düsseldorf; near it is situated the ancient and interesting ruin of *Hohen-Syburg* (p. 22).

Beyond *Burbach* the Giessen line enters the Duchy of Nassau and ascends the valley of the *Dill* to *Wetzlar*, where it unites with the Lahn Railway.

Wetzlar (**Herzogliches Haus*), formerly a free imperial town, is picturesquely situated on the *Lahn*, and commanded by the ruined castle of **Kalsmunt*, which together with the **Metzeburg* are the finest points in the environs. The most ancient (N. W.) part of the **Cathedral*, the so-called Heidenthurm, was erected in the 11th cent.; the remainder dates from the 14th—16th. Here Goethe resided for some months in 1372, and Wetzlar and its environs were the scene of the events which suggested his "Sorrows of Werther".

The line continues to ascend the valley of the Lahn, and after crossing the frontier of Hessen-Darmstadt near *Dutenhofen*, unites with the Main-Weser line at Giessen.

The valleys of the Sieg, Heller, Dill and Lahn have for centuries been noted for their richness in iron; in some places lead, copper and silver mines are also worked.

Those interested in agriculture should here observe the manner in which the hills are frequently cultivated. The underwood is cleared every 16—20 years, and the soil employed as arable land during a period of 3 years.

Before Giessen is reached the ruins of *Gleiberg* and *Fetzberg* are seen on the l.

Giessen (*Einhorn; Rappe; Prinz Carl;* good beer and fine view at the *Felsenkeller*), situated on the Lahn, is principally of modern origin, and the seat of a university, founded in 1607 (400 students).

About 3 M. to the l. of stat. *Butzbach* rise the considerable ruins of the castle of *Münzenberg*, destroyed in the thirty years' war. The higher (145 ft.) of its two towers commands an extensive view.

Nauheim (**Hôtel de l'Europe*, R. and B. 1 fl. 18 kr.; *Curhaus; Hôtel Henkel, Hôtel de Paris*), a watering-place with a saline spring, situated on the N. E. slopes of the Taunus Mts., is a handsome looking place when viewed from the station, especially when the warm fountain plays, the milky and foaming mineral water of which rises to the height of 56 ft. The "green table", lately introduced, forms one of the principal attractions of the place, which is visited by about 3000 patients annually The *Johannisberg*, a wooded eminence, 1 M. from the Cursaal, surmounted by the tower of an ancient monastery, commands an extensive prospect.

Friedberg (*Hôtel Trapp; Simon*), once a free Imperial town, is surrounded by walls of considerable extent, and possesses two handsome Gothic churches. On the N. side stands a fine, well-preserved watch-tower, near which is situated the beautiful Palace garden.

As the train approaches *Frankfurt*, the Taunus Mts. are seen on the r. *Bonames* is the station for the baths of *Homburg*.

Frankfurt, see R. 39.

13. The Rhine from Cologne to Bonn.

Comp. Map R. 4.

By Railway, express in 40 min., ordinary in 1 hr.; fares: 20, 15 and 10 Sgr. — By steamboat in $2^1/_2$ hrs. (down in $1^1/_4$ hr.), fares: 8 or 5 Sgr. Conveyances see p. 25.

N. B. In the following routes (13—24) *r.* and *l.* are used to indicate the position of towns, villages etc. with regard to the steamboat-passenger ascending the river.

As the majestic city of Cologne, with its cathedral, numerous towers and lofty railway-bridge gradually disappears, the castle of **Bensberg** comes in sight, situated on an eminence 9 M. to the l. It was erected by the Count Palatine John William, and is now employed as a Prussian military school. At the foot of the hill on which the castle stands, is a monument erected by the present emperor of Austria in 1854, to the memory of about 2000 Austrian soldiers who fell at the battle of Jemappes in 1794. About $^3/_4$ M. to the E. rises the *Erdenburg*, an eminence surmounted by the remnants of an old wall, believed to be of ancient Germanic origin. A few miles farther on is (l.) *Mondorf*, at the old influx of the Sieg. Opp. to the island of *Graupenwerth*, at the mouth of the Sieg, lies the village of *Grau Rheindorf*.

On the hillside, about 9 M. from the confluence of the Sieg and Rhine, are seen the buildings of the ancient Benedictine Abbey of Siegburg, now employed as a lunatic-asylum. Siegburg is a stat. on the Cologne and Giessen railway: diligence several times a day from Bonn in $1^1/_4$ hr. (9 Sgr.).

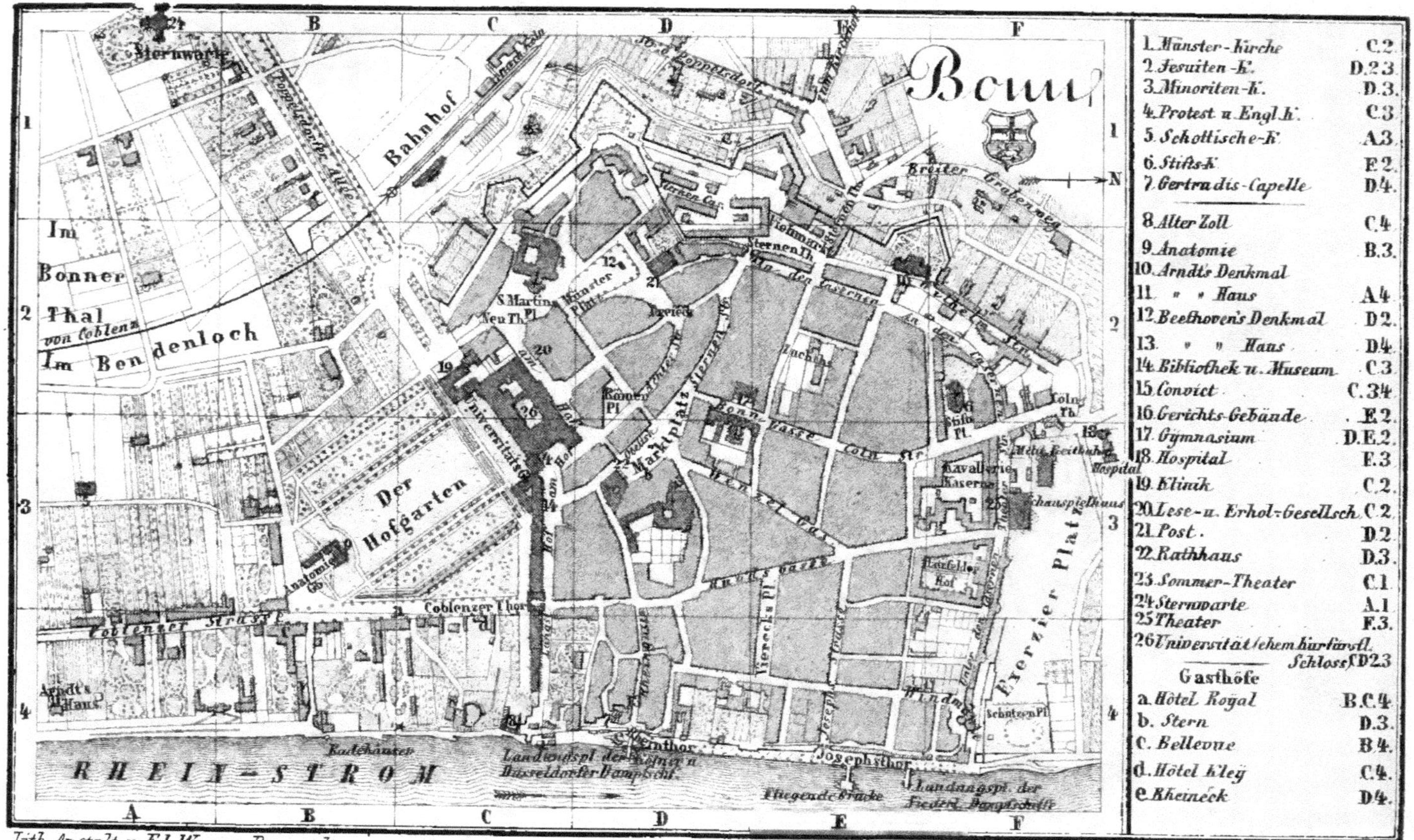

Lith. Anstalt v. Ed. Wagner, Darmstadt

To the l. the church of **Schwarz-Rheindorf** is seen peeping from among the trees; it is a curious structure, consisting of two churches, one above the other, consecrated in 1511 by Archbishop Arnold of Wied. It shows no trace of the pointed-arch style, and possesses a particular value in the history of architecture. The arcade which almost entirely surrounds the church, with its numerous pillars whose bases and capitals exhibit the most various styles of decoration, is well worth the inspection of architects and lovers of art. The lower church contains interesting frescoes of the 12th cent. To the r. the *Jesuitenhof*, then the *Wichelshof.* As the steamboat approaches Bonn, the charms of the Rhineland gradually begin to present themselves to the view.

14. Bonn.

Hotels. *Star, in the market-place, well conducted, excellent table d'hôte. *Royal Hotel, R. 20, L. 6, A 6 Sgr.; Bellevue, outside of the Coblenz gate, with gardens on the bank of the Rhine, R. 16—20, L. 5, B. 8, A. 6 Sgr.; *Hôtel Kley, at the Coblenz gate, with garden extending to the river, R. 15, L. 4, B. 8, D. 15 Sgr.; it is at the same time a good restaurant and boarding house, pension $1^1/_3$ Thlr. per diem and upwards. — *Rheineck, opp. the steamboat pier, R. 12, B. 7, D. 15, A. 5 Sgr. Rheinischer Hof, Schwan, good second-class house. *Hôtel Garni:* Château du Rhin.

Restaurants. Clouth, in the Sandkaul; *Nettekoven, in the Neugasse, Bavarian beer. *Voss and *Perrin, both in the Wenzelgasse.

Cafés. Schweizer Caffehaus next to the Jesuits' church; Laubinger, confectioner in the market-place, opp. to the Star Hotel.

Newspapers and restaurant in the *Lese- und Erholungs-Gesellschaft*, opp. to the University; the *Academic Reading-room* coutains upwards of 200 newspapers and periodicals; visitors must be introduced by a member.

Bath. Warm and Shower baths at Räss's, 8 Sgr. Cold river-baths in the Rhine, 3 Sgr. On the r. bank, Swimming-baths 5 Sgr.; after 5 p. m. boats cross every half-hour at the upper end of the town.

Carriages. For a drive in the town, 1—2 pers. 5, each additional person $2^1/_2$ Sgr., box 1 Sgr.; $^1/_2$ hr. $7^1/_2$—10 Sgr.

Railway station near the Poppelsdorf avenue (p. 47).

Telegraph Office Fürstenstrasse 38.

English Church Service performed by a resident chaplain in the University church.

Visitors whose time is limited should inspect the exterior of the Münster church (p. 46), the monument of Beethoven (p. 46), the Collection of Rhenish and Westphalian antiquities (p. 46); the frescoes in the Aula (p. 45), the Scientific Museum in the palace at Poppelsdorf (p. 46), the view from the Kreuzberg (p. 47), and the "alte Zoll" (p. 46).

The lofty tower of the Münster church, the handsome new residences on the Rhine above the town, the long extended buildings of the University, peeping from among the trees, and the grounds of the "*alte Zoll*" give a cheerful and pleasing aspect to the town, when viewed from the steamboat.

Bonn (*Bonna,* or the *Castra Bonnensia*) frequently mentioned by Tacitus (Hist. IV, 20, 25, 62, 70, 77. V. 22), was one of the first Roman fortresses on the Rhine, probably founded by Drusus, and the head-quarters of the 1st, 5th, 15th, 21st, and and 22nd Legions, and of the Austrian cohort. It was celebrated for its Temple of Mars and the *Ara Ubiorum*, which is believed by some to have stood here (*Tacit. Ann. I, 39, 57.*). One of the two bridges, which Florus says that Drusus constructed across the Rhine, was at Bonn, the other at Mayence. The former stood at the end of the Steinweg or Roman Street at the *Wichelshof*, on the N. side of the town, as was proved by excavations made in 1818. In the year 70 A.D. Claudius Civilis, the leader of the Batavi, who had taken up arms against the Romans, forced his way as far as Bonn, and gained a victory, *Bonnense prœlium*, as Tacitus records (Hist. IV, 20.).

Under Constantine the Great, whose mother Helena is said to have founded the Münster, Bonn seems to have been a flourishing place. About the middle of the 4th cent. it was destroyed by the Alemanni. The Emperor Julian shortly afterwards caused the walls to be rebuilt, but the town did not regain its former importance till 1268, when the Archbishop Engelberg of Falkenburg transferred his residence and the seat of his temporal government thither. An ancient tombstone, as well as the oldest seal belonging to the town, bears the name of *Verona*, which was the appellation given to that part of the town occupied by the citizens, whilst the name of *Bonna* was applied to the military portion. In later ages the name of Verona does not again occur. The German kings, Frederick of Austria (1314), and Charles IV. (1346) were crowned in the Münster at Bonn.

Tbe Protestant tendencies of the Archbishops of Cologne, Hermann of Wied and Gebhard of Waldburg in the 16th cent., principally manifested by the latter in his marriage with the nun Agnes of Mansfeld, for which sacrilegious act he was declared apostate and banished from his Electorate, brought the town of Bonn into great trouble; for Gebhard, being as much soldier as priest, collected an army and made war against the prelate who had been elected in his stead; but he was compelled to retire to the castle of *Godesberg*, a stronghold belonging to the father of Agnes, which was besieged and blown up, thus terminating his turbulent career. In the war of liberation of the Netherlands, in the 30 years' war, and especially in the Spanish war of succession, Bonn suffered repeatedly from sieges. The Electors of the house of Bavaria were always at this period in alliance with France against the house of Austria. The siege of 1689 was conducted by the Elector Frederick III. of Brandenburg (King Fred. I.)

at the head of the Imperial and allied troops. Amongst other celebrated generals, Alexander of Parma, Montecuculi, Marlborough, Opdam, and Coehorn took part about the same time in the operations against the town, the fortifications of which were finally dismantled in 1717, in accordance with the peace of Baden.

Under the magnificent sway of the Electors of the 18th century Bonn rose to great opulence, and one of them, Max Frederick of Königseck, founded an *Academy* in 1777, which three years later was raised to a *University* by his successor. It only subsisted however till 1794, when the town fell into the hands of the French.

During the French dominion Bonn suffered much, and its population decreased from 9500 to 7500; the number of inhab. is now 19,425 (3000 Prot., 500 Jews, 800 Students, 900 Soldiers). The present **University** was founded by the king of Prussia in 1818. Whole streets of handsome houses have since then sprung up, especially on the S. side of the town; the more ancient portion consists of a few narrow streets on the N. side which, however, present no objects of interest.

The lectures, with the exception of those on natural science and agriculture, are delivered in the **Schloss** (Pl. 27), which the Elector Clemens August erected in 1730 as a residence. The buildings were much injured by the French, but have been completely restored by the Prussian government. They occupy considerably more than half of the S. side of the town (1400 ft. in length), and present a very imposing appearance. They are terminated on the E. side by the Coblenz gate. Besides the lecture-rooms they contain a well-arranged library of 200,000 vols., adorned with a large collection of busts, among which are those of Niebuhr, Schlegel, Welcker, and Arndt; a valuable *Numismatic collection* (4000 Greek and Roman coins); the *Museum of Antiquities* (see p. 46); the *Physical cabinet*; an admirable *Clinical institution*, and the *Aula* or Hall, containing frescoes emblematical of the four faculties, theology, jurisprudence, medicine, and philosophy, painted by Cornelius and his pupils, Hermann, Förster, and Götzenberger in 1824–35. Admission to the Aula on application to the door-keeper, who lives to the l. under the university-halls (fee 5 Sgr.). The academical *Museum of Art*, containing many valuable casts, statues, &c., has lately been transferred to the academical riding-school. The library and museum of art are always accessible (attendant's fee 10 Sgr. for 1 pers., 20 Sgr. for a party). What was formerly the courtchapel of the Electoral palace is now converted into a Protestant place of worship. Divine service, according to the rites of the Church of England, is performed on Sundays by a resident chaplain.

The **Museum of Antiquities** (*Museum vaterländischer Alterthümer*) is an extensive and valuable collection of monuments and other objects belonging to the Roman period, found in the Rhenish province and Westphalia, and greatly enriched by the excavations at the Wichelshof already mentioned (p. 44). One of the most interesting objects is a Roman altar, dedicated to Victory, 6 ft. in height, and hewn out of shell-limestone. It bears the inscription "*Deæ victoriæ sacrum*", and is decorated with high-reliefs; it is believed by many to be identical with the *Ara Ubiorum*, mentioned by Tacitus. The numerous inscriptions on the various monuments in the collection embrace almost the entire field of Roman mythology, and some of them contain allusions to the Gallic and even to the ancient German religious rites. Of tombstone-inscriptions one of great historical importance is that of Marcus Cælius, in which the battle of the Teutoburg Wood (*bellum Varianum*) is mentioned; a Greek gravestone, found at Bonn, is also very remarkable. The entrance hall contains a number of ancient and other capitals.

The grounds at the E. side of the Coblenz gate, terminating in an old bastion, known by the name of the ***Alte Zoll**, deserve a visit for the sake of the fine prospect they afford of the Rhine, Seven Mountains, &c.

The finest of the churches is the ***Münster** (Pl. 1), built in the transition style. It was formerly an archdeanery of St. Cassius and St. Florentius, and, like many of the Rhenish churches, traces its foundation back to the time of Constantine the Great, having been, as we are told by an ancient tradition, founded by St. Helena, the pious mother of the emperor. The choir, with its towers, and the crypt, which a glass door separates from the choir, as well as the cloisters with their tastefully decorated pillars, date from the year 1157, and the remainder of the edifice from 1270. The interior only contains two *Basreliefs* worth inspection, the Nativity and Baptism of Christ on the altars to the r. Not far from the chief portal is the *Sarcophagus* of the archbishop Engelbert von Falkenburg (d. 1275). The ancient chapter-house adjoining the church is now converted into a residence for the clergyman.

The other churches offer few attractions to detain the traveller. The *Minoritenkirche* contains an altar-piece by Spielberg, representing the baptism of the Franconian king Clovis by St. Remigius, and possesses a fine organ.

The bronze ***Statue of Beethoven** (Pl. 19), in the Münsterplatz, was executed by Hähnel, an artist of Dresden. The house where the celebrated composer was born is in the Bonngasse.

The fountain-pillar in the market-place was erected in 1777 by the townspeople in honour of the Elector Max Frederiek, to whom the town was indebted for its university, and for many acts of kindness and generosity.

A gate on the S. E. side of the Münsterplatz leads into the *Hofgarten* and the **Poppelsdorfer Allee**, the principal promenade of the town, which consists of a quadruple row of beautiful horse-chesnuts, $^3/_4$ M. in length. To the r. of the avenue is the Railway Station, and beyond it to the l. the handsome new **Observatory** with its tower and six smaller turrets.

At the extremity of the avenue is situated the **Poppelsdorfer Schloss,** formerly a country residence of the Electors, presented to the university by Fred. William III. It contains the *Natural history collection,* consisting of upwards of 150,000 specimens, among which the minerals and fossils are particularly worthy of inspection, as they serve to illustrate the geology of the Rhine and the volcanic formation of the Seven Mountains (R. 16) and Eifel (R. 33). The valuable *Zoological cabinet*, in the rotunda, is also well arranged. The "*Grottensaal*", or Grotto-hall, fitted up in the time of the Electors, contains numerous models in explanation of mining operations, of the Rhine, the Seven Mountains, &c., which may be purchased. The custodian's lodge is on the l. hand side of the entrance (fee $7^1/_2$ Sgr., for a party 15—20 Sgr.). The *Botanical Garden* at the Schloss (open to the public on Tuesdays and Fridays, at other times fee as above) is of considerable extent and well-kept; the large hot-houses deserve inspection. Opposite to it are the buildings of the *Agricultural Academy*, with lecture-rooms, collections, and the residence of the director.

Above the village of Poppelsdorf, $^3/_4$ M. from the Schloss, rises the ***Kreuzberg** (400 ft.), surmounted by a white church which forms a conspicuous object in the landscape. It belonged to a monastery erected here by the Elector Ferdinand of Bavaria (d. 1650), which no longer exists, and contains the so-called *Holy Steps,* of Italian marble (in the chapel behind the altar) constructed by the Elector Clemens August (d. 1761). These steps, 28 in number, must only be ascended on the knees, and are a duplieate of the *sancta scala* at the Lateran at Rome, superstitiously believed to be the identical steps of the hall of the Prætorium at Jerusalem ascended by the Saviour when he appeared before Pilate. A vault under the church presents a very ghastly spectacle. Here are preserved the bodies of 25 monks, robed in the cassocks in which they lived. They were the Servite monks belonging to the monastery, whose corpses the peculiar dryness of the soil has preserved from decay. The tower commands a beautiful and extensive view.

On returning from the Kreuzberg the road to the l., about half-way along the Poppelsdorf avenue, leads to the ***Cemetery,** situated near the Sternenthor. (If the principal E. gate be closed, the visitor may gain admittance by a small gate to the r.)

Tombstones. By the wall on the r. *Monument to Niebuhr* (d. 1831), erected by the late king Fred. William IV. to his "teacher and friend". Farther along the same walk, on the r., the monuments of *Ernst von Schiller*, the son, and of *Charlotte von Lengefeld*, the widow of the poet. The *Chapel in the middle of the cemetery is a beautiful little structure in the late Romanesque style, built about the year 1200, and transferred in 1847 from Ramersdorf (s. below) to its present site.

15. The Rhine from Bonn to Remagen.

By railway in 40 min. — By steamboat in 1¾ hr. (down in 1 hr.); piers at Bonn, Königswinter and Rolandseck: small-boat stations at Obercassel, Plittersdorf (Godesberg) and Unkel. The steamboat is, on account of the beauty of the scenery, far preferable to the railway.

Shortly after the steamboat has quitted Bonn, the beauty of the scenery rapidly increases, and the imposing group of the Seven Mountains is approached. l. *Ramersdorf*, with woods in the background, was formerly a lodge of the knights of the Teutonic order. The original building having been burned down with the exception of the chapel, the latter, which was unsuitable for the new structure, was taken down and subsequently re-erected in the cemetery at Bonn.

l. **Obercassel** (**Zur Wolfsburg*). On the Rabenlei in the vicinity, a basalt quarry yields an excellent paving stone, the so-called table-basalt.

r. **Plittersdorf,** stat. for Godesberg, situated 1 M. to the S.W.

l. **Niederdollendorf,** on the bank of the river; **Oberdollendorf,** ½ M. inland, at the entrance of the valley of Heisterbach (p. 201).

To the r. rises the handsome castle of *Godesberg*, situated on an eminence, 1½ M. from the Rhine.

r. **Rüngsdorf;** the country residence with the tower belongs to M. Camphausen, Prussian minister in 1848.

l. **Königswinter** (146 ft.) (**European Hotel; *Berlin Hotel;* opp. to the pier, of the first cl., Cologne prices; **Hôtel Rieffel,* unpretending, near the N. end of the principal street, R. and B. 16, D. 12 Sgr.; **Düsseldorfer Hof, Pension*, 1⅙ Thlr. per diem, at *R. Schmitz's, opp. to the floating baths; or at Bonn's opp. the post-office, similar charges), is a small modern town, clean and well-to-do, inhabited principally by stone-cutters, and a favourite resort of the inhabitants of Bonn and Cologne. The railway stat. *Mehlem* (p. 51) is on the opposite bank, about ½ M. from the river. Excursions among the Seven Mountains see R. 16. Omnibus to Honnef 5 Sgr.

Porterage. Travelling-bag from the steamboat into the town 2½, to Honnef (p. 56) 5 Sgr., trunk into the town 2½, to Honnef 6 Sgr. Guide to the Drachenfels to carry small packages 7½, to Heisterbach or Petersberg 8, to the Oelberg, Löwenburg or other hills 12½; for half a day 10, for a whole day 20 Sgr. The guides are forbidden by the police to demand fees or refreshment-money in addition to the above charges.

Donkeys. (Stand on the road to the Drachenfels, ½ M. to the E. of the steamboat pier). Drachenfels or Wolkenburg 10, Drachenfels and Wolkenburg 15, Heisterbach 15, Petersberg 15, Löwenburg 20, Oelberg 20, Oelberg and Heisterbach 25 Sgr., for a whole day 1 Thlr. 5 Sgr. If the traveller remain 1—2 hrs. at any of the above places, 5 Sgr. must be paid in addition to the above charges for the ride back, for every additional hour 2½ Sgr. If the donkey be brought to the door of the traveller's hotel, 2½ Sgr. extra is charged. The guides and donkey-boys are strictly prohibited from demanding any additional fee.

l. The castle of **Drachenfels** (dragon's rock), situated 855 ft. above the level of the Rhine, was newly erected by Arnold, Archbishop of Cologne at the commencement of the 12th cent., and was held as a fief from him by the counts of the castle. Henry, Count of Drachenfels (d. 1348), made an agreement with the chapter of the cathedral of Cologne to supply them with the stone of which the cathedral is constructed; the quarry still bears the name of *Dombruch*, or Cathedral quarry. The wine yielded by the vineyards on its slopes is known by the appellation of *Drachenblut,* or Dragon's blood. In the 30 Years' war the half-ruined castle was occupied by the Swedes, but was taken from them by the Duke Ferdinand of Bavaria, Elector of Cologne, who completed its destruction to avoid the necessity of placing a garrison in it.

The cavern among the vineyards, which is visible from the Rhine about half-way up the hill on the side facing the river, is said once to have housed the dragon, slain by Siegfried, the hero from the Low Countries, who, having bathed himself in its blood, became invulnerable.

The ascent of the Drachenfels is best accomplished from Königswinter, and occupies about 50 min. The road (guide quite unnecessary) leads between the two hotels straight to the foot of the hill (7 min.), where, at the donkey-station, it turns off at a right angle, and is, at the commencement, somewhat steep. About half-way up a booth is reached, where minerals found in the vicinity may be purchased. A little farther on, the path divides. They both lead to the top; that to the r. round the rock with view of the Rhine, the old path to the l. through wood. The *inn at the summit has sleeping accommodation for about 20 persons at 20 Sgr. each; B. 7½ Sgr.; board and lodging at 1½ Thlr. per diem.

The obelisk near the top was erected in 1857 to replace an old monument to Prussian soldiers who fell during the passage of the Rhine in 1814, and records the gratitude of the nation for the 42 years of peace which has since then been vouchsafed to them.

The summit commands one of the noblest prospects on the Rhine: to the E. are seen several of the seven peaks, to the S.E. the basaltic heights at the back of Honnef, among others the Minderberg (p. 63) and the Hemmerich (p. 53), which gradually slope to the plain of the Rhine. Immediately beneath, on the r. bank, lie the villages of Rhöndorf, Honnef, Rheinbreitbach, Unkel, and Erpel; on the l. bank Remagen and the Gothic church on the Apollinarisberg, and in the background the heights of the Eifel with the ruins of Olbrück and Tomberg; in the vicinity are Oberwinter, the islands of Grafenwerth and Nonnenwerth, the arched ruin of Rolandseck, and near it the farmhouse of Roderberg. Farther to the r. the Kreuzberg, Bonn, and even Cologne are visible.

"The castled crag of Drachenfels
Frowns o'er the wide and winding Rhine,
Whose breast of waters broadly swells
Between the banks which bear the vine;
And hills all rich with blossom'd trees,
And fields which promise corn and wine,
And scatter'd cities crowning these,
Whose far white walls along them shine,
Have strew'd a scene which I should see
With double joy wert *thou* with me.

"And peasant girls with deep blue eyes,
And hands which offer early flowers,
Walk smiling o'er this paradise;
Above, the frequent feudal towers
Through green leaves lift their walls of gray,
And many a rock which steeply lowers,
And noble arch in proud decay,
Look o'er this vale of vintage bowers;
But one thing want these banks of Rhine —
Thy gentle hand to clasp in mine!

"The river nobly foams and flows,
The charm of this enchanted ground,
And all its thousand turns disclose
Some fresher beauty varying round:
The haughtiest breast its wish might bound,
Through life to dwell delighted here;
Nor could on earth a spot be found
To nature and to me so dear,
Could *thy* dear eyes in following mine
Still sweeten more these banks of Rhine!"

BYRON.

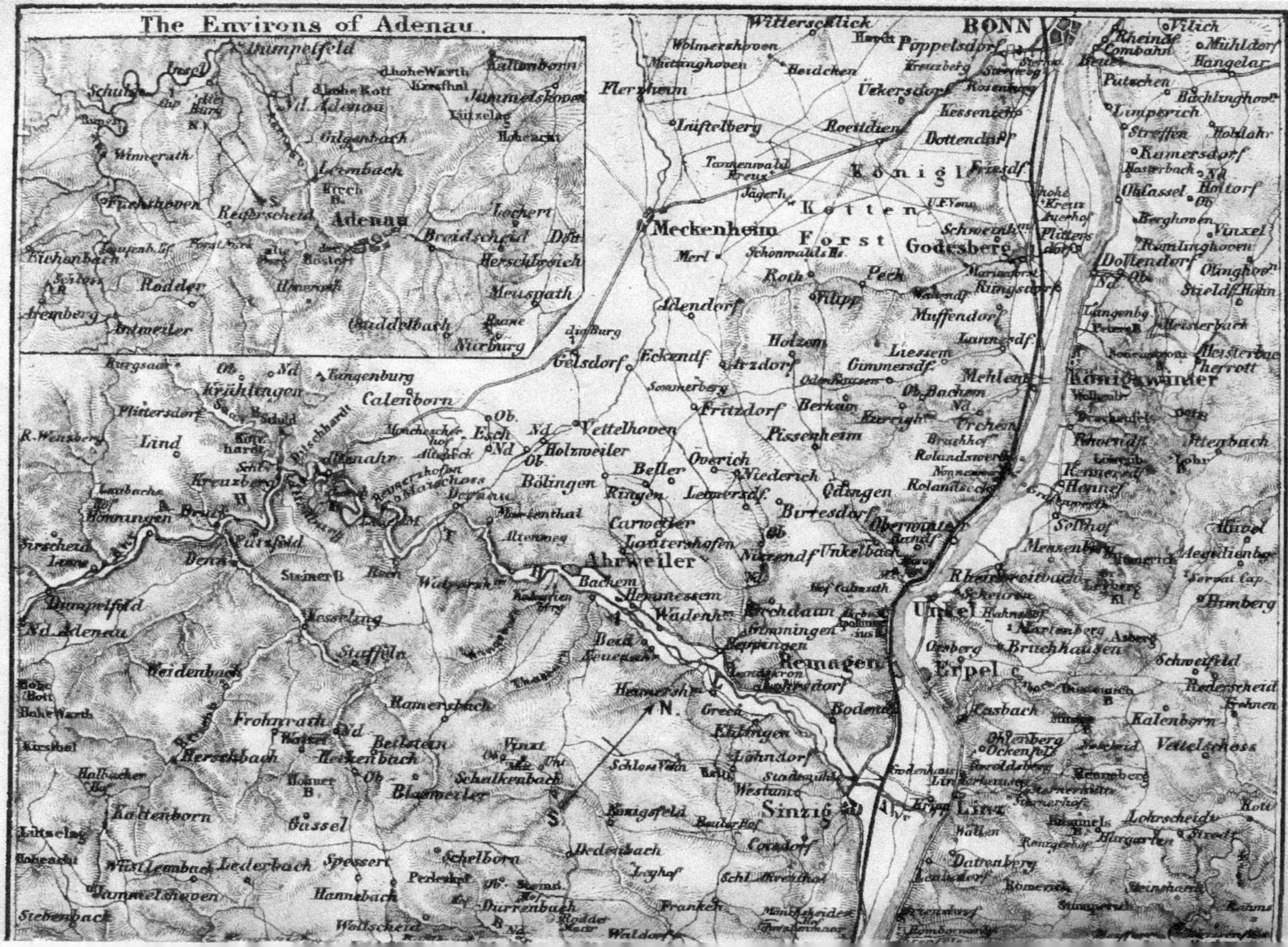
The Environs of Adenau.
BONN
Poppelsdorf
Witterschlick
Meckenheim
Königl. Kotten Forst
Godesberg
Königswinter
Ahrweiler
Remagen
Sinzig
Linz
Unkel
Erpel
Adenau
Altenahr
Calenborn
Gelsdorf
Mehlem
Honnef
Dümpelfeld
Kalenborn
Vettelschoss
Rolandseck
Heimersheim
Bodendorf
Nürburg
Kaltenborn
Ramersbach
Oberwinter
Vilich
Beuel
Limperich
Friesdorf
Dottendorf
Kessenich
Flerzheim
Lüftelberg
Adendorf
Fritzdorf
Vettelhoven
Holzweiler
Bölingen
Lind
Kreuzberg
Staffeln
Frohnrath
Herschbach
Blasweiler
Gassel
Lederbach
Dedenbach
Dattenberg
Bruchhausen
Schweifeld
Lohrscheid
Mayschoss
Rech
Dernau
Walporzheim
Breidscheid
Meuspath
Quiddelbach
Hümpelfeld
Reifferscheid
Leimbach
Wimmerath
Fuchshofen
Rodder
Antweiler
Pissenheim
Gimmersdorf
Muffendorf
Lannesdorf
Oedingen
Birresdorf
Lantershofen
Carweiler
Ringen
Beller
Niederich
Leimersdorf

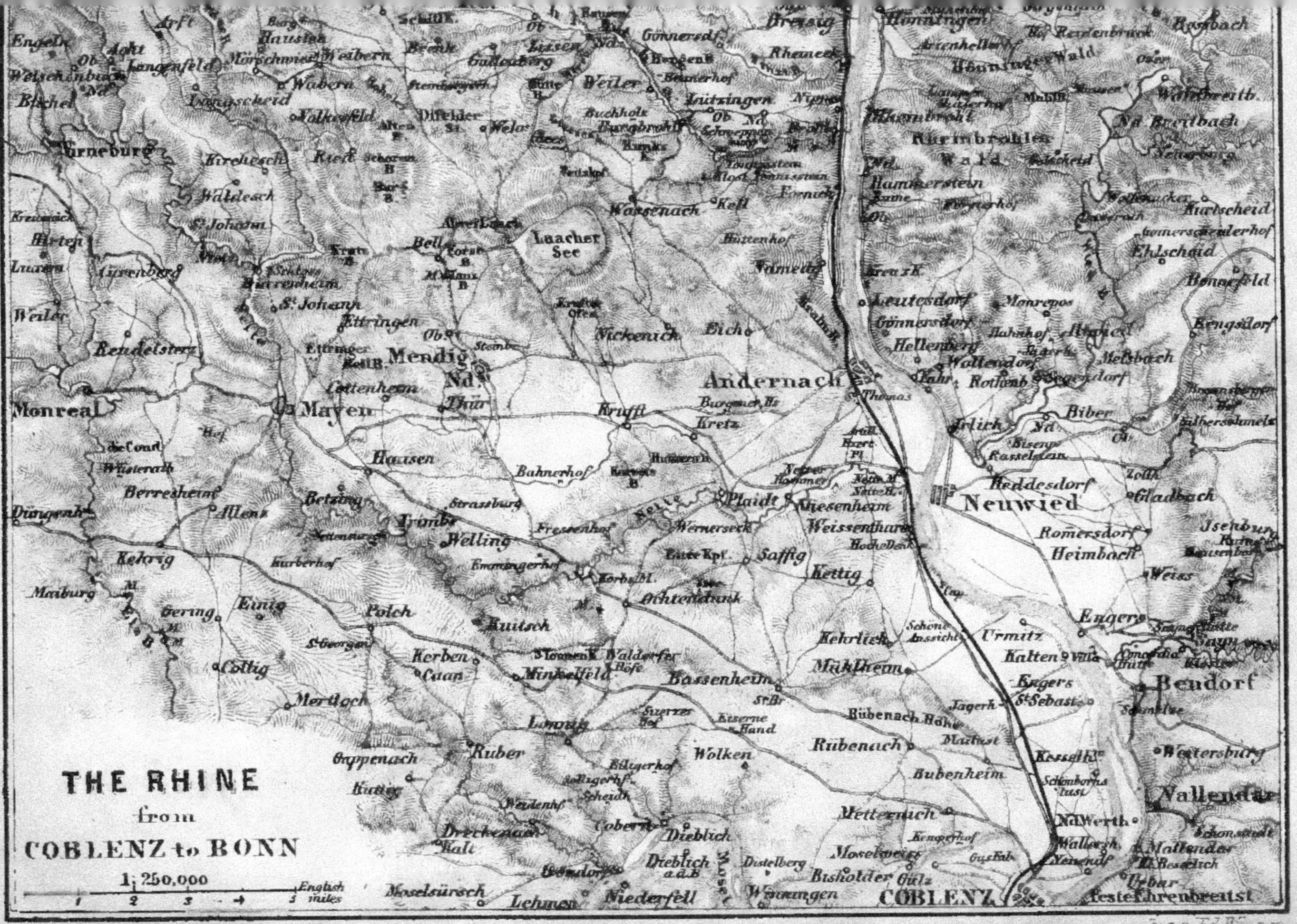
THE RHINE
from
COBLENZ to BONN
1:250,000
English miles
Andernach
Neuwied
Mayen
Mendig
Laacher See
Coblenz
Bendorf
Vallendar
Monreal
Engers
Polch
Lith. geograph. Anst. v. Ed. Wagner, Darmstadt

r. **Mehlem** (*Stern; Krone; Goldenes Schiff,* on the Rhine with garden, pension 1 Thlr.) was the birthplace of the celebrated artist of the Cologne school, John of Mehlem. Railway stat. and flying bridge to Königswinter (see p. 48).

r. **Rolandseck** (steamboat and railway stat. **Hôtel Rolandseck; *Roland's Hotel*, also a hydropathic establishment; **Hôtel Billau*, near the steamboat pier; **Railway-station restaurant*, charges all according to a fixed tariff; magnificent view from the terrace. On the hill rises the solitary arch of the ruin of *Rolandseck*, $^3/_4$ M. from the station; the path ascends by the Hotel Roland (donkey 10 Sgr.). The *view from this basaltic rock, 340 ft. above the Rhine, is less extensive than that from the Drachenfels, but is still more picturesque, as the Drachenfels itself, the Wolkenburg, and other wooded heights of the Seven Mountains form the foreground of the landscape. In the distance, to the S., the castle of Olbrück is visible.

The castle is believed to have been built by the knight Roland, peer of France and paladin of Charlemagne, who fell in the battle of Ronceval. He is called by Eginhard (the secretary of Charlemagne) the guardian of the north coast, and his dominions are described as having extended to that part of the Rhine where the mountains begin. The castle is mentioned in a document of 1040—1045 as *Rulcheseck*. In the time of the Archbishop Frederick it was already a ruin, but was partly restored by him in 1120 to defend his dominions against Henry IV. The fortress stood till the close of the 15th cent., when, in the contests between the deposed Archbishop Ruprecht of the Palatinate assisted by Charles the Bold of Burgundy, and the Emperor Frederick III., it fell entirely to decay. A beautiful legend is connected with th castle and convent, which probably suggested Schiller's "*Ritter Toggenburg*". It may be thus briefly narrated:

The brave knight Roland, whilst scouring the Rhine in search of adventure, found himself the guest of Count Heribert, the lord of the Seven Mountains, at his castle of Drachenburg. According to the custom of the times, the daughter of the host, the peerless Hildegunde, welcomed him with the offering of bread, wine and fish. Her beauty rivetted the gaze of the ardent young knight, and Hildegunde and Roland were shorly affianced lovers; but, as the course of true love never did run smooth, an interruption soon came to their happiness. Roland was summoned by Charlemagne to the crusade. Time sped on, and anxiously did Hildegunde await the return of her betrothed; but instead of his arrival sad rumours came. The brave Roland was said to have fallen by the hands of the Infidels, and the world no longer possessing any charm for the inconsolable Hildegunde, she took refuge in the "Kloster" in the adjacent island of Nonnenwerth. The rumours, however, of the death of her betrothed were unfounded. Though desperately wounded, he recovered and hastened to the halls of Drachenburg to claim his bride, but instead of being welcomed back by that fondly remembered smile, he found that his love was for ever lost to him. In despair he built the castle, of which one crumbling arch alone remains, and there in solitude he lived, catching an occasional glimpse of a fair form passing to and fro to her devotions in the little chapel of the Kloster. At length he missed her, and soon the tolling of the bell and a mournful procession conveyed to him the heart-rending intelligence that his beloved Hildegunde was now indeed removed from him for ever. From that moment Roland never spoke again; for a short time he dragged on his wretched existence, but his heart was broken, and one morning his sole attendant found him rigid and lifeless, his glassy eye still turned towards the convent-chapel.

The new tower, $\frac{1}{2}$ M. to the W. of the ruin, affords a more extended prospect, comprising Godesberg, the lower hills of the Seven Mts., and the plain between Bonn and Cologne, which are not visible from Rolandseck. The key of the tower may be procured from the proprietor, Herr vom Rath, who lives opposite to Roland's Hotel. About $\frac{1}{2}$ M. from the tower is situated the *Roderberg*, a crater, $\frac{1}{4}$ M. in diameter and 60 ft. in depth. On the rounded margin of this crater the pumice-stone is everywhere visible; the bottom is now converted into arable land, belonging to the farm-house of *Bruchhof*, which lies in the middle. The building on the island of **Nonnenwerth**, or *Rolandswerth*, was once a nunnery, the date of whose foundation reaches back to the ages of tradition. It is first mentioned in a document of the 12th cent. The old building was burned down in 1673, since which date the present was erected. In 1802 the nunnery was suppressed by Napoleon, and would have suffered the fate of the other religious establishments which fell into his hands but for the interposition of Josephine, who procured permission for the nuns to retain possession of their loved island, though no addition to the sisterhood was allowed. The building has since gone through many vicissitudes and passed into various hands; it is now an educational estab., conducted by Franciscan nuns.

On the wide plain to the l. lie the villages of *Rhöndorf*, *Honnef*, *Rheinbreitbach*, and *Scheuern*.

r. **Oberwinter** (*Fassbender*) once belonged to the Duchy of Jülich. The retrospective view from this point is one of the finest on the Rhine. Rolandseck and the Drachenfels with its ruined castle, the rugged cliffs of the Wolkenburg and the entire range (upwards of 30) of the peaks of the Seven Mountains, at the r. extremity of which is the flattened summit of the Löwenburg surmounted by a ruin (the isolated sharp peak still farther to the r. is the Hemmerich), form a mountain chain of incomparable beauty, whilst the lovely island of Nonnenwerth and the grand river itself constitute the foreground of the picture.

In 1846 a considerable landslip took place on the bank opp. to Unkel. One half of a hill (the *Birgeler Kopf*) moved down towards the Rhine; the barren, rugged walls of the other portion show distinctly where the slip took place, and the otherwise regular strata of basalt have been dislodged from their original position.

l. **Unkel** (*Clasen;* steamboat stat.), a handsome village, between which and Remagen the Rhine describes a wide curve; both banks are studded with handsome country residences. Below the Apollinarisberg to the r. a railway is seen emerging

NONNENWERTH a. ROLANDSECK

from the hills, which conveys the basalt from the quarries to the river.

r. *Remagen* and the *Apollinarisberg* see R. 18.

16. The Seven Mountains (*Siebengebirge*).

One day suffices to visit the most remarkable and beautiful points in this district, unless the tourist travel for geological purposes. *Königswinter* is assumed as the starting point; to *Heisterbach* 3 M., to the *Great Oelberg* 3³/₄ M., to the *Drachenfels* (p. 49) 3³/₄ M., thence to *Königswinter* 1¹/₂ M., altogether 12 M. Charges for guides and donkeys see p. 49. Guide not absolutely necessary if the map and the following directions be consulted.

The district of the **Seven Mountains** extends E. from the Rhine little more than 3 M., and is from N. to S. about 9 M. in length, Königswinter being the central point of the W. side. It consists of a group of peaks, cones and long extended ridges of rounded forms, and is covered partly with high-wood, partly with luxuriant herbage. They are all the result of volcanic agency and have been upheaved through the grauwacke rocks.

"Is consequence of a powerful but local force in the interior of our planet, elastic gases either force up dome-shaped and unopened masses of trachyte mixed with felspar and dolerite (Puy de Dôme, Seven Mountains) through the earth's crust, or the raised strata are so broken through and inclined outwards that on the opp. inner sides a steep wall of rocks is formed."
HUMBOLDT.

The Seven Mountains consist partly of trachyte (*Drachenfels* 1001 ft., *Wolkenburg* 1009 ft., *Lohrberg* 1355 ft.), partly of basalt, a more recent formation than trachyte (*Oelberg* 1429 ft., *Löwenburg*, consists of dolerite, 1413 ft.; *Nonnenstromberg*, a ridge 300 yds. in length, 1036 ft.; *Petersberg* 1027 ft.). These seven peaks, from which the mountains derive their name, are seen simultaneously only in the neighbourhood of Cologne; as Bonn is approached the Löwenburg is hidden by the Nonnenstromberg. Besides these seven summits there are also many others, such as the sugar-loaf shaped *Hemmerich* (1114 ft.), consisting of trachyte, which overtops the lower mountains of the S. side, the *Rosenau* (999 ft.) and the *Stenzelberg* (886 ft.), which adjoins the Nonnenstromberg on the N. The surface of the Rhine at Königswinter is 146 ft. above the level of the sea, so that the different heights of the mountain tops above the Rhine may easily be calculated. The view from the *Drachenfels* is the most picturesque, that from the *Oelberg* the most extensive (comprising even the Taunus). For the geologist a tour through this district presents many objects of interest (see above), for the botanist fewer. The former should not omit to provide himself with the admirable geological map of this district by *H. v. Dechen* (proportion 1 : 25,000).

A much frequented path leads from Königswinter half-way up the **Petersberg** (1027 ft.) (the chapel on the summit commands a fine view; near it a *restaurant), then round the W. and N. slopes of the hill, chiefly through wood, to ***Heisterbach,** once a Cistercian Abbey, beautifully situated in a mountain ravine. The gate through which the visitor enters the avenue of fruit-trees still bears the arms of the abbey, a *Heister* (young oak) and a *Bach* (brook); at the side stand St. Benedictine and St. Bernhard (comp. R. 34) as guardians. Of the Romanesque church only the external part of the high-choir, with its slender and elegant basaltic pillars, is still extant, forming a singularly picturesque ruin. The Abbey was originally a magnificent building, erected in 1202—1233, but was sold and almost entirely pulled down about 60 years ago. The blocks of trachyte of which it consisted were employed in the construction of the locks on the North Canal (R. 54). Some of the finest old German pictures in the Pinakothek of Munich were formerly brought from the church of Heisterbach. Refreshments may be procured at the farm-buildings. The whole of the abbey-lands are the property of the Count zur Lippe whose family burial-ground is at the foot of the hill.

The path to the Great Oelberg turns to the r. by the E. wall of the Abbey, $^3/_4$ M. farther to the r. again, and after $1^1/_2$ M. more the **Stenzelberg** (886 ft.) is reached, where the most extensive quarries of trachyte in the Seven Mts. are worked. The stone is columnar and almost always arranged in perpendicular masses, but is far inferior in eleganee and regularity to the basaltic columns (p. 63).

The path to the l., which leaves the road a little farther on, must now be taken; it soon emerges from the wood, and crosses the fields to a red house, the school of *Heisterbacherrott.* The broad road to the r. must now be taken and the wood is soon re-entered; 3 M. from Heisterbach the foot of the hill is reached, at the point where our path joins the Königswinter road (see p. 55). Here the turning to the l. must be taken, and a steep winding path will bring the pedestrian to the top in about 20 min. The ***Great Oelberg** (1429 ft.) is a basaltic mountain through which the trachyte has been upheaved. The prospect from the summit is the most extensive on the lower Rhine, and the foreground is at the same time highly picturesque, differing in many respects from the view from the Drachenfels. The entire wooded tract of the Seven Mountains lies like a raised map before the eye of the spectator, the Rhine is seen glittering between the valleys which intersect its banks, and its course may be traced as far as Cologne; in the

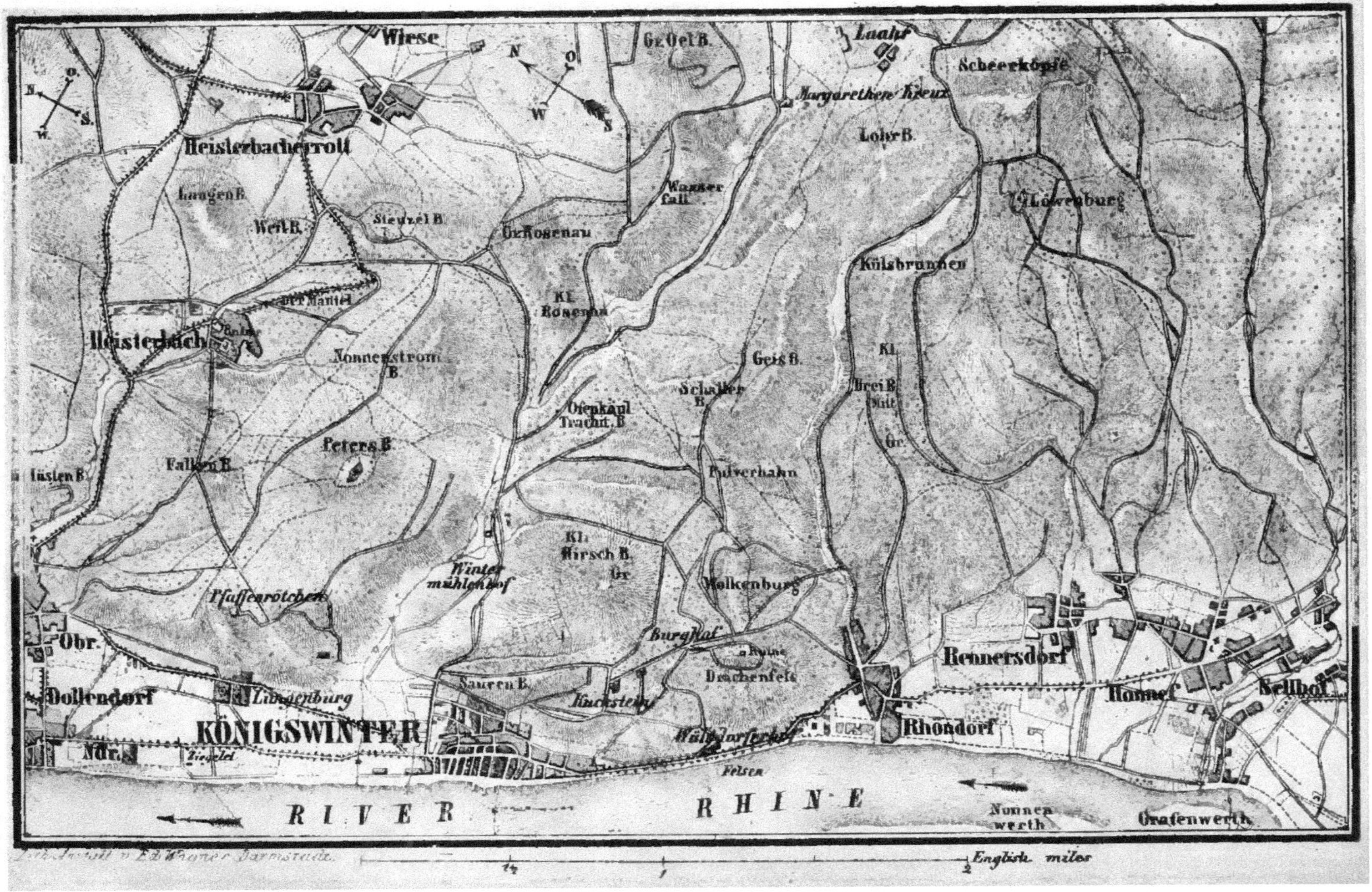
Wiese
Gr. Oel B.
Laahr
Scheerköpfe
Margarethen Kreuz
Heisterbacherrott
Lohr B.
Langen B.
Weil B.
Steuzel B.
Gr. Rosenau
Wasser fall
Löwenburg
Külsbrunnen
Kl. Rosenau
Der Mantel
Heisterbach
Nonnenstrom B.
Geis B.
Schaller B.
Kl.
Brei B.
Mitt.
Gr.
Petersb.
Pulverhahn
Kl. Hirsch B.
Gr.
Winter mühlenhof
Wolkenburg
Pfaffenrötchen
Obr.
Burghof
Ruine
Drachenfels
Rennersdorf
Saurenb.
Kuckstein
Dollendorf
Königswinter
Ndr.
Ziegelei
Rhöndorf
Honnef
Bellhof
Felsen
RIVER RHINE
Nonnenwerth
Grafenwerth
English miles

distance to the S. the Taunus, and to the N.E. the heights in the neighbourhood of Düsseldorf bound the prospect.

From the Oelberg to Königswinter $3^3/_4$ M. The above-mentioned road, which the road from Heisterbach joins at the foot of the hill, leads in a W. direction straight to Königswinter. About half-way, two broad tracks diverge to the l., leading to the quarries of the *Ofenkaulen-Berg*, which yield the so-called oven-stone, a trachyte conglomerate.

After descending from the summit of the Oelberg, the road continues in a S. direction to *St. Margarethenkreuz* (St. Margaret's cross) ($^1/_2$ M.), a hamlet which derives its name from a cross decorated with a relief of St. Margaret with a crucifix and the enchained dragon.

From the Oelberg to the Drachenfels. About 100 yds. to the S. of the Cross of St. Margaret a path through the wood diverges from the road to the r. and leads in a W. direction along the N. brow of the mountain-chain to the Drachenfels, about 3 M. distant. The path, which finally passes the quarries of the Wolkenburg and turns to the l. on the S. side of that hill, cannot be missed.

Following the road from St. Margaret's Cross in a S. direction, the village of **Lahr** is reached ($^1/_2$ M.), at the first houses of which the path to the r. must be ascended, then the first path to the l. between two houses, then for $^1/_2$ M. along the heights. The path now descends to the r. into a narrow pass between the *Lohrberg* (1355 ft.) on the r., and the *Scheerköpfchen* (1215 ft.), the largest mass of trachyte in the Seven Mts., to the l.; $^1/_2$ M. farther is the *Löwenburger Hof*, where refreshments may be procured, situated 100 yds. from the Rhöndorf road, and 300 yds. from the summit of the ***Löwenburg** (1413 ft.), a ruin on a wooded peak consisting of dolerite, a volcanic product which must have been ejected in a liquid state, and now lies above the trachyte and grauwacke. The castle, the extensive ruins of which are visible from the Rhine, was once the scene of the conferences which Hermann, Elector of Cologne and Count of Wied, held with the reformers Melancthon and Bucer, before he became a convert to Protestantism. Here, too, in the troublous times of 1583, the Elector Gebhard, Truchsess of Waldburg, resided with his consort, the beautiful Countess Agnes von Mansfeld, whom he had abducted from the convent of Gerresheim. The summit commands a fine view.

The way from the Löwenburger Hof to *Rhöndorf* (3 M.) cannot be missed. It descends gradually through a narrow, and sometimes swampy mountain dale, and is shaded by groves of oaks and beeches. The heights which bound the path on the N. are the *Geisberg*, *Schullerberg*, *Bolverhahn*, and finally the *Wolkenburg* and *Drachenfels*, all of which are composed of trachyte. The ancient fortress which once stood on the Wolkenburg has long since given place to the quarries on the N. side. **Rhöndorf** (*Beul*) is 1 M. distant from Königswinter, and the same distance from Honnef (see below). On the side wall of the small church of Rhöndorf is a well preserved tombstone of the last knight of Drachenfels, with coat of arms, and the date 1530, brought from the old Abbey of Heisterbach.

In the rich and fruitful plain, 1½ M. broad and 3 M. long, which lies between the Seven Mts. and the Rhine, are situated the flourishing villages of *Rheinbreitbach*, *Honnef*, and *Rhöndorf*. The mildness of the climate and the beauty of the country attract numerous visitors to this district in summer, especially to **Honnef,** which is gradually becoming the Interlaken of the Rhine. Besides a number of country residences which have here sprung up of late, there are several boarding houses: **Dr. de Berghes* at Honnef, pension 1⅙—1⅓ Thlr.: *Hôtel Klein* (D. exc. W. 15 Sgr.), *Zum Siebengebirge*, both good and moderate inns; *Clouth*, at **Rheinbreitbach** (pension 1 Thlr. and upwards).

Excursions from Rheinbreitbach: to the *Breitbacher Kreuz*, near the village, commanding a pleasing view; to the **Haanenburg* (2¼ M.), property of a merchant of Cologne, by a broad path through the vineyards, fine view from the top of the tower, and beautiful walk back, round the building and over the *Heidekamm;* to the "Giants' Graves" (Hünengräber), 1½ M. from Honnef. Near the Haanenburg are the copper mines of *Marienberg*, and 1½ M. farther N. the copper and lead mines of the *Virneberg*, once worked by the Romans. From the Virneberg a path through a fir-wood leads to *Farinasruhe* and thence to the *Menzenberg* (1½ M.).

Excursions from Honnef. One of the most delightful is a walk of 2 hrs., by the farmhouse of *Zicklenburg*, to *Menzenberg*, the slopes of which yield the best red wine of the district, past the *Hager Hof*, a large farmhouse, by the foothpath to Rheinbreitbach and back to Honnef by the road. A shorter walk (1½ M.) may be taken to *Menzenberg*, passing the vineyards of the so-called *Hager Köppelchen* (fine view). The churchyard of Honnef also commands a pleasing prospect. — The *Löwenburg* (p. 55) is best ascended from Honnef (3½ M.), as the path to it offers a succession of beautiful views. Way back from the Löwenburg by Rhöndorf (3¾ M.) to Honnef (1 M.) see p. 55.

17. The Valley of the Ahr.

Comp. Map R. 15.

Distances. From Remagen to Ahrweiler 9 M. (Bodendorf 3, Heppingen 3, Ahrweiler 3); from Ahrweiler to Altenahr 7¼ M. Diligence several times a day in 1½ hr. Carriage from Remagen to Altenahr and back, for 1—4 pers., 1-horse 3⅙, 2-horse 4⅓ Thlr., inc. tolls and driver's fee (comp. p. 61).

A footpath ($4^1/_2$ M.), leading from Remagen to Heppingen, effects a saving of $1^1/_2$ M. At the Apollinarisberg the turning to the l. must be taken, leading through some quarries, and about 500 paces will bring the pedestrian to the road. After $^1/_2$ M. the turning to the r. must be taken, and the path soon enters a copse, on emerging from which the *Köhlerhof* ($1^1/_2$ M.) lies to the l. By proceeding in a straight direction, two new houses (1 M.) are reached, where a road to the l. leads to the Landskron ($1^1/_2$ M.) and the straight road to Heppingen ($1^1/_2$ M.).

The full-flavoured dark red wines produced by the vineyards of the valley of the Ahr, in good seasons upwards of 600,000 gallons (the most celebrated are those of *Walporzheim*, *Ahrweiler*, and *Bodendorf*), are well-known under the name of *Ahrbleichert*.

Millions of "*Rümpchen*" (cyprinus phoxinus), small fish 1—2 in. in length, are annually caught in the Ahr, boiled in saltwater, and packed in willow-bark for exportation. They are served with vinegar and oil, and are esteemed a great delicacy.

The *Ahr* rises at Blankenheim in the Eifel, traverses a winding and generally narrow valley, 54 M. in length, and falls into the Rhine below *Sinzig*. Near the wooden bridge over the Ahr near Sinzig, the road which leads to the Ahrthal diverges from the main road to Coblenz and traverses an open country, the hills which enclose the valley being as yet low and far apart, passing the villages of *Bodendorf*, *Lohrsdorf*, *Heppingen*, *Wadenheim*, *Hemmessem*, and *Ahrweiler*. As yet there is no trace of the wildness which characterizes the upper part of the valley; the land is on the contrary fertile and well-cultivated: the slopes exposed to the S. are covered with vineyards, and the heights on the opposite bank with wood.

The **Landskron** (856 ft.) is a basaltic peak which attains a greater height than the other hills which bound the lower part of the valley. The castle of Landskron, on the summit, is said to have been founded in 1205 by Philipp the Hohenstaufe, when on his way to be crowned at Aix-la-Chapelle, that he might from this point carry on his hostilities against the Archbishopric of Cologne, which supported the claims of the Emperor Otto IV. The castle, in the 14th and 15th centuries the property of a race of knights of the same name, and in 1667 destroyed by the French. The richly endowed chapel on the S.W. side of the summit has been spared; a basaltic grotto serves as sacristy. Near it is a quantity of massive basalt, curiously deposited above columnar basalt. The view from the Landskron comprises the Ahrthal from Ahrweiler to the Rhine, the higher peaks of the Seven Mountains, to the S. part of the Eifel with the castle of Olbrück, and to the W. the ruin of Tomberg near Meckenheim. Seen from the W. side, from the road below, the hill with the white chapel and ruin on the top is a very picturesque object in the landscape.

At the foot of the Landskron, on the S. side, lies the village of **Heppingen** (3 M.), with two pleasant mineral springs.

Near **Wadenheim**, $1\frac{1}{2}$ M. farther, a new spring, the *Apollinarisbrunnen*, was enclosed in 1853. On the opposite (r.) bank of the Ahr are the **Baths of Neuenahr**, opened in 1858, and rapidly rising into importance. The supply of water 96—114° Fahr.) is abundant, and strongly resembles in its component parts the springs of Ems, of which Neuenahr is probably destined some day to be a formidable rival. This water is especially efficacious in pulmonary complaints, gout, and scrofula. The bathing establishment, with which a *pension* is combined, is replete with every comfort and convenience, and the beauty and repose of the situation offer great attraction to the traveller in search of retirement, as well as to the valetudinarian. On a lofty peak (1008 ft.), at the foot of which the village of *Beul* and Bad Neuenahr lie, rises the *Castle of Neuenahr*, destroyed as early as 1371, and once the seat of a younger branch of the Counts von der Are, who became extinct in the 16th cent. Ahrweiler is $2\frac{1}{4}$ M. distant from Neuenahr or Wadenheim. The small church of *Heimersheim*, $2\frac{1}{4}$ M. to the E. of Neuenahr, is, like that of Sinzig, built in the late Romanesque style, and contains some old stained glass.

Ahrweiler (**Krone; *Stern;* Bavarian beer at the restaurant of *J. Kreutzberg*), a cheerful little town surrounded by old walls. The Gothic church was founded in 1275 (the summit of the tower and roof repaired subsequent to 1689), and the town probably enclosed by walls about the same date. In the feud between the chapter of the cathedral of Cologne and the deposed Archbishop Ruprecht of the Palatinate the town successfully stood a siege in 1473, and in a later feud between the same chapter and the deposed Archbishop Gebhard, Ahrweiler sided with the former. In 1646 and 1689 it suffered greatly from the devastations of the French, and on the latter occasion was, with the exception of 10 houses, entirely burned to the ground. A fine view may he obtained from the *Calvarienberg*, an eminence $\frac{1}{2}$ M. to the S., surmounted by an extensive building, formerly a Franciscan monastery, now an Ursuline nunnery, and much frequented as an educational establishment.

Near the entrance to the narrower part of the valley lies the village of **Walporzheim** (*St. Petrus*) ($\frac{3}{4}$ M.), where the best Ahr-wine is produced. The vineyards are kept with the utmost care.

A rocky ravine is now entered, penetrating the jagged and cleft slate mountains; on the l. rushes the Ahr, and on the r. rises almost perpendicularly a black wall of slate-rock, from which a single ridge called "*die bunte Kuh*" projects. To the r. of the road are the ruins of the old nunnery of *Marienthal* ($1\frac{1}{4}$ M.), abandoned at the commencement of the French Revolution.

About $^3/_4$ M. farther, before entering the village of **Dernau,** a footpath, far preferable to the dusty road, leads through the valley, which here widens a little, along the bank of the Ahr, passing an old stone bridge, which however must not be crossed, to the village of **Rech** (1 ½ M.). Here the valley again contracts. The river Ahr winds through a wild and rocky district, the road following its course, rounding the precipitous *Saffenburg*, and leading to **Mayschoss** (1 ¼ M.) and the **Lochmühle** (½ M.), where travellers may find tolerable accommodation for the night. (S., R. and B. 22 Sgr.)

The pedestrian may, if he please, choose a different way from Rech to the Lochmühle. Close to the bridge (on the r. bank), a path ascends to the r. through the vineyards (closed from the end of August till the middle of October) to the ridge of the hill, the summit of which is occupied by the fragments of the **Saffenburg** (794 ft.). It is related of the "brave" French commander of the castle, when it was besieged in 1703 during the Spanish war of succession, that, when summoned to surrender the place, he replied that he was not at all disinclined to do so, but begged that, to save his honour, three cannon-shots should first be discharged against the castle. His wish was complied with, and he was then enabled "honourably" to evacuate the castle, which was blown up in the following year. On the W. side of the Saffenburg the path descends rapidly and joins the road at the bridge of Mayschoss, close to the *Lochmühle* (Inn, see above). [From the bridge at Rech over the Saffenburg to the Lochmühle is a walk of about 35 min.; by the road by Mayschoss a few min. more.]

Near the Lochmühle is a cutting in the rock, the walls of grauwacke being 40 ft. in height, beyond which the hamlets of *Lach* and *Reimerzhofen* are reached, and a little farther on, the road passes through a tunnel, 92 yds. in length, on emerging from which the clean little village of **Altenahr** (*Caspari; Winckler*) comes in sight.

It is, however, far preferable to leave the road at *Reimerzhofen,* 1 M. from the Lochmühle, and follow the footpath which ascends through the vineyards (closed during the vintage-season), leading to the *Cross* (15 min.) which is visible from the road. It stands on a rocky ridge, 350 ft. above the stream, and commands the finest *view in the whole valley, surpassing that from the castle of Altenahr, as the latter itself forms the foreground of the wild and rocky landscape. The path descends on the other side of the hill to *Altenahr* (8 min. walk), passing a decayed gate-way which forms the entrance to the *Castle of Altenahr.* The latter is perched like an eagle's nest on the summit of a grand and rugged wall of rock, 348 ft.

above the village, and was once the seat of the powerful Counts of the Are and Hostaden or Hochsteden. Conrad, Archbishop of Cologne, the last of the elder branch of the family, laid the foundation-stone of the cathedral of Cologne in 1248. The castle fell into the hands of the French in 1690, was occupied by a Bavarian garrison in the Spanish war of succession, and finally, in consequence of the peace of Utrecht (1714) was blown up, like the castles of Saffenburg and the Landskron, to prevent its becoming a harbour for robbers. Admission 3 Sgr., or for a single visitor 5 Sgr.; the custodian is generally at the ruin, but it is safer to inquire for him in the village.

One of the finest points of view is the ***Horn**, above Altenahr; to Altenburg 15 min., thence to the pavilion with guide an ascent of 45 min.

The short distance between the "*bunte Kuh*" and *Altenahr* is undoubtedly by far the most beautiful part of the valley, which, however, offers many fine points of view above Altenahr (diligence from Altenahr to Adenau daily in 2 hrs.). One of the best views is obtained from the bridge over the Ahr; farther on, to the l., are the rugged rocks of the "*Teufelskanzel*" (*Devil's Pulpit*) and then the grand mass of rocks known by the name of the *Old Castle*. The bright-looking castle, picturesquely situated on a rugged peak near **Kreuzberg** is a private residence. At **Dümpelfeld**, 6 M. from Altenahr, the road leaves the Ahr, and leads in a straight direction to **Adenau** (**Halber Mond*), the principal village of the district, in the vicinity of which are the two highest points of the Eifel, the basaltic peaks of **Nürburg** (2118 ft.), 4½ M. to the S., surmounted by a ruined castle with a lofty tower, and the ***Hohe Acht** (2340 ft.), 6 M. to the E., the latter of which commands an extensive and magnificent view over the whole of the Eifel as far as the mountains of the Rhine, and even the cathedral of Cologne. Near the top there is a small hut for protection against the weather. The guide from Adenau, provided with a telescope, 10 Sgr. The traveller may, if he please, drive nearly to the summit of the Hohe Acht (in 1½ hr., charge 2½ Thlr.). From the Hohe Acht N.E. to *Kaltenborn* 3 M., to *Leimbach* 3 M., to *Kempenich* (Comanns) 3¾ M. From here the castle of Olbrück is 3¾ M. distant (to the N.E.), the Laacher See (R. 19) 10½ M., but the road is uninteresting. Carriage from Adenau over the Hohe Acht to Laach and Andernach 7 Thlr.; from the Hohe Acht to Kempenich 2 hrs., to Laach 2 hrs., thence to Andernach in 1½ hr., the whole drive occupying 5½ hrs. Or a carriage may be taken from Adenau over the Hohe Acht by Virneburg and Mayen (R. 19) to Andernach in $4\frac{1}{2}$ hrs., fare 6 Thlr. From the Hohe Acht by Virneburg (*Müller*) to Mayen is a walk of about 15 M.

On the Ahr itself, which the road leaves at *Dümpelfeld* (see p. 60), there are two other fine points, at **Schuld**, 3 M. to the W. of Dümpelfeld, and at **Antweiler** (*Neubusch*), near which are situated the ruins of the castle of *Aremberg*, once seat of the Dukes of Aremberg. Antweiler lies 6 M. to the W. of Adenau.

18. The Rhine from Remagen to Coblenz.

Comp. Map R. 15.

Distance from Remagen to Sinzig 3 M., Nieder-Breisig $2\frac{1}{4}$ M., Brohl $2\frac{1}{4}$ M., Andernach $4\frac{1}{2}$ M., Neuwied 3 M., Coblenz 9 M., total 24 M. — By railway, see R. 36, in 1 hr.; fares: 30, $22\frac{1}{2}$ and 15 Sgr. — By steamboat (fares: 16 or 10 Sgr.) in $3\frac{1}{2}$ hrs. (down in 2 hrs.); piers at Remagen and Neuwied; small-boat stations at Linz, Niederbreisig, Brohl, Leutesdorf, Andernach, Urmitz and Engers. The steamboat is far preferable to the railway on account of the beauty of the scenery.

Remagen (**Hôtel Fürstenberg*, R. 15—20, B. 8, D. 20, A. 5 Sgr.; **König von Preussen;* **Hôtel Monjau*), steamboat and railway stat. — Tariff of charges for carriages fixed by the police (inc. tolls and fees): to Ahrweiler 1-horse $1\frac{1}{3}$ Thlr., 2-horse 2 Thlr., the drive back 20 Sgr. or 1 Thlr.; to Altenahr $2\frac{1}{2}$—3 Thlr., drive back 20 Sgr.—$1\frac{1}{3}$ Thlr., if the carriage be kept for the whole, day 4—$5\frac{1}{2}$ Thlr.; Laacher See and back (1 day) 3—$4\frac{2}{3}$ Thlr., or by Andernach 4—6 Thlr. These charges are mentioned in such detail as Remagen is the best place for head-quarters between Bonn and Coblenz for making excursions.

The small town of Remagen was known to the Romans as *Rigomagus.* A milestone bearing the date 162, found in 1763 when the high road was in course of construction, records that the old Roman road which formerly passed here was begun under the Emperors M. Aurelius and L. Verus. It indicates the distance from Cologne as being 30,000 Passus, which is tolerably correct. Several of these stones are exhibited in the museum at Bonn.

The choir of the *Church* was, as an inscription on the outer door records, erected in 1246. The interior contains several old frescoes. The churchyard-wall, next to the exterior of the W. side of the choir, consists of Roman concrete-masonry.

The *Portal* next to the Rom. Cath. parsonage is worthy of inspection. The grotesque sculptures which it bears are very ancient, and are interpreted as signifying that the animals and persons they represent are excluded from the sacred edifice.

Below Remagen, on an eminence on the road-side rises the ***Apollinarisberg**, a beautiful Gothic church, erected by the Count of Fürstenberg-Stammheim (d. 1859), under the direction of *Zwirner*, the late eminent architect of the cathedral of Cologne. The old building in front of the church was formerly a rich deanery of Siegburg, much resorted to by pilgrims. The church, which is a perfect gem in its way, is open daily from 9½ to 12, and 2 to 4 o'clock; on Saturdays and the eves of festivals from 9½ to 12, and from 2 to 4. Admission on Sundays and holidays 2½ Sgr. It is adorned with 10 large frescoes in the best style of German art. The view, from this point, of the Rhine from Hönningen to Königswinter, and the Seven Mountains in the background is one of singular beauty.

****Frescoes.** On the l. on entering the church, representations from the life of the Saviour; on the r. scenes from the life of the Virgin. In the transept to the S., St. Apollinaris consecrated bishop, and miraculous resuscitation of a girl; on the N., destruction of idols, death and glorification of the saint, and a Crucifixion. In the choir on the r., coronation of the Virgin, on the l. the Resurrection. In the choir-niche the Saviour with Mary and John the Baptist, St. Peter and St. Apollinaris with the four Evangelists. — The crypt contains the old sarcophagus of the saint, belonging to the 14th cent., and surmounted by a modern statue.

Opposite to Remagen, near **Erpel**, rises the *Erpeler Lei* (625 ft.), a basaltic cliff, the quarries of which are the most profitable on the Rhine, as the stone is at once transferred to the vessels on the river. The columns, however, do not present the same elegance as those of the Minderberg and Dattenberg quarries (p. 63). Above Erpel lies (l.) *Kasbach*, surmounted by the ivy-clad ruins of *Ockenfels*, then **Linzerhausen**.

(l.) **Linz** (**Nassauer Hof*), an ancient walled town which formerly belonged to the Electorate of Cologne The fine old church in the round-arch style, dating from the beginning of the 13th cent., contains an admirable picture painted in 1463, representing the Annunciation and Crucifixion on the outer wings, the Annunciation and Coronation of the Virgin on the inner, and the Nativity, Adoration, Presentation in the Temple &c., in the centre compartment. The picture has recently been cleaned and retouched. The churchyard commands a fine view to the S. W., in the direction of the confluence of the Ahr with the Rhine; the round tower of the castle of Olbrück stands out on a mountain peak in the distance. The environs of Linz yield a considerable quantity of red wine, and during the vintage the little town is the central point of the busy scene.

The extensive ***Basalt Quarries** at *Dattenberg* and on the *Minderberg* near Linz well deserve inspection, especially the latter. The road to the Minderberg ascends the valley to the E., leading to the *Sternerhütte*, copper, vitriol, and zinc works. (Near it is a castle of the Prince of Salm-Kyrburg; above it the *Renneberg* with a tower on the summit). From the Sternerhütte the path ascends to the l. and the quarry soon comes in view. It is a spacious hall of the most beautiful black prismatic basaltic pillars, some of them upright, others heaped together in confused masses, varying from 3 to 10 inches in diameter, and sometimes attaining a length of 20 ft.; when struck they produce a clear metallic ring. These masses resemble numerous charcoal piles closely crowded together, and form a huge wall, suggesting by its beauty the celebrated Fingal's Cave in the island of Staffa. The *view from this height (1328 ft.) is considered by many to equal that from the Oelberg (p. 54). The pedestrian is recommended to return by the *Kasbachthal;* guide unnecessary; should he be in doubt, he may ask the way at the large farm-house on the hill. The whole circuit may be made from Linz in about 3 hrs.

The columns in the quarry of Dattenberg (1½ M. from Linz) are as high as those in the quarry of Minderberg, but much thicker and more massive. A fine view is obtained from the foot of the ruined castle in the grounds of Herr von Mengershausen, of the windings of the Ahr, with the basaltic peak of the Landskron (p. 57) in the background.

The stone yielded by these quarries is admirably adapted for pavements and the foundations of buildings, but, as it attracts moisture, is unsuitable for the upper parts. It is exported in large quantities to Holland, where it is employed in the construction of dykes.

To the E. of Linz rises the *Hummelsberg* (1345 ft.), on the summit of which stands a cross, erected by the burghers of Linz in commemoration of the battle of Leipzig. Another cross on the *Kaisersberg*, nearer the Rhine, was erected in 1840 to commemorate the battle of Belle-Aliance. On both of these hills are also productive basalt quarries.

From the village of (r.) **Krippe** on the Rhine a path leads past the manor of *Godenhaus* to the *Mineral Spring of Sinzig*, which contains carbonate of soda and is free from iron. The path joins the high road on the l. bank of the Ahr, not far from the bridge below Sinzig.

Between Remagen and Nieder-Breisig the Rhine makes a long circuit, which both the railway and the road cut off. The beautiful church of (r.) *Sinzig* (on the railway, 1½ M. from the river) is visible from tbe steamboat.

The village of (l.) *Dattenberg*, peeping out of a ravine, is opposite to the confluence of the *Ahr* (R. 17) and the Rhine. On the same bank **Leubsdorf**, with an ancient royal abode, a small building with four towers, and near it **Ariendorf.**

On an eminence to the l. rises the castle of **Arenfels,** with gilded pinnacles and weathercocks, erected by Henry of Isenburg, and named by him after his consort the Countess of Are. It is now the property of Count Westerholt, by whom it has been restored. A tall round stone tower of peculiar construction surmounts the castle. The grounds which extend along the brow of the hill command a series of fine views.

l. **Hönningen** (* *Kraus*) and **Rheinbrohl** (*Krone*), with a handsome Gothic * *Church*, built of grauwacke, are two villages of some importance, situated in a fertile plain, beyond which the mountains to the l. rise more abruptly from the river.

r. **Nieder-Breisig** (steamboat aud railway stat.), near the S. extremity of which part of an ancient Templars' lodge is still to be seen. About $1^3/_4$ M. above the village a path ascends the wooded hill surmounted by the castle of

r. ***Rheineck.** The road winds up the N. and W. sides of the hill, at the foot of which, far below, lies the hamlet *Thal Rheineck.* The square tower, 65 ft. in height, on the S. side is the sole remnant of the old castle, which was dismantled by the French in 1689, destroyed by the troops of the Electorate of Cologne in 1692, and finally burned to the ground in 1785. The new castle, built in the round-arched style, belongs to Herr von Bethmann-Hollweg, and was erected in 1832 by the eminent architect Lassaulx. The interior is tastefully and comfortably fitted up, and contains several modern pictures and frescoes of merit. Permission to inspect it is seldom refused (1 pers. 5—7½ Sgr.; a party 20 Sgr.—1 Thlr.). The *view from the garden, which is always open to the public, comprises the whole course of the Rhine from far above Andernach to the Apollinarisberg, with the peaks of the Seven Mountains rising in the background, and is scarcely surpassed by the prospect from the Drachenfels.

Rheineck has been since the most ancient times a boundary between several different races. In the time of Cæsar the Eburones inhabited the district below, aud the Treviri that above this point; opposite to the former lay the dominions of the Sygambri, and to the latter those of the Ubii; higher up were the Usipetes and Tenchteri. At the present day Brohl forms a strongly defined line between the upper and lower Rhenish dialects, and here too the picturesque head-dress of the country girls is first observed.

To the r. the *Brohlbach* falls into the Rhine at the village of **Brohl** (*Nonn*) (steamboat and railway stat.), which extends along the hill-side and up the valley, adjoining the hamlet of **Nippes.** Here is the depôt for the tuffstone found in the valley.

l. **Nieder-Hammerstein,** the vineyards of which yield a good wine, then **Ober-Hammerstein** (*Burg Hammerstein*), near which a large rocky peak (grauwacke) rises abruptly from the river, surmounted by the ruined castle of *Hammerstein.* Here the Emperor Henry IV. resided for some time when persecuted by his son Henry V., and here he kept the imperial insignia till their removal by his usurping successor. During the 30 Years' war the castle was in turn occupied by the Swedes, the Spaniards, the troops of Cologne, and those of Lothringia, and was finally destroyed in 1660 at the instance of the archbishopric of Cologne, being deemed too powerful a neighbour to be tolerated.

On the heights, about $4\frac{1}{2}$ M. to the E. of the Rhine, the course of the well-known Roman intrenchment, which was constructed as a protection against the attacks of the Germanic tribes, is distinctly visible, and may be traced from Monrepos as far as the Seven Mountains. The table-land above Hammerstein in the immediate vicinity of the intrenchment still bears the name *Marsfeld* (field of Mars), where Roman coins and other relics are frequently found.

Above (r.) **Fornich** rises the *Fornicher* or *Weghübler Kopf*, recognizable from a great distance by the solitary group of trees rising from the bushes on the summit. It is the nearest volcanic peak to the Rhine, and the lava stream, divided into huge pillars close to the road, is visible from the steamboat.

(r.) **Namedy,** a small village at some distance from the river, possesses a small but elegant Gothic church of the 15th cent., divided into two parts by a row of slender pillars; near it is the castle of the ancient knights of Namedy. On the l. extends the considerable village of **Leutesdorf** (*Eisen*), surrounded by productive vineyards planted among the rocks. As Andernach is approached the mountains which confine the river commence to recede.

The ancient and picturesque town of (r.) **Andernach** (* *Hackenbruch;* steamboat and railway stat.), with its old bastions, Roman gate and high watch-tower, was known to the Romans by the name of *Antonacum* (*Statio ante Nacum*, station before the Nette). It was an ancient frontier fortress, and the head-quarters of the *præfectus militum Arinsensium*, of the *Legio XXI. rapax*, and the *Legio XXII. primigenia*, of the *Cohors Ticinensis* and the *Cohors Asturiensis.* It was conquered by the Allemanni in 335, but retaken by the Emperor Julian in 359. In the middle ages it was an Imperial town, and was taken by the Electorate of Cologne in 1496; in 1698 it was burned down by the French.

They also destroyed the *Schloss*, erected in 1109 by Frederick I., Archbishop of Cologne, and defended against them by the troops of the Elector of Brandenburg; the extensive ruins rise from the deep fosse near the Coblenzer Thor. On the pointed and vaulted *Stadtthor* (town-gate) the traces of violent attempts to destroy it are still visible.

The *Pfarrkirche*, with its four towers and richly decorated portals, is a fine specimen of the late Romanesque style

(1206); the choir was erected in 1120. On the vaulting of the nave are seen the Imperial arms, with those of the town and of Hermann IV., Archbishop of Cologne (d. 1508). The choir was re-decorated in 1856. The carved wooden pulpit was brought in 1807 from the Abbey of Laach (p. 72).

The tall round *Watch-tower* on the Rhine, with its octagonal summit. was erected in 1414—68. The wide breach on the W. side was made by the French cannonade in 1668.

The volcanic products of the neighbourhood of Andernach, millstones of lava (p. 70), tuffstone, trass, &c., form an important branch of commerce, and are exported to all parts of the world. The lava quarries are at *Niedermendig*, near the *Laacher See* p. 72), 7½ M. to the W. of Andernach, and are best reached from here, returning to the Rhine by the valley of Brohl (p. 70).

Above the small village of (l.) *Fahr* are the ruins of the *Teufelshaus* (devil's house) or castle of *Friederichstein*, begun in the 17th cent., but never completed. It received the above appellation from the serfs who were employed in its construction, on account of the arduousness of the tasks imposed on them. Farther up, on a fertile eminence surrounded by fruit-trees, stands the Romanesque *Feldkirche.* At the small fishing village of **Irlich**, a short railway connects the river with the extensive *Rasselstein* foundry, the first puddling-work erected in Germany (in 1824). Between Irlich and Neuwied the *Wiedbach* falls into the Rhine.

The steamboat now touches at the cheerful and industrial little town of **Neuwied** (**Anker*, *Wilder Mann*, both on the Rhine; *Brüdergemeinde.* Steamboat pier on the l., railway stat. to the r. on the opposite bank, ½ M. from the river). At the lower extremity of the town are situated the handsome palace and park of the Prince of Wied. The town was founded in 1653 by Count Frederick of Wied, on the site of the village of Langendorf, which had been destroyed in the 30 Years' war. Under his protection the town, which is divided into squares by streets 40 ft. in breadth, rapidly increased in importance. Its population is now 7000, consisting of Protestants, Rom. Catholics (2000), Moravian Brothers, Anabaptists, Quakers, aud Jews, who all live together in great harmony. Starch, chicory, and tin-wares are the principal products of the place.

The Pheasantry, an isolated building in the park, contains a collection of **Objects of natural history*, brought by Prince Maximilian from Brazil in 1817, and from N. America in 1836. Admission at any hour may be obtained by applying to the porter at the entrance gate of the palace (fee 10 Sgr., for a party 20 Sgr.). A small collection of Roman antiquities in a room adjoining the road is only interesting from the fact that they were all found in the vicinity of Neuwied. The coins in the collection are of various dates down to 260, when the camp which stood here was probably destroyed by the Franks. The excavations made in 1819 and 1857 at the village of Niederbiber have been since filled up, and the traces of the Roman camp have disappeared under the plough.

The community of **Moravian Brothers**, also called *Herrenhuter* from the village of Herrenhut in Saxony, where they had established themselves after their expulsion from Moravia during the 30 years' war, occupies a separate part of the town. Their establishments are well worthy of inspection, and afford an insight into the habits of this remarkable sect. As is well known, they were originally the followers of John Huss, and as is usual in all cases of religious persecution they increased enormously in numbers after the death of their leader. They now form what may be called a religious republic, having their own laws both for public and private life, which are administered by their elders, or religious chiefs. In their manners and habits they are grave and austere, which has gained for them the appellation of the Quakers of Germany. The unmarried brothers live in a separate building and carry on different trades, the profits of which are devoted to the community. Of these manufactures the best known are the faience stoves, and deer-skin gloves. Visitors are readily admitted, but are first conducted to the magazine, where they are expected to make some purchase. The establishment for the sisters is conducted in a similar way; they are easily recognized by their peculiar white head-dresses, fastened with ribbons of various colours, according to the situation in life of the wearers — girls dark red, young unmarried women pink, married women blue, and widows white. At stated seasons "love-feasts" are celebrated in the church, accompanied by singing, prayers, and a sermon, during which tea is partaken of. The educational portion of the establishment is justly celebrated, and is frequented by pupils from all parts of Germany, as well as from England. There are many other schools at Neuwied which also enjoy a high reputation.

(The country-seat of *Monrepos* (1008 ft.) 6 M. from Neuwied, the white walls of which stand out in striking contrast to the wooded slopes on which it stands, forms a conspicuous point in the background of the landscape.)

Opposite to the park the (r.) *Nette* falls into the Rhine. The mountain with the two peaks which rises to the W. is the *Plaidter Hummerich* (909 ft.). On the road and railway is (r.) the *Netterhof*, important on account of its numerous corn, oil, bone, and other mills.

r. **Weissenthurm**; at one end of the village rises a tall square watch-tower, erected by Kuno von Falkenstein in 1370, being the extreme point of the dominions of the Electors of Treves, which here adjoined the territory of the Archbishops of Cologne.

On an eminence above the village stands a small obelisk to the memory of the French General *Hoche*, who here crossed the Rhine in 1797 with the army, and shortly afterwards died suddenly at Wetzlar at the age of 30. The inscription records that it was erected by the army of the Sambre and Meuse to its general, but it was really erected by his widow (d. 1859), and has been repaired by the Prussian government.

(r.) *Der gute Mann*, formerly a hermitage, with a new chapel, near which are some lime-kilns and a manufactory for the preparation of the Engers stone (see below); then **Urmitz** and **Kaltenengers**

Near (l.) **Engers** (**Römerbrücke*; steamboat stat.) may be seen some fragments of old wall (concrete-masonry, in which coins of Constantine have been found), perhaps remnants of the counterpoise of a Roman bridge or of a tête-de-pont. At this spot there is reason to believe that Cæsar's second passage of the Rhine took place.

Engers, formerly called *Kunostein-Engers*, was in ancient times the capital of the Engersgau. The Archbishop Kuno von Falkenstein erected (in 1386) a fortified castle here with a round tower (the ivy-clad trunk of the latter rises below the palace), which was intended to protect the navigators of the Rhine from the rapacious Counts of the Westerwald. On its site stands the present château (lately converted into a Prussian military school), erected by the Elector Johann Philipp von Walderdorf in 1758.

Near (l.) **Mühlhofen**, where the *Saynbach* falls into the Rhine, rise the smelting furnaces of the Foundry of Sayn, and farther from the river the *Concordia Foundry*.

On the hill-side, about 1½ M. inland, the ruins of the Castle of Sayn, destroyed by the French in the 30 Years' war, are visible from the steamboat. Below it is situated **Schloss Sayn**, a modern residence of the Prince of Sayn-Wittgenstein-Berleburg, open in absence of the family on Thursdays till 5½ p.m. (Admission-card 2½ Sgr.; proceeds devoted to charitable purposes). The château is magnificently fitted up, and contains a small but select *collection of modern pictures. The hill on which the extensive ruins of the old castle are situated has been laid out as a park. The summit commands a beautiful prospect, similar to that from the Friederichsberg (see below).

Near the château are the extensive royal iron-works of Sayn (**Burg Sayn*), the buildings of which consist almost entirely of cast-iron and glass.

Above the valley rises the **Friederichsberg**, laid out as a park by the government of Nassau, and much resorted to in summer. The views obtained from the heights of the rich and orchard-like plain of the Rhine, and the narrow ravines of the romantic valley of Sayn are extremely beautiful and well repay the ascent. Farther up the valley (3½ M.) are situated the ruins of the castle of *Isenburg*, the ancient family seat of a still flourishing race.

On the S. W. wooded slopes of the circle of hills which encloses the beautiful *Engersgau*, rises the church-spire of *Heimbach*, near which are the ruins of the ancient abbey of **Rommersdorf**, with fine cloisters and chapter-house, erected about 1200. Some of the pillars are of verde antico.

Between *Sayn* and *Engers* a peculiar kind of pumice-stone conglomerate is dug up in the open fields. It is cut into squares and dried, and is much valued as a building material for inner walls, on account of its durability and lightness. The bed is in some places 20 ft. in depth. Geological research has suggested the idea that, before the Rhine broke through the chain of mountains near Andernach, the basin of Neuwied was a deep lake. The pumice-stone ejected from the volcanoes of the l. bank of the Rhine (p. 70) was probably washed down by the rain into the lake, where, in combination with a clayey binding material, it formed the deposits which now yield the above-mentioned stone.

l. **Bendorf** (*Rheinischer Hof; Beringer*), surrounded with fruit-trees, and possessing a curious old Romanesque church;

farther up (r.) the villages of **St. Sebastian** and **Kesselheim,** opp. to the island of *Niederwerth.* Partly concealed by the island lies (l.) the busy little town of **Vallendar,** with a handsome new church, built by Lassaulx.

In the valley behind Vallendar are the remains of the nunnery of *Schönstatt* with its well preserved Gothic towers, abandoned in 1567, afterwards destroyed by the Swedes, and now converted into a cloth factory. From this point the road to the l. leads through a beautiful wooded valley to the wealthy Nassovian village of **Höhr** (*Müllenbach*), with its extensive potteries.

On the long island of (r.) **Niederwerth** stands the dilapidated-looking village of the same name, with a convent-church built in 1500, containing a carved altar-piece and fragments of good stained glass. Edward III. of England once resided here for a short time in 1337, and had several interviews with the Emperor Louis and other princes.

l. **Mallendar,** a great portion of which formerly belonged to the knights of the Teutonic Order; on an eminence above the village stands the *Haus Besselich*, once the property of the Knights Templar, and afterwards an Augustine nunnery till 1804, when it was secularized and passed into private hands. The garden commands a fine view. On the hillside, higher up the river, is seen the village of *Urbar*, surrounded by fruit-trees.

r. **Wallersheim,** and above it **Neuendorf,** chiefly inhabited by raft-men. The smaller rafts generally lie here for some time and receive considerable additions until they reach the dimensions of 850—900 ft. in length and 180—250 ft. in breadth; they are furnished with a number of wooden huts on the middle for the accommodation of the crew, which frequently numbers 150—160 men. It is said that a raft proprietor must have a capital of at least 45,000*l.*, one third of which consists of wood in the forest, one third timber on the water, and one third is requisite for the expenses of transport from the Upper Rhine to Dordrecht in Holland.

The steamboat now passes the influx of the Moselle, commanding a view of the lofty arches of the bridge, glides beneath the rocks and bastions of Ehrenbreitstein, and finally stops at Coblenz (R. 20).

19. Brohlthal, Laacher See, Lava quarries of Niedermending.

(Comp. Map R. 15.)

Distances. From Brohl (p. 64) to Tönnisstein 4½ M., to Wassenach 2¼ M., to the Abbey of Laach 3 M., to Niedermendig 3 M., to Mayen 3 M. Diligence twice a day between Mayen and Coblenz in 3 hrs., to the Neuwied station in $2^3/_4$ hrs. The Laacher See may be most conveniently visited by carriage from Andernach; a two-horse carriage from Andernach to Niedermending, Laach (where dine), Tönnisstein, Brohl, and back to Andernach, costs 3 Thlr., the drive occupying about $5^1/_2$ hrs.

The ***Brohlthal** has been for more than half a century the object of the unwearied investigations of many celebrated geologists. It is a beautiful winding valley enclosed by high, wooded mountains, traversed by a rapid brook, and studded with numerous mills and other houses, but the principal object of interest is the extensive bed of *Tuffstone*, 15—20 ft. in thickness, of which the whole of the bottom of the valley consists. It is a soft whitish-grey or pale yellow stone with sponge-like pores and much veined with pumice stone, very similar to the Italian puzzolana earth, and is believed to be the product of volcanic mud-streams. It is sometimes found covered with softer, sandy substances, such as loose pumice stone and volcanic ash, and sometimes on the surface of the earth, where it has been exposed by the action of the weather. The tuffstone was in very early times used as a building material, and almost all the churches from this part of the Rhine down to Holland were constructed of it, the cornicings and carved work being hewn out of the trachyte of the Drachenfels (which however is more easily weathered than the tuffstone). In more modern times it has never been employed for building purposes, except in the case of the church of Apollinarisberg (p. 62). The tuffstone, however derives its principal value in commerce from the "*trass*", or cement made from it. When pounded down and mixed with lime it possesses the invaluable property of hardening under water, and is exported in large quantities to Holland, where it is used in the construction of the dykes. (Geologists should consult the admirable *Geognostic-orographic maps of the neighbourhood of the Laacher See*, by *Oeynhausen*, pub. at Berlin, 1847.)

The numerous mineral springs in the vicinity of the Laacher See, and especially in the Brohlthal, may serve as a proof that the volcanic agency has not yet altogether ceased. They are formed by the carbonic acid gas which rises from the fissures of the slate rocks and impregnates the springs to such an extent, that they form probably about one half of the water which the Brohlbach conveys to the Rhine.

The period when the beds of tuffstone were formed cannot possibly be determined, as even the pumice-stone, the most recent volcanic production, which frequently covers the former, belongs to an epoch far more remote than any recorded in human history. The fact that the Romans, the earliest annalists of this part of the world, buried their dead in those same pumice-stone beds (at Andernach for example), serves to prove their antiquity. It is, however, a remarkable fact that the remains of plants contained by the tuffstone belong to species which still exist.

The tuffstone quarries are seen on both sides of the valley, and are partly open, partly subterranean, forming extensive galleries, supported by natural pillars left for the purpose. Here and there, where these galleries have fallen in, the pillars which have been left standing, are covered with the most luxuriant vegetation, favoured by the decomposition of the stone, and enhance the beauty and variety of the valley. A good high-road leads through the valley from Brohl to Ober-Zissen (p. 74), and a tolerable carriage-road from Tönnisstein (see below), to the Abbey of Laach and Niedermendig.

At the entrance of the Brohl valley, on the N. side, the traveller passes a paper-mill, surrounded with gardens and grounds. About $1\frac{1}{2}$ M. farther, the small castle of **Schweppenburg**, probably erected in the 16th cent., rises from an eminence in the middle of the valley. The garden contains a Roman altar found here. About $\frac{3}{4}$ M. farther up the valley, which here diverges to the S. is the *Heilbrunnen*, a mineral spring with a saltish but refreshing taste, similar to that of the Kreuzbrunnen of Marienbad.

One mile from Schweppenburg, the road to the l. leads through a side-valley to the Laacher See, while that which continues in the valley in a straight direction leads to Olbrück. On the former road, soon after the Brohlthal is left, the traveller reaches the **Tönnissteiner Brunnen**, the water of which is strongly impregnated with carbonic acid gas, and, when mixed with wine and sugar, forms an agreeable and refreshing beverage. The marble basin was constructed in 1700 by Joseph Clemens, Elector of Cologne, and the grounds were laid out by his successor Clemens August.

Seven minutes' walk from Tönnisstein the road (to regain which the pedestrian must retrace his steps from the springs and recross the bridge) passes the ruins of the (l.) Carmelite monastery of *Antoniusstein* (hence the corruption "Tönnisstein"), leads through the village of **Wassenach** (*Laacher Hof*), and descends through the wood towards the Laacher See. On the r. rises the wooded *Veitskopf* (1228 ft.) a volcanic peak with a double crater opening on the W. side, and a broad and rapidly descending stream of lava. The view from this point of the lake surrounded by wooded hills is very striking.

On the S. W. bank rises the Benedictine Abbey of ***Laach,** founded by the Count Palatine Henry II. in 1093, and secularized in 1802, once one of the wealthiest and most celebrated in Germany. In 1863 it became the property of the Jesuits, who have converted it into an educational establishment. The church, completed in 1156 (no longer used for divine service), with its dome, five towers, and crypt, in the Romanesque style, and richly decorated, is an object of almost equal interest to architects and the unprofessional traveller. The beautiful cloisters, restored in 1859, belong to the close of the 12th cent., and the curious monument of the founder, the foremost pillars of which are monoliths of calc sinter, to the end of the 13th. The church is the property of, and is kept in repair by Government. What was formerly a large summer-house in the orchard is now converted into an inn of small pretensions. Excellent pike fishing may be enjoyed on the lake, and a traditional fish of 40 lbs. is made an additional incentive to the angler. As the fishing is farmed, whatever fish is captured must be purchased if carried away. Boats with the services of fishermen acquainted with the lake may be procured at the inn, which also affords tolerable refreshment and accomodation.

The ***Laacher See** (846 ft.) is nearly round, averaging 1 2/3 M. in diameter, and is about 6 M. in circumference. It is the largest of the crater-tarns (R. 33) of the Eifel and was probably one of the more recent results of the volcanic agency in this district. It is not itself a crater, but is believed to have been formed by a series of volcanic eruptions which took place in the vicinity, especially by the upheaving of the Veitskopf (p. 71). There are several craters in the hills which surround the lake, the principal of which is the *Krufter Ofen* (1443 ft.), 1 M. distant, the barren, brownish-red slag walls of which sink towards the lake.

The road leads along the W. side of the lake, but the E. side is by far the more interesting for the geologist. At the N. E. corner, 3/4 M. from the Wassenach road, on the l. side of the footpath, and near a barren spot to the r. of the meadow, is a "*mofette*" (comp. R. 33) in a bed of clay, about 20 ft. above the level of the water, where dead mice, birds, squirrels, &c. are constantly found, having been suffocated by the carbonic acid gas which continually issues in greater or less volumes from the hole, affording another proof that the volcanic agency is not yet completely extinct (comp. p. 53). The lower strata of the air in this cavity are overpowering even to human beings, of which the traveller may satisfy himself by bending down his head.

After an inundation in the 12th cent. which threatened the destruction of the Abbey lands, the Benedictines caused a shaft to be sunk on the S. side of the lake, by which the water is conveyed under ground to the Nette. A similar shaft constructed in 1845 has lowered the level of the lake by about 23 ft.

The extensive basalt-lava ***Quarries of Niedermendig** (*Müller*) are situated about 3 M. to the S. of the Laacher See. The subterranean galleries, which extend over an area of 3 M. in length and 1½ M. in breadth, reach as far as the Krufter Ofen (p. 72), but the lava-stream which was probably ejected by the *Forstberg* (1842 ft.) is the largest at Niedermendig, where it is intersected by numerous and spacious halls, supported by huge pillars. These pits, which were probably worked by the Romans, are almost all connected with each other, and communicate with the surface of the earth by means of wide, walled shafts for ventilation and the transport of the stone. A guide (10 Sgr.) precedes the visitor with a torch; the inspection occupies about an hour. The temperature in these mines is so low that even in the height of summer huge icicles are suspended from the roof, and masses of ice are seen in all directions. The lava is not only used for millstones, but on account of its extreme hardness and durability forms an excellent material for paving and building purposes. The deserted galleries are used as beer-cellars, and to them the beer of Mendig is indebted for its celebrity.

At **Mayen** (**Müller; Post*), the district town (diligence twice a day to Coblenz in 3 hrs., to the Neuwied station in 2¾ hrs.), there are also lava-quarries, which, however, are more open and of a less depth than those above described. The lava-bed in which they are worked is the outlet of the sunken volcano of **Ettringer-Beller-Kopf** (1287 ft.), 1½ M. N. from Mayen. The E. side of the crater commands a fine view of the fruitful plain which lies between Mayen and Andernach, and of the valley of the Rhine. The rugged walls of the S. extremity of the lava-field are to be seen at the *Reifer Mühle* in the valley of the Nette, about 1½ M. below Mayen, and in the vicinity of the slate quarry of *Radscheck*.

From Laach to Mayen another road leads by *Bell*, the same distance (6 M.) as by Niedermendig, passing the remarkable brickstone (similar to tuffstone) quarries of Bell. Beyond them rises the ***Forstberg** (1842 ft.), the crater of which opens towards the N. W. The *Hochstein*, a mass of rock on the W. side, commands a fine view of the Laacher See, the Eifel, and the Rhine as far as the Seven Mountains. Below the Hochstein is an old artificial grotto, the origin of which is unknown. From the Forstberg the road leads by *Ettringen* and the above mentioned *Ettringer-Beller-Kopf* to Mayen.

From the Laacher See to the Rhine (or from Niedermendig) are three different ways: 1st, the old road to *Andernach* (9 M.), which offers little variety, passing the villages of *Nickenich* and *Eich* a little to the r.; 2nd, the high-road to Andernach (10½ M.) by *Kruft* (in the valley are seen the ruins of *Korretsburg*), *Plaidt*, and *Miesenheim*, where the Andernach road diverges from that to Neuwied: the latter leads in a N. E. direction, passing the *Netterhammer* and joining the Coblenz road at the *Netterhaus* near the Neuwied station; 3d, to *Coblenz*, which by the direct road (by *Ochtendung*, *Bassenheim* and *Rübenach*) is 15 M. distant. About 1½ M. from Niedermendig it passes the **Church of St. Genovefa**, where according to the old tradition the saint was discovered in the wilderness by her husband Siegfried, Count Palatine of Hohensimmern. The church contains monuments of both. Near the brook which crosses the road not far from the church, numerous mineral springs bubble up on the road-side (p. 71).

Instead of diverging to the l. to Tönnisstein (p. 71), the traveller may keep the road in the Brohl valley, which will bring him to **Burgbrohl** (**Salentin*) (1 M.), a picturesquely situated village with an old castle, once the seat of a family of the same name. The huge masses of calcareous tuff of which the rocks here consist, have been gradually deposited by the mineral springs, like the thermal tuff of Carlsbad. The road next passes through **Nieder-Zissen** (**Burchartz*) (3 M.), **Ober-Zissen** (1¼ M.) and **Hain** (*Rademacher*) (1 M.); 1 M. further the castle of **Olbrück** (1456 ft.) is reached. The latter is one of the highest points in this district, and commands an extensive view of the volcanic peaks of the Eifel, the hilly country in the direction of the Rhine, and the Seven Mountains. The only part of the castle which is still in good preservation is the lofty square tower, a conspicuous object in the landscape when viewed from the Seven Mountains and the plain of the Rhine. The peak on which it stands consists of clink-stone or phonolite, also a volcanic product. From the *Perler Kopf* (1800 ft.), 3 M. to the W. of Olbrück, the prospect is still more extensive. [From Olbrück S. W. to *Kempenich* (p. 60) 3¾ M., thence to the *Hochacht* (p. 60) 10½ M.].

The traveller who wishes to return to the Rhine by a different route is recommended to take the path at *Nieder-Zissen* (see above) which ascends to the N., traversing a low wood (the *Scheiderwald*), passing the volcanic peak (2¼ M.) of *Herchenberg* (997 ft.), the summit and E. slopes of which consist of tuffstone, the W. side of slag, and the S. of cleft pillar-like lava; 1¼ M. farther **Ober-Lützingen**, 1¼ M. **Nieder-Lützingen** (**Paulsen*), then turning to the l. by the chapel, over the ridge of the mountain, and finally through wood bearing to the r., the castle of **Rheineck** (p. 64) (2 M.) is reached, the entire distance from Nieder-Zissen being 6¾ M.

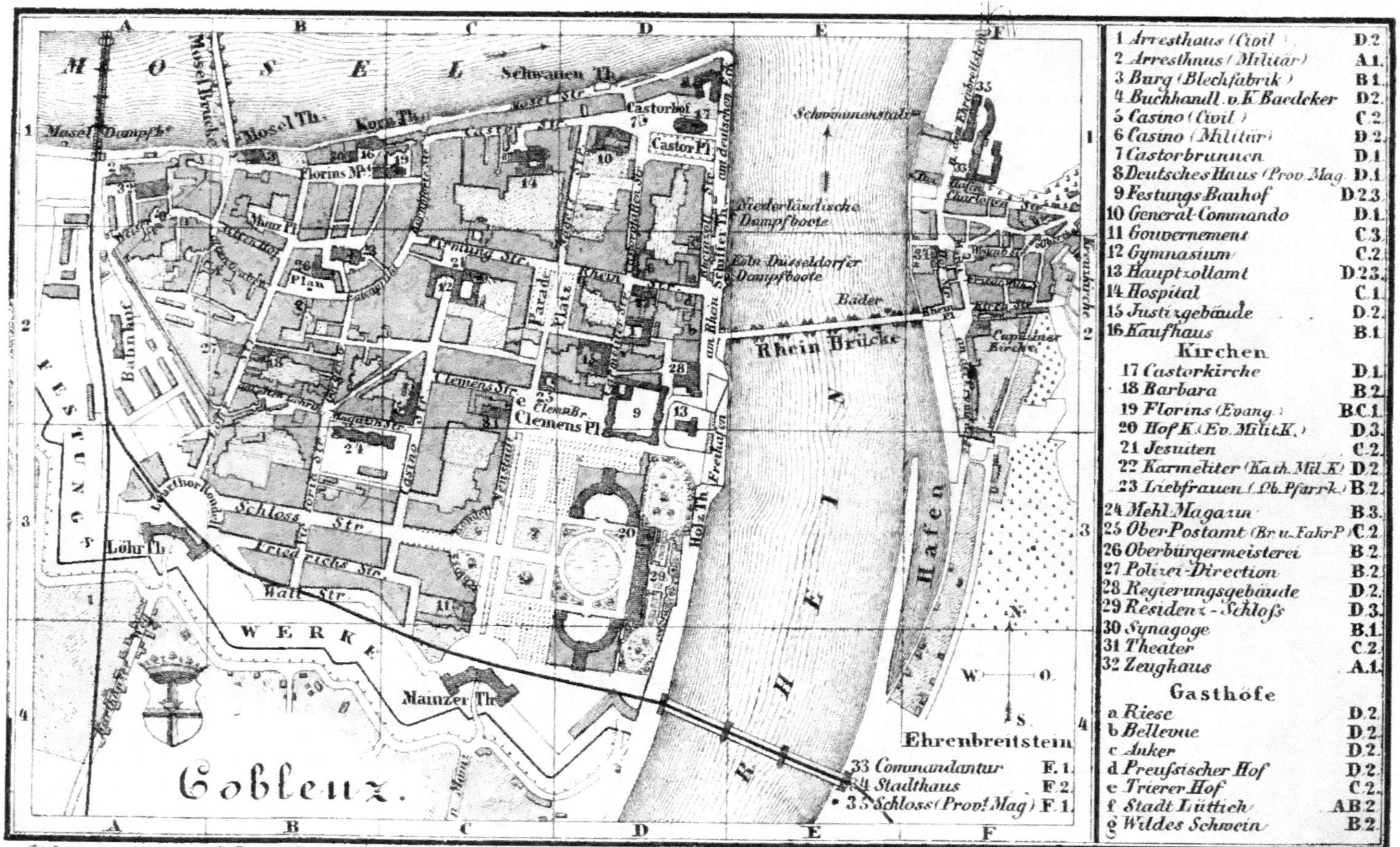

Lith. geogr. Anst. v. Ed. Wagner, Darmstadt

This path passes at Nieder-Zissen by the foot of the *Bausenberg* (1056 ft.), which rises to the N. of the village, 450 ft. above it. Its summit is one of the finest and most distinctly defined craters in the vicinity of the Laacher See, its inner wall, 79 ft. in height, opening to the N. W. The lava stream may be traced 3 M. in a N. E. direction, down to the valley of the *Pfingstbach* at *Gönnersdorf*, where it terminates in huge columnar masses of rock.

20. Coblenz.

Hotels. On the Rhine: *Giant (Pl. a) and *Bellevue (Pl. b) (R. 15—20 Sgr., L. 5. B. 10, D. 24, A. 6 Sgr.). — *Anker (Pl. c) (R. and B. 22 Sgr.; *Hôtel de Prusse (Pl. d.) (R. and B. 19 Sgr.). — In the town: *Hôtel de Trèves (Pl. e) in the Clemensplatz, quiet (R. 15, B. 8, D. 20, A. 5 Sgr.). — *Hôtel de Liége (Pl. f), not far from the station and the Moselle steamboat wharf; Wildes Schwein (Pl. g); Traube. — In Ehrenbreitstein; White Horse, with garden commanding a fine view of the Rhine and Coblenz.

Cafés. *Trinkhalle, on the Rhine-promenade, ¾ M. from the Holzthor: in summer a Café on the Rhine-wharf, opp. the steamboat piers; both of these command fine views. Hubaleck, opp. the post-office. Beer in all.

Newspapers in the Casino; strangers introduced by a member.

Porterage from the steamboat to one of the hotels *on the Rhine:* 2 Sgr. for every box, 1 Sgr. for smaller packages; *into the town* 3 or 2, to Ehrenbreitstein 4 or 2½ Sgr.

Military Music on Sundays at 11½, and Wednesdays at 12 o'clock, in the Clemensplatz.

Baths in the Rhine, attached to the bridge of boats; in the Moselle on the l. bank (ferry 1 Sgr.). Swimming-baths in the Rhine, a little below the bridge; charge for a single bath (excl. of towel etc.) 5 Sgr.

Railway Station on the W. side of the town, within the ramparts.

Telegraph-office in the Schloss Rondel, No. 11.

Carriages. One-horse: for a drive 1—2 pers. 5, 3 pers. 7, 4 pers. 8 Sgr.: for an hour 15, for each following hour 7½ Sgr.; to *Laubbach* (p. 90) 10, there and back, with one hour's stay, 15 Sgr.; to *Capellen* (Stolzenfels) 17½, there and back, with one hour's stay, 27½ Sgr.; for half a day 1 Thlr. 7½, or including the *Königsstuhl* 1 Thlr. 27½ Sgr. To the *Karthause* (p. 79) as far as the *Schöne Aussicht* and back, with one hour's stay, 1 Thlr. To the top of Ehrenbreitstein and back, with 2 hours' stay, 1 Thlr. 7½ Sgr.; to *Arenberg* (Calvarienberg worth a visit, view magnificent) and back, with 2 hours' stay, 1 Thlr. 5 Sgr.; to *Niederlahnstein* 22½, there and back, with one hours' stay, 27½ Sgr., for half a day 1½ Thlr.; to *Ems* (R. 22) 2 Thlr. 5 Sgr., there and back, with stay of ½ day, 2 Thlr. 20 Sgr.; for the whole day 3 Thlr. 10 Sgr.; to *Sayn* (p. 68) and back, with two hours' stay, 1 Thlr. 22½ Sgr. — Two-horse carriages cost one half more. Bridge toll (4½—6 Sgr.) may be saved by taking a carriage in Ehrenbreitstein for excursions on the r. bank of the river. Stands *on the Rhine* near the "Giant", near the *Mainzer Thor* and in *Ehrenbreitstein* near the bridge. N.B. Carriages from the hotels, and those not furnished with a number have no fixed charges.

English Church Service performed by a resident chaplain every Sunday in the English Chapel in the Palace.

Moselle-steamboats comp. R. 32. The following two-days' excursion includes the most beautiful points on the Moselle. By steamboat to *Alf*, by carriage to *Bertrich* 1⅔ Thlr., or to the *Falkenlei*, near the village of *Kenfuss*, about 2½ Thlr., visiting, on the way back to Bertrich, the *Cheese-grotto*, waterfall, Bertrich itself and environs, and returning the same evening to Alf. On the following morning by steamboat back to Coblenz, arriving in the afternoon.

Travellers whose time is limited are recommended to walk down the Rhine from the steamboat wharf to the Moselle, then to the l. along the bank of the latter and through the gate, inspect the Castorbrunnen and Castorkirche (p. 77), the Moselle bridge (p. 78), the S. gates of the town (p. 79), the view from the Karthause (p. 79), and on the way back the Cemetery, all of which may be accomplished in 4 hrs. *Ehrenbreitstein, see p. 80, *Stolzenfels R. 24.

Coblenz, at the confluence of the Moselle and the Rhine, is the capital of the Rhenish Province and the seat of the highest civil and military authorities. Population, including a garrison of about 5000 men, 27,767 (3752 Prot., 415 Jews); pop. of Ehrenbreitstein 4287.

No town on the Rhine can vie with Coblenz in the beauty of its situation, and many circumstances contribute to its importance. It stands at the confluence of perhaps the two most lovely streams in the world; equidistant from the important towns of Cologne and Mayence, it forms a half-way resting place to travellers from both, and it is necessarily the depôt at which the commerce of the Moselle, the Rhine, and the Lahn is concentrated; when to these advantages is added its great importance in a military point of view, that it is a favourite residence of the amiable sovereign who has endeared herself to her Coblenz subjects by a thousand acts of generosity, that it is the resort of crowds of the pleasure-seeking of our own and other countries, it may be readily understood that Coblenz stands unrivalled amongst the cities of this beautiful and highly-favoured province.

The side of the town which faces the Rhine consists of a row of handsome buildings, commencing with the palace, government buildings, and other houses mostly of modern construction, and terminating with the venerable and imposing Church of St. Castor and the sadly unpicturesque building which formerly belonged to the Teutonic order. The side next to the Moselle, extending as far as the railway bridge, has a much poorer aspect, but is far from devoid of interest.

Coblenz was the *Confluentes* of the Romans, and belonged to a series of fortresses erected by Drusus on the l. bank of the Rhine in the year B.C. 9, as a protection against the incursions of the neighbouring Germanic tribes. It is also mentioned by *Ammianus Marcellinus* (d. 390) as being the only Roman fortress on this part of the Rhine in his time. At the junction of the two rivers several coins of Roman emperors were discovered in 1844, when the new wharves were in course of construction.

Till the establishment of the Rhenish Towns' Confederation, Coblenz was a place of little importance. In the 30 Years' war it was in turn besieged and garrisoned by the Swedes, the French, and the Imperial troops. In 1688, although the greater part of the town was destroyed by the French cannonade, it successfully resisted the attacks of Marshal Boufflers. On the completion of the palace in 1786 it became the residence of the Elector of Treves, but a few years later (Oct. 23rd, 1794) it was taken by the French, who exacted a contribution of 4 million francs and made it the capital of the Department of the Rhine and Moselle. On the 1st of January, 1814, the French were compelled by the allies to evacuate the town, and in the following year it became subject to the crown of Prussia.

The ***Church of St. Castor** (Pl. 2), close to the junction of the two rivers, was founded by Louis the Pious in 836; the present structure dates from 1208, and is said to present the earliest example of what is called the "Lombard style" in the Rhenish Provinces. The sharp-arched vaulting belongs to the year 1498. The N. choir contains a remarkably fine monument of the *Archbishop Kuno von Falkenstein* (d. 1388, see p. 68); it is a Gothic sarcophagus-niche with a fresco (adoration of the Saviour, on the r. St. John and St. Castor, and on the l. the archbishop kneeling, Mary and Peter) ascribed to the then celebrated master Wilhelm of Cologne. The two fine frescoes in the choir were painted by Settegast in 1849 and 1852. The *Monument of St. Riza*, who according to an ancient tradition was a daughter of Louis the Pious, is a modern work. The new *Portal* was erected in 1862.

Opposite to the entrance of the church stands the **Castorbrunnen** (Pl. 4), erected by the last French prefect in commemoration of the French campaign against Russia, with the inscription: "*An 1812. Mémorable par la campagne contre les Russes. Sous le préfecturat de Jules Doazan.*" The Russian general St. Priest, who entered the town on the 1st of January, 1814, with exquisite irony caused the words: "*Vu et approuvé par nous Commandant Russe de la ville de Coblence, le 1. jan. 1814*," to be added.

Adjacent to the Castorplatz is the residence of the commander-in-chief of the Rhenish province, a large and straggling pile with no claim to architectural beauty, but possessing some interest from the associations with which it is connected. It was formerly the seat of the Counts of Leyen, and in 1791 afforded an asylum to the Counts of Provence and Artois. In 1800 it became the seat of the French prefect, and in 1804 (17th—20th Sept.) was visited by Napoleon and his consort.

A few steps northward bring the visitor to the Mosel-strasse, by following which, passing the crane and under the bridge, he will reach the *Wolfsthor.* On entering the town by this gate, and passing the *Metternicher Hof*, birthplace of Prince Metternich, on the r., he reaches the ***Moselle-bridge** with its 14 arches, erected by the Elector Balduin in 1344 (the tower was added in 1832), and commanding a fine view of Ehrenbreitstein. Across it are conveyed the conduit-pipes which supply the town with water from the heights of Metternich, a village 2 M. distant. Above the bridge is the new railway-bridge, and 3 M. beyond it the blue roofs of Rübenach with its tall spire are seen glittering in the distance.

On re-entering the town, the ancient *Archiepiscopal Palace* (*Burg*, Pl. 11) stands on the l. It was erected in 1276; the handsome staircase of the tower belongs to the more recent additions. It is now converted into a manufactory of japanned tin-wares.

With the exception of St. Castor's, the churches offer few objects of interest. The **Liebfrauenkirche,** or Church of Our Lady, was founded in the 13th cent., but not completed till the 15th. The Gothic choir, with its lofty pointed windows, was added in 1405, the upper parts of the towers were renewed after the siege of 1688. — The **Carmelitenkirche,** erected in 1673, has recently been fitted up as a garrison-church. The (Prot.) **Florinskirche** was built at the commencement of the 12th cent., the choir added subsequently to 1356. Near the latter is the **Kaufhaus,** or Merchants' Hall, erected in 1480 as a Town-hall, and used as such till 1805.

The **Schloss,** or palace, in the "Neustadt", is a building of considerable extent, but no architectural pretensions. It was erected by Clemens Wenceslaus, the last Elector of Treves (d. 1812) in 1778—86, and occupied by him till 1794. Soon after his departure the French successively converted it into a hospital and a barrack. In 1845 it was restored by the Prussian government, and since 1850 has been a frequent residence of the Prince and Princess (now King and Queen) of Prussia. A suite of apartments in the building is assigned to the use of the President of the Rhenish Province, and the N. wing contains the military protest. church and the English chapel. The latter was liberally placed at the disposition of the English residents by the Princess (now Queen) of Prussia, who not unfrequently attends the service.

In the middle of the Clemensplatz (military music see p. 75), adjoining the Esplanade with its numerous trees, rises a fountain-obelisk, erected by Clemens Wenceslaus in 1791, and dedicated "*vicinis suis*". Opposite to it, and adjoining the Hôtel de Treves, is the *Theatre* (Pl. 20).

The handsome S. gates, the **Mainzerthor** and the **Löhrthor**, belong to the fortifications of the town, and serve as barracks for the artillery and pioneers. A glance at the ramparts from the drawbridges in front of the gates will convey an idea of the fortifications of the town, which are, however, of far less importance than the strongly fortified outworks of Ehrenbreitstein, the Karthause, and the Petersberg. The new ***Promenade**, which the traveller will reach in 5 min. from the Mainzer Thor by traversing the glacis to the l., extends for upwards of 2 M. along the bank of the river, and well deserves a visit on account of the beautiful view it affords. The new and handsome iron ***Railway Bridge** is seen to the l., as the glacis is quitted.

The fortifications on the *Karthause*, on the r. bank of the Moselle, consist of **Fort Alexander** on the summit, and lower down **Fort Constantine**, the latter occupying the site of an ancient Carthusian monastery. The road which ascends the hill between rows of trees and leads to the Hunnsrücken was, before the construction of the road along the bank of the Rhine, the high-road to Bingen and Mayence. The view about half-way up is singularly beautiful; in the foreground is the rich plain of the Rhine and the island of Oberwerth, and the background consists of a semicircle of picturesquely shaped hills with the castles of Stolzenfels and Lahneck.

On the side of the Karthause facing the Moselle, about 150 paces S. from the military rifle-practice ground, is a spot railed in and furnished with seats ("**die schöne Aussicht*") which affords a strikingly beautiful glimpse of the peaceful and lovely valley of the Moselle. If the road along the brow of the hill be now followed in the direction of the fortifications, the traveller will reach a broad road planted with poplars, which continuing nearly on the same level, leads round the fortifications of Fort Alexander, affording a succession of fine views, and joining the main road near Fort Constantine.

The ***Kühkopf** (1159 ft.), the wooded summit to the S. of the Karthause, is about 1½ M. distant from the exercising-ground, and commands a splendid and peculiar prospect, especially from the Luisen-Linde (a large lime-tree named after the Princess Louisa of Prussia, now Grand-duchess of Baden), from which three navigable rivers, the Rhine, the Moselle, and the Lahn, are visible at the same time. About ½ M. beyond the point where the path from the Kühkopf joins the road, another road (for pedestrians only) descends to Stolzenfels (p. 90).

At the foot of the fortifications of Fort Alexander, on the N. side, is situated the ***Cemetery,** with its numerous monuments and weeping willows, where, among other illustrious dead, lie the remains of the poet Max von Schenkendorf (d. 1817).

Beyond the bridge over the Moselle rises the slight eminence of *Petersberg*, crowned by the fortifications of **Fort Franz**, which commands the town, the roads to Treves and Cologne, and the entire intervening plain. Two smaller outworks, to the r. and l. of the principal fort, and connected with it by subterranean passages, and a third in the plain near Neuendorf, complete this portion of the fortifications and form an extensive camp capable of affording shelter to 100,000 men. The full complement of the garrison in time of war is fixed at 15,000, but owing to the admirable arrangements of the works 5000 men (Alexander and Constantine 2000, Franz 500, Town 800, Ehrenbreitstein 1200 and Asterstein 500) would be sufficient to defend the town against an enemy of far superior force.

Within the walls of Fort Franz, to the l. on entering, a plain marble slab, enclosed by four corner-stones, indicates the grave of the French General *Hoche* (p. 67), whose remains were brought from Wetzlar to Coblenz and here interred, and near it his companion in arms *Marceau* ("*soldat à 16 ans, général à 22 ans*"), who fell at Altenkirchen in 1796. The monument of the latter as well as his remains were, on the construction of the fortification in 1819, removed to their present position at the foot of the hill, on the l. hand side of the Cologne road, about $^3/_4$ M. from the Moselle bridge. Byron's well-known lines:

"By Coblenz, on a gentle rise of ground,
There is a small and simple pyramid,
Crowning the summit of the verdant mound;
Beneath its base are hero's ashes hid
Our enemy, — but let not that forbid
Honour to Marceau!" &c.

refer to the monument in its original position.

The fertile plain which extends between Coblenz and Andernach is celebrated in history as the scene of Cæsar's first passage of the Rhine (near Engers), B. C. 55, the contests between Charles the Bald and Louis the German in 871, the devastation of this district by the Normans in 882, the sieges of the 30 Years' war in 1631—1636, the murderous and destructive campaign of Louis XIV., the Spanish war of succession, and the French revolutionary war of 1794—1797. — About 1 M. to the N. W. of Marceau's monument is situated **Schönbornslust**, once a villa of the Elector of Treves, and the residence of the Bourbon princes and other illustrious fugitives during the first French revolution.

21. Ehrenbreitstein.

Cards of admission ($2^1/_2$ Sgr.) must be procured at the office of the commandant (Pl. 33), the first door to the r. after crossing the bridge over the dock. Visitors are received at the top and conducted over the fortress by a soldier. Two hours suffice for the walk from Coblenz to the summit and back. The view from the *Pfaffendorfer Höhe* (p. 82) is similar to that from Ehrenbreitstein; no permission necessary.

Opposite to the influx of the Moselle rises the majestic fortress of ***Ehrenbreitstein**, justly termed the Gibraltar of the Rhine, situated on a precipitous and rugged rock, 377 ft. above the Rhine and 566 ft. above the level of the sea. The castle which formerly occupied the site of the present fortification is said to have been presented by the Franconian king Dagobert to the Archbishops of Treves, and it is known that the latter were confirmed in their possession by the Emperor Henry II. in 1018. It was subsequently greatly enlarged and strengthened at various periods, and became a fortress of great importance. It has only twice succumbed to an enemy, once having been taken by stratagem, and once reduced by famine. On the first of these occasions it fell into the hands of the French in 1631, under whose protection the Elector Christoph von Sötern had placed himself. The Elector having found a pretext for drawing off the greater part of the garrison, the French crossed the Rhine at Bingen, marched across the hills from Lorch to Montabaur, and entered the fortress in the rear. Five years later it again came into the possession of the Imperial general Johann von Werth.

During the French revolutionary war, Ehrenbreitstein was besieged four different times, in 1795, 1796, 1797, and 1798, and was finally surrendered, Jan. 27th, 1799, by the brave Colonel Faber, after all the provisions had been consumed. Immediately after its occupation by the French, they added several new intrenchments on the N. side, but in consequence of the peace of Luneville they blew up the entire works and evacuated it in 1801. At the second peace of Paris, 15 million francs were paid according to treaty by the French to the Prussian government for the restoration of the fortifications, which were recommenced in 1816 under the direction of General Aster, and completed 10 years later, at a total expense of not less than 8 million dollars (1,200,000*l.*). The new fortress extends over a part of the narrow table-land to the N. of the rock, and justly excites the admiration of connoisseurs from all parts of Europe.

A bridge of boats, 470 yds. in length, connects Coblenz with the small town of Ehrenbreitstein. On the pillars of the gateway are indicated the heights attained by the Rhine during recent inundations; the highest was that of 1845.

The way to the fortress leads through the town. On entering the gate beyond the drawbridge the visitor passes a handsome building on the r., erected in 1747 by the Electors of Treves as a residence for the governors of the place. It now serves as a provision magazine. A little beyond it the road ascends to the r. into the fortress, passing the old *Pagenhaus* (or institution for pages) of the Electors of Treves, and the *Helfenstein*, or lower part of the fortification. The steep flight of steps on the side facing the Rhine is now no longer used.

On three sides Ehrenbreitstein is, according to military criticism, inaccessible, and the N. side, where alone it could be attacked, is defended by a double line of bastions, which would have to be taken successively before an enemy could enter in that direction. The view from the top is one of the finest on the whole Rhine. It comprises the rich and fruitful plain of the Rhine from Stolzenfels to Andernach, and the numerous volcanic peaks of the Maifeld and Eifel (R. 33). Immediately below are the Rhine, the Moselle, and the triangular town of Coblenz.

The **Asterstein** on the *Pfaffendorfer Höhe*, to the S. of Ehrenbreitstein, is connected with the latter, and forms a part of the fortifications of the r. bank of the Rhine. The tower on the W. slope was erected in honour of the Grand-duchess of Baden, daughter of the present king of Prussia.

Coblenz and Ehrenbreitstein were visited by Goethe in the summer of 1774, and he resided for some time in the last house in Ehrenbreitstein on the l. before entering the fortress, at that time the residence of the Chancellor de la Roche. The poet gives a pleasing description of his visit in the 3rd part of his "Fiction and Truth."

22. From Coblenz to Wetzlar.

Ems and the Valley of the Lahn.

Comp. map. R. 24.

By railway direct, since the completion of the new railway bridge at Coblenz, to Ems in 1/2, to Wetzlar in 2 3/4—3 hrs. Carriage-road and footpath to Ems see p. 83; carriages p. 75.

On quitting the Coblenz station the train leaves the Left-Rhenish line, and passing the Löhr and the Mainzer Thor (p. 79) approaches the Rhine. From the railway-bridge a pleasing glimpse is obtained of the town, the palace, and the fortress of Ehrenbreitstein. Passing the villages of *Pfaffendorf*, *Horchheim* and *Niederlahnstein*, and crossing the *Lahn* opposite to the beautifully situated castle of Stolzenfels, the train stops at **Oberlahnstein** (p. 91; *Railway refreshment-room; to Rüdesheim and Wiesbaden see R. 23), where carriages must frequently be changed.

The train now slowly skirts the base of the wooded eminence on which the castle of *Lahneck* (p. 92) stands, and remains on the l. bank of the Lahn till Nassau is reached.

Besides the railway, a good road leads from Ehrenbreitstein to Ems by Niederlahnstein, thence ascending the picturesque valley of the Lahn on the r. bank of the river, passing several iron-foundries and the village of *Fachbach*, a distance of 12 M. (by carriage in 2 hrs.) The footpath from Ehrenbreitstein over the hills (*Arzheim* 1 M., signpost 3 M. farther, *Fachbach* $1^1/_2$ M., thence to Ems $1^1/_2$ M., total distance 7 M.) may be found without a guide.

Hotels in Ems. Englischer Hof, at the W. end; Russischer Hof, in the centre of the town. Four Seasons, and Europäischer Hof, near the Cursaal. Darmstädter Hof, near the old Curhaus. Guttenberger Hof, on the l. bank of the Lahn, good table d'hôte; Hôtel de France, both near the station. Besides these hotels there are a great number of lodging-houses: Panorama, Pariser Hof, Prince of Wales, Stadt London, etc. on the l. bank of the river.

Carriages. To *Arnstein* and back 6 fl.; *Braubach* 5 fl., back by *Lahnstein* 7 fl.; *Coblenz* 5 fl., and back 7 fl.; to *Ehrenbreitstein* $4^1/_2$ fl., and back 6 fl.; *Nassau* and back $3^1/_4$ fl., for the whole day $5^1/_2$; *Lahnstein* $3^1/_3$ fl. and back 5 fl., for the whole day 6 fl. These charges include tolls and driver's fee.

Donkeys. To *Ehrenbreitstein* $1^1/_2$ fl.; *Braubach* $1^1/_2$ fl. (to *Marksburg* 18 kr. more); *Nassau* $1^1/_3$ (to the castle 18 kr. more); *Arnstein* 1 fl. 48 kr.; *Fachbach* and *Nievern* 40 kr.; *Mooshütte* 30 kr., to the highest point 40 kr., same and back by Dausenau 1 fl. These charges all include the return-ride; the donkey-boys expect a fee of a few kreuzers. Two-donkey carriages at somewhat more than double the above charges.

Telegraph Office during the season in the Fürstenhof.

English Church Service during the season in the English Chapel on the l. bank of the Lahn.

Ems was known to the Romans, as is proved by the vases, coins, &c., found at various times in the vicinity, and is mentioned in a document of 1354 as a warm bath under the inspection of the governments of Hessen-Darmstadt and Oranien-Nassau, to the latter of which it has exclusively belonged since 1803. It is a curious fact, showing to what an extent Germany was formerly cut up into small principalities, that from the bridge over the Lahn, which commands but a limited view, the dominions of 8 different independent princes could be seen.

The village (3000 inhab., $^1/_3$ Rom. Cath.) has within the last few years completely altered its aspect. For many years it was limited to a row of lodging-houses on the r. bank of the river, but by degrees a new Ems has sprung up on the l. bank, consisting of a group of handsome and commodious residences, which are in some respects far preferable to those on the r. bank, being less exposed to the sun, and, what is of no little moment to the invalid, more retired, and farther removed from the bustle of the promenade and Curhaus (rail. stat. also on the l. bank). Among the plantations at the back of the (l.) *English Church*, higher up the hill, is seen the *Schweizer Haus* (Swiss House), a café commanding a pleasing view. On the wooded summit of the *Mahlberg-Kopf* stands a tower, much resorted to for the sake of the view (comprising Stolzenfels), and reached by pleasant, shady walks. Way back by the *Lindenbach* (*Inn), past some silver works, re-entering the valley of the Lahn about 1½ M. below Ems.

The principal buildings are the *Bath-establishment* with the four towers, the old *Curhaus*, connected by an elegant open hall, used as a bazaar, with the Cursaal, where the usual seductions of an elegant ball-room, supper and reading-rooms, with apartments devoted to gambling are offered to the unwary traveller. The new *Bath-house* on the l. bank is a large square building with two court-yards and gardens in the middle, and two mineral springs, the water of which is pumped up by steam. The baths in this establishment are better and more comfortably fitted up than those of the old Curhaus, the latter being only separated by partitions which do not reach to the ceiling. It also contains a new "inhaling-apparatus." A covered iron bridge connects this bath-house with the walks on the r. bank of the Lahn.

The most celebrated springs are the *Kesselbrunnen* (117° Fahr.), the *Krähnchen* (79—85°), and the *Fürstenbrunnen* (93—95°), all enclosed in the hall belonging to the old Curhaus. The principal ingredients of the waters are bi-carbonate of soda and chloride of sodium, and they are most efficacious in pulmonary and female complaints. About 150,000 bottles are exported every year. The annual number of guests who visit Ems is about 5000 (in 1823 only 1200), most of them belonging to the higher classes. The height of the season is from the middle of July to the end of August. In the evening between 6 and 8 o'clock the grounds of the Curhaus are thronged by a fashionable crowd, which assembles at the same hours in the morning, to drink the waters.

On the E. side of Ems the **Bäderlei*, a rugged group of slate rocks, rises precipitously from the street. Half-way up are the *Hanselmann's caves*, not unlike small casemates and embrasures, sinking deep into the grauwackian strata (origin unknown). The *Mooshütte* at the top commands a fine view. (Way up by the old Curhaus.) The *Winterberg* commands a fine view; a Roman watch-tower and the remnants of an intrenchment were discovered on the summit in 1859.

The railway to Limburg keeps the l. bank of the Lahn till within a short distance of Nassau (11 min. from Ems). Shortly after leaving Ems the train passes **Dausenau,** where an old octagonal tower indicates the ancient fortification of the valley. Near stat. *Nassau* the Lahn is crossed by an iron bridge, beyond which Haupt's Hydropathic establishment is seen on the r., and a new hospital on the l.

Nassau (*Krone*) was the birth-place of the celebrated Prussian minister Baron von Stein (d. 1831). In 1815 he caused a Gothic tower to be added to his residence in commemoration of the war of liberation. Above the entrance are the arms of the family and the well-known words of Luther: "Eine feste Burg ist unser Gott" (our God is a sure stronghold). The library contains portraits of Maximilian I., Charles V., Luther, Frederick the Great, Blücher, &c. In the upper rooms are preserved commemorative tablets on which the most eventful days of the years 1812—1815 (war of liberation) are recorded in gilt letters. The tower, which was the favorite resort, and is replete with reminiscences of its former illustrious owner, may also be visited (fee 18 kr.). The property now belongs to Count Kielmannsegge, the son-in-law of the minister.

The remains of the Baron von Stein are interred in the family vault at **Frücht**, a village on the heights between Ems and Braubach (p. 93). The forester has the keys of the vault, which is built in the form of a chapel (fee 18 kr., for a party 30 kr.—1 fl.).

On the opposite bank of the Lahn, which is crossed by a handsome *Suspension bridge*, rises a wooded eminence, surmounted by the ruins of the *Castle of Nassau* (fine view from the tower), family seat of the House of Nassau, erected about 1100; below it is the ruined *Burg zum Stein.* The hill is encircled with promenades. A small open pavilion on a projecting rock commands a beautiful view.

The road to Wiesbaden (no diligence) passes at the foot of the hill, then enters a beautiful valley, after which it crosses the high land to *Schwalbach* (R. 33) and *Wiesbaden* (R. 37).

Soon after leaving Nassau the train passes the old castle of *Lungenau*, formerly the seat of an Austrian family of that name which became extinct in 1603. The watch tower and outer walls are well preserved; within the latter a modern dwelling house has been erected. On the opposite bank of the Lahn rises the monastery of *Arnstein*, with its church and other buildings, picturesquely situated among trees on a rocky eminence. The castle, which was built by the powerful Counts of Arnstein about the middle of the 13th cent., was in the following century converted by the last of the family into a monastery, and secularized in 1803. The still habitable buildings were up to 1861 employed as a house of correction for Roman Catholic clergymen. Near **Obernhof** are old lead and silver mines, now worked by an English company.

The train next passes *Kalkofen*, the "*alte Haus*", the fragment of an ancient nunnery on the heights of the l. bank, and **Laurenburg**, a village with a small palace and ruined castle, in very early times the residence of the Counts of Nassau.

Before reaching the church, a path to the l. ascends to the village of **Scheid** (1¼ M.) on the hill, and, about 8 min. walk farther, again leaves the main road and descends to the r. into the valley of the Lahn to **Geilnau** (1½ M.). The Lahn describes a circuit of many miles between Laurenburg and Geilnau, which the path just described cuts off. The mineral spring (no inn) of Geilnau is situated 1½ M. above the village, and its waters are exported in large quantities, but it is never resorted to by the patients in person. The valley between Geilnau and Balduinstein is extremely picturesque.

The train proceeds in the valley of the Lahn and after passing through the *Cramberg tunnel* stops at stat. **Balduinstein** (*Noll*), where the grand ruins of the castle of the same name are seen rising from a narrow ravine behind the village. High up on the r., a little farther off, the castle of ***Schaumburg** overlooks the valley from a wooded basaltic peak. It was once the seat of the princes of Anhalt-Schaumburg, the last of whom died in 1812, and now belongs to his grandson the Archduke Stephan, who has resided in it since 1848, and greatly enlarged and improved it. The library contains many works of value, and a collection of minerals occupies the groundfloor of the new part of the building. Live bears, eagles, and deer are also kept. The hot-houses contain many rare and beautiful plants. Refreshments (good and moderate) to be had at the farm-buildings. The footpath from Balduinstein to the castle of Schaumburg is somewhat steep, by the carriage-road a gentle ascent of 15—20 min.

Stat. **Fachingen** (*inn*) derives importance from the celebrated Brunnen of that name, from which 300,000 bottles of mineral water are annually exported. The process of filling and corking the bottles is an interesting sight.

Dietz (**Holländischer Hof; Hôtel Lorenz*), a clean little town, picturesquely situated on the Lahn, and surmounted by an old castle (of the counts of Dietz), now converted into a house of correction. The prisoners are employed in cutting and polishing marble (found in the neighbourhood) ornaments of various kinds which may be purchased in the magazine. Permission to see the process, which is worth inspection, must be procured from the director of the establishment. The bridge which here crosses the Lahn is an interesting old structure; it is supported by pillars erected on two others which lie unbroken in the bed of the river like the fallen tower of the castle of Heidelberg.

Beyond Dietz, on the l. bank of the Lahn, is situated

Schloss Oranienstein, erected in 1676, and still the frequent residence of the Duke of Nassau. It was for several years occupied by the Prince William V. of Oranien-Nassau, the exiled stadtholder of the republic of Holland, and great-grandfather of the present king.

Limburg (**Preussischer Hof*, near the post-office, R. 36 kr., D. 48 kr., B. 18 kr.; **Nassauer Hof*, and *Deutsches Haus*, near the bridge) on the *Lahn*, which is here crossed by a bridge erected in 1315, lies 3 M. to the N.E. of Dietz. High above the town rises the **Dom*, or Cathedral, with its 5 towers: *Basilica St. Georgi erecta 909*, as the inscription above the portal records. The present structure, however, one of the finest churches in the transition style, belongs to the year 1235, and is the cathedral of the bishop. The interior contains a very ancient font, and in the N. transept a monument to the Emperor Conrad I. (d. 918), founder of the original building.

Beyond Limburg the banks of the Lahn become less abrupt for a short distance. To the l. *Dietkirchen*, which boasts of the oldest church in the Duchy, is situated on a rocky eminence rising precipitously from the Lahn. Stat. *Eschhofen;* then

Runkel (*Wied'scher Hof*), an ancient town situated on both banks of the Lahn, with an extensive old castle of the princes of Wied, a portion of which is still habitable. Near stat. *Vilmar* are considerable marble quarries; then *Aumenau*, with ironstone mines, and after a rapid succession of tunnels, bridges and viaducts,

Weilburg (**Deutscher Hof;* **Traube; Schwan*), once the residence of the Dukes of Nassau-Weilburg, who became extinct in 1816. Their château, erected in 1711, is picturesquely situated on a rocky eminence rising abruptly from the Lahn. To the l. is seen the mouth of a tunnel, constructed in 1845 to facilitate the navigation of the river at this point.

The following stations are *Löhnberg*, *Stockhausen*, *Braunfels*. The small town of Braunfels, the residence of the Prince of Solms-Braunfels, is situated on the height to the S. Stat. *Albshausen*.

Wetzlar see p. 41.

23. From Coblenz to Wiesbaden.

Railway journey. (*Comp. Map R.R. 24, 27 and 45.*)

By the direct railway, crossing the Rhine at Coblenz, in 3 hrs.; fares: 2 Thlr. 17, 1 Thlr. 22½, 1 Thlr. 6 Sgr. Return-tickets, valid for 5 days, must be stamped for the return-journey at the booking office. Passengers who break their journey must get their tickets checked on leaving the train. Views of the Rhine to the *right*.

[For the detailed description of the localities mentioned on the following pages comp. R.R. 24, 25 and 34).

From Coblenz to Oberlahnstein see preceding Route.

Stat. **Oberlahnstein** (*Hôtel Weller; Hôtel Lahneck*), where the line to Ems and Wetzlar diverges. As the train proceeds, a view of the village of *Rhense*, and the fertile slopes and woods beyond, is obtained. Stat. *Braubach*, at the foot of *Marksburg*, is opposite to the picturesque village of *Brey*, above which are situated *Nieder-* and *Ober-Spay*. Beyond stat. *Osterspay*, above which rises the castle of *Liebeneck*, the river describes a long curve; on the opposite bank, at a considerable elevation, stands the *Jacobsberger Hof*. The train next passes through the village of *Filsen*, opposite to the *Mühlbad*, commands a fine view of *Boppard*, one of the most beautifully situated of the Rhenish towns, and reaches stat. *Camp*. The convent of *Bornhofen* and the foot of the "Brothers" *Sterrenberg* and *Liebenstein* are now skirted. Above stat. *Kestert*, on the opposite bank, lies the pleasant village of *Hirzenach*. Beyond stat. *Welmich*, at the base of the "*Mouse*," the imposing ruins of *Rheinfels* on the l. bank, rising above the town of *St. Goar*, come in sight.

Stat. **St. Goarshausen** at the entrance of the *Swiss Valley*, commanded by the "*Cat*," is next reached. The train then penetrates the rocks of the *Lurlei* and *Rossstein* by means of two tunnels, on emerging from which the handsome town of *Oberwesel*, on the opposite bank, commanded by *Schönburg*, comes into view. Opposite stat. *Caub*, at the foot of the castle of *Gutenfels*, is situated the *Pfalz* in the middle of the Rhine. Farther up the river, on the l. bank, lies the ancient town of *Bacharach*, behind which rise the picturesque ruins of *Stahleck*. The next ruin on the opposite bank is that of *Fürstenberg*, beyond which lies the village of *Rheindiebach*. The train now intersects the village of *Lorchhausen*, skirts the base of the ancient castle of *Nollingen*, at the entrance of the *Wisperthal*, and stops at

Stat. **Lorch.** On the opposite bank, above the village of *Niederheimbach*, rises the round tower of *Heimburg*, and farther on, the picturesque castle of *Sooneck*. Again on the l. bank *Trechtingshausen*, and beyond it the castle of *Falkenburg*, at the entrance of the *Morgenbachthal;* then the *Clemenscapelle* and above it the picturesquely situated *Rheinstein*. The train now halts at stat. *Assmannshausen*, the usual point whence the Niederwald is visited; a thermal spring (95° Fahr.) discovered here by the Romans, occasionally attracts invalids. Skirting the base of *Ehrenfels*, and passing the *Binger Loch*, the *Mouse Tower* on an island in the Rhine, and *Bingen*, at the influx of the *Nahe*, the train next stops at

Stat. **Rüdesheim.** Steam ferry to *Bingerbrück*, fares 7 kr. or 4 kr. On the opposite bank rises the wooded *Rochusberg* with its chapel. To the l., on the brow of the hill, are situated the village and convent of *Eibingen.* To the l. of stat. *Geisenheim,* lies the castle of *Johannisberg*, with the village of the same name, 2 M. distant; the castle is easier of access from stat. *Winkel*, whence it may be reached in 20 min. To the l. the castle of *Vollraths*, another wine-growing locality of the highest reputation, and to the r. the village of *Mittelheim.* Opposite stat. *Oestrich*, on the l. bank at some distance from the river, is situated *Nieder-Ingelheim.* To the l. of the line lies the village of *Hallgarten*, amidst vineyards of high repute; to the r. the château of *Reichartshausen;* to the l. the lunatic asylum of *Eichberg,* the abbey of *Eberbach*, and the celebrated Steinberg vineyard. Beyond stat. *Hattenheim* the train passes the *Marcobrunn* vineyards, opposite to which three picturesque and fertile islands are situated in the Rhine. To the l. of the village of *Erbach* rises the handsome tower of *Scharfenstein* near *Kiedrich*, and farther on, *Bubenhausen*, an eminence commanding a noble prospect.

From stat. **Eltville** (*Rheinbahn Hotel*, at the stat.), a diligence runs twice daily in summer to *Schlangenbad* and *Schwalbach.* On the brow of the hill to the l. is seen the spire of *Rauenthal.* The line continues to intersect a series of vineyards, and passes several handsome country residences. Opposite stat. *Niederwalluff*, on the l. bank of the river, is situated the chapel of *Budenheim*, whence the **Leniaberg* (refreshments at the forester's), commanding a fine survey of the Rheingau, may be ascended in $1/2$ hr. The *Nürnberger Hof*, an inn on the heights to the l., is another favourite point of view. Beyond stat. *Schierstein*, to the r., is the *Rheinhütte* foundry, where the line quits the bank of the Rhine. Passengers for Castel and Frankfurt proceed direct from stat. *Mosbach* to stat. *Curve*, without changing carriages. The N. entrance of the ducal park of Mosbach is in the immediate vicinity of the station. To the r. are situated the extensive new barracks of *Biebrich*, beyond which, on the opposite bank of the Rhine, rise the spires of Mayence. The line now runs parallel with the Taunus railway, and a pleasing view is obtained of the town of *Wiesbaden*, the *Platte*, the *Neroberg* and the *Greek Chapel.* To the l. the buildings of the gas-works. The stations of the Nassovian and Taunus lines are contiguous.

24. The Rhine from Coblenz to St. Goar.

Comp. Map R. 24.

Distances: from Coblenz to Capellen $3\frac{3}{4}$ M., Rhense $2\frac{1}{4}$ M., Niederspay (opp. to Braubach) $1\frac{1}{2}$ M., Boppard $4\frac{1}{2}$ M., Salzig 3 M., Hirzenach $2\frac{1}{4}$ M., St. Goar $3\frac{3}{4}$ M.; total distance 21 M. — By railway on the *left bank* see R. 35, on the *right bank* by Oberlahnstein to St. Goarshausen in 1 hr. — By steamboat in $2\frac{1}{2}$ hrs. (down in $1\frac{1}{2}$ hr.). *Piers* at Oberlahnstein, Boppard and St. Goar; *small-boat* stations at Capellen, Spay, Camp, and Hirzenach.

After passing through the bridge of boats the steamer passes the once electoral, now royal palace on the r., and beyond the new railway bridge, the picturesque village of **Pfaffendorf** with its pointed spire to the l.

In a valley to the r., partially concealed by the island of *Oberwerth* is situated the pleasant Hydropathic estab. of *Laubbach*, under the management of Dr. Petri (charges $8\frac{1}{2}$—20 Thlr. per week for board, lodging, and med. attendance). The vineyards of (l.) **Horchheim** (**Holler*) produce a good red wine; the plain between this village and the mouth of the Lahn is rich and fruitful (l.). **Niederlahnstein** (*Douqué*) lies on the r. bank of the Lahn, which is navigable as far as Weilburg, and serves as a highway for the products of Nassau, such as iron-ore, mineral water, etc.

Above the village of (r.) **Capellen** (**Stolzenfels; *Bellevue*) rises the royal castle of ****Stolzenfels,** the highest point of which is 410 ft. above the Rhine. A broad and winding road of easy access leads to it, spanned at one point by a handsome viaduct. Two Roman mile-stones are passed on the road, and after entering the *Klause* (now stabling), a drawbridge is crossed and the castle attained. The public are readily admitted, and great numbers of visitors avail themselves of the privilege (fee 10 Sgr. for 1 pers.; 20 Sgr.—1 Thlr. for a party). As only a certain number are conducted round the castle at a time, visitors are not unfrequently kept waiting outside, but the time is hardly misspent in the enjoyment of the exquisite view obtained from the S.E. corner tower, immediately contiguous to the entrance. — Capellen is a *Railway* and *Steamboat-station;* a steam ferry-boat plies between the stations of Capellen and Oberlahnstein. Carriage from Coblenz to Capellen see p. 75; boat from Capellen down to Coblenz 20 Sgr. Donkeys to be had at the foot of the hill, to the castle 8, there and back 12 Sgr.; to the Kühkopf 20 Sgr., there and back 1 Thlr. Stolzenfels is $3\frac{3}{4}$ M. from Coblenz, and the Königsstuhl $1\frac{1}{2}$ M. farther.

The castle of Stolzenfels was greatly strengthened, if not entirely built, by Arnold von Isenburg, Archbishop of Treves,

STOLZENFELS

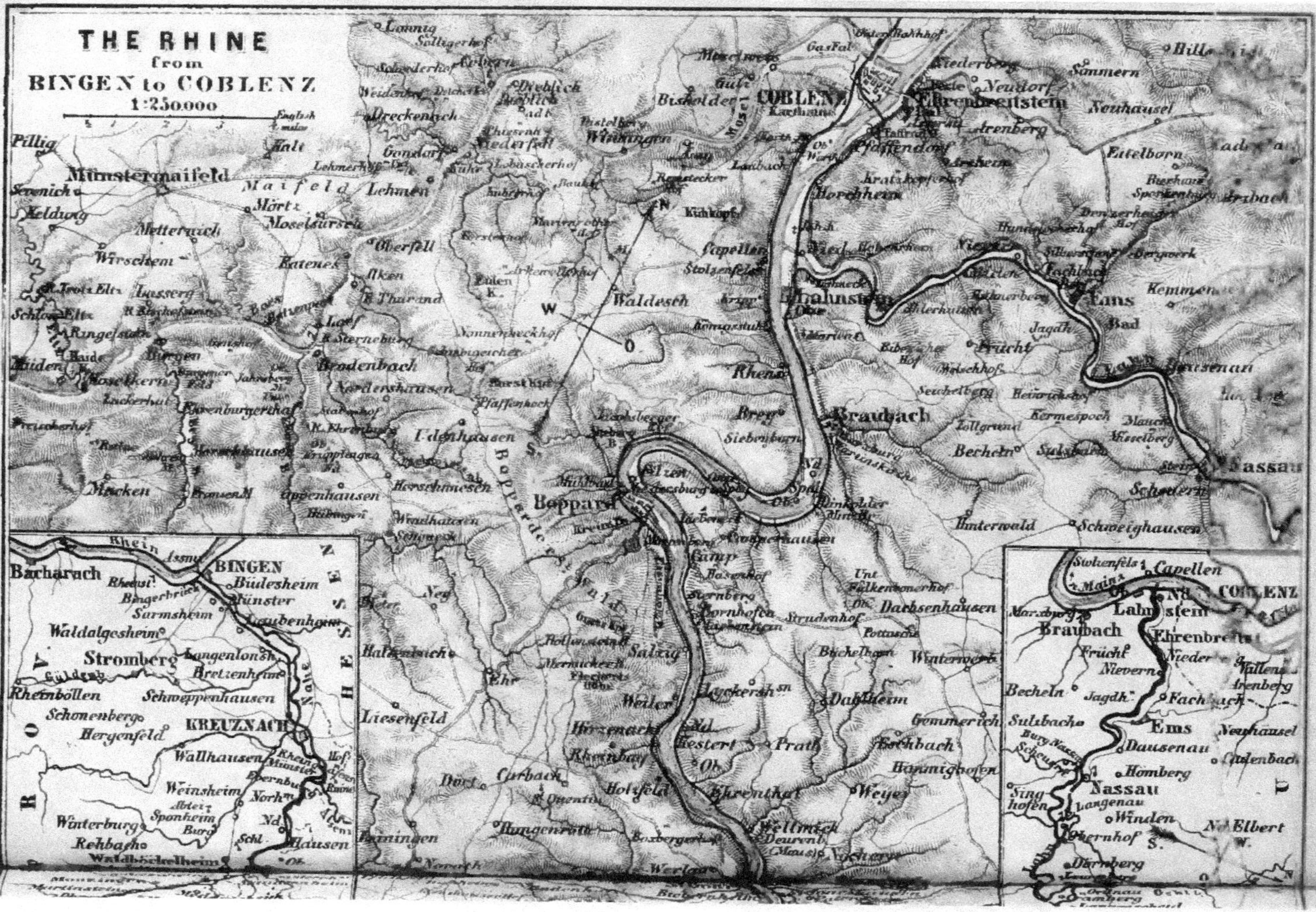

THE RHINE
from
BINGEN to COBLENZ
1:250.000
English miles
COBLENZ
Ehrenbreitstein
Neuhäusel
Münstermaifeld
Maifeld
Lehmen
Winningen
Moselkern
Brodenbach
Waldesch
Capellen
Stolzenfels
Lahnstein
Ems
Nassau
Braubach
Rhens
Boppard
Salzig
Hirzenach
Udenhausen
Liesenfeld
Becheln
Gemmerich
Weyer
Schweighausen
Dachsenhausen
Bacharach
BINGEN
Büdesheim
Stromberg
KREUZNACH
Waldalgesheim
Rheinböllen
Schwepenhausen
Wallhausen
Weinsheim
Winterburg
Rehbach
Dausenau
Homberg
Singhofen

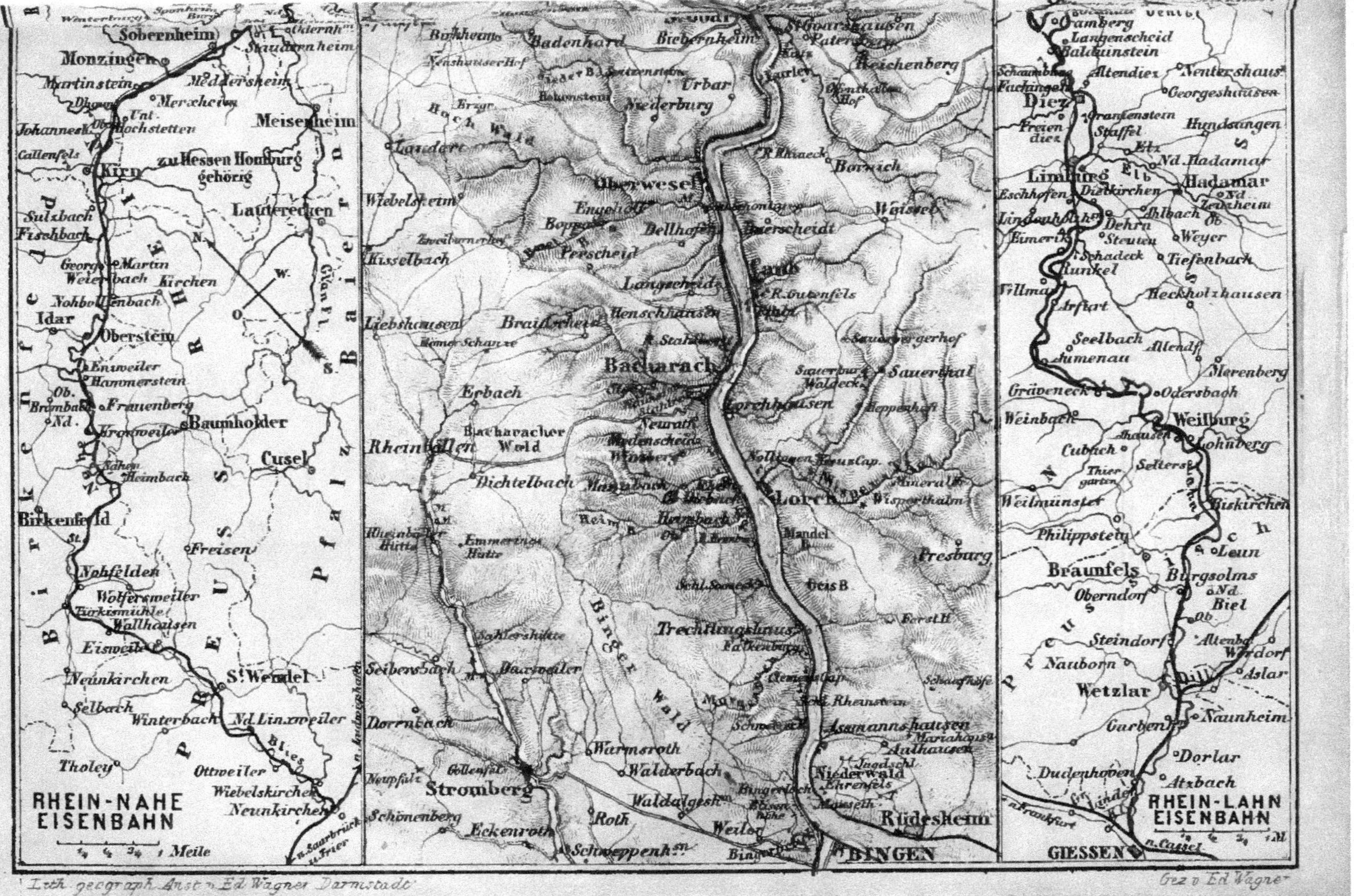
RHEIN-NAHE EISENBAHN
Meile
RHEIN-LAHN EISENBAHN
BINGEN
GIESSEN
Rüdesheim
Stromberg
Bacharach
Oberwesel
Lorch
Diez
Limburg
Weilburg
Wetzlar
Braunfels
Hadamar
Kirn
Oberstein
Idar
Birkenfeld
Baumholder
Cusel
Meisenheim
Sobernheim
Monzingen
St. Wendel
Neunkirchen
Tholey
Binger Wald
Lith. geograph. Anst. v. Ed. Wagner Darmstadt
Gez. v. Ed. Wagner

in 1250, and was in the middle ages frequently a residence of the archbishops. Till 1688 it was garrisoned by the Electors of Treves, when it met the usual fate at the hands of the French, whose visit to this fair land is recorded, not by the monuments they have left, but by the number of monuments they have destroyed. In 1802 the ruin was purchased by the town of Coblenz, and (1823) presented to the late king Fred. William IV., at that time crown-prince. Since then it has been completely restored at an expense of upwards of 53,000*l*.

The Chapel, a small but elegant building, is decorated with *frescoes on a gold ground by *E. Deger*, representing the Creation, Fall, First Sacrifices, &c. — On the outer wall, above the garden-hall, is a fresco by *Lasinsky:* the emperor Rupert and his nephew the Count of Hohenzollern visiting the Archbishop of Treves at Stolzenfels, Aug. 20th, 1400. — At the side of the entrance flight of steps, stands an ancient sculptured chimney-piece with reliefs, bearing the arms of the city of Cologne. — The walls of the "Rittersaal" are illuminated with six *frescoes, by Professor Stilke of Düsseldorf, representing the principal attributes of chivalry: 1. Faith is typified by Godfrey de Bouillon at the Holy Sepulchre after the conquest of Jerusalem; 2. Rudolph of Habsburg sitting in judgment on the knightly bandits represents Justice; 3. Minstrels accompanying king Philip of Swabia and his consort Irene on a pleasure excursion on the Rhine is symbolical of Poetry; 4. Love is pourtrayed by the Emperor Frederick II. welcoming his bride Isabella of England; 5. Hermann von Siebeneichen, sacrificing his life to safe the emperor Fred. Barbarossa, is the type of Loyalty; and (6) the blind king John of Bohemia at the battle of Cressy, of Bravery. — The larger "Rittersaal" contains a valuable and extensive collection of goblets, armour, and weapons; among the latter the swords of Napoleon, Murat, Blücher, Tilly, Kosciusko, &c. — The upper rooms contain a modern picture of Gutenberg, at three different periods of his life, about 50 small pictures by old masters, *Dürer, Holbein, van Dyck, Rembrandt*, &c., an ancient Byzantine cross, antique furniture, &c.

View. At Stolzenfels the narrowest and most romantic part of the valley of the Rhine, which begins with the castle of Ehrenfels below Bingen, may be said to terminate. The view from the castle is scarcely surpassed by any on the Rhine, and comprises the Marksburg, Braubach, Rhense, Oberlahnstein, and a part of the lovely valley of the Lahn. Opposite to the castle is situated the *Allerheiligenberg*, surmounted by a pilgrims' chapel, a spot of much pious resort. At the confluence of the Lahn and Rhine, at the extremity of a fertile plain, stands the Romanesque *Church of St. John*, and below it the village of *Niederlahnstein*. Farther down the river is the island of *Oberwerth*, on which a convent formerly stood, long since converted into a country house. — The magnificent fortress of Ehrenbreitstein, the strongest on the Rhine, is one of the most conspicuous objects in the landscape; opposite to it is Fort Constantine, and between them lies the town of Coblenz; farther distant is visible the small town of Vallendar with its handsome church.

(l.) **Oberlahnstein** (*Hôtel Weller; Hôtel Lahneck*), mentioned in an old document as early as 890, is surrounded with remnants of ancient walls, towers, and fosses. The *Schloss*, once a residence of the Electors of Mayence, was founded in 1394; the new part of the building belongs to the last century. On the bank of the Rhine is a depôt for iron-ore of various descriptions. (Railway to Ems see p. 82, station at the steamboat pier.)

Behind Oberlahnstein rises the castle of **Lahneck,** beautifully situated on a rocky eminence above the Lahn. It was purchased some years ago by an Irish gentleman, who is gradually restoring it with great taste and judgment; when completed it will present an almost unique specimen of a restored Rhenish castle. The old feudal proprietors would hardly recognize their ancient strongholds in the generality of the modern, so-called restorations.

About $1\frac{1}{2}$ M. above Capellen is the **Königsstuhl** (king's seat), situated between the high road and the Rhine, but partially concealed by trees from the steamboat passenger. The original structure was erected in 1376 by order of the Emperor Charles IV., but during the French dominion fell so completely to decay, that at the beginning of the present century almost all traces of it had disappeared. It was of an octagonal shape, 24 ft. in diameter and 18 ft. high, and rested on 9 pillars, the 9th being in the centre. The top was encircled by a stone seat, where the Electors held their meetings. The present building was constructed in 1843 partly out of the old materials. The situation was chosen on account of its vicinity to the dominions of the four Rhenish Electors, Braubach belonging to the Palatinate, Rhense to Cologne, Stolzenfels to Treves, and Lahnstein to Mayence. Here many emperors were elected, decrees made, and treaties concluded, and here the Emperor Maximilian took the oaths, when on his way to his coronation at Aix-la-Chapelle. Near the Königsstuhl is a mineral spring discovered in 1857 in the bed of the Rhine.

On the rich and fruitful bank of the Rhine, opposite to the Königsstuhl, a small white chapel, situated near the S. gate of Oberlahnstein, is visible among the trees, where, Aug. 20th, 1400, the Rhenish Electors deprived the Bohemian king Wenzel of the imperial crown. On the following day they crossed the river to the Königsstuhl, and elected the Count Palatine Rupert III. in his stead.

Above the Königsstuhl ($\frac{3}{4}$ M.) lies the small town of (r.) **Rhense** (*Königsstuhl; Siebenborn*), once belonging to the Electorate of Cologne, and still surrounded by the walls and fosses constructed by the Archbishop Frederick III. of Cologne in 1370. — Small boat to Coblenz 20—25 Sgr. A footpath to Boppard ascends to the r. at the signpost, on leaving the town by the S. gate.

The building about 1 M. above Rhense, on the same bank of the river, was erected by a company as silver smelting-works, but has never been used; beyond it, surrounded by fruit-trees, lies the small village of (r.) **Brey.**

(l.) **Braubach** (*Philippsburg* at the upper, *Arzbächer* at the lower end of the village; *Deutsches Haus*, with beer-garden, near the station), invested with municipal privileges by the Emperor Rudolph in 1276, is commanded by the imposing castle of **Marksburg**, 480 ft. above the Rhine. It was called the *Braubacher Schloss* previously to 1437, when Count Philipp of Katzenelnbogen founded a chapel in it, which he dedicated to St. Mark, after whom the castle has ever since been named. From 1651 to 1803 it was the property of Hessen-Darmstadt, and subsequently of Nassau. It now serves as a state-prison, and is garrisoned by about 20 men. The summit affords a pleasing survey of the grassy dales in the rear and of a limited portion of the Rhine. Several Swedish cannons of the 30 Years' war, as well as French guns, are exhibited to the visitor. (Castellan's fee 12 kr. for 1 pers., 18—24 for a party.)

Two paths ascend to the fortress, one at the back, and another (cart-track) at the upper end of the town, passing the ancient *Chapel of St. Martin*, and leading round the E. side of the hill. The entrance is on the N. side. The little town with its old watch-tower, towngate and church rising from among poplars, with the castle in the background, forms a charming picture, though somewhat defaced by the railway embankments.

From this point a road leads over the hills to the Baths of Ems, about 7½ M. distant. Refreshments to be had at the *Lahnsteiner Forsthaus*, not far from *Frücht*, Fine view of Dausenau and the valley of the Lahn in descending.

In the first valley above Braubach is a chalybeate spring called the *Dinkholder Brunnen;* the second is traversed by a path which ascends the hill, commanding a fine view, and leads to Welmich (7½ M.), emerging from the wild and rocky ravine at the back of the village near the "Mouse" (p. 96).

Above Braubach are the (r.) villages of **Nieder-** and **Oberspay,** connected by an avenue of walnut-trees, beyond which the river is ascended in a W. direction.

On the wooded heights above the village of (l.) **Osterspay** stands the picturesque little castle of **Liebeneck.**

From Liebeneck to Camp (p. 95) a path leads across the high tableland which commands a most striking view of the Rhine from Salzig to below Boppard, and the heights of the Hunnsrücken, of which the Fleckertshöhe (see p. 94) is the most conspicuous. In the opposite direction this path is less agreeable, as the ascent is steep and leads through sunny and shadeless vineyards.

At (l.) **Filsen** the river resumes its S. direction. On an eminence to the r. stands the *Jacobsberger Hof*, 500 ft. above the Rhine, formerly a Jesuits' college, now the property of the Grammar School of Coblenz; from this point a much-frequented mountain-road leads to *Rhense,* 3 M. distant, cutting off the circuit of 6 M. which the river here forms.

(r.) **Boppard** (**Post*, in the town; **Spiegel*, on the Rhine; *Rheinischer Hof*), the *Baudobriga* of the Romans, was once a town of the empire, and from 1501 belonged to the Electors of Treves. The name seems to indicate a Celtic origin. The *Notitia dignitatum utriusque imperii,* a statistical review of the Roman empire in the 2nd cent., mentions Boppard as the residence of the *præfectus militum ballistariorum,* and stones found in the neighbourhood indicate its once having been a station of the 13th Legion. The wall of defence which encloses the interior of the town in a rectangular form, though much damaged, is evidently of Roman origin and is constructed of the concrete building-material so frequently employed in those ages. The outer and far more extensive wall belongs to the middle ages. Boppard, like St. Goar and Bacharach, once boasted of an establishment of the Templar knights, the traces of which may be recognized in the fragments of walls with round-arched windows, situated at the upper end of the town. Knights Templar of Boppard are mentioned among the crusaders at the siege of Ptolemaïs.

The *Pfarrkirche,* erected in the late Romanesque style, about 1200, is remarkable for its peculiar vaulted roof and the curious construction of the supporting arches. The *Carmeliterkirche* contains a good marble relief representing the Trinity, a monument of a Countess von Eltz (d. 1500). The old monastery of *St. Martin* and the adjacent *Franciscan convent* have been converted by the Prussian Government into a Reformatory for juvenile criminals.

Marienberg, the large building which rises from the midst of an orchard at the back of the town, was formerly a Benedictine nunnery, but is now converted into a hydropathic establishment. Below Boppard, on the bank of the river, is situated the *Mühlbad,* a private water-cure estab., the property of Dr. Heusner, the government physician of the district. Average weekly charge in both the above, for board, lodging, baths, and medical attendance, 12½ Thlr.

The finest excursion from Boppard is to the ***Fleckertshöhe** (1663 ft.), about 6 M. distant, and 1½ M. to the l. of the road leading to the Hunsrücken, which must be left at the fir-wood, soon after passing the mile-stone marked "0,84". The top is indicated by a stone pillar. The view is very extensive, and comprises the Seven Mountains, the Eifel, the Hochwald, Idar and Taunus, and Monrepos (p. 67). A small portion only of the Rhine is visible near Ehrenthal (p. 96). On the S.W. side, about ½ M. from the top, refreshments may be procured at the *Mermicher Hof.* The traveller may avail himself of the diligence from Boppard to Simmern to reach the above-mentioned fir-wood, where his path diverges to the l. Pedestrians on their route southwards may, instead of returning to Boppard, proceed to *Weiler* and *Hirzenach.*

The road from Boppard to the Moselle (9 M.) leads through the village of *Buchholz* (1229 ft.), to which a guide (10 Sgr.) should be taken. About 1½ M. beyond *Herschwiesen,* a road to the l. descends to the *Ehrenburg* (p. 125); thence through the Ehrenburger Thal to Brodenbach.

Above Boppard, to the l., is situated the village of **Camp** (**Anker; Rheinischer Hof*), so called from the remains of an intrenchment on the hill ascribed to the Romans, but more probably dating from the 30 Years' war. (Path over the hills to Liebeneck and Braubach see p. 93). A shady road planted with walnut-trees leads along the bank of the Rhine from Camp to the convent of

(l.) **Bornhofen**, with a Gothic church erected in 1435, which, even at the present day, is a favourite resort of pilgrims. On a rocky eminence above the convent, and surrounded by vineyards, stand the twin castles of

Sterrenberg and **Liebenstein**, better known as "the Brothers," and connected with each other by a sharp chine of rocks. Few are unacquainted with the legend of these castles, which may thus be briefly told:

Conrad and Heinrich, the two sons of the noble knight Bayer von Boppard, the owner of Liebenstein, were enamoured of their foster-sister, the beautiful Hildegarde. Heinrich by an exercise of rare generosity tore himself away and joined the crusades, leaving his brother Conrad to win the prize of which he too hastily deemed him worthy. That his son and the fair bride might still be near him, the old knight built the castle of Sterrenberg for their reception, but his death occurring before its completion the nuptials were deferred for a year. During this period Conrad's heart grew cold towards Hildegarde, and hearing of the valiant deeds of his absent brother against the infidels, his soul burned to share his honours, and wearied of an inactive life, he joined the crusades. Hildegarde now passed her days in the lonely castle of Liebenstein, brooding over her sad lot, not doubting the affection of Conrad, but weeping over the uncertainty of his return. Suddenly Conrad returned to Sterrenberg with a lovely Grecian bride, and the outraged Hildegarde, stunned by the blow, shut herself up in the loneliest chamber of her dreary abode, and refused to see any one but her attendant. Late one evening a stranger knight demanded the hospitality of the castle; he proved to be the chivalrous Heinrich, who, hearing of his brother's perfidious conduct, resolved to avenge his foster-sister's wrongs. He accordingly challenged Conrad to single combat, but before the brothers' swords had crossed, Hildegarde's figure interposed between them and insisted on a reconciliation, to which they reluctantly consented. Hildegarde then retired to the convent of Bornhofen, situated at the base of the rock on which the castles stand. Conrad's Grecian bride soon proved faithless, and he, overcome with shame and remorse, threw himself on his generous brother's breast, exclaiming that no consolation was now left him but his friendship. Thus their estrangement ended, and the brothers continued to live together in harmony and retirement at Liebenstein, whilst Sterrenberg was for ever deserted.

The castle of *Sterrenberg* was held as early as the 12th cent. as a fief of the empire by the knights of Boland, and afterwards came into the possession of the Electors of Treves. The date and cause of its abandonment are unknown. It lies on the extreme verge of the rocky height, and is separated from Liebenstein by a thick massive wall. The castles deserve inspection on account of the grandeur and extent of their ruins and the view they command of the rocky ravines in the vicinity.

(r.) **Salzig** (so called from the weak saline spring which it possesses) is situated in the midst of a vast orchard, whence whole ship-loads of cherries are annually exported to the Lower Rhine, Holland, and even to England. Farther up, on a fertile promontory to the l., lies the village of **Nieder-Kestert** (*Stern*).

(r.) **Hirzenach** (*Comes*); in the rear of the village are slate-quarries; the house on the summit of the hill, above the village, is a quarrymen's tavern. The small new Gothic edifice at the upper end of the village is a synagogue. The handsome building which was once a deanery, and the church, built about 1170, formerly belonged to the Abbey of Siegburg. (l.) **Ehrenthal**, a small village inhabited by the miners who work in the lead-mines in the vicinity.

(l.) **Welmich**, a picturesquely situated village, with a small Gothic church, is commanded by the ruined castle of *Thurnberg* or *Deurenburg* in the background. This stronghold, commenced by the Archbishop Bœmund of Treves, and completed by his successor Kuno von Falkenstein in 1363, was derisively called the **Maus** (mouse) by the Counts of Katzenelnbogen, in contradistinction to their "Cat," but Kuno enjoyed such a reputation for courage that he was feared by cats and mice alike. Here he died in 1388. The ascent is somewhat fatiguing, but the pedestrian is well rewarded by the fine view from the summit, especially in the direction of St. Goar. The interior of the castle is in a good state of preservation, and contains a few points of interest to the architect.

(r.) **St. Goar** (*Lilie; Krone*) owes its name and origin to a chapel, founded in the time of Siegbert, king of Austrasia (570), by St. Goar, who preached the gospel here, and was afterwards revered as a saint and invoked by the boatmen when in danger.

St. Goar was till 1794 the capital of the Hessian "Lower Grafschaft" of Katzenelnbogen (comp. p. 97), and has a more imposing appearance than any other Rhenish town of the same size, for which it is principally indebted to the extensive ruins of Rheinfels in the background. The Protestant church, built about 1468, contains, among other monuments, that of the Landgrave Philipp (d. 1583) and his countess in marble. A flaw in the altar is said to have been made by Gustavus Adolphus in 1632, who, indignant at the damage done to the church by the Spaniards, violently struck the altar with his sword. The crypt on the E. side once contained the bones of St. Goar. — The Roman Cath. church is adorned with an old stone effigy of the saint with an inscription.

A curious old custom prevailed here till the commencement of the steamboat traffic in 1827. It is said to have dated from the time of Charlemagne, and was called the "*Hänseln,*" or Initiation. Every traveller who visited the town for the first time was conducted to a ring attached to the wall of the Custom-house, to which he was secured. He was then obliged to submit to the water or the wine-ordeal. If the former was selected, the luckless traveller had to submit to a good ducking; the more agreeable alternative consisted in drinking a goblet of wine to the health of Charlemagne, the sovereign of England, the reigning prince, and the members of society who enforced obedience to the ancient custom. The traveller was then crowned and invested with the rights of a citizen and member of the society. The crown and the goblet, together with the book in which the names of the travellers were inscribed, are now in the possession of the landlord of the "Lilie."

Rheinfels, the Ehrenbreitstein of the middle ages, rises at the back of the town to the height of 368 ft. above the Rhine, and is incomparably the handsomest and most imposing ruin on the whole river. It was founded in 1245 by Count Dethier III. of Katzenelnbogen, the friend of the Emperor Frederick II., and a new Rhine-toll was here established. Ten years later a confederation of 26 Rhenish towns, dissatisfied with the newly imposed burden, attacked the castle, but after a fruitless siege of 15 months they were compelled to withdraw their forces. Under the Hessian Landgrave Philipp it was considerably strengthened in 1568, and in 1692 it was bravely and successfully defended by the Hessian General von Görtz against the French General Count Tallard with an army of 24,000 men. In 1758 the garrison was surprised and the castle taken by the French, who kept it garrisoned till 1763. Thirty years later, notwithstanding the great strength of the place, the Hessian commander basely deserted it, and the castle, with its valuable stores of ammunition and provisions, fell into the hands of the French revolutionary army, Nov. 2nd, 1794. Three years later it was blown up and sold for the insignificant sum of 60*l.* The ruin now belongs to the king of Prussia. The interior contains little worthy of note; view from the summit limited. The custodian lives in St. Goar, but is generally at or near the castle (fee 5 Sgr.).

(l.) **St. Goarshausen** (*Adler*, R. 36, B. 20, D. 48, S. 30, A. 18 kr., beer, and baths in the Rhine; *Rhein. Hof*) may be advantageously selected as head-quarters for excursions to the Swiss valley, Lurlei, Reichenberg, Oberwesel, Caub, Bacharach, &c., and offers many attractions to the traveller in search of repose. The upper part of the town consists of a neat row of houses, most of them new, and built close to the river, from the inundations of which they are protected by a dyke. The ferry to St. Goar is at the upper end of the place; charge for 1 pers. 2½ Sgr., for several together 1 Sgr. each.

(l.) The castle of *Neu-Katzenelnbogen*, commonly called the **Katz** (cat), which rises behind St. Goarshausen, was erected by Count Johann of Katzenelnbogen in 1393, and when the family became extinct in 1470, came into the possession of the Princes of Hessen, and was occupied by a Hessian garrison till 1806, when it fell into the hands of the French, to whom, like so many of the Rhenish castles, it is indebted for its destruction. (Guide with the keys from St. Goarshausen, 18 kr.)

On the brink of the ravine at the back of the castle lies (r.) the village of **Patersberg**, $1^1/_2$ M. beyond which, and 3 M. from St. Goarshausen, are situated the handsome ruins of the castle of **Reichenberg**, erected in 1280 by Count Wilhelm I. of Katzenelnbogen, and afterwards, during the Hessian dominion, the seat of the governor of the district. Since 1818 it has been a ruin, but is in a better state of preservation than most of the Rhenish castles. The portal with its granite pillars in the castle-yard has a Moorish look, and the interior with its lofty columns and pointed vaulted roof is picturesque and striking. The road to Reichenberg leads through the *Haselbach Valley* (Brewery), the mouth of which is immediately below St. Goarshausen, where a carriage may be procured for the excursion. Pedestrians may make a beautiful round by ascending through the **Swiss Valley* at the back of the town, a rocky and well-wooded ravine, $1^1/_2$ M. in length, to Patersberg, thence to Reichenberg, and back to St. Goarshausen by the road through the Haselbach valley. Those who wish to ascend the Lurlei, must take the "Promenadenpfad" for foot-passengers leading to the top of the hill, the last part of the way through wood, a few hundred paces beyond which is a signpost indicating the way to the Hühnerberg, a pavilion commanding a fine view of St. Goar and St. Goarshausen. From this point the road to the Lurlei leads towards a group of bushes, where it finally diverges to the r. From the Lurlei a path leads down to the Rhine.

25. The Rhine from St. Goar to Bingen.

Comp. Map R. 24.

Distances from St. Goar to Oberwesel $4^1/_2$ M., Caub 3 M., Bacharach $1^1/_2$ M., Rheindiebach $1^1/_2$ M., Lorch (Niederheimbach) $^3/_4$ M., Rheinstein $3^3/_4$ M., Bingen 3 M.; total distance from St. Goar to Bingen 18 M. — By steamboat (preferable on account of the beauty of the scenery) in $2^1/_2$ hrs. (down in $1^1/_4$ hr.); piers at St. Goar and Bingen, small-boat stations at St. Goarshausen, Oberwesel, Caub, Bacharach, Lorch and Niederheimbach. By railway on the *left* bank from St. Goar to Bingen, on the *right* bank from St. Goarshausen to Rüdesheim, in 1 hr.

From Niederlahnstein to Bingen the r. bank of the river belongs to the Duchy of Nassau, the l. to Prussia.

Immediately above St. Goar, and nearly in the middle of the stream, is situated the "Bank," a sunken ledge of rocks running out from the bank to the r., and causing a species of whirlpool (*Gewirre*) which not unfrequently proves destructive to the rafts if not skilfully managed. Even those of considerable size are often partially submerged when passing this spot, being drawn down by the undercurrents.

To the l. rise the rugged and imposing rocks of the **Lurlei**, 420 ft. above the Rhine. On the N. side of the precipice a steep path, furnished with benches at intervals, leads to the summit. The ascent may be accomplished in about 25 min.; view limited. The well-known legend of the siren who had her dwelling on the top of the rock, and, like other sirens of old, enticed the sailors and fishermen to their destruction in the rapids at the foot of the precipice, has been a theme for the poet and painter in all ages. The famous echo is not audible on the deck of the steamer; the pedestrian alone can awaken it successfully. The sharp angle formed by the Lurlei is penetrated by a railway tunnel.

To this rocky basin the salmon-fishery of St. Goar is principally confined. The cool, shady depths and sandy bottom of the river at this point appear to be peculiarly suited to the habits of the fish. It is tantalizing to the angler to know that they are only captured in nets, thrown from boats of peculiar construction, and the epicure may hear with emotion that the yield which formerly amounted to 8000 lbs. per annum is now diminished by the increase in steamboat traffic to 1000 lbs. It is of course in great demand, and frequently realizes a price of 3*s.* per pound. The river is here narrower and deeper (72 ft.) than at any other part.

In the bed of the river opposite to the *Rossstein*, a rocky point to the l., penetrated by a railway tunnel, a ridge of rocks is visible when the water is low, known by the name of the "*Seven Virgins.*" As hardly a rock or ruin exists without its legend, so it is said that these rugged masses were once seven fair maidens, condemned by the river-god for their fickleness to this dreadful metamorphosis.

(r.) **Oberwesel** (**Goldener Pfropfenzieher*, at the lower end of the town, R. and B. 16 Sgr.; the sign-board, now in the coffee-room, was painted by the well-known Düsseldorf painter Schrödter in commemoration of the frequent visits of Düsseldorf artists to this place; *Trierscher Hof; Rheinischer Hof*, on the river). Oberwesel, the *Vosavia* of the Romans, was once a town of the empire, but was made over by Henry VII. to his brother, the Archbishop Balduin of Treves. To the S. of the town rises the conspicuous **Frauenkirche* (Church of our Lady), a fine specimen of Gothic architecture erected at the beginning of the 15th cent. The rood-loft (*lectorium*) which separates the choir from the nave deserves particular inspection. The ancient wood-carvings of the high-altar, contemporary with the date of the foundation, and two pictures said to have been painted in 1504, are also objects of interest. One forms an altar-piece in the N. chapel, the lower portion representing the landing of the 11,000 virgins (see St. Ursula Church at Cologne); the other on the N. wall represents the Last Judgment in a series of small pictures. The N. chapel contains monuments of several knights and counts of Schönberg. — The old gate-way ("*Eselsthurm*") in the field near the church was formerly the town-gate.

The *Chapel* on the town wall, on the side next to the

Rhine, commemorates the alleged murder of the boy Werner by the Jews in 1286. According to the legend, his body was flung into the river, and miraculously floated up the stream to Bacharach where it was canonized (p. 101).

Oberwesel is one of the most beautiful spots on the Rhine. The rocky ravines which intersect the mountains in the vicinity, are favourite subjects for the pencil of the artist; they also yield excellent wines, the most esteemed of which is produced in the *Engehölle* valley, and is the best in the Prussian dominions.

Above Oberwesel rise the picturesque ruins of (r.) **Schönburg,** the cradle of a once mighty race. It was the birth-place (1615) of the Count Frederick Hermann of Schönberg, better known as Marshal Schomberg, who fought under the Prince of Orange, and in 1668, when in the French service, compelled the Spaniards to acknowledge the House of Braganza. In 1668, on the revocation of the Edict of Nantes, he was obliged to quit the French service, after which he became minister of state under the Elector of Brandenburg, governor of Prussia, and finally passed over to England with the Prince of Orange, and fell in the memorable battle of the Boyne, in 1690. His remains are interred in Westminster Abbey. In the 30 Years' war the castle fell into the hands of the Swedes, and in 1689 was demolished by the French. The family became extinct in 1713, and the ruin now belongs to Prince Albrecht of Prussia.

The small town of (l.) **Caub** (**Grünewald; Nassauer Hof*) is a place of some importance on account of its productive subterranean slate-quarries, which are efficiently worked under the inspection of the Government of Nassau.

The stately castle of **Gutenfels,** on a height in the background was, with the town itself, sold by the knights of Falkenstein to the Palatinate. Here the English Earl of Cornwall, who was elected emperor of Germany in 1257, fell in love with the beautiful countess Beatrix of Falkenstein, whom he afterwards married, on the death of his first wife in 1269. In 1504 the castle was fruitlessly besieged during 6 weeks by the Landgrave William of Hessen, a fact recorded in rhyme on a stone tablet in the wall near the Rhine custom-house. In 1804 the castle became the property of Nassau, in 1805 it was dismantled by order of Napoleon, and in 1807 was finally abandoned to decay. The schoolmaster Müller at Caub has the keys. A still more extensive view than that afforded by the castle is obtained from the pavilion on the *Adolphshöhe*, 15 min. to the S. of Caub.

Above Caub appears the ***Pfalz,** or *Pfalzgrafenstein,* rising from the middle of the Rhine, reminding the traveller of the castle of Chillon on the lake of Geneva, and likened by some to a stone ship for ever at anchor on the Rhine. It is a small hexagonal building, standing on a ridge of rock, and was erected by the Emperor Ludwig the Bavarian at the commencement of the 13th cent., as a convenient tollhouse for waylaying and exacting tribute from the passing vessels. The entrance is on the E. side through a portcullis, several feet above the rock; the S. corner bears the Lion of the Palatinate. The well in the narrow courtyard, which is surrounded by a sort of vaulted cloister, is sunk to a much greater depth than the bed of the Rhine:

In 1194 the Emperor Henry VI. wished to marry the daughter of the Count Palatine Conrad to one of his friends or relations, but the young princess had already gained the affections of Henry of Brunswick. The father dreading the Emperor's wrath, would not consent to the alliance, but caused a tower to be built in the middle of the river below Bacharach, where he kept his daughter a close prisoner. Her mother, however, secretly aided the Prince of Brunswick in gaining admittance to the tower, where his union with the princess was privately solemnized. When the princess was about to give birth to a child, her mother disclosed the whole affair to her husband the Count, who, finding his opposition no longer availing, in the exercise of his capricious authority, passed a law that all future Countesses Palatine should repair to the Castle to await their accouchements. Such is the ancient and improbable tradition connected with the Pfalz, whence it also derives its name.

Here on New Year's night, 1814, the 1st Prussian army-corps under York, and a division of Russian troops under Langeron, effected the passage of the Rhine. At the same place a body of Prussian troops crossed the river in 1793 on their way to France.

(r.) **Bacharach** (*Post*), called *Ara Bacchi* in the middle ages, was celebrated in early times for its wine, and was up to the 16th cent. one of the greatest wine-marts of the Rhine. Pope Pius II., better known as Æneas Silvius, caused a cask of the wine of Bacharach to be annually brought to Rome, and the town of Nürnberg obtained its freedom in return for a yearly tribute of 4 tuns to the Emperor Wenzel. To this day a vessel laden with the wine of Bacharach is annually dispatched to the fair of Frankfurt.

On a slight eminence (accessible by a path on the S. side of the church of St. Peter) stands the ruined *Church of St. Werner*, erected about 1428 in the most beautiful and elaborate Gothic style, and in the form of a trefoil; it commemorates the canonization of the boy Werner, who, according to a tradition, was barbarously murdered by the Jews. Behind it (10 min. walk) rises the castle of Stahleck (see p. 102).

The *Church of St. Peter*, or so-called Templar's Church, is built in the late Romanesque style, and is distinguished by the symmetry of its proportions. A tower of the ancient House of the Templars is still to be seen in the yard of the post-house.

In the adjacent valley of Steeg are situated the ruins of the old castle of **Stahlberg.** The valley in latter times has received the appellation of "*Blücherthal,*" from having been in 1814 the scene of a skirmish between a body of French soldiers and the troops of Blücher.

From Bacharach by Stromberg to Kreuznach. Pedestrians ascending the Rhine who are already acquainted with this part of the river may vary their route very agreeably by taking the following walk (7½ hrs.) over the hills. From Bacharach to the Rheinböller Foundry 9 M., to Stromberg 6 M., and to Kreuznach 7½ M. The last stage being the least interesting the traveller may prefer to take a carriage from Stromberg to Kreuznach (1 Thlr.). The route is as follows, guide unnecessary: from Bacharach through the valley of Steeg (Blücherthal, s. above) to *Steeg* (1 M.). At the tower (½ M.) with the small pond the road ascending to the l. must be taken. On the table-land (2½ M.) the road leads in a straight direction, bearing to the l.; ¾ M. farther a wood is entered, on emerging from which (¾ M.) the road descends to the l. to the village of *Rheinböllen* (2 M.), with conspicuous church-spire. The road next leads through plantations to the *Rheinböller Iron-works* (*Inn), 1¼ M. beyond the village. The narrow and wooded ravine of the *Güldenbach* is now traversed, on the r. slope of which is situated the modern castle of *Carlsburg*, and, farther on, the *Sahler Foundry*. Before entering Stromberg (*Fustenburg*), the castle of *Goldenfels* is seen rising on an eminence to the r.; beyond Stromberg the extensive ruins of *Fustenburg*. *Schweppenhausen* 1½ M., and *Windesheim* 1½ M., are the two following villages. Where the road begins to descend into the valley of the Nahe, 1½ M. from Kreuznach, a fine distant view is obtained. (Diligence from Bacharach to Rheinböllen twice daily in 2 hrs., fare 10½ Sgr.)

Above Bacharach rise the ruins of the once strongly fortified castle of **Stahleck,** the cradle of the Counts Palatine, and till 1823 their principal residence. The French besieged and took the castle and town eight times in the years 1620—40, and finally destroyed the castle in 1689. The extensive ruins now belong to the Dowager Queen of Prussia, a descendant of the Counts Palatine. View fine but limited.

On a rocky eminence to the r. rise the handsome ruins of **Fürstenberg,** made over to the Palatinate in 1243 as a fief of the city of Cologne. In 1292, when Adolph of Nassau was on his way to his coronation at Aix-la-Chapelle, so bold were the vassals of the robber-knight of the castle, that they demanded the usual toll of the emperor, and on its refusal, fired into the vessel. It was taken in 1321 by the Emperor Lewis from his opponent Frederick, and presented to his consort Margaret of Holland. In 1632 it fell into the hands of the Swedes, and in 1689 was destroyed by the French. Since 1847 it has been the property of the Princess Frederick of the Netherlands, sister of the King of Prussia. The brook which falls into the Rhine at the foot of the castle was in ancient times the boundary between the dominions of the archbishops of Mayence and Treves.

(l.) The village of **Lorchhausen.**

Through the **Wisperthal** to *Schlangenbad* and *Schwalbach,* a beautiful walk of 21 M.; from Lorch to the *Kammerberger Mühle* 6 M., the *Laukenmühle* 2¼ M., *Geroldstein* 2¼ M., *Niedergladbach* 3 M., *Hausen* 3 M., *Schlangenbad* 3 M.; or from Geroldstein by *Langenseifen* to *Schwalbach* 10½ M.

In the valley of the *Sauer*, which unites with the Wisper, 3/4 M. above Lorch, is situated the **Sauerburg,** 4 1/2 M. from Lorch or Caub, one of the strongholds of Sickingen, destroyed by the French in 1689. In the neighbouring farm-house the last of the Counts of Sickingen, descending in direct line from the celebrated Knight of this name, died in 1836 in the most abject poverty.

(l.) The small town of **Lorch** (**Schwan*, at the upper end of the place, R. 48 kr., B. 24 kr., D. exc. W. 1 fl., wine and cuisine good, pension 2 1/3 fl. per diem; *Rhein. Hof*), the *Laureacum* (?) of the Romans, mentioned in an old document as early as 832, was formerly the residence of a number of knights who founded a peculiar institution for the education of their sons, which was known under the name of "Schul-junkerschaft," and thither the scions of the Rhenish nobility were sent to be trained. The lofty and handsome *Church* belongs to the 12th cent., and possesses the finest bells in this district, which formerly was considered to belong to the Rheingau. The old carved wooden altar, a fine font of 1464, several monuments of knightly families of the Rheingau, especially that of *Joh. Hilchen*, the companion in arms of Sickingen, are worthy of inspection. The inscription on the latter records that Hilchen distinguished himself against the Turks, and, as field-marshal in 1542—44, against the French. His house, decorated with carved stone-work in front, erected in 1546, is the most conspicuous building in the village.

Above Lorch rises a rugged cliff called the *Kedrich*, or "*Devil's Ladder*," which one of the knights of Lorch is said to have scaled with the assistance of the mountain sprights, and thus to have gained the hand of his lady-love. Opposite to it, on the r. bank of the *Wisper*, which here falls into the Rhine, stands the ruined castle of **Nollicht** or **Nollingen,** rising 565 ft. above the Rhine.

The long village of (r.) **Niederheimbach** with the ruined castle of *Hohneck* or **Heimburg** next comes in view. This is the best station to disembark at for travellers ascending the river and intending to visit Rheinstein (3 M.), Assmannshausen and the Niederwald (comp. p. 107). Extensive retrospective view as far as Bacharach.

The valley of the Rhine now becomes somewhat narrower. To the r. rises the slender tower of **Sooneck,** commanding the entrance of a mountain ravine. The castle, built by Archbishop Willigis of Mayence about the year 1015, was dismantled by the Emperor Rudolph as a robbers' stronghold, and again restored in the 14th cent. The ruin now belongs to the Prussian Royal family, and has been partially restored.

(r.) **Trechtingshausen** (*Stern*). On an eminence beyond the village rise the ruins of *Reichenstein*, more commonly called **Falkenburg,** destroyed by the French in 1689. In 1252 this robbers' castle was dismantled by the Rhenish Confederation, but was restored in 1261 by its owner, Philipp von Hohenfels, who recommenced his lawless calling of a freebooter. The Emperor Rudolph of Habsburg afterwards besieged and dismantled this stronghold, as well as many others, and relentlessly consigned to the gallows the tribe of robbers of high and low degree, whom he found in possession of them. At the foot of the hill is the entrance to the **Morgenbachthal*, which for a short distance ($1\frac{1}{2}$ M.) is one of the most romantic side-valleys of the Rhine.

At (l.) **Assmannshausen** (*Anker; Krone*), celebrated for its red wine, the river makes a bend. At the mouth of a ravine below the village the much esteemed *Bodenthaler* wine is produced. In the vicinity traces of Roman baths have been discovered. Path to the Niederwald see p. 107.

On the bank opposite to Assmannshausen, rise the towers and pinnacles of **Rheinstein,** 250 ft. above the Rhine. Its origin is unknown, but it is mentioned as early as 1279, and was subsequently to 1348 frequently a residence of the archbishop Kuno von Falkenstein. After this date we hear nothing more of the name. In 1825—29 Prince Frederick of Prussia caused the castle to be completely rebuilt on a new plan; his remains (d. 1863) are interred in the chapel on the S. side. The **Collection* of old armour, objects of art, and stained glass, is open to the public (fee $7\frac{1}{2}$ Sgr. for 1 pers., 15—20 Sgr. for 4 pers.). The view from the castle, as well as that from the Swiss house, to which the public are not admitted, is limited.

In the vicinity of the castle stands the **Clemenskirche,** the origin of which is also unknown. It is indebted for its complete restoration to the Princess Frederick of Prussia.

Shortly after leaving Assmannshausen the steamboat reaches the **Bingerloch**, a rapid caused by the narrowness of the rocky channel, the widening of which has been the work of ages, from the Roman period till the years 1830—32, when the last blasting operations took place. A monument, erected in 1832, on the roadside on the l. bank, records the fact that the passage was made ten times wider than before by the Prussian government in the reign of Fred. William III. The ascent of the rapid is still attended with considerable difficulty in the case of heavily laden vessels, but in the descent the only craft liable to danger are the large rafts, the navigation of which requires extreme caution.

Above the rapids rises the tower of (l.) **Ehrenfels,** erected about the year 1210 by Philipp von Bolanden, a governor of the Rheingau, the frequent residence of the archbishops of

Lith. Anst v Ed. Wagner Darmstadt

RHEINSTEIN

Mayence in the 15th cent., much damaged by the Swedes in 1635, and finally dismantled by the French in 1689. The steep slopes of the *Rüdesheimer Berg* yield the well-known wine of that name, and terrace rises above terrace to secure the soil from falling. The entire hill is covered with walls and arches, the careful preservation of which may serve to give an idea of the value of the vines. According to an old tradition Charlemagne is said to have observed from his palace at Ingelheim that the snow always melted first on the Rüdesheimer Berg, and that he therefore caused vine-plants to be brought from Orleans and re-planted here.

Opposite to the castle, on a quartz-rock in the middle of the Rhine, is situated the **Mouse-tower,** which derives its name from the well-known legend of the cruel Archbishop Hatto of Mayence; at the expense of the story, however, it must be confessed that in all probability the real name was *Mauth-Thurm*, or Tower of Customs, and that it was erected in the middle ages by some of the robber-knights of the Rhine. The ruins have been recently covered with stucco and converted into a watch-tower, whence signals are made to vessels descending the river, which are required to slacken their speed when vessels are proceeding in the contrary direction through the Binger Loch.

The valley of the Rhine now suddenly expands, and the Rheingau, a district which was once in all probability a lake, is entered. Immediately below (r.) *Bingen* the *Nahe* unites with the Rhine. Bridges over the Nahe, and stations of the Rhenish and Rhine-Nahe lines, see p. 109.

26. Bingen.

Hotels on the Rhine: Victoria Hotel, White horse, charges in both: R. 1 fl., L. 18 kr., B. 30 kr., D. 1 fl. 12 kr., A. 18 kr.; *Bellevue more moderate; Englischer Hof and Deutsches Haus on the Rhine.

Restaurants. Soherr, in the Market-place. Beer at the Ehrenfels on the Rhine, adjacent to the Bellevue.

Railway to *Mayence* and *Cologne* see R. 36, to *Saarbrücken* see R. 28, (from *Rüdesheim*) to *Wiesbaden* or to *Oberlahnstein* see R. 23.

Bingen (pop. 5612) was known as early as the Roman period. The rebellious Treviri fought here against the legions of Cerialis in the reign of Vespasian. Tacitus (Hist. IV, 70) relates that Tutor, the chief of the Treviri, retired from Mayence to Bingen, where he crossed the Nahe and destroyed the bridge, but the cohorts of Sextilius pursuing him and discovering a ford over the Nahe, crossed the river, attacked and defeated him.

Bingen was also a point from which two Roman military roads led to Cologne and Treves, and was protected by a fort which probably stood on the site now occupied by the castle of ***Klopp**, destroyed by the French in 1689. The entrance to the castle, which stands in private grounds, is at the back of the White Horse Hotel; the gardens, to which strangers are admitted (fee 12 kr.), command a pleasing prospect on all sides.

The seven-arched **Bridge** over the *Nahe* was constructed by Archbishop Willigis on the foundations of the old Roman bridge; it was afterwards partially destroyed, but again restored. The Nahe here forms the boundary between the dominions of Hessen-Darmstadt and Prussia.

The Gothic **Pfarrkirche**, or Parish Church, dates from the 15th cent., and contains an ancient font erroneously conjectured to belong to the Carlovingian period. The **Town Hall** was restored in 1863 in the mediæval style.

The **Rondel*, about 1½ M. on the road from Bingen to the Hunnsrücken, which diverges from the Coblenz road soon after the bridge is crossed, commands a beautiful prospect in three directions, even surpassing that from the Rochusberg, as Bingen itself and the castle of Klopp form a beautiful foreground to the picture. Instead of crossing the bridge and following the road the whole way, the pedestrian may cross the Nahe near the church; after passing a country-house and the old custom-house buildings, he will reach the road to the Hunnsrücken leading to the Rondel, a spot planted with trees and easily recognizable from a considerable distance. Near it is the *Elisenhöhe,* another fine point of view, 400 ft. above the Rhine.

The finest points, however, and the most frequented in the neighbourhood, are the *Rochuscapelle* (E.) and the *Scharlachkopf* (S.E.), each ½ hr. walk from the town. The carriage road to the former, which cannot be missed, leaves the street at the back of the Englische Hof, and after 100 yds. ascends to the l., leading past the cemetery.

The ***Rochuscapelle**, or Chapel of St. Roch, situated on an eminence 360 ft. above the Rhine, founded in 1666 at the time of the plague, destroyed in 1795, and restored in 1814, commands a noble prospect of the entire Rheingau. The interior of the chapel contains a picture representing St. Roch leaving his dismantled palace, painted in commemoration of the restoration of the sacred edifice, and presented by Goethe and others. At the festival of St. Roch (first Sunday after Aug. 16th), admirably described by Goethe, thousands of persons congregate here, and celebrate certain ecclesiastical solemnities, to which the jovial ringing of glasses and open-air dances form a somewhat incongruous accompaniment. The chapel is generally opened in summer at 7 p.m. Near the E. entrance a stone pulpit has been erected for open-air sermons.

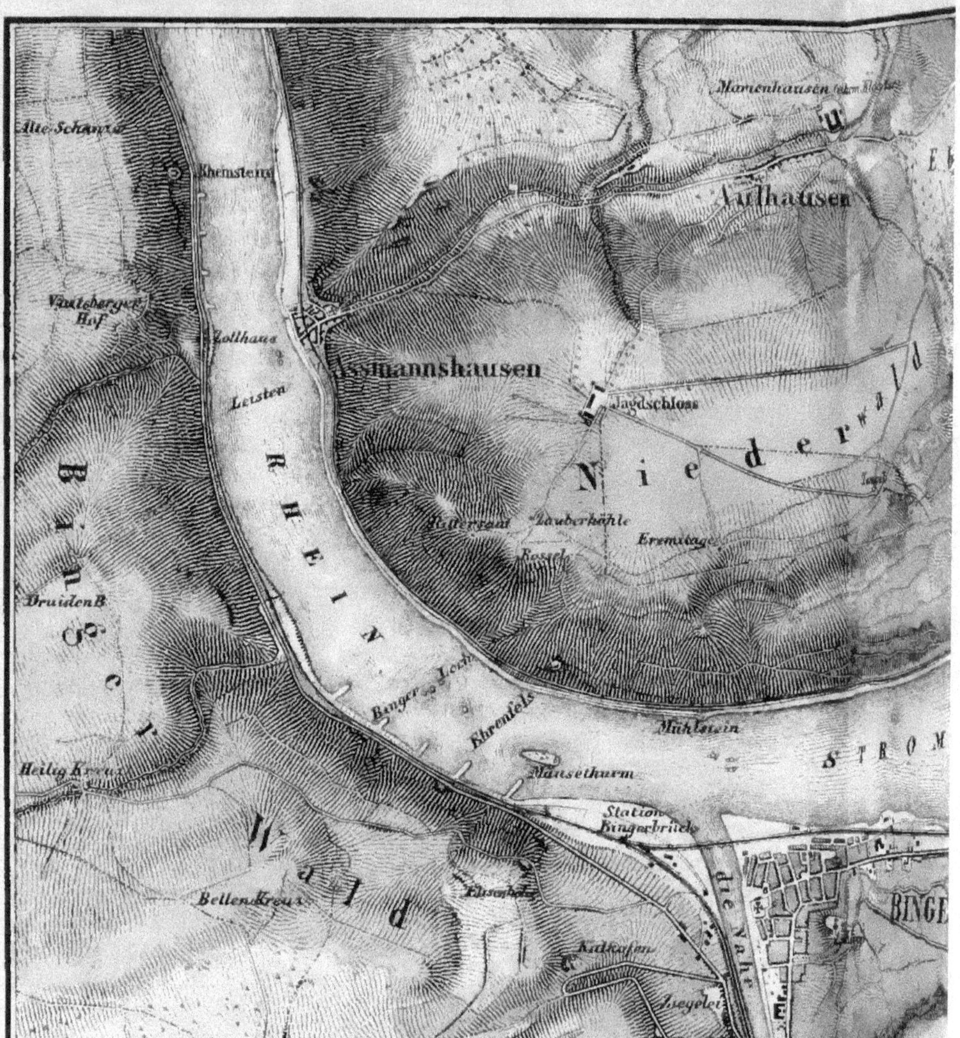

Originalaufnahme des Gross Hess Generalquartiermeisterstabes

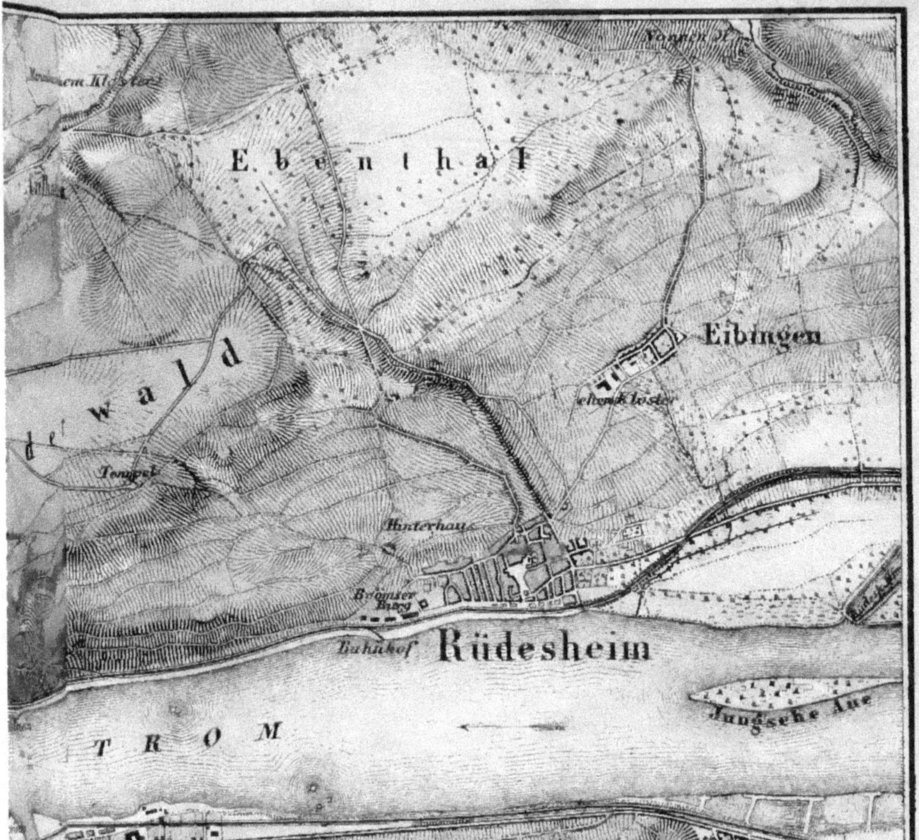

stab = $\frac{1}{40000}$

34

From the Rochuscapelle a carriage road leads over the hill on the same level to the ***Scharlachkopf,** about $1^1/_2$ M. to the S.W. The view is very fine, and quite different from that afforded by the chapel; it commands the valley of the Nahe and the populous Palatinate, dotted with numerous villages, and bounded by the Donnersberg. The Rhine is only visible from the influx of the Nahe to the Mouse tower. A shady road through a fragrant grove leads from here along the N.W. side of the hill, and brings the pedestrian in about 25 min. to the road to the chapel; in 10 min. more he will reach the town.

27. The Niederwald.

Tariffs of Rüdesheim and Assmannshausen. Donkey with guide from Rüdesheim to the Temple on the Niederwald (or from Assmannshausen to the castle) 48 kr.; to all the points of view, the castle and Assmannshausen (or *vice versâ* from Assmannshausen to Rüdesheim) 1 fl. 24 kr. Guide alone at half the above charges. Horse with guide 12—24 kr. more. Two-horse carriage to the Niederwald and castle $3^1/_2$ fl., including Assmannshausen, $4^1/_2$ fl.; the same excursion, including the Johannisberg, $6^1/_2$ fl. — Boats from *Rüdesheim* to Rheinstein, waiting 2 hrs. at the castle, and returning to Assmannshausen, 1 fl. 54 kr.; to Assmannshausen alone 1 fl. 6 kr.; the number of persons is not limited, the boatman must take as many as his boat will accommodate without additional charge. — Ferry from Rüdesheim to Bingen for 1—3 pers. 12 kr., for each additional pers. 4 kr. more; from Assmannshausen to Rheinstein for 1—3 pers. 15 kr., for each additional pers. 5 kr. more. The wealthier inhabitants of the place, however, generally pay the boatmen so that they always receive at least 30 kr. for each passage. Steam ferry-boat between the stations of Rüdesheim and Bingerbrück; fares 2 or 1 Sgr.

Bingen boatmen's tariff. From Bingen to Assmannshausen 1—6 pers. 1 fl. 10 kr., Rheinstein 1 fl. 30 kr., Rheinstein and Assmannshausen 1 fl. 48 kr., for each additional pers. 6 kr.; return fare one-half more. The boatmen must be provided with numbered badges, and there must always be two in each boat; want of respect towards the passengers, or attempts to overcharge are severely punished.

Plan. By water from Rüdesheim or Bingen to Rheinstein, where the boat must await the traveller's return from the castle; thence to Assmannshausen, the walk from which over the Niederwald to Rüdesheim may easily be accomplished in $2^1/_2$ hrs. Guide perfectly unnecessary. The path ascending to the Schloss cannot be missed, the only place where a difficulty may arise is between the Schloss and the temple, but one of the boys at the former will readily show the path for a few kreuzers. Riders are advised to take their donkeys or horses only as far as the Schloss, where they should be immediately dismissed, as the descent may be accomplished with the greatest ease by the most ordinary walker. [From Bingen to Rheinstein on foot (ferry across the Nahe at the church) is about 3 M.]

The **Niederwald** is a wooded height, the S. slopes of which are covered with vineyards rising abruptly from the Rhine, and is one of the most favorite points of view on the Rhine. The ascent is generally made (after Rheinstein has been visited) from Assmannshausen, where the road enters a valley, on the S. slopes of which the celebrated Assmannshäuser red wine is produced. A gradual ascent of $^1/_2$ hr. will bring the pedestrian to *Aulhausen* (near it the former nunnery of *Marienhausen*, now employed as farm-buildings). At the village church the path leaves the road through the valley, and in 20 min. more the **Jagdschloss** (hunting-castle) is reached, which, with the whole of the Niederwald, belongs to the Duke of Nassau (**Restaurant*, wines good, also R. 48 kr). — A nearer path leads from Assmannshausen, ascending rapidly to the r. by the figure of a saint (3 min.), in 35 min. to the Jagdschloss.

From the Jagdschloss the traveller takes a boy (6—12 kr.), to open the Zauberhöhle and Rossel. The "*Zauberhöhle*" (magic cave), ½ M. to the S.W. of the Schloss,. is a short dark passage, at the extremity of which is a semi-circular chamber with three windows, commanding views, through cuttings in the wood, of the Clemenscapelle and Falkenburg, the castle of Rheinstein and the Swiss house. Five min. walk farther in the same direction is the ***Rossel** (759 ft. above the river), an artificial ruin, built on the highest point of the Niederwald, commanding a beautiful and extensive prospect; to the W. the valley of the Nahe with the Donnersberg and the Soonwald in the background; to the r. the wooded heights of the Hunnsrück. Far below the Rhine is seen rushing past the ruin of Ehrenfels through the Bingerloch by the Mouse Tower. On the opposite bank lies Bingen with the castle of Klopp, sheltered by the wooded and vine-clad Rochusberg. In the valley of the Nahe are seen numerous villages, and Kreuznach in the distance. Below the mouth of the Nahe is Rheinstein, with the Swiss house; beneath the latter the Clemenskirche surrounded by trees, and beyond it the Falkenburg. From the Rossel to Rüdesheim is a walk of 1¼ hr.

From the Rossel the path leads in a S.E. direction to the (2 min.) *Adolphshöhe*, exactly opposite the influx of the Nahe, the *Hermitage* (10 min.) and a stone seat (5 min.) where the path to the r. must be taken, which in 10 min. more leads to the ***Temple** (628 ft. above the Rhine), an open circular building, supported by pillars, situated on the brow of the hill, and commanding a new and magnificent view, including the entire Rheingau, bounded on the S.E. by the Taunus mountains, on the S. by the Melibocus, and on the W. by the distant Donnersberg.

From this point the road proceeds to the l., reaching a signpost (5 min.), where the path to the l. must be taken, which will bring the traveller to Rüdesheim in ½ hr. The track to the r. is a steep and stony path for pedestrians only, and descends through the vineyards, but is little shorter than the other; during the vintage, commencing about the end of

August, this path is closed. Distance from Rüdesheim to the Temple 45 min.; thence to the Jagdschloss 40 min.; down to Assmannshausen by Aulhausen 40 min.

28. From Bingen to Saarbrücken.

Comp. Map R. 24.

Distance 94 M. By the Rhine-Nahe line to Neunkirchen (p. 197) in $3^1/_2$ hrs.; from Neunkirchen (by the Prussian Saarbrücken line) to Saarbrücken in $^1/_2$ hr.; fares from Bingerbrück to Saarbrücken: 4 Thlr. 4, 2 Thlr. 26, 1 Thlr. 26 Sgr. — The terminus station is at *Bingerbrück* on the l. bank of the Nahe, close to the station of the Rhenish railway, about 2 M. from Bingen. Tickets may also be procured at the *Bingen* station. Steam ferry-boat between Bingerbrück and Rüdesheim.

The finest points on this route are the tract between *Kreuznach* and *Norheim*, and the environs of *Oberstein*. The most remarkable part of the line in an engineering point of view is between *Fischbach* and *Birkenfeld*, where there are 10 tunnels and 20 bridges over the Nahe. The rocks through which the cuttings are made consist chiefly of porphyry and dark red melaphyr, many of which are very precipitous and most grotesquely shaped.

The line commences at **Bingerbrück** on the l. bank of the Nahe and passes the foot of the Hunnsrücken mountains, traversing vineyards and a fertile tract of country, passing the old tower of *Trutzbingen*, erected in 1494 by a prefect of Kreuznach, and several small stations, the most important of which is *Langenlonsheim* (*Weisses Ross*).

Kreuznach and environs, s. R. 29.

After leaving the station the train crosses the Nahe, winds round the E. side of the town, passing the saline spring of *Carlshalle*, on the r., the jagged porphyry precipice of the *Gans*, and, on the l. bank, the buildings of the mineral spring of *Theodorshalle*. Near the bridge, which crosses to the l. bank of the river, rises, on the l., almost perpendicularly the rugged cliff of the Rheingrafenstein (comp. R. 29).

Beyond the station of *Münster am Stein* the line passes through a deep cutting, on emerging from which the Rheingrafenstein is again visible on the l., and, separated from it by the Alsenz, which here falls into the Nahe, the ruins of **Ebernburg* (p. 113), now converted into an inn.

Immediately afterwards the train passes between the Nahe and the jagged and precipitous cliffs of *Rothenfels* (900 ft.), the best view of which may be had from the train by looking back on the l. side, after passing through two long tunnels, and before reaching the village of *Norheim*.

The line now follows the picturesque windings of the valley, passing the villages of *Niederhausen* on the r., and *Oberhausen* on the l., and a steep rock rising on the r., surmounted by the ruins of *Böckelheim*, in which the Emperor Henry IV. was kept a prisoner by his son Henry V. in December, 1105, in order to compel him to give up the imperial treasures, kept in the castle of Hammerstein at Andernach on the Rhine. The village of *Waldböckelheim* lies in a side valley, about 2 M. from the station of that name.

Half an hour's walk from Waldböckelheim are situated the castle and abbey of **Sponheim,** the seat of one of the oldest families of the Rhenish noblesse. The church built in the Romanesque style is an object of interest for lovers of art.

On emerging from the tunnel beyond *Boos* (r.), the traveller will observe on the l. the considerable ruins of ***Dissibodenberg**, a monastery founded by the Irish bishop Dissibodus (d. 560), the first propagator of Christianity in this district. It was abandoned to decay in 1560, and is now converted into tastefully laid out pleasure grounds, which afford a good survey of the valley of the Nahe and the *Glan,* which here falls into the Nahe.

Staudernheim (**Salmen*) is in the dominions of the Landgrave of Hessen-Homburg, and lies on the r. bank of the river, and is connected with the station by the "Landgrave-bridge."

Sobernheim (*Adler; Hoheburg*), a small town of some antiquity, enclosed by a town-wall.

Monzingen (*Pflug*) lies on the hillside to the r., and yields one of the best wines of the Nahe. The next station is that of *Martinstein,* curiously built on a rock to the r., with a church on an eminence surrounded by a fine group of trees. Beyond it is a valley opening on the r., in which the grand ruins of **Dhaun* are situated.

***Dhaun,** a castle of an old family of the Rhenish noblesse which became extinct in 1750, was erected in the 12th cent., and in later years greatly enlarged and improved. It is situated about $6^1/_2$ M. from stat. Monzingen, and $3^3/_4$ M. from Kirn (see below). A relief over one of the doors, representing an ape in the act of giving an apple to a child, commemorates the fact that a child of one of the Counts was carried off by an ape, but fortunately recovered. Magnificent view of the valley of the Nahe as far as Lemberg, and of the Simmerthal and the dark ravines of the Soonwald.

The traveller who takes the road from Monzingen to Dhaun should again descend into the valley of the Nahe by *Johannesberg* (see below), the church of which contains monuments of members of the above-mentioned family.

On an eminence to the r. is situated the church of *Johannesberg.* The valley here becomes narrower; the train passes through a tunnel and reaches **Kirn** (**Post*). It contains a very old church, with a Romanesque nave, and Gothic choir, added in the 15th cent. The town is commanded by the ruined castle of *Kyrburg* (*Restaurant), once the residence of the Princes of Salm-Kyrburg, the last of whom perished by the guillotine in Paris in 1794.

About $1^1/_2$ M. up the valley of the *Hahnebach,* which unites with the Nahe at Kirn, are situated the ruins of **Stein-Callenfels,** curiously perched on the side of the rock like a swallow's nest. In the background is seen the white castle of **Wartenstein;** thence by *Oberhausen* to *Dhaun,* and from Dhaun by *Johannesberg,* or through the wood to *Kirn,* a pleasant walk of $3^1/_2$ hrs.

After traversing an opener and less romantic tract, the line again enters a more mountainous district at *Sulzbach*, where the melaphyr cliffs become more abrupt, and confine the river in narrower limits. After passing *Fischbach*, a bridge, a tunnel, and another bridge, the train comes in view of *Oberstein*, situated most picturesquely on the opposite bank. The station is at some distance from the town. Inn on the r. bank (**Heindl*, R. and B. 15, D. 10, S. 8 Sgr.). On the l. bank are the shops where the agates (see below) are sold at moderate prices. Below Oberstein are huge masses of conglomerate, the "*Fallen rocks*," on the r. side of the road, which have become detached from the steep hillside and now stand leaning against it.

Oberstein is the finest point in the valley of the Nahe. The precipitous melaphyr cliffs, 400 ft. in height, on the l. bank of the river, confine the town within very narrow limits. On their summits are situated the ruins of two castles, belonging to the Barons of Oberstein, who became extinct in 1670. Half-way up is the **Protestant church*, curiously built (12th cent.) into the face of the rock. It contains an old tombstone, said to belong to the founder, and a picture of the Oberstein family. The flight of steps which lead to the church are opposite to the bridge; the sexton lives in the last house on the l., as the visitor ascends. The new Gothic Roman Cath. church, constructed of dark red melaphyr, lies on the r. bank of the Nahe.

Oberstein has a population of 3500 ($^1/_4$ Rom. Cath.), the greater portion of which is occupied in cutting and polishing agates, which were formerly found here in great abundance. They are now, however, much more scarce, and large quantities are imported from Brazil and Montevideo. A process has recently been discovered, by which colourless agates are converted into onyxes, sardonyxes &c., by the addition of colouring matter. On the *Idarbach*, which falls into the Nahe near Oberstein, there are upwards of 50 polishing mills; **Idar** (*Gorlitz*), $1^1/_2$ M. to the N.W. of Oberstein, contains a sort of merchants' hall in which these wares are sold at officially regulated prices. In Idar and Oberstein upwards of 100 so-called goldsmiths are engaged in setting the stones in silver and other metals. — Beautiful excursion to the *Wildenburg* ($1^1/_2$ hr.) by the *Katzenloch;* guide necessary.

On leaving Oberstein the train passes through a rapid succession of tunnels and cuttings. The town of **Birkenfeld** (*Emmerich*), situated 3 M. to the r. of the station, is the capital of the principality of Birkenfeld, and now belongs to the Duchy of Oldenburg. At *Wallhausen* the line attains its greatest height (1225 ft.), the culminating point (watershed) between the Nahe and Saar. It now descends to the district-town of **St. Wendel** (*Jochem*), which contains a fine old Gothic church with pulpit of 1462. On emerging from the tunnel (450 yds.) of *Wiebelskirchen*, the train reaches **Neunkirchen**, and joins the Saarbrücken line. From this point to *Saarbrücken*, see R. 45.

29. Kreuznach and its Environs.

(*Comp. Maps R.R. 45 and 24.*)

Hotels. *Pfälzer Hof, next to the post-office; Adler, both in the town. — Berliner Hof, near the bath-island. Bath-establishments and hotels on and near the bath-island: Curhaus, Englischer Hof, Kauzenberg, Oranienhof, Rheinstein, Hof von Holland, Ebernburg, &c.

Carriage fares (to the following places and back with 4 hrs. stay): Münster am Stein one-horse $1^2/_3$ Thlr., two-horse $2^1/_2$ Thlr.; Rheingrafenstein and Münster am Stein 2—3 Thlr.; Eberuburg 2—3 Thlr.; Altenbaumberg 2—3 Thlr.; Rothenfels $2^1/_3$—3 Thlr.; Dissibodenberg $2^1/_2$—4 Thlr.; Stromberg $2^1/_2$—$3^1/_2$ Thlr.; Rheinböller Hütte 5 Thlr.; Schloss Dhaun 5 Thlr. Bridge and road tolls are included in the above. Driver's fee optional.

Donkeys at the Curhaus (to the following places and back with halt of $^1/_2$ day): Münster am Stein 1 Thlr., Rheingrafenstein 1 Thlr., Ebernburg 1 Thlr., Rothenfels 1 Thlr. A ride to the *Gans, Rheingrafenstein, Ebernburg*, and back to *Kreuznach*, costs about $1^1/_4$ Thlr. The pedestrian would require about 4 hrs. to make this beautiful round. He is recommanded, when on the summit of the Kühberg, not to keep the carriage road, but to diverge to the r. by the signpost. The path leads through wood and along the brow of the hill, commanding a succession of fine views and a survey of the deep ravine of the Salmen.

Railway to Bingen and Saarbrücken, see R. 28.

Nahe-wines. The best are yielded by the vineyards of the Scharlachberg and Kauzenberg, of Norheim, Monzingen, Ebernburg, Münster am Stein, Wiuzenheim and Bosenheim.

***Statuettes** made of an imitation of ivory (stucco saturated with stearic acid) at *Cauer's*.

English Church Service during the season.

Kreuznach (11,000 inhabitants; $^1/_3$ Rom. Cath.) has within the last 20—30 years become a place of importance on account of its baths, which are particularly beneficial in cases of scrofula, and is visited by about 6000 patients annually. The baths are situated on and near the **Badeinsel** (bath island), near the bridge over the Nahe. A row of handsome houses has lately been erected here, among which is the *Curhaus*, with a bath-establishment, conversation-hall, &c. The island is in the morning and evening resorted to by the visitors, who assemble here to drink the waters of the *Elisabeth spring* (containing iodine and bromine), situated at the S. extremity, and to enjoy the grounds and promenades. Temporary stalls abound with all those objects with which the traveller is usually tempted, the most conspicuous among them being the really beautiful agate wares peculiar to the neighbourhood (p. 111). The **Church** on the island was ereeted in 1768 to replace that destroyed by the French in 1689. The ruins of the Gothic choir (1333) of the latter have been fitted up as an English Chapel.

On the N.W. side of the town, on the l. bank of the Nahe, rises the **Schlossberg**, a hill laid out in private gardens and pleasure grounds; the vineyards on its S. slopes yield an excellent wine. The summit, whieh is surmounted by the ruined castle of *Kauzenberg*, seat of the Sponheim family, destroyed by the French in 1689, commands a fine view of the Nahe valley from the Rheingrafenstein to Bingen. A lion hewn in stone brought here from Dhaun (p. 110) commemorates the gallant conduct of Michel Mort, a butcher of Kreuznach, who sacrificed his life to save his Prince, Johann von Sponheim, in the battle of Sprendlingen ($4^1/_2$ M. to the E. of Kreuznach), which the latter fought in 1279 against the Archbishop Werner of Mayence. Kreuznach was from the 13th to the 15th cent. the capital of the dominions of the Counts of Sponheim, and afterwards became subject to the Electors Palatine.

In the valley of the Nahe, 1 M. above Kreuznach, in Prussian territory, but the property of the Grand-duke of Hessen, are situated the saline springs of *Carls-* and *Theodorshalle*, the baths in connection with which are a private undertaking (*Hôtel Rees; Foreith;* R. in both 3—5 Thlr. per week).

At **Münster am Stein**, $2^1/_2$ M. from Kreuznach, are extensive salt-works belonging to the Prussian Government, and warm saline baths (87° Fahr.). Good accommodation may be had at the springs, or in the village (*Curhaus; Hôtel Löw*).

Here the ***Rheingrafenstein,** a porphyry cliff, rises almost perpendicularly from the Nahe to the height of 420 ft. The river should be crossed near the saline springs (to the l. a *restaurant), opposite to which a somewhat steep but easily accessible path leads to the top, which commands a fine view. The boldly situated ruined castle, built in the 11th cent., was once a residence of the "Rheingrafen" (or Rhenish counts), but was blown up by the French in 1689. The new castle, farm-buildings, vineyards, &c., are now the property of the Prince of Solms-Braunfels, who sometimes resides here in the summer. (Direct path from Kreuznach to the Rheingrafenstein, see R. 45.)

The ***Gans** (1070 ft.), $^3/_4$ M. to the N.E. of the Rheingrafenstein, commands a still more extensive view, comprising the Nahethal as far as Bingen, a portion of the Rheingau, the Rochuscapelle, Johannisberg, and the course of the Rhine; far below are the Rheingrafenstein and Ebernburg, and in the distance to the l. the Donnersberg; in the valley the village of Münster am Stein, farther up Norheim, and on the opposite bank of the river the barren cliffs of Rothenfels.

Opposite to the Rheingrafenstein, to the W., is situated the ruined castle of ***Ebernburg,** once the stronghold of Franz von Sickingen (d. 1523, see p. 103), and which at that time often served as an asylum for outlaws and fugitives. Under his roof several of the early Reformers found shelter from persecution, and Ulrich von Hutten here composed his letters to Charles V., to the German nobility and nation. Shortly after

Sickingen's death the castle fell into the hands of the Electors of Treves, Hessen, and the Palatinate. It was fortified by the French in 1689, but, in accordance with the stipulations of the peace of Ryswyck in 1698, it was again dismantled. Out of the ruins rises a pinnacled building of strange appearance, built by the present owner, and employed as an *inn. It contains portraits of Sickingen and his wife, of Ulrich von Hutten, and others. The weapons, bullets &c., found in the old well (295 ft. deep), as well as several old sculptures, are to be seen in the castle yard. The prospect is fine, especially that of the valley of the *Alsenz*, with the ruins of *Kronenburg* in the background.

The view from the ***Rothenfels**, a porphyry cliff, rising precipitously from the valley to the height of 900 ft., surpasses those commanded by the Gans and Ebernburg, as it embraces the valley of the Nahe as far as the Lemberg and the Alsenzthal to the Moschellandsberg. The distant view is quite as extensive as that from the Gans. The footpath leading to it ascends from the saline springs through shady woods. Donkeys and conveyance, see p. 112.

Two delightful but more distant excursions may be taken from Kreuznach to the Dissibodenberg, and Dhaun (p. 110), which may best be reached by railway. — From Kreuznach by Stromberg to Bacharach, see p. 101.

30. From Saarbrücken to Treves and Luxembourg.

By railway to Treves in $2^3/_4$ hrs.; fares: 2 Thlr. $15^1/_2$, 1 Thlr. $22^1/_2$, 1 Thlr. 5 Sgr.; to Luxembourg in $3^1/_2$ hrs.; fares: 3 Thlr. 27, 2 Thlr. 16, 1 Thlr. 24 Sgr.

The line follows the course of the *Saar*, the most picturesque parts of which are between Saarbrücken and Saarlouis, and afterwards between Mettlach and Saarburg.

Saarlouis (**Rheinischer Hof; Zwei Mohren*), a Prussian fortress built by Vauban within *one* year, in consequence of a bet with Louis XIV., and the birthplace of the unfortunate Marshal Ney; the house in which he was born is indicated by a marble tablet.

The next stations are *Dillingen*, *Beckingen*, and *Merzig* (Trierscher Hof), at the last of which are the remnants of a pointed-arched piazza of the 12th cent.

At *Mettlach* (before reaching which a long tunnel is passed through) are the buildings which once belonged to a Benedictine abbey, founded in the 7th cent., now occupied by the extensive stone-ware manufactory of Villeroy and Boch, one of the most important in Germany.

At Mettlach the Saar makes a considerable circuit, which the line avoids by means of the above-mentioned tunnel. The N. point of the hill which it penetrates ($4^1/_2$ M. to the N.W. of Mettlach, reached by a pretty, shady walk) is called the ***Clef**, which affords a fine survey of the two arms of the valley of the Saar, separated by a narrow strip of land, on which stands the ruined castle of *Montclair*, destroyed as early as 1350 by the Elector Balduin of Treves.

One mile W. from the Clef lies the village of *Orscholz* (*Thiellemanns) from which a carriage road leads to *Weiten*, $2^1/_2$ M. to the N. A mile farther in the same direction is the old castle of *Freudenburg*, and 1 M. beyond it a signpost indicates the way to the village of **Castell**. Near it, on a bold rock overhanging the Saar, is an old chapel restored by the late king Fred. William IV. in 1830, when Crown-prince, and to which he caused the bones of his ancestor, the blind king John of Bohemia who fell at Cressy in 1346, to be transported. The castellan lives in the village below.

At the Prussian village of **Nennig** (8 M. to the W. of Freudenburg) is a remarkably fine Roman **Mosaic-floor*, 50 by 33 ft. It represents 8 different pictures, the principal being a combat of gladiators surrounded by groups of animals and athletes.

The line still keeps the r. bank of the Saar, and its lofty embankments traverse the grauwackian hills, between which the river flows. As the train approaches Saarburg, the above-mentioned chapel of *Castell* is seen rising on a precipitous rock on the l. bank.

Saarburg (*Post*, carriage to Castell [see above] $2^1/_3$ Thlr.; **Trierscher Hof*) is picturesquely situated in a basin formed by the surrounding hills, and overtopped by the considerable ruins of a castle of the former Electors of Treves. The *Leuk*, which here unites with the Saar, forms a waterfall, 60 ft. in height, near the "Post."

The line still continues in the valley of the Saar, passing several wine-producing villages, till it reaches **Conz**, the *Consitium* of the Romans, immediately below which the valley of the Moselle is entered. The bridge over the Saar at Conz is mentioned by the Roman poet Ausonius (d. 392) in his poem entitled "Mosella," but the present structure was erected by Clemens Wenceslaus, the last Elector of Treves, the original bridge having been destroyed by the French under Marshal Crequi, on their retreat on the 11th of August, 1675, when defeated by the imperial confederates under George William of Brunswick.

The railway here crosses the Moselle by a massive stone bridge. On the l. bank the line to Treves diverges; the station is near the old Moselle bridge. **Treves**, see p. 117.

The Luxembourg line next passes the village of *Igel*. The celebrated **Monument of Igel* (p. 121), the most beautiful Roman relic on this side of the Alps, is visible from the train. Above Igel are extensive gypsum and lime quarries. Before reaching stat. *Wasserbillig* the line crosses the frontier of Luxembourg; scenery picturesque; the *Sauer* (*Sure*) here unites with the Moselle, after having for a considerable distance towards the N. formed the boundary between Prussia and

Luxembourg. Near stat. *Mertert* the line quits the valley of the Moselle and ascends that of the *Sire*. After passing several minor stations, the train crosses the *Pulverthal* by a viaduct 800 ft. in length and 100 ft. in height; the station, which is situated on the r. side of the Petrusthal, is connected with the town by means of a handsome bridge.

Luxembourg, formerly *Lützelburg* (*Hôtel de Cologne; Hôtel de Luxembourg*), a fortress of the German confederation with a Prussian garrison (6000 men) and a pop. of 12,170, is the capital of the duchy of the same name, now subject to the king of Holland. The situation of the town is at once peculiar and picturesque. The upper portion is perched upon a rocky table-land, connected with the open country towards the W. only, whilst the other three sides are bounded by abrupt precipices, 200 ft. in height, at the base of which flows the *Petrusbach* and the *Alzette* (*Alzig*); beyond these streams again rise equally abrupt walls of rock. In this narrow ravine lies the lower portion of the town, distinguished by its industrial animation, and consisting of *Pfaffenthal*, the N. suburb, and *Clausen* and *Grund*, the S. suburbs separated by a rocky ridge termed *le Bouc* (*Bock*). The valley of the Alzette, studded with numerous habitations, and occasionally intersected by the walls of the fortress, forms a natural fosse. The view of the town with its variety of mountain and valley, gardens and rugged rocks, handsome military edifices and groups of trees, as seen from the Treves road, is singularly striking. This imposing aspect is enhanced by the gigantic railway viaducts, and the handsome, colossal bridge which connects the railway station with the opposite side of the valley.

The fortifications combine the massive proportions of modern structures of this description with the boldness of ancient mountain castles. The most interesting portion is the *Bouc* (*Bock*), a narrow projecting ridge, honeycombed from top to bottom with casemates, loopholes and embrasures, by which the valley of the Alzette is commanded in all directions. On this ridge is constructed the road to Treves, descending from the upper part of the town by numerous windings.

The construction of these works has during a period of 500 years gradually progressed under various possessors, — Henry IV., Count of Luxembourg, afterwards German emperor as Henry VII. (d. 1312), his son John, the blind king of Bohemia (killed at the battle of Cressy in 1346), the Burgundians, the Spaniards, the French (whose eminent military engineer Vauban, under Louis XIV., reconstructed a great portion of the fortress), and finally the German Confederation. Luxembourg is designated by Carnot as "*la plus forte place de l'Europe après*

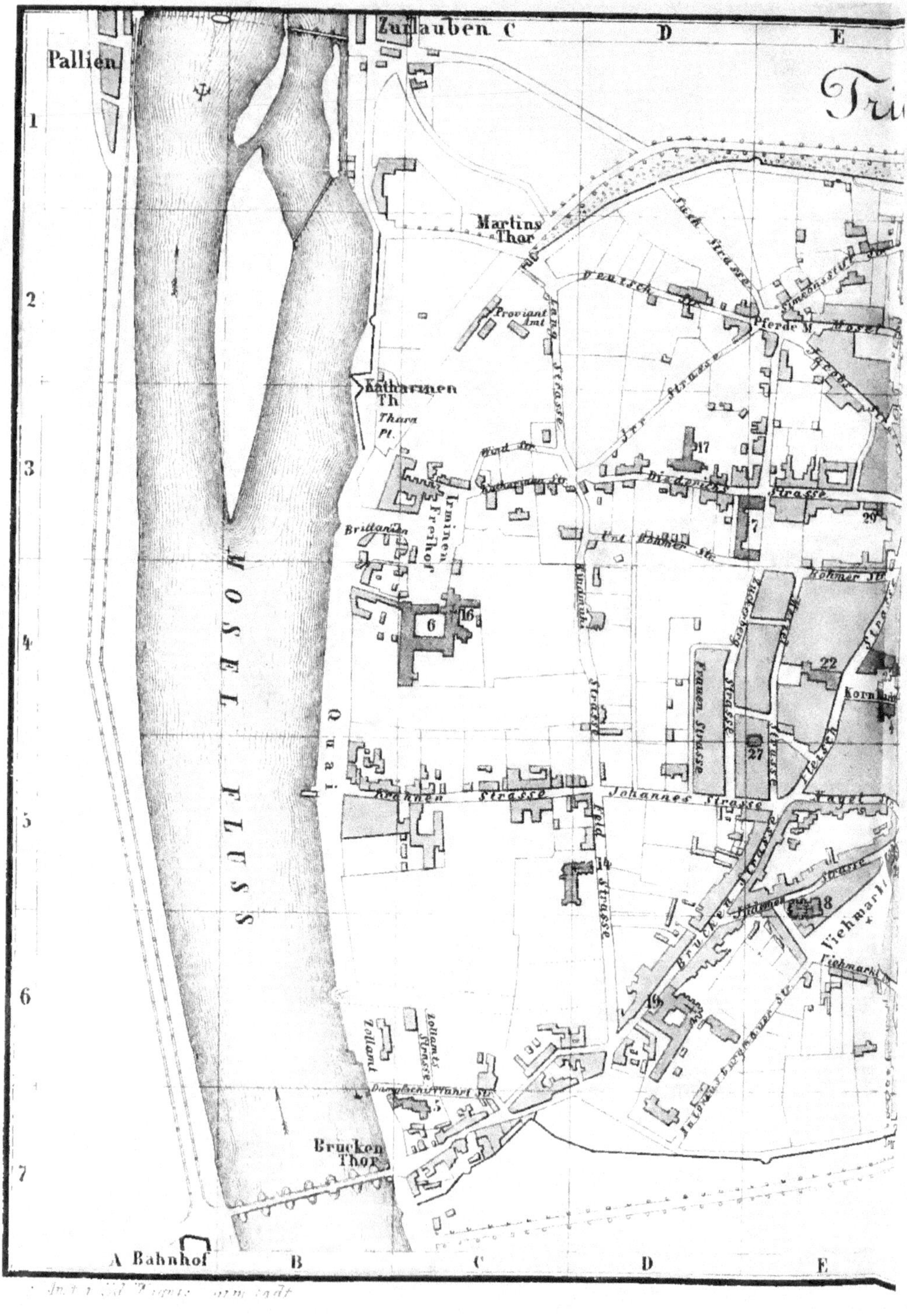
Zurlauben
C
D
E
Pallien
Tri
1
2
3
4
5
6
7
Martins Thor
Sack Strasse
Deutsch Str.
Pferde M.
Mosel
Proviant Amt
Katharinen Th
Thara Pl.
Wind Str.
Irminen Freihof
Brittanien
Dietrich Strasse
Böhmer Str.
Frauen Strasse
Fleisch Strasse
Kornmarkt
MOSEL FLUSS
Quai
Krahnen Strasse
Johannes Strasse
Feld Strasse
Brücken Strasse
Viehmarkt
Zollamt
Zollamts Strasse
Dampfschiffahrt Str.
Brücken Thor
A Bahnhof
B
C
D
E

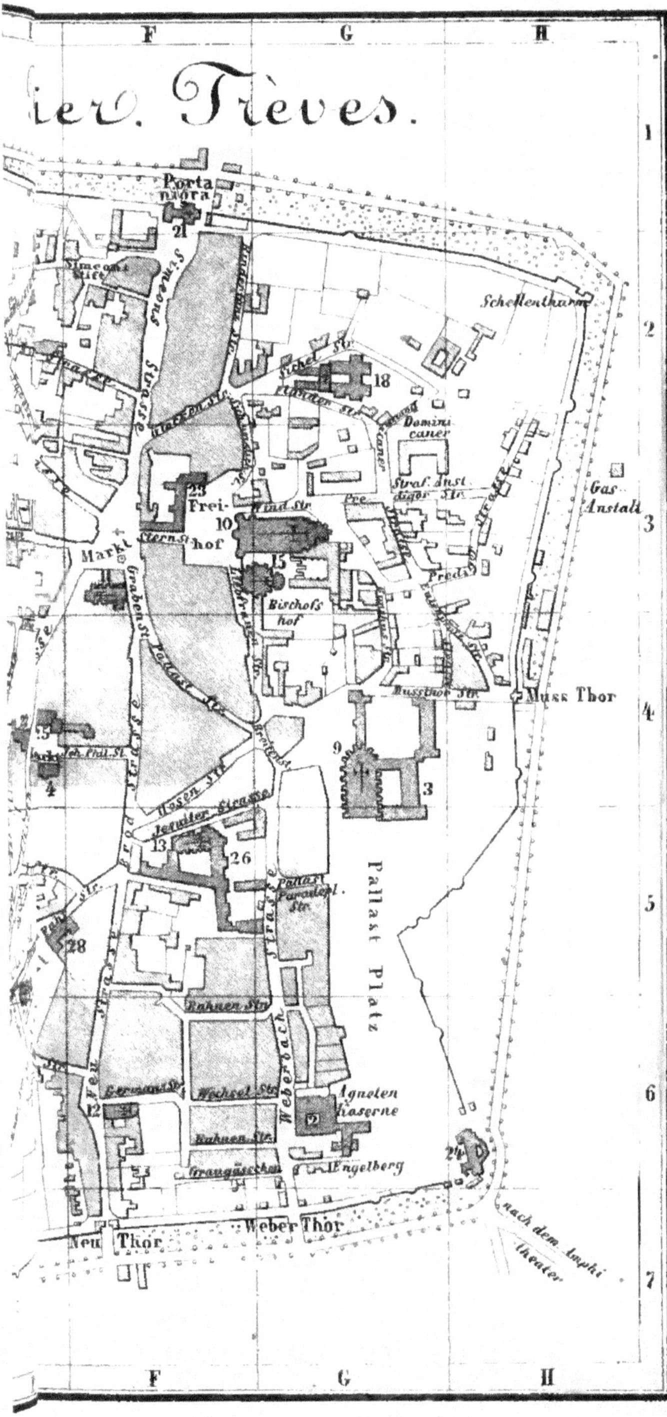

1. Bibliothek städtische in № 26 Gymnasium — F. 5.

Casernen

2. Agneten C. — G. 6.
3. Pallast C. — G. 4. 5.
4. Casino — E. 4.
5. Dampfschifffahrts Geb — C. 7.
6. Hospital — C. 4.
7. Justiz Gebäude — D. E. 3.

Kirchen

8. St Antonius K. — E. 5. 6.
9. Basilica — G. 4. 5.
10. Dom — F. G. 3.
11. St Gangolph K. — F. 3.
12. Gervasius K. — F. 6.
13. Jesuiten K. (Dreifaltigkeits K.) — F. 5.
14. St Joseph K. — C. D. 5.
15. Liebfrauen K. — F. G. 3.
16. St Paulus K. — C. 4.

Klöster

17. Clarissen Kl. — D. 3.
18. Welschnonnen Kl. — G. 2.
19. Landarmenhaus — D. 6.
20. Museum in № 26 Gymnasium — F. 5.
21. Porta nigra — F. 1.
22. Postamt — E. 4.
23. Regierungsgebäude — F. 3.
24. Römische Bäder — H. 6.
25. Stadt u. Kaufhaus — E. 4.
26. Seminar u. Gymnasium — F. 5.
27. Synagoge — E. 4. 5.
28. Theater — E. F. 5.
29. Vertheidigungsthurm — E. 3.

Gibraltar, le seul point d'appui pour attaquer la France du côté de la Moselle."

Beyond the fortifications and the delightful environs Luxembourg possesses little to arrest the traveller. Of the magnificent castle of the Spanish Governor Count Mansfeld (1545—1604) no vestige is left, with the exception of a *Gateway* in the lower part of the town, into which several Roman reliefs and inscriptions are built. The celebrated Mansfeld Gardens and parks now only nominally exist in a walk along the E. slope of the hill, in the vicinity of the Treves Gate, which however merits a visit on account of the striking view it commands. The traveller who has sufficient leisure will be well repaid by a walk through the entire valley.

31. Treves.

Hotels. *Trierscher Hof (Pl. a), R. 20, L. 5, B. 10 Sgr. *Rothes Haus (Pl. b) (similar prices), formerly senate-house. *Luxemburger Hof (Pl. c) and *Stadt Venedig (Pl. d), both good second-class houses with moderate charges.

Cafés. Fischer, in the market-place. Bellevue and Schneider's Hof, both on an eminence on the l. bank of the Moselle, commanding a magnificent view, $^3/_4$ M. distant from the ferry at *Zurlauben* at the lower end of the town; back to Treves by Zurlauben, passing the entrance to the Pallien-Thal, a pretty glimpse of which is obtained through the arch of a bridge built by Napoleon.

Carriages. Two-horse carriages 4 Thlr. per diem; to *Igel* (p. 115) 2 Thlr., one-horse 1 Thlr. 10 Sgr.

Railway station on the l. bank of the Moselle. Railway to Saarbrücken, see R. 30, and to Luxembourg.

Telegraph Office near the Neuthor.

Steamboat to *Coblenz*, see p. 121.

Treves (Ger. *Trier*), said to be the oldest town in Germany, was the capital of the Treviri, a race of the Belgic Gauls, conquered B.C. 56 by Cæsar, who converted it into a Roman colony under the name of *Augusta Trevirorum.* The new colony increased rapidly in importance, and was on more occasions than one the residence of the Emperors. Under Constantine the Great it was the capital of the whole of Gaul, and had its senate, magistrates, nobility, and priesthood; and with its arts, sciences, and extensive commercial relations became no mean rival of Imperial Rome itself. The relics and remnants of buildings belonging to that age with which the vicinity abounds, are incontestibly the finest on this side of the Alps.

Upon the introduction of Christianity by Constantine, Agricius of Antioch was in 328 elected first Bishop of Treves, which for nearly 15 centuries continued to be the residence of the bishops, archbishops, and electors, till Clemens Wenceslaus, the last elector, transferred his residence to Coblenz in 1786.

On Aug. 10th, 1794, the French took the town, exacted

from it a contribution of $1\frac{1}{2}$ million francs, and in 1802 abolished all the monasteries and religious establishments. Till 1815 Treves was the chief town of the Department of the Saar, when it was made over to Prussia. Its population is 17,240 (1500 Prot., and 2000 soldiers). The vine-clad hills in the environs, the wooded heights, the rich and fruitful plain in which the town, with its red sandstone walls and numerous towers, is situated, form a most picturesque and striking landscape.

The most important and at the same time the most interesting and best preserved of the Roman antiquities of Treves is the ***Porta Nigra** (*Römerthor, Simeonsthor,* Pl. 21) at the N. end of the town. The dimensions of this magnificent relic are: length 115 ft., height 74—93 ft., breadth including the wings 167 ft. It consists of three different stories, with two gateways, 23 ft. in height, and is constructed of huge, uncemented blocks of lias sandstone, blackened by time. In 1035 this structure was converted into a church, and the lower story filled up, and in this state it remained till 1817, when it was restored to its ancient condition and use as a gateway by the Prussian government. In the part formerly used as the choir a collection of Roman antiquities is exhibited by the custodian of the baths.

Next in interest are the ***Roman Baths** (Pl. 24), entered from the Promenade and also through a wicket-gate from the Esplanade (5 Sgr.), forming the S.E. corner of the town. They were as late as 1817 almost entirely buried beneath a mass of earth and rubbish, but this has been removed by the Prussian government, and the spacious apartments, halls, and channels for hot air, carefully and tastefully constructed of large bricks and small blocks of limestone, are now completely exposed to view and preserved from the farther ravages of time. The summit is reached by a steep spiral stair-case, and affords a good survey of the structure itself and the town.

On a rising ground about 500 yds. from the Baths is the ***Amphitheatre,** termed by the inhabitants the *Käskeller* (cheese-cellar), situated among vineyards. This arena, still in excellent preservation, has a diameter from N. to S. of 225, and from E. to W. 156 ft., and was capable of accommodating 57,000 spectators. Here Constantine the Great sullied his fame in the year 306 by causing several thousand captive Franks, with their leaders Ascarich and Ragais, to be torn to pieces by wild beasts, which barbarous scene was repeated in 313, when thousands of the Bructeri were sacrificed for the amusement of the people. The ten apertures in the walls, which led to the vaulted dens (*caveæ*) where the wild beasts were kept, are still to be seen. The * *Villa Recking,* above the Amphitheatre, affords the best view of the town, as well as of the amphitheatre itself. Pleasant walk to the village of *Clewig* (1 1/2 M.).

The * **Basilika** (Pl. 9) is a building said to date from a period prior to the time of Constantine, the purposes of which antiquarians have been unable to determine with precision; some suppose it to have been a theatre, others an imperial residence. In the early part of the middle ages it was the seat of the Governors of the town, but at the commencement of the 12th cent. was, with the supreme jurisdiction of the town, transferred to the bishops, and constituted a part of the episcopal palace, afterwards erected by them. When the town became Prussian, it was converted into a barrack, but in 1846 was restored to its ancient condition by the late king Fred. William IV. In 1856 it was fitted up and consecrated as a Protestant church. The entire length is 220 ft., breadth 98 ft., and height of the hall 97 ft.; the N. side is built in a semicircular form, and the interior is lighted by a double row of windows.

In the time of the Romans the * **Bridge** over the Moselle was situated in the middle of the town. It was partially destroyed by the French in 1689, and in 1729 the remnants were employed in the construction of the present bridge, which crosses the river at the S.W. extremity of the town.

In the Diedrichstrasse, at the fourth house from the market-place on the l., are the old walls of a building, now employed as a coach-house, believed to have been a Roman tower of defence (*propugnaculum*) (Pl. 29), but in reality dating from the 6th or 7th cent.

Among the older ecclesiastical buildings only two are worthy of note, the Cathedral, and the adjacent Liebfrauenkirche, both situated near the Basilika. The * **Cathedral** (Pl. 10) was once, according to an ancient tradition, a palace of the Roman emperors, and the birthplace of St. Helena, the mother of Constantine the Great. It is difficult to convey an idea of its architectural merit, as no less than six different styles have been combined in its construction: Corinthian columns of the time of Constantine contrast with Romanesque and Gothic arches; the grotesque styles of the 17th and 18th centuries, and the unsuitable Ionic pillars erected in 1849 to support the organ, form, with the recent external and internal decorations, an incongruous though not unimposing whole. Fragments of the pillars of Odenwald granite, which once decorated the portion of the structure where the grand choir now begins, lie in front of the W. Portal. The entire length of the edifice, exclusive of the treasury, is 314 ft., breadth 135 ft., and height 90 ft.

It contains three aisles and two choirs. The different periods of the architecture, beginning with the Roman period, are well exhibited in the interior of the church. In its vaults repose the remains of 26 archbishops and Electors. The finest of the monuments is that of Johann III. (*von Metzenhausen*, d. 1540), on the wall of the N. aisle. On the tombstone of the Elector Richard III. (*von Greifenclau*, d. 1531), the successful opponent of Protestantism, are small medallions with likenesses of the Elector on the l., and his most violent antagonist, Franz von Sickingen (p. 103), on the r. side. This church is the depositary of some highly prized relics. Foremost may be named the "Holy Coat" without seam, the exhibition of which at rare intervals attracts enormous crowds of pilgrims. A nail from the Cross and a portion of the Crown of Thorns are also objects of superstitious veneration. By the steps leading to the High altar are statues of *Constantine* and *St. Helena*, and on the pulpit, reliefs in stone of 1572, representing the 8 Beatifications and the Last Judgment.

Adjacent to the cathedral, and connected with it by beautiful cloisters restored in 1847, is the ***Liebfrauenkirche** (Pl. 15), a church of inconsiderable dimensions, but deservedly admired as one of the most exquisite specimens of Gothic architecture in Germany. It was completed in 1243, five years before the foundation-stone of the cathedral at Cologne was laid. The form of the structure is circular, intersected by a lofty vaulted cross, and supported by 12 slender pillars, on which the 12 apostles are represented, painted probably in the 15th cent.; they may all be seen simultaneously from a slab of slate in the pavement, about 8 yds. from the entrance, which the sacristan points out. The church contains numerous monuments of ecclesiastical dignitaries, and the mummy of Bishop Theodulf, who died in the 6th cent. The **Portal* is richly decorated with sculptures, symbolical of the Old and New Testament.

The **Town Library**, in the buildings of the Grammar School (Pl. 26), contains a considerable collection of rare and valuable works, amongst them the bible of Faust and Gutenberg of 1450, and the Catholicon of 1460; of the MSS. the most interesting is the Codex aureus, which contains the four Gospels, presented by Ada (d. 809), the sister of Charlemagne, to the Abbey of St. Maximin, within the precincts of which she was afterwards interred. It is illuminated with strictly allegorical paintings; the binding is superbly ornamented with precious stones and a cameo of uncommon size, representing the Familia Augusta.

The **Museum** (Pl. 20) in the same building may be visited on account of the valuable collection it contains of fossils and volcanic productions from the Eifel, and a great number of coins and antiquities of the Roman period and the middle ages.

By far the most interesting Roman monument on this side of the Alps must now be mentioned — the celebrated ***Igeler Säule**, or Igel Monument, popularly termed "*Heidenthurm*" (heathens' tower), situated in the middle of the village of that name, about 20 yds. to the r. of the Treves and Luxembourg road. It is a square sandstone column, 71 ft. in height, and 16 ft. broad at the base, probably erected in the 2nd cent.; it bears a number of reliefs, carvings and inscriptions on the different panels. Antiquarians differ in their conjectures concerning the origin and purpose of this fine relic, and its inscriptions have been variously interpreted. It was, however, in all probability a monument erected by the rich mercantile family of Secundini, who lived in this vicinity, to the memory of one their sons, who, as some of the allegorical reliefs seem to intimate, perished by drowning, and, as another relief exhibits a man and woman in the act of joining their hands, it may also have been intended to commemorate a happier and more auspicious event.

Another object of almost equal interest is the ***Mosaic floor** of a Roman villa, discovered in 1852 at *Nennig,* a village on the r. bank of the Moselle, see p. 115.

32. The Moselle from Treves to Coblenz.

Steamboats four times a week, in summer daily, down the river in 10—12 hrs., up in $1\frac{1}{2}$ day. When the river is very low they do not ply. Fares: Cabin, 4 Thlr., steerage $2\frac{2}{3}$ Thlr. These boats are smaller but not inferior in comfort and accommodation to those on the Rhine.

From Treves to Coblenz by water is about 150 M., by land half that distance. To the traveller in search of the picturesque, the course of the river presents the greatest attractions. The scenery, though not on so extensive a scale, is hardly inferior to that of the Rhine; indeed there are those who yield the preference to the softer and more varied charms of the lesser stream. The fall from Treves to Coblenz is 204 ft.

The villages on the banks, other objects of interest, and the best points for inland excursions are here enumerated:

l. *Pfalzel* (*Palatiolum*), where Adela, daughter of King Dagobert, founded a convent in 655.

r. *Ruwer* on the river of the same name, the *Erubrus* of the Roman poet Ausonius (d. 392).

l. *Ehrang*, the *Quint* (ad quintum, i. e. 5 M. from Treves) with extensive iron-foundry, and *Issel*.

l. *Schweich* (*Dany), with ferry to the Treves and Coblenz road.

r. *Kirsch;* beyond is *Longwich*.

l. *Riol* (*Rigodulum*), where the Roman general Cerialis conquered the rebellious Treviri, and took their leader Valentinus prisoner (*Tacit. hist. IV. 70*).

l. *Trittenheim*, birthplace of Johann Trithemius, an eminent historian, and abbot of Sponheim.

r. **Neumagen** (*Claeren*, *Hain*), the *Noviomagum* of the Romans, where Constantine had a castle (the "*inclita castra Constantini*" of Ausonius), few traces of which now remain. The church is believed to have been partly constructed (1190) with the stones of the castle.

l. *Pisport* (*Pisonis Portus*) is celebrated for its wine.

l. *Minheim* nearly opposite to

r. the *Ohligsberg*, *Dusemond*.

l. The *Brauneberg*, another celebrated wine district.

r. **Mühlheim** (**Karsch*), a village of some importance.

l. **Lieser** (*Heyder*), with several country houses in the vicinity, at the mouth of the brook of the same name.

l. *Cues* was the birthplace of the learned Cardinal Nicolaus Cusanus (d. 1464), where he founded a hospital to which he bequeathed his library, containing some valuable MSS., a considerable number of Codices and some rare old impressions.

r. **Berncastel** (**Drei Könige*), capital town of this district, partly burned down in 1857; ruined Castle of *Landshut*. Diligence daily to Treves in 6, to Kreuznach in 9 hrs.

From Berncastel a footpath, commanding a fine view, crosses the hill to Trarbach, which may be reached in $1^{1}/_{4}$ hr. At the highest point, 1100 ft. above the river (40 min. walk), stands a direction post. To the r. of the path may still be seen traces of extensive intrenchments, made partly by the French. The descent to Trarbach is stony and somewhat steep. Distance by water 15 M.; steamboat down in $1^{1}/_{2}$ hr., up in 3 hrs.

r. *Graach*, and beyond it *Zeltingen* (de Wilde), both celebrated for their wine.

l. **Uerzig** (**Post*, *Berres*) at the beginning of the road leading to Wittlich and the Eifel (p. 126). Below the village is a tower built into the rock, formerly a castle of the family von Urlei, afterwards a hermitage.

l. *Cröff* (*Comes*); opposite to it,

r. *Wolf*, with ruins of an old monastery on the height.

r. **Trarbach** (*Gräfinburg*), completely burned down in 1857, is the busiest and wealthiest town on the whole river; it is commanded by the ruin of the *Gräfinburg*, erected in the middle of the 14th cent. by the Countess Laurette von Starkenburg with the ransom she exacted from Balduin, archbishop of Treves, for his release from the Castle of Starkenburg, where she had caused him to be confined as a punishment for an attempted infringement of her rights. The castle was dismantled by the French in 1734.

Opposite to Trarbach, at the foot of vine-clad slopes, lies

l. **Traben** (**Claus*), on the wide table-land above which may be seen the traces of the extensive fortification of Montroyal, constructed by Louis XIV. in 1686, and levelled in 1697 in accordance with stipulations made in the Treaty of Ryswyck. Fine view.

r. *Enkirch* (*Immich), from which a footpath leads over the hill to Zell in 1½ hr.; distance by water 9 M.

l. *Reil* (Barzen).

r. *Pünderich* (Schneiders). On the l. bank, opposite to the landing place, a steep path ascends to the r. through vineyards to ***Marienburg**, a ruined castle or monastery, which may be reached in ½ hr. The view is one of the most beautiful on the Moselle; at the top refreshments may be procured. The descent on the other side of the hill to Alf may easily be accomplished in less than ½ hr., while the whole distance by the river is about 12 M., which the steamboat performs in 1 hr. with, and 2 hrs. against the stream. A tolerable walker, disembarking at Pünderich, may without difficulty cross the hill and regain the boat at Alf.

r. *Briedel* (*Theisen).

r. **Zell** (*Melchiors; Fier*), principal town of the district, surrounded by remnants of an old wall and tower.

r. *Merl*, view of the Marienburg.

l. **Alf** (**Theisen; Bad Bertrich*) beautifully situated at the mouth of the lovely valley of the Alf. The walk from Alf to Pünderich is particularly recommended to those ascending the river.

A day may be advantageously devoted to the *Baths of Bertrich*. and its volcanic environs. The road from Alf to Bertrich (5 M.; carriage there and back 1⅓—2 Thlr.) leads through the romantic *Valley of the Alf*, enclosed by precipitous rocks, 700 ft. in height, passing the ruins of the *Burg Arras*, and some extensive iron-works.

Bertrich (**Werling; *Klering; Adler; *Post*), a watering-place much frequented by the inhabitants of the banks of the Moselle, is visited annually by upwards of 1000 patients. The warm springs (90° Fahr.) contain a considerable quantity of Glauber's salt, and are especially efficacious in cases of gout, rheumatism, and nervous maladies. Bertrich is a place of rising importance. It is delightfully situated in a secluded valley, enclosed by wooded hills, and offers many attractions to the valetudinarian who would fain be free from the allurements of the gaming table and the other excitements which must too often retard the cure at the more fashionable watering-places. On an eminence called the *Römerkessel*, where the Roman relics now to be seen in the garden of the bath-establishment were found, stands a small Protestant chapel.

About $^1/_2$ M. to the W. of Bertrich the road twice crosses the *Uesbach*. At the second bridge, in the hill to the l., is the so-called ***Käskeller** (cheese-cellar), a grotto composed of basaltic columns, each of which is formed of 8 or 9 spheroids, exactly resembling cheeses. Near it is a *Waterfall*, 50 ft. in height. A basaltic stream of lava is visible in several places in the bed of the Uesbach.

The new road to Lutzerath leads at a considerable elevation on the l. bank of *Uesbach* as far as a crescent ($^1/_2$ M.), whence it ascends to the r. in a zigzag direction to the village of *Kenfuss* (1 M.). A footpath to the r., to the rear of the gardens of the village, leads in 6 min. to the ***Falkenlei** (1276 ft.), a semi-conical hill, the S. side of which is a precipice 160 ft. in height, exhibiting the geological constitution of the interior. At the bottom lie solid masses of lava; and at the top scoriae and slag, in which numerous caves and clefts have been formed. The summit affords an extensive view of the numerous volcanic peaks of the Eifel, the highest of which are the *Hohe Acht* (2340 ft.), the *Nürburg* (2118 ft.), with a tower on its summit, and the *Hohe Kelberg* (2070 ft.), to the N. On the W. the prospect is circumscribed by the long isolated ridge of the *Mosenberg* (p. 132). *Lutzerath* (1259 ft.), a post station on the Coblenz and Treves road, is $4^1/_2$ M. distant from the Falkenlei. Diligence twice a day between Bertrich and Lutzerath.

On the Moselle, opp. to Alf, lies

r. *Bullay*, whence a precipitous path leads to the (50 min.) **König*, commanding an extensive prospect. Descent in 30 min. to Merl (p. 123).

l. *Aldegund* (Andries) with ancient church.

r. *Neef*, surrounded by fruit trees. A footpath over the hill, on the summit of which the churchyard of Neef and the *Chapel of St. Peter* are situated, leads in $^3/_4$ hr. to *Eller*, cutting off the long circuit which the Moselle here describes. At the extremity of the bend lies

l. *Bremm* (*Amelinger).

r. *Stuben*, a monastery erected in the 12th cent. and secularized in 1788; finally abandoned to decay in 1793.

l. **Eller** (*Gietzen; Maintzer*) with old castellated houses and farm-houses belonging to the feudal ages; path over the hill to Cochem in 2 hrs. The banks of the river are however particularly beautiful at this point, and the traveller is recommended not to leave the boat.

l. **Ediger** (*Maass*), a small town, surrounded with old fortifications; on the height the ruins of the *Kreuzkapelle*.

l. *Senhals*, where Roman coins and relics have been repeatedly discovered.

r. **Beilstein**; the castle on the heights was once the residence of the counts, now princes, of Metternich-Winneburg.

r. *Bruttig*, birthplace of the celebrated grammarian Petrus Mosellanus, professor at Leipsic, who died in 1524.

l. *Ober-* and *Nieder-Ernst*. Between them a handsome new church and school-house.

r. *Valwig;* the rocks are here very picturesque and resemble the Lurlei on the Rhine.

l. **Cochem** (*Union; *Kehrer*), principal town of the district, with ruins of a castle which frequently served as a residence of the Archbishops of Treves in the 14th and 16th centuries. Picturesquely situated on an eminence are the buildings which formerly belonged to a Capuchin monastery. Beyond it, on the summit of a mountain, rise the ruins of the castle of *Winneburg*, the most ancient seat of the Metternich family. Cochem is one of the most beautifully situated places on the Moselle.

l. *Clotten* (Thomas) with an old castle; depôt for the slate of *Müllenbach*, a village 9 M. to the N.W., with numerous and remarkable subterranean quarries.

Treis (*Castor; Raueiser*) with a modern church. Opposite to it lies

l. **Carden** (*Brauer*), where, in the 12th cent., a church was founded by St. Castor, which in the 12th cent. was enlarged and converted into a handsome three-towered *Stiftskirche* in honour of the saint.

l. *Müden.* Footpath to Schloss Eltz in $^3/_4$ hr.

l. *Moselkern* (Deiss) at the mouth of the *Eltz.*

In the narrow and winding valley of the Eltz, about 4 M. to the N.W. of Moselkern, stands ***Schloss Eltz**, an ancient residence of the noble family of Eltz. The castle is most picturesquely situated, and presents one of the best preserved specimens of a feudal residence of the middle ages in Germany, which the traveller is strongly recommended to visit. Many of the rooms are furnished in the ponderous style of bygone ages, and the walls hung, if not adorned, with a collection of family portraits, ancient armour, &c. In the Rittersaal (knights' hall) a book is kept in which visitors may record their names, and, if so disposed, inspect the autograph of the Prince of Wales, who during his sojourn in Germany visited this delightful spot. Opposite to Schloss Eltz are the ruins of *Trutz-Eltz*, erected by Archbishop Balduin to command the castle, with the counts of which he carried on a protracted feud. About 3 M. farther up the valley lie the ruins of the fine old castle of *Pyrmont*. The road from Moselkern to Schloss Eltz through the valley is very rough, and only adapted to the hardy pedestrian. The stream must be crossed 13 times, a stepping-stone here and there affording but an indifferent footing, but if a prospect of wet feet does not deter the pedestrian, the beauty of the walk will amply repay him. Another footpath runs along the brow of the hill on the r. bank of the Eltz, but is much overgrown with brushwood and to be traced only with difficulty. By carriage the excursion can only be made from **Münstermaifeld** (*Maifelder Hof*), a venerable town of some importance, 3 M. to the N.E. of Schloss Eltz. The church was founded as early as 642; the front with the towers appears as if it appertained to some old fortress rather than to a sacred edifice. — Diligence daily to Coblenz in 3 hrs.

Below Moselkern a tall round tower rises on the hill to the l., a remnant of *Burg Bischofstein*, erected in 1270.

l. **Hatzenport** (*Hattonis porta*) (*Moritz). Opposite to it lies

r. **Brodenbach** (*Joh. Probst*), from which a road ascends through a mountain ravine to the ruins of ***Ehrenburg** (2 M.), situated on an isolated peak, the finest ruin on the Moselle. Road to Boppard on the Rhine, see p. 94.

l. The *Tempelhof* or *Sternberg*, a ruined Gothic castle, situated in the midst of vineyards.

r. *Alken*, an ancient borough connected by walls and towers with the old castle of *Thurant*, on the height above, built by the Count Palatine Heinrich in 1197. It was besieged in 1246—48 by the Archbishops of Treves and Cologne, during which time upwards of 600,000 gallons of wine are said to have been consumed by the besiegers.

r. *Oberfell; Kühr* (*Günther).

l. *Lehmen* (*Zirwas).

r. *Niederfell* (*Fasbender).

l. *Gondorf* (Haupt) with a country-seat erected by the Elector Johann von der Leyen in 1560.

l. **Cobern** (*Fischer*). Above it stands the *Niederburg*, once the seat of the knights of Cobern. Higher is situated the *Ober-* or *Altenburg*, in the interior of which is the **Chapel of St. Matthias*, celebrated for the beauty of its architecture. It is built in the form of a hexagon, and, according to tradition, owes its origin to a crusader in the early part of the 13th cent.

r. *Dieblich* (*Nörtershäuser) possesses a handsome new church.

l. **Winningen** (*Krone*), a small market-town, where the best wine of the Lower Moselle is produced, below it, r. *Lay*, and l. *Güls* with a handsome church, situated in the midst of an vast orchard.

r. *Moselweis*, completely surrounded by fruit-trees.

r. **Coblenz** (R. 20). Steamboat-passengers disembark above the railway bridge.

33. The Volcanic Eifel.

An excursion into the *Vorder-Eifel*, the most remarkable part of this mountainous district. may be advantageously combined with the tour of the Moselle as follows. 1st day: from Coblenz by steamboat to *Alf* (p. 123) in 7—8 hrs.; ascend the *Marienburg* ($1^1/_2$ hr.); on foot in 2 hrs. to *Bertrich* (or in an open carriage), inspect the *Falkenlei* and *Käskeller* ($1^1/_2$ hr.), pass the night at Bertrich. 2nd day: on foot through *Hontheim*, *Strotzbüsch*, *Trautzberg* and *Strohn* to *Gillenfeld* (12 M.), to the *Pulvermaar* and back (2 M.), to dinner at Gillenfeld; in the afternoon to *Schalkenmehren*, *Weinfelder Maar*, *Mäuseberg* and *Daun* (10 M.). 3d day: by carriage to *Gerolstein* and back to Daun in 8 hrs.; afternoon on foot to *Manderscheid* (9 M.). 4th day: environs of Manderscheid, and on foot to *Wittlich*, or, if the traveller's time be limited, to *Uerzig*, 6 M. farther, where on the following morning he may take the boat (in summer daily) to Coblenz. A 6th day would be well spent in visiting Treves (by diligence from Wittlich, twice daily in 4 hrs.).

The *Moselle* between Coblenz and *Alf* has been already described in the preceding route. From the *Grotto of Cheeses* a road leads in a S. W. direction to *Hontheim* ($2^1/_4$ M.), thence to *Strotzbüsch* ($4\frac{1}{2}$ M.), and through *Trautzberg* to **Strohn** ($1\frac{1}{2}$ M.), a village in the valley of the Alf. The **Wartesberg** (1498 ft.), one of the largest volcanic mountains in the Eifel, extends along the E. side of the valley, commencing at Strohn and terminating at *Sprink* (1 M. farther S.). The crater, which it undoubtedly possesses, is difficult to recognize on account of the extensive masses of slag by which it is concealed.

Gillenfeld (1263 ft.) (**Klasen-Otto*; *Caspari*) is situated $1\frac{1}{2}$ M. farther up the valley. On the heights, 1 M. to the E. of Gillenfeld, lies the ***Pulvermaar** (1249 ft.), an extinct crater of a nearly circular form, now filled with water 330 ft. in depth. It is enclosed on three sides by wooded hills, and is the most beautiful, and, with the exception of the Laacher See (p. 72), the largest of these crater-lakes of the Eifel; it occupies an area of about 90 acres. The banks consist of volcanic sand, tufa and scoriae. On the S. side of the lake rises the volcanic *Römersberg* (1468 ft.). [*Manderscheid* lies $7\frac{1}{2}$ M. to the S.W. of Gillenfeld; the road leads by *Eckfeld* and *Buchholz*; $\frac{1}{2}$ M. beyond Buchholz the pedestrian, having skirted the wood for a short distance, must enter it and proceed to the *Belvedere*, p. 131.]

The road to *Saxler* and Schalkenmehren leads through several peculiar volcanic valleys. The village of **Schalkenmehren**, $3\frac{3}{4}$ M. to the N. of Gillenfeld, and the same distance from Daun, is situated on the banks of the *Schalkenmehrer Maar* (or *tarn*) (1301 ft.), covering an area of 50 acres; on the E. side is a peat-bog. The *Alf* flows out of the tarn on the S. side. At the inn a good dish of pike may generally be procured, but not desirable accommodation for the night.

The road to Daun leads along the W. bank of the lake, and ascends the natural barrier which separates it from the *Weinfelder Maar* (1475 ft.) The latter is nearly square (area 45 acres), and has no visible outlet. On its N. bank rises the *Weinfelder Kirche*, a cemetery-chapel for the village of Schalkenmehren.

The pedestrian should now leave the direct road to Daun, and ascend to the l. on the N. W. bank of the tarn. There is no regular path, but he must proceed in a W. direction along the hill about half-way up: in about $\frac{1}{2}$ hr. from the Weinfelder Kirche he will reach the *Gemündener Maar* (1246 ft.), the smallest of these tarns, situated 150 ft. above the bed of the *Lieser*. The summit of ***Mäuseberg** (1735 ft.), the N. side of which rises somewhat abruptly from the Gemündener Maar, commands a remarkably fine view of a great portion of the Eifel.

The three above-mentioned tarns ("*Dauner Maare*") lie in an extensive tract of volcanic formations, consisting chiefly of slag-sand, scoriæ and occasionally of volcanic tufa. The greatest breadth of this tract is from E. to W., from the village of *Mehren* to the slopes of the valley of the Lieser; the only spot in it where the grauwacke is visible is low down on the margin of the Weinfelder Maar.

From the Mäuseberg the traveller must descend the heights which bound the Gemündener Maar on the E., and cross the mountain-ridge, on the N. side of which he will reach the footpath which leads from the Weinfelder Kirche (skirting a portion of the tarn) to Daun; then descend to the high road (from the Mäuseberg to the road 1 M.) near the village of **Gemünden,** from which the road leads through the valley of the *Lieser* to Daun, 1½ M. farther.

The little town of **Daun** (1254 ft.) (* *Grethen*, R. and B. 15 Sgr.; carriage to Gerolstein, Manderscheid, or Lutzerath 2½ Thlr.; diligence every morning to Lutzerath to meet the Coblenz and Treves coach; night-diligence to Wittlich) is the principal place in this district, picturesquely situated on the brow of a mountain, and commanded by a modern building founded on the ruins of the castle of the counts of Daun, celebrated in the annals of Austrian warfare. Their arms are still to be seen over the entrance of the building which is now the residence of the royal head-forester.

To the N. about 1½ M. from the town, rises precipitously the long, scorified ridge of a crater, called the *Dauner-Lei* (Lei = cliff), from which a lava-stream of considerable size descends westward towards the Lieserthal. About 4½ M. to the W. of Daun rises the *Nerother Kopf* (2000 ft.), another volcanic cone, surmounted by a ruined castle.

The vicinity of Daun, especially in a N. W. direction, possesses peculiar interest for the geologist. Here he finds, more than in any other part of the Eifel, evidences of volcanic agency in many places covered with minerals, which, in all probability partly issued from the beautifully and distinctly formed craters. The district in which these formations occur in such abundance covers an area of about 50 sq. M., extending N.W. to *Hillesheim* and *Steffen*, from the former place down the Kyllthal as far as *Birresborn*, and then E. to Daun, and from Daun N. to *Dockweiler* and *Dreis*. The cones, which protrude from the surrounding grauwackian and calcareous formations, are partly of a basaltic nature, but far more frequently consist of slag, with well preserved craters or traces of them.

Proofs of the former volcanic activity of this region are

The Volcanic Eifel

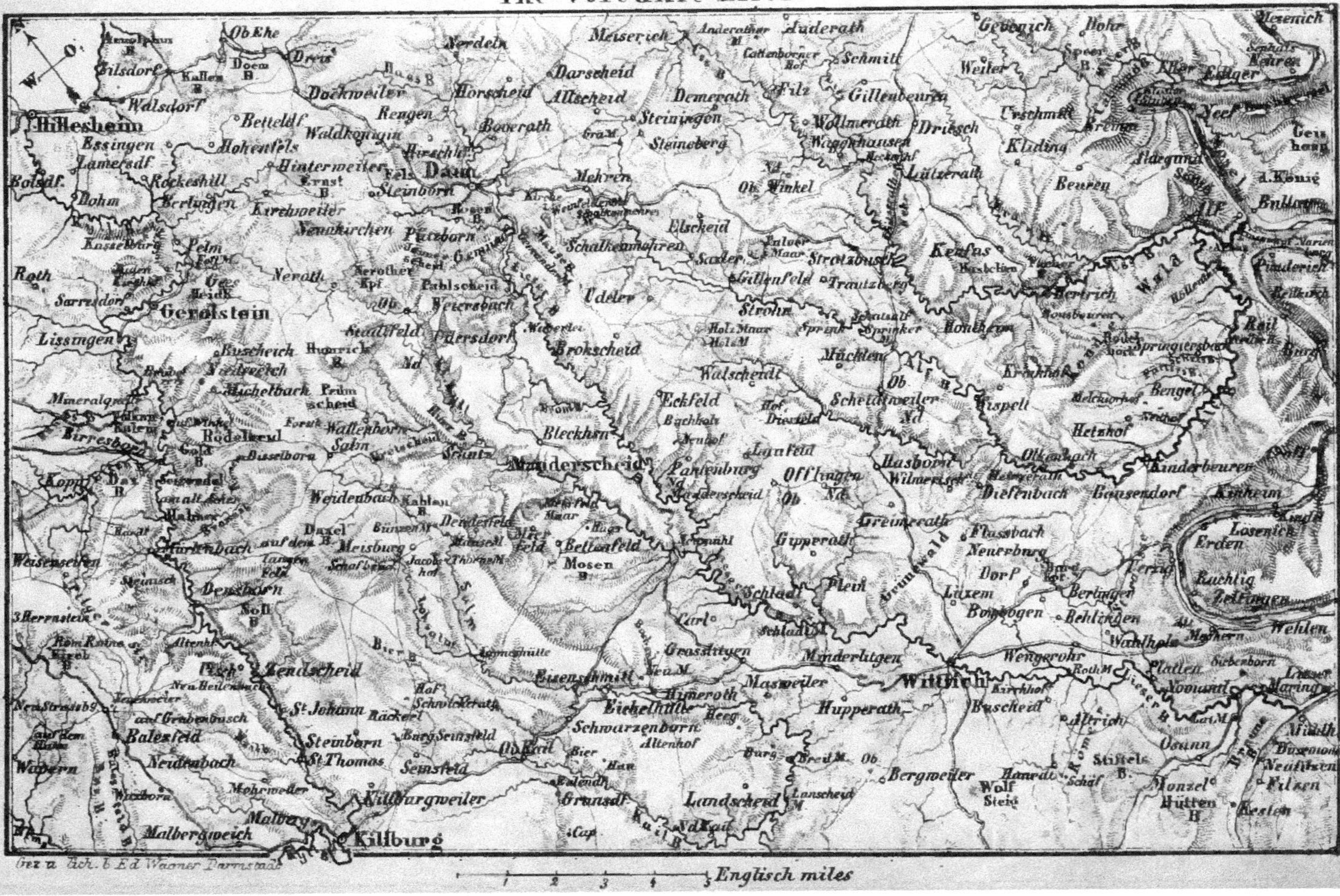

most distinctly visible at the **Scharteberg** (2094 ft.), situated to the S. of *Kirchweiler.* The summit of this mountain consists of blistered-looking masses of slag which surround the extinct crater. About 100 ft. lower the lava-streams commence, extending towards the N., S. and E. The last of these streams, though for the most part covered with scoriæ and volcanic sand is not only easily recognized in its distance and extent by the protrusion of isolated rocks, but may be more minutely inspected at the quarries of *Steinborn.* The lowest part consists of a porous and very slightly cleft basaltic lava, the upper of slag, 3—5 ft. in thickness, above the latter is a layer of scoriæ and volcanic sand, 20 ft. thick, and, next to the surface of the earth, basaltic lava (comp. p. 73).

The most considerable of these craters is the basin in which the village of **Hohenfels** (1½ M. to the N. of Kirchweiler, see below) lies. The heights which surround the village are entirely composed of masses of lava, often descending precipitously towards the interior; the highest part is 1825 ft., and the bed of the brook which issues from the crater 1334 ft. above the level of the sea.

From the **Erensberg** (2134 ft.) (the highest point of this part of the Eifel, situated to the N. of the road between Steinborn and Kirchweiler), the principal stream of lava, which begins 200 ft. below the summit, extends in a N. direction, past *Dockweiler*, nearly as far as *Dreis.* On the E. and S. margins of the *Dreiser Weiher*, a boggy meadow situated in a hollow on the road-side, 7½ M. to the N. of Daun, are frequently found masses containing olivine (some of them 1½ ft. in diameter and weighing 30 lbs.), ejected by volcanic action, and occurring in the deposits of the less compact volcanic products which surround all these basaltic and lava cones. From the summit of the Erensberg a fine view is obtained, and the ascent is recommended.

Travellers who desire to visit the most remarkable points in the vicinity of Daun in the shortest possible time, should early in the morning, cross the hill from Daun into the valley in which *Neunkirchen* and *Steinborn* are situated; to the r. of the latter rises the *Felsberg*, and to the l. the *Rimmerich*, two craters with lava streams; a little farther are the slag-mountains of *Neroth* (p. 128). From Steinborn the path which ascends a side-valley to the l. must be taken, leading along the southern slope of the lava-stream above described, and crossing the *Scharteberg* to the *Erensberg*; then by *Hinterweiler* and *Hohenstein* into the Kyllthal to *Pelm* and *Gerolstein.*

The whole walk, for which a guide (15 Sgr.) is almost indispensable, occupies 5—6 hrs.

Except in a geological point of view the high road from Daun to Gerolstein (12 M.) presents no objects of interest to the pedestrian, till the Kyllthal at *Pelm* is reached, 3 M. from Gerolstein. Where time is limited, a carriage should be taken from Daun to *Neunkirchen*, *Steinborn* (with mineral spring), *Kirchweiler*, the highest point of the road, and **Pelm,** a village on the *Kyll*, beautifully situated at the foot of the ***Casselburg** (1464), the considerable ruins of which look down into the valley from a wooded basaltic peak, 300 ft. above it. It was originally the seat of the knights of Castelberg, subsequently of the Counts of Manderscheid, and at a later period of the Duke of Aremberg, and is now the property of the state. In the *Försterhaus*, at the entrance to the castle, good and moderate accommodation may be obtained. The summit affords a fine prospect of the Kyllthal.

In the immediate vicinity of the castle, to the N. W., rises a lava cone, the N. base of which eonsists of grauwacke, and the S. of caleareous stone. Between this cone and the Casselburg are deposits of scoriæ and volcanic sand, and on the S. side of the latter the calcareous stone is partly covered with variegated sandstone.

The high and precipitous calcareous rocks (dolomite) on the r. bank of the **Kyllthal*, extending from Pelm to beyond Gerolstein, give a grand and picturesque appearance to the valley; indeed, in more respects than one, this is the finest part of the whole Eifel, and abounds with fossil crabs, coral, and shell-fish, belonging to the period when the whole of this district was covered by the sea. The valley diverging in a S. direction from Pelm to *Gees* is particularly rich in these specimens, which may be purchased from the schoolmaster at Pelm, or Frau Scholz at Gerolstein.

Gerolstein (1218 ft.) (**Schreiber;* carriage to Daun $2\frac{1}{2}$ Thlr.; *Clemen*) is a village built on the narrow strip of land between the rocks and the stream, and is commanded by the ruins of a castle of the Counts of Manderscheid. At the summit of the limestone mountain opposite is a small crater, the *Papenkaul*, from which a narrow stream of lava descends into the Kyllthal, and along the r. side of the valley as far as *Saresdorf*.

About 3 M. farther down the valley, some distanee before reaching **Birresborn,** are situated the *Mineral springs* of the same name, under a roof supported by pillars, on the r. bank of the Kyll. It is the strongest and best-known of the mineral waters of the Eifel, and is celebrated for its salubrious qualities.

On a hill in the Gerolstein wood on the l. bank of the stream (not to be found without a guide), is a hole, the *Brudeldreis*, 2 ft. broad and 1½ ft. deep, from which a stream of carbonic acid gas issues. In wet weather the hole is filled with water, and the gurgling sound of the gas forcing its way up may sometimes be heard 300—400 yds. off. At the margin the bodies of mice, birds, &c., are frequently found suffocated by the powerful fumes of the gas.

According to the plan proposed at p 126, the traveller would now return to Daun, and proceed S. to *Manderscheid*, 9 M. distant. That part of the road which leads through the Lieserthal offers many picturesque points of view. It passes the village of *Gemünden* (1½ M.); the *Maar* (p. 127), on the height to the l., is about 5 min. walk from the road. From this point the ascent of the *Mäuseberg* may be made in less than ½ hr.

Below *Weyersbach* (1½ M.) in the Lieserthal are seen the vast and lofty masses of lava enclosing the village of *Uedersdorf*, which lies 277 ft. above the bed of the Lieser. They are believed to have proceeded from two extinct volcanoes, one to the S. of Uedersdorf, the *Weberlei* (1453 ft.), and the other (1698 ft.) to the N. W.

Manderscheid (1170 ft.) (**Pantenburg*), a village of some importance, lies on the table-land between the *Lieser* and the *Little Kyll*. On the S. side, in a singularly picturesque and striking situation, are two **Castles*, perched on cleft and jagged slate-rocks which rise precipitously from the Lieser. They were the seat of the Counts of Manderscheid (whose family became extinct in 1780), and are still well preserved. In the beauty and grandeur of their situation they are surpassed by none of the castles on the Rhine.

High up in the wood at the back of the castle, a bare spot is visible called the "*Belvedere*," a favorite resort of the inhabitants of the neighbourhood on account of the view which it commands. The ascent occupies nearly 1 hr.: the bridge over the Lieser below must be crossed, and the road followed which gradually ascends through the wood, and at the top crosses the fields in the direction of the church-tower of *Buchholz*; the wood must now be skirted on the S. then in a W. direction, and finally entered. The view from the summit is peculiar and grand, but less picturesque than that from the bridge over the Lieser, or from the N. slopes of the valley. From the Belvedere a footpath descends in the direction of the valley, but it is a very dangerous one, and the traveller should return by the same road to Manderscheid (Diligence from Manderscheid through Wittlich to *Treves;* to *Bonn* through Daun, Kelberg, and Altenahr).

The following path (3 hrs. walk) between Daun and Manderscheid is recommended in preference to the road, as the walk from Manderscheid to the Belvedere (see above) is hereby saved. The pedestrian leaves the high road at Gemünden, and ascends to the l. passing the Gemündener and Weinfelder Tarns. On the E. side of the latter he continues to skirt the height (far below lies the Schalkenmehrer Maar, p. 127), through wood and across moor. In the distance is seen the church-spire of *Buchholz* (see above), but before it is reached two gullies and the villages of *Brockscheid* and *Eckfeld* must be passed. On reaching Buchholz the path to the r. by the church must be taken, leading to a sign-post indicating the way to Manderscheid to the l., and the "Waldweg" to the r., which leads to the *Belvedere*.

The finest and most remarkable point of the volcanic mountains of the Eifel is the *Mosenberg*, 3 M. to the W. of Manderscheid. The mountain with its three peaks cannot be mistaken. About ³/₄ M. from Manderscheid, before descending into the valley of the *Little Kyll*, the traveller must take the road to the l. leading to Bettenfeld, the continuation of which may be distinctly seen on the Mosenberg opposite.

The ***Mosenberg** (1626 ft.) is a long lava-mountain extending from N. to S., and has four craters, the lava-walls of which rise in the most grotesque shapes to the height of 50 ft. The masses of basalt and slag which form the summit have here protruded through the grauwacke to a height of 240 ft. The N. crater was formerly filled with water, but was drained in 1846 and now yields peat. The S. crater has an opening from which a huge lava-stream (³/₄ M. in width) has issued, and may be traced as far as *Horngraben*, where it reaches the bed of the *Little Kyll;* the lava-cliffs here rise perpendicularly to the height of 100 ft. The view is very extensive and well repays the fatigue of the ascent. The village of **Bettenfeld** lies on the table-land 1 M. to the W. of the Mosenberg.

About 1½ M. to the N. of the Mosenberg lies the **Meerfelder Maar**, formerly one of the largest of these volcanic lakes, but now almost entirely drained. The scoriæ and volcanic sand of the Mosenberg extend as far as the heights round the Meerfelder Maar, but may easily be distinguished from the volcanic productions of the latter, being mingled only at one spot. Meerfeld, on the W. side of the Maar, is ³/₄ M. from Bettenfeld, and 3 M. to the W. of Manderscheid.

From the Mosenberg a path leads S. into the valley to *Neumühl* (3 M.), where the *Little Kyll* falls into the *Lieser.* The scenery of the valley, at all times pleasing, at some points reaches almost to grandeur. The pedestrian, as before stated, may effect a saving of 3 M. by taking this road instead of returning to Manderscheid.

The road from Manderscheid to Wittlich (13 1/2 M.; carriage 2 Thlr.), descends in numerous windings to *Neumühl* (3 M.), and ascends the opposite slopes in the same way; it then leads for a short distance through wood and reaches the unfertile moor on the table-land. At the villages of *Gross-* (4 1/2 M.) and *Minder-Litgen* (2 1/4 M.) the land becomes more fertile.

Beyond Minder-Litgen the road winds down into the valley, 3 M. below, but by following a footpath, 1/2 M. from the village, half the distance is saved. The *view over the rich and fertile plain which sinks towards the Moselle, and the mountains of the latter, rendered more picturesque by the red sandstone which here takes the place of the grauwacke, is a pleasant conclusion to the tour.

Wittlich (**Post*), district-town on the Lieser, is situated in a fertile country where tobacco is much cultivated. Diligence twice a day to Treves in 4 hrs.

A good road leads from Wittlich E. through *Bombogen*, where two basaltic cones rise from the plain, to *Uerzig* (* Post) on the Moselle, 6 M. distant.

34. The Rhine from Bingen to Mayence.

The Rheingau.

Railway on the l. bank of the Rhine, see R. 35, to Mayence in 3/4 hr.

Railway on the r. bank of the Rhine, see R. 23. If time permits, it is preferable to ascend by

Steamboat in 2 1/2 hrs. (down in 1 3/4 hr.) to Mayence; piers at Bingen, Eltville and Biebrich, small-boat stations at Rüdesheim, Geisenheim, Oestrich and Walluf.

Pedestrians will be amply repaid by the walk from Rüdesheim to Eltville; this tract, the garden of the Rhine, is replete with interest. If a carriage be employed, the driver should be expressly told to include the castle of Johannisberg in the excursion, otherwise the traveller will lose one of the finest points on the Rhine.

Those who are already acquainted with the banks of the river may vary their tour by proceeding from *Geisenheim* to *Schloss Johannisberg* (1 1/2 M.); thence, passing *Schloss Vollraths*, to *Hallgarten* (3 M.); by the *Steinberg* and across the *Bos* to *Eberbach* (2 1/4 M.); by the Lunatic Asylum of *Eichberg* to *Kiderich* (3 M.); thence to Eltville (1 1/2 M.). The path leads chiefly through vineyards, destitute of shade, but the castle of Johannisberg, the view from the Bos, the monastery of Eberbach and the Gothic chapel at Kiderich will amply reward the pedestrian.

Rüdesheim (**Darmstädter Hof*, R. and L. 1 fl., D. 1 fl., B. 24 kr., A. 18 kr.; **Rheinstein*, an excellent second-class house; *Massmann; *Rheinischer Hof; *Scholl,* confectioner and restaurateur, near the station). The celebrated wine of the place is yielded by the vineyards immediately behind the town. At the lower extremity is situated the castle of ***Brömserburg,** or *Niederburg*, the property of Count Ingelheim. It is a massive rectangular stone tower, 105 ft. long, 83 ft. broad, and 60 ft. high, and is said to have been once a Roman fort. The three vaulted stories belong to the 13th cent. Till the beginning of the 14th cent. it was a residence of the Archbishops of Mayence; subsequently it became the property of the knights of Rüdesheim, and was occupied by the celebrated Brömser family, whose family residence is in the vicinity of the castle, and still well preserved. One of these knights who had distinguished himself by destroying a dragon in the Holy Land, and had escaped out of the hands of the Saracens, vowed that, if he ever returned to Rüdesheim, he would devote his only daughter Gisela to the Church. The latter had during her father's absence formed an attachment to a young knight of a neighbouring castle, and heard with dismay her father's fatal vow. The old crusader was inexorable, and Gisela in a fit of despair threw herself from the tower of the castle into the Rhine. According to popular belief her pale form still hovers about the ruined tower, and her lamentations are heard mingling with the moaning of the wind.

The **Oberburg,** or **Boosenburg,** an old tower to the rear of the *Brömserburg*, was for 300 years the property of the Counts Boos; it now belongs to Count Schönborn.

On the opp. bank of the Rhine rises the *Rochusberg*, surmounted by the *Rochuscapelle*, a conspicuous object in the landscape, at the foot of which is situated the *Villa Landy;* farther on are the villages of *Kempten* and (rail. stat.) *Gaulsheim.*

The clean little town of **Geisenheim** (**Stadt Frankfurt; Wyneken*) contains a handsome red sandstone church of the 15th cent. with a modern portal and openwork Gothic towers. The country residence of the *Zwierlein* family contains a collection of stained glass which deserves inspection. The garden contains about 600 different species of vines. The wine of this district, especially the Rothenberger, is highly esteemed.

On the hill behind Geisenheim, near the village of **Eibingen,** is seen the former nunnery of that name, founded in 1148, secularized in 1802, and again appropriated to divine worship in 1835. Farther to the N. E. are the remnants of another convent, founded in 1390. About $^3/_4$ M. farther N. ($2^1/_4$ M. from Rüdesheim) is the convent of *Marienthal*, picturesquely situated in a forest.

***Schloss Johannisberg,** situate on a vine-clad eminence, 340 ft. above the Rhine, is a conspicuous object in the land-

Rheingau

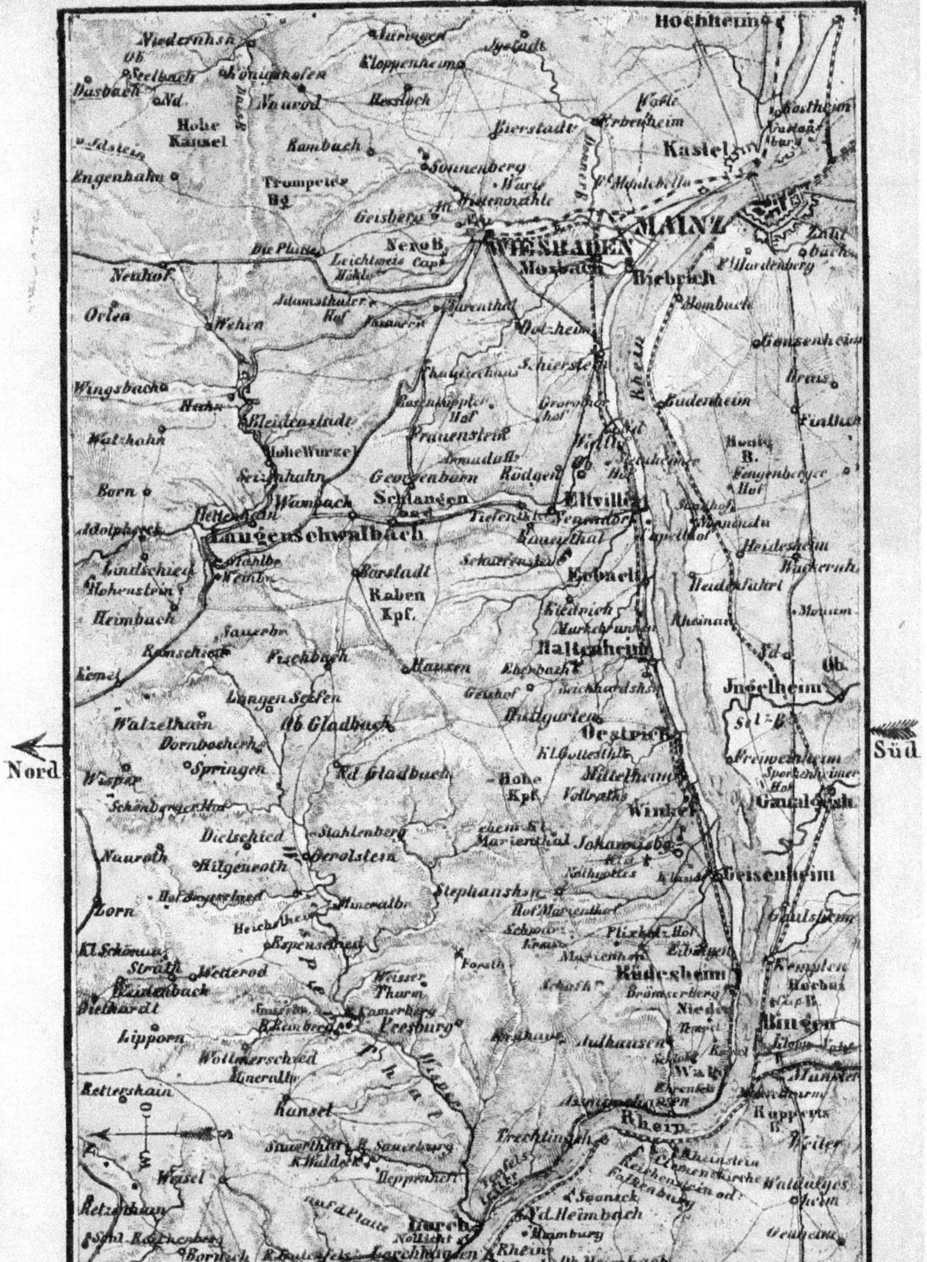

Hochheim
Kastel
Mainz
Wiesbaden
Mosbach
Biebrich
Bierstadt
Erbenheim
Sonnenberg
Kloppenheim
Naurod
Rambach
Heßloch
Igstadt
Königshofen
Niedernhsn
Hohe Kanzel
Engenhahn
Trompeter Bg.
Geisberg
Neroß
Neuhof
Orlen
Wehen
Dotzheim
Schierstein
Rhein
Budenheim
Gonsenheim
Finthen
Wingsbach
Bleidenstadt
Hohe Wurzel
Watzhahn
Born
Wambach
Schlangen
Georgenborn
Frauenstein
Rödgen
Eltville
Langenschwalbach
Adolphseck
Lindschied
Hohenstein
Heimbach
Bärstadt
Raben Kpf.
Rauenthal
Kiedrich
Erbach
Heidesheim
Hattenheim
Fischbach
Hausen
Eberbach
Hallgarten
Oestrich
Ingelheim
Walzelhain
Dornbacherhg.
Springen
Ob. Gladbach
Nd. Gladbach
Hohe Kpf.
Mittelheim
Winkel
Gaualgesh
Nord
Süd
Wispar
Dickschied
Hilgenroth
Stahlenberg
Gerolstein
Johannisbg
Geisenheim
Stephanshsn
Zorn
Espenschied
Strüth
Wetterod
Weisser Thurm
Presburg
Rüdesheim
Bingen
Lipporn
Wollmerschied
Dielkardt
Rettershain
Kunsel
Rhein
Trechtingshsn
Sauerburg
Weisel
Lorch
Nd. Heimbach
Ob. Heimbach
Caub
Bacharach
Stahleck
Nauheim
Oberwesel
Steeg
Mershütte
Stromberg
English miles
1 2 3 4 5 6 7 8
10 Kilomètres

scape, and visible from a great distance: The castle with its two wings was erected in 1716 by the Abbot of Fulda, on the site of a Benedictine convent founded by an Archbishop of Mayence in 1106. On the secularization of the Abbey of Fulda in 1802, the castle became the property of tho Prince of Orange, in 1805 it was presented by Napoleon to the French Marshal Kellermann, and in 1814 it was given by the Emperor of Austria to the late Prince Metternich as an imperial fief. The vineyards, which occupy an area of about 40 acres, and yield an annual income of 6—7000*l.*, are most carefully cultivated, and once took the lead among the vineyards of the Rhine; but of late years there has been a great rivalry between the two estates of Johannisberg and Steinberg, in some years the latter realizing the higher price. The *view from the balcony of the castle is very fine (fee 24 kr.; good Johannisberger in the restaurant at 5 fl. per bottle), and comprises the whole course of the Rhine from Mayence to Bingen. The *Chapel,* founded in the 12th cent., and restored at a more recent date, contains a monument to the eminent historian and tutor to the Prince, *Nic. Vogt,* who died a senator of Frankfurt, but was interred here by his own wish.

At the foot of the Johannisberg lies the "*Klause*" (hermitage), the remnant of an ancient nunnery, founded in the 12th cent. In the vicinity is a hydropathic and pine-cone-bath establishment. Winkel is 1, and Geisenheim $1\frac{1}{2}$ M. distant.

Mittelheim, with the borough of **Winkel** (*Rheingauer Hof*), forms one long street, long enough, according to Goethe, to exhaust the patience of all who traverse it. At the W. extremity is situated a country residence of *M. Brentano-Birkenstock* of Frankfurt, mentioned in Goethe's "Correspondence of a Child", and containing various reminiscenees of the poet

At **Oestrich** (*Iffland*) the inhabitants of the Rheingau formerly swore allegiance to the newly elected Archbishops of Mayence, who came here for the purpose, and were obliged first to confirm the rights and privileges of the land. The village with its projecting crane, and the castle of Johannisberg in the background, forms a most picturesque scene.

On the hill-side behind Oestrich lies the village of **Hallgarten** in the midst of vineyards, and near it the well preserved castle of *Vollraths,* erected about the year 1362 by a member of the family *von Folraz,* in whose possession it continued till a few years age.

Before reaching the village of **Hattenheim** (*Laroche*), the road passes *Schloss Reichartshausen*, situated in a small park (1 M. from Oestrich), once a depôt for the wines of Eberbach, now the seat of Count Schönborn.

Between Hattenheim und Erbach lie the three islands of *Sandau*, *Langwertherau*, and *Rheinau*. On the l. side of the road between these two villages is situated the *Markbrunnen* (or boundary-well) adjacent to which are the vineyards, now intersected by the railway, which yield the Markobrunner, one of the most highly prized Rhenish wines.

Erbach (*Engel; Wallfisch*), mentioned as early as 980, is concealed from the steamboat passenger by the long island of *Rheinau*. At the W. extremity of the village is situated the country residence of the Princess Albrecht of Prussia.

A broad path leads inland from Erbach to the once celebrated and richly endowed Cistercian Abbey of **Eberbach**, founded by St. Bernhard of Clairvaux in 1131, and situated in one of those lonely valleys which this order always selected for the site of their monasteries. Hence the Latin proverb:

Bernardus valles, montes Benedictus amabat,
Oppida Franciscus, celebres Ignatius urbes.

The Abbey was secularized in 1803 and soon afterwards converted into a House of Correction. The building was erected at various periods from the 12th to the 15th cent. The Romanesque convent-church, consecrated in 1186, and recently restored, contains a number of **Monuments*, most of them of Abbots of the 12th—19th cent., and interesting in an artistical as well as historical point of view. The handsome Gothic monument which encloses the gravestones of the Archbishop of Mayence Gerlach (d. 1371) and Adolph II., Count of Nassau (d. 1474), particularly deserves inspection. The *Refectory*, belonging to the 13th cent., is now occupied by wine-presses, and the cellars below are employed by the Duke of Nassau for the celebrated "Cabinet" wines, the most choice production of the vineyards of the Rheingau. In the immediate vicinity is the celebrated **Steinberg** vineyard, carefully cultivated by the industrious monks of Eberbach ever since the end of the 12th cent. It covers an area of upwards of 60 acres, and now belongs to the Duke. The ***Bos** (obsolete word = hill), an eminence close to the monastery, commands a magnificent prospect, embracing the whole of the Steinberg vineyard. To the E. of the Eberbach valley are seen in the distance the handsome buildings of the *Asylum of Eichberg*.

At **Eltville** or **Elfeld** (*Rheingauer Hof; Engel*; *Rheinbahn Hotel*), formerly the capital of the Rheingau, the German king Günther of Schwarzburg resigned his royal dignity, when hard pressed and besieged by his opponent Charles IV. In the 14th and 15th centuries Eltville was a residence of the Archbishops of Mayence, to which they often resorted to escape from civic broils, and contained the archiepiscopal mint. Here too was erected one of the first printing-presses in 1465, 50 years after the first invention of the art, and before the death of Gutenberg. The tall and handsome watch-tower with the arms of the founder, and the adjoining castle-wall are the sole remnants of a castle erected by Balduin, Archbishop of Treves, in 1330, who was at that time High-steward of Mayence; the church-spire belongs to the same date. Eltville is also a favorite residence of several members of the German nobility, whose country-seats give a handsome appearance to the place. Diligence to Schlangenbad and Schwalbach see p. 89.

About 1½ M. to the N. W. lies the large village of **Kiederich** (**Fischer; Pape; Krone*) formerly a favorite resort of pilgrims, where the church of *St. Valentine*, and the * *St. Michaelscapelle*, erected in 1440 in the later Gothic style, restored in 1858, are well worth a visit. Near Kiederich is situated the *Gräfenberg*, one of the most celebrated vineyards of the Rheingau, surmounted by the castle of *Scharfenstein*, erected by the Archbishops of Mayence at the close of the 12th cent., dismantled by the Swedes in 1632, and finally by the French in 1682.

Beyond Eltville several country-residences, situated in carefully kept vineyards, are passed; the island opposite is tastefully laid out as a pleasure-ground. The church-spire of *Rauenthal* is visible on the hills in the background. The *Rauenthaler Höhe (p. 155), one of the finest points of view in the Rheingau, may be reached from Eltville in ½ hr. The road from Eltville or Niederwalluf to *Schlangenbad* and *Schwalbach* unites at *Neudorf* (Krone) with the Biebrich and Schlangenbad high-road.

At the village of **Niederwalluf** (**Schwan; Gartenfeld*), mentioned in an old record as early as 770, the rich wine-tract of the Rheingau terminates. The entire district was in ancient times surrounded by a thick and impenetrable barrier, formed by a belt of trees, 50 yds. in width, planted close together, their branches being so interwoven as to form a gigantic hedge.

At the ancient village of **Schierstein** (*Drei Kronen*), which stands in the midst of one vast orchard, M. Habel, the keeper of the Ducal archives, has a collection of pictures and antiquities which deserves a visit. About 1½ M. inland are situated the ruins of the castle of *Frauenstein* and the village (*Weisses Ross*) of that name.

Biebrich (**Rheinischer Hof; Bellevue; European Hotel;* prices as in Mayence, p. 38; *Krone*, where good beer may be procured; *Löwe*. English Church service on Sundays in the Ducal chapel), which, with the adjoining village of **Mosbach,** forms one town, and is the summer residence of the Duke of Nassau. At the upper end of the town is situated a large new barrack, and at the lower, the Ducal palace, erected in 1706 in the "renaissance" style. The group of statues with which the centre is adorned was much injured in 1793 during the siege of Mayence, by the French batteries on the island of Petersau, whilst the Palace was occupied by Prussian troops. The garden and park, nearly 1 M. in length, are well kept, and abound with beautiful walks. The extensive hot-house, constructed in 1850, containing arbours, seats, and fountains, forms a delightful winter-garden. The small castle in the palace-garden, built in the middle ages on the site of the old imperial palace *Biburk*, once the residence of Louis the Pious, is fitted up in the Gothic style, and contains monuments of the Counts of Katzenelnbogen, brought from the Abbey of Eberbach (p. 136). Biebrich is connected with the Taunus railway by a horse-railway, with Wiesbaden by the Rheingau line, and also by an omnibus (24 kr. with luggage) which runs to meet the steamboats.

Soon after leaving Biebrich the steamboat passes between two islands, that of *Ingelsheimer Au* on the r. and *Petersau* on the l.; on the latter, where he had a summer residence, the emperor Louis the Pious, the son and successor of Charlemagne, expired, June 20th, 840, in the 64th year of his age. His body was conveyed to Metz and there interred.

The steamboat-pier at Mayence is at the lower end of the town, below the bridge of boats, and a considerable distance from the railway station, situated on the Rhine at the upper end. Conveyances etc. see below.

35. Mayence.

Hotels. On the Rhine: *Rhenish Hotel, R. 1, L. 18, B. 36, D. 1 fl. 30, A. 24 kr.; *Hôtel de Hollande, somewhat more moderate; English Hotel; Victoria Hotel. — Hôtel de Cologne; *Hôtel de Mayence, R. 48 kr., D. 1 fl., A. 18 kr., restaurant on the ground-floor; Stadt Coblenz; Hôtel Taunus. — In the town: Karpfen, opp. the post-office; Schützenhof, opp. the cathedral; *Landsberg, Löhrgasse. — In *Castel*, near the station: *Hôtel Barth. R. 1 fl., B. 30, A. 18 kr.; Taunus Hotel, more moderate; both of these hotels are conveniently situated for travellers arriving or departing by the Taunus line. Anker, a good third-class house.

Cafés. Rheinisches Kaffehaus, opposite to the Rhine bridge; near it, Café Français. In the Theaterplatz, Café de Paris.

Restaurants. Volk, in the Emmeransgasse (only in the evening), good wines, game of all kinds according to the season. Rothes Haus, in the Theaterplatz. Café de Paris. Anker (see above), in Castel, Bavarian beer.

Baths, cold and warm, near the railway station. Swimming-bath outside of the Neuthor.

Military music on Wednesdays at 12 o'clock in the Schillerplatz, performed by the band of the Prussian garrison; on Thursdays in the Palace-square by the Austrian band. Once a week, from 5 to 8, military concert in the new Anlage (p. 145).

Railway Stations. Trains for Cologne (R. 36), *Ludwigshafen* (R. 55), *Frankfurt* (by direct way R. 40) and *Darmstadt* (R. 41) start from the Mayence station on the Rhine, at the upper end of the town; for *Frankfurt* and *Wiesbaden* from Castel (p. 167). — Steam ferry-boat, omnibus and carriages from station to station see below.

Steamboats (see Introd.). The steamboats for the *Lower Rhine* have their landing-place below the railway bridge, at Mayence as well as at Castel, where they are in direct correspondence with the Taunus Railway.

Carriages in Mayence. One-horse for $^1/_4$ hr., 1—2 pers. 12 kr., 3—4 pers. 18 kr., by the hour 48 kr. or 1 fl. Two-horse carriage about $^1/_4$ more.

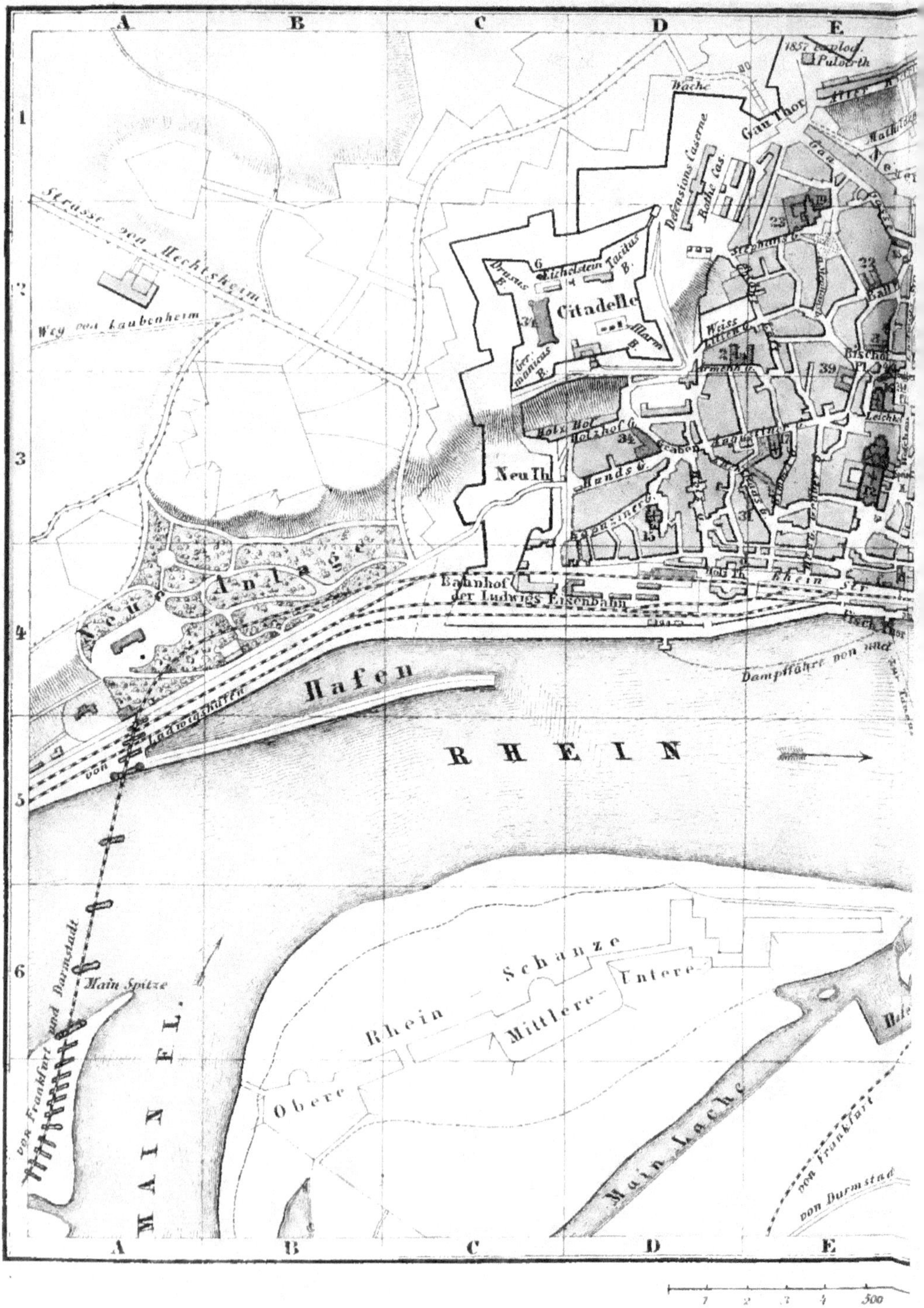

A
B
C
D
E
1
2
3
4
5
6
1857 explod. Pulverth
Wache
Gau Thor
Strasse von Hechtsheim
Weg von Laubenheim
Defensions Caserne
Rothe Cas.
Stephans G.
Citadelle
Drusus B.
Eichelstein
Tacitus B.
Germanicus B.
Alarm B.
Weiss Lilien G.
Bischof Pl.
Holz Hof
Holzhof G.
Augustiner G.
Neu Th.
Hunds G.
Kapuziner G.
Neue Anlage
Bahnhof der Ludwigs Eisenbahn
Holz Th.
Rhein Str.
Fisch Thor
Dampffähre von und
Hafen
RHEIN
Main Spitze
von Frankfurt und Darmstadt
MAIN FL.
Schanze
Obere
Rhein
Mittlere
Untere
Main Lache
von Frankfurt
von Darmstad
1
2
3
4
500

Mainz. Mayence.

1.	Actienbrauerey	F. 1.
2.	Armenhaus u. Waisenhaus	D E. 2
3.	Bischöffl. Pallast	E. 2
4.	Casino (Hof z. Guttenberg)	F. 3
5.	Deutsches Haus	G. 4
6.	Eigelstein	C. 2.
7.	Entbindungs Anst.	G. 2
8.	Fruchthalle	F. 2
9.	Gymnasium	F. 2
10.	Justiz Pallast	F. G. 3
11.	Kaufhaus	F. 4

Kirchen

12	Dom	E. 3.
13	St. Christoph	F. 3
14.	St. Emmeran	F. 2
15	St. Ignatz	D. 3
16	St. Johannes	E. 3
17.	Liebfrauen K.	E. 3
18	St. Peter	G. 3
19	St. Stephan	F. 12
20	St. Quintin	F. 3.

Klöster

21	Carmeliter Schule	F. G. 3 4
22	Engl. Fräulein St.	E. 2
23	Frauenkl. zum guten Hirten	E. 12

Monumente

24	Guttenberg	E. 3.
25	Schiller	F. 2.
26	Regierungs Pall.	F. G. 2.
27	Stadthaus	F. 3
28.	Schloss jetzt Lagerhaus mit: Alterthümer Museum, Bibliothek, Gemälde Saml., Naturalien Cab., Röm. germ. Museum	H. 4.
29	Theater mit der Industriehalle	F. 3
30.	Invalidenhaus	E. 3.
31.	Zuchthaus	D E. 3

Militair Gebäude

32.	Artillerie Direct.	G. 3
33	Artillerie Bauhof	H. 3
34	Casernen	D. 3 G. 3 F. 3. F. 12 C. 2
35.	Festungs Gouvernem.	E. F. 2
36.	Festungs Command.	G. 2
37	Fortifisat. Bauhof	G. H. 2 3.
38	Garnisons Spital	F. 1.
39.	Genie Direct.	E. 2 3.
40	Militair Casse	E. 2 3
41	Zeughaus	G. 4.

Hôtels

a.	Rhein Hof	F. 4.
b.	Holländischer H.	F. 4
c	Englischer	F. G. 4
d.	Kölner	D. 4
f.	Stadt Coblenz	E. 4
h	Karpfen	F. 4
i	Mainzer Hof	F. 4
k.	Landsberg	F. 4

in Castel

l.	Barth	G. 6.
m.	Taunus	G. 6.
n.	Anker	G. 6.

For waiting, half the above charges. Trunk 6 kr., smaller packages free. Bridge-toll (16 kr.) charged extra. — In Castel charges somewhat higher.

Porterage. From the steamboat or station to the hotels on the Rhine: Trunk under 50 lbs. 6 kr., over 50 lbs. 9 kr., smaller packages 3 kr., or several together 6 kr. To *Castel*, see p. 42.

English Church in the Clara Strasse. Chaplain resident.

The **Town-gates are closed** at 10 p.m., and admission is denied to all except travellers arriving by the public conveyances, or persons furnished with a card from the military head-quarters of the town.

The traveller whose time is limited had better inspect the town as follows; Cathedral and monuments (p. 141), Gutenberg monument (p. 143), Eigelstein (s. below), collections in the Palace (p. 144), and spend the evening in the new Anlage (p. 145), in Wiesbaden (p. 149), or in the Palace-garden at Biebrich.

Mayence, or *Mainz,* lies below the confluence of the Main and the Rhine, and is amongst the most interesting of the Rhenish towns in an historical point of view. Its important strategic situation has in all ages attracted the attention of the different nations to whom the Rhine has belonged. As early as B.C. 38, Vipsanius Agrippa caused a camp to be pitched on the spot where Mainz now stands, for the security of his line of defence against the Germanic tribes. In the year B.C. 14, Augustus sent his son-in-law Drusus to the Rhine as commander-in-chief, and to him Mayence owes its foundation. The camp which he pitched was called the *Castellum Magontiacum*, and occupied the whole of the table-land between Mainz and Zahlbach, as is proved by the abundant Roman remains still to be seen in the vicinity of the town. In order the more effectually to secure the passage of the Rhine, a second *Castellum* was soon afterwards constructed on the opposite side of the river by Drusus, from which the present *Castel* derives its origin and name. Many traces have been recently discovered of the four roads which led from the *Castellum Magontiacum* in different directions, and milestones which belonged to them are exhibited with other Roman relics in the Palace (p. 144).

Within the walls of the **Citadel** is the ***Eigelstein,** a monument erected by the 2nd and 14th Legions in honour of Drusus ("*exercitus honorarium tumulum excitavit*". Sueton. Claud. 1.). The name is believed to have been derived from the *aquila* or *aigle*, with which the tower was formerly surmounted. The external masonry has long since disappeared, and the height and form of the monument have undergone many changes. It is now a grey circular mass of stone, 42 ft. in height; the interior was furnished with a spiral stair-case in 1689; the summit commands a view of the town and environs. Cards of admission at the *Platz-Commando* (military head-quarters) in the Schillerstrasse. The visitor is accompanied by a soldier who shows the tower (fee 12 kr.).

Excavations made in the former half of the last century led to the discovery of the hexagonal reservoir which supplied the Roman fortress with water, and was situated near the Gauthor, on the spot now occupied by the "*Entenpfuhl*" (duck-pond). An ***Aqueduct**, of which 62 pillars, some of them 30 ft. in height, still exist, out of the 500 it is said once to have been supported by, conveyed the water to this basin. Remains of the pillars are to be seen near *Zahlbach*, 3/4 M. to the S. W. of Mayence, not far from the *Stahlberg*. In an acacia-plantation on a rising ground to the l., once the burial-ground of the Romans, a number of Roman tombstones have been erected on the spot where they were discovered. The spring which the aqueduct conneeted with the Castrum is called the *Königs-Born*, and is situated at *Finthen* (*Fontanæ*) on the road to Bingen, 5 M. from Mayence.

Mayence, with other places, claims to have been the scene of Constantine's vision of the Cross, as described in his letter to Eusebius, in 311, when he set out with his legions on his expedition against Maxentius. But besides this traditional distinction Mayence may unquestionably claim to be the oldest Archiepiscopal See in Germany, and the English traveller may be interested to know that the first Archbishop was St. Boniface, a native of England, who was raised to this high dignity by Pope Zachary in 746. He is generally called the Apostle of the Germans. It has been erroneously asserted that Boniface was of royal descent, but he was the son of a wheelwright, and so little ashamed of his parentage that he bore wheels in his arms, which out of compliment to him have been invariably assumed by his successors in the See of Mayence. The founder of the Rhenish Towns' Confederation (1254) was a citizen of Mayence, and his native town thus became the central point of this powerful and influential society. It was at that time celebrated for its commercial prosperity, which gained for it the title of the "Golden Mainz." Two centuries later it was deprived of its extensive privileges by the Archbishop Adolf of Nassau, and from that time it lost its freedom and remained subject to the Archiepiscopal jurisdiction.

On Oct. 22nd, 1792, the French republicans under Custine, wearing their red Jacobite caps, entered the town almost without a blow, but it was retaken by the Prussians under Kalkreuth in the following year. It became French in 1797 by the peace of Campo Formio, and was the capital of the department of Donnersberg till 1814, when it was assigned to the Grand-duchy of Hessen. Population 42,000 (7000 Prot., 3000 Jews).

Mayence is the strongest **Fortress** of the German Confederation. It is surrounded by a threefold line of fortifications: 1st, the chief rampart consisting of 14 bastions with the citadel already mentioned; 2nd, a line of advanced forts, connected by glacis; 3d, by still more advanced intrenchments, erected partly by the Prussian, partly by the Austrian engineers, of which the prineipal are the *Weissenauer Lager*, the *Hartenburg*, and the *Binger Thurm*. On the N. side of the town stands the vast *Military Hospital*, facing the Schlossplatz. In time of peace the garrison consists of 3000 Prussian, and a similar number of Austrian troops; in time of war the number is trebled.

The ***Dom,** or Cathedral, was founded in 978 by Archbishop Willigis. Six times it suffered more or less from fire, and on each occasion was restored and enlarged in the style of the age; it therefore affords specimens of the architecture of the 13th, 14th, and 15th centuries, and is in this respeet well worthy of inspection. During the siege of 1793 every thing of a combustible nature in it was destroyed by fire. At the commencement of the French period it served as a hay magazine, but was restored to its sacred uses in 1804. On Nov. 9th, 1813, after the retreat of the French at the battle of Leipsic, 6000 men took up their quarters in the edifice, and again the benches and wood-work became a prey to the flames. During the siege of 1814 it was ignobly employed as a slaughter-house by the garrison, and subsequently as a salt and corn magazine. Since then it has been kept sacred as a place of worship, and is indebted for its restoration to the architect Moller of Darmstadt. The E. round towers belong to the most ancient part of the structure, and the E. fronton and choir to the beginning of the 12th cent.; the W. choir was erected in 1239, and the cloisters in 1412. The octagonal "*Pfarrthurm*" is surmounted by a cupola of cast iron, designed by Möller. The two brazen gates on the N. side, at the entrance from the market place, formerly belonged to the Liebfrauenkirche. The inseriptions which they bear were engraved in 1135, and record the various privileges granted to the town by the Archbishop Adalbert I. out of gratitude for his liberation from the hands of Henry V., and an enumeration of his grievances and the eause of his imprisonment.

The vaulted *Interior* of the ehurch, which rests on 56 pillars, is richer in tombstones and monuments of Electors, Archbishops, and other dignitaries, than any other church in Germany. The most interesting of these are the following, beginning with the aisle on the r., at the N. entrance. (The attendance of the sexton is quite unnecessary). The monument of the Canon von Breidenbach, 1497; von Gablentz, 1572. — N. aisle. On the 1st pillar, the monument of Albert of Brandenburg, Elector of Mainz, and Archbishop of Magdeburg (the statue admirably executed, and said to be a faithful likeness), 1545; in a chapel opposite, the monument of the family of Brendel von Homburg, a well-executed Adoration of the Cross in stone, 1563; on the 4th pillar, Adalbert of Saxony, administrator of the Archbishopric, 1484; on the 6th pillar, opposite to the pulpit, the Elector Dethier of Isenburg, 1482; on the altar at the side, St. Boniface (p. 140), a relief of 1357. — S. aisle. On the 7th pillar, the Elector Damian Hartard v. d. Leien, 1678; on the 4th pillar, the *Elector Berthold von Henneberg, 1504, the finest monument in the cathedral, and said to have been executed at Rome.

On the l. side of the entrance to the cloisters, a stone-tablet is built into the wall, with an inscription to the memory of *Fastrada*, the third wife of Charlemagne, who died at Frankfurt in 794, and was interred in the church of St. Alban's (destroyed in 1552 by the Markgrave Albrecht of Brandenburg), whence the tablet was removed to its present position.

The S. part of the transept contains more modern monuments, amongst which the only object deserving of particular inspection is the fine head of Saturn which surmounts the monument of the Canon von Breidenbach-Bürresheim. The well-executed monument of the Archbishop Conrad II. von Weinsberg belongs to the year 1396.

The Memorie, or Chapter-house, erected in 1248, adjoins the cathedral, and now forms an entrance-hall to the Cloisters, constructed in 1412. The latter are the best preserved of all structures of this description in the Rhineland; they served as a place of exercise for the clergy, and afforded an opportunity for the observance of the monastic rule: "*post cœnam stabis, seu passus mille meabis.*"

The *Memorie* and the recently restored *Cloisters* contain several monuments worthy of note. On the S. wall is **Schwanthaler's monument to Frauenlob*, a female figure decorating a coffin with a wreath, erected by the ladies of Mayence in 1842, in memory of the Minnesänger Count Heinrich von Meissen (d. 1318), surnamed *Frauenlob* (women's praise), "the pious minstrel of the Holy Virgin, and of female virtue and piety." Beyond it, on the E. wall, is a remarkable **Sculpture*, brought in 1839 from the Capuchins' garden, representing the reconciliation of the clergy with the townspeople after the insurrection of 1160, in which the Archbishop Arnold lost his life. Near it is an older tombstone of Frauenlob, erected in 1783, a copy of the original of 1318, which had been accidentally destroyed by some workmen.

The cathedral is open in the morning till 11½ o'clock, and in the afternoon from 2 to 6. The view from the summit of the tower (283 ft.) is similar to that from the Eigelstein, but less extensive than the prospect commanded by the Stephansthurm (p. 145).

Near the cathedral is the *Gutenbergsplatz*, so called by order of Napoleon in 1804. It is adorned with a ***Statue of Gutenberg** (d. 1468) (Pl. 24), designed by the Danish sculptor Thorwaldsen and executed at Paris, the expenses being defrayed by subscriptions from all parts of Europe.

The **Theatre** (Pl. 29) was erected in 1833 by Moller, and is, excepting the instances at Dresden and Carlsruhe, the only modern edifice of the kind, the use of which is indicated by its external form. The **Hall of Industry** in the E. wing is a kind of bazaar, principally of wares manufactured in the place. The furniture and leather goods of Mayence have long enjoyed a high reputation.

The **Fruchthalle** (Pl. 8), or Fruit-market, lies to the W. of the theatre, and is one of the largest buildings of the kind in Germany. The interior can be converted into a concert or ball-room by the addition of a moveable ceiling and floor, and is capable of containing 7—8000 persons.

If the traveller now return to the theatre and follow the broad Ludwigsstrasse in a W. direction, he will reach the **Schillerplatz** (formerly *Thiermarkt*), a rectangle planted with lime-trees, bounded on the S. side by the *Government buildings*, and on the W. by the *Prussian Barracks* and *Military Casino*, where a bronze **Statue of Schiller** was erected in 1862. The pillar of the fountain is said to have been brought from the palace of Charlemagne at Ingelheim, and the Schillerplatz itself was in Roman times the *Forum gentile*, or market-place of the fortress.

(A new, broad street leads from the Schillerplatz to the **Kästrich,** a vine-clad eminence formerly occupied by a powder-magazine, accidentally blown up in 1857, where a new quarter with a terrace, commanding an extensive view of the town and its environs, is in course of construction.)

Near the N. extremity of the Schillerstrasse are the *Government buildings,* passing which and turning to the E., the traveller enters the **Grosse Bleiche**, the longest (800 yds.) street in Mayence, which bounds the old part of the town and leads to the Rhine. On the N. side of this street are situated the *Residence of the Commandant* and the old *Library buildings*. In the small square to the l. is the *Neubrunnen*, a pillar with symbolical reliefs, erected at the commencement of the last century; the base is adorned with representations of river-gods. The building with the gilt horse, farther down the street, formerly the stables of the Electors, is now used as cavalry-barracks.

On the r. at the E. extremity of the street, where it enters the large Palace square, is situated the **Church of St. Peter** (Pl. 18), erected in 1751, and formerly Court-church of the Electors. The interior contains little to interest the traveller.

The **Palace** of the Electors (Pl. 3) forms the N.E. point of the town. It was erected in 1627—1678 and was the residence of the Electors till 1792; during the French war it served as a hay-magazine, and afterwards as a depôt for the cargoes of vessels. It is now occupied by different collections of objects of interest. That of Roman monuments is the richest in Germany. These, as well as the picture-gallery, are open to the public on Wednesdays from 2 to 5, and on Sundays from 9 to 12 o'clock. At other times cards of admission (12 kr.) may be procured at the "Octroi" at the S. side of the building.

The *Roman antiquities consist of altars, votive-tablets, sarcophagi, and tombstones of Roman soldiers with sculptures and inscriptions. — The Roman-Germanic Museum contains upwards of 2000 casts of relics of the Roman-Germanic period down to the time of Charlemagne. The Collection of coins contains between two and three thousand Roman specimens, about 1800 of the town of Mayence from Charlemagne to the fall of the Electorate, and 1500 of modern times. — The Library possesses 100,000 vols., among which are old impressions by Gutenberg, Faust, and Schöffer, dating from 1459—1462. The Natural hist. collection is also one of considerable value, especially the zoological portion.

The *Picture-gallery belongs to the town and the Art-union; the best paintings were presented by Napoleon I. The following by well-known masters are among the most interesting: 1st Room: 98. Cattle by *Snyders*, the figures by *Rubens*; 97. The Duck-stealer, by *Murillo*. 2nd Room: 4. Filial affection, by *Titian*; 75. The Rape of Europa, by *G. Reni*. 3d Room: 185. Woman in the ancient German costume, by the younger *Holbein*; 6. Adam and Eve, by *Albrecht Dürer*; 108—110. St. Hieronymus, Adoration of the infant Jesus, and the young Tobias, three fine pictures by *Gaudenzio Ferrari*. 4th Room: 173. Portrait of a Cardinal, by *Velasquez*. 5th Room: 96. David anointed king by Samuel, by *Rubens*. 7th Room: 5. Adoration of the shepherds, by *Luc. Giordano*; 121. Coronation of the Virgin, by *Agostino Carracci*. The 8th Room contains modern pictures. 9th Room: 27. John in the wilderness, by *Agost. Carracci*; 3. Madonna receiving the scapulary, by *Annib. Carracci*; 92. St. Franciscus, by *Guercino*.

Opposite to the Electoral Palace, to the S., is situated the *House of the Teutonic Order*, now fitted up as a **Grand-ducal Palace** (Pl. 5), connected with which is the **Arsenal** (Pl. 41), containing collections of old armour and weapons, as well as large stores of modern engines of warfare, but of little interest to persons who have visited more important collections. Cards of admission may be procured gratis at the Artillery-office at the corner of the Grosse Bleiche and the Bahnhofstrasse.

On an eminence to the N. W. of the Citadel is situated the **Church of St. Stephen** (Pl. 19), erected in 1318, and restored in 1857. It contains three aisles of nearly equal height, a form rarely seen in the churches of the Rhineland. The octagonal tower (210 ft.), the base of which is 100 ft. above the Rhine, commands the finest view in the whole town. To procure admission the visitor must ring at the door of the N. tower. The interior contains but few objects of interest. The *Cloisters* are remarkable for their tastefully constructed ceilings and windows.

The ***Cemetery,** once the burial-place of the Roman legions, and of the most ancient Christian church (St. Alban's), is situated on an eminence in the vicinity of Zahlbach (p. 140), and deserves a visit on account of the beauty of its situation, as well as of the monuments it contains.

The **Neue Anlage** (* *Voltz's* Restaurant), or new public grounds, are situated on a slight eminence, near the Neuthor, on the site of the electoral *Lustschloss Favorite*, where on July 25th, 1792, the well-known manifesto of the Duke of Brunswick addressed to the French nation was framed by a large assembly of princes. The fine view from the grounds embraces the town, the river, and the Taunus mountains.

The *Mainspitze* (or promontory of the Main), opposite to the Neue Anlage, is occupied by a bombproof fort commanding the two rivers. Near it are the remnants of a hexagonal star-fort, erected by Gustavus Adolphus. At this point the river is crossed by the railway-bridge of the Aschaffenburg-Darmstadt-Mainz line, opened Nov. 22nd, 1862.

Mayence is connected with **Castel** (see p. 167) by a bridge of boats, 740 yds. in length (toll 2 kr.), below which, when the water is low, remnants of pillars may be seen, probably the supports of the wooden bridge built by Charlemagne in 793—803, afterwards ignited by lightning and burned to the water's edge. The greater number of the 17 water-mills are attached to these foundation pillars. Castel is also strongly fortified its, line of fortifications being connected with those of Mayence. By railway from Castel to Wiesbaden in 20 min., to Frankfurt in 1 hr., see p. 166.

36. From Mayence to Cologne.

Railway journey. (Comp. Maps R. R. 24, 15 and 4.)

By the Hessian-Ludwig Railway to Bingen, thence by the Rhenish line to Cologne; by express in 4 hrs. 35 min., by ordinary trains in 5¼—5¾ hrs.; fares: 4 Thlr. 25, 3 Thlr. 15, or 2 Thlr. 10 Sgr. Return tickets are valid for 3 days for the 3d cl., and for 5 days for the 1st and 2nd cl.; passengers provided with the latter may break the journey twice, provided they get their tickets stamped on leaving the carriage. — 50 lbs. of luggage free. — View of the Rhine to the r. only.

The train traverses the fortifications of Mayence, and near stat. *Mombach* passes opp. to *Biebrich* (p. 137). The district between Mayence and Bingen is flat and uninteresting. The first station of importance is

Nieder-Ingelheim (*Post; Löwe; Hirsch*), where a celebrated palace of Charlemagne, described by ancient historians and poets as an edifice of great magnificence, once stood. Mosaics, marble sculptures, and other works of art, were sent in 784 by Pope Hadrian I. from the palace of Ravenna to adorn the building. The granite columns of the fountain at the castle of Heidelberg (p. 183) were once in the palace of Ingelheim, and other relics from it are to be seen at Mayence, Eberbach, &c. At Ingelheim the convocation of the bishops of Mayence, Cologne, and Worms, who dethroned Henry IV., assembled on Dec. 30th, 1105.

An obelisk on the S. side of the village marks the road begun by Charlemagne, and completed by Napoleon. From this point a fine prospect of the entire Rheingau is obtained. The red wines of Ingelheim and *Heidesheim* (*Friederich) opposite to Eltville (p. 136) enjoy a high reputation. In the district between this and Mayence are numerous quarries of limestone, composed of innumerable snail-shells (*Litorinelli*), which is conveyed by the returning coal-barges to the Lower Rhine and Holland, and burned in the numerous lime-kilns on the banks of the river.

On the opposite (r.) bank of the river rises the castle of *Johannisberg* (p. 134). The train now skirts the base of the *Rochusberg* and stops at the station of

Bingen (R. 26), where the finest scenery of the Rhine commences. (For a more minute description of the banks of the river between Bingen and Coblenz see RR. 24, 25). The *Nahe* is now crossed at some distance below the old stone bridge, and **Bingerbrück** (*Hôtel Rheinstein; Ruppertsberg*) reached. Opp. to it is the *Mouse Tower* (p. 105), and in the immediate vicinity, the station of the *Rhine-Nahe* line (R. 27). As the train leaves Bingerbrück, a beautiful retrospective view of the distant Rheingau may be obtained.

From **Bacharach** to Oberwesel, see pp. 101, 100. The delightfully situated town of **Oberwesel** is next reached; station at the upper end of the town, near the *Church.* After passing through two tunnels, the traveller obtains a glimpse of the **Lurlei* (p. 98) on the r. bank. The train now enters a tunnel penetrating the rocks near the "Bank," on emerging from which it stops at

St. Goar (p. 96); beyond the town the base of the ancient fortress of *Rheinfels* is skirted. On the opp. bank, above the village of *Welmich*, rises the *Maus* (p. 96); farther down, the castles of *Liebenstein* and *Sterrenberg*. The station of **Boppard** is in the rear of the town. Beyond Boppard the village of *Osterspay* and the picturesque, white castle of *Liebeneck* are seen on the r. bank. The train next passes through the village of *Brey*, opp. to *Braubach* and the castle of *Marksburg* (p. 93), and the small but ancient town of *Rhense*, beyond which, to the r. is situated the *Königsstuhl* (p. 92). Stat. *Capellen* is situated at the foot of *Stolzenfels*, and opp. to the castle of *Lahneck* and *Oberlahnstein* (railway to Ems and Limburg, see R. 22), with which it is connected by a steam ferry-boat. — Opp. to the island of *Oberwerth* the train quits the bank of the Rhine, skirts the base of *Fort Constantine* and traverses the fortifications of

Coblenz, see R. 20. From the station little or nothing can be seen of the town. As the train crosses the Moselle a fine view is obtained of Ehrenbreitstein to the r., rising above the arches of the stone bridge. At the foot of the fortified *Petersberg*, to the l., is situated the monument of Marceau (p. 80). A pleasing view is now obtained of *Neuwied*, commanded by the château of *Monrepos*, to the r.; above the village of *Weissenthurm*, to the l., rise the monument of General Hoche (p. 67) and the ancient boundary tower. The station of

Neuwied (p. 66) is situated 1 M. from the town, which lies on the opposite bank. The train next crosses the *Nette*, passes the *Netterhof* (p. 67) and stops at the station of

Andernach (p. 65), 3/4 M. distant from the town; the church, the ancient tower and walls are the most conspicuous objects. The *Lunatic Asylum* (l.) was once the Augustine nunnery of St. Thomas. Beyond Andernach the train runs close to the river and commands a beautiful view in both directions; farther on, it passes the *Krahnenberg*, where, on the construction of the line, the remains of a Roman villa were discovered, and intersects the lava-stream of the Fornicher Kopf (p. 65) (to the r. the castle of *Namedy* is visible). Opp. to stat. *Brohl* is situated the church of *Rheinbrohl* (Brohlthal, etc., see R. 19); the train then skirts the base of the castle of *Rheineck* and passes stat. *Nieder-Breisig*, opp. to (r.) the castle of *Arenfels*, where the bank of the river is quitted. The next station is

Sinzig (**Hôtel Baur; Deutsches Haus*) a small and very ancient town, surrounded by high walls, 1½ M. from the river. The ruins of the Franconian palace, afterwards Imperial residence, which stood here, and from which various decrees of Pepin, the emperor Henry III., and others were issued, have been converted into a picturesque modern Gothic villa. The *Helenenberg*, to the l. of the line and S. of the town, derives its name from a tradition that the empress Helena once founded a chapel on it. The handsome **Church*, in the finest transition style, the round predominating, is constructed of tuffstone and dates from the 13th cent. A natural mummy called the "holy Vogt", found in the churchyard 200 years ago, is exhibited in a glass case in one of the chapels. A worthless picture, painted in 1708, alludes to Constantine's vision of the Cross (p. 140), the scene of which, according to some traditions, was at Sinzig. The choir contains a fine winged picture on gold ground by a Dutch master (John Foeten, 1480), restored in 1855. (*Ahrthal*, see R. 17; diligence from Sinzig twice a day to Ahrweiler in 1½ hr., see p. 56).

Remagen (and tbe Apollinarisberg, see pp. 61, 62) is one of the stations (Sinzig the other) for the Valley of the Ahr (R. 17). Here the train re-approaches the river; beautiful retrospective view. Farther on, the scene of the landslip of the *Birgeler Kopf* is intersected by the line, where, as well as at Rolandseck, the peculiar formation of the mountains is exposed to view by the railway cuttings. Beyond the village of *Oberwinter* the train reaches

Rolandseck (* *Railway refreshment-rooms;* magnificent view, see p. 51), a favorite resort of the inhabitants of Bonn and Cologne. — *Mehlem*, the station for *Königswinter* on the r. bank, is ¼ M. from the Rhine; ferry to Königswinter in 5 min.

Most of the handsome residences of **Godesberg** (* *Blinzler*), opposite to the station, belong to wealthy merchants of Cologne, Elberfeld, &c. The *Draischbrunnen*, a weak alkaline, chalybeate spring, was known to the Romans, as is proved by a votive-tablet to Aesculapius, found in the vicinity. Half a mile to the N. of the station, on an eminence (275 ft.), stands the handsome castle-tower (100 ft.). At the foot of the hill a Roman colony is said formerly to have existed, and at the summit a fort, founded by the emperor Julian (360), a temple, and afterwards a Christian church. The castle was erected in the 13th and following centuries by the archbishops of Cologne, principally as a protection against the incursions of the citizens of Cologne (p. 27). In 1583 it was defended by Count Adolf of Neuenahr against the Bavarians, who fought in support of the newly chosen Archbishop Ernst of Bavaria against the deposed Gebhard of Waldburg, who had turned Protestant. They succeeded in storming the castle, and blew it up; the tower alone has escaped destruction. Fine view from the summit. The ruin now belongs to the queen of Prussia.

As Bonn is approached, to the r. stands the **Hochkreuz**, an obelisk 30 ft. in height, erected in 1332—49 to the memory of a knight who fell in a duel at this spot. The train now crosses the Poppelsdorf avenue and enters the station of

Bonn, see R. 14. On leaving the station, the *Cemetery* with its chapel are seen to the r., and the *Kreuzberg* to the l. *Roisdorf* possesses a mineral spring, similar to that of Selters. Near stat. *Sechtem* the wine-growing district terminates. The former royal hunting-residence *Falkenlust*, connected with Brühl by an avenue, is now private property.

Brühl (**Pavillon;* **Belvedere*; **Barion*, on the Cologne road). The train stops opposite to the royal *Palace* of Brühl, a handsome building, erected by the Elector Clemens August in 1728. During the French period Marshal Davoust resided in it for several years, and it was afterwards assigned to the 4th cohort of the French Legion of Honour. For many years it was untenanted and fell to decay, but was restored in 1842 by the late king Fred. William IV. The halls contain old portraits of Rhenish electors and other princes. The garden and park are favorite resorts of the inhabitants of Bonn and Cologne.

After passing stat. *Kalsçheuren*, the train skirts the W. side of the city, passes by the Town Garden and the goods station, traverses the fortifications and a portion of the town, and finally enters the station of

Cologne, see R. 10.

37. Wiesbaden.

(Comp. Map. R. 34)

Hotels. Hôtel Victoria, *Taunus Hotel (R. and L. $1^1/_2$ fl., A. 24 kr.), both near the railway stations. — With baths: *The Four Seasons Hotel, *Eagle, *Rose, *Nassauer Hof, all of the first class. — Hôtel de France, *Grüner Wald (Green Wood), more moderate. — *Table d'hôte in the Cursaal, at 1 o'cl. 1 fl., at 5 o'cl. $1^3/_4$ fl.

There are also numerous **Bathing-establishments:** *European Hotel, at the Kochbrunnen, well fitted up, English Hotel, *Bear, *Römerbad, Engel, *Schwan, Krone, &c. The charges vary with the season. In the Römerbad, for example, from October to April a bedroom is let for

2 fl. per week, in May and September for 5 fl., in June and Aug. for 7 fl., and in July for 9 fl.; a bath in the 7 winter months costs 15 kr., in the 5 summer months 24 kr. Tea and coffee are the only refreshments supplied in these establishments.

Restaurants. *Christmann, Lugenbühl; Restaurant Francais, all in the untere Webersgasse, near the Theaterplatz; Spehner; Café Hartmann; table d'hôte in all during the season. Beer at Christmann's (see above), at the *Bierstadter-Berg, $^1/_2$ M. to the S. E. of the Cursaal, and at Duensings near the station.

Newspapers in the Reading-room of the Cursaal; the guests of the establishment can procure cards of admission gratis from the directors.

Military Concert in the Curgarten from 4 to 6 p.m., and frequently later in the evening by gas-light.

Cursaal. During the height of the season "*Réunions dansantes*" on Saturdays, for which separate cards of admission are necessary. *Concerts* on Fridays, performances by musicians of the highest class; adm. 1—3 fl.

Theatre, 3—5 times a week at $6^1/_2$ o'clock.

Carriages. From the station to the town 1—2 pers. 30, 3-4 pers. 48 kr. (inc. trunk, travelling bag, and hat-box); each additional trunk 6 kr. A drive in the town 1—2 pers. 18, 3—4 pers. 24, $^1/_2$ hr. 24—36, 1 hr. 1 fl. 12—1 fl. 24 kr.; two-horse carriages about $^1/_3$ rd more. To the *Greek Chapel* and back 1 fl. 30—1 fl. 48 kr.; to the *Platte* and back 4—5 fl.; to *Schlangenbad* 5—7 fl.; to *Schwalbach* 6—8 fl.

Donkeys, on the Sonnenberg road, opp. to the Berliner Hof, 30 kr. per hour (inc. fee); to the *Platte* and back 1 fl. 24 kr.

Railway Stations of the Taunus line (R. 40) and the Right-Rhenish or Nassovian line (to Oberlahnstein, Ems, Limburg, Wetzlar, comp. RR. 22, 23) at the E. extremity of the Rheinstrasse.

Telegraph Office Bahnhofstrasse 1.

The **Mineral Waters** are drunk from 5 to 8 a.m., seldom in the evening.

English Church Service is performed by a resident chaplain in the new English church is the Wilhelmstrasse.

Wiesbaden (pop. 20,797, 6022 Rom. Cath.), the capital of the Duchy of Nassau, and principal residence of the Duke, is one of the oldest watering-places in Germany. "*Sunt et Mattiaci in Germania fontes calidi trans Rhenum, quorum haustus triduo fervet*" is the account given by Pliny (*hist. nat. XXXI. 2*) of Wiesbaden. On the *Heidenberg*, which rises to the N. of the town, traces of a Roman fortress (500 ft. in length, and nearly as broad) were discovered in 1838, which according to the inscriptions was garrisoned by the 14th and 22nd Legions. The *Heidenmauer* (heathens' wall), 650 ft. long, 10 ft. high, and 9 ft. thick, among the stones of which fragments of ruined temples, votive-tablets &c. may be recognized, now forms a sort of town-wall on the N. W. side, and was perhaps a connecting line between the fort on the Römerberg and the town. Urns, implements, weapons, and tombstones of Roman soldiers, found here on different occasions, are exhibited in the Museum (p. 152).

Wiesbaden lies on the S. W. spurs of the Taunus mountains, 90 ft. above the Rhine, and is surrounded by handsome villas standing in pleasure-grounds tastefully laid out. These are most numerous in the vicinity of the Cursaal and the railway stations, and are principally designed for the accommodation of visitors. The annual number of strangers who visit Wiesbaden amounts to (1863) 35,000, of whom one-third are passers-through. It also attracts about 1600 winter residents by the various public institutions of art and science it contains. It is needless to say that there is a considerable difference between the summer and winter prices.

On leaving the station (at the S. E. end of the town) the traveller enters the Wilhelmstrasse, planted with trees and about ½ M. in length, bounding the entire E. side of the town. At its extremity on the l., is the *Theaterplatz*, three sides of which are occupied by the *Hotel of the Four Seasons*, the *Hotel Zais*, the *Nassauer Hof*, and the *Theatre;* on the r. is the square in front of the *Cursaal*, embellished with two handsome fountains. On each side of the square are long and spacious colonnades, where every description of fancy article is on sale.

The ***Cursaal** is the chief resort of visitors. The principal hall is embellished with niches containing copies of celebrated antiques. The orchestra galleries are supported by handsome pillars of the red and grey marble of the country. To the r. and l. are spacious and magnificently decorated saloons, dedicated to play(open from 11 a.m. to 11 p.m.), dining, ball, drawing, and reading rooms. To the rear of the building are tastefully laid-out pleasure-grounds, much frequented in the afternoon as a promenade; a good band is in frequent attendance, and the scene is highly animated and gay. In the midst of a fish-pond of considerable size a fountain throws a jet of water upwards of 100 ft. Paths laid out in a delightful grassy dale lead past the *Dietenmühle* (good inn), where a Hydropathic estab. (Dr. Genth, director) has been recently opened, to the ruin of *Sonnenberg* (1½ M.) and the *Rambacher Capelle*, 1½ M. farther, where remains of a Roman camp were excavated in 1859.

The **Kochbrunnen**, or boiling spring, is the most important of the warm springs (156° Fahr.), and is connected with the Curgarten by means of a long iron *Trinkhalle* or Pump-room, in the form of a veranda. The **Hygeia group*, near the spring, was executed by Hoffmann of Wiesbaden in 1850.

The warm spring in the garden of the Adler (Eagle) Hotel is also provided with a pump-room. Another spring (122° Fahr.) in the *Schützenhof* is enclosed in a large vaulted building belonging to the Roman period, where Roman relics have been found. The principal ingredient in the water is chloride of sodium.

The most conspicuous building in the town is the Gothic

Protestant Church with five lofty towers, opposite to the palace, built of polished bricks in 1852—1860. The **Roman Cath. Church** is also a handsome modern structure in the round-arch style, with vaulted network ceiling. The altar-piece to the r., a Madonna and Child is by *Steinle*, that to the l., St. Boniface, by *Rethel.*

The other buildings worthy of note are the *Ducal Palace*, the *Palace of the Dowager Duchess*, constructed in the style of the Alhambra, situated on the height near the Cursaal, and the *Ministerial buildings*, in the Florentine palatial style.

The **Museum** in the so-called "*Schlösschen*" in the Wilhelmstrasse contains a collection of Roman and other antiquities (open to the public Mon., Wed. and Frid. 3—6 p.m.) on the ground-floor, amongst which the Mithras-altar, with remarkably well preserved sculptures, discovered at Heddernheim (*Novus Vicus*) on the Nidda, 4½ M. to the N. W. of Frankfurt, deserves particular inspection. Among the curiosities of the middle ages is a gilded and carved wooden altar of the 13th cent., which formerly belonged to the Abbey of Marienstadt near Hachenburg. On the ground-floor to the r., a *Picture Gallery* (Sun., Mon., Wed. and Frid. 11—4) has begun to be formed. The first floor contains an admirably arranged collection of *objects of Natural History*, especially of geological specimens from the Duchy of Nassau, and Gerning's celebrated *Collection of Insects* (Mon., Wed. and Frid. 2—6, also Wed. 11—1). — The *Library* in the upper story (open on Mon., Wed. and Frid. from 9 to 12 and from 2 to 5). contains some valuable old MSS., among which may be mentioned "The Visions of St. Hildegard", a parchment MS., illuminated with curious miniatures of the 12th cent. and "The Visions of St. Elisabeth of Schönau", with painted and gilt letters.

The *Collection of Antiquities and objects of art* from Italy, the property of Prince Emil v. Wittgenstein, is open to the public Mon., Wed. and Frid. afternoon.

Wiesbaden possesses several excellent educational establishments, the most important of which are the *Chemical Laboratory of Fresenius*, the *Agricultural institution* on the old Geisberg, *Schirm's Commercial School*, the *Grammar School*, &c.

On the *Neroberg*, 1 M. to the N. of the town, where, according to an obscure tradition, the Emperor Nero once had a palace, is situated the ***Russian-Greek Chapel**, erected by the Duke as a Mausoleum for his first wife, the Duchess Elizabeth Michailowna, a Russian princess who died in 1845. From the portal a fine view is obtained of Wiesbaden and Mainz, to the S. the Melibocus, and S. W. the long ridge of the Donnersberg. The Chapel is constructed of sandstone in the form of a Greek cross, and is richly decorated, principally in the round-arch style. It is surmounted by one large, and four smaller cupolas, all richly gilded, on the highest of which is a Russian double cross, 183 ft. from the ground, secured by hanging gilt chains, in the style of the Kremlin at Moscow. The interior consists entirely of marble, white and coloured. A rich Altar-screen (*Ikonostas*), with representations of numerous saints, especially those revered in Russia, separates the choir, which is only accessible to the priests and their attendants, from the body of the chapel. The altar itself, with a Crucifix of crystal, is only visible during divine service. A pentagonal recess on the N. side contains a magnificent monument to the Duchess. The recumbent effigy is of white marble, and rests on a sarcophagus, at the sides of which are statuettes of the 12 Apostles, and at the corners Faith, Hope, Charity, and Immortality, executed by Professor Hopfgarten of Berlin. Divine service, according to the ritual of the Greek church, is performed here every Sunday at 10 a.m., but the public are excluded. At other times the chapel is shown by the sacristan who lives near (fee for 1 pers. 24 kr., for a party of 3—4, 1 fl.). Near the chapel is a well-kept *Russian Burial-ground*, containing several monuments.

About $^3/_4$ M. to the N. W. beyond the chapel is an open temple supported by pillars, which commands a fine view. Promenades and walks of all kinds traverse the wood in every direction, and extend as far as the *Platte* (see below). At the base of the hill on the S. is the *Hydropathic Establishment of Nerothal.*

The ***Cemetery,** on the hill-side opposite to the Neroberg, and 1 M. from the Cursaal, contains many handsome monuments, several of which are Russian. To the r. of the building used for depositing the coffins, stands the monument of the Hanoverian General *von Baring*, the defender of La Haye Sainte at the battle of Waterloo. A fragment of a pillar on the E. wall bears the name of the Polish General *Uminsky* (d. 1851). A chapel is in course of construction over the grave of the *Duchess Pauline* (d. 1856), who, according to her own wish, was interred here.

The ***Platte,** a hunting-residence of the Duke, stands on a height (1511 ft.), about $4^1/_2$ M. to the N. of Wiesbaden, and is frequently visited for the sake of the view. The above-mentioned walks on the *Neroberg* are connected with the Platte, and abundantly provided with signposts. The carriage drive is the old Limburg road. (Far below in the valley to the l. is situated the ancient nunnery of *Clarenthal*, founded in 1296 by the Emperor Adolf of Nassau and his consort Imagina of Limburg; above it, the former *Fasanerie*, or pheasantry). The view from the platform of the building extends over the Westerwald, Spessart, Odenwald, Donnersberg, the entire valley of the Rhinc as far as the Haardt mountains, with Maycnce iu the foreground. The large telescope enables thc spectator distinctly to recognize the people crossing the bridge of boats. The interior of the shooting-box contains no objccts of arts, with the exception of some pictures of animals, hut is appropriately fitted up. Near it is a good inn. The pedestrian may descend from the Platte in a S. E. direction to the Sonnenberg (p. 151) about $3^1/_2$ M. distant. The path leads past an oak plantation to the l. of the high road, and is distinctly visible from the platform. Wicsbaden lics $1^1/_2$ M. to the S. W. of the Sonnenberg.

Wiesbaden is connected with *Mosbach* (p. 137) by a road planted with a quadruple row of horse-chesnuts. Half-way to the village is the *Adolphshöhe*, a rcstaurant, which affords a survey of the Rheingau as far as the Rochuscapellc at Bingen.

Another fine view is obtained from the *Chausseehaus* or Forester's house, on the old Schwalbach road, about 3 M. from Wiesbaden, where the road to Georgenborn and Schlangenbad diverges. — Excursion to the Taunusmountains see R. 40.

38. Schwalbach and Schlangenbad.

(Comp. Map R. 34.)

Hotels in Schwalbach. *Alleesaal; *Post; *Duke of Nassau, R. 1 fl., L. 15, B. 30 kr., D. exc. W. 1 fl. 12 kr.; Taunus Hotel; *Hôtel Wagner; *Russischer Hof, D. 48 kr. in the two latter.

Boarding Houses (without dinner). Among others may be mentioned: Neglein, Kranich (telegr. office and starting point of the Wiesbaden omnibus), Wiener Hof, Stadt Hanau, Einhorn, Victoria, Bellevue, Tivoli (large and well fitted up, but somewhat expensive) Panorama, Widow Grebert, Pariser Hof (dinner), Stadt Coblenz, Englischer Hof. — *Dinner* may be procured from the Duke of Nassau Hotel, Hôtel Wagner, Dieffenbach's Restaurant or the Pariser Hof; price from 1 fl. to 36 kr.

Reading Room in the Alleesaal.

Baths in the Badhaus (from 5 a.m. till $1^1/_2$ p.m., 1 fl.). Kranich, Stadt Mainz, Engl. Hof, Einhorn, Baltzer 54 kr. per bath. *Contribution to the band* 2 fl. for the season.

Carriages and Horses have no fixed charges; donkeys according to a printed tariff.

Diligence to *Wiesbaden* in 2 hrs., at 7 a.m. and $1^1/_4$ p.m., to *Schlangenbad* (in 1 hr.) and *Eltville* (in 2 hrs.) at 8 a.m. and $5^1/_2$ p.m. in summer only; to *Diez* (p. 86) at 8 p.m. in 4 hrs. — Omnibus to *Wiesbaden* at $7^1/_2$ a.m. in $2^1/_2$ hrs.

Telegraph Office in the "Kranich".

English Church Service in the Lutheran Church during the season.

Langen-Schwalbach, commonly called *Schwalbach*, is situated on the Wiesbaden and Coblenz road, $10\frac{1}{2}$ M. to the N. W. of Wiesbaden and 25 M. S. E. of Ems. The three principal springs, the *Stahlbrunnen* in one of the valleys, and the *Wein-* and *Paulinenbrunnen* in the other, are connected by by means of walks and shrubberies. The Bath-establishment is at the Weinbrunnen; the water, which is strongly impregnated with iron and carbonic acid gas, is adapted for internal as well as external use, and is especially efficacious in nervous and female complaints.

The village itself $\frac{3}{4}$ M. in length, is situated in a beautiful wooded ravine. The annual number of visitors is upwards of 3000. The *Paulinenberg*, *Platte*, the ruins of (2 M.) *Adolphseck* (Kling) and (6 M.) *Hohenstein* (Ziemen) are very favorite resorts. — A good road leads from *Schwalbach* through the *Wisperthal* to *Lorch* (21 M.) on the Rhine.

Schwalbach is usually approached from Wiesbaden, from Eltville by Schlangenbad (diligence twice daily) or from Ems (railway to Diez, thence by carriage [no diligence] in 4 hrs.)

The new high-road from *Wiesbaden to Schwalbach* (diligence at $8\frac{1}{2}$ a.m. and 10 p.m. in $2\frac{1}{4}$ hrs., omnibus at $5\frac{1}{2}$ p.m. from the Taunus Hotel, opp. the rail. stations), soon after Wiesbaden is left, quits the old road leading by the Chausseehaus and the *Hohe Wurzel* (1600 ft.), and enters the *Aarthal*, which it follows, passing by *Bleidenstadt*, till *Schwalbach* is reached.

The road from *Biebrich to Schlangenbad and Schwalbach* (carriage to Schlangenbad in $1\frac{1}{2}$, to Schwalbach in $3\frac{1}{4}$ hrs.) leads by *Schierstein* and *Neudorf* (Krone), where it unites with the road from Eltville; it then passes the former convent of *Tiefenthal* (now a mill), and traverses a picturesque valley, enlivened by numerous mills. The pedestrian is recommended to make a circuit of $1\frac{1}{2}$ M. by Rauenthal; about $\frac{1}{4}$ M. beyond Neudorf a signpost indicates the road to the l., leading to **Rauenthal** (*Nassauer Hof*), celebrated for its wine, situated on the ridge of the hill. On leaving the S. side of the village the tourist will see a cross, 50 yds. beyond which he must turn to the r. and then ascend to the l.; in a few minutes he will reach the *Rauenthaler Höhe* (1668 ft.), which commands a magnificent view of the entire Rheingau from Mayence to below Johannisberg, with the handsome buildings of Eltville in the foreground.

On the N. side of Rauenthal a good path leads along the hill-side to Schlangenbad. Those who prefer to return to the high road must turn down to the r. by the signpost, $\frac{1}{4}$ M. from the village, and a descent of $\frac{1}{4}$ hr. more will bring them to the road; $1\frac{1}{2}$ M. farther, **Schlangenbad** ($4\frac{1}{2}$ M. from

Schwalbach) is reached (**Nassauer Hof*, D. 1 fl. 12 kr., R. at fixed rates; *Hôtel Victoria*, D exc. W. 1 fl. — The refreshment rooms in the upper and lower *Curhaus*, and on the terrace, belong to the landlord of the Nassauer Hof). The baths are visited principally by ladies. The water (84°—90° Fahr.), only used externally, is clear and free from odour, and is smooth and oily to the touch; it is most efficacious in skin complaints, convulsive affections, nervous weakness, and similar maladies. For a minute and masterly description of the whole of this locality, the reader is referred to the work of Sir Francis Head, "Bubbles from the Brunnens of Nassau." Suffice it here to say that Schlangenbad, unlike Ems in its circle of hills, is situated in a richly wooded valley, refreshed by a constant current of air, which invigorates the enervated frame. Paths of easy ascent are cut in all directions through the woods, affording enjoyment even to those whose pedestrian powers are limited. Instead of the day being devoted to the excitements of "roulette" and "rouge et noir", it is passed in healthful recreation and the pure enjoyment of exquisite scenery and a delightful and invigorating atmosphere.

According to a tradition the springs were discovered by a cow-herd, 200 years ago, who found his herd diminishing, and going in search of the truant animals found them luxuriating in the warm spring. The Bath establishment was erected by the former lord of the soil, the Landgrave Carl of Hessen-Cassel, and surrounded by pleasure grounds. The terrace at the Curhaus and the grounds connected with it are the only public places of resort for visitors. Schlangenbad also possesses a whey-cure establishment.

From Schlangenbad to Wiesbaden the new carriage-road by Georgenborn (7½ M.) is the best route for pedestrians. The road ascends in an E. direction to **Georgenborn** (1152 ft.). From the highest point a magnificent prospect is enjoyed of the neighbourhood of Frankfurt as far as the confluence of the Main and Rhine, the Rhine from Worms to Bingen, and in the background the Donnersberg. A road leads from the village to the *Chausseehaus* (p. 154), about 2¼ M. distant; thence to Wiesbaden by the old Wiesbaden and Schwalbach road (3¾ M.).

The high-road from Schlangenbad by *Wambach* to Schwalbach (4½ M.) rises considerably for about 2 M., commanding a fine view from the culminating point, and then descends to *Schwalbach.*

39. Frankfurt.

Hotels. Outside of the town, conveniently situated between the Taunus and Main-Weser stations: *Westendhall, R. 1 fl. and upwards, L. 18, B. 30 kr., D. exc. W. 1 fl. 12 kr., A. 24 kr.; also a café-restaurant. In the town: *Hôtel de Russie (of the highest class) and *Roman Emperor, in the Zeil; *Hôtel d'Angleterre, in the Rossmarkt, R. 1½ fl. L. 24,

Fran

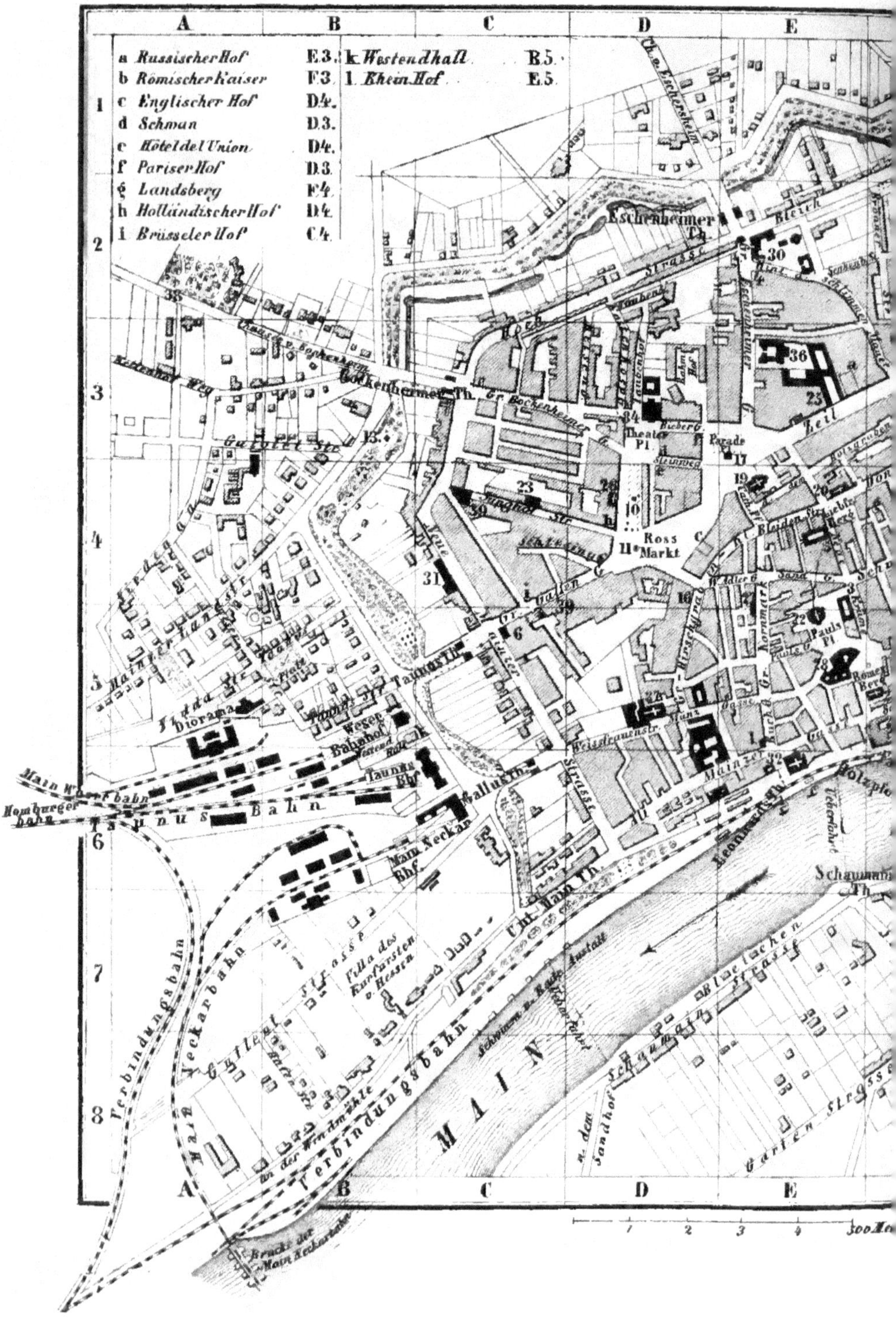

A B C D E
a Russischer Hof E3.
b Römischer Kaiser F3.
c Englischer Hof D4.
d Schwan D3.
e Hôtel de l'Union D4.
f Pariser Hof D3.
g Landsberg F4.
h Holländischer Hof D4.
i Brüsseler Hof C4.
k Westendhall B5.
l Rhein Hof E5.
1 2 3 4 5 6 7 8
Eschenheimer Th.
Bockenheimer Th.
Theater Pl.
Parade
Ross Markt
Pauls Pl.
Diorama
Taunus Bahn
Homburger bahn
Main Weser bahn
Main Neckar Bhf.
Taunus Bhf.
Gallus Th.
Unt. Main Th.
Verbindungsbahn
Main Neckarbahn
Villa des Kurfürsten v. Hessen
An der Windmühle
Gutleut Strasse
MAIN
Schaumain
Garten Strasse
Brücke der Main Neckarbahn
Sandhof
Zeil
Mainzer Thor
Leonhards Th.
Taunus Str.
Mainzer Landstr.
Gr. Bockenheimer G.
Kl. Hirschgr.
Weissfrauenstr.
Holzpforte
1 2 3 4 300 Met

kfurt.

Lith. Ast. v. Ed. Wagner, Darmstdt.

B. 42 kr., D. 1½ fl., A. 30 kr. — *Swan, B. 1 fl., L. 18, B. 18, B. 36, A. 24 kr., excellent table-d'hôte at 1, inc. W. 1 fl. 45 kr., and Hôtel de l'Union (similar prices), near Goethe's monument. — *Holländischer Hof, in the Goethe-Platz, R. 1 fl. 20 kr., L. 18, B. 36, A. 24 kr., at the same time a café-restaurant. *Landsberg, R. 1 fl., L. 18 kr.; good dinner at 1, inc. W. 1 fl. 30, B. 36, A. 18 kr,; Rheinischer Hof, in the Buchgasse; Pariser Hof, in the Paradeplatz, all second-class houses. Grüner Baum, grosse Fischergasse, and Stadt Darmstadt in the same street, very moderate.

Cafés. Milani, next door to the theatre; Holland, in the Goetheplatz; Parrot, next to the Post office; Café neuf, in the Schillerplatz.

Confectioners. Röder, opposite to the Goethe-monument; good ices 12 kr.; Bütschli, kleiner Hirschgraben 8; Knecht. by St. Paul's Church.

Restaurants. Jouy, Gallengasse, good but dear. *Jacoby, in the Stiftsstrasse, near the Zeil; wine good. Westendhall at the Taunus station; Ostendhall at the Bavarian station. Beer may be procured at the following restaurants: *Eysser, by the Main-Weser station; in the town: *Zum Guttenberg in the Gallengasse, not far from the stations.

Newspapers in the Bürgerverein (p. 165).

Theatre (Pl. 34), representations nearly every day.

Railways. *Taunus-line* and *Hessen-Ludwig-line* see R. 40, *Main-Neckar-line*, R. 41, *Main-Weser-line*, for *Homburg* (p. 170). The three stations adjoin each other, and are situated on the W. side of the town. The *Bavarian station* is on the E. side, outside of the Allerheiligenthor. The *Offenbach station* is in Sachsenhausen, on the l. bank of the Main.

Omnibus from the station to the town 12 kr., for each box 6 kr. From the town to the station 6 kr. for a passenger without luggage, 12 kr. for a passenger with ordinary luggage, for each additional box 6 kr.

Fiacres from the station to the town for 1—2 persons with ordinary luggage 24 kr., 3 pers. 30 kr., 4 pers. 36 kr.; for each box 6 kr. By time: (1 horse) for ¼ hr. 1—2 pers. 12 kr., 3—4 pers. 18 kr.; (2 horses) 18 and 24 kr. For longer periods at somewhat reduced rates. N.B. The *unnumbered* vehicles have no fixed tariffs.

Telegraph-offices. The *Frankfurt* and *Prussian* offices are at the Exchange, the *Bavarian* Paulsplatz No. 2. At the *Taunus station* despatches within the limits of this line only are received.

Valets de place 1¾—2 fl. per diem.

Shops, the best in the Zeil. Böhler, Zeil, 54, ornaments of carved stag's horn. Ihlée, Zeil 63, small bronze objects (Ariadne). Antonio Vanni, Kruggasse 8, depôt of casts from antiques and modern sculptures. Jos. Milani, Bleidenstrasse 6, Sartorio, grosser Kornmarkt, fruit-merchants. Toys at Albert's, Zeil 36.

Baths. *Warm-baths* at the Leonhardsthor and at the island, 48 kr. *Cold-baths* at the Untermainthor 12 kr.; also *swimming-bath*, 12—16 kr.

Military music at the W. end of the Zeil at 12 o'clock; on Wednesday at the Goetheplatz. The garrison consists of Austrian, Prussian, Bavarian, and Frankfurt troops.

English Church Service performed every Sunday by a resident chaplain in the French Church in the Goetheplatz.

Collections and Exhibitions:

**Ariadneum* (p. 164), or *Bethmann's Museum*, daily 10—1 o'clock; fee 18—24 kr.

Exhibition of the Art-union (Pl. 23), Junghofstr.; adm. (9—6 o'clock) 30 kr.

Town-library (p. 162). Mond, Wed. and Frid. from 2—4, Tues. and Thurs. from 10—12.

**Diorama* near the Main-Weser-station; adm. 1 fl., or 36 kr.

**Kaisersaal*, in the Römer (p. 159), open from the beginning of May till the end of September, on Mon., Wed. and Frid. from 11—1 o'clock.

Senckenberg natural hist. society (p. 164); the collections open on Wed. 2—4, and Frid. 11—1, gratis; at other times for a fee of 24 kr.

Städel picture-gallery (p. 165) daily 11—1 gratis, at other times for a fee of 30 kr.

**Zoological garden* (p. 166); adm. 30 kr.; concert on Wed., Sat. and Sund.

Those whose time is limited should inspect the Städel Gallery (p. 165), the Kaisersaal (p. 159), the Dom (p. 161), Dannecker's Ariadne (p. 164), the monuments of Goethe, Gutenberg and Schiller.

Frankfurt on the *Main* (Pop. 82,000; 11,000 Rom. Cath. and 4500 Jews) was formerly a free town of the Empire, and is now one of the free towns of the German Confederation, the seat of the Diet, and garrisoned by 4500 troops. Old watch-towers at different points in the vicinity indicate the extent of the ancient city in which the German emperors were formerly elected and crowned. Frankfurt is situated in a spacious plain bounded by mountains, on the river Main, navigable for ships of a considerable size, and forming a source of great commercial advantage to the city, which ranks among the handsomest and most opulent in Germany.

The town is surrounded by the "Anlagen", or public grounds, in which are situated many substantial and tastefully built residences. An air of wealth and importance pervades the entire city, affording a striking indication of the success and extent of its commercial relations.

Frankfurt dates its origin from the time of Charlemagne. In 794 the emperor held a convocation of the bishops and dignitaries of the empire in the royal residence "*Franconofurt*" (ford of the Franks). Louis the Pious granted to the town certain privileges, and from the time of Louis the German it gradually rose to importance. In 1249 Frederick II. sanctioned the Easter Fair. By the Golden Bull of Charles IV. Frankfurt was destined to be the *Town of Election of the German Empire*, and the majority of the emperors were here chosen. After the dissolution of the Empire in 1806, Frankfurt, together with Aschaffenburg, Hanau, Fulda and Wetzlar, was made over as a Grand-duchy to Carl von Dalberg, Primate of the Rhenish Confederation, and formerly Archbishop of Mayence. By the Congress of Vienna it was finally recognized as a free city.

On entering the town the first object which attracts the eye is the ***Monument of Gutenberg**, erected in 1858, a large galvano-plastic group with sandstone pedestal, a work of great merit, executed by Ed. v. d. Launitz. The central figure with the types in the l. hand represents Gutenberg, that on his r. Fust, and on his l. Schöffer. On the frieze are 13 likenesses of celebrated printers, Caxton among others. In the four niches underneath are the arms of the four towns where the art of printing was first principally practised, Mainz, Frankfurt, Venice, and Strasbourg. On four separate pedestals are female figures emblematical of Theology, Poetry, Natural History, and Industry. The heads of four animals, which serve as water-spouts, represent the four quarters of the globe and indicate the universal diffusion of the invention. In the Junghofstr. in the vicinity is the **Permanent Exhibition of Art*.

In the "Allee" bounding the N. side of the town, the ***Monument of Goethe** is a prominent object. The poet in modern costume holds a wreath of laurel in his l. hand. The half-reliefs upon the pedestal are emblematic of Goethe's literary activity. In the front (S. side) are represented Natural Science, Dramatic and Lyric Poetry; on the E. side Orestes and Thoas (Iphigenia), Faust and Mephistopheles; on the N. side to the r. Götz von Berlichingen, Egmont, and Tasso, on the l. the Bride of Corinth, the god and the bayadere, Prometheus, and the Erl-king with his child; on the W. side to the r. Mignon with Wilhelm Meister, and on the l. Hermann and Dorothea.

The house in which Goethe was born (Pl. 16) is in the Hirschgraben, near the Rossmarkt, and has a tablet affixed to it with the inscription: *Johann Wolfgang Goethe was born in this house on the 28th of August, 1749.* The arms over the door, three lyres placed obliquely and a star, were chosen by Goethe's father on his marriage with the daughter of the senator Textor, from their resemblance to a horse-shoe, the grandfather of the poet having been a farrier by trade. In the attics facing the court the poet lived in 1773—75, and there his time was occupied with "Götz" and "Werther"; they were also the scene of those boyish exploits and more serious adventures which render his biography so interesting. The house has been recently purchased by a society ("deutsches Hochstift") and is being suitably restored. Entrance free.

Among edifices possessing an historical interest the ***Römer** (Pl. 28) is entitled to the first mention. It was purchased by the city for a Town-hall in 1405. The lower part serves as a depôt for merchandize during the fairs. On the first floor is the **Kaisersaal* (Imperial Hall), where the newly chosen emperor dined with his electors, and showed himself from the balcony to the people assembled on the Römerberg (p. 160). It was restored in 1840 and embellished with a series of portraits in oil of the emperors. This collection was formed at the expense of princes, societies, and private individuals, to replace the miserable old frescoes which formerly disfigured the walls.

From the Kaisersaal the visitor is conducted into the red-tapestried *Wahlzimmer* (election-room), which has been left in its original condition, and contains a portrait of Leopold II. The senate now holds its meetings here. The allegorical and burlesque ornaments which embellish the ceiling, as well as the entire internal arrangements of the building, date from 1740.

One of the chief objects of interest preserved amongst the archives in this collection is the celebrated Bull of the Emperor Charles IV., known as the "Golden Bull", promulgated at Nürnberg in 1306. It is considered by the Germans as the basis of many of their most highly prized political privileges. "Bulla" was the name originally given to the little ornament worn as a kind of amulet round the necks of the Roman youth, occasionally used as a seal. In course of time the word was applied to the documents themselves, to which impressions of seals in gold, silver, and lead were appended, and the imperious edicts issued from the Vatican, which have sometimes shaken the world, came to be known as Bulls. Golden Bulls are very rare, and those of silver even more so. The British Museum possesses a fine series in lead.

The *Römerberg*, or market-place in front of the Römer, which up to the end of the last century no Jew was permitted to enter, was the scene of those public rejoicings which Goethe so admirably describes in his Life.

His masterly pen depicts to the life the glee of the people, when the Hereditary Marshal rode up, according to the old custom, to a heap of oats and filled a silver-handled measure with the grain for the supply of the imperial stables. The Hereditary Chamberlain next made his appearance with a basin, ewer and towel for the use of his imperial master. That part of the ceremony performed, the Hereditary High-steward raised the popular excitement to a still higher pitch; the dignitary rode through the crowd to the large temporary kitchen erected in the square, and cut a slice from the ox which was roasting whole on this festive occasion, and brought it back in a silver dish for the use of the imperial table. It was now the turn of the Hereditary Cup-bearer to fetch from the fountain some of the wine with which it flowed. The imperial table was thus supplied; upon this all eyes were anxiously strained to catch a glimpse of the Hereditary Grand-treasurer, whose duty was to ride forth and scatter largesse among the people, and finally to throw amongst the eager crowd the richly embroidered purses which had contained the coins, and which were suspended on each side of his saddle in the place of pistol-holsters. The scrambling and jostling which now ensued afforded immense amusement to the spectators, but the scene did not reach its climax till the Emperor and his nobles retired from the balcony, which was the signal for the commencement of the most unbounded ebullitions of extravagance on the part of the populace. Finally a rush was made upon the kitchen, which was speedily demolished, and a fierce onslaught commenced upon the roasting ox.

Behind the Römer is situated the **Church of St. Paul** (Pl. 22), a circular building completed in 1833 in the new Romanesque style, which served in 1848-9 as the session-house for the "German National Assembly for remodelling the Constitution," but was again fitted up as a place of worship in 1852.

Opposite to this church is the **Börse** (Exchange) (Pl. 3), erected in 1844 after the designs of *Stüler* in the round-arch style. The building is of grey sandstone with intermediate layers of red. Two statues, "Hope" by Wendelstätt, and "Prudence" by Zwerger, adorn the E. side. Those on the W. side are emblematical of Commerce by sea and by land, and between them are represented Europe, Asia, Africa, America and Australia, executed by Launitz and Zwerger. The hall of the exchange is in the old Indian style. From eight black marble pillars project eight white fan-like roofs, ornamented with painted bas-reliefs, and terminating at the top in large gilded rosettes. A considerable portion of the mercantile community of Frankfurt assembles here daily from 12 to 2 o'clock, the most animated time being about 1, when the tumult of business attains its highest pitch.

The S. side of the Rõmerberg is bounded by the Gothic **Nicolaikirche** (Pl. 21), a small but elegant structure belonging to the 13th cent., restored in 1847. The altar-piece, executed by Rethel, represents the Resurrection.

A few steps southwards from the Rõmerberg lead the traveller to the **Saalhof** (Pl. 29), a gloomy building of 1717, situated on the Main, the old chapel of which, lately restored, is said to have formed a portion of the ancient palace of the Carlovingian kings. The site of the latter, on the river, a little below this spot, was in 1200 occupied by a chapel of the Virgin, converted in 1219 into the Rom. Cath. church of **St. Leonhard**; the Gothic choir of 1434 was restored in 1808. On the spire may still be seen the imperial eagle, bestowed by Louis the Bavarian in acknowledgment of services rendered to him in defiance of the papal ban. In the chapel on the r. by the choir is an altar-piece representing the liberation of St. Leonhard, painted in 1813 by the Bavarian court-painter Stieler, and presented to the church by Carl von Dalberg.

Retracing his steps to the Rõmerberg, and turning eastwards, the traveller soon reaches the (Rom. Cath.) ***Dom** (St. Bartholomäus. Pl. 8). It was founded in 1238, the choir erected in 1315—18, and the tower (260 ft.), which is still unfinished, in 1415—1512 (admission 6 kr.). The church was restored in 1855, and all the sculpture painted and gilt. Entrance on the N. side. On the wall to the right are tombstones of the families of Holzhausen and Sachsenhausen, equestrian effigies of the 14th cent. At the high-altar the ceremony of the coronation of the emperors was performed by the Elector of Mayence. To the r. is the *Wahlkapelle* (election-chapel), where the electors held their final deliberation, at the entrance to which stands the beautiful monument to the German king, Count Günther von Schwarzburg, who died at Frankfurt in 1349, where he had taken refuge from his opponent Charles IV. The 18 coats of arms on the border belong to the families who erected the monument. The original inscription is in old German, and the new one in Latin. The wall paintings are of 1427, renovated in 1856. The high-altar-piece (by Veit, 1851) represents the coronation of the Virgin. The sacristy to the l. contains a Descent from the Cross, attributed to *Dürer;* and a Holy Family, to *Rubens.* In the chapel on the r. by the choir is a Sepulchre with the sleeping watchmen underneath, an old sculpture of the 13th cent.; next to it is an altar-piece representing St. Bartholomäus, and a small painting (by *Roose*) of the Adoration of the Magi. The cathedral is generally open till 12 o'clock, but visitors are prohibited from walking about during divine service. If the doors are closed, admission may be obtained by ringing at the N. portal (fee 9 kr.; for a party 24 kr.).

On a corner house opposite to the E. side of the cathedral is an old stone effigy of Luther with an inscription. The great reformer is said to have addressed the people from this house, when on his journey to Worms (p. 198).

The churches of *St. Catherine* (Pl. 19), the *Liebfrauenkirche* (Pl. 20), and others, contain no objects of interest.

To the S. E. of the cathedral is the handsome old **Bridge** over the Main, built of red sandstone in the year 1340. The railroad under the first arch connects the E. and W. railway-stations. In the middle of the bridge a statue of Charlemagne, executed in red sandstone by Wendelstätt and Zwerger, was erected in 1844. Near it a cock is seen perched on an iron pole. According to an old tradition, the architect vowed that the first living being which crossed the bridge should be sacrificed to the devil, and a hapless cock became the victim. On the restoration of the bridge in 1740 the architect indulged his exuberant fancy by placing grotesque stone carvings on the W. parapet on the Sachsenhausen side; they represent two artillerymen loading a gun, and beyond them the river-god Moenus.

Beyond the bridge lies **Sachsenhausen,** a suburb of Frankfurt, chiefly inhabited by gardeners and vintners. It was founded by Charlemagne, who assigned it as a residence for the more unruly of the conquered Saxons, from whom the place derives its name. To the l., on the Main, is seen the *Deutsch-Ordenshaus* (Pl. 14), or House of the Teutonic Order (erected 1709). It is with the church the property of the Arch-duke Maximilian, the Grand-master of the Order, and is now employed as a barrack for the Bavarian troops.

On the r. bank of the Main is a row of large barrack-like houses called *Zur schönen Aussicht,* at the upper end of which is situated the **Town-library** (Pl. 2) with the inscription: *Studiis libertati reddita civitas.* The entrance hall contains a *marble statue of Goethe in a sitting posture, executed by P. Marchesi of Milan in 1838, and presented to the library by three citizens of Frankfurt. *Prehn's Picture-gallery* (Tues. and Thurs. 10—12) contains 855 small pictures, most of them copies. The library itself (72,000 vols.) in the upper rooms contains many literary curiosities, as well as several Egyptian, Greek, Roman and German antiquities.

Behind the library is situated the *Fremden-Hospital* (Pl. 15), or Strangers' Hospital, destined for the reception of servants and journeymen; near it is the old *Jewish Burial-place* and *Jews' Hospital*, founded by the Rothsehild family in 1830, at the entranee to the dark and narrow **Judengasse** (Jews' street) with its gloomy, dirty and antiquated houses, its numerous passages and brokers' shops.

As early as the 12th cent. many Jews settled in Frankfurt, but on account of the tyrannical treatment to whieh they were subjected they founded the above mentioned street in 1462, where till 1806 the whole community lived. In the evening, and on Sundays and holidays, this street was closed with gates and bars, and no Jew ventured into any part of the town under a heavy penalty. In spite of this tyrannical and oppressive treatment, many of the denizens of these unwholesome purlieus flourished, and among them the now enormously opulent family of *Rothschild*. Their offiees are now in a eorner house between the Zeil and the Judengasse, not far from the beautiful new *Synagogue* (Pl. 33), built in the oriental style in 1855.

In a N. W. direction from the new synagogue is situated the ***Zeil**, the finest street in Frankfurt, consisting almost exclusively of handsome shops and warehouses, and bounded at the W. end by the *Hauptwache* (chief guard-house), and at the E. by the Police-station.

To the rear of the Hauptwache, in the Schiller (formerly Parade) Platz, stands **Schiller's Monument**, erected in 1864.

Opposite to the Police-station, to the N. W., is the Schäfergasse, in which the *Old Churchyard* is situated, where, to the r. on entering, the tombstone of Goethe's mother may be seen, as well as many others of eminent persons.

In front of the Friedberger Thor stands the **Hessian Monument**, erected by Frederick William II. of Prussia "to the memory of the brave Hessians who fell victorious on this spot, December 2nd, 1792, fighting for their fatherland." It consists of masses of roek heaped together, on which a pillar stands, surmounted by a helmet, sword, and a ram's head, the latter being emblematieal of the attack made by the Hessians on Frankfurt, at that time occupied by the French under Custine. On the sides are brazen tablets recording the names of the fallen, and a Latin inscription announcing that the monument was erected by Fred. William, King of Prussia, "the admiring witness of their bravery."

On the opposite side of the road is situated the ***Ariadneum**, or *Bethmann's Museum* (Pl. 1; admission see p. 157), a circular building lighted from the top, containing amongst various objects of art Dannecker's exquisite group of **Ariadne* on the panther, the artist's master-piece, and deservedly the pride and boast of Frankfurt. The casts in the museum of Achilles, Silenus with the young Bacchus, Germanicus, the Gladiator, Laocoon, Apollo Belvedere, Venus de Medici, and Diana of Versailles, are all taken from the original antiques. Here are also preserved casts of the features of the Emperor Nicholas and the Prince Lichnowsky, who was brutally murdered near this spot during the revolution of 1848.

The road to the l. of the Hessian monument leads to the new ***Cemetery**, about $^1/_2$ M. distant, where the remains of many celebrities of modern times are interred. It contains numerous well executed monuments and tombstones, among which may be mentioned the vault of the *von Bethmann* family (E. side farthest to the l.), which contains an admirable bas-relief by Thorwaldsen, executed at an expense of 34,000 fl., to the memory of a member of the family, who died in consequence of his exertions in rescuing a boy from drowning in the Arno at Florence. The vault being closed, visitors must apply to the sexton, who lives at the gate (fee 30 kr.). Near it is a monument to another member of the same family, a well executed marble relief representing the angel announcing the resurrection to the women.

On the N. side of the cemetery a new burial-ground was laid out in 1845, near the middle of which stands a monument "to those who fell on Sept. 18th, 1848." Among the names recorded on its white marble tablets is that of the murdered Prince Lichnowsky. At the W. end of the enclosure are interred about 30 of those who fell at the barricades on the same occasion; their graves are marked by crosses and inscriptions. Near the latter is a large *Temple*, erected by the Elector William II. (d. 1847) to his consort, the Countess Reichenbach. The S. E. side of the cemetery is bounded by the burying-ground of the Jewish community (open on Tues. and Thurs. afternoons).

If the traveller now retrace his steps, enter the public walks (p. 158), which occupy the place of the old fortifications, and turn to the r., he will reach the *Eschenheimer Thor*, the only gate which has preserved intact its ancient exterior. In the immediate vicinity are the buildings of the **Senckenberg Society** (Pl. 30; adm. see p. 157), which comprise a hospital, anatomical theatre, botanical garden, and contain a considerable collection of natural curiosities, the most valuable of which are those brought by the traveller Rüppel from Egypt, Nubia, Abyssinia, and the Red Sea.

The large house adjoining the above-mentioned buildings was the residence of the Archduke John in 1848-9, in his capacity of Regent of the Empire, and is now the property of the *Bürgerverein* (citizen's club) (Pl. 4), to which strangers may be introduced by a member. The entrance hall contains a good copy of a celebrated portrait of Goethe by Tischbein. The Palace of the Prince of Thurn and Taxis (Pl. 36) in the same street, where the *Diet* now holds its sessions, may be recognized by the sentinels posted at the gates.

One of the handsomest buildings in the town is the new *Saalbau*, erected by the "Deutsches Hochstift" and containing spacious concert and assembly rooms. — The new *Lunatic Asylum*, on the Eschenheimer road, merits the inspection of professional men.

The institution to which Frankfurt is perhaps most indebted for its reputation as a cradle of the fine arts is the ***Städel Art-institute** (Pl. 31; adm. see p. 157) in the Mainzer Strasse, near the railway stations. It was founded by a citizen of Frankfurt, *Joh. Fred. Städel* (d. 1816), who bequeathed his collection of pictures and engravings, his houses and a sum of 1,200,000 florins (100,000*l.*) to the town, for the purpose of founding a School of Art. The latter is frequented by about 200 students, and was formerly under the management of Veit, now under that of Passavant and Steinle. The collection consists of pictures, 30,000 engravings, and drawings by eminent masters, as well as many excellent casts, and is valued at 480,000 fl. (40,000*l.*). The gallery is adorned with many valuable productions of the old masters, especially those acquired since the death of the founder, but the institution is more particularly celebrated for its collection of works by modern artists, which is second to none in the Rhenish cities.

****Städel Gallery** (adm. see p. 157). Catalogues for the use of the public in all the rooms. Entrance hall: Coloured engravings from *Raphael's* paintings in the Vatican at Rome; sketch by *Cornelius* of the Last Judgment, the original of the fresco in the Ludwigskirche at Munich.

1st Room, beginning on the r., Italian School: (N.) 29. Mars and Venus, by *Paolo Veronese*. (W.) 22. Portrait, by *Sebastiano del Piombo*; 25. *Four priests at the throne of the Virgin, by *Moretto*, purchased in 1847 for 35,000 fl. (S.) 36. Mary and Child adored by the infant John, by *Perugino*. (E.) 24. Mary and Child, St. Sebastian, and St. Anthony, by *Moretto*; *28. Portrait of the Doge M. Antonio Memmo by *Tintoretto*. (N.) 42. Mary with John the Baptist and St. Sebastian, by *Innocenzio da Imola*.

2nd Room contains chiefly pictures by modern artists; the following are the most remarkable: (N.) 332. Ezzelin in prison after the battle of Cassano in 1259 exhorted to repentance by monks, by *Lessing*; 332. Alpine scene, by *Funk*; 326. The Tiburtinian Sibyl, by *Steinle*; 336, Daniel in the lions' den, by *Rethel*; 341. Lake scene, by *Pose*. (E.) 334. Landscape scene, house in flames, by *Lessing;* *331. Huss before the Council of Constance, in the background Count Chlum, the friend of the reformer, a large picture occupying almost the entire E. wall, by *Lessing;* 333. Wood landscape, by *Lessing;* 349. Sheepfold, by *Verboeckhoven;* 339. Storm at sea on the Norwegian coast, by *Achenbach.* (N.) 347 (above the door). Norwegian mountain scene, by *Saal.*

3rd Room. * *Overbeck's* celebrated picture of the Triumph of religion in the arts occupies the entire E. wall. Being a most elaborate work, and replete with portraits of eminent persons it must be studied with the aid of the catalogue. (N.) 67. Scenes from the life of John the Baptist, by a pupil of *Roger of Bruges.* (W.) 102. Father with sick child, by *Holbein the Younger.* (S.) 106. *Dürer's* portrait of his father; 106. Portrait, by *Dürer.*

Fresco Room: (N.) 357. The arts introduced into Germany by Christianity, by *Veit.* Casts of the bronze doors of the Baptistery at Florence (which Mich. Angelo said deserved to be the gates of Paradise).

4th. Room contains principally Dutch pictures of no great value. (E.) 122. Child sitting on a stool, by *Rubens.* (N.) 146. Portrait, by *Rembrandt.* (S.) 124. Portrait, by *Van Dyck.* (W.) 145. Portrait, by *Rembrandt.* — The 1st room in the wing of the building contains smaller pictures by older Frankfurt artists, and some Dutch pictures. 2nd Room: 330. The wise and foolish virgins, by *Schadow;* 335. Job and his friends, by *Hübner;* drawings of *Steinle's* "Sermon on the mount" in the chapel of Rheineck (R. 18); scenes from Dante, Ariosto, &c. by *Schnorr.*

The ***Zoological Garden** (adm. see p. 157) is situated on the Boekenheimer road, about $\frac{1}{4}$ M. from the gate. The grounds are tastefully laid out, and eontain a valuable eolleetion of animals, birds, &c.

40. From Frankfurt to Mayence and Wiesbaden.

Taunus Railway. Excursion to the Taunus.

By Railway to Castel (Mayence) in 1 hr.; to Wiesbaden in $1\frac{1}{4}$ hr., Fares to Mayence 1 fl. 48, 1 fl. 9, 42 kr.; to Wiesbaden 2 fl. 15, 1 fl. 24, and 51 kr. Views on the r. Omnibus &c. see p. 32.

Sinee the eompletion (1862) of the railway-bridge at Mayenee, the most direet route (in 1 hr.; fares 1 fl. 54, 1 fl. 12, 45 kr.) to Mayenee is by the *Hessian-Ludwig* railway, viâ *Niederrad*, the *Forsthaus*, with wood-walks, a favorite resort of the Frankfurters, *Schwanheim*, *Keltersbach*, *Raunheim*, *Rüsselsheim* and *Bischoffsheim;* before entering the last of these stations the line unites with the Mayenee-Darmstadt railway; eomp. p. 172.

The *Taunus railway* is one of the oldest in Germany, having been opened in 1838. Immediately on leaving the town the train passes the *Gallenwarte*, one of the towers whieh mark the territory of Frankfurt. Beyond *Bockenheim* the *Nidda*, often mentioned in the history of the French revolutionary war, is crossed, and the busy little Nassovian town of **Höchst** is reaehed. The ehurch of *St. Justinus* at the latter place is interesting in an arehiteetural point of view. It was built in 1090 in the form of a piazza, the Gothic choir added in 1443. By a branch railway from Höchst to Soden (p. 169) in 12 min.; fares: 30, 18, 12 kr.

Stat. **Hattersheim.** As the train proceeds, a good view on the N. side is obtained of the principal peaks of the Taunus, the *Altkönig,* behind it to the r. the *Great Feldberg,* and to the l. the *Little Feldberg* (p. 169). The *Hofheimer Chapel,* much visited by pilgrims, is also a conspicuous object in the landscape.

Near **Flörsheim,** to the r., are situated the handsome buildings of the watering-place of *Weilbach* (sulphur-springs). A pleasing view may be obtained by ascending the "*Kanzel*" (pulpit), a hill surmounted by four trees, 1/2 M. above *Diedenbergen,* and 3 M. to the N. of Weilbach. To the N. are seen the peaks of the Taunus, to the S. the Melibocus, to the S.W. the Donnersberg, a part of the Rheingau, and then the towns of Frankfurt, Worms, Oppenheim, and Mayence; to the N. W. are Johannisberg and the towers of Geisenheim.

The line now traverses the foot of the long range of vine-clad hills of **Hochheim** (*Schwan*), where, in the best vineyards, each plant is not unfrequently valued at a ducat (9s. 6d.). The most potent wine is yielded by the vineyards surrounding the old *Domdechanei* (deanery), now a shooting-box of the Duke of Nassau. At the point where the vineyards of Hochheim begin, stands (close to the line on the r.) a monument in the English-Gothic style, bearing the inscription "*Königin-Victoria-Berg*" (Victoria-Vineyard) in gold letters, and the English arms in silver, erected by the owner, a speculative wine merchant of Mayence, to attract the attention of English travellers.

On entering **Castel** (p. 145), the line intersects the fortifications. Station near the Rhine bridge. *Omnibus* to Mayence, without luggage, 18 kr.; carriage for 1 person 30, for 2 pers. 36, for 3 pers. 42, and for 4 pers. 50 kr.; each box 6 kr.; all these fares include bridge-toll. A steam ferry-boat plies between Castel and Mayence (fares: 4 and 2 kr.), on the arrival of each train. (Tickets for the Taunus line can be procured at the Mayence booking-office). *Porterage* from railway-station to steamboat: each box 6 kr., travelling-bag 3 kr.; from station to carriage 3 kr. for each package, no charge made if the vehicle belong to Castel; from *Castel to Mayence,* for each box 10 kr., travelling-bag 6 kr., several smaller packages together 10 kr.; bridge-toll (2 kr.) is extra.

The train again intersects the fortifications of Castel, and leaving *Fort Montebello* on the l., stops near Biebrich (see p. 137), and a few minutes later at Wiesbaden (see R. 37).

The station (adjoining that of the so-called *Right-Rhenish* line, in contradistinction to the older Rhenish, now *Left-Rhenish* railway) is at the extremity of the *Wilhelmsstrasse*, which consists of new and spacious residences on the l. and an avenue on the r., and terminates in the square in front of the *Cursaal*.

Excursion to the Taunus.

A pedestrian may in two days visit the finest points of this fertile district. Leaving the train at *Hattersheim*, he should first visit *Hofheim* (2¼ M.), inspect the chapel (½ hr.), and then proceed to *Eppstein* (5¼ M.) and its castle; next to *Königstein* (5 M.); in the evening to the castle and the Falkenstein (or with guide from Eppstein to the *Rossert* and Königstein, 7 M.). — Early next morning the traveller should walk to the summit of the *Great Feldberg* (5 M.) by the smaller mountain of the same name; then to the *Altkönig* (3 M.), and back to Königstein (3½ M.); dine, and in the afternoon walk to Soden, about 3 M. distant, and there take the train to *Frankfurt* (½ hr.). — A third day may be well employed in walking from Soden to *Cronthal*, *Cronberg*, *Ober-Ursel*, *Homburg*, a distance of about 10 M.; thence to Bonames, and by rail to Frankfurt. Even in half a day a glimpse of this mountainous district may be obtained by starting from Frankfurt immediately after an early dinner, and proceeding by rail to *Soden* (½ hr.), visit the grounds and bath-establishment, ascend the *Cronberg* (1 hr.), take coffee at the Schützenhof under the chesnut trees, visit the *castle, and, leaving the latter on the N. side, proceed to *Falkenstein* (2 M.), the keys of which are kept in the village at the foot of the hill; walk to *Königstein* (¾ M.); thence on foot or by omnibus to *Soden*, and by train to *Frankfurt* in ½ hr.

The road from stat. **Hattersheim** (**Nassauer Hof*) on the Taunus line to *Hofheim* is destitute of shade, but the view from the *Chapel* (p. 167) well repays the ascent.

The road through the *Lorsbacher Valley* to Eppstein passes through luxuriant meadows, carpeted with flowers, enclosed by shady slopes, and watered by the rapid *Schwarzbach*. At the extremity of the valley, above the old village of **Eppstein**, the castle of the same name is seen situated on a precipitous rock. It was in ancient times the seat of a powerful family, which numbered among its members five archbishops and electors of Mayence between the years 1059—1284. The Protestant church contains several monuments of the family, which became extinct in 1535. The castle is now in private hands, and the grounds connected with it are tastefully laid out. Near Eppstein is the inn *Zur Oelmühle*, charges as in Frankfurt.

The ***Rossert** (1563 ft.) may be ascended best from the Eppstein side, and affords a fine prospect of the valleys of the Rhine and Main.

The road from Eppstein to Königstein leads through a picturesque mountain ravine to *Fischbach* (1½ M.) after which it crosses a high table-land as far as *Schneidhain* (2 M.), and then ascends to **Kœnigstein** (**Löwe*), 1½ M. farther. Above the village are the ruins of the fortress of the same name (1321 ft.), demolished by the French in 1596. From 1581 it

Taunus

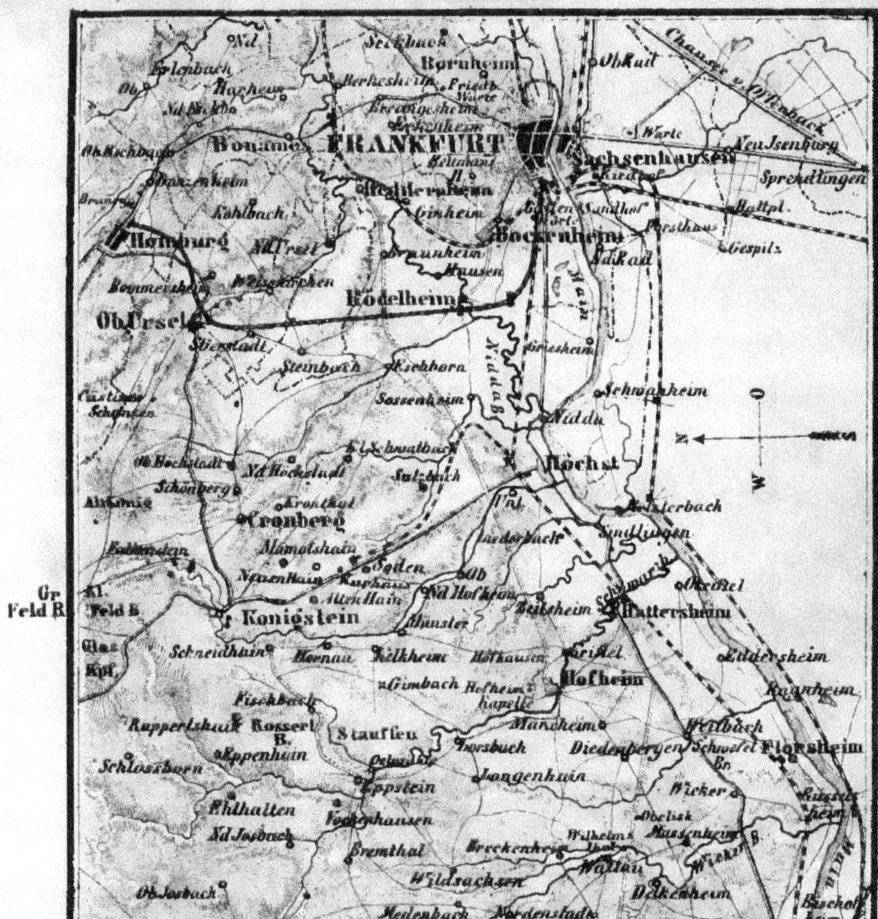

Bornheim
Bonames
FRANKFURT
Sachsenhausen
Neu Isenburg
Sprendlingen
Homburg
Bockenheim
Rödelheim
Ob. Ursel
Steinbach
Eschborn
Sossenheim
Schwanheim
Nidda
Höchst
Chaussee v. Offenbach
Main
Nidda B.
Cronberg
Soden
Königstein
Hattersheim
Hofheim
Eddersheim
Flörsheim
Staufsen
Eppstein
Langenhain
Wallau
Delkenheim
Hochheim
Bischofheim
Nordenstadt
Kloppenheim
Erbenheim
Kastel
Sonnenberg
Rambach
Bierstadt
MAINZ
WIESBADEN
Biebrich
Mosbach
Schierstein
Frauenstein
Budenheim
Gonsenheim
Finthen
Neuhof
Wehen
Orlen
Engenhahn
Rhein
Gr Feld B.
Kl. Feld B.
Schlossborn
Ruppertshain
Rossert B.
Fischbach
Eppenhain
Ehlhalten
Kelkheim
Hornau
Schneidhain
Medenbach
Wildsachsen
Bremthal
Breckenheim
Diedenbergen
Marxheim
Zeilsheim
Kriftel
Okriftel
Sindlingen
Kelsterbach
Schwalbach
Sulzbach
Kronthal
Schönberg
Mammolshain
Neuenhain
Altenhain
Münster
Naurod
Niedernhausen
Königshofen
Igstadt
Mombach
Walluf
Geisberg
Nerob.
English miles

belonged to the eleetors of Mayenee, whose arms may still be seen above the entrance. After the re-eapture of Mayenee in 1753 (R. 31), the eastle was employed as a state-prison. The platform affords a similar *view to that from the Falkenstein (see below). The Duke of Nassau possesses a handsome villa in the vieinity. Hydropathic estab. Omnibus to Soden see p. 168; diligenee to Höehst 3 times daily.

About 1½ M. to the E., the ruined eastle of *Falkenstein* (1532 ft.) erowns the summit of a well wooded hill, and eommands a fine view. It was the family possession of the powerful arehbishop Kuno of Treves (R. 40), and was built at the commeneement of the 13th eent.

Guide to the Feldberg 40 kr.; donkey with guide 1 fl. 12 kr., or, ineluding the eastle of Falkenstein, 1 fl. 24 kr. (The services of a guide may however be easily dispensed with). About 1½ M. from Königstein the pedestrian must leave the Frankfurt and Limburg road, and turn to the r., eross the *Little Feldberg* (2547 ft.), about 1 hour's walk, and in ¼ hr. more the ***Great Feldberg** (2708 ft.) is reaehed. It is the highest peak of the Taunus; the summit consists of quartzose roek, and the slopes of tale and elay-slate. In fine weather the view from the top is very extensive; it eomprehends the Rhine and the Main to the E. as far as the Inselsberg, the Rhöngebirge, and Spessart; to the S. Melibocus, Königsstuhl, Mereurius near Baden, and the Vosges; to the W. the Donnersberg, Hunnsrüek, and the mountains of the Moselle; to the N. the Seven Mountains and those of Westphalia. Refreshments and if need be, a night's lodging may be proeured at the "Feldberghaus." The bloek of quartz whieh crowns the summit is mentioned in an old doeument as early as 812, under the name of *Brunhildenstein*. A triangular stone plaeed here indieates the frontiers of Nassau, Frankfurt, and Hessen-Homburg. On the declivity the ruin of *Ober-Reiffenberg* is situated. (From the Feldberg to Homburg with guide in 3 hrs.)

The **Altkönig** (2428 ft.) is 1¼ hour's walk to the N. of the Great Feldberg. The ascent is somewhat fatiguing, but possesses considerable interest for the antiquarian. The summit is surrounded by a gigantie double wall, eonstructed of loose stones, erroneously aseribed to the Romans, but more probably ereeted by the aneient inhabitants of the country as a plaee of refuge in time of war. The higher of the walls is in a good state of preservation.

A good road deseends S. from Königstein to **Soden** (* *Hôtel Franz* near the Curhaus; * *Europ. Hof*, hotel and bath-estab.; *Frankfurter Hof*, a quiet house; *Holländ. Hof; Hôtel garni zum Stolzenfels*), 3¾ M. distant. It is a flourishing little watering-place (3000 patients annually) with handsome *Curhaus* and tastefully-arranged gardens and grounds. The villas in the environs, most of them in the Swiss style, belong to citizens of Frankfurt. Omnibus between Königstein and Soden in the morning only; diligence between Soden and Königstein 3 times daily in 35 min., fare 18 kr.; between Höchst and Königstein 3 times daily, fare 35 kr. Railway between Soden and Höchst see p. 168.

About 2 M. to the E. of Königstein is situated the **Cronberg** (**Schützenhof*), celebrated for the productiveness of its orchards. The castle above the town, a ruin of considerable extent, commands a magnificent *view of the surrounding mountains and plain; it well repays the ascent to the summit of the tower, which is accomplished by 132 wooden steps (the adventurous scrambler may reach the highest point of the belfry by means of a ladder). Königsberg, or Cronberg, being both situated in the heart of the Taunus, are the best head-quarters for pedestrians who desire to become better acquainted with this beautiful mountain district. Omnibus 3 times daily to Weisskirchen, stat. on the Homburg railway. The mineral baths of **Cronthal** (1¼ M. to the S.), now little frequented, are delightfully situated in the midst of a chesnut grove, and are noted for the salubrity of the air. Rooms 5 fl. and upwards per week; table d'hôte 42 kr.

About 10 M. to the E. of Königstein or Soden lies **Homburg** *(Four Seasons, Russian, English, Imperial,* and *Hessian Hotels)*, the capital of the Landgrafschaft of Hessen-Homburg, and of late years a much frequented watering-place (average annual number of visitors 8000). It is situated on one of the hills at the foot of the Great Feldberg, and is, independently of the baths, a place of no importance. The activity of the place is almost entirely centred in the * *Curhaus* and avenues which lead to the chalybeate springs, ¾ M. distant.

The palace of the Landgrave of Hessen-Homburg is situated here, but, with the exception of some family portraits and a small collection of Roman relics found at the Saalburg, contains nothing worthy of note.

For the antiquarian, the **Saalburg** is an object of considerable interest. It is the remnant of an old Roman fort, situated on a wooded ridge of the Taunus (1304 ft.), about 5 M. to the N. of Homburg, a few hundred yds. to the l. of the road to Usingen. It belonged to the extensive line of fortifications, known under the name of *Limes imp. Rom.*, which protected the Roman possessions from the incursions of the Germans, and was undoubtedly built by Germanicus to replace that erected by Drusus, destroyed A.D. 9, after the defeat of Varus *(posito castello super vestigia paterni praesidii in monte Tauno expeditum exercitum in Cattos rapit. Taciti Annal. I. 36)*. Ptolemy mentions it as *Arctaunon*. It consists of a square, 705 ft. by 465 ft., with rounded corners, and surrounded by two deep fosses. In the centre stands the *Prætorium*, 153 ft. by 132 ft., with foundations of sandstone;

here are also two large blocks of sandstone forming the pedestal of a large bronze statue, traces of which were found among the ruins some years ago.

By railway from Homburg to Frankfurt in $^3/_4$ hr.; fares 1 fl., 36 kr., 21 kr.

41. From Frankfurt to Heidelberg.

Main-Neckar line. Station to the S. of the Taunus station (p. 157). To Darmstadt in $^1/_4$ hr., to Heidelberg in 2 hrs. more. Fares to Darmstadt 1 fl. 6, 42, and 30 kr.; to Heidelberg 3 fl. 33, 2 fl. 21, and 1 fl. 33 kr.; to Mannheim in the same time and at the same fares as to Heidelberg. Exp. trains dearer. Omnibus &c. see p. 32. The seats on the E. (left) side of the train should be selected for the sake of the view.

As soon as the train has crossed the Main bridge, it diverges to the l. on the Offenbach branch, and passes (l.) the castle-like farm-house of Herr von Bethmann. The country between Frankfurt and Darmstadt presents few features of interest.

Darmstadt (* *Traube*, R. and A. 1 fl. 6, B. 36 kr.; *Darmstädter Hof; Hôtel Köhler*, the nearest to the station; **Alte Post*, opp. to the Palace; **Stengel's Café*, opp. to the stat.), the capital and residence of the court of the Grand-duchy of Hessen, with a pop. of 32,000 (2500 Rom. Cath.), was up to the close of the 18th cent. the capital of the Grafschaft of Katzenelnbogen, and a place of no importance. The Grand-duke Ludwig I. (d. 1830) erected the new part of the town with its broad streets and handsome houses, and to him alone Darmstadt is indebted for its present prosperity. In 1844 the *Ludwigsdenkmal* was erected by his "grateful people" to the memory of this prince. The summit of the column (fee 18 kr.) commands a good view of the town and its environs, but the surrounding country is flat and uninteresting.

The *Schloss*, the greater part of which was erected about the middle of the last century, is situated at the extremity of the Rheinstrasse, which leads from the station into the town. It contains a valuable *Library* of 200,000 vols. as well as some MSS. and typographical curiosities (open to the public 9—12 a. m. and 2–4 p. m.). The collections of pictures, relics, costumes, coins, &c. are open on Tues., Thurs., and Sund. 10—12; admission at other times may be procured for a fee of 1 fl.

The ***Picture-gallery**, in the upper story of the palace, contains about 700 paintings, many of them of considerable value. 1st Room. 79 The Castle of Heidelberg, by *Schirmer;* 666. Sunset, by *Lessing.* — 2nd Room. (W.) unnumbered: Landscape, by *Chr. Morgenstern;* The treachery of Judas, by *C. H. Hoffmann.* — 3rd Room. Old German School: 136. The dying Mary, by *Schoreel.* (N.) 201. Portrait, by *Holbein.* (E.) 672. Madonna, by *Memling.* — 4th Room. Dutch pictures: 678. Portrait of the painter Erasmus Quellyn, by *Van Dyck;* 419. Christ scourged, by *Rembrandt.* (W.) 284.

Nymphs of Diana returning from the chase, by *Rembrandt;* the nymph with the red robe is a portrait of the painter's first, and the nymph with the hares of his secoud wife; 686. Portrait, by *Van Dyck.* — 5th Room. 691, 692. Portraits by *Van Dyck;* 366. Portrait, by *Rembrandt* of his second wife. — 6th Room. (N.) 420. Portrait, by *Van der Helst;* 271. Woman combing a boy's hair, by *Rembrandt;* 415. Madonna, by *Van Dyck.* — 7th Room. French pictures of no great value. — 8th Room. (N.) 558. Sleeping Venus, by *Titian.* — 9th Room. 594. Carthusian monk, by *Titian;* 572. St. Michael, by *Raphael;* 573. Peter's denial, by *Domenichino;* 580. Portrait by *Titian.* (E.) 592. St. Franciscus, by *Guercino;* 628. Sketches of the "Marriage at Cana" in the Louvre, by *Paolo Veronese.* (N.) St. John, by *Raphael.* — The adjoining room contains a cabinet of natural history, with a valuable collection of fossils and skeletons of antediluvian animals, among others that of a mastodon, found at Eppelsheim, in Rhenish Hessen.

In the middle story; 1st Room. Roman antiquities. *Mosaic pavement of a Roman bath, dug up at Vilbel in 1849. — 2nd Room. Carved ivory and alabaster ornaments, coins, &c. — 3rd Room. Armour and weapons. — 4th Room. Model of the Schloss, ancient costumes, &c. — 5th Room. Drawings and engravings.

"It is not saying too much to assert that masterpieces of art, and curiosities of all conntries and all ages are here to be met with." Goethe, 1814.

To the N. of the Palace is the *Herrengarten*, consisting of public grounds and walks. To the r. on entering it is the *Theatre*, and to the l. the *Exercierhaus*, now a military magazine. Between these two buildings are erected statues of the Landgrave *Philip the Generous* (d. 1567) and his son *George I.* (d. 1590), the founder of the Grand-ducal family. In the *Herrengarten* to the r. is a mound railed in and surrounded by shrubs, under which rest the remains of the Landgravine Henrietta Carolina (d. 1774), mother of the queen of Fred. William II. of Prussia; the unpretending urn erected on the spot by Frederick the Great bears the inscription: "*Femina sexu, ingenio vir.*"

To the E. of Darmstadt are beautiful and extensive woods and plantations. Picturesque walks (N. E.) to the shooting-box and park of *Kranichstein* (3 M.); (S. E.) to the *Ludwigseiche*, or Ludwig's oak ($4^1/_2$ M.), which commands an extensive view of the Odenwald, Spessart, Vogelsberg, Taunus, and Melibocus; (S.) to the *Ludwigshöhe* and *Marienhöhe* (2 M.), and to **Frankenstein* ($7^1/_2$ M.)

From Darmstadt to Mayence direct by rail. in 1 hr. Fares 1 fl. 42 kr., 1 fl., and 39 kr. Country flat and uninteresting. The Rhine is crossed above the influx of the Main by the handsome new bridge, completed in 1862.

On the mountains to the l. of the station *Eberstadt* stands the stately ruin of *Frankenstein*, and beyond *Bickenbach* (p. 175), the zinc-covered tower of the *Alsbacher Schloss*.

At the station of **Zwingenberg** (**Löwe*, R. 36, B. 18 kr.) commences the picturesque Bergstrasse, leading to Heidelberg.

The ***Bergstrasse** runs through orchards and pleasant villages along a range of hills, partly wooded and partly covered with vineyards, on which here and there are situated ruined castles. To the W. between the road and the Rhine, a distance of 10—12 M., is extended a wide and fertile plain. Though wanting in water, tbis district is one of the most beautiful in Germany, but the traveller will scarcely be able to appreciate it from the windows of a railway-carriage. The name of "Bergstrasse" is given to the W. slopes of the Odenwald, and is not confined to the road (*Strasse*). One of the highest points is tbe ***Melibocus**, or **Malchen** (1630 ft.) The ascent from

Zwingenberg is easy (1 hr.), and should be undertaken. Guide (unnecessary) 24 kr., or for the whole day 1 fl. The excursion may also be made by carriage (4 fl.); if the traveller desire, he may then drive on to the Felsberg (p. 175), and back by Reichenbach (p. 176) to Zwingenberg (6 fl.). — Pedestrians may easily make the ascent without a guide by attending to the following directions: The road leads E. from the *Löwe* at Zwingenberg and ascends the hill, then to the r., following the water-conduit for about 8 min; a good path then leads over the *Luzieberg*; in 25 min. more the carriage-road, furnished with direction-posts, is regained. Where the high wood terminates, a path leads to the l., by a young beech-wood, to the tower (80 ft.) on the summit, erected in 1777 by Ludwig IX., Landgrave of Hessen.

The Melibocus consists entirely of granite. The view embraces the valley of the Rhine from Speyer to Mayence, the Vosges, and the Donnersberg; the Main as far as the Taunus and Vogelsberg. A little to the W. of, and some 20 ft. lower than the tower is the best point of view, which commands a prospect of the entire plain from Mannheim to Darmstadt. The keys of tower must be procured at the forester's (Heyl) at Zwingenberg; in fine weather he is generally on the spot (fee for 1 pers. 9 kr., for a party 30 kr.). — From the Melibocus to the Auerbacher Schloss direct in 3/4 hr.

The next station is **Auerbach** (**Krone*, R. 48 kr., weekly 3—4 fl., B. 20, D. 48 kr., a pleasant resting-place; *Nack's* restaurant at the mill in the middle of the village, and at the "Schloss" in favourable weather; refreshments at the *Fürstenlager*), a picturesque village with a small castle and park in the vicinity, the property of the Grand-duke. This place is a favorite summer resort of families from the neighbouring towns, and even from the N. of Germany; good head-quarters for pedestrians who wish to explore the Bergstrasse and the W. part of the Odenwald (p. 175).

The **Auerbacher Schloss* (2 M. from the Melibocus, same distance from Auerbach) is situated on an eminence (1024 ft.), and is said to have been founded by Charlemagne. It was afterwards the property of the monastery of Lorsch (see p. 174), and then of the Electorate of Mayence. In 1674 it was taken and blown up by Turenne, but the two towers stood till 1806, when one of them fell, and was rebuilt in 1852. In the castle-yard a number of old Hessian warriors held a festival in 1840 to commemorate the campaigns in which they had served together from 1792 to 1815, principally under their leader Prince Emil; this event is recorded by a stone tablet on the wall. The view is less extensive but more picturesque than that from the Melibocus. The custodian (usually on the spot) opens the tower-gate (fee 9—30 kr.).

A broad road leads through a beech-wood from the castle to the *Hochstädter Valley*, by a mineral spring and a mill, to the *Neun Aussichten* (9 views), the *Champignon*, and the *Fürstenlager* (3½ M.); thence to *Schönberg* (1½ M.), from which a delightful view may obtained from the castle-garden and church. From Schönberg through the valley of the same name to Bensheim (1½ M.)

Bensheim (*Sonne; Post*), a busy little town in a picturesque situation, besieged in vain during eleven days in 1504 by the Landgrave of Hessen and the Dukes of Brunswick and Mecklenburg, as an inscription on the gate-way records.

To the r. in the plain, on the *Weschnitz*, 3 M. distant, lies the market-town of **Lorsch**, with the ruins of a Monastery, founded by Charlemagne, to which in 788 he banished Tassilo, duke of Bavaria, who had been condemned to death as a traitor. The *Church* was erected about the year 1090.

Near **Heppenheim** (**Halber Mond*) on the l., S. of the road, is situated the *Landberg*, a hill surmounted by three trees, where the Counts of Starkenburg used to hold their tribunals. The church of Heppenheim was founded by Charlemagne, according to an inscription bearing the date of 805.

The **Starkenburg** (1½ M. from Heppenheim), erected in 1064 by an abbot of Lorsch, captured by the Swedes and Spaniards in the 30 years' war, and besieged in vain by Turenne in 1645 and 1674, has only lately been quite abandoned. It gives the name to a province of Hessen. Fine view from the tower.

Immediately after passing Heppenheim the train enters the dominions of Baden. At *Hemsbach*, the following station, is a country seat of a member of the Rothschild family.

Before entering **Weinheim** (*Pfälzer Hof*, R. 48, B. 24 kr., ¼ M. from the station; *Carlsberg*, in the market-place) the train crosses the *Weschnitz*. Weinheim with its handsome new church, is the most considerable and beautifully situated town on the Bergstrasse. Its towers and fosses, and the old buildings, which once belonged to the Templar and Teutonic knights, bear testimony to its former importance. *Hubberger*, the best wine of the Bergstrasse, is produced near Weinheim.

To the E. stands the old castle of **Windeck**, the property of the monastery of Lorsch in the 12th cent., afterwards of the Palatinate, commanding a remarkably beautiful view. Delightful walks through the valleys of *Gorxheim* and *Birkenau*. At the entrance to the former village is erected a stone, in memory of the peasants of the district who were driven out of their valleys and cruelly massacred by the French in 1799.

At *Gross-Sachsen*, said to have been founded by Charlemagne, the line leaves the Bergstrasse, and turns S. E. to **Ladenburg** (*Adler*), the *Lupodunum* of the Romans, the walls and towers of which, as well as its fine old Gothic church, give it an air of importance. The stone bridge which here crosses the Neckar was the scene of several skirmishes during the revolution of 1849; some of the cannon balls are still to be seen in the walls of the station-buildings.

At stat. *Friedrichsfeld* (omnibus to Schwetzingen, see p. 29) the Mannheim train diverges to the r., while the Heidelberg line runs parallel to the Mannheim and Heidelberg Railway.

Between Weinheim and Heidelberg the peculiar beauty of the Bergstrasse is seen to the best advantage, and this stage (12 M.) should, if possible, be performed on foot. The road leads through the villages of *Gross-Sachsen* (good red wine), *Schriesheim* with the *Strahlenburg* in the background, *Handschuchsheim* and *Neuenheim* (*Waldhorn), where Heidelberg

(R. 43) at the foot of the hill with its imposing castle, and the Königsstuhl in the rear, first bursts on the view. On the l. side of the road rises the precipitous *Heiligenberg*.

42. The Odenwald.

(Comp. Map p. 172.)

Pedestrian tour of one day. From *Bickenbach* to the *Felsberg* in 2 hrs., thence to Lindenfels in $3^1/_2$ hrs., and by carriage in $2^1/_2$ hrs. through the valley of the *Weschnitz* to *Birkenau* and *Weinheim*, or, if possible, from Birkenau to Weinheim on foot over the *Wagenburg* in $1^1/_2$ hr.

Tour of three days. 1st day, as above as far as *Lindenfels*; 2nd day, across the *Dromm* to *Waldmichelbach* in $3^1/_2$ hrs., thence by *Ober-* and *Unter-Schönmattenwag* to *Hirschhorn* in $3^1/_2$ hrs. (or by *Schönau* to *Neckarsteinach* in 5 hrs.); 3d day, from *Hirschhorn* to *Neckarsteinach* in 2 hrs., and thence to *Heidelberg* in $2^1/_2$ hrs.

Tour of four days. 1st day, as above to Lindenfels; 2nd day, by *Gumpen* to *Reichelsheim* in $1^1/_2$ hr., by carriage through *Gersprenz* and *Michelstadt* in 3 hrs. (or on foot through *Ostern* and *Mossau* in $3^1/_2$ hrs.) to *Erbach*; 3nd day, to *Beerfelden* in $2^1/_2$ hrs. (better by carriage thus far), then through the *Gammelsbacher Thal* to *Eberbach*; 4th day, to *Hirschhorn* in 2 hrs., to *Neckarsteinach* in 2 hrs., and thence to *Heidelberg* in $2^1/_2$ hrs.

The *Odenwald* is the wooded mountain district which extends between Darmstadt and Heidelberg, a distance of 40 M., and is 24—30 M. in breadth. Its valleys and finest points of view are well worth visiting, but are, as well as its inns, inferior to those of the Black Forest.

The best known summit of the Odenwald is the **Melibocus** (see p. 172); the ascent is usually made from Bickenbach or Zwingenberg.

Bickenbach (next station to Zwingenberg) is the best point for commencing a ramble in this district; thence E. (post-omnibus 3 times daily, 14 kr.) to ($1^1/_2$ M.) *Jugenheim* (*Rindfuss), a picturesquely-situated village, in the middle of which a road through a gate to the r. ascends through well kept grounds, past the ruins of a monastery, to the residence of Prince Alexander of Hessen, a general in the Austrian army: fine view from the terrace. The pedestrian should next ascend to the r. through the grounds, and, at the sign-post indicating the way to the *Felsberg*, turn to the l. round the hill which commands a pretty glimpse of the château and the plain of the Rhine. A quarter of an hr. more conducts him to another sign-post, where the path turns to the l. through shady plantations; in another $^1/_4$ hr. the path to the l. must be ascended, which in about $^1/_2$ hr. leads to a sign-post. About 300 yds. farther a path diverges from the carriage road to the r., passes a fir-wood, and leads (in 20 min.) to the Forester's house on the ***Felsberg** (1578 ft.), where refreshments and tolerable accommodation for the night may be obtained. The view to the E. embraces a great part of the Odenwald, and extends to the Spessart and Aschaffenburg (much more extensive than from the Melibocus); to the W. and N. lie the plains of the Rhine and Main as far as the Donnersberg and Taunus, but they are partially hidden by the Melibocus and Frankenstein. A good road leads from the Felsberg to the Melibocus (4 M.) which cannot well be missed; the Auerbacher Schloss (p. 173), 4 M. distant, may also be visited from the Felsberg. The road to it, termed the "*neun Krümme*", is picturesque, and leads first through wood, then across some fields to the village of *Balkhausen*, then to the l. through a wood which it finally skirts.

Near the Forester's house (5 min.) lies the *Altarstein*, a nearly cubic block of syenite, and lower down, in a small gully, is seen a column (*Riesensäule*, 32 ft. long) of the same material, both of which must have been quarried on the spot, but when and by whom is unknown. The *Felsenmeer* (rocky sea), on the road to Reichenbach, and 5 min. walk from the "Riesensäule," consists of weathered and rounded blocks of syenite which lie scattered about in huge and confused masses on a sloping space, in breadth about 200, and in length about 500 paces — an island of rocks surrounded by forest and extending almost to the valley. This phenomenon is accounted for by the smaller and looser masses having been washed away by the rain and the action of the elements, the larger and more solid alone remaining.

The path now descends a somewhat steep hill to **Reichenbach** (** Traube)*, a village on the *Lauterbach*, 4 M. to the N. E. of Bensheim (p. 173). [Travellers wishing to return from this point to the Bergstrasse should not omit to visit *Schönberg* (*Rettig) (beautiful view from the church), and the castle and grounds of Count Erbach-Schönberg.]

The road here crosses the brook and leads up the valley on the way to Lindenfels; it should, however, again be left in about $^1/_4$ hr., and the path pursued to the r., past some old copper mines, to the *Hohenstein*, a group of quartzose rocks commanding a very pleasing prospect of the valley and mountains. In 5 min. more the hill should be ascended to the l., then past some houses of *Unter-Reidelbach*, and back to the above-mentioned main road, which is not again to be diverged from. The whole walk from Reichenbach to Lindenfels traverses picturesque valley-scenery, but does not offer much variety.

About 1$^1/_4$ M. from the point where the traveller regains the high road, he passes through the small village of *Kolmbach*, and about $^3/_4$ M. farther reaches a point marked by

Odenwald und Bergstraße

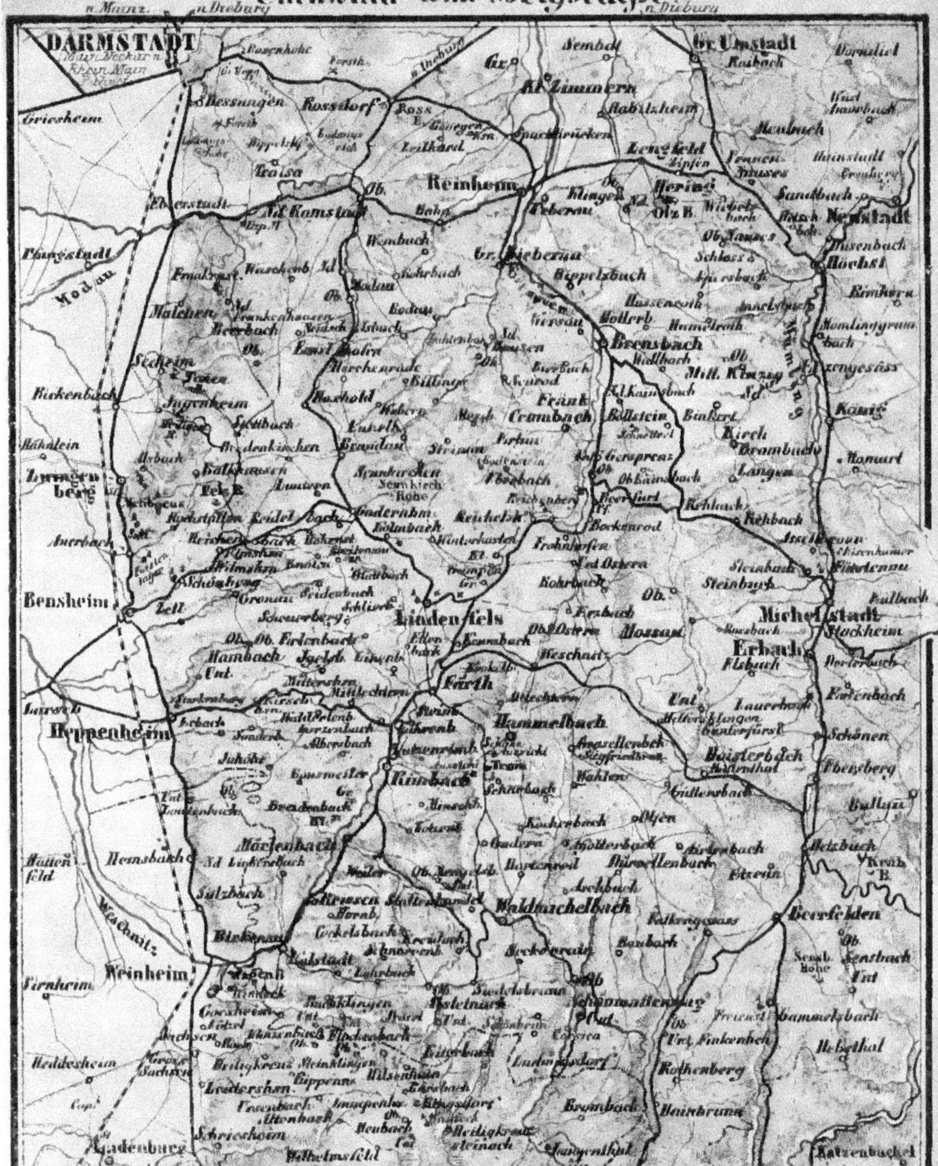

benches and a group of trees, from which a fine view is obtained of the extensively wooded, but fertile mountain district; Lindenfels with its stately ruined castle stands out picturesquely in the foreground; beyond is the broad valley of the Weschnitz, thickly sprinkled with villages; the back-ground is formed by a chain of mountains, above which rises the tower on the Königsstuhl near Heidelberg.

The road now leads through a beautiful beech-wood, interspersed with boulders of granite, to **Lindenfels** (**Harfe; Hess. Hof)* picturesquely situated on an eminence, and commanded by the considerable ruins of the castle. The latter was formerly the property of the Palatinate, but dismantled by Turenne in 1674. Near it are black-lead mines.

On the beautiful *Waldberg*, to the E., is situated a small circular wooden temple, called the **Ludwigshöhe*, 1¼ M. distant from Lindenfels, which commands a fine view of the neighbourhood; and by ascending for another ¼ hr., the pedestrian may reach a point from which the Spessart is visible.

From Lindenfels to Heppenheim (p. 174) on the road to Fürth is a walk (at first with guide, 18 kr.) of 2 hrs.; the path leads by Eulsbach, Erlenbach, Mittershausen and Kirchhausen.

From Lindenfels to Weinheim by carriage (4 fl.) through the valley of the *Weschnitz* in 2½ hrs. Pedestrians should descend to the S. of Lindenfels; after 10 min. the path leads to the l. through the wood; in 25 min. more, over a slight eminence, covered with fir-wood, and ½ M. farther **Fürth** is reached (*Löwe;* good beer at *Hess's*, opp. to the inn), a small town about 11 M. from Weinheim. The footpath (shorter than the road) leads by *Fahrbach* in 1 hr. to *Rimbach* (*Nic. Geist), then by the road through *Mörlenbach*, *Reissen*, and *Birkenau* to Weinheim.

Between **Birkenau** *(Birkenauer Hof)* and Weinheim (2 M.) the road winds through the narrow and romantic valley of the *Weschnitz*, enclosed by granite rocks. But the path over the **Wagenberg* (4M.) is far preferable. Near the W. end of Birkenau, on the l. bank of the Weschnitz opposite to the pump, the path ascends; in about 25 min. it enters the corner of the wood and turns sharp off to the l.; ½ M. farther it leaves the broad road which leads into the valley of Gorxheim, and ascends a steep hill to the r., and, after 200—300 yards, to the r. again; then about 1½ M. along a tolerably level path through the wood, round the N. E. slope of the Wagenberg to the castle of Windeck (p. 174), and finally a descent of ¾ M. to Weinheim. This walk commands a series of the most beautiful views, first of the entire Weschnitz Thal to Lindenfels, with the basaltic peak of *Otzberg*, looking like a ruined castle, in the background; then, as the traveller proceeds round the mountain, the broad valley of the Rhine, with Weinheim and Windeck in the foreground, and a great part of the Palatinate as far as the Donnersberg and the Haardt mountains, come gradually in sight. The Melibocus and Felsberg at the commencement, and the Wagenberg at the end, are undoubtedly the finest points in the whole excursion.

Travellers wishing to spend several days in the Odenwald, may remain the first day in Lindenfels and ascend the Ludwigshöhe (see p. 177), and proceed the next morning on foot to Fürth (3 M.). The footpath thence to the *Dromm* cannot well be missed (but it is safer to take a guide as far as the wood, ½ hr.). After 20 min. the turn to the r. must be taken, and 5 min. farther a narrow footpath to the r., which for a short distance skirts the wood, crosses the brook, and then enters the wood and ascends; after 25 min. a large meadow in the wood is reached, which the path skirts; 25 min. more brings the pedestrian to the **Dromm** (1780 ft.), one of the most elevated points of the Odenwald, commanding a good survey of the valley of the Weschnitz, and in the distance the plain of the Rhine. The house on the summit must then be passed and the ridge of the mountain followed (½ M. from the house, a fine view of the valley of the Rhine is obtained from some rocks among the bushes on the r.). Then a gradual descent to the little town of *Waldmichelbach* (*Gärtner, near the Prot. church).

From Waldmichelbach the traveller may take the high road to *Ober-Schönmattenway*, but here he should leave it, and walk through the rich pastural valley of the *Lax* by *Unter-Schönmattenwag*, *Corsika*, and *Langenthal* to *Hirschhorn.* The path cannot be missed. Another path leads from Waldmichelbach by *Siedelsbrunn* and *Heiligkreuzsteinach* to *Schönau* (12 M.), a small but ancient town which stands on the ruins of the once rich and celebrated monastery of the same name. It was founded in 1136, and in 1560 given by the Elector Palatine Frederick III. to some French refugees who built the village. From Schönau through the romantic valley of the *Steinach* to *Neckarsteinach* in 1 hr.

From Waldmichelbach an interesting path leads by *Siedelsbrunn* in 1½ hr. to *Oberabsteinach,* and through the *Löhrbacher Thal* in 1½ hr. to *Birkenau* (p. 177).

Hirschhorn *(*Berthold; Langbein)* lies in a remarkably picturesque situation at the foot of the stately castle of the same name, once the property of the powerful family *von Hirschhorn,* by whom the Carmelite monastery at the foot of the rock was built; the chapel still stands, and contains many tombstones of members of the family. The view of the town and castle from the road to Neckarsteinach is extremely beautiful.

Neckarsteinach (**Harfe*; see p. 186) is situated on the Neckar and commanded by four castles, the highest of which, the *Mittelburg*, has been restored in the old style. From Neckarsteinach by Neckargemünd to the Wolfsbrunnen and Heidelberg Castle, see p. 186.

Those who may wish to penetrate still more deeply into the Odenwald, visit *Erbach*, and ascend the *Katzenbuckel*, should proceed on the second day from *Lindenfels* to *Reichelsheim* (4 M.), a prettily situated village, commanded by the Castle of *Reichenberg*, visible at a great distance.

Half an hour's walk to the N. of Reichelsheim, in a wild and lonely wooded mountain district, lies the ruined castle of *Rodenstein*, popularly believed to be haunted by the wild huntsman and his comrades.

From Reichelsheim the traveller is recommended to take a carriage to *Gersprenz*, *Michelstadt* (Hydropathic estab.), and *Erbach*, a drive of 3 hrs. (or on foot from Reichelsheim to *Ostern*, *Obermossau*, and *Erbach* in $3^1/_2$. hrs.) **Erbach** (*Burg Wildenstein*; *Krone*) is situated in the Mümlingthal, about 12 M. to the E. of Lindenfels. The castle of Count Erbach contains a considerable *collection of ancient armour, once worn by well-known historical characters, old fire-arms, relics, vases, &c. In the chapel may be seen the stone coffin in which the bones of Charlemagne, his wife Emma, and her sister Gisela once reposed. An ancient helmet, found on the battle-field of Cannæ, is also an object of interest (fee 24 kr.)

From Erbach to *Beerfelden* (*Breimer), a distance of $7^1/_2$ M., and thence down the *Gammelsbacher Thal* to Eberbach ($7^1/_2$ M.), the traveller had better proceed by carriage, as the wooded valley presents but little variety. From *Eberbach* (*Krone) the ascent of the **Katzenbuckel** (2094 ft.), the highest point of the Odenwald, is usually made. The watch-tower (keys at the forester's at Katzenbach) commands a fine prospect of the valley of the Neckar, Baden, Württemberg as far as the Alb, and the Black Forest.

The district between Eberbach and *Hirschhorn* (6 M.) is wild and romantic. The valley of the Neckar is narrow, and enclosed by steep, well-wooded mountains. From Hirschhorn by Neckarsteinach to Heidelberg see above.

43. Heidelberg.

Hotels. At the station: *Hôtel Schrieder (*Kühne*), R. from 1 fl., L. 15, B. 36, D. 1 fl. 30, A. 24 kr.; Victoria see p. 180. In the town, 1 M. from the station: *Prince Charles, and near it the *Adler (Eagle), in the Kornmarkt; *Russischer Hof (also Hôtel garni); *Europäischer Hof (*Schrieder*) in the Anlage; *Badischer Hof, Hauptstrasse; *Holländischer Hof, at the Neckar bridge. Charges in all these hotels nearly the same: R. 1 fl., L. 12, B. 30 kr., D. exc. W. 1 fl. 12, A. 24 kr. — Second-class inns: Bayrischer Hof, R. 48 kr., D. 1 fl., B. 24 kr., is at the same time a restaurant; *Darmstädter Hof, both near the station. In the town: *Ritter and Prinz Max, Müller's Victoria Hotel (Hôtel garni) in the Anlage.

Cafés. Wachter; Thiele; Krall, corner of the Hauptstr. and the Friedrichsstr.; good beer at the Bremeneck, in the Burgweg.

Newspapers at the Museum in the Ludwigsplatz, opposite to the University.

Swimming baths at the Neckar, at the Mannheimer- and Carls-Thor (12 kr.). River baths near Werle's Oil mill.

Omnibus between the town and the station (or steamboat-wharf) 6 kr., with luggage 12 kr.

Carriages (Stands in the Ludwigsplatz and Kornmarkt): between the station and town for 1—2 pers. 12 kr. each, for 3—4 pers. 9 kr. each, boxes 6 kr. each. *By time:* $^1/_4$ hr. for 1—2 pers. 18 kr., for 3—4 pers. 24 kr.; 1 hr. 1 fl. or 1 fl. 12 kr. — To the *Castle* 2 fl.; *Wolfsbrunnen*, and back by the road 2 fl.; *Wolfsbrunnen* and *Castle* 3 fl.; *Castle* and *Molkencur* $3^1/_2$ fl.; *Castle*, *Molkencur*, and *Wolfsbrunnen* $4^1/_2$ fl.; *Castle*, *Molkencur*, *Königsstuhl* and *Wolfsbrunnen*, for 2 pers. $8^1/_2$ fl., for more than 2 pers. 11 fl.; to *Schwetzingen*, for the whole day $5^1/_2$ fl., half a day $3^1/_2$ fl.; to *Neckarsteinach*, for the whole day 6, half day 4 fl.

Donkeys to the *Castle* 24 kr., back 12 kr.; to the *Castle*, *Molkencur* and back 1 fl. 12 kr.; to the *Wolfsbrunnen* 1 fl., there and back 1 fl. 12 kr.; to the *Königsstuhl* $1^1/_2$ fl., there and back $1^3/_4$ fl.; to the *Königsstuhl* and back by the *Wolfsbrunnen* 2 fl. 24 kr.; for waiting 30 kr. per hour. Donkey-stands on the path leading from the Kornmarkt to the Castle.

Railways. To *Bruchsal*, *Durlach*, *Carlsruhe*, &c. from the Baden station, to *Darmstadt* and *Frankfurt* from the Main-Neckar station, adjoining the first-named. Railway to Würzburg opened as far as Mosbach.

Telegraph Office at the Railway station and in the Ludwigsplatz, No. 10.

Steamboats to Heilbronn (somewhat tedious) in 12 hrs. (down in 6—8 hrs.). By railway to Heilbronn or Stuttgart in $4^1/_4$ hrs.

English Church near the Badischer Hof.

The traveller whose time is limited should proceed at once from the station to the Riesenstein, Molkencur, and Castle ($1^1/_2$ hr.) according to the following directions: opposite to the station the "*Pariser Weg*" must be followed for about 240 paces, then the hill to the r. is ascended through the "*Wolfsschlucht*" in $^1/_2$ hr. to the *Rondel* (crescent), then a new broad carriage-road to the l. leads (in 5 min.) to the *Kanzel* (pulpit), which commands a magnificent prospect of the town and castle. The quarries are next reached, and, after avoiding a road to the l. (which leads to the town), the traveller, by pursuing the road in a straight direction for about 1 M., will reach the *Molkencur*, and, $^3/_4$ M. farther, the *Castle*. The descent should be made by the Burgweg, across the Kornmarkt, through the town past the theatre to the Anlagen, and thence to the station. A short street leads from the large church in the market-place to the bridge (p. 185), which also commands a delightful prospect.

Few towns can vie with Heidelberg in the beauty of its environs and its richness in historical associations. The Count Palatine Otto of Wittelsbach (1228—53) transferred the seat of his government and family from Stahleck (p. 102), near Bacharach, to Heidelberg, which thus became the capital of the Palatinate, and continued for nearly 5 centuries to be the seat of the Electors, till Carl Philipp in 1720, on account of some differences with the Protestant portion of the community, transferred the seat of government to Mannheim. Since 1802 Heidelberg has belonged to the Grand-duchy of

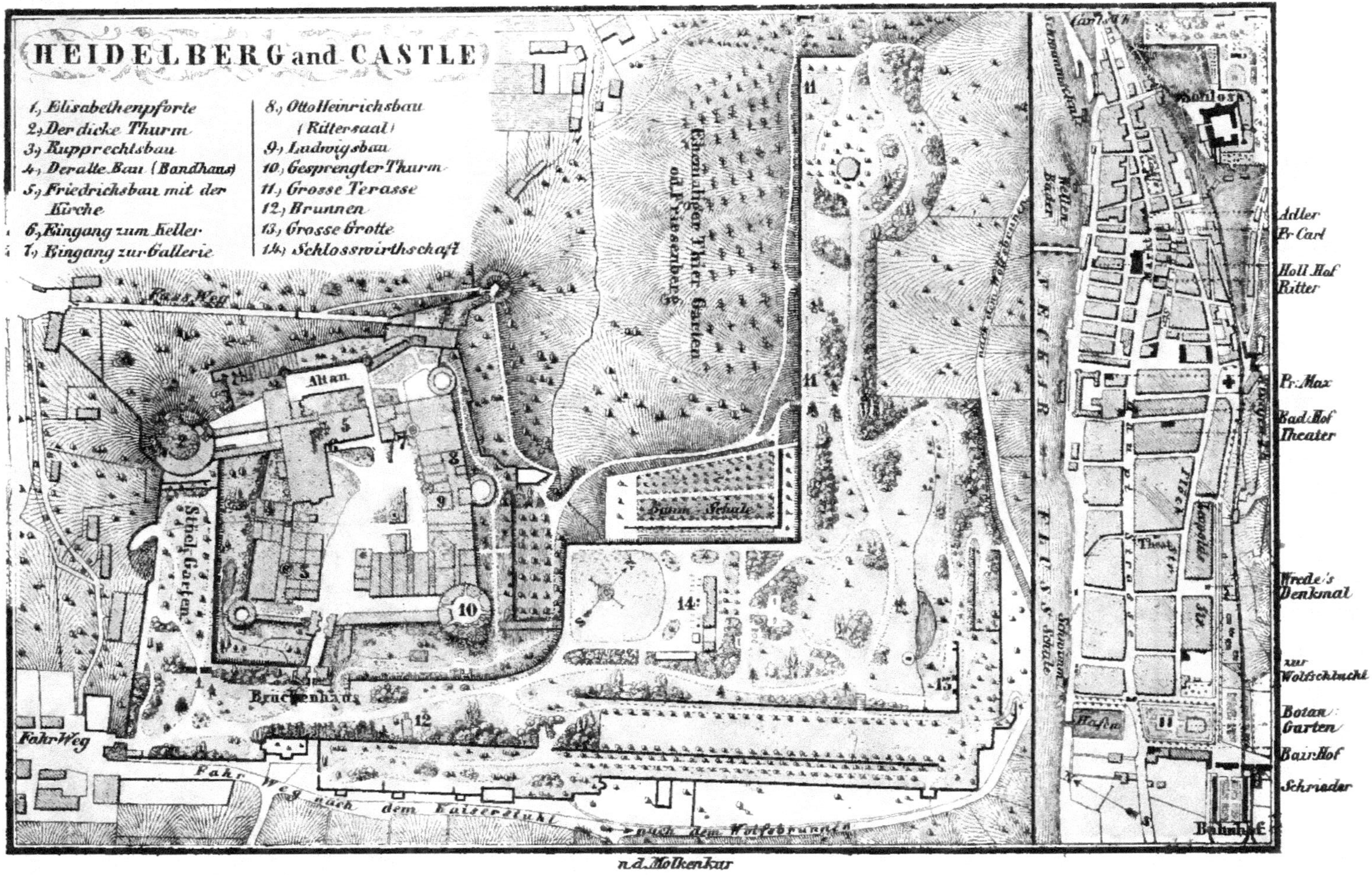
HEIDELBERG and CASTLE
1, Elisabethenpforte
2, Der dicke Thurm
3, Rupprechtsbau
4, Deralte Bau (Bandhaus)
5, Friedrichsbau mit der Kirche
6, Eingang zum Keller
7, Eingang zur Gallerie
8, Otto Heinrichsbau (Rittersaal)
9, Ludwigsbau
10, Gesprengter Thurm
11, Grosse Terasse
12, Brunnen
13, Grosse Grotte
14, Schlosswirthschaft
Ehemaliger Thier Garten od. Friesenberg
Altan
Stück Garten
Baum Schule
Bruckenhaus
Fahr Weg
Fuss Weg
Fahr Weg nach dem Kaiserstuhl
nach dem Wolfsbrunnen
n.d. Molkenkur
NECKAR FLUSS
Wellen Bäder
Schwimm Schule
Schloss
Haupt Strasse
Plöck
Leopolds Str.
Theat. Str.
Hafen
Bahnhof
Adler
Pr. Carl
Holl. Hof
Ritter
Pr. Max
Bad. Hof
Theater
Wrede's Denkmal
zur Wolfschlucht
Botan. Garten
Bair. Hof
Schrieder

Baden. Its prosperity has of late years been considerably augmented by the completion of the railway, and the consequent increase in the influx of visitors.

Heidelberg is the key of the mountainous valley of the Neckar, which below the town widens and is at length united with the Rhine, but the town itself is limited to the narrow confines between the river and the castle hill. It consists of one long street (1 ¼ M.), extending from the Mannheimer to the Carls-Thor, and has a population of 16,288 (⅓ Rom. Cath.). On the N. side flows the river, and on the S., running for some distance parallel with the town, is the "*Anlage*," a public walk, planted with trees, where of late years a number of handsome residences have been erected. The two monuments near the station record the names of the founders of this walk; in the immediate vicinity is the old *Churchyard of St. Anne*, in which the remains of many eminent men repose.

Near the E. extremity of the Anlage, on the l., is the Protestant Church of *St. Peter*, where Hieronymus of Prague, the companion of Huss, expounded his doctrines to the people in 1406. Farther on is the *Jesuits' Church*, and in the market-place the *Church of the Holy Ghost*, erected at the commencement of the 15th cent., under the Count Palatine Rupert; the choir contains the tombstone of King Rupert, and his queen Elizabeth, sister of Frederick of Zollern, the first Elector of Brandenburg. Opposite to this church is the inn of the *Ritter St. George*, built in 1592, and interesting as being almost the only house which remained intact in the devastation of 1693 (p. 182).

The **University** (800 students), after that of Prague the oldest in Germany, the celebrated *Ruperto-Carolina*, cradle of the sciences in S. Germany, was founded in 1386 by the Elector Rupert I. For its present extent and arrangements, it is indebted to the learned Charles Frederick of Baden, who in 1802 provided it with eminent professors, as well as scientific collections and institutions.

The greater number of the lectures are held in the *University buildings* in the Ludwigsplatz, erected in 1693. The *Library* is a separate building, and contains 200,000 vols. and 1800 MSS. It is open daily from 10 to 12, and on Wed. and Sat. also from 2 to 4 o'clock. The scientific collections, though valuble to the student, possess little interest for the passing traveller.

The town itself contains little worthy of note, and the tourist should devote every spare hour to exploring the **Castle** and its environs. It is situated on a wooded slope of the Königsstuhl, 320 ft. above the Neckar, and probably owes its origin to Ludwig der Strenge (the Severe), son-in-law of Rudolph of Habsburg, about the close of the 13th cent. The *Ruprechtsbau* was crected by the Elector Rupert III., who in 1400 was elected by the council of electors at Rhense (p. 92) to be Roman emperor; this fact is indicated by the imperial cagle placed above the arms of the Palatinate on this part of the building. The Elector Frederick I., "the Victorious", the Frederick the Great of his age, enlarged the building. The Electors of the 16th and 17th centuries, especially Otto Heinrich (1555—59), Frederick IV. (1583—1610), and Frederick V. (1610—21), king of Bohemia and husband of Elizabeth, daughter of James I. of England, made splendid additions to the edifice. It suffered much in the 30 years' war, but was restorcd by Carl Ludwig (1650—80). It was this prince, who, when hard pressed during the devastations of the Palatinate in 1673, wrote to Turenne, saying that such barbarities could not possibly be perpetrated by the command of the "most Christian king," and perhaps arose from some personal feelings against himself, which he should be most willing to satisfy by meeting the Marshal in single combat. The Marshal, however, declined the proffered challenge. In the Orleans war the French general Melac, contrary to the stipulation, caused the castle to be blown up in 1689. (Picture by Dietz in Carlsruhe).

The town uud its habitants, however, met with the most barbarous usage in 1693 at the hands of the French, to whom, owing to the treachery or cowardice of the commandant, the castle and town surrendered after little or no resistance. The massacre of the inhabitants, and destruction of the castle and habitations, immediately commenced. After the most savage and almost incredible barbarities, to which the greater portion of the peaccable inhabitants fell victims, the town was left a heap of smouldering ruins, and the castle entirely dismantled.

After this feat of arms so tarnishing to his fame, the "most Christian king" Louis XIV. caused a medal to be struck, bearing the words: "*Heidelberga deleta.*" The Castle was struck by lightning in 1764, and the scanty remnants left by the French burned to the ground. The walls alone remained, but so vast is their extent that to this day they form the most imposing and magnificent ruin in Germany. The towers, turrets, buttresses, balconies, the lofty gateways and fine old statues, the courts and grounds, render it the *Alhambra of the Germans.* Nor are the splendour of the structure and the beauty of its situation its sole attractions; its ivy-clad ruins are connected with innumerable historical

HEIDELBERG

associations of the deepest interest, and the striking contrast here presented between the eternal rejuvenescence of nature and the instability of the proudest monuments of human skill, has called forth many a poetic effusion.

There are several footpaths which lead from the town to the Castle; the shortest is the *Burgweg*, leading from the Kornmarkt to the *Great Balcony*, an ascent of about 12 min. A carriage road leads from the Klingelthor, at the E. extremity of the walk which commences at the station, to the Castle in 15 min. By this road the visitor is led first into the garden, and then to the l. through the *Elisabethen-Pforte*, erected by the Elector Frederick V. in honour of his consort Elizabeth of England, to the *Stückgarten*, the extreme W. point of the grounds, commanding an extensive view as far as the Haardt mountains. The "*dicke Thurm*" (thick tower), at the W. corner, was once the festive Hall of Frederick V., and statues of him and his brother Ludwig V., are seen peering forth from ivy-clad niches.

To the r. on entering the *Schlosshof* (castle yard) is a fountain with granite columns, which once adorned the Palace of Charlemagne at Ingelheim (p. 146). To the l. is the *Ruprechtsbau*, with the imperial eagle, and above the entrance a wreath of five roses supported by two angels, one of whom is in the act of putting a pair of half-opened compasses into one of the roses — an allegory which has never been satisfactorily interpreted. The small hall contains a collection of old armour, bullets &c., found in the castle. Visitors who wish to gain an idea of the magnitude of the whole edifice, should explore the extensive, and partly subterraneous passages which connect this point with the "Thick Tower," and afterwards inspect the castle chapel and the cellar. (Fees for conducting visitors over the entire ruin, including the "Great Tun": for 1 pers. 24, for 2–3 pers. 36, for every additional pers. 12 kr.)

The **Otto Heinrichsbau* (1556) to the E. especially deserves a careful inspection. The decorations in the front facing the court are admirably executed in the purest Italian "renaissance" style, and are remarkable for the accuracy of their proportions; the designs are ascribed to Michel Angelo. Over the door is the bust of the Elector Otto Heinrich, who erected this part of the castle, as its name implies, and higher up in twelve niches are statues of mythological characters; over the windows are medallions of Roman emperors, and in the four lower niches are placed, somewhat incongruously, statues of Joshua, Samson, Hercules, and Mars.

The *Friedrichsbau* (1601) seems by the superfluity of its

decorations to strive to excel all the rest of the edifice in magnificence. The front is embellished by statues of 16 Electors Palatine, from Otto of Wittelsbach (1184), to Frederick IV. (1607); above them to the l. is a statue of Charlemagne. In the corner, to the l., is the entrance to the cellar, which contains the celebrated *Heidelberg Tun*, constructed in 1751, capable of containing 49,000 gallons. Near it stands a grotesque wooden figure of Perkeo, court-jester of the Elector Charles Philip, probably placed there to commemorate some frolic of olden times, and a second large tun bears some amusing inscriptions.

The * *Graimberg Gallery* in a suite of rooms on the first floor of the Friedrichsbau (admission 12 kr.; for parties of 6 and upwards 9 kr. each), contains a considerable collection of portraits of princes, chiefly of the Palatinate, documents, coins, a cork model of the castle, relics found in the tomb of the emperor Rupert in the church of the Holy Ghost, ornaments, ecclesiastical antiquities &c. The gallery, as a whole, possesses considerable value and historical interest, though many of the objects are in themselves insignificant.

A vaulted passage leads through the Friedrichsbau to the * *Great Balcony* (1610), which commands a beautiful prospect of the Neckar to the N. Beneath the balcony is a long vaulted gateway leading to the steps which descend to the footpath to the town.

The "*gesprengte Thurm*" (blown-up tower) at the E. extremity of the castle, in the fosse to the r. of the bridge leading into the castle-yard, is of so massive a construction that, when the French attempted to blow it up in 1689, the only result of the explosion was, that an enormous portion became detached from the rest and fell bodily into the ditch, where it still remains. The Tower is 82 ft. in diameter, and the walls are 20 ft. thick; beneath it are long casemate passages.

The present castle-garden was laid out in 1804, and abounds with the most delightful walks presenting new and ever-varying views. One of the finest points is the * *Great Terrace* to the N.E., erected in 1615, which commands a fine prospect of the Castle itself. On the path from the Castle to the terrace is a wine and coffee-garden, where a band generally plays on summer afternoons.

To reach the Molkencur, the traveller must ascend the steps opposite to the "gesprengte Thurm", and then turn to the r. among ivy-clad walls; another flight of steps is then ascended which lead to the broad carriage road, a little below the Rondel. The Friesenweg, so called on account of an inscription on the rock in memory of the artist *Ernst Fries* of Heidelberg, to the l. of the Rondel, then leads through an avenue of chesnuts past the so-called *"Old Castle"* on the *Jettenbühl*, inhabited in the 12th cent. by Conrad of Hohenstaufen, the brother of Barbarossa, but completely destroyed by lightning in 1537, to the **Molkencur** (whey-cure), an inn situated 288 ft. above the Castle, and a very favorite resort. The view is similar to that from the Castle but more extensive.

The ***Königsstuhl**, also called the *Kaiserstuhl* in commemoration of the visit of the emperor Francis in 1815, is 851 ft. higher than the Castle, and 1752 ft. above the level of the sea. It is ascended by a very steep flight of steps from the road, about 1 M. from the Molkencur, but it is also accessible by a good carriage road in $^3/_4$ hr. The watch-tower on the top, 89 ft. in height, commands a most extensive view of the Rhine, Neckar, Odenwald, Haardt mountains, Taunus, the Black Forest as far as the Mercuriusberg at Baden, and even the cathedral-spire of Strasburg.

From the Molkencur a broad carriage-road leads to the W. round the *Riesenstein* (giant-stone), past some sandstone quarries, to the so-called ***Kanzel** (pulpit), 1 M. distant, and, a few hundred yards farther, to the ***Rondel** (crescent), from both of which, especially the latter, the most extensive prospect may be enjoyed. From the Rondel a path to the r. descends through the Wolfsschlucht to the station (1 M.). The pedestrian may, if he pleases, continue his walk along the brow of the hill $1^1/_4$ M. farther to the *Neuhof* (*Inn), but the view remains the same. In this case the road back will bring him through the wood to the **Cemetery** (fine view from the front of the chapel), $^3/_4$ M. from the railway station.

To the E. of the Castle a road leads to the **Wolfsbrunnen** (3 M.), once a favorite resort of Frederick V. and his bride (p. 182). According to an ancient tradition, the beautiful enchantress Jetta was here killed by a wolf; hence the name. The five ponds fed by the spring contain trout, a dish of which may be had at the inn. The view from this point is far inferior to those in the more immediate vicinity of the town.

The handsome **Bridge** over the Neckar was constructed by the Elector Carl Theodor in 1788, and is embellished with statues of the Electors and one of Minerva. In 1799 it was bravely and successfully defended by the Austrians against the attacks of the French.

On the r. bank of the Neckar is the ***Philosophenweg**, a beautiful walk extending for 3 M. along the brow of the *Heiligenberg*, chiefly through vineyards, commanding splendid views of the town, the castle, the valley, the plain of the Rhine with the cathedral of Speyer and the beautiful outlines of the S. Haardt mountains. This path is reached by taking the first street (*Hirschgasse*) which ascends the hill, about $^3/_4$ M. beyond the bridge. The way back leads through *Neuenheim* (p. 174); or the walk may be taken in the opposite direction. At Neuenheim the river is crossed by a ferry (4 kr.); the swimming-bath is at the landing place on the l. bank of the river, and not far from the station.

Excursions (carriages and railways p. 180) may also be made to **Neckargemünd**, about 6 M. distant, situated on the l. bank of the Neckar at the confluence of the *Elsenz*. Beyond it, on a wooded eminence to the r., rises the Castle of **Dilsburg**, in vain besieged by Tilly in the 30 years' war, and about the commencement of the present century employed as a state prison. The next place of note is the old town of **Neckarsteinach** (* *Harfe*) (p. 179), about 10 M. distant from Heidelberg. It was once the seat of the valiant race of the Steinachs, which became extinct in 1653. The four old castles still bear testimony to the power of these knights. The church contains numerous monuments of members of the family, several of whom bore the surname of Landschaden (land-devastation), perhaps on account of the numerous feuds in which they were engaged. In the *Steinbach*, which here unites with the Neckar, pearl-muscles of considerable value are occasionally found.

Excursion to *Speyer*, *Mannheim*, and *Schwetzingen*, see RR. 44 and 48.

44. Mannheim and Schwetzingen.

Hotels. On the Rhine near the steamboat wharf: European Hotel (R. 1 fl., L. 18, B. 30, A. 24 kr.). In the town: *Pfälzer Hof (Hotel of the Palatinate) similar prices. *Deutscher Hof (German Hotel). — *König von Portugal and Schwarzer Löwe for travellers of modest pretensions. Weisses Lamm, inn and beer-house, clean and moderate; Goldene Gans.

Restaurants. Stern near the theatre; Café Français; Mohrenkopf, Rosenstock, the two latter generally possess good bills of fare at moderate charges. Drei Glocken, near the Strohmarkt, moderate and respectable beer-house.

Railway Station in Mannheim for the *Darmstadt*, *Frankfurt* and *Heidelberg* trains, in Ludwigshafen for those to *Mayence, Speyer, Neustadt*, &c.

Conveyances. Omnibus from the Mannheim station to that of Ludwigshafen without luggage 22 kr., each box 6 kr.; cab from station to station 1—2 persons 45 kr., 3 pers. 51 kr., 4 pers. 1 fl. 8 kr.

Steamboat. The wharf is $^3/_4$ M. distant from the Ludwigshafen, and $1^1/_2$ M. from the Mannheim station. A straight road leads from the latter to the wharf past the theatre and the Jesuits' church to the Observatory, and then to the l. through the Palace gardens.

Porterage from station or steamboat to cab or omnibus 3 kr. for each package.

English Church Service during the season.

Mannheim was founded in 1606 by the Elector Frederick IV. of the Palatinate, but when still in its infancy was destroyed by the French in 1689. For its subsequent importance it was indebted to the Elector Charles Philip, who on account of ecclesiastical differences with the townspeople of Heidelberg transferred his residence to Mannheim in 1721. The siege

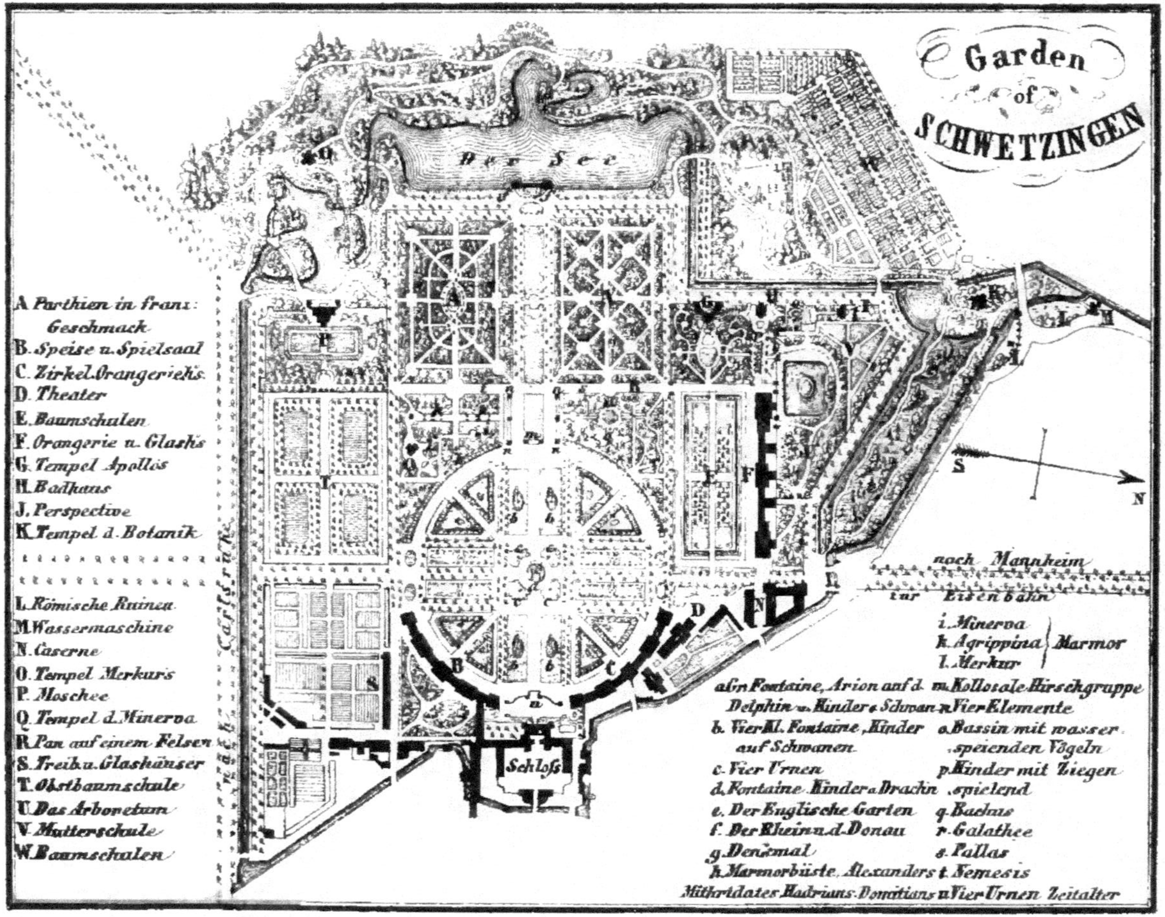
Garden of SCHWETZINGEN
Der See
Schloss
Carlsruh
nach Mannheim
zur Eisenbahn
S
N
A. Parthien in franz: Geschmack
B. Speise u. Spielsaal
C. Zirkel Orangeriehs.
D. Theater
E. Baumschulen
F. Orangerie u. Glashs
G. Tempel Apollos
H. Badhaus
J. Perspective
K. Tempel d. Botanik
L. Römische Ruinen
M. Wassermaschine
N. Caserne
O. Tempel Merkurs
P. Moschee
Q. Tempel d. Minerva
R. Pan auf einem Felsen
S. Treib u. Glashäuser
T. Obstbaumschule
U. Das Arboretum
V. Mutterschule
W. Baumschulen
i. Minerva
k. Agrippina
l. Merkur
Marmor
a. Gr. Fontaine, Arion auf d. Delphin u. Kinder a. Schwan
b. Vier Kl. Fontaine, Kinder auf Schwanen
c. Vier Urnen
d. Fontaine Kinder a. Drachn
e. Der Englische Garten
f. Der Rhein u. d. Donau
g. Denkmal
h. Marmorbüste Alexanders Mithridates Hadrians Domitians
m. Kollosale Hirschgruppe
n. Vier Elemente
o. Bassin mit wasser speienden Vögeln
p. Kinder mit Ziegen spielend
q. Bachus
r. Galathee
s. Pallas
t. Nemesis
u. Vier Urnen Zeitalter

of 1795 occasioned considerable damage to the town; in 1799 the fortifications were demolished.

Mannheim has a population of 26,914 (1/2 Prot.), and is the most regularly built town in Germany, being divided into 100 square compartments like a chess-board. The streets have no names, but are designated as Square *(Quadrat)* A. B. C. &c., with the exception of the *Planken*, a street planted with trees, which extends from the Rhine to the Heidelberg gate. The extensive traffic in tobacco, madder, spelt, and fruit, which is here carried on, has rendered Mannheim, which is conveniently situated at the confluence of the Neckar and Rhine, the most important commercial town of the Upper Rhine. The harbour of the Rhine is connected with that of the Neckar and with the Baden station by means of rails laid down through the town.

The spacious **Schloss,** erected in 1720—1729, and partially destroyed in 1795, contains (in the gateway, to the l.) a number of *Roman monuments*, with remarkable inscriptions, statues, small Etrurian sarcophagi, &c.; in the first floor of the same wing is a *Picture-gallery*, where a few Dutch pictures are to be seen, together with a considerable collection of engravings and casts of celebrated antiquities, and a cabinet of natural history. The Grand-duchess Stephanie (d. 1860), adopted daughter of Napoleon I. and widow of the Grand-duke Charles (d. 1818), formerly resided in the palace. Mannheim is also the chief residence of the nobility of the Palatinate.

The **Theatre**, completely restored in 1854, ranks among the best in Southern Germany, and is admirably decorated. Schiller's first pieces, the "Robbers," "Fiesco," "Kabale und Liebe," were here represented under his own direction. — *Schiller's Monument*, in the "Schillerplatz", was erected in Nov. 1862 by voluntary contributions collected in Mannheim.

Mannheim possesses several handsome modern churches and other edifices, but offers few objects of attraction to the passing traveller, who may far more advantageously employ his time at Speyer with its magnificent cathedral, in the beautiful environs of Heidelberg (see R. 43, railway in 1/2 hr.), or in the celebrated garden of Schwetzingen.

Train from Mannheim to *Friedrichsfeld*, about halfway to Heidelberg, thence by carriage (one-horse there and back 1 fl. 45 kr.) or omnibus (in summer 4 times a day) to **Schwetzingen** (*Erbprinz; Hirsch*). The * *Gardens*, laid out by the Elector Charles Theodore in the middle of the 18th cent., cover an area of 112 acres of land, and contain handsome avenues in the old French style, as well as portions laid out in the fashion of an English park. The whole may be seen in about 2 hrs. The objects most worthy of note are as follows, beginning on the l. (services of a guide quite unnecessary): Temple of Minerva, the Mosque (with fine view from the highest minaret, 140 ft., fee 12 kr.), Temple of Mercury; view from the large pond (near the colossal statues of the "Rhine" and "Danube") through an opening in the wood of the Haardt Mts.; Temple of Apollo, Bath-house (fee 12 kr.), bird fountain, Roman aqueduct and orangery.

The *Schloss*, or palace, built by the Elector Carl Ludwig about the middle of the 17th cent., contains nothing of interest.

45. The Bavarian-Rhenish Palatinate.

Donnersberg and Haardt.

The following **Plan of excursion** comprises the entire mountainous district of the Rhenish Palatinate. Travellers whose time is limited should take the railway (p. 224) from Ludwigshafen to Speyer, where they may inspect the cathedral; thence in 1 hr. to *Neustadt* in the centre of the Haardt.

From this point a pleasant excursion may be made by taking the railway to *Frankenstein* (3/4 hr.), and then proceeding on foot through the Isenachthal by the Hartenburg and monastery of Limburg (p. 191) to Dürkheim (13½ M.). Or still better — from Neustadt with 1-horse carriage (1 fl.) to Frankenstein in 2½ hrs.; inspect the villa, and then drive on to the Hartenburg in 2 hrs.; on foot to Limburg (3 M.), and 1½ M. farther to Dürkheim. Those who are already acquainted with Speyer may prefer to go direct from Ludwigshafen to Dürkheim by omnibus, or 1-horse carriage (3½ fl.) in 2 hrs.

At Dürkheim the finest part of the vine-clad *Haardt mountains* begins, to explore which about 3 days are required. 1st day: from *Dürkheim* to *Neustadt*, the *Hambacher Schloss*, and *Edenkoben*. 2nd day: along the brow of the hill to *Eschbach*, the *Madenburg*, over the mountain to *Trifels*, to *Annweiler* and *Willgartswiesen*. 3d day: *Dahn* and environs, through the Lauterthal to *Hinter-Weidenthal* and the *Kaltebach*, where the diligence which runs between Landau and Zweibrücken stops daily. From Zweibrücken a branch line joins the main line between Ludwigshafen and Saarbrücken at Homburg; thence in 2 hrs. to Neustadt, in 3 hrs. to Ludwigshafen.

The remaining part of this prosperous district, though less celebrated as a wine-country, is scarcely less beautiful. In order to appreciate it, the traveller is recommended to commence the tour from Kreuznach; on the 1st day by the Rheingrafenstein, Ebernburg, through the Alsenzthal to *Dielkirchen;* 2nd day, over the Donnersberg to *Grünstadt,* and thence by carriage to *Dürkheim;* on the 3d, 4th and 5th days as above.

The finest wines of the Palatinate are produced at Königsbach, Ruppertsberg, Deidesheim, Forst, Wachenheim, Dürkheim, Ungstein, and Callstadt; the red wine of the last named place resembles Burgundy. In good years the Palatinate yields upwards of 20 million gallons of wine. Pedestrians should observe that the footpaths through the vineyards are closed in Sept. and Oct.

Maps and views of the Palatinate and of the cathedral of Speyer may be procured at *Gottschick-Witter's*, bookseller at Neustadt.

Kreuznach, the *Rheingrafenstein* and *Ebernburg* are described in R. 29. The path to the Gans and Rheingrafenstein cannot well be missed. It leaves the high road at the Hotel *zum Rheinstein*, opposite to the bath-island, and ascends in 1 hr. to the *Rheingrafensteiner Hof*, then through the grounds to the *Gans*, and in ½ hr. more to the *Rheingrafenstein;* the latter part of the path is however somewhat difficult to find without a guide. From the Rheingrafenstein ¼ hour's walk brings the pedestrian to the foot of the porphyry rock, opposite to which lies the village of **Münster am Stein** (R. 29).

The river *Nahe* is here the boundary between Prussia and Bavaria. On an eminence on the r. bank lies the **Ebernburg** (**Inn*). The road now ascends the Alsenzthal in S. direction,

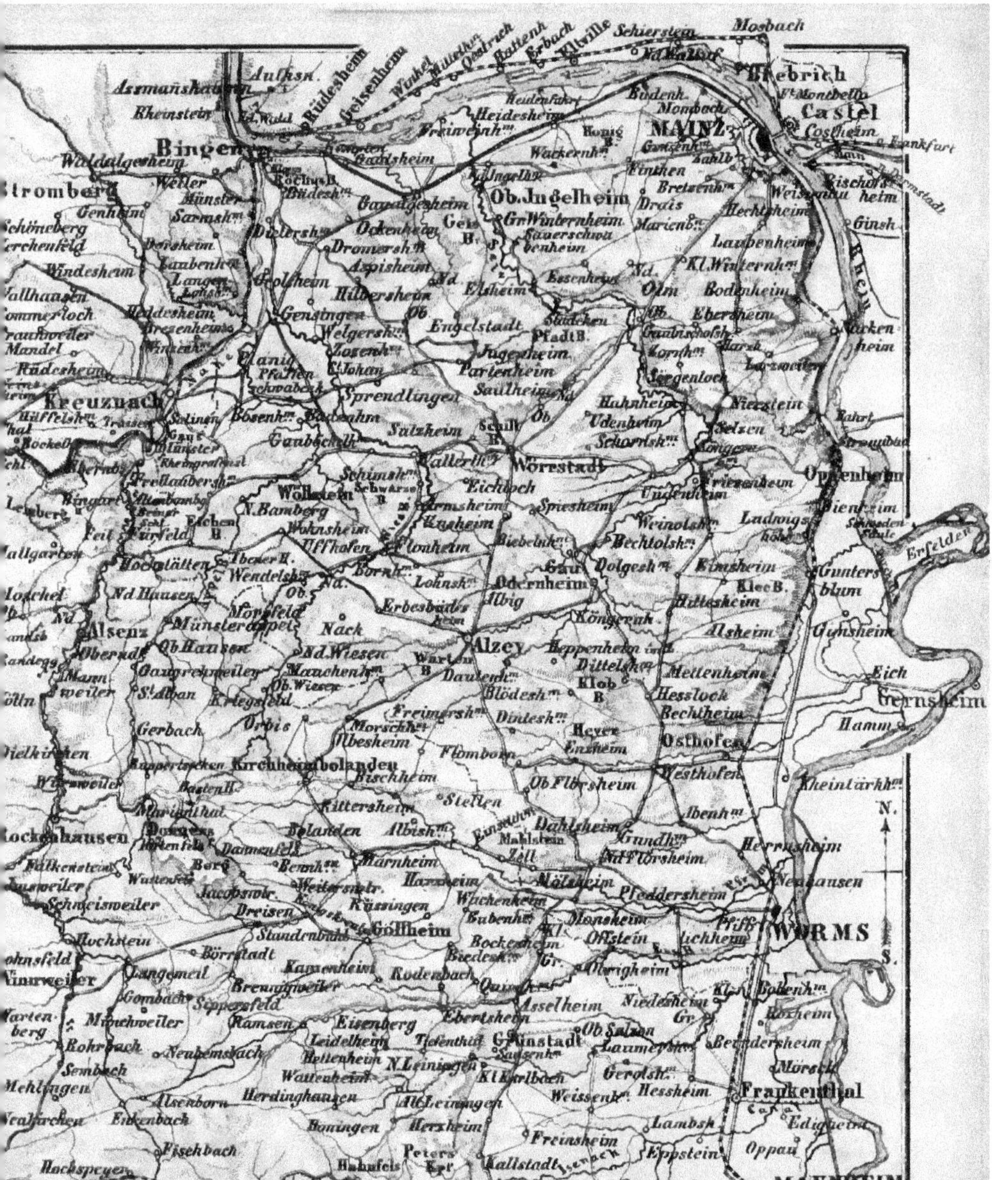
Mosbach
Schierstein
Biebrich
Castel
MAINZ
Costheim
Frankfurt
Bingen
Stromberg
Rüdesheim
Geisenheim
Heidesheim
Ob.Ingelheim
Gaualgesheim
Kreuznach
Sprendlingen
Wörrstadt
Oppenheim
Nierstein
Alzey
Alsenz
Kirchheimbolanden
Göllheim
Eisenberg
Grünstadt
WORMS
Frankenthal
MANNHEIM
Oggersheim
Dürkheim
Wachenheim
Deidesheim
Neustadt
Lambrecht
Hassloch
Schifferstadt
Mutterstadt
Ludwigshafen
Gernsheim
Pfeddersheim
Osthofen
Westhofen
Rhein
N.
S.
1 2 3 4 5 Englisch miles
bez. u. lith. b. Ed. Wagner

passing *Altenbamberg* (with old castle on the heights, destroyed by the French in 1669) to **Alsenz** (*Post*) (7½ M.). Farther on in the picturesque and populous valley, near *Mannweiler*, are the ruins of the castle of *Randeck*, situated on a wooded eminence. The next village is *Köln*.

Dielkirchen (**Hoster*), 6 M. from Alsenz, is a good halting place for the night, the inn being good and moderate, unless the traveller should feel disposed to proceed to *Dannenfels*, 10 M. farther. The road continues in the Alsenzthal for 1½ M. more, and as it approaches **Rockenhausen** (* *Post*), diverges to the l. to *Marienthal* (3¾ M.). The footpath leading from Dielkirchen to the Marienthal is not difficult to find and saves about 1½ M. Guide from Dielkirchen over the Donnersberg to Dannenfels (36—48 kr.) not absolutely necessary.

Marienthal possesses a fine Gothic church of 1478, which has lately been restored in the old style; it contains several good monuments of the counts of Grafenstein. At the **Bastenhaus**, ¾ M. from Marienthal, the pedestrian must leave the road and follow the track which ascends to the r., along the course of the *Appelbach*. Where the path divides that to the l. must be taken which leads out of the wood. Although the flat summit of the Donnersberg now lies before the traveller, he must still bear to the l., as the way to the top is somewhat circuitous. The inns at Marienthal and the Bastenhaus are tolerable.

The ***Donnersberg** (2126 ft.), dedicated in ancient times to the god *Thor*, was called by the Romans *Mons Jovis*. The upper part of it consists principally of red porphyry. From a great distance the mountain may be easily recognized by its shape, being an extensive table-land, bounded by precipitous slopes, and entirely clothed with luxuriant beech-wood.

A large farmhouse, the *Donnersberger Hof*, erected on the ruins of an old monastery, formerly occupied the summit, but it was removed in 1854 by the Bavarian government, and the site planted with wood. Ten minutes' walk from the spot where the building stood is the *Hirtenfels*, a shady seat among the rocks on the E. side of the table-land, commanding a most beautiful view of the course of the Rhine upwards nearly to Speyer, of the Haardt mountains to the S., and the Odenwald (Melibocus) and the Taunus (Feldberg, Altkönig) to the E. The view from the *Königsstuhl*, a porphyry rock farther to the W., on which the Franconian kings and the counts of the Wormsgau are said to have held their tribunals, is less attractive, and only extends over the wooded hills.

The path which descends on the E. side is shaded by beautiful beech, ash, and maple trees, and leads in about $1/2$ hr. to the village of *Dannenfels* (* *Gümbel*), a romantic spot in a grove of remarkably fine chesnut trees. The road, now destitute of shade, leads across an undulating plain to *Bennhausen* ($2\,1/4$ M.), *Weitersweiler* ($1\,1/4$ M.), and *Dreysen* ($1\,1/4$ M.), where the "*Kaiserstrasse*," constructed by Napoleon, is crossed. **Göllheim** (*Hirsch*), $1\,3/4$ M. farther, is a small town of considerable antiquity, at the entrance of which is situated a handsome new chapel, designed by Voit of Munich; near it is an ancient elm, under which stands the *Königskreuz*, a crucifix much injured by the French republicans in 1794. On the r. side is the inscription:

"*Anno milleno trecentis bis minus annis*
In Julio mense rex Adolphus cadit ense"

to which is added by way of postscript, that the monument was renewed by Count Ludwig of Nassau in 1611. The old inscription on the E. side is almost illegible.

Under this tree, on July 2nd, 1298, the emperor Adolph of Nassau (p. 201) expired amid the noise and turmoil of battle, pierced by the sword of his antagonist Albert of Austria. The contest, which had commenced at the *Hasebühl*, $1\,1/2$ M. to the S., was terminated on this spot by the death of the emperor. The cross and the wall into which it is built, were shortly afterwards erected by a member of the imperial family.

Dürkheim is about 15 M. distant from Göllheim by the road through Grünstadt, and 12 M. by the footpath by *Eisenberg* and *Leiningen*. The intervening district is undulating and fertile but uninteresting. The traveller who starts from Dielkirchen early in the morning, crossing the Donnersberg, and reaching Grünstadt on foot (as no carriages are to be had at Göllheim), must either pass the night there, and proceed by omnibus on the following morning, or take a carriage the same evening to Dürkheim (one-horse 2 fl.)

Grünstadt (*Jacobslust;* diligence 24 kr., in the morning, and omnibus to Dürkheim; 1-horse carriage 2 fl.) was till the time of the first French revolution the residence of the counts of Leiningen. Their castles of *Alt-* and *Neu-Leiningen*, the ruins of which are seen on a hill at some distance, were destroyed in 1690. The *Obere* and *Untere Hof*, the residences of the counts in Grünstadt, are now employed for industrial and educational purposes. The road, which lies very high, next traverses a succession of extensive vineyards. *Herxheim*, *Callstadt*, and *Ungstein* are noted for their wines.

Dürkheim (**Hôtel Reitz*, at the E. side of the town, R.

1 fl., B. 20 kr., D. 1 fl.; * *Vier Jahreszeiten*), with a pop. of 7000, was almost entirely rebuilt after the destruction of the castle of the counts of Leiningen by the Elector Palatine Frederick in 1471, and again after the French devastation of 1689. During the subsequent century it was the prosperous and animated residence of the princes of Leiningen-Hartenburg, till their castle was burned down by the French in 1794. Its site is now occupied by the Town-hall. Dürkheim is one of the most important places in the Palatinate, and is beautifully situated amidst the vineyards of the Haardt mountains. The grape-cure and the neighbouring saline baths of *Philippshalle* attract numerous visitors in autumn. Ludwigshafen (p, 224) is 12 M. distant, Neustadt 9 M., Grünstadt $7^1/_2$ M., Kaiserslautern (p. 196) 21 M. Omnibuses run daily in all directions; to Neustadt five times a day in 2 hrs., fare 30 kr. One-horse carriage to Neustadt 3 fl.; diligence twice daily, 24 kr.

On a precipitous height at the entrance of the *Isenachthal*, $1^1/_2$ M. to the W. of Dürkheim, are situated the stately ruins of the ancient Benedictine monastery of ***Limburg**, a palatial building, ornamented with a handsome piazza, belonging to the 11th cent. It is one of the principal objects of attraction in the environs of Dürkheim, and is frequently visited from Mannheim. It was once the castle of the Salic count Conrad the Elder, who was elected king of Germany in 1024 as Conrad II. His eldest son Conrad having lost his life while hunting, the king resolved to convert his castle into a place of worship, an act of devotion which he believed would be favourable to the repose of his son's soul. He accordingly laid the foundation-stone of the church in presence of his Queen Gisela, July 12th, 1030, at 4 o'clock in the morning, as the old chronicles tell us, and, at a later hour on the same day, the foundation-stone of the cathedral of Speyer. Twelve years later the edifice was completed and placed in the hands of the Benedictines. The abbots chose the Hartenburg counts of Leiningen for their protectors, but subsequent quarrels induced Count Emich VIII. to take possession of and destroy the abbey in 1504. It was partially restored in 1515—1554, but was finally secularized by the Elector Palatine Frederick III. in 1574, and since then has gradually fallen to decay.

The ruin now belongs to the town of Dürkheim, and is surrounded by public walks and grounds (refreshments to be procured at the top). The S. W. tower, which belongs to the 13th and 14th centuries, commands a fine view; a portion of the cloisters of the same date and the vaults on the E. side are still well preserved. In three different directions delightful prospects are obtained, especially that to the E. over the vast Palatinate, extending like a garden beyond the mountains of the Odenwald. To the N. W. the view is bounded by the red ruins of the **Hartenburg** (* *Hirsch*), a castle founded by the counts of Leiningen about the year 1200, completed in 1510 and destroyed in 1794. Its extensive vaults and huge dismantled towers resemble those of the castle of Heidelberg. A large grass-plat (gymnastic ground) on the E. side of the castle, surrounded with handsome lime-trees, commands a fine view of the valley.

To the N. E. of Limburg is situated the Kastanienberg, on the wooded slopes of which a part of the *Heidenmauer* may be seen; above it rises the *Teufelsstein*, a mass of rock, 12 ft. in height, which possibly once served as an altar. The Heidenmauer (heathens' wall) is a stone wall, 8—12 ft. in height, constructed of loose stones heaped together, and enclosing a space on the summit of the Kastanienberg of 60—100 ft. in diameter. The novelist Cooper derived the materials for his tale "The Heidenmauer" from this locality. The wall, like that on the Altkönig (p. 169), is incontestibly of ancient Germanic origin. The *Peterskopf* (1530 ft.), 2¼ M. to the N. W. of the Teufelsstein, commands an extensive and beautiful view.

On the verge of the W. mountain-basin, a path leads by the village of *Seebach* (1½ M.), with an ancient convent and well preserved church of the 12th cent., through vineyards (closed in Sept. and Oct.) to **Wachenheim** (*Krone*), 2¼ M. farther. By the high road from Dürkheim to Wachenheim the distance is not above 1½ M.

On the W. side of Wachenheim lie the ruins of the *Wachtenor Geiersburg*, once the property of the Salic dukes, afterwards of the Counts Palatine, destroyed in 1689. On the S. side are situated handsome villas and well-kept grounds, belonging to the wealthy wine-merchants of the district. The next village on the road is *Forst* (¾ M.), and 1½ M. farther **Deidesheim** (* *Bairischer Hof*), both celebrated for their wine; the rich wine-merchants constitute the sole aristocracy of the country.

Pedestrians should leave the high road a little to the S. of Deidesheim, and turn to the r. through vineyards, skirting the brow of the hill, to *Königsbach* (2 M.), and, ¾ M. beyond it, *Gimmeldingen*; about 2 M. farther the castle of *Winzingen* is reached, the ruins of which are covered with ivy, and surrounded by private pleasure-grounds (not open to the public). Near it are the * *Wolf'sche Anlagen*, behind the village of

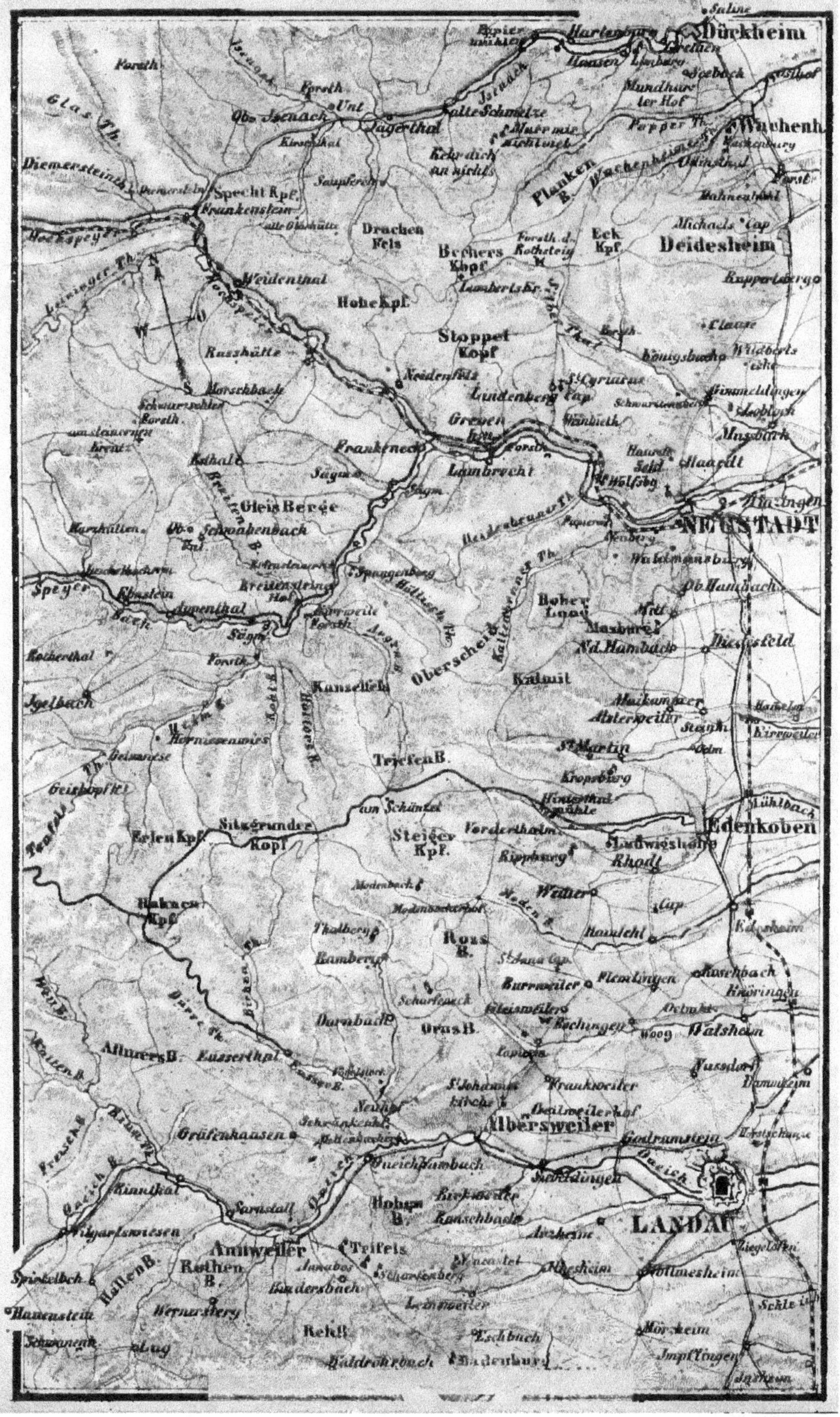
Dürkheim
Hartenburg
Jägerthal
Frankenstein
Weidenthal
Drachen Fels
Hohe Kpf.
Stoppel Kopf
Deidesheim
Lambrecht
Gleis Berge
NEUSTADT
Kalmit
St. Martin
Edenkoben
Steiger Kpf.
Rhodt
Albersweiler
Annweiler
Trifels
LANDAU

Haardt, near the church, which are always accessible to visitors. From the highest part of the grounds near the *Hermitage* a fine view is obtained over the entire plain of the Rhine; Speyer, Mannheim, and even the red sandstone arches of the castle of Heidelberg may be distinguished. At the foot of the hill lies Neustadt, 1½ M. distant. *Neustadt, Maxburg, Edenkoben, Landau,* see R. 55. The *Maxburg* lies 3 M. to the S. W. of Neustadt. From the Maxburg a steep path leads to *Mittel-Hambach* at the foot of the hill, from which the road leads through the plain to **Edenkoben** (3 M.).

The pedestrian should now proceed along the slopes of the wooded and vine-clad mountains to the large and wealthy village of **Rhodt** (1½ M.), on an eminence near which are situated the ruins of *Rietburg* or *Rippburg*. At the foot of the hill is the *Ludwigshöhe*, a handsome villa, erected by king Ludwig I. of Bavaria, commanding a noble prospect, but the interior is destitute of artistic decoration. About 6 M. to the W. is situated the "*Schänzel*," on the *Steigerkopf* (1919 ft.), an important military point, bravely and successfully defended against the French by the Prussian general von Pfau, to whose memory a monument has been erected on the spot.

The road next leads through the villages of **Weiher** (1½ M.) and **Burweiler** (1½ M.); above the latter lies the picturesque, white *Anna-Capelle*; ¾ M. farther is **Gleisweiler** (1000 ft.), sheltered from the N. and W. winds, at the foot of the *Teufelsberg* (2500 ft.); it possesses an extensive *Hydropathic Estab.*, containing likewise grape, whey, and (strange to English ears) cowhouse-air cures (also an hotel); weekly charges, incl. medical attendance, 17½—28 fl.; pleasant excursion to *Scharfeneck*, a ruin 4½ M. to the S.W. — **Frankweiler** (*Schwan*) (1½ M.) and **Siebeldingen** (1½ M.) are the next villages. The *Queich* (p. 223) is now crossed. The mountains on the r. bank of the Queich are considered to belong to the *Vosges*, of which the Haardt constitutes the N. spurs.

After passing *Ilbesheim* (2¼ M.), with the ruined castle of *Neucastel*, the road leads to **Eschbach** (*Engel*), a village at the foot of the Madenburg (to visit which the traveller should engage the services of a guide), and thence to Trifels.

The ***Madenburg**, 1½ M. to the S.W. of Eschbach, is the grandest and most extensive ruin in the Rhenish Palatinate. The castle formerly belonged to the counts of Leiningen, afterwards to the archbishopric of Speyer, and was burned down by the French general Montclar in 1680. It commands a noble prospect — the finest in the whole Palatinate — comprising the plain of the Rhine from Strasburg to the Melibocus, and in the distance the heights of the Odenwald and Black Forest. The cathedral spire of Strasburg, the towers of Carlsruhe, Speyer, Mannheim, and Worms, are all visible to the naked eye. But what lends a peculiar charm to the scene is the view of the adjacent chain of the Vosges, with its numerous volcanic and forest-clad peaks, from many of which bare masses of variegated sandstone rise in grotesque forms, often resembling old ruined castles.

A walk of 4½ M. in a N.W. direction along the high mountain slopes, through fragrant pine, fir and beech woods, will now bring the pedestrian to the ruins of the Castle of ***Trifels** (1422 ft.), where Richard Coeur de Lion was confined for more than a year by the Emperor Henry VI., until his liberation was effected by the instrumentality of the faithful Blondel. Trifels was not unfrequently occupied by the German emperors; its walls protected the unhappy Henry IV., when he was excommunicated by the Pope in 1076, deserted by his nobles and pursued by the unnatural hostility of his own son. The castle also served as a prison for Adalbert, archbishop of Mayence, who was closely confined here by Henry V., but released by the citizens of Mayence, as the inscription on the brass gates of the Cathedral records. Here too were frequently kept the imperial insignia and treasures. After the 30 Years' war the castle fell gradually into decay, so that at the present day nothing is left but the tower (30 ft.) and fragments of the walls. The view resembles that from the Madenburg, but is less extensive. On a mountain of the same height as that on which Trifels stands, rises the *Münz*, a square tower (70 ft.), the ascent to which is made in 1 hr. from Annweiler, a village at the foot of the hill on the N.W. side. — A still finer prospect is obtained from the tower on the *Rehberg*, 3 M. distant from Annweiler.

Annweiler (*Trifels*; *Rother Ochse; Post;* good beer at the *Bairischer Hof*) is a small town, possessing a handsome modern *Town-hall*, designed by Professor Voit of Munich, but contains no objects of interest to the traveller (Omnibus twice daily to Landau, p. 223). From this point the road ascends the beautiful **Annweiler Thal*, a narrow dale enclosed by wooded slopes and mountain peaks from which grotesque masses of variegated sandstone project, giving a most picturesque appearance to the valley.

The finest portion of the valley is comprised between Annweiler and **Willgartswiesen** (**Lamm*), a distance of 6 M. The grandest and most remarkable broken masses of coloured sandstone, rising from the woods and bushes, are those in the vicinity of **Dahn** (*Pfalz*), which, with the assistance of a guide, may be reached in 2 hrs. from Willgartswiesen. Before entering the village tbe extensive ruins of the old castle of *Dahn* are seen situated on a wooded sandstone rock, which, as well as the castle itself, is so overgrown with underwood that it is difficult to distinguish the one from the other. The steps and passages are partly cut out of the solid rock. The highest point affords a good survey of the surrounding mountains, and is worth a visit, as the ascent does not occupy more than 20 min.

In the immediate vicinity of Dahn is the *Jungfernsprung* (virgin's leap), a rock of considerable height, overhanging the road to Kaltebach, with which various traditions are connected. About 3$^3/_4$ M. farther in the valley of the *Lauter*, where similar rocky formations are frequently met with, lies **Kaltebach,** a post-station on the high road between Landau and Zweibrücken. Beyond this point the country offers few objects of attraction to the traveller. He may now return to the Rhine by the Zweibrücken diligence or by the omnibus.

Another circuit may be made by again turning E. from Dahn, following the high road by *Busenberg, Erlenbach* with the castle of *Barbelstein,* and *Birkenhördt,* to **Bergzabern** (*Huber*), a small old-fashioned town, 12 M. from Dahn, from which an omnibus runs to the railway stat. *Winden,* 4$^1/_2$ M. distant.

Instead of descending from the hill at *Gleisweiler,* the traveller may, if he prefer it, proceed along the heights, which offer a succession of fine views, to *Albersweiler* and *Annweiler* (12 M.); here he may take a carriage to *Dahn,* return in the evening to Annweiler, and proceed the next day to *Trifels, Madenburg* and the railway stat. *Landau.*

46. From Mannheim to Saarbrücken.

Ludwigshafen-Bexbach and Prussian Saarbrücken line.

To Neustadt in 1, Kaiserslautern in 2, Homburg in 3, and Saarbrücken in 4 hrs. Fares 6 fl. 7, 3 fl. 48, and 2 fl. 35 kr. The station at Ludwigshafen, opposite to Mannheim, is $^3/_4$ M. distant from the Rhine bridge, and 2$^1/_4$ M. from the Mannheim station. Carriage from one station to the other, 1—2 pers. 45 kr., 3 pers. 1 fl., 4 pers. 1 fl. 12 kr.; omnibus 22 kr., to Mannheim 16 kr.

During 1 hr. the train traverses fields of corn and tobacco. Stations *Mutterstadt*, *Schifferstadt*, junction of the branch line to Speyer (p. 200), which may be reached in 15 min.; *Böhl*, from which a view of the distant Donnersberg may be obtained; *Hassloch*, a large, flourishing village with 5000 inhabitants. As the *Haardt mountains* are approached, the *Maxburg* (p. 223), on an eminence to the l., comes in view, to the r. the ruin of *Winzingen*, and beyond it, farther to the r., the extensive vineyards of *Königsbach*, *Ruppertsberg*, *Musbach*, and on the mountain-side the long village of *Haardt* (p. 193).

At **Neustadt** is the junction of the Maximilian, Ludwig, and Bexbach lines, see p. 224. The latter now enters the mountain district of *Westrich*. For an hour the train winds through the narrow, well-wooded, and picturesque valley of the *Speyerbach*, the variegated sandstone rocks of which are penetrated by 12 tunnels. Beyond Neustadt, on an eminence to the r., are situated the red ruins of *Wolfsburg*, below which stands a castellated cloth-factory. The next station is *St. Lambrecht-Grevenhausen* (*Weber), the numerous cloth-factories of which owe their origin to French emigrants. On a neighbouring height are the ruins of *Neidenfels*. At the following stat. *Frankenstein* (*Krone; *Hirsch), the valley is remarkably wild and picturesque; to the r. is the rock called the *Teufelsleiter* (devil's ladder). In a secluded valley diverging to the r. lies the ruin of *Diemerstein*, now converted into private pleasure-grounds. (From Frankenstein to Dürkheim see p. 188.) The station of *Hochspeyer*, the highest on the line, lies nearly 100 ft. higher than Neustadt. The last tunnel is about 1400 yds. in length.

Kaiserslautern (**Schwan*) is one of the most important places in the Palatinate, and is situated in the hilly tract of Westrich. It was once a residence of the Emperor Frederick Barbarossa, who erected a magnificent palace here in 1153, the site of which is now occupied by a house of correction. His memory is still greatly revered in Kaiserslautern, as he presented a wood to the town, which produces an annual revenue of 30,000 fl. The Protestant church also owes its foundation the same monarch. The churchyard contains a monument to the memory of soldiers of Napoleon who were natives of the place. Here the Prussian troops under the Duke of Brunswick, after their return from Champagne, repulsed the French under Pichegru and Hoche in Nov., 1793. [Diligence to Kreuznach through the Alsenzthal (p. 189) in 8 hrs.]

The tract of country between Kaiserslautern and Homburg is remarkably flat. The line (together with the Kaiserstrasse, p. 146) skirts the turf-moor and the foot of the hills.

Landstuhl (*Engel; Krone*) was once the seat of the Sickingen family, whose strong castle, with its massive walls, 24 ft. in thickness, now lies in ruins above the town. Franz von Sickingen was besieged in this stronghold by the electors of the Palatinate and of Treves, and lost his life by the falling of a beam. His bones lie in a vault under the church.

The monument erected to his memory was destroyed by the French, but portions of it are still to be scen at the church. The large Rom. Cath. *Orphan Asylum* is a modern building.

The next station of importance is **Homburg** (*Carlsberg; Post*), among the buildings of which the handsome Rom. Cath. church is a conspicuous object. The castle of *Carlsberg*, $1\frac{1}{2}$ M. to the E. of the town, was built by Duke Charles II. of the Palatinate in 1780, and destroyed by the French in 1793.

Branch line (23 min.; fares 30, 18, 12 kr.) to **Zweibrücken** (*Pfälzer Hof; Zweibrücker Hof; Lamm*), formerly the principal residence of the Dukes of the Zweibrücken-Palatinate, and known in the literary world as the place where the *Editiones Bipontinæ* of Latin and Greek authors were published. When Charles X. (Gustavus) of the house of Zweibrücken ascended the Swedish throne, the Duchy became subject to Sweden, which it continued to be till the death of Charles XII. in 1719. Stanislaus Lesczinsky, the fugitive king of Poland, resided here for some time, and to him belonged the neighbouring grounds of *Tschiflik*, on the road to Pirmasenz, now quite fallen to decay.

Beyond *Bexbach* the line enters a rich mining and coal-district in the Prussian dominions. The foundry of the brothers Stumm at **Neunkirchen** (*Jochum*, near the bridge) employs about 800 hands, and yields 5000 tons of iron-wares annually. At Neunkirchen is the junction of the Rhein-Nahe and Saarbrücken lines.

Beyond Neunkirchen the train passes through the *Bildstock tunnel* (500 yds.). The numerous cuttings which have been made in this vicinity, expose to view the strata of coal, with intervening layers of slate and sandstone, containing many remarkable fossils (*sigillaria*), which are rarely met with in such abundance. In many of the cuttings from 40 to 50 fossil trunks of trees of various diameters have been found. Some of the coal-mines are situated on the main line, others are connected with it by branch railways. They all belong to the Prussian government, at whose expense they are worked. The number of hands employed is about 13,000, and the yield upwards of 2 million tons of coals annually, worth 800,000*l*. These mines form the entire source of the industry of the district. Glass-houses, sal-ammoniac, Prussian-blue, and other manufactories abound.

Between the stations of *Sulzbach* and *Duttweiler*, in the wood $\frac{1}{4}$ M. to the l. of the line, is situated the "**brennende Berg**" or burning mountain, a coal-bed which ignited spontaneously about 160 years ago. A slow combustion is still taking place, and the whole bed, 400 by 40 yds., is gradually sinking. Smoke may be seen, especially after rain, issuing from the fissures, in which eggs are sometimes cooked by visitors.

Saarbrücken (**Zix*) on the *Saar*, which here becomes navigable, is a Prussian town on the French frontier, connected by a bridge with the suburb of **St. Johann.** The palace was up to 1793 occupied by the princes of Nassau-Saarbrücken; the palace-church contains monuments of the family.

At **Arnual** in the immediate neighbourhood is a **Church* built in the best Gothic style, containing a remarkably fine font, pulpit, and interesting old monuments of the above mentioned princely family, whose vaults were formerly at Arnual.

From Saarbrücken to *Metz* by railway in $2^1/_2$, to *Paris* in 12 hrs.

47. Worms.

Worms (**Alter Kaiser*, or Old Emperor, near the cathedral, R. 42, A. 18 kr.; *Rhenish Hotel*, at the steamboat wharf, $^3/_4$ M. from the town; *Liebfrauenberg*), one of the most ancient towns in Germany, is situated $^3/_4$ M. from the Rhine to which its walls formerly extended, and is rendered worthy of a visit by its Cathedral, the baptistery of which contains some good statues. The Burgundian conquerors of the Rhineland (431), the Franconian kings, and afterwards Charlemagne and his successors, frequently resided at Worms. Here the war against the Saxons was brought to a close in 772; here the May assembly was often held, and the great contest concerning the investiture of the bishops with ring and staff was here terminated by the Concordat between the emperor Henry V. and Pope Calixtus II. Many other historical events of interest are also connected with this venerable city.

As early as 1255, Worms belonged to the Confederation of the Rhenish towns, and in the time of Frederick Barbarossa contained a pop. of 70,000 souls; at the commencement of the 30 Years' war this number was reduced to 40,000, and at the present period to 10,726 ($^2/_3$ Prot.). All the suburbs were levelled in 1632 by order of the Swedish Colonel Haubold, and in 1689 the town suffered the most cruel devastation at the hands of Melac and the young Duc de Crequi. A proclamation had been issued that on a certain day the whole town, with the exception of the cathedral, should be committed to the flames. The dismayed inhabitants accordingly sought an asylum in the sacred edifice with their most valuable property, which thus became an easy prey to the enemy. On May 31st, 1689, the town was set on fire, and, with the exception of the cathedral and synagogue, soon became one smouldering heap of ruins. Traces of the fire may still be observed on the cathedral walls.

The * **Dom,** or *Cathedral,* was consecrated in 1016 in presence of the emperor Henry II., but underwent extensive alterations towards the close of the 12th cent. The whole structure, with its four slender towers, two cupolas and choir, is, more particularly in its exterior, one of the finest Romanesque churches in existence. Quaint figures of animals and masks are visible upon the towers, of which the N.W. was erected by Bishop Reinhardt in 1472, to replace the old one, which had fallen in. To the same datc belongs the S. pointed arched **Portal*, in the pediment of which may be seen the figure of a woman adorned with a mural crown and mounted on a animal, whose four different heads (angel, lion, ox, and eagle) are symbolical of the four Evangelists. The whole is evidently emblematical of the victorious Church, and has no reference, as some suppose, to the frightful execution of the tyrannical Brunhilde, consort of the Austrasian king Sicgbert, which took place here in 613, under the direction of Clotaire II. of Soissons.

The interior of the cathedral is destitute of ornament, but the very ancient *Sculpture*, representing Daniel in the lions' den, in the first S. chapel on the r., together with the *Tombstone of the three Franconian princesses*, belonging to the 13th cent., and removed from the Nunnery to its present position in the N. aisle, may afford some interest to the visitor.

The *Baptistery*, to the l. of the S. Portal, contains some large **Sculptures*, admirably executed, most perfect in detail, and in excellent preservation. They formerly belonged to the cloisters constructed in the 15th cent., but on the demolition of the latter in 1813, they where removed to their present position; they represent the Annunciation, Descent from the Cross, Resurrection, Nativity and Genealogy of Christ. Beyond them is the *Tombstone* of the knight Eberhard von Heppenheim, a well-executed figure in armour kneeling before a crucifix. The font formerly belonged to the ancient chapel of St. John, which was taken down in 1807. The paintings in the old Byzantine style of the two patron saints of the Church, St. Peter und St. Paul, and of other saints, alone escaped the French conflagration. The objects in this chapel deserve the minutest examination, and may be seen on application to the sexton (fee 18 kr.) who lives in the square, a few hundred yards from the S. portal of the church.

It may perhaps interest those who are versed in German legendary lore to know that the open space in front of the cathedral was the scene of the quarrel between Brunhilde and Chrimhilde, as recorded by the Nibelungenlied in the 14th Adventure.

The handsome sub-structure of red sandstone on the N. side of the cathedral was formerly the episcopal residence, rebuilt in 1727, after having been destroyed by the French in 1689, and again despoiled by the republicans in 1794. It was here that the diet of April, 1521, was held, in which Luther defended his doctrines in presence of Charles V., six electors, and a numerous assembly. Here too a last and ineffectual attempt at a reconciliation between the Protestants and the Rom. Catholics was made by order of the emperor Ferdinand, the Protestant cause being defended by Melancthon and the Rom. Catholic by the Dean Jacob von Eltz.

The **Synagogue** near the Mainzer Thor is an object of interest to antiquarians, though externally of unimposing appearance. The Jewish community of Worms is one of the oldest in Germany, and is said to have existed as early as 588 B. C., at the time of the first destruction of the Temple by the Babylonians.

Heil's Garden is worth a visit on account of the magnificent palms and rare plants which the hot-houses contain.

In the Mainzer suburb, destroyed by the Swedes and the French, the ***Liebfrauenkirche**, or Church of our Lady, $^3/_4$ M. from the cathedral, alone escaped. The broad path to the r. which leads to it, diverges from the high-road about 100 yards from the Mainzer Thor, and passes the old churchyard, bounded on the S. by fragments of walls connected with the old church. The church was erected at the close of the 15th cent. to replace an older edifice which occupied the same site; the key-stone of the vaulted roof bears the arms of the different corporations of Worms who caused it to be built. The only object of interest which the interior contains is a curious old piece of painted sculpture in the N. aisle. The *Portal* is decorated with well-executed statues, representing the wise and foolish virgins, the death of the Virgin and her coronation by the Saviour. Service on Saturdays and those days which are dedicated to the Virgin.

The well-known second-class wine called *Liebfrauenmilch* is yielded by vineyards in the immediate vicinity of the church. Near the old watch-tower *Luginsland*, and at the *Catetloch* on the S. side of the town, a wine scarcely inferior to the above is produced.

In former times the Rhine flowed round a meadow known to this day by the name of the *Rosengarten*, on the r. bank of the river, opposite to Worms. With it are connected many ancient German traditions, preserved in the poetry of Siegfried and the Nibelungen, to appreciate which, however, a thorough acquaintance with the old German language and literature is requisite.

48. Speyer.

Speyer (**Wittelsbacher Hof; Rheinischer Hof;* **Bregenzer's* Restaurant near the cathedral), the principal town of the

Bavarian Palatinate, seat of Government and a bishopric, "city of the dead emperors," has a pop. of 11,000 ($^3/_5$ Prot.). It was known to the Romans as *Noviomagus*, *Neomagus*, *Nemetæ*, or *Augusta Nemetum*, and as, by the partition of Verdun (843), it became with Worms and Mayence a portion of Germany, it has frequently been the residence of German monarchs. It especially rose to importance under the Salic kings, who resided at their palace of Limburg near Dürkheim (p. 191), 18 M. from Speyer.

The ****Cathedral** (open till 11 a.m., and from 2 to 6 p.m.) was founded in 1030 by Conrad II. as a burial place for himself and his successors, and completed by his son Henry III., and grandson Henry IV. (1061), all of whom found their last resting-place within its precincts. The remains of Henry IV., however, who had been excommunicated by Pope Gregory, were not conveyed here till 5 years after his death, during which period his body remained unburied in the Chapel of St. Afra, on the N. side of the cathedral, which he himself had erected. His son Henry V., the last of the Salic imperial family, is also interred in the cathedral, as well as Philip of Swabia, Rudolph of Habsburg, Adolph of Nassau, and Albert I. of Austria, by whose hand Adolph fell at Göllheim (p. 190). After the murder of Albert I., the Emperor Henry VII. caused the remains of the two rival monarchs to be deposited side by side in the same vault. Here too lie the remains of Gisela, the pious consort of Conrad II., Bertha, the queen of Henry IV., and Beatrice, the wife of Barbarossa, with her daughter Agnes. The cathedral was in 1146 the scene of the zealous and fiery preaching of St. Bernhard, whose fervency in the cause of the Cross induced Conrad III. to join the crusades.

The cathedral suffered much by a great conflagration in 1450, but was soon restored. On May 31st, 1689, the sacred edifice was laid waste by the fire and sword of the French soldiery, who in their eagerness for spoil did not even respect the resting-places of the dead. The tombs of the emperors were broken open and ransacked, the finest towers in the town were blown up, the inhabitants driven out, and the town itself, after having been filled with combustibles, committed to the flames and completely destroyed, whilst the most frightful atrocities were practised by the hirelings of the "most christian" Louis XIV. The demolition of the imperial monuments was again repeated in 1693 by the order of the French intendant Henz, and by a singular coincidence, exactly 100 years later, on the same anniversary, the despoliation of the tombs of the French kings at St. Denis was perpetrated under the direction of one Hentz, a representative of the people, and the ashes of Louis XIV., the devastator of the Palatinate, were the first to suffer what appeared to be a righteous retribution.

In the following year (1794, Jan. 10th – 20th) the cathedral was subjected to a new devastation. Everything of a combustible nature, crosses, altars, prayer-books &c. were burned in a heap in front of the sacred edifice, while the republicans danced demoniacally round the pile. The church was further desecrated by being converted into a magazine, and was actually, at the close of the last century, on the point of being put up to public auction at a valuation of 8000 fr., a degrading fate it was happily spared. Napoleon ordered it in 1806 to be rededicated to public worship, but in the absence of funds it still continued to be used as a store-house. In 1822 it was completely restored by the assistance of the king Maximilian, and again devoted to its sacred purposes.

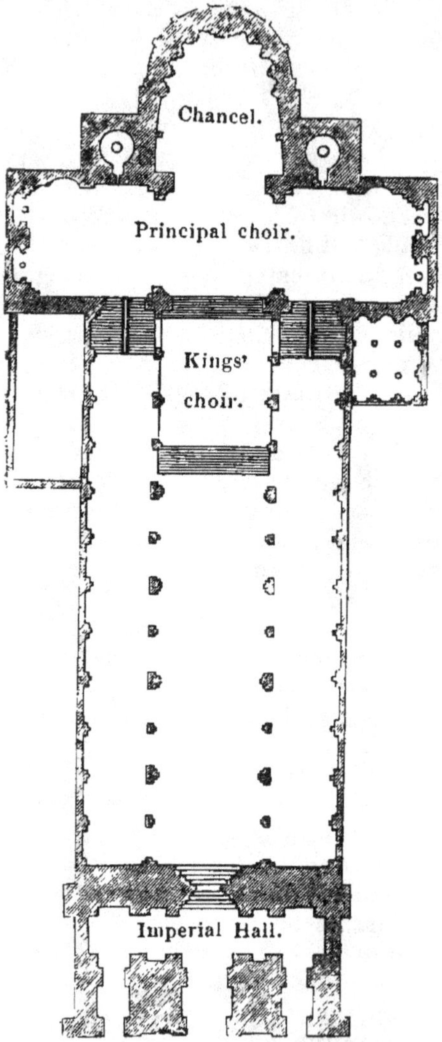

The crypt, under the transept and choir, is in all respects the same as it was in 1039; the choir, with the two E. towers, belongs probably to a date subsequent to 1068, while the upper parts of the church are believed to have been erected after a fire in 1159. The whole edifice is a grand and massive, but simple specimen of the Romanesque style.

The *Front* of the cathedral was newly constructed from the designs of the eminent architect Hübsch of Carlsruhe in 1854—58, as well as the W. spire (225 ft.) and the Kaiser-Halle (Imperial Hall). The large circular window in front has a head of the Saviour crowned with thorns in the centre on a gold ground, and in the corners the emblematic figures of the four Evangelists, an angel (Matthew), winged lion (Mark), ox (Luke), and eagle (John). Over the principal gate is the imperial double eagle, and over the side entrances the lion of the Palatinate. In the entrance (Imperial) hall under the W. towers, in niches of gold mosaic, were placed in 1858 statues of the emperors interred in the *Kings' choir;* on the r. Conrad II., Rudolph of Habsburg, Adolph of Nassau, and Albert of Austria; on the l. Henry III., Henry IV. (in the robes of a penitent), Henry V., and Philip of Swabia. The four reliefs are by *Pilz:* Conrad laying the foundation-stone of the cathedral; Rudolph and the priest with the host; Rudolph receiving the tidings of his election to the imperial throne; the same emperor taking the cross from the altar at his coronation at Aix-la-Chapelle. Over the principal inner portal is represented the consecration of the church to the Virgin, on the l. St. Bernhard and St. Stephen, on the r. John the Baptist and the painter Schraudolph.

The entire length of the Cathedral is 475 ft., and the breadth of the body 130 ft.; the transept is 190 ft. in length, and the body of the church 100 ft. high; externally the length is exactly 200 yds., and the breadth of the front 58 yds. In the interior from the entrance-choir to the kings' choir is 90 yds., the kings' choir 30, and the principal and foundation choir 56 yds. long; the breadth of the nave is 60 and that of the chief choir about 87 yds. The central portion of the edifice is double the height of the aisles.

Two inscriptions in the church itself, over the W. side-doors, are to the following effect: *This house of God, destroyed by fire in 1689, was rebuilt in 1772 by the Archbishop Imperial Count of Limburg-Styrum, despoiled in 1794, again restored in 1820 by Maximilian Joseph I., King of Bavaria. Maximilian II., King of Bavaria caused it to be embellished with paintings by Johann Schraudolph and adorned by Joseph Schwarzmann, completed in 1853.*

In the kings' choir, on broad pedestals, stand two large stone **Statues;* on the r. *Rudolph of Habsburg*, of Tyrolese marble by Schwanthaler, is represented in a sitting posture with a sword in his r. hand and a helmet at his feet, as the restorer of peace and order after the sad interregnum. The features bear a faithful resemblanee to a genuine tombstone of the emperor, which still exists in the vaults of the church. The statue on the l., executed in sandstone by Ohmacht, represents the emperor *Adolph* in a kneeling position.

On the r. and l. sides of the passage to the principal choir two reliefs, formerly in the vaults, were built into the walls in 1853; each contains full-figured likenesses of four emperors, partially gilt, and bearing old Latin inscriptions.

The frescoes in the nave, finished in 1852, are 32 in number, and are among the finest specimens of modern German art.

****Frescoes**, executed by *Joh. Schraudolph*, assisted by *C. Schraudolph* and others, since 1845; the decorations by *Joseph Schwarzmann*. Nave. *N. wall:* 1. Adam and Eve; 2. Abraham's promise; 3. David's vision; 4. The birth of the Virgin; 5. Her bethrothal; 6. Visited by the angel; 7. Adoration of the Magi; 8. The circumcision; 9. Mary finds Jesus in the Temple; 10. Joseph's death; 11. Jesus teaching; 12. The risen Saviour. *S. wall:* 1. Noah's thankoffering; 2. Moses at the bush; 3. Prophesying of Jeremias; 4. Mary's sacrifice; 5. The Angel's greeting; 6. The nativity of Christ; 7. Simeon's prophecy; 8. The flight to Egypt; 9. Jesus at Nazareth; 10. Marriage at Cana; 11. Crucifixion; 12. Descent of the Holy Ghost. On the vaulted cupola: the Lamb, Abel, Abraham, Melchisedech, the manna, Isaiah, Jeremiah, Ezekiel, Daniel, and the Evangelists. S. side-choir: Stoning of Stephen; above it Stephen before the council; to the l. the consecration of the deacons and beheading of the martyr Stephen; on the wall at the back: prayer of the same saint. N. side-choir: Vision of St. Bernhard; above it, arrival of St. Bernhard in Speyer; on the r., his prayer at the altar, and under it the presentation of the banner of the Cross; on the back part of the wall: Miraculous cure of a boy; Departure of the saints. Foundation choir: Mary and John; Death of Mary; Her interment, ascension and coronation.— The coloured sketches and cartoons are exhibited in a room above the S. baptistery (adm. 12 kr.); entrance from the S. side-choir. On the exterior a gallery without balustrades extends round the whole cathedral and not only affords a fine view of the neighbourhood, but gives the visitor an opportunity of inspecting the frescoes in the nave and choir from above. The sexton (30 kr.) acts as guide. — The crypt, restored in 1857, under the choir, is in an architectural point of view well worth visiting.

The ancient **Churchyard** of the cathedral is now converted into grounds planted with trees. On the S. side of the building is the *Oelberg* (Mt. of Olives), a curious mass of stone, with emblematical representations in sandstone, surrounded by five insulated Gothic pillars, the whole erected in 1441. It was originally a chapel in the ancient cloisters, of which no trace is now left, and represented the garden of Gethsemane and the capture of the Saviour. Near it under the trees is the *Domnapf,* or cathedral-bowl, a large vessel of sandstone, once marking the boundary between the episcopal and civic jurisdiction. Every new bishop was obliged, after having vowed to respect the freedom of the town, to fill this vessel with wine, which was then emptied to his health by the townspeople. To the E. of the choir rises from among the trees the *Heidenthürmchen* (Heathens' Tower), the foundation of which is ascribed to the Romans. It belonged in all probability to the old town-wall built by Bishop Rudger in 1080. It contains the bones of some antediluvian animals and relics of the middle ages. In a N.E. direction from the cathedral is an open hall enclosed by railings called the *Hall of Antiquities*, in which Roman and other relics found in the Rhenish Palatinate are preserved.

The Cathedral is bounded on the E. by the broad Maximilian road; on the W. by a fine old tower called the **Altpörtel,** the sole relic of the once free Imperial town; the imperial eagle which formerly adorned its summit has long since disappeared.

The devastations of the French in Speyer have left few other relics of antiquity. A mouldering wall by the Protestant church is all that remains of the ancient imperial palace called the **Retscher,** where 29 diets were held, from one of which, under Charles V., emanated in 1529 the celebrated "Protest" from which the "Protestants" derive their appellation. The bishops, who like those of Cologne were not permitted to live in the town, resided up to the commencement of the 17th cent. in the Madenburg (p. 193), and afterwards in Bruchsal.

From Speyer travellers may descend the Rhine in $^3/_4$ hr. to *Ketsch* (Inn) by small boat (48 kr. and upwards according to the number of the party), whence a good footpath, traversing a pine-forest, leads to Schwetzingen (p. 186) in $^1/_2$ hr.

49. From Heidelberg to Carlsruhe.

Baden Railway. By express in $1^1/_4$ hr., by ordinary trains in 2 hrs. Fares by express 2 fl. 42 and 1 fl. 51 kr.; by ordinary trains 2 fl. 12 kr., 1 fl. 30 kr. and 1 fl.

The line traverses the wide and fertile plain, bounded on the E. by a low range of hills, and intersects fields, meadows, and small plantations, and here and there passes villages peeping out from among innumerable fruit-trees. The train has scarcely left the station before the new cemetery-chapel, and behind it the slender tower of the Königsstuhl come in sight. **Langenbrücken** (*Ochs; Sonne*), the third station, possesses sulphur baths, and near it, to the r. of the line, is *Kislau*, formerly a hunting-castle of the archbishops of Speyer, now a penitentiary for women. Opposite to it, at some distance off, lies *Mingolsheim*, where in 1622 Count Ernst of Mansfeld, the ally of the Elector Frederick V., gained a victory over the Bavarians under Tilly.

Bruchsal (**Badischer Hof*, R. 48, B. 24, A. 18 kr.; *Zähringer Hof*), formerly a residence of the archbishops of Speyer, now the seat of a court of justice held in the Schloss. The castellated building to the l. of the line is a prison, capable of containing 408 criminals in separate cells. The church of *St. Peter* contains monuments of the last bishops of the place.

At Bruchsal is the junction of the *Württemberg West-line* and the *Baden State-railway*, which is connected by means of the former line with the *Württemberg North-line* (to Stuttgart in 2—3 hrs.).

On the Michaelsberg, near *Unter-Grombach,* is situated the *Michaelscapelle,* and on an eminence near *Weingarten* the tower of the ruined castle of *Schmalenstein.*

Durlach (**Carlsburg,* R. and B. 54 kr.), the ancient capital of the Duchy of Baden-Durlach, was, with the exception of 5 houses, burned to the ground by the French in 1688. The lofty watch-tower of the *Thurmberg,* visible for many miles round, commands a magnificent view as far as Strasbourg. Here the line to *Pforzheim* diverges to the l.

The train now proceeds by the side of the straight high-road, planted with rows of poplars, past the old Benedictine monastery of *Gottsau* (on the r.), now an Artillery-barrack. The station of Carlsruhe deserves a moment's attention on account of the excellence of its design and arrangement. On the W. side stands a fine *Statue of the state-minister Winter* in the posture of an orator.

50. Carlsruhe.

Hotels. *Erbprinz, in the Langestrasse, very attentive landlord, R. 1 fl., L. 18, B. 24, A. 24 kr.; *English Hotel, and *Hôtel Grosse, in the market-place, similar prices. — *Goldner Adler, the second hotel to the l. on entering the town by the Ettlinger Thor, moderate. Grüner Hof, to the E. of the station.

Café-Restaurant. *Hoeck (Grüner Hof). Beck, Carl-Friedrichsstrasse; beer at Kappler's, Neff's, etc.

Carriages. One-horse, for 1—2 pers. for 1/4 hr. 12 kr. To the station to meet the early train (before 6) 1 fl.

Telegraph Office in the Kreuzstrasse, No. 14.

Military Music daily from 12 to 1 in the Schlossplatz.

English Church Service in the Chapel of the Stiftung, near the Mühlberg gate.

Carlsruhe, the capital and residence of the court of the Grand-duchy of Baden, with a population of 27,000 (10,000 Rom. Cath., and 1000 Jews), is situated 3 M. from the Rhine, on the skirts of the Hardwald, and is indebted for its origin to some differences between the Margrave Carl Wilhelm and the towns-people of Durlach. He commenced in 1715 to lay out the grounds of the town round his hunting-castle, which soon gave place to the present palace. The plan of the town resembles a fan, the palace being the centre from which the streets radiate. Carlsruhe is a quiet, clean and well-built town, in which three distinct architectural styles may be observed. 1st: that of the beginning of the last century, — the older French style; 2nd: imitations of the Greek and Roman styles; 3d: the modern Romanesque (circular) School, of which the talented architect *Hübsch* is a warm supporter.

The *Ettlinger Thor* (Pl. 45) near the station, adorned with half-relief sculptures, emblematical of the union of a part of

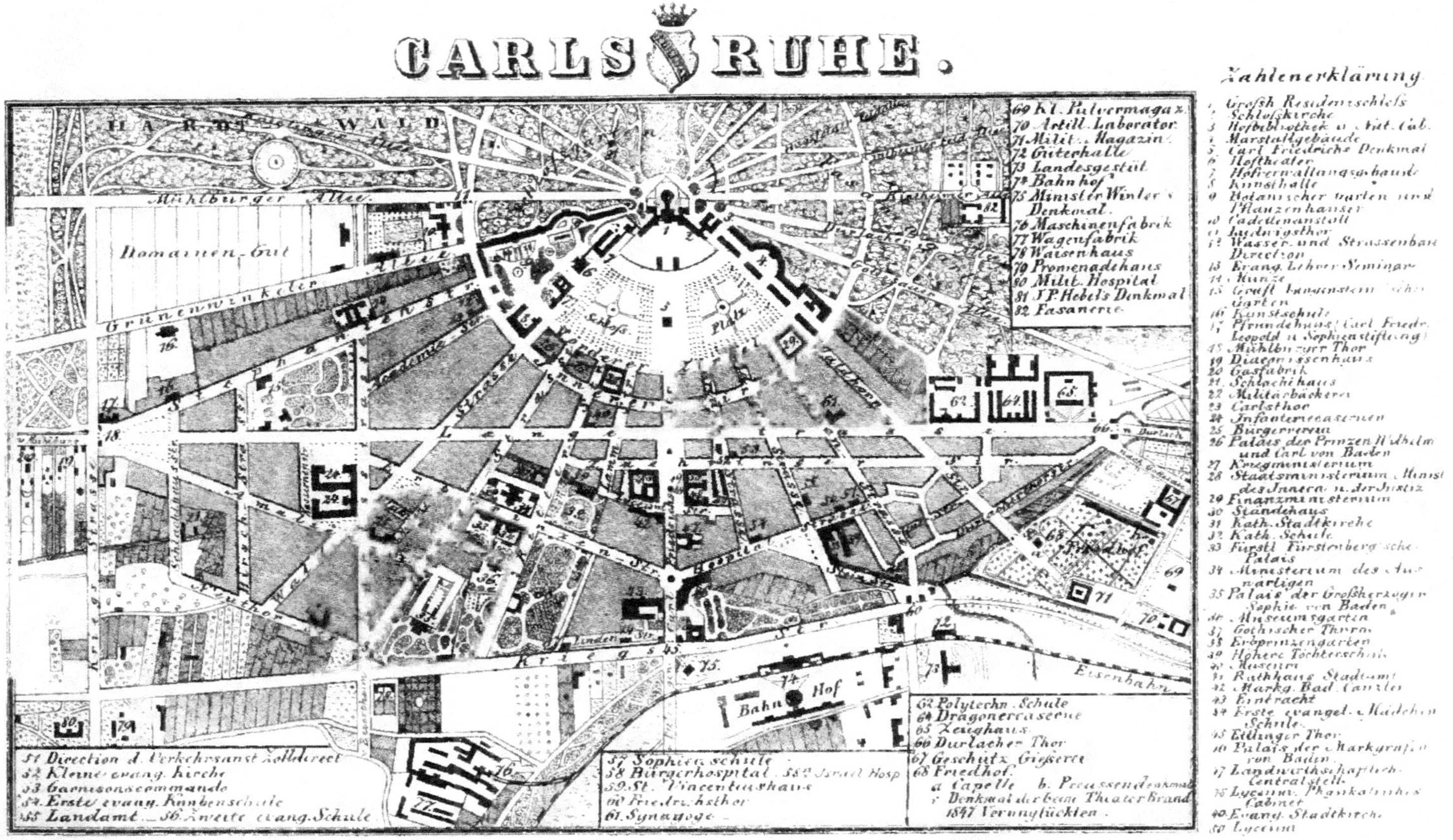
CARLSRUHE.
HARDT WALD
Mühlburger Allee
Domainen-Gut
Grünenwinkeler
Lange Strasse
Kriegs Str.
Linden Str.
Eisenbahn
Bahn Hof
Platz
69 Kl. Pulvermagaz.
70 Artill. Laborator.
71 Milit. Magazin
72 Güterhalle
73 Landesgestüt
74 Bahnhof
75 Minister Winter's Denkmal.
76 Maschinenfabrik
77 Wagenfabrik
78 Waisenhaus
79 Promenadehaus
80 Milit. Hospital
81 J.P. Hebel's Denkmal
82 Fasanerie
51 Direction d. Verkehrsanst. Zolldirect.
52 Kleine evang. Kirche
53 Garnisonscommando
54 Erste evang. Knabenschule
55 Landamt _ 56 Zweite evang. Schule
57 Sophienschule
58 Bürgerhospital
59 St. Vincentiushaus
60 Friedrichsthor
61 Synagoge
62 Polytechn. Schule
64 Dragonercaserne
65 Zeughaus
66 Durlacher Thor
67 Geschütz Giesserei
68 Friedhof
a Capelle
b. Preussendenkmal
c Denkmal der beim Theater Brand 1847 Verunglückten
Zahlenerklärung
1 Grossh. Residenzschloss
2 Schlosskirche
3 Hofbibliothek u. Nat. Cab.
4 Marstallgebäude
5 Carl Friedrichs Denkmal
6 Hoftheater
7 Hofverwaltungsgebäude
8 Kunsthalle
9 Botanischer Garten und Pflanzenhäuser
10 Cadettenanstalt
11 Ludwigsthor
12 Wasser- und Strassenbau Direction
13 Evang. Lehrer-Seminar
14 Münze
16 Kunstschule
17 Pfründehaus (Carl Friedr. Leopold u. Sophienstiftung)
18 Mühlburger Thor
19 Diaconissenhaus
20 Gasfabrik
21 Schlachthaus
22 Militärbäckerei
23 Carlsthor
24 Infanteriecasernen
25 Bürgerverein
26 Palais der Prinzen Wilhelm und Carl von Baden
27 Kriegsministerium
28 Staatsministerium, Minist. des Innern u. der Justiz
29 Finanzministerium
30 Ständehaus
31 Kath. Stadtkirche
32 Kath. Schule
33 Fürstl. Fürstenberg'sche Palais
34 Ministerium des Auswärtigen
35 Palais der Großherzogin Sophie von Baden
36 Museumsgarten
37 Gothischer Thurm
38 Erbprinzengarten
39 Höhere Töchterschule
40 Museum
41 Rathhaus Stadtamt
42 Markg. Bad. Canzlei
43 Eintracht
44 Erste evangel. Mädchen Schule
45 Ettlinger Thor
46 Palais der Markgrafen von Baden
47 Landwirthschaftlich. Centralstell.
48 Lyceum. Physikalisches Cabinet
49 Evang. Stadtkirche
50 Lyceum

the Rhenish Palatinate with Baden, forms the N. limit of the town. The objects of interest to the traveller are almost all comprised in the *Carl-Friedrichsstrasse*, which runs from the above-mentioned gate to the palace. They present themselves in the following order: the *Obelisk*, with the arms of Baden and bust of the Grand-duke Carl (1811—1818), with inscription; to the r. of the monument the *Palace* of the Margrave Wilhelm; on the l. side of the market-place the *Town-hall* (Pl. 41), and on the r. side the *Prot. Church* (Pl. 49), with its five Corinthian pillars, resembling a Greek temple; *Statue of the Grand-duke Ludwig* (1818—1830); *Pyramid* in honour of the founder of Carlsruhe, the Margrave Carl (d. 1738); in front of the palace the **Bronze statue* of the Grand-duke Charles Frederick (d. 1811), executed by Schwanthaler; at the corners of the pedestal are four female figures, personifying the four divisions of the Duchy, the whole well-designed, the statue itself being particularly well executed.

The **Schloss** (Pl. 1), or palace, erected in 1750, is built in the form of a semi-circle, and is surmounted by the *Bleithurm* (140 ft.), open on Frid. from 4 to 6 p.m., whence a good survey of the town and the Hardwald may be made. The dining-hall, ball-room, throne-room and other apartments are magnificently fitted up. The *Court-library* (Pl. 3) occupies the E. wing; a *Cabinet of Nat. History* (open Wed. and Sat. 10—12 and 3—5 o'clock) in the same part of the building, contains among other curiosities the remains of several antediluvian animals, and a valuable collection of shells. The well-appointed ducal stables are also on the same side.

In the crescent to the W. of the Schloss is situated the **Court-theatre**, a handsome modern building, erected in 1847—1853, to replace the former, which had been burned down. In the pediment to the r. are reliefs of Goethe, Schiller, and Lessing, and on the l. of Mozart, Beethoven, and Gluck; in the centre the Muse of dramatic Poetry.

An arched passage in the W. wing of the Schloss leads to the **Palace-garden**, the grounds of which extend into the Hardwald. About 300 yds. to the N.W. of the Bleithurm, in the middle of a small alley, is a bust of the poet *Hebel*, with quotations from his poetry. To the l. of the entrance of the garden are situated the extensive hot-houses fitted up as a **Winter-garden**, containing a palm-house, pond for the Victoria regia, orangery, green-houses, &c. The adjoining *Botanical garden* (Pl. 9) is open daily (Sat. and Sun. excepted), before 12 and after 2 o'clock; adm. to the hot-houses on Mon. and Frid. only, 9—12 and 3—5 o'clock; to procure admittance at other times application must be made to the committee.

Adjacent to the botanical garden is the ***Hall of Art** (Pl. 8), erected by Hübsch (1836—1845) in the modern Romanesque style. It contains collections of pictures, casts and antiquities, open to the public on Wed. and Sun. 11—12 and 2—4 o'clock; at other times for a fee of 30 kr. Frommel's catalogue (42 kr.) gives a full description of everything contained in the Hall. The director is the eminent painter K. F. Lessing.

The stair case is adorned by some fine frescoes by *Schwind*. That on the wall at the back represents the consecration of the cathedral at Freiburg by Duke Conrad of Zähringen; the flag-bearer is a portrait of the Grand-duke Leopold, holding the crown-prince by the hand, the crowned female figures are the Grand duchess and the princesses.

The collection of pictures is, on the whole, one of considerable value, especially those by modern German masters, but those of the older schools, among which are several attributed to *Murillo, Rembrandt, Michel Angelo*, &c., are of inferior worth.

The **Polytechnic School** (Pl. 62), an excellent educational intitution, possessing a considerable laboratory and attended by about 500 pupils, is situated near the Durlacher Thor at the E. end of the Langestrasse, and was erected by Hübsch. Over the entrance are two stone statues by *Raufer*, of Keppler, who represents the mathematical, and Erwin of Steinbach the architectural sciences. In the immediate vicinity of the Durlacher Thor, a little way back from the street, stands the *Arsenal* (Pl. 65), bravely defended in the revolution of 1849 by the townspeople against the insurgents.

The *Finanz-Ministerium* (Pl. 29), at the E. corner of the Schlossplatz, was also erected by Hübsch, as well as the *Landesgestüt* (national stud) near the station, the arrangements of which are worthy the notice of those who are interested in such establishments.

The **Cemetery** of Carlsruhe deserves a visit on account of the taste and care displayed in the arrangement of the grounds, as well as from its tombstones and monuments. Among the latter may be mentioned the *Preussen-Denkmal, a handsome monument in memory of the Prussians who fell in the revolution of 1849, erected in 1851 from designs furnished by the late king Fred. William IV. himself.

Railway from Carlsruhe to the Rhine, by *Mühlburg* to *Maxau* in ½ hr.; fares 27, 18, 12 kr.

51. From Carlsruhe to Baden.

By the Baden Railway in 1—2 hrs. Fares 1 fl. 42 kr., 1 fl. 9 kr., or 48 kr. As the train approaches Rastadt a fine view of the Black Forest may be obtained from the E. side of the train.

As the train leaves the station, the statue of the minister Winter (p. 206) is seen on the r., and beyond it *Kessler's* extensive engine manufactory. Farther on, at some distance to the r., lies the village of *Bulach* with its handsome church with two spires, erected by Hübsch. To the l., on a well-wooded eminence, lies the industrial little town of **Ettlingen** (*Hirsch; Krone*) with large velvet and paper manufactories.

From stat. *Muggensturm* an omnibus (also diligence twice daily, 36 kr.) runs to Gernsbach (p. 214) in the Murgthal, the mountains enclosing which bound the view to the l. The heights of the Black Forest now gradually come in sight, the most conspicuous of which is the Mercuriusberg with its tower. In the foreground are the ruins of the castle of Ebersteinburg (p. 215). As the train approaches Rastadt, the statue of Jupiter on the palace is seen high above the green ramparts of the town.

Rastadt (**Post; Kreuz;* **Löwe;* **Laterne;* the two latter are second-class houses), with a pop. of 6000, was burned down by the French in 1689, but soon after rebuilt by the celebrated imperial general, the Margrave Ludwig of Baden, and continued to be the residence of the Margraves till the line became extinct.

In 1840 Rastadt was destined to be a fortress of the Confederation, and is garrisoned by Austrian, Baden and Prussian troops.

The handsome *Palace*, completed by the Margravine Sibylla Augusta (p. 215), now employed as a barrack, the garden being converted into an exercising-ground, stands on an eminence and is surmounted by a gilded statue of Jupiter. It contains a collection of Turkish trophies, taken by the Margrave Ludwig Wilhelm, arms, caparisons &c., besides a number of family portraits. The tower commands an extensive view (castellan's fee 24 kr.). In one of the apartments the articles which formed the basis of the peace concluded at Baden in Switzerland between France and Austria, which terminated the war of succession, were signed by Prince Eugene of Savoy and Marshal Villars. A congress was also held here in 1797—1799, which, however, led to no result, and at its close the two French delegates were barbarously murdered in the adjacent wood near the Rheinauer Thor; the pepetrators of the outrage were never discovered.

The fortress of Rastadt served in 1849 as a last place of refuge to the remnant of the Baden insurgents, about 6000 in number, among whom were adventurers of all nations. After a resistance of three weeks, they at last surrendered to the Prussian troops, July 23rd, 1849. Curiously euough, the revolution had also begun at Rastadt, on May 11th, in the same year.

The train now crosses the *Murg*. Farther on, between Rastadt and *Oos*, the hunting-seat *Favorite* may be seen in the midst of shrubberies. At Oos the Baden branch diverges from the main-line, and in 10 min. the latter place is reached.

52. Baden and its Environs.

Hotels. *Victoria-Hotel, in the Leopoldsplatz. Baden Hotel (with baths), at the entrance to the town. *English Hotel, at the Promenadenbrücke. *European Hotel, opposite to the pump-room. These four Hotels are of the 1st class; charges: R. $1^1/_2$ fl. and upwards, L. 24, B. 42, D. inc. W. at 5 o'clock 1 fl. 48, A. 24 kr. Russischer Hof, *Zähringer Hof (with baths), Französischer Hof, Hôtel Royal, Hirsch (with baths), Darmstädter Hof (with baths), charges somewhat more moderate than in the first mentioned. — *Stadt Baden, immediately on leaving the station, R. 48 kr. to 1 fl. 12 kr., L. 18, B. 28, D. at 1 o'clock 1 fl. 12, at 5 o'clock 1 fl. 36, A. 18 kr. — *Stadt Strassburg, Hotel and Café, at the end of the new promenade, R. 1 fl., B. 24, D. exc. W. at 1 o'clock 1 fl., at 6 o'clock 1 fl. 24 kr. — Engel, at the Gernsbacher Thor, more moderate. Bär in the Lichtenthal (p. 212), $1^1/_2$ M. from the Conversationshaus, very moderate. — The best wines of the country are Affenthaler (red), Klingenberger and Markgräfler (white).

Cafés. Café-Restaurant in the Conversationshaus. A la Fleur, near the Russ. Hof. Café de Hollande on the new Promenade, &c. At the following beer may procured: Haug, and Görger, at the station. Geist, at the Gernsbacher Thor. Krone.

Telegraph-office at the station.

Theatre. Performances in summer by a French company, in spring and autumn by that of the Carlsruhe theatre.

Carriages. The following charges include drivers' fees. *Ebersteinschloss* 5, or returning by Gernsbach $5^1/_2$, *Ebersteinburg* 4, *Fremersberg* 3, same by the Jagdhaus 4, *Jagdhaus* 3, *Seelach* 3, *Geroldsau* to the *waterfall* 4, *Favorite* $3^1/_2$, *Gernsbach* $4^1/_2$, *Rothenfels* $4^1/_2$, *Yburg* 5, to the *old castle* (allowing time to inspect it) and back 4 fl. (Should any of the above excursions occupy more than 6 hrs. the charge is increased by one half). *Ebersteinschloss, Gernsbach, Rothenfels, Kuppenheim, Favorite* 7 fl., *Forbach* 9 fl., same through the Murgthal 10 fl., *Wildbad* 18 fl., *Rippoldsau* 20 fl. — By time: $^1/_4$ hr. for 1—2 pers. 24 kr., 3—4 pers. 30 kr.; $^1/_2$ hr. 36—45 kr.; $^3/_4$ hr. 48 kr.—1 fl.; 1 hr. 1 fl.—1 fl. 15 kr.; 2 hrs. 1 fl. 48 kr.—2 fl. 12 kr., &c. — *Donkeys:* $^1/_2$ day 1 fl. 12 kr., whole day 2 fl. Carriage and donkey-stands opposite to the English Hotel, at the end of the avenue leading to the Conversationshaus, opposite to the Baden Hotel, and in the Leopoldsplatz. Omnibus from the station into the town 12 kr. inc. luggage.

English Church Service in the Spital Kirche.

Baden has the reputation of being an expensive watering-place, and such it probably is to those who frequent the first-class hotels, atteud the numerous Matinées musicales (adm. 5—20 fr.), and are led away by the seductive attractions of the gaming-tables; but all the charms and enjoyments of the place may be participated in without any very serious inroad being made upon the purse. The expenses of a single visitor need not exceed 100—120 fl. per month, for Baden affords, in common with large towns, the opportunities of regulating the expenditure in accordance with the resources at command. A respectable private lodging in a good situation may be procured for 6—10 fl. a week; breakfast in the lodging-houses costs 12—15 kr.; dinner at a restaurant 42 kr. (e. g. at Frau *Zerr's*, Leopoldstrasse 154, at any hour after 12 o'clock, price as above; or at Frau *Göringer's*, in the new Promenade, or at *Buhl's*). A bath costs 12—36 kr. according to circumstances. The water may be drunk in both the pump-rooms without charge, other kinds of mineral water, with whey and goats' milk, are supplied in the new pump-room at fixed charges.

The visitor who wishes to spent only one day at Baden should, after devoting an hour or so the *Old castle*, take the following drive: by *Hauen-Eberstein* to the *Favorite*, by *Kuppenheim*, *Rothenfels* (good hotel and bath-house, and seat of the Margrave Wilhelm), *Gaggenau*, *Ottenau*, *Gernsbach* through the *Murgthal*, the *Ebersteinschloss*, *Lichtenthal*, and back to *Baden*. This drive, comprising the most remarkable points in the environs of Baden, costs for a one-horse 6, for a two-horse carriage 8 fl., and requires about 6 hrs. The visitor would thus have time enough to visit the "Morning-cure"

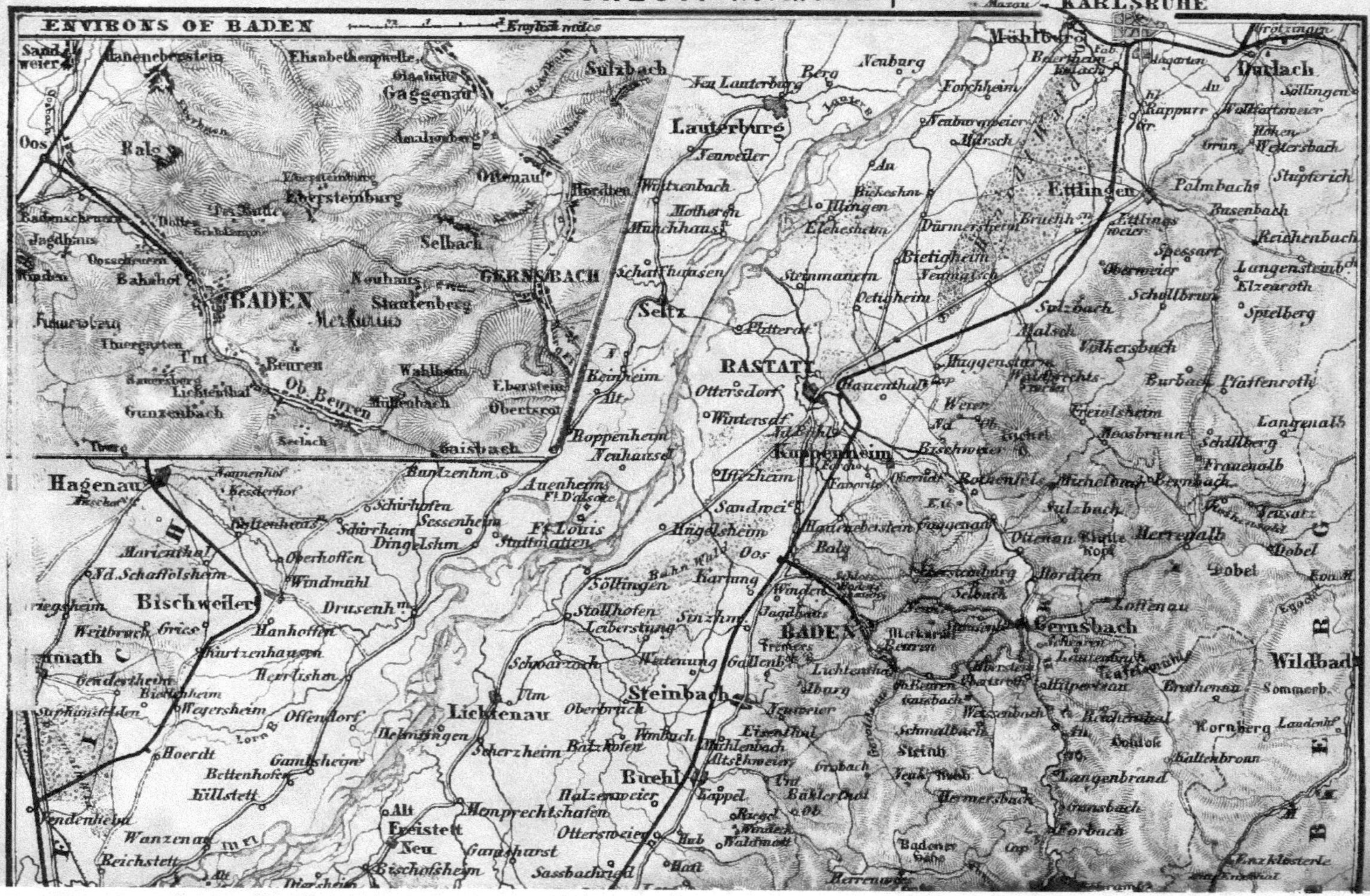
THE BLACK FOREST. Northeren part
ENVIRONS OF BADEN
English miles
KARLSRUHE
Durlach
Ettlingen
Mühlburg
Lauterburg
Seltz
RASTATT
Kuppenheim
Hagenau
Bischweiler
BADEN
GERNSBACH
Gernsbach
Sulzbach
Gaggenau
Ebersteinburg
Selbach
Oos
Steinbach
Lichtenau
Buehl
Wildbad
Herrenalb
Freistett
Bischofsheim
Wanzenau
Reichstett

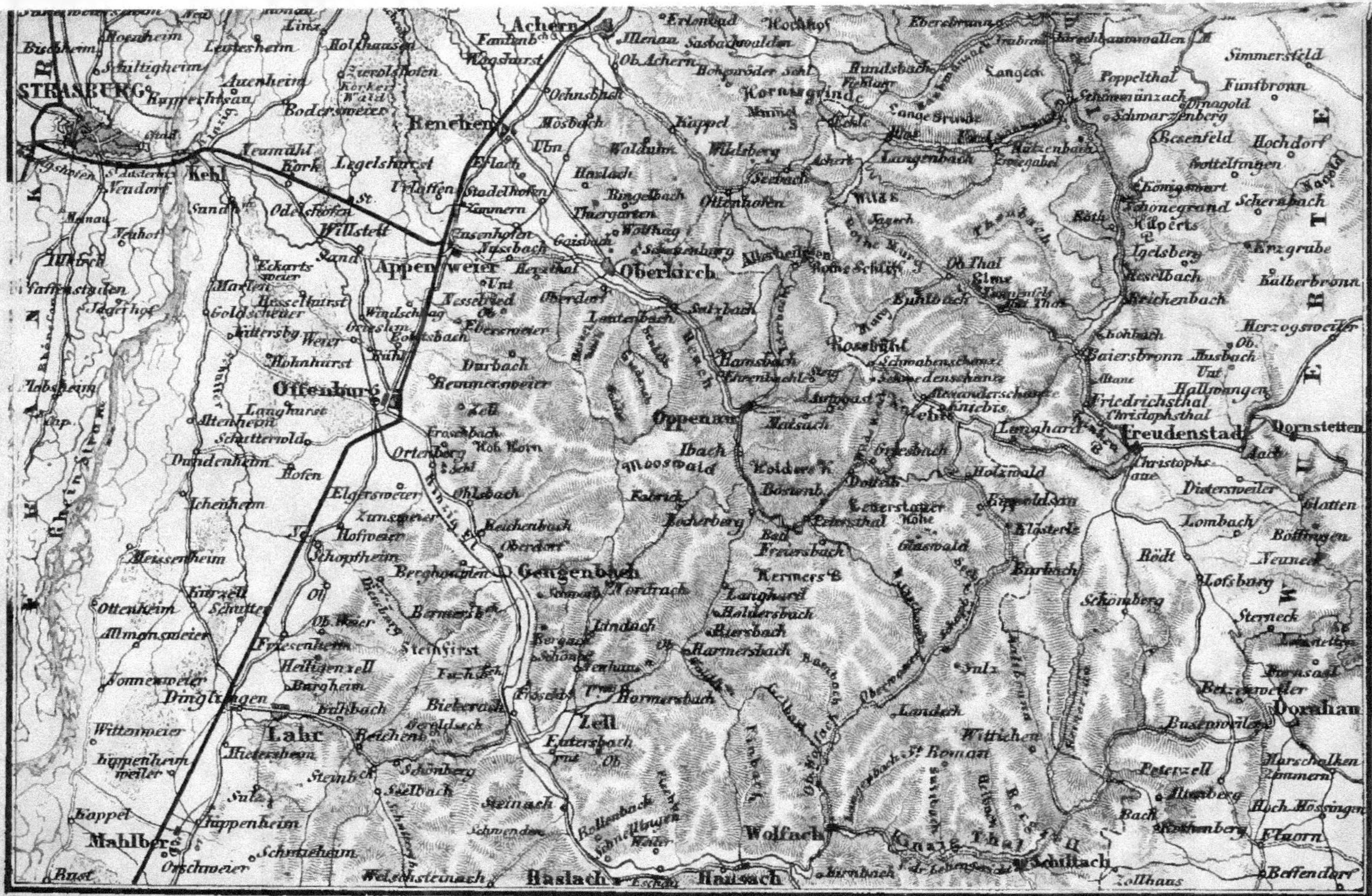

Lith. Anst. v. Ed. Wagner, Darmstadt

Geograph. Meilen

1:435,000 der Natur

Gez. v. Ed. Wagner

10 English miles

in the new Pump-room (6—8 a.m.) and see the "Corso" after 6 p.m. in the "Lichtenthaler Allee." The animated scene in front of the Conversationshaus does not commence till after 7. The drive may be shortened by 1 hr. by omitting the *Rococo Favorite* (p. 215).

The pedestrian may walk from Baden to the castle of *Eberstein* and *Gernsbach* in 3 hrs., and then take the diligence (36 kr.), or the omnibus (30 kr.) which runs every morning and evening by *Ottenau*, *Gaggenau*, *Rothenfels*, and *Bischweier*, to the station at *Muggensturm*.

Baden (generally called *Baden-Baden*, to distinguish it from the places of the same name near Vienna and in Switzerland) lies at the entrance of the Black Forest, among picturesque and well-wooded hills in the delightful valley of the *Oos* or *Oel-Bach*. It vies with Heidelberg and Freiburg in the beauty of its situation, which is scarcely inferior to any in Upper Germany. The climate is mild and salubrious, and the efficacy of the waters was known even to the Romans, who called it *Aurelia aquensis*. For six centuries it was the seat of the Margraves of Baden, among whom Hermann III. (d. 1190 in the Crusades) was the first who resided in the old castle. The new castle, immediately above the town, was erected by the Margrave Christoph in 1479, but both town and castle suffered so much in the 30 Years' war, and especially in the war of the Palatinate (1689), that the Margraves soon after transferred their residence to Rastadt.

The town is not large (pop. 7000), but the influx of visitors is very great, amounting to upwards of 40,000 annually, and even in winter about 200 strangers reside here. The French language and manners predominate.

The *Oosbach* separates the bathing from the town-population. The former confine themselves almost exclusively to the grounds which extend along the l. bank of the stream, the *Conversationshaus* and the *Pump-room* being the central points of attraction. The ***Pump-room** ("Trinkhalle") was erected in 1842, and decorated with 14 frescoes by Götzenberger, representing traditions of the Black Forest, but unfortunately somewhat faded. Admittance free. A few paces farther is the **Conversationshaus**, magnificently fitted up, and containing drawing-rooms, dining, concert and gaming-rooms. The latter are open from 11 a.m. till 12 at night, and the fact that the lessee pays a rent of about 11,000*l.*, and has besides to defray all the expenses of the establishment, will afford some idea of the extent to which play is indulged in. The shady alley which leads from the E. side of the Conversationshaus to the English Hotel is the bazaar of Baden, which, as well as the other walks in the vicinity, is the rendezvous of the gay world from 3 to 4, and during the open air concerts after 7 p.m.

A handsome avenue, which commences near the Conversationshaus leads in a S.E. direction to the ($1\frac{1}{2}$ M.) Convent of **Lichtenthal** (*Bär; Ludwigsbad; Gräff*'s brewery), founded in 1245 by Irmengard, grand-daughter of Henry the Lion, and widow of Hermann IV. of Baden, as is recorded by the picture in the choir of the church, where the beautiful tombstone of the foundress is also to be seen. At the side-altars are the richly decorated skeletons of the martyrs St. Pius and St. Benedictus. The convent has fortunately escaped the devastations of war and the ravages of time, and is still occupied by nuns, who pass their days in the strictest seclusion. The **Todtencapelle* (mortuary chapel) which stands apart in front of the church, belongs to the 13th cent., and was formerly the church of the convent. It contains tombstones of the Margraves of Baden-Durlach, and altar-pieces by the old German master Hans Baldung, surnamed Grün. The *Orphan Asylum*, situated within the precincts of the convent, was founded by the wealthy and benevolent tailor *Stulz*, who was afterwards ennobled under the name of von Ortenberg. The *Gunzenbachthal*, the second valley which diverges from the road in a S. direction, is a favourite haunt of mineralogists.

The **Theatre**, erected in 1861, at the entrance of the Lichtenthal avenue, and adjoining the Conversationshaus, is magnificently fitted up. Near it is the **Statue** of the Grand-duke Leopold, in the Leopoldsplatz, also erected in 1861.

Among the churches of Baden the only one worthy of note is the ***Pfarrkirche**, or *Stiftskirche*, belonging to the 15th cent., "*in sæculo VII. exstructa, in ecclesiam collegiatam erecta 1453, incendio vastata 1689, reparata 1753.*" The choir contains *monuments of the Rom. Cath. Margraves of Baden, commencing with Bernhard I. (d. 1431).

The most interesting are those of *Leopold Wilhelm* (d. 1671 at Warasdin in Hungary), the celebrated general who fought against the Turks with Stahremberg and Montecucoli — a recumbent effigy on a sarcophagus supported by two Turks; *Frederick*, bishop of Utrecht (d. 1517), a knightly figure in armour; *Ludwig Wilhelm* (d. 1707 at Rastadt; see p. 209), the greatest general of his time, who commanded in 26 campaigns without sustaining a single defeat, and was the companion of Prince Eugene in the Turkish wars (executed by *Pigal*, the sculptor of the monument of Marshal Saxe at Strasburg, but overloaded with ornaments and devoid of good taste).

The handsome new **Protestant Church** is situated on the S.E. side of the town, on the r. bank of the Oos.

The **Old Churchyard**, at the Gernsbacher Thor, with a statue of a *Gravedigger* on a lofty pedestal, contains several well-known names, among others those of the poet *Ludwig Robert* (born at Berlin 1778, d. 1832) and the French general *Guilleminot* (d. 1840). There is also a curious representation of the Mount of Olives, with Christ praying and the sleeping disciples. Above the entrance gateway is a relief (1482) of the head of the Saviour on a grave-cloth. The large new **Cemetery** also contains several handsome monuments.

Behind the Pfarrkirche are the sources of the **Hot Springs,** thirteen in number, which issue from the rocks of the palace-terrace, ealled the Schneckengarten, and are conducted by means of pipes to the different bathing-establishments of the town. Their temperature ranges from 115° to 153° Fahr., and they yield upwards of 90 gallons per minute. The principal spring, called the *Ursprung,* is enclosed by ancient Roman masonry, and the handsome building erected over the spot in 1847 is fitted up for *Vapour baths à la Russe.*

A part of the old Pump-room has been fitted up as a **Hall of Antiquities** (12 kr.), in which many Roman relics found in the neighbourhood are exhibited, among others a mile-stone bearing the name of Marcus Aurelius (Caracalla), stones dedicated to Neptune, Minerva, and Hercules, the original of the altar of Mercury on the Stauffenberg, and tombstones of Roman soldiers.

The so-called **Neue Schloss,** situated on a hill above tbe town, was founded in 1479, enlarged in 1519, dismantled in 1689, and afterwards partially restored. It is now used as a summer-residence by the Grand-duke, but contains few objects of interest, with the exception of the subterranean vaults and rooms, furnished with iron and stone doors, sometimes called Roman baths, sometimes dungeons of the *Vehmgericht* (Secret Tribunal). There are unmistakeable traces of ancient baths, but whether they owe their origin to the Romans or not, is involved in uncertainty (fee 18 kr.).

From the new castle a carriage-road ascends N. to the *Old castle;* about $1/2$ M. from the former, at the thatched summer-house, a broad foot-path branches off to the r. through the fragrant fir-wood; sign-posts are placed at intervals; $1/2$ M. farther, at the *Sophienruhe,* a clear spring of water, the path crosses the road. Another $1/4$ hr. will bring the pedestrian to the castle.

The **Old Castle,** probably founded in the 10th or 11th cent., was, till the erection of the new castle, the seat of the Margraves, and afterwards of several of the dowager Margravines, but since its destruction by the French in 1689 it has been a complete ruin. The chapel of St. Ulrich, to the l. on entering, is now converted into an inn. The view from the top of the tower is one of singular beauty; in the distance lies the whole expanse of the valley of the Rhine from Worms to beyond Strasburg (the town itself is bidden), and in the fore-ground the lovely valley of Baden with its bright shining villas and rich-pasture land, presenting a striking contrast to the sombre hue of the fir-woods.

Near the old castle lie cleft masses of porphyry, resembling in one place the ruined walls of a castle, in another a gigantic tower, and in another a sea of rocks. At its base is a good broad path leading to the *Teufelskanzel* (devil's pulpit, see below), and another to the summit of these rocks. Sign-posts are placed in all directions.

On a rocky eminence about 2 M. to the N.E. of the old castle are situated the ruins of the castle of **Alt-Eberstein,** of Roman origin, and once like the Yburg (p. 215) a Roman watch-tower. An old Rhenish tradition relates that the Emperor Otto I., being unable to take the castle by storm, induced the count to leave it by inviting him to a tournament and dance at Speyer, treacherously intending to attack the stronghold in his absence. The count being informed of this scheme by the emperor's daughter during the dance, immediately hurried back to his castle, the capture of which was prevented by his timely return. The tradition very properly ends with the marriage of the heroic count and the daughter of the emperor. A beautiful prospect, similar to that from the old castle, is obtained from this point; it comprises the richly cultivated lower Murgthal, with the flourishing villages of Kuppenheim, Bischweier, Rothenfels, Gaggenau and Ottenau.

The road from the old castle to *Gernsbach* (6 M.) leads through the wood to the S. of the old castle, and passes the *Teufelskanzel.* About $1^1/_4$ M. from the castle a cross is reached; here the path leads in the direction of the village of *Eberstein,* and then descends to the r.; about 1 M. farther the wood to the r. must be entered, and the Murgthal soon comes in view. In 25 min. more the *Neuhaus* is reached, below which a broad road descends to the r. to *Staufenberg* ($1^1/_4$ M.), then through the valley to *Gernsbach* ($1^1/_2$ M.). From Baden to Gernsbach by the new carriage road by Lichtenthal and Oberbeuren is a distance of 9 M.

Gernsbach (**Stern*, R. 30, B. 18 kr.; **Löwe; *Pfeifer's* pine-cone bath-etab. above the village, where the path to Schloss Eberstein diverges, pleasant quarters for a prolonged stay) on the *Murg,* a small commercial town, inhabited principally by wood-merchants. The new row of houses on the r. bank of the Murg, opposite to the bridge, was built to replace those burnt down by the insurgents in 1849. Drive to Rothenfels and the Favorite, see p. 210, to Muggensturm (p. 210), to Forbach (p. 251) in the Murgthal (p. 250); one-horse carriage to Baden 2 fl., there and back $3^1/_2$, two-horse 3 fl. Wildbad is about 8 M. distant from Gernsbach, carriage 6—10 fl.; diligence daily at 4 p.m.; fare 2 fl. 6 kr.

A path follows the stream in a S. direction, passing the

Klingel Chapel, and leading to the * **Ebersteinschloss** (2 M.), a castle founded in the 13th cent., afterwards destroyed, and in 1798 restored by the Margrave Frederick, under the name of "*Neu-Eberstein*." It stands on a wooded eminence in a most delightful situation, high above the Murg. The view which it commands of the valley to Weissenbach and Hilpertsau, and in an opposite direction to Gernsbach, is magnificent, and comprises a large portion of the beautiful Murgthal. The interior contains a number of ancient relics, weapons, armour etc., and in one of the apartments a collection of pictures of the 16th cent. Refreshments may be had from the castellan. This point is generally visited from Baden (3 hrs. on foot, 2 hrs. by carriage) by the carriage-road passing Lichtenthal and *Beuern*, and leading through beautiful wood scenery.

Half-way between Oos and Rastadt, to the E. from the railway near Kuppenheim (p. 210), and 6 M. to the N.W. of Baden, a large building is seen rising among the woods, the **Favorite,** a castle belonging to the Grand-duke, and erected in 1725 by the Margravine Sibylla, wife of the Margrave Ludwig Wilhelm. After the death of the latter, this remarkably talented and beautiful woman, after having for 19 years superintended the education of her sons, retired to this castle, where she spent the remainder of her life in acts of penance and devotion. In the *Hermitage* in the park are preserved some relics of this singular character. The castle served as a residence for the Prince, now king of Prussia, in 1849, during the transformation of Rastadt into a fortress of the Confederation. The steward who lives in the park shows the château (fee 24 kr.), and supplies visitors with refreshments.

To the N.E. of Baden rise the Great and the Little **Stauffen.** The former (2240 ft.) is generally termed the **Mercuriusberg,** on account of the votive tablet to Mercury found on the top and now exhibited at Baden, bearing the inscription: IN H. D. D. DEO. MERCVR. ER. C. PRVSO. (*in honorem domus divinæ Deo Mercurio C. Pruso erexit*). The tower (136 steps) commands a magnificent * view (comp. panorama sold here for 24 kr.) of Strasburg, the town and environs of Heidelberg, Baden and its environs, the Murgthal &c. Refreshments may be procured on the top. The road to the Mercuriusberg (2½ hrs. from Baden) diverges at the *Teufelskanzel* to the r. from the Gernsbach road, and winds up to the summit. A good walker should return by the *Schaafberg* or the *Steinbruch* (quarry), although the path is somewhat fatiguing.

In the opposite direction, 7 M. to the S.W. of Baden, lies the ancient *Yburg*, like *Alt-Eberstein* (p. 214) once a Roman watch-tower and stronghold, and still in a good state of preservation. The massive ruins, surrounded by dark fir-wood, form a magnificent foreground to the picture of the broad valley of the Rhine beyond. A good-carriage road leads to the castle. From *Geroldsau* a footpath leads by *Malschbach* and the wooded ridge of the *Iwerst* to the Yburg in about 1½ hr. From the latter to *Steinbach* (see below) 1½ M.

One of the finest excursions in the vicinity of Baden is to ***Allerheiligen** (see p. 254) by *Achern*. Carriages to be had at the *Krone* or *Adler* at Achern; charges for the whole excursion, 5—6 fl.; if not farther than the *Neuhaus* (p. 254), 4 fl. 30 kr. Travellers who desire to return from Allerheiligen to Achern (2 hrs. drive) by another road, should rejoin their conveyance near the waterfall, and drive in 1¼ hr. to *Oppenau*, then down the Renchthal in 2 hrs. to *Lautenbach* and *Oberkirch* (*Adler, good Klingenberger wine, which is produced here), and thence to the station of *Appenweier* or *Renchen*. A carriage from Achern for the complete tour costs 7—10 fl. Carriages from Allerheiligen, see p. 254; *Mummelsee* and *Hornisgrinde*, see p. 251.

53. From Baden to Strasburg.

(Comp. Map R. 52.)

By the Baden Railway in 2—3¼ hrs.; fares: by express 3 fl. 37 and 2 fl. 34 kr., ordinary trains 3 fl. 14, 2 fl. 18 and 1 fl. 31 kr. Best views to the l.

At *Oos* is the junction of the Baden branch with the main line. To the l. are seen the mountains of the Black Forest in picturesque groups, and farther on, the grey tower of *Yburg* (see above), situated on a flattened mountain peak. Near the second station of Steinbach, on a barren hill to the l., stands a red sandstone monument, erected in memory of *Erwin*, architect of Strasburg cathedral, who was born at Steinbach, and died at Strasburg in 1318. In the neighbourhood the *Affenthaler*, one of the best red wines of Baden, is produced.

Bühl (Rabe) possesses one of the most ancient churches in the whole country. On the mountains are seen the ruins of the castle of *Windeck*, once the seat of a powerful race which became extinct in 1572. Near Bühl are two unpretending and inexpensive watering-places, the *Hubbad* (2 M.), with mineral springs and hydropathic estab., and the *Erlenbad* (3 M. from Achern), a warm saline spring of 70° Fahr. The former lies to the N., and the latter to the S. of Windeck.

The high mountain to the l. of the station *Ottersweier*, with the pile of stones on its summit, is the *Hornisgrinde* (p. 251),

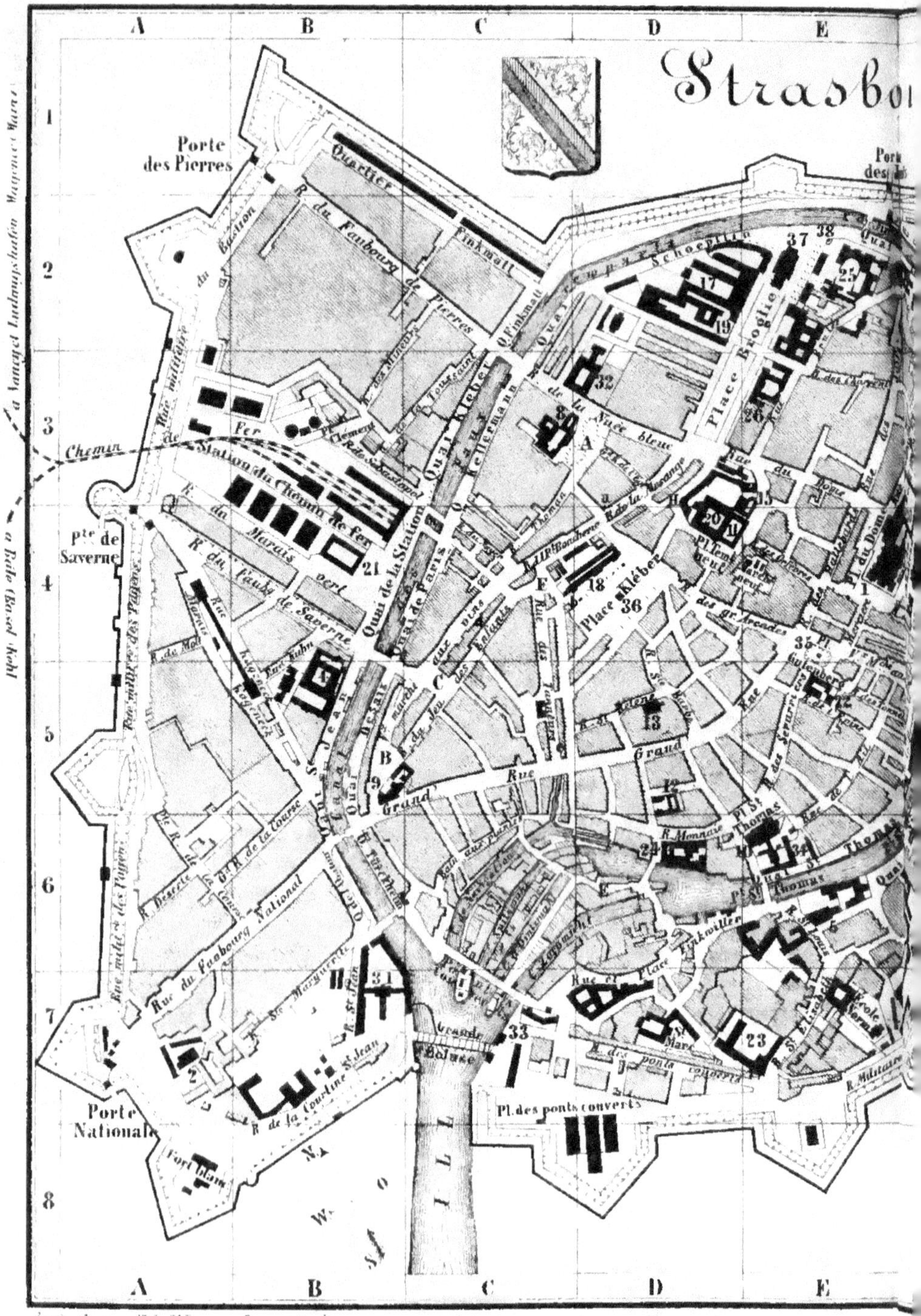

Porte des Pierres
Quartier
Finkmatt
R. du Faubourg de Pierres
Rue militaire du Bastion
Chemin de Fer
Station du Chemin de fer
Pte de Saverne
R. du Marais vert
R. du faub. de Saverne
Quai de la Station
Quai de Paris
Quai Kléber
Place Kléber
Place Broglie
Quai Schoepflin
Rue de la Nuée bleue
Rue des Grandes Arcades
Grand Rue
Rue militaire des Paysans
Rue du Faubourg National
Porte Nationale
Fort blanc
Pl. des ponts couverts
Grande Ecluse
R. des ponts couverts
Quai St. Thomas
Pl. St. Thomas
R. Monnaie
Rue et Place Finkwiller
R. Militaire
Ecole Normale
Pl. Gutenberg
Quai St. Jean
R. de la Courtine
R. Ste. Marguerite
a Bâle (Basel) Kehl
A
B
C
D
E
1
2
3
4
5
6
7
8

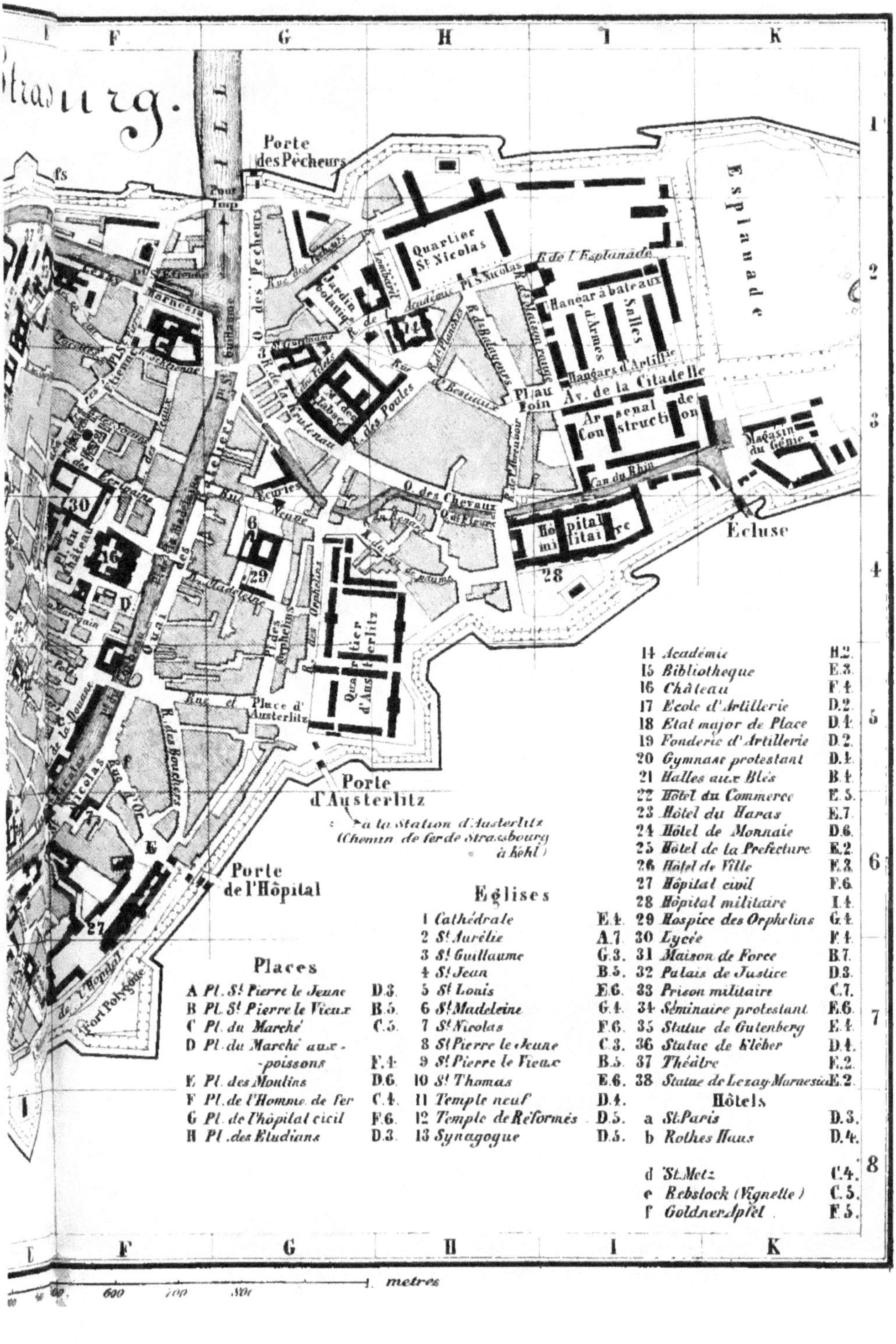

F
G
H
I
K
1
2
3
4
5
6
7
8
Porte des Pêcheurs
Esplanade
Quartier St. Nicolas
R. de l'Esplanade
Hangar à bateaux
Salles d'Armes
Hangars d'Artillie
Av. de la Citadelle
Arsenal de Construction
Magasin du Génie
Écluse
Hôpital militaire
O. des Pêcheurs
Jardin botanique
Pl. S. Nicolas
Pl. au Foin
O. des Chevaux
Rue Neuve
R. des Poules
Quartier d'Austerlitz
Place d'Austerlitz
Porte d'Austerlitz
à la Station d'Austerlitz (Chemin de fer de Strassbourg à Kehl)
Porte de l'Hôpital
R. des Bouchers
Pl. des Orphelins
Quai
Fort Polygone
Pl. du Château
Marnesia
Places
A Pl. St. Pierre le Jeune D.3.
B Pl. St. Pierre le Vieux B.5.
C Pl. du Marché C.5.
D Pl. du Marché aux-poissons F.4.
E Pl. des Moulins D.6.
F Pl. de l'Homme de fer C.4.
G Pl. de l'hôpital civil F.6.
H Pl. des Etudians D.3.
Eglises
1 Cathédrale E.4.
2 St. Aurélie A.7.
3 St. Guillaume G.3.
4 St. Jean B.5.
5 St. Louis E.6.
6 St. Madeleine G.4.
7 St. Nicolas F.6.
8 St. Pierre le Jeune C.3.
9 St. Pierre le Vieux B.5.
10 St. Thomas E.6.
11 Temple neuf D.4.
12 Temple de Réformés D.5.
13 Synagogue D.5.
14 Académie H.2.
15 Bibliotheque E.3.
16 Château F.4.
17 Ecole d'Artillerie D.2.
18 Etat major de Place D.4.
19 Fonderie d'Artillerie D.2.
20 Gymnase protestant D.4.
21 Halles aux Blés B.4.
22 Hôtel du Commerce E.5.
23 Hôtel du Haras E.7.
24 Hôtel de Monnaie D.6.
25 Hôtel de la Prefecture E.2.
26 Hôtel de Ville E.3.
27 Hôpital civil F.6.
28 Hôpital militaire I.4.
29 Hospice des Orphelins G.4.
30 Lycée F.4.
31 Maison de Force B.7.
32 Palais de Justice D.3.
33 Prison militaire C.7.
34 Séminaire protestant E.6.
35 Statue de Gutenberg E.4.
36 Statue de Kléber D.4.
37 Théâtre E.2.
38 Statue de Lezay-Marnesia E.2.
Hôtels
a St. Paris D.3.
b Rothes Haus D.4.
d St. Metz C.4.
e Rebstock (Vignette) C.5.
f Goldner Apfel F.5.
600
metres

the highest point (3612 ft.) of the lower part of the Black Forest. From the Erlenbad a new road leads to the summit by *Sassbachwalden* and the Brigittenschloss in 3 hrs.

At **Sassbach**, $1\frac{1}{2}$ M. to the N. of Achern, the French marshal Turenne fell in an engagement he had just commenced with the imperial general Montecucoli, but which on his death was discontinued, the French army retreating across the Rhine. The spot is marked by a grey granite obelisk, erected by the French in 1829, on which the marshal's victories are recorded. A French *invalide* has the charge of the monument, which is visible from the railway; the ground on which it stands belongs to the French government.

In the market-place of **Achern** (**Krone; Adler;* carriage to Allerheiligen 7—8 fl.; beer at *Huber's*) stands a handsome monument in memory of the Grand-duke Leopold (d. 1852). The town possesses also an admirably conducted *Lunatic Asylum*, capable of accommodating 400 patients. To the E. the view is bounded by the *Hornisgrinde.* Beyond *Renchen* the spire of Strasburg Cathedral becomes visible in the distance to the W.

At *Appenweier* [whence a diligence (2 fl. 48 kr.) runs daily in summer into the Renchthal as far as Rippoldsau (p. 255) in $6\frac{1}{2}$ hrs.] the Strasburg railway diverges from the main line, passing the stations of *Kork* and *Kehl,* and traversing a district rendered marshy by the frequent inundations of the *Kinzig* which falls into the Rhine at Kehl.

Kehl (**Post* or *Weisses Lamm; Rehfuss,* R. 1 fl.; *Salmen,* at the station), formerly only a fortified "tête de pont" of Strasburg, possesses a handsome new *Church* of red sandstone.

At Kehl the junction line between the Baden and the French railways crosses the Rhine by means of an iron bridge, immediately below the bridge of boats.

The bridge rests on four pillars, is furnished with a turning or swing-bridge on each bank, and terminates at either end in a cast-iron portal. The pillars on the French and German sides respectively record the names of the French emperor, the reigning Grand-duke, and the engineers and other officials entrusted with the construction of the bridge.

The train now passes the Desaix-monument (l., see p. 222), skirts the cemetery (r.) and stops at a station near the S.E. gate (*porte d'Austerlitz*) of Strasburg. It next describes a wide circuit round the S. side of the town and near the village of *Königshofen* joins the Bâle-Strasburg line (comp. R. 56). The formalities of the "douane" are the same at the "porte d'Austerlitz" as at the principal station.

54. Strasburg.

Hotels. *Ville de Paris (Pl. a) a handsome new building; R. from 2 fr., L. 1 fr., B. $1\frac{1}{2}$ fr., D. exc. W. 3 fr., A. 1 fr. *Maison Rouge (Pl. b).

Hôtel d'Angleterre near the stat., well spoken of. Vignette (Pl. e, *Grand'-Rue* 119); La Pomme d'or (Pl. f) in the Rue d'Or; Badischer Hof.

Cafés. *Café Cadé in the Kleberplatz; *Café Adam, or du Broglie; Café de l'Europe and Café de l'Univers both near the Kleberplatz; Café Hauswald, not far from the Railway station.

Public Gardena. Jardin Lips and Jardin Kämmerer, both outside the Porte des Juifs; music and other entertainments in the evening 2 or 3 times a week. The *Orangerie*, a well-kept garden belonging to the town, situated in the Ruprechtsau, about 3 M. distant, affords an agreeable promenade.

Cabs or *Citadines* 1—2 persons for $^1/_4$ hr. 50 cent., $^1/_2$ hr. 90 cent., from the Strasbourg station to the Rhine bridge 1 fr.

Railway Station on the N.W. side of the town for the Paris, Bâle, Mayence and Kehl lines; on the last-named line there is also a station at the Austerlitz Gate.

Pâtés de foie gras at Henry's, Meissengasse, Doyen, Münstergasse, or Hummel, Schlossergasse; prices from 5 to 40 fr. according to size. The geese's livers not unfrequently attain a weight of 2—3 lbs. each.

Travellers whose time is limited should ascend the tower of the Cathedral (see below), inspect the cathedral itself, and visit the Church of St. Thomas (p. 221).

English Church Service in the Hôtel de Paris.

Gates closed at 11.

Strasburg (Ger. *Strassburg*), the *Argentoratum* of the Romans, formerly capital of Lower Alsace and one of the most important towns on the Rhine, now the capital of the French Department of the Lower Rhine, lies on the *Ill*, about 3 M. from the Rhine with which it is connected by a small and a large canal. On the 30th of Sept., 1681, in a time of peace, Strasburg was seized by Louis XIV., and France was confirmed in the possession of the city by the peace of Ryswyk in 1697. Since then the fortifications have been greatly enlarged, so that it is now one of the strongest fortresses and the third largest arsenal in France. Garrison upwards of 6000; pop. 79,000, of whom nearly one half are Protestants.

The Emperor Maximilian I., in writing of Strasbourg, describes it as the strong bulwark of the holy Roman kingdom, and praises it highly for the good old German honesty, constancy and bravery of its inhabitants. The town has to this day a German air, and although it has been under French dominion for 170 years, the ancient language and customs of the townspeople still prevail.

The ***Cathedral** (Pl. 1) (always open except from 12 to 2 o'clock) was first founded by Clovis in 510, but having been destroyed by lightning in 1007, the foundation of the present edifice was laid by Bishop Werner of Habsburg in 1015, and the interior completed in 1275. In 1277 the erection of the **Façade* was commenced by Erwin of Steinbach and his daughter Sabina, to the latter of whom the church is indebted for the magnificent decorations of the **Portal.* Above it in niches are the equestrian statues of Clovis, Dagobert, Rudolph of Habsburg, and (since 1823) Louis XIV. The sculptures above the portal belong chiefly to the 13th and 14th centuries. The upper part of the spire was erected by Johann Hültz of Cologne at the commencement of the 15th cent. in the capricious and variegated modern Gothic style, and finally completed in 1439. The upper part of the S. tower is entirely wanting. Few cathedrals offer so good an opportunity for tracing the progress of the Gothic style from the time when it took its origin from the modern Romanesque style (choir, crypt and part of transept) to its highest and purest perfection (the body of the church completed in 1275, and the façade of 1277—1339); and to its decline (the platform between the towers of 1365, and the top of the spire of 1439).

The entire length of the edifice is 175 yds., and the breadth 65 yds.; the middle nave is 95 ft. in height and 42 ft. in breadth. Some of the stained-glass windows are admirably executed; the Magi with the Virgin Mary in the north aisle are modern. The pillars and columns of the interior are elegant. and are embellished with statues, but on the whole the church is somewhat destitute of ornament. The *font* in the N. transept dates from 1453 and the **pulpit*, richly decorated with sculpture, from 1486. The Chapel of St. John (to the l. by the choir) contains a monument to *Bishop Conrad of Lichtenberg*, under whose auspices the construction of the façade began. The Chapel of St. Mary (S. aisle) contains a sculpture representing the interment of the Virgin, executed in 1480.

The celebrated astronomical **Clock*, constructed by Schwilgué in 1838—1842 in the S. transept, is a highly curious and ingenious piece of workmanship. Some paintings and portions of the old clock have been used in the erection of the new.

The globe beneath shows the course of the stars, behind it is a perpetual almanac, on the l. a piece of mechanism exhibiting ecclesiastical reckoning of time, and on the r. the geocentric opposition and conjunction of the sun and moon; above it is a dial determining the intervening time, and still higher is shown the course of the moon through the heavens. The exterior of the clock attracts spectators at all times, but especially at noon. On the first gallery an angel strikes the quarters on a bell which he holds in his hand; higher up is a skeleton, representing time, which strikes the hour of 12, and round it are figures which strike the quarters and represent man's progress through the various stages of boyhood, youth, manhood and old age. Under the first gallery the symbolic deity of each day of the week steps out of a niche, Apollo on Sunday, Diana on Monday, and so on. In the highest niche the 12 apostles move round a figure of the Saviour, bowing as they pass. On the highest pinnacle of the side-tower is perched a cock which flaps its wings, stretches its neck and crows, awakening the echoes of the remotest nooks of the cathedral.

Two old inscriptions on a pillar near the clock commemorate the zeal and piety of *Johann Geiler of Kaisersberg* (d. 1510), one of the most learned men and undaunted preachers of his time.

On the Romanesque S. **Portal* were erected, in 1840, statues of the great architect Erwin and his talented daughter Sabina. The sculpturing on this portal by the latter has been skilfully renovated and deserves the minutest inspection. Above the doors is represented the death, interment, resurrection and coronation of the Virgin, and on the middle pillar the Saviour and king Solomon. Beneath is Solomon's Judgment, and on the r. and l. figures emblematical of Christianity and Judaism. There are also several statues by Sabina on pillars in the S. aisle next to the transept.

On the N. side is the Chapel of St. Laurentius with its beautiful gateway of the 15th cent., adorned with restored sculptures of the martyrdom of the saints.

The ***Cathedral-Tower** rises in front of the structure to such a height that the spectator almost feels dizzy as his eye attempts to reach so vast an altitude. Near the r. hand Portal, round the corner, is a door leading to a staircase of easy ascent. A few steps up, the custodian dwells, from whom a ticket (15 cent.) must be procured. The visitor then ascends 330 steps to the platform, 230 ft. above the street, which commands a fine view of the old-fashioned town with its planted ramparts and promenades. To the l. is seen the Black Forest from Baden to the Blauen; on the W. and N. the entire chain of the Vosges, and on the S. the insulated Kaiserstuhl (p. 253), rising from the plain, and beyond it in the extreme distance rises the magnificent chain of the Jura. The services of the door-keeper are unnecessary in ascending to the platform, though a fee is generally expected. From the platform another staircase leads to the summit of the spire, the so-called "*Lantern.*" The entrance to it is closed by an iron grating, which is not opened to the visitor without a special permission from the mayor.

The ancient residence of the Bishops, opposite to the S. Portal of the Cathedral, with terrace facing the Ill, was purchased by the town at the period of the Revolution and presented in 1806 to Napoleon. From 1814—1848 it served as a royal residence, and in 1853 was presented to Napoleon III.

From the cathedral the attention of the traveller is next directed to the Church of St. Thomas. His way leads across the *Place Gutenberg,* where a handsome bronze **Statue** was erected in 1840 to the memory of the great printer who conducted his first experiments in the newly-discovered art at Strasburg in 1436. The four bas-reliefs are emblematical of the power and blessing of the invention of printing in the four quarters of the globe, and comprise likenesses of many celebrated men.

The ***Church of St. Thomas** (Pl. 10; the sacristan lives at the back of the choir) was founded in 1031; the choir, of plain Gothic construction, was commenced in 1270, and the main-body of the church with its five aisles was erected in the Gothic style in 1313—1330. It is now appropriated to the use of a Protestant congregation. The choir where the high-altar formerly stood contains a magnificent monument in marble, erected by Louis XV. to *Marshal Saxe;* it is the work of the sculptor Pigalle, and the result of twenty years' labour. The marshal is represented descending into the tomb held open to receive him by Death, while a beautiful female figure personifying France strives to detain him; at the side Hercules is represented in a mournful attitude leaning upon his club; on the l. side are the Austrian eagle, the Dutch lion and the English leopard, with broken flags beneath them, commemorating the victories gained by the marshal over the three united powers in the Flemish wars. The whole is an allegory in accordance with the questionable taste of the age, but as a work of art it is masterly and original.

The church also contains busts and monuments of celebrated professors of the University of Strasburg, among others of Schöpflin, Koch and Oberlin, brother of the well-known pastor of that name. In a side-chapel may be seen two mummies, found in 1802, and said to be the bodies of a Count of Nassau-Saarbrücken and his daughter, who probably died in the 16th cent.

The **New Church** (*Temple neuf, Pl. 11*) which belongs to the 16th cent., once the property of the Dominicans, now appropriated to the Protestant service, contains the tombstone of the celebrated Dominican Joh. Tauler (d. 1361) and some curious old frescoes of a death-dance, probably of the 14th or 15th cent.

Near the New Church is the *Town Library* (Pl. 15) which possesses a rich collection of curious ancient works and documents. In the entrance-hall some Roman and other antiquities are to be seen.

The square called the *Broglie,* after a marshal of that name, is bounded on the N.E. by the **Theatre** (Pl. 37), completed in 1821, with a Portico adorned with statues of 6 of the Muses. Representations in French only, on Sund., Tues., Thurs. and Frid.

Opposite to the theatre on the r. are the residences of the prefect of the town and the general of the troops garrisoned here. The *Statue* (Pl. 38) of the Marquis de Lezay-Marnesia, by Grass, was erected in 1857. Farther on is the **Town-hall** (Pl. 26, entrance from the Rue brulée) which contains a small collection of pictures open on Sund., Tues. and Thurs. from 2 to 4; at other times on payment of a fee of 1 fr.

The *Rue brulée*, which runs in a S.E. direction parallel with the Broglie, has received its appellation from the circumstance of 2000 Jews, who refused to be baptized, having been burned, Feb. 14th, 1349, on the spot where the Hôtel de la Préfecture now stands.

The *University*, inaugurated in 1621, once numbered Goethe among its students; it was here that the great poet and scholar completed his law studies and took the degree of doctor in 1772. It is now converted into an *Academy*, and deserves a visit on account of its *Museum of natural history*, a collection of more than ordinary value and interest. It is open to the public on Thurs. from 2 to 4, and on Sund. from 10 to 12; at other times adm. may be procured for a fee of 1 fr.

On the Place d'Armes (Parade-Platz) is erected a bronze *Statue* to the memory of *General Kleber*, at the foot of which reclines an Egyptian sphynx, and on the sides are two reliefs. The *Café Cadé* is on the N.W. side of the Place, next to the Guard-house.

The *Kehl* railway-station is about 4 M. distant from Strasburg, and connected with it by a junction line lately completed. In the immediate vicinity of the Porte d'Austerlitz are the spacious **Artillery Barracks** (*St. Nicholas*) and near them the *Arsenal de construction*, one of the largest dépôts of ammunition in France.

A few minutes after leaving the town by this gate the traveller passes the *Cemetery* and catches a glimpse of the green ramparts of the *Citadel*, constructed by Vauban in 1682—1684, which lies to the l. of the road. On the other side of the bridge over a branch of the Rhine stands a *Monument* erected by Napoleon to the memory of *General Desaix*, who fell in the battle of Marengo in 1800.

Junction line to Kehl see p. 217; fares 1 fr., 70 and 50 c.

55. From Strasburg to Mayence.

Comp. Maps to the R.R. 52 and 45.

By Railway in $5^3/_4$—8 hrs. Fares to Weissenburg 6 fr. 55, 4 fr. 5 and 2 fr. 65 c.; from Weissenburg to Mayence 6 fl. 27, 3 fl. 51 and 2 fl. 33 kr.

Through-passengers by exp. train are exempt from the *visite* of passports and luggage. Travellers unacquainted with the r. bank of the Rhine should select the Baden line.

At Wendenheim this line diverges from the Paris railway, and taking a N.E. direction, crosses the *Zorn* at the *Hördt* station. The country is flat; on the r. in the distance are the mountains of the Black Forest from the Hornisgrinde (R. 63. a.) to below Baden. Station *Bischweiler*, cloth factories, and in the neighbourhood hop-gardens.

After passing *Marienthal,* where up to 1789 there was a convent, the town of **Hagenau** (*Post; Blume; Wilder Mann*) is reached. It was formerly a free town of the German empire, and part of the walls and fortifications, erected by Frederick Barbarossa in 1164, still exist. The lofty church of St. George belongs partly to the 13th cent. The large building on the N. side is the prison.

The train next traverses the *Hagenauer Wald,* and after passing some smaller stations arrives at **Weissenburg** (*Ange*), where the passengers by ordinary trains must change carriages. Here the Bavarian branch commences.

At Weissenburg the line traverses the now fallen intrenchments, called the *Weissenburger Linien,* constructed by Marshal Villars in 1705, during the Spanish war of Succession, and extending on the r. bank of the Lauter to Lauterburg near the Rhine. The *Lauter* and the Bavarian frontier are next crossed.

The next station of importance is **Landau** (**Pfälzer Hof; Schwan*), a fortress of the German Confederation, with a pop. of 7000 (1/2 Prot.), and a garrison of 4500 Bavarians. Landau has long been a fortified town; it was seven times besieged and captured in the 30 Years' war, seized in 1680 by Louis XIV., regularly fortified by Vauban in 1686, changed hands several times between 1702 and 1713, and was under the French dominion from the peace of Rastadt (1714) till 1814. Above the town-gates are suns (that over the French gate wears a pleasant expression, while that over the German has an angry look), above which may be read the vain inscription of Louis XIV., "*Nec pluribus impar.*" An omnibus runs from the station to Gleisweiler (p. 193) in 1 hr., and twice daily to Annweiler (p. 194).

The train next crosses the *Queich,* the ancient frontier between Alsace and the Palatinate, and the boundary between the Vosges and the Haardt Mountains.

Edenkoben (**Schaaf,* good, R. and B. 1 fl.), the next place of consequence, is a cheerful little town which boasts of a sulphur spring, a grape-cure establishment, and, in the background, a royal villa, the *Ludwigshöhe* (p. 193). On an eminence at the foot of the *Kalmit* (2097 ft.) are situated the ruins of the *Kropsburg,* formerly a nobleman's castle, now occupied by several poor families.

On a hill to the l. of the next stat. *Maikammer* lies the handsome and imposing castle of * **Maxburg,** property of the King of Bavaria. The ruins, out of which the new structure was erected, were of vast extent, and some Roman remains discovered on the spot lead to the supposition that one of the

Roman *castra stativa* was here stationed to command Upper Germany. The old castle is said to have been built by the Emperor Henry II., but fell into the hands of the bishops of Speyer as early as 1100. In an insurrection of the peasantry in 1525 it was stormed and demolished by the insurgents, who, however, were subsequently compelled to rebuild it at their own expense. In 1552 it was burned by the Margrave Albert of Brandenburg, but for its complete destruction it was indebted, like most of the castles in the Palatinate, to the "most christian" king Louis XIV.

Neustadt (**Löwe*, at the station, R. 54, B. 24, D. 48, A. 18 kr.; **Schiff;* **Krone*) is the largest town in the Haardt. The handsome Gothic church, erected in the middle of the 14th cent., the choir of which serves as a place of worship for the Rom. Catholics and the nave for the Protestants, contains several monuments of the Counts Palatine, the founders of the town. The gutters on the roof terminate in heads of apes, pigs, geese, &c., and are called by the inhabitants *Höllenkinder* (children of hell). The Rom. Cath. *Church of St. Ludwig*, a handsome Gothic structure, was consecrated in 1862. From the **Schiesshaus*, 1/4 M. from the station, a fine prospect of the environs may be enjoyed. On the height, 1 M. to the N., are situated the ruins of *Burg Winzingen* (p. 192); 1 1/2 M. farther the *Wolfsburg*, commanding a pleasing prospect. An agreeable excursion of half a day may be made to *Mittel-Hambach* by carriage (1-horse 4 fl.), thence to the Maxburg on foot, and back; from Mittel-Hambach to the villa of *Ludwigshöhe* near *Rhodt*, to the watering-place *Gleisweiler* (p. 193), and back to Neustadt.

Neustadt is the junction of the Maximilian, Ludwig and Bexbach (Saarbrücken) lines, and is a favorite resort of invalids undergoing the grape-cure.

The Ludwig-railway here turns E. and enters the great plain of the Rhine, where vineyards, tobacco and corn fields are extended before the traveller's eye.

Ludwigshafen (**Deutsches Haus*, R. 36 kr., B. 24 kr., D. inc. W. 1 fl.; *Hôtel Wolff; Railway refreshment-room;* good beer at *Pschorr's*), formerly the tête-de-pont of the old fortress of Mannheim, scene of many a bloody contest during the revolution, and, as late as 1849, cannonaded from Mannheim by Baden insurgents, is a town of very recent construction, having been founded in 1843, but has already attained to considerable commercial importance. The wharf is one of the best on the Rhine, and is lined with long rows of warehouses and magazines connected with the railway by tram-ways. *Mannheim* on the opposite side of the river, see R. 44.

At the next stat. *Oggersheim* there is an extensive plush manufactory, after which the train passes the flourishing little town of **Frankenthal** (*Hôtel Otto*), founded by Calvinists from the Netherlands, driven out of their country by the Spaniards in 1554, and who, on account of religious differences, emigrated from Frankfurt to this place in 1562. The town is connected by a canal (constructed 1777) with the Rhine, which is 3 M. distant. — Omnibus to Dürkheim (p. 190) in 2½ hrs.

Near **Worms** (p. 198) the line crosses the Bavarian-Hessian frontier, and afterwards passes close to the *Cemetery*, in which a tombstone surmounted by a helmet is a conspicuous object — one of the monuments erected in 1848 to veterans of Napoleon, which are so frequently met with in the churchyards of the larger towns on the l. bank of the Rhine.

In the distance to the l. is situated **Hernsheim**, with the white castle of the Dalbergs, one of the oldest and most respected families in the time of the German Empire. The buildings, grounds and church of Hernsheim are worth a visit. In the latter many members of the above-mentioned family repose, among others the prince-primate Carl von Dalberg, once Grand-duke of Frankfurt (d. 1817), and Emmerich Joseph von Dalberg (d. 1833), the ambassador of Baden in Paris, created Duke by Napoleon for his services in furthering the emperor's alliance with Marie Louise.

Guntersblum (*Krone*), a small town belonging to the Count of Leiningen, possesses a venerable church with helmeted towers, a large Town-hall, and on the N. side a palace and grounds of the Count. In the great plain between Guntersblum and Oppenheim the election of the Emperor Conrad II. took place in 1024.

Near **Oppenheim** (*Ritter*), the ancient *Bonconica*, the line traverses vine-clad hills. The red church of *St. Catherine* on the hill is a striking object; near it is the gloomy-looking Castle of *Landskron*. This very ancient town became a portion of the Rhenisb Confederation in the 12th cent.; in 1689 it was, with the exception of one house, burned to the ground by the French. The W. choir (1439) of * *St. Catherine's Church* was also destroyed; but the E. portion, which dates from the 13th cent. was spared. It was restored in 1838—43, and is now a remarkably fine Gothic structure. A charnel-house on the N. side of the churchyard contains numerous bones of Spaniards and Swedes killed in the 30 Years' war. In many of the skulls the holes made by the bullets may be seen. The sexton (fee 12 kr.) lives up the stair on the l. of the S. entrance.

The *Landskron*, connected with the town by a wall, is all that remains of a once famous Imperial stronghold of that name. It was constructed by the Emperor Lothar, and restored by the Emperor Ruprecht, who died here in 1410. Subterranean passages connect it with the town. The top commands a good view of the plain of the Rhine, N.E. the Taunus, S.E. Melibocus and the mountains of the Bergstrasse.

The two modern towers which rise from among the ruins, the one serving as a clock-tower, the other erected by a private individual, have a curious effect.

Nierstein (**Anker*) is distinguished for the careful culture of its vineyards. The green vines planted on a red soil have a very picturesque effect. The wine yielded by them is reckoned among those of the Rhine, while that of Oppenheim belongs to the Palatinate wines. The chapel of the family *von Herding* is embellished with frescoes of some merit by Götzenberger. On the height to the l. rises an ancient watch-tower.

On a chain of low, productive, vine-clads hills to the l. lie the villages of *Nackenheim*, *Bodenheim*, and *Laubenheim*, and near Mayence (see R. 35) the handsome village of *Weissenau*, which forms a part of the fortifications of that town.

56. From Strasburg to Bâle.

Comp. Maps to RR. 52 and 62.

Alsace Railway. By express in 3½, by ordinary trains in 5—6 hrs.; fares: 15 fr. 80, 11 fr. 85, 7 fr. 80c. Railway or Paris time is 22 min. behind Bâle and Strasburg time. Second-class carriages generally bad. View on the W. side only. Refreshment-room on the line at Colmar not good. Return-tickets are now issued between Cologne and Colmar (valid for 5 days), and between Cologne and Mühlhausen, Bâle and the other Swiss stations (valid for one month).

A peculiar kind of wine ("*straw wine*") is made in Alsace from the finest grapes which are kept in straw through the winter till March, when they are picked and pressed. The price varies from 5 to 10 fr. per bottle.

The banks of the Rhine between Bonn and Bingen are scarcely richer in ruined castles than these eastern slopes of the Vosges. The railway is so far distant from the hills that the mere outlines only are visible; there are, however, several fine points of view, especially between Schlettstadt and Colmar.

The population of Alsace clearly betrays its German origin, and, though the French language gains ground in the larger towns and is the language of the upper classes, that of the country-people is still German, and to many of them French is totally unintelligible. Sermons and school-instruction are German, and will probably continue so for many years, though there are few children who do not possess some acquaintance with the French tongue.

Soon after Strasburg is left, the junction line to Kehl and the Baden railway diverges to the l. at *Königshofen*. After traversing a broad fertile plain which yields abundant crops of tobacco, and passing a succession of unimportant stations, the train approaches the mountains.

Schlettstadt (*Bock*), onee a free German town, was taken by the Freneh and fortified by Vauban. Over the ramparts peeps the red-sandstone tower of the *Münster*, founded by the Hohenstaufen in 1094.

At the entrance of the *Leberthal* is situated the castle of *Kinsheim;* near stat. *Orschweiler* is another ruined eastle, and on a detaehed peak of the Vosges, before stat. *St. Hippolyte* (p. 232) is reached, rise the ruins of the *Hohkönigsburg.*

Rappoltsweiler (called "Rappschwier" by the inhabitants), the French *Ribeauvillé* (*Lamm*), is a manufacturing town with 8000 inhabitants, and lies 3 M. from the station at the entrance of a beautiful valley and at the foot of vine-clad hills. High above the town on a rugged precipice is perched the castle of *Hohen-Rappoltstein*, with lofty tower; lower are the ruins of *Niederburg*, or *St. Ulrich*, celebrated for its tasteful architecture, and *Girsberg*, or "*Der Stein*", remarkable for the boldness of its situation. The castle of St. Ulrich well merits a visit on account of the fine views it affords.

At the entrance of the valley of the *Weiss*, 4½ M. to the r. of the railway, lies the small town of **Kaisersberg** (**Krone*), with a castle of the same name, destroyed during the 30 Years' war. The town was founded in the first half of the 13th cent. by the emp. Frederick II. of the house of the Hohenstaufen, who were at the same time dukes of Swabia and Alsace. The *Church* belongs to the same period, and contains some ancient wood-carving, an Entombment and an altar-piece of some merit.

Colmar (*Trois Rois; Clef*) was once a free German town and in 1474 so powerful that the inhabitants refused to open the gates to Charles the Bold, who, by a treaty with the Arehduke of Austria, had become master of Alsace, the Sundgau and the Breisgau, and was then on his way to the siege of Neuss (p. 39). It has now a pop. of 22,000 and is the capital of the Department of the Upper Rhine and seat of the *Cour impériale.* The most considerable building is the *Münster*, founded in 1360, but still incomplete.

The environs of Colmar possess some historieal interest; here Louis the Pious fell into the hands of his degenerate sons, who, after holding a deliberation at Colmar (then only a farm-house), lured the army of Louis to the "red field," where the latter was defeated and taken by his son Lothaire to a monastery at Soissons.

Omnibus to Breisach and Freiburg see p. 244.

The castle of *Hohenlandsberg*, situated on a well-wooded height, the most extensive mountain-fortress of Alsace, was destroyed by the Freneh in 1635. Near stat. *Egisheim* are seen three ruined castles of the 10th and 11th eenturies, termed the "*Three Exen,*" i. e. the castle of *Hohen-* or *Dreien-Egisheim*, with the towers of *Dagsburg*, *Wahlenburg* and *Wek-*

mund, birthplace of Pope Leo IX., who was a count of Egisheim and Dagsburg.

Ruffach (*Ours*), the *Rubeacum* of the Romans, is built round the castle of *Isenburg*, one of the oldest in Alsace and frequently the seat of the Merovingian kings of France. The Church of *St. Arbogast* belongs to the end of the 12th cent.

To the r. are situated the industrial towns of *Gebweiler* and *Sultz*, overtopped by the *Gebweiler Belchen* (*Ballon de Guebwiller*, 4417 ft.), the highest peak of the Vosges, the summit of which commands a magnificent view. Beyond stat. *Bolweiler* the picturesque and rocky slopes of the Vosges gradually disappear.

From *Lutterbach* a branch-line diverges to **Thann** (*Löwe*; *Krone*), a manufacturing town with 4000 inhab., situated at the entrance of the romantic valley of St. Amarin (p. 234). The * *Church of St. Theobald* (1445), with its bold open-work tower (1516), is a remarkably elegant Gothic structure. The most striking view of it is obtained from the *Engelburg* (demolished by Turenne in 1674), which commands the town and the mouth of the valley, and whose tower, overturned bodily, lies prostrate like a giant cask. The interior of the church contains some good carving, statues and fine stained-glass windows rescued from the ravages of the first French revolution.

At *Dornach* the *Thur*, the boundary between Alsace and the Sundgau, is crossed, and near *Mühlhausen* the *Rhine-Rhone Canal*.

Mühlhausen (*Ville de Paris; Lion Rouge; Cicogne*) in the *Sundgau*, formerly a free town of the German Empire, from 1515 to 1798 in alliance with Switzerland, and since then belonging to France, is the most considerable manufacturing town of the Upper Rhine, and has a population of 30,000, to which may be added about 7000 workmen who come daily from the neighbouring villages. The situation of Mühlhausen on the *Rhine-Rhone Canal* is very advantageous. Its ancient architectural remains have given place to manufactories, and the antiquarian will find but few objects of attraction in the town, with the exception perhaps of the *Town-hall*, erected in 1551 and restored in 1846, which contains some tolerable frescoes. Another relic of olden times is the picturesque house with projecting tower which adjoins the Town-hall. At the entrance to the town from the Railway station are the handsome new buildings and halls belonging to the "*Société commerciale*", containing a scientific and industrial museum. At Mühlhausen a line diverges to the W. to *Belford*, whence one branch goes direct to Paris, and another to Besançon, Dijon and Lyons.

To the l. the *Blauen* (p. 247) stands out conspicuously from the Black Forest. The train now skirts a succession of vine-clad hills, and passes stat. *Rixheim*. To the l. of *St. Louis*, the seat of the French custom-house authorities, rises the ancient fortress of *Hüningen*, constructed by Vauban under Louis XIV. (1679), and demolished by the Austrians in 1815. The red open-work towers of the cathedral of Bâle now come in sight.

57. The Vosges. *Northern part.*

From Strasburg to Saarburg.

Paris Railway. To Zabern in 1 hr.; fares 4, 3 and 2 fr. The 1st class carriages are scarcely equal in comfort to those of the 2nd class on the Baden line. Station and conveyances see p. 218.

At *Wendenheim*, the first station, the line diverges from the l. bank of the Rhine. After passing several unimportant places, the rocky heights and ruined castle of *Hoh-Barr* appear on the l.; near them the slender tower of *Geroldseck*, and to the r. the ruin of *Greifenstein.*

Zabern or *Saverne* (* *Sonne*), the *Tabernæ* of the Romans, afterwards the capital of the Wasgau, is now a quiet little town with about 6400 inhabitants. Long before entering the town the stately *Schloss* is a conspicuous object. It was erected in 1667 by a bishop of Strasburg, afterwards inhabited by the Cardinal de Rohan, also Bishop of Strasburg, the calumniator of Marie Antoinette in the well-known and mysterious affair of the necklace. By an imperial decree of 1852 the building is now appropiated to the use of the widows and daughters of members of the Legion of Honor. In front of this building stands an *Obelisk* erected in 1666, which records the distances (in German miles) from Saverne of upwards of 100 different towns.

Near the station, on the road to the town, a pretty figure of "*Hora*" has been erected over a fountain, with a tablet on which the day of the month is daily inscribed by order of the police. The road to the hotel crosses the *Rhine-Marne-Canal.* According to an old historian, the town was in 1550 surrounded by a wall with "as many towers as there are weeks in the year", but these have long since disappeared, and the spot has nothing to recommend it as a halting-place.

Above the town rises the tower of the old stronghold of *Greifenstein*, and near it is the *Grotto of St. Veit,* a chapel and hermitage constructed in a large cave of sandstone, and a favorite resort of pilgrims. On the other side of the mountain, situated on a wooded eminence, are the extensive ruins of the castle of ***Hoh-Barr,** which appears to form a portion of the variegated sandstone and conglomerate rocks on which it stands. An inscription over the gate records that the castle was restored by Count Manderscheid-Blankenheim, Bishop of Strasburg, in 1583. As late as 1744, during the war of succession, the castle was still habitable, but it has subsequently completely fallen to decay, and is occupied by a forester, from whom refreshments may be procured. By means of a ladder the venturesome traveller may clamber to the top of huge and otherwise inaccessible rocks, which command a view of the plain of Strasburg as far as the Black Forest, and a part of the Vosges.

The railway here traverses the chain of the Vosges at the narrowest part; near Saverne it penetrates into the narrow and picturesque valley of the *Zorn*, through which the high-road, the railway, the Marne-Canal and the brook itself run side by side. The train passes bridges, high embankments, viaducts and tunnels in rapid succession between Saverne and Saarburg.

Lützelburg (**Jespère* near the station, good beer), the only station between Saverne and Saarburg, is the first Lothringian village in the Meurthe Department, and prettily situated. On the opposite side of the brook, on a projecting rock, rises the *Lützelstein*, or *Castle of Lützelburg*, fortified up to the beginning of the last century; beneath it is the railway tunnel.

The line now leaves the valley of the Zorn. A handsome bridge spans the stream which descends from a valley on the l., and a second arch crosses the *Rhine-Marne-Canal*, which here passes over to the r. side of the valley, but soon rejoins the line at the remarkable tunnel of *Ertzweiler* (*Archwiller*), upwards of 1 ½ M. in length, by means of which both the canal and the railway penetrate the mountain. At the E. extremity the line lies immediately under the canal, but at the W., it runs by the side of it. The vast fertile plains of Lothringia now lie stretched before the traveller.

Saarburg (**Hôtel du Sauvage*) on the *Saar*, which here becomes navigable, is a small town enclosed with walls and gates (not to be confounded with Saarburg near Treves, in the Prussian dominions). It forms the boundary between the two languages, French being spoken in the upper part of the town and principally German in the lower. The names above the shops are chiefly German. The ancient fortifications were dismantled in 1552 by the Margrave Albert of Brandendenburg. The place would become one of the utmost importance in case of a war on the Rhine, and has in consequence been provided with extensive provision magazines. (Railway to Paris in 10 hrs.)

The following excursion through the Vosges will well repay the pedestrian; it should not however be undertaken without a guide (Paul Zuber at Saverne can be recommended, fee 3 fr.). From Saverne an ascent of 3/4 hr. to *Hoh-Barr* (p. 229), then the descent through *Hager* to *Haberacker* (in 1/2 hr.), where refreshments may be obtained at the Forester's house. The ruin of *Ochsenstein*, above the latter, was till 1789 the property of the Landgraves of Hessen-Darmstadt.

The path now lies through forest, past some houses called *an der Haardt* (3 M.), to the *Chapel auf der Hueb* (1 1/2 M.), then 1 1/2 M. down a steep declivity into a narrow grassy valley, after which the ascent again commences; in 1/4 hr. more a cross is reached, where the path to the l. must be taken, which in about 20 min. conducts the traveller to the *Dachsburg*. The castle which formerly stood on this high and solitary rock, which commands a fine view, was destroyed by the French in 1675, and almost all traces of it have vanished, with the exception of the Chapel. In the wood may still be seen some remains of Roman fortifications, where as the spot is but rarely visited, Roman relics are still frequently found.

At the foot of the rock lies the village of **Dachsburg**, called *Dabo* by the French. Belated travellers had better apply to the clergyman for a night's lodging, as the inns are bad.

The road to Lützelburg now leads past *Schaefershof* (3 M.), and at the *Neumühl* (1 1/2 M.) it enters the beautiful dale of the Zorn bounded by well-wooded mountains. In the middle of the valley are several mills (1 1/2 M.), the way to which is indicated by a cross, and which afford better accommodation than the wretched inns of Dachsburg. One mile farther the railway bridge already mentioned (p. 230) is reached, and 2 M. beyond it Lützelburg. The finest points of this excursion are the Hoh-Barr, and the valley of the Zorn from Neumühl to Lützelburg.

58. The Vosges. *Southern part.*

Four days suffice for a hasty glance at the Vosges Mountains. This period may be most advantageously allotted as follows, the traveller taking the last train but one from Strasburg to *St. Hippolyte*, which is assumed as the starting point. 1st day: *Hohkönigsburg*, *Markirch*, *Rappoltsweiler* (24 M.). 2nd day: Along the vine-clad slopes to *Kaisersberg* (6 3/4 M.); pass afternoon in exploring the town and its environs; in the evening proceed to *Orbey* (6 3/4 M.). 3d day: *Lac blanc, Reisberg, Münster, Metzeral* (21 3/4 M.). 4th day: Over the *Herrenberg* to *Wildenstein*, through the beautiful valley of *St. Amarin* to the village of the same name (21 M.). On the following morning omnibus to *Thann* in 1 hr. These four days enable the pedestrian to inspect the most beautiful points of these magnificent highlands, generally but too seldom visited. The unfrequency of the inroads made by travellers upon this district may constitute, in the eyes of some, not one of its least considerable charms.

From Strasburg to St. Hippolyte in $1^3/_4$ hr.

From the station of Benfeld an omnibus runs three times a day to *Barr*, whence the ***Ottilienberg** or **Mont Ste-Odile** (2466 ft.), mentioned by Goethe in his biography, may be ascended in $2^1/_2$ hrs. Guide unnecessary. as the path is furnished with direction-posts.

St. Hippolyte (*Krone*), a small and old fashioned town, about $2^1/_2$ M. from the station, lies at the foot of the mountain crowned by the Hoh-Königsburg. Of the four roads leading from the S. W. gate of the town, that in the direction of the castle is the one to be selected; it leads at first through vineyards; $^3/_4$ M. higher the traveller must turn to the l.; after another mile the road passes a chestnut-wood, where the real ascent commences; in 10 min. the *Lower Forester's House* is reached; a steep ascent of another mile brings the pedestrian to the *Upper Forester's House*, where refreshments may be procured; in 20 min. more the summit is reached.

The ***Hoh-Königsburg**, which stands at a height of 1700 ft. above the level of the sea, is, after the castle of Heidelberg, the largest German fortress of the middle ages. Its huge walls of red sandstone towering above the green of the chestnut-wood present a most picturesque appearance. Nothing certain is known of its origin, but it has evidently been the result of the labour of many centuries. The lions over the principal entrance are the arms of the House of Hohenstaufen.

As early as the year 1462 the castle was partially destroyed by the Bishop of Strasburg and the Archduke of Austria, on account of depredations committed by the count; it was afterwards restored, but was burned by the Swedes in 1633. Since then this once magnificent pile has been a ruin, and with the surrounding woods and fields is now the property of a banker at Colmar.

The footpath to the entrance leads round the castle to the r., and from it a correct idea of the extent of the ruin can best be formed. From the platform of the S. W. round tower (to which a footpath to the l. leads) the most extensive prospect may be enjoyed; far beneath is the *Leberthal;* on the opposite hill-side the *Frankenburg;* and the wide and populous plain of the Rhine is seen stretching on the E. to the mountains of the Black Forest and the Kaiserstuhl, and on the W. to the Vosges. In clear weather the snow-clad peaks of the Bernese Alps are sometimes visible; if seen very

Vogesen. (Vosges.)

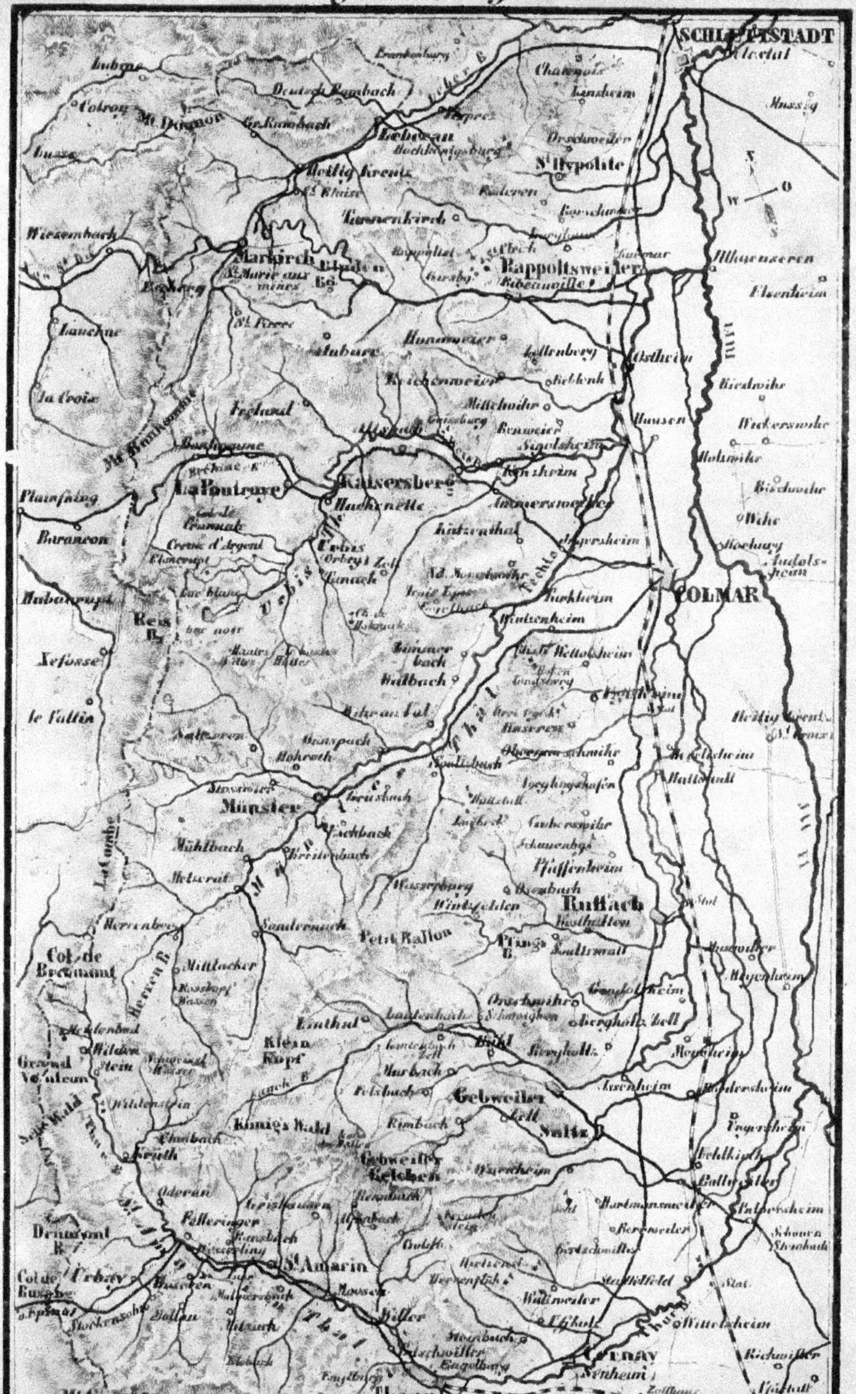

distinctly, it is a sign of rainy weather. Neither the road from St. Hippolyte to the Hoh-Königsburg, nor that from the castle to the Leberthal can well be missed; travellers wishing to return by the latter must take the path to the r., about $1/2$ M. after passing the Upper Forester's house, which will bring them to the high road; 3 M. farther is the Leberthal, an industrial, as well as picturesque and well-wooded valley watered by the *Leber* (*Lièpvre*). An hour's walk up the valley then takes the traveller past *Leberau* (*Lièpvre*) to *Heilig-Kreuz* or *Ste. Croix-aux-mines* (good beer at *Schmidt's*), both busy, animated villages; 2 M. farther **Markirch,** or *Ste. Marie-aux- mines* (*Hôtel du Commerce*), the principal town of the valley (pop. 12,000) is reached.

From Markirch a good high-road leads across the *Bludenberg* or *Bressoir* (3840 ft.) to Rappoltsweiler, a distance of about 10 M. About $1/2$ M. from Markirch the traveller may effect a considerable saving by taking the old road, which diverges from the new at a house on the road-side to the l., and leads by a row of cherry-trees and through a narrow lane, till it rejoins the high-road about $1\,1/2$ M. farther on. The view looking back on the Leberthal is picturesque, but on ascending it disappears. Near the top is a stone with coat of arms and date 1779, beyond which the road runs through the wood almost the whole way to **Rappoltsweiler** (see p. 227). The road from here to Kaisersberg (6 M.) leads through the vineyards on the hill-side to *Hunaweier*, $1\,1/2$ M. farther to *Reichenweier* or *Riquevihr* (* *Krone*, exeellent wine), and thence to **Kaisersberg.**

From Kaisersberg the traveller next turns his steps W. to *Hachimette*, $4\,1/2$ M. up the broad valley of the *Weiss.* Five min. after passing the last-named village, the path diverges to the l. to **Orbey** (2 M.) (*Croix d'Or*, above the Church), a French mountain village, where the night may be passed. A coach runs every morning to Kaisersberg and Colmar (p. 227), returning in the evening.

About 6 M. to the W. of Orbey, near the summit of the granite-ridge which forms the boundary between the Wasgau and Lothringia, are situated two mountain lakes, the ***Lac blanc** and the **Lac noir.** The former, which derives its name from the quartz at its bottom, is about 3 M. in eircumferenee, and is enclosed on two sides by high and precipitous walls of rock, and on a third by immense fragments of granite lying in a eonfused mass. The Lae noir, of about half the size, lies $3/4$ M. farther to the S. It probably owes its appellation to the blaekish sand of its banks or to the dark firwood by which it is surrounded. Both lakes are drained by the *Weiss*, which, united with the Fecht, falls into the Ill below Colmar. The gullies in which the lakes are situated are frequently partially covered with snow the whole year round.

On the W. side of the Lac blanc rises perpendicularly a huge wall of granite, the ***Reisberg** (3160 ft.), the summit of which may be reached from the lake in $^3/_4$ hr. Here the traveller is rewarded by a most extensive and magnificent view; before him lie Lothringia and a great part of the Vosges, the Black Forest and the entire plain of the Rhine. Farther S. a portion of the Münsterthal is visible, in the foreground the Lac noir, and in the distance the Alps. The way from Orbey is not difficult to find, but it is advisable to take a guide and a supply of provisions, as these desolate heights can boast of no inn. From the top of the Reisberg to *Les-hautes-huttes* is a distance of about 3 M.

Travellers who do not care to visit the above-mentioned lakes and the Reisberg can walk direct from Orbey to Münster (12 M.). The path first ascends through beautiful well-watered meadows to *Les-basses-huttes* (3 M.); here it diverges to the r., by a house, across a small bridge towards a round hill; $^3/_4$ M. farther the path again turns to the r., ascends, then runs across a stony moss-covered field towards a cross, and finally leads to a house surrounded by fir wood (*Les-hautes-huttes*); a short way beyond this, another cross stands at the summit of the ridge, which is nearly half-way between Orbey and Münster. From this point a good view of the Reisberg, and the granite walls of the Lac blanc, which seem quite near, is obtained.

The S. slope of the ridge, which the pedestrian now descends, is barren and stony, and forms a striking contrast to the N. side. Towards *Sultzeren* (good beer at Jaekele's), however, the valley is more attractive; $^3/_4$ M. farther is *Stossweier*, and about 2 M. beyond it Münster. The whole walk well repays time and trouble.

Münster (*Storch; Krone*) is a busy little town of some importance and very ancient origin, with a pop. of 4600. It owes its origin to the Benedictine abbey built here in 660 by king Childerich. The beautiful and fertile valley in which the town is situated is watered by the *Fecht*, and its inhabitants are principally German protestants.

A most interesting walk may be taken from Münster to Wildenstein in the valley of St. Amarin, a distance of 14 M. The way to the height which separates the valleys of the Fecht and the Thur cannot well be missed, nor from this point to Wildenstein is the road difficult to find; however, it is safer to take a guide from Münster (2 ½ fr.) or at all events from Metzeral

To Breitenbach and Metzeral the road is excellent, at the latter place there is a tolerable inn near the bridge, opposite to which the traveller must diverge to the r. and follow the valley of the Fecht for about 2 M., after which a bridge is crossed and a good road leads in about 10 min. to the *Forest-house,* where refreshments may be procured.

Here the path quits the main road, and, branching off to the r. through the *Königswald* and across the *Herrenberg*, follows a sort of wooden causeway made to facilitate the process of dragging the timber down from the forest. After a two hours' ascent through the wood, the "*Herrenberger Wasser*" at the top is at last reached, near which there is a shepherd's hut; 1 M. beyond the latter is a second hut, at the commencement of the W. slope of the hill, and near it a good spring of fresh water. All trace of the path is now entirely lost, but by descending into the wood which must be traversed for some little distance to the right, the road will again be reached. From the summit to Wildenstein is about 3 M. Path very rough. Pedestrians desirous of taking this excursion in the opposite direction should not fail to take a guide at least as far as the shepherd's hut.

Wildenstein (* *Sonne*), a village prettily situated in the upper part of the St. Amarinthal (pop. German Rom. Cath.), the most beautiful valley of the Vosges. An hour's walk above the village, beyond the *Wildenstein glass-house*, the *Thur* is precipitated over a rock, 30 ft. in height, forming a waterfall termed the *Bain des Payens* or *Heidenbad.*

In the forenoon an omnibus runs from Wildenstein to Wesserling in 1 hr., but the valley is so romantic that walking is far preferable. The road passes a small waterfall. In the middle of he valley a precipitous and well-wooded rock rises abruptly before the traveller; it derives its name of *Schlossberg*, (Castle-mountain) from the ruined *Fortress of Wildenstein*, which belonged in former times to the Abbey of Murbach, but in the 30 Years' war was surrendered to a French general; in 1634 it was betrayed to the Lothringian troops, and 10 years later it fell into the hands of General von Erlach, the commander of the troops of Weimar, by whom it was finally dismantled.

From a considerable distance the zinc-covered spire of *Krüth*, situated about 3 M. from the castle, is a conspicuous object. About 1 ½ M. farther lies the village of *Oderen*, prettily situated on an eminence in the valley. The chapel on the E. side of the village contains a number of curious votive tablets.

The next village through which the road leads is *Felleringen*, and $^1/_2$ M. beyond it is **Wesserling**, picturesquely situated on a hill. The latter is a place of recent origin, being a colony of cotton-spinners, and in this respect one of the most important places of the kind in France. The beautiful grounds and handsome residences of the manufacturers bear testimony to the productiveness of their labour.

The road here joins the coach-road to *Remivemont* and *Epinal.* On the W. declivity of the mountain, which here separates the Wasgau from Lothringia, on the *Col de Bussang*, 6 M. from Wesserling, is the source of the *Moselle.*

From Wesserling an omnibus runs five times a day in $1^1/_4$ hr. to the railway station of Thann, passing *St. Amarin* (*Goldener Löwe), a celebrated resort of pilgrims, and the point from which the *Gebweiler Belchen* is generally ascended, but not without a guide; descent to Gebweiler on the other side. *Thann* see p. 228.

59. From Baden (or Strasburg) to Freiburg.

Comp. Map R. 62.

Baden Railway. From Baden $2^3/_4$—$4^3/_4$ hrs.; fares: express 5 fl. 27 and 3 fl. 42 kr., ordinary 4 fl. 36 kr., 3 fl. 6 kr. and 2 fl. — From Strasbourg in $2^3/_4$—$4^1/_2$ hrs.; fares: express 5 fl. 42 and 4 fl. 7 kr., ordinary trains 5 fl., 3 fl. 36 and 2 fl. 32 kr. Best views to the the l.

From *Baden* to *Appenweier* see p. 216. From *Strasburg* to *Appenweier* see p. 217.

The main line continues to run parallel with, and at a short distance from the mountains. In the distance to the l., on a rising ground, stands the Grand-ducal castle of *Staufenberg*, founded in the 11th cent. by Otto of Hohenstaufen, Bishop of Strasburg, and still in a good state of preservation.

Offenburg (**Fortuna*, R. 48 kr., B. 24 kr., D. inc. W. at $12^1/_2$ o'clock 1 fl., Durbacher wine good; * *Schwarzer Adler*) on the *Kinzig*, contains a statue, by the sculptor Friedrich, of Sir Francis Drake, "*the introducer of the potato into Europe, 1586.*" It was formerly an imperial town, and till the peace of Pressburg, seat of government of the district of *Ortenau* or *Mordnau*, which in ancient times belonged to the Duchy of Allemania or Swabia, while the *Uffgau*, in which Baden-Baden lies, was considered French-Rhenish territory. The *Breisgau* adjoins the Ortenau on the S.

After crossing the *Kinzig*, the train passes within sight of the castle of *Ortenberg*, which lies on a hill to the l. (see p. 257). *Dinglingen* is the nearest station for the town of **Lahr** (*Post* or *Sonne; Krone*), one of the most flourishing commercial places in the Duchy, situated in the Schutterthal, 1 1/2 M. from the railway.

On a high and precipitous peak, rising out of a distant mountain ravine, stand the ruins of the castle of *Hohengeroldseck*, destroyed by the French marshal Crequi in 1697. By an act of the Rhenish Confederation, the domains belonging to the castle, though not comprising more than 45 sq. M., were recognised as a free state, and their possessor dignified with the title of Prince. By the Congress of Vienna in 1815, the Princes of Hohengeroldseck lost their independence and became subjects of Austria, and afterwards of Baden.

Kippenheim, the birthplace of the rich tailor *Stulz* (p. 212), possesses a monument to his memory To the r. in the distance stretches the chain of the Vosges, among which the *Hohkönigsburg* (p. 232) is a conspicuous object.

The castle of *Mahlberg*, on an eminence above the small town of the same name, was, in remote times, one of the seats of the old Baden government; in the middle ages it belonged to the house of Hohenstaufen. The town was founded by Conrad III. about the middle of the 12th cent.

Not far from stat. *Orschweier,* the village of *Ettenheim* lies at the entrance of the Münsterthal; its large old church is a conspicuous object. This village possesses a mournful interest as the spot where the unfortunate Duc d'Enghien was seized on the night of March 14th, 1804.

Near stat. *Kenzingen* the line twice crosses the *Elz.* Above *Hecklingen*, on a slight eminence, are seen the ruins of the castle of *Lichteneyg*, once the seat of the Counts of Tübingen.

Near *Riegel* the *Dreisam* unites with the Elz. The entire plain at this point was, until lately, a marsh, but the water of the Dreisam is now drawn off by the *Leopolds-Canal* and emptied into the Rhine. The isolated mountain to the r. is the *Kaiserstuhl* (p. 243), raised by volcanie action, and consisting principally of basalt. Its S. and E. slopes are fertile and thickly populated.

The line now traverses the plain between the Kaiserstuhl and the slopes of the Black Forest, and commands an extensive view of the chain of hills by which Freiburg is enclosed. The *Schauinsland* (p. 243), *Belchen* (p. 248) and *Blauen* (p. 247), which, next to the Feldberg (p. 259), are the highest points of the Black Forest, are visible in the distance, rising from the mountain chain in the rear of the spire of the Münster of Freiburg.

At **Emmendingen** (*Post*), in the churchyard, Goethe's sister Cornelia (d. 1777) is interred. Beyond the town, on an eminence to the l., are to be seen the extensive and still well-preserved ruins of *Hochburg*, dismantled by order of Louis XIV. in 1689.

Between Emmendingen and *Denzlingen*, with its curious open-work tower, the train crosses the Elz. From this point a beautiful view is obtained of the valley of the Elz, opening to the N. E., at the entrance of which is situated the little town of *Waldkirch* (p. 257), with its slender white tower and ruined castle, at the N. W. base of the *Hohen-Kandel* (3886 ft.).

Near Freiburg, on the l., stands the old watch-tower of the now completely ruined castle of *Zähringen*, once the seat of a powerful race, which became extinct in 1218 by the death of Count Berthold V. (p. 240). The Counts of Hochberg, as well as the present Grand-duke of Baden, are descendants of the Dukes of Zähringen.

60. Freiburg and its Environs.

Comp. Map R. 62.

Hotels. *Zähringer Hof, opp. the station; *Hôtel Fehrenbach (spacious apartments); Hôtel Müller, *Deutscher Hof. Of the second class: *Pfau, near the station, comfortable house. *Wilder Mann, not far from the Schwabenthor. Charges nearly the same in all: R. 48 kr.—1 fl., B. 24 kr., D. at 12½ o'clock 1 fl., A. 18 kr. — *Heil. Geist, opp. to the west-portal of the Münster, R. 36, B. 20, D. 48 kr. — *Röm. Kaiser for those of moderate requirements.

Cafés. *Kopf, where beer may be procured; Gramm, by the Schlossberg.

Newspapers in the Museum, near the post-office; strangers introduced by a member.

Swimming-baths at the foot of the Lorettoberg; bath 12 kr.

Carriages: ¼ hr. for 1 pers. 12, 2 pers. 15, 3 pers. 18, 4 pers. 21 kr.; ½ hr. 24, 30, 36, 42 kr., and so on; for a whole hour 48—66 kr.

Telegraph-office at the railway station.

Höllenthal (p. 94). *Diligence* three times a day, Two-horse carriage to the Höllensteig and back in 6 hrs. for 7 fl.

English Church Service in a room at the post-office buildings.

The traveller whose time is limited should follow the street to the r. leading from the station, through the town as far as the Schwabenthor, and then ascend the *Schlossberg*, which may be done in 20 min. On the way back he should visit the *Münster*, *Merchants' Hall* (exterior only), traverse the broad Kaiserstrasse, and return to the station by the Deutscher Hof.

Freiburg (in the *Breisgau*), situated about 12 M. distant from the Rhine, vies with its sister-towns Baden and Heidelberg in the beauty of its situation, and the magnificence of its environs. The heights of the Black Forest, the picturesque groups of mountains in the vicinity, the populous and fertile plain, bounded by the vine-clad Kaiserstuhl, and the lovely valley of the Dreisam, all combine to render the situation one of singular beauty.

For nearly 300 years Freiburg was subject to the Imperial house of Habsburg; it suffered much in the 30 years' war; in 1677 it was taken by the French and fortified by Vauban, and was confirmed to them by the peace of Nymweg in 1678; by the peace of Ryswyk in 1697 it was given back to Austria, was conquered by Villars in 1713, after an obstinate defence; again restored to Austria by the peace of Rastadt in 1714, besieged and taken by the French in 1745, and finally, after the destruction of the fortifications, once more made over to Austria by the peace of Aix-la-Chapelle. The whole of the *Breisgau* was an hereditary possession of the house of Austria, Freiburg being the capital, but was annexed to Baden by the peace of Pressburg in 1806, and thus restored to the descendants of the house of Zähringen, to which it originally owed its foundation.

Notwithstanding its antiquity it contains few buildings worthy of note, with the exception of the Münster and the Merchants' Hall, for which paucity it is indebted to its almost complete destruction in 1747 by the French under Marshal Coigny.

All the streets of the town are supplied with streams of pure water from the Dreisam, which gives them an agreeable freshness in summer. The pop. is 17,000, 2000 of whom are Protestants, who have settled here within the last twenty years. Freiburg is still the seat of many old and wealthy families of the Austrian nobility.

The jurisdiction of the archiepiscopal see extends over the whole of the Grand-duchy of Baden and the Hohenzollern principalitics. The archbishop is also the head of the church of the Upper-Rhine, comprising the bishoprics of Rothenburg, Freiburg, Mainz, Fulda and Limburg.

The **University**, founded in 1456 by the Archduke Albert IV., is frequented almost exclusively by subjects of Baden, and is one of the best Rom. Cath. institutions in Germany. The lectures are chiefly held in the *New University*, formerly a Jesuits' college (in the street leading from the station to the Kaiserstrasse), and the medical lectures in the *Old University*, not far from the new. The latter contains a *Zoological collection* of considerable value (fee 18 kr.), and in the former is a remarkable *Anatomical museum* (men only admitted), containing specimens interesting only to the professional visitor, but which by a strange inconsistency are explained by a female attendant. Entrance opp. to the monument of Berthold Schwarz.

In front of the old university stands the handsome statue of the Franciscan monk *Berthold Schwarz*, the inventor of gunpowder in 1340. Opposite to it is the Franciscan Church, with fine cloisters.

The ***Münster** is almost the only perfect Gothic church in Germany, and is deservedly admired for the symmetry of its proportions and its tasteful decorations. The structure, which is of red sandstone, much darkened by age, was probably commenced by Conrad of Zähringen in 1122; the transept and the lower part of the side-towers, which are in the Romanesque style, appear to belong to the most ancient portion of the edifice. The body of the church, the W. side and the spire (385 ft.), the finest part of the whole building, date from 1236. The tower is supported by a square foundation, and is of an octagonal form, terminating in a bold pyramid of the most exquisite fret-work masonry. Beneath it is the principal entrance or *Portal*, richly decorated with sculptures; on the r. side the 7 sleeping virgins, the 7 free arts, St. Margaretha and St. Catharina; on the l. the 7 watchful virgins, and figures of saints. In front of the Portal are three columns, supporting very inferior statues of the Virgin, St. Alexander, and St. Lambert, the patron of the church.

The designs of the older part of the edifice were taken from those of the Münster at Bâle, while those for the more recent portions undoubtedly served as a model for the construction of the Strasburg Cathedral. The N. side of the aisle is less richly decorated than the S. side. Round the entire building are placed numerous statues of saints, prophets, and allegorical figures in niches. The beauty of the S. entrance is unfortunately marred by a portico erected in the 17th cent.

The interior of the Münster (320 ft. long, 95 ft. broad, and 85 ft. high), produces a deep impression with its magnificent stained-glass windows belonging to different dates. The best time to visit it is from 8 to 9 a.m., and from 11 a.m. to 7 p.m., as at these times there is no service. The services of the sacristan (18 kr.) had better be engaged, as several pictures &c. cannot be seen without his assistance. The most interesting objects are generally shown in the following order, beginning on the r.

South Aisle. Good stained-glass windows of the 15th cent. The four Evangelists in stained glass, executed by *Helmle* in 1822. An old tombstone with haut-relief of Berthold V. of Zähringen, the last of his line (d. 1218). In the *Holy Sepulchre Chapel* the Saviour on a sarcophagus, with a small aperture in the chest opened on Good Fridays to receive a portion of the host; under it the watchmen of the sepulchre asleep, valuable old sculptures. The eight small stained-glass representations of scenes from the Passion, designed by Dürer, and executed by Helmle, in 1826, are remarkable for the beauty of their colouring. The figures on the carved wood-work of the side-altars are old. That on the l. with the adoration of the Magi, executed in 1505, especially deserves inspection.

Choir Chapels. The capitals of the pillars at the entrance are decorated with quaint figures of sirens, griffins, monks and women, — burlesques in the taste of the middle ages. The stained glass in these chapels is much damaged. — Altar-pieces: 1st chapel. *Winged picture, St. Augustin, Antonius and Rochus in the middle, and St. Sebastian and Christoph on the wings, by an unknown master. — 2nd chapel (University Chapel). The *Nativity and the adoration of the Magi. Next to it a portrait of a priest, in Holbein's style, worthy of inspection. — At the back of the high-altar, a *winged picture by *Hans Baldung*, surnamed *Grün* (1516), representing the Crucifixion, to the l. St. Hieronymus and John the Baptist, to the r. St. George and St. Laurentius. The chapel to the l. behind the high-altar contains a Byzantine *crucifix* of the time of the Crusades, with silver-gilt figure of the Saviour. — Another chapel to the l. contains a carved wooden **Adoration* of the 15th cent., in a large Gothic frame-work.

Choir. At the entrances to the r. and l., haut-relief sculptures of the dukes Berthold III. and IV., of Conrad III. and Rudolph of Zähringen. On the wall a quaint monument of *General de Rodt* (d. 1743). — High-altar piece by *Hans Baldung*, painted in 1516, with coronation of the Virgin in the centre, and the twelve apostles at the sides; at the extreme sides the Annunciation, Visitation, Nativity, and Flight into Egypt. Episcopal chair richly carved.

North Aisle. In the chapel of the Mount of Olives a stone relief of the Last Supper (1805), and four small *stained-glass windows with scenes from the Passion, designed by Dürer, and executed by the brothers Helmle. — Statue of the *Archbishop Boll* (d. 1836), by Friederich. — Monument to the *Archbishop Demeter* (d. 1842). Near the latter a sarcophagus containing bones of ancient Counts of Zähringen, transferred in 1829 from the abbey of Thennenbach (see below). — In the closed *Chapel of St. Alexander* may be seen the skeleton of the saint in a robe richly embroidered with gold, silver and jewels, presented by Pope Innocent X. in 1650.

On the W. wall are circular stained-glass windows, those to the l. new, and those to the r. old. The *pulpit*, executed by the sculptor Kempf in 1561, is said to be hewn out of a solid block of stone.

Tower. Entrance in the church to the r. by the portal; adm. by card 6 kr., fee for the warder of the tower 12 kr., who also shows the mechanism of the clock by *Schwilgué*. The ascent is recommended, more for the sake of examining the beauty of the architecture than for the view, which is similar to that from the Schlossberg.

Opposite to the S. portal of the Münster is the **Merchants' Hall**, erected in the 15th cent. The front rests on five pillars, forming a circular hall, above which is a balcony with two projecting towers, covered with coloured tiles and painted arms in relief; on the outer wall, small statues of the emperors of Austria &c. with inscriptions. The hall in the interior is now used for concerts, balls and other festivities.

The **Prot. Church**, at the N. extremity of the Kaiserstrasse, in the Romanesque style, was erected in 1839, with the materials taken from the ruined abbey of Thennenbach. Nearly opposite to it are the barracks built by the Austrian government in 1776, and farther to the E. the *Hall of Art* *and Harmony*, and the well-conducted *National Asylum for the Blind.*

The old Gothic Fountain in the middle of the Kaiserstrasse, with its old and new statues of saints, knights and bishops in niches, is worthy of inspection. A second fountain farther S. in the same street has a monument of Berthold III., the founder of Freiburg (1120), and bears inscriptions recording the names of the various benefactors of the town.

Near the **St. Martinsthor** is a figure painted on the wall, representing St. Martin dividing his cloak with a beggar. The inscription on the gateway commemorates the bravery displayed by the townspeople against the French in 1796.

On leaving the town by the **Schwabenthor**, a broad footpath to the l. leads through vineyards to the ***Schlossberg** (400 ft.), once strongly fortified with two castles, destroyed by the French in 1744, during the Bavarian war of succession. The ruins of these strongholds, with their huge, massive walls, rocky vaults, fosses &c., are now converted into pleasure grounds. On the highest rock is an inscription recording the gratitude of the burghers of Freiburg to the Dukes of Zähringen, who founded the town, and to their descendant the Grand-duke Ludwig. The iron indicator, supposed to point to the different objects visible from the top, cannot be implicitly relied upon. The view is preferred by many to those from the castles of Baden and Heidelberg; to the E. lies the green and animated Kirchzarter Thal, irrigated by the Dreisam; in the background the entrance to the Höllenthal; nearly due S. rises the Schau ins Land (see p. 243), to the r. of it the peak of the Belchen (p. 248), the second highest of the Black Forest; S. W. the Schönberg (2000 ft.), and in front of it the Chapel of Loretto (see below), to the W. the blue chain of the Vosges, and the Rhine. From the plain rises the Kaiserstuhl (p. 243), sloping southwards into a richly cultivated plain bounded by the extensive range of the spurs of the Black Forest mountains. In the foreground lies Freiburg itself with its elegant open-work Münster-tower.

From the large crescent ("*Kanonenplatz*") a path through a gate leads to *Schaichs Schlösschen*, a restaurant where good beer may be procured. This is also the shortest way back to the town.

The ***Lorettocapelle,** mentioned above, lies about 1 M. to the S. of the town, and deserves a visit for the sake of the view it affords of the lovely Günthersthal, with its ancient monastery, which is not visible from the Schlossberg. It was in this valley that the Imperial General Mercy successfully defended his entrenchments against the columns of Turenne in 1644.

On market-days (Thurs. and Sat.) the peculiar costume of the peasantry of the Black Forest may be seen to advantage at Freiburg.

Excursion to the Höllenthal, see p. 258.

One of the principal heights of the Black Forest is the **Schau ins Land,** or **Erzkasten** (3930 ft.), which may best be visited as follows: by carriage (1-horse 3 fl.) to the *Molz-Bauer*, in the Kappeler Thal, in $1^1/_4$ hr.; thence on foot to the summit in $2^1/_2$ hrs.; down in $2^1/_2$ hrs. to the Baths of Littenweiler, where dine, and in the afternoon back to Freiburg (3 M.) on foot or by omnibus.

Excursion from Freiburg. — *Bad Littenweiler* (charges moderate) lies not far from the Dreisam, at the entrance of the *Kappeler Thal,* and is visited for the sake of its powerful chalybeate waters, which are better adapted for baths than for drinking. Also a whey-cure establishment.

From the baths S. into the Kappeler valley to Kappel ($1^1/_2$ M.), to *Molzbauer* ($1^1/_2$ M.), then a steep ascent; 2 M. farther the road leads to the r. by a cottage, and then in a straight direction for 1 M. to 4 cottages (refreshments); $^3/_4$ M. beyond them the path makes a steep ascent, and 2 M. more bring the pedestrian to the spot where landslips took place in 1849 and 1855. A little to the left the path ascends the hill, passing a spring of delicious water, and reaching the ridge of the mountain in about 20 min.; a walk of 10 min. more to the r. brings the pedestrian to the cross at the top, which commands a magnificent view. About 2 M. to the S. is a group of houses called *an der Halde,* the highest of which to the r. is the *Rössle*, a good, clean country inn. The Feldberg (p. 259) is 7 M. to the E. of this point; the Belchen the same distance.

Beautiful walks from Freiburg to the *Schönberg* ($4^1/_2$ M. to the S. W., through the Günthersthal, p. 242), to the *Kybfelsen* (5 M. to the S. E.; at the entrance to the wood before reaching the Günthersthal, the road to the l. must be taken, see sign-post), back by the Günthersthal and Lorettoberg. Longer walks may be taken to the *Rosskopf* (2290) ft.) N. E., and thence to the *Jägerhäusle,* or the castle of *Zähringen* (p. 74).

An excursion to the **Kaiserstuhl** may be best made as follows: by carriage (1-horse 3 fl.) in 2 hrs. to *Oberschaffhausen*, at the foot of the Kaiserstuhl; with guide in 1 hr. to the *Neun Linden* (1763 ft.), the summit of the hill, commanding a most beautiful view of the Black Forest and the Vosges; then without guide in 1 hr. to *Bickensohl* (good wine at the "Stubenwirth"), and by *Achkarren* in $1^1/_2$ hr. to *Breisach,* whence the diligence runs twice a day in 3 hrs. to Freiburg (1 fl.), or in the same time to Colmar (2 fr.).

The high road from Freiburg to Breisach traverses the *Mooswald,* a boggy, wooded district between *St. Georgen* and *Thiengen*, and then leads S. round fertile slopes, raised by volcanic action, past *Munzingen* and the *St. Apollonius-Capelle.* At *Ober-Rimsingen* is the château of Baron Falkenstein.

Breisach, or **Alt-Breisach** (*Post*), the *Mons Brisiacus* of the Romans, is situated at the S.W. extremity of the Kaiserstuhl, and is visible from a considerable distance. As late as the 10th cent., the Rhine is said to have flowed round the town, which was in early times a fortification of great importance, and was regarded as the key of Germany. From 1331 it belonged to Austria, in 1638 it was taken, after a dreadful siege, by the Swedes under Bernhard of Weimar, and was after his death garrisoned by the French; in 1700 it again came into the possession of Austria; in 1703 it was taken by Tallard and Vauban, and in 1714 restored to the Austrians. In 1740 a change in the course of the Rhine proved so detrimental to the fortifications, that they were afterwards abandoned and partly demolished by the Austrians, and in 1793 completely destroyed by the French. At a later date they were again partially restored, but were again levelled by the government of Baden. There is an old saying with regard to Breisach:

Limes eram Gallis, nunc pons et janua fio;
Si pergunt, Gallis nullibi limes erit!

The town, now of no importance, is situated on a rock rising precipitously several hundred feet above the Rhine, and surmounted by the Gothic Münster of **St. Stephen*, erected at the close of the 13th cent. The interior contains a fine old rood-loft belonging to the same date, and an altar-piece of carved wood, representing the coronation of the Virgin, executed in 1597. The communication with the opposite side of the Rhine is maintained by means of a flying-bridge. The high-road to *Colmar* (omnibus twice a day in 3 hrs.) leads past *Fort Mortier* and **Neu-Breisach** (*Hôtel de France*), strongly fortified in 1700 by Vauban.

Colmar, see p. 227.

61. From Freiburg to Bâle.

(*Comp. Map R. 62.*)

By the Baden Railway in $1\frac{1}{2}$–$2\frac{1}{2}$ hrs. Fares: express 3 fl. 6, and 2 fl. 6 kr.; ordinary trains 2 fl. 33, 1 fl. 45, and 1 fl. 6 kr.

The course of the railway is within a short distance of the W. spurs and vine-clad slopes of the Black Forest. To the r. are the S. slopes of the Kaiserstuhl (p. 243). Beyond *Schallstadt* the castle of *Staufenburg* (p. 249) is visible in the distance to the l., situated on an eminence at the entrance of the Münsterthal, which is terminated by the Belchen (p. 248). Stat. *Krotzingen* (* Post), The little town of *Heitersheim*, once the seat of the Master of the Order of St. John of Malta in Germany, lies 1 1/2 M. from the station.

Müllheim (* *Kittler*, R. 42 kr., B. 20 kr., at the station; *Engel*, *Krone* in the town), celebrated for the Markgräfler wine which is here produced, especially from the vineyards near *Auggen*, and on the slopes of the hills as far as *Grenzach*, above Bâle. Omnibus to *Badenweiler* (see below) on the arrival of every train, in 3/4 hr., fare 36 kr. Travellers who arrive late in the evening are recommended to pass the night at Müllheim, as the hotels at Badenweiler are occasionally full.

To the W. of Müllheim, 1 1/2 M. from the station, lies **Neuenburg**, on the Rhine, besieged in 1633—34 by Bernhard von Weimar, who here ended his heroic career, not without suspicion of poison.

At **Schliengen** (* *Krone*) the line approaches the Rhine, which is here divided into several arms by fertile islands. Near the stat. *Kleinkembs* it runs close to the river, and penetrates the "*Isteiner Klotz*," a limestone cliff immediately overhanging the water. The short distance between *Bellingen* and *Efringen* is remarkable for the windings of the line, which here runs along an embankment high above the Rhine. At *Eimeldingen* (825 ft.) the train crosses the *Kander* (p. 247), beyond which a splendid view is suddenly disclosed of the course of the Rhine, Alsace, and the Jura beyond Bâle. Near the stat. *Leopoldshöhe* lies the old fortress of *Hüningen*, on the opposite bank of the river. The terminus at *Klein-Basel* is 3/4 M. from the Rhine-bridge, to which a broad street leads direct, and 2 M. from the Swiss central-station at Bâle.

Bâle, see R. 64.

62. Badenweiler and its Environs.

Bürgeln, Blauen, Belchen, Münsterthal.

Hotels. *Römerhaus, R. 48 kr., B. 24 kr., D. 1 fl. 12 kr. *Stadt Carlsruhe, R. 40 kr., B. 20 kr., D. incl. W. 1 fl. 12 kr. — Badischer Hof, moderate. — Single travellers may find good and cheap accommodation at the *Ochs* and *Wilder Mann* at Oberweiler, a village at the foot of the Badenweiler hill, or at the *Löwe* and *Schwan* at Niederweiler, on the road to Müllheim. Good wine and refreshments in the inn at Vögisheim, a village between Müllheim and Auggen, and 4 M. from Badenweiler, with which it is connected by a shady walk.

Omnibus from the station at Müllheim to Badenweiler in 1 hr., but the distance may be walked in nearly the same time, as the road ascends the whole way. Those who wish to employ the omnibus are recommended to engage a seat immediately on leaving the train.

Donkeys at Badenweiler: to the station 40 kr., Blauen 1 fl. 20 kr., Belchen 3 fl., Bürgeln 1 fl. 20 kr., Kandern 1 fl. 48 kr., Sophienruhe 18 kr., Alte-Mann 24 kr.

Holly walking-sticks, carved, at Noll's, in Oberweiler.

Badenweiler, situated on the W. spurs of the Black Forest, 1314 ft. above the level of the sea, and 695 ft. above the Rhine, commands an extensive view of the vast plain of the Rhine as far as the Vosges. This pleasant little watering-place was until recently but little frequented, except by the inhabitants of the neighbouring towns, but has of late lost much of its pristine simplicity (300 patients in 1863).

The principal rendez-vous of the gay world is the ***Cursaal**, which contains concert, ball, drawing and reading-rooms. In front of this edifice stands a small fountain with two bas-reliefs of Jesus and the Samaritan woman, and Moses striking the rock. One pipe yields thermal (82° Fahr.), and the other common water. At the back of the Cursaal is a *Restaurant, where a band plays in the morning and evening, and where the keys of the Roman baths are kept.

Adjoining the Cursaal is a small ***Park** extending up the hill, which is surmounted by the ruins of the **Castle**, originally built by the Romans for the protection of the baths below, and destroyed by the French in 1688. The fragments of the walls are completely enveloped in ivy; view magnificent.

That the springs were known to the Romans was proved in 1784 by the discovery of the ***Roman baths** (fee 12 kr.), which are in good preservation, and are among the finest specimens known. Their entire length is 324 ft., breadth 100 ft., and the partitions, flooring, steps &c. are all well preserved. The larger apartments all contain two baths, cold baths (*frigidaria*) 33 by 21 ft., and warm (*tepidaria*) 29 by 25 ft.; there are also vapour baths (*laconica*), vestibules (*atria*), anointing-rooms (*unctoria*) &c. An inscription on the altar records that the baths were dedicated to "*Diana Abnob*(*a*)," or the Diana of the Abnoba, or Black Forest mountains.

The environs of Badenweiler afford the most delightful **sylvan walks*. A signpost on the Kandern road, immediately at the back of the village, indicates the way to the *Sophienruhe;* the traveller ascends the hill in about 17 min. to the crescent, then to the l., in 2 min. more to the l. again, and then, slightly descending to the l., a few hundred steps farther the ***Sophienruhe** is reached. It is a large open space on the outskirts of the wood, in a S. E. direction from Badenweiler, and about 200 ft. above the village; the view is still more picturesque than that from the old castle, which forms with Badenweiler itself a beautiful foreground to the landscape.

On returning, 2 min. from the Sophienruhe, a good broad path ascends to the ***Alter Mann** ($^3/_4$ M.), a rocky elevation, accessible only by bridges and steps, about 100 ft.

THE BLACK FOREST Southern part.

zu Bädeker's Rheinlande

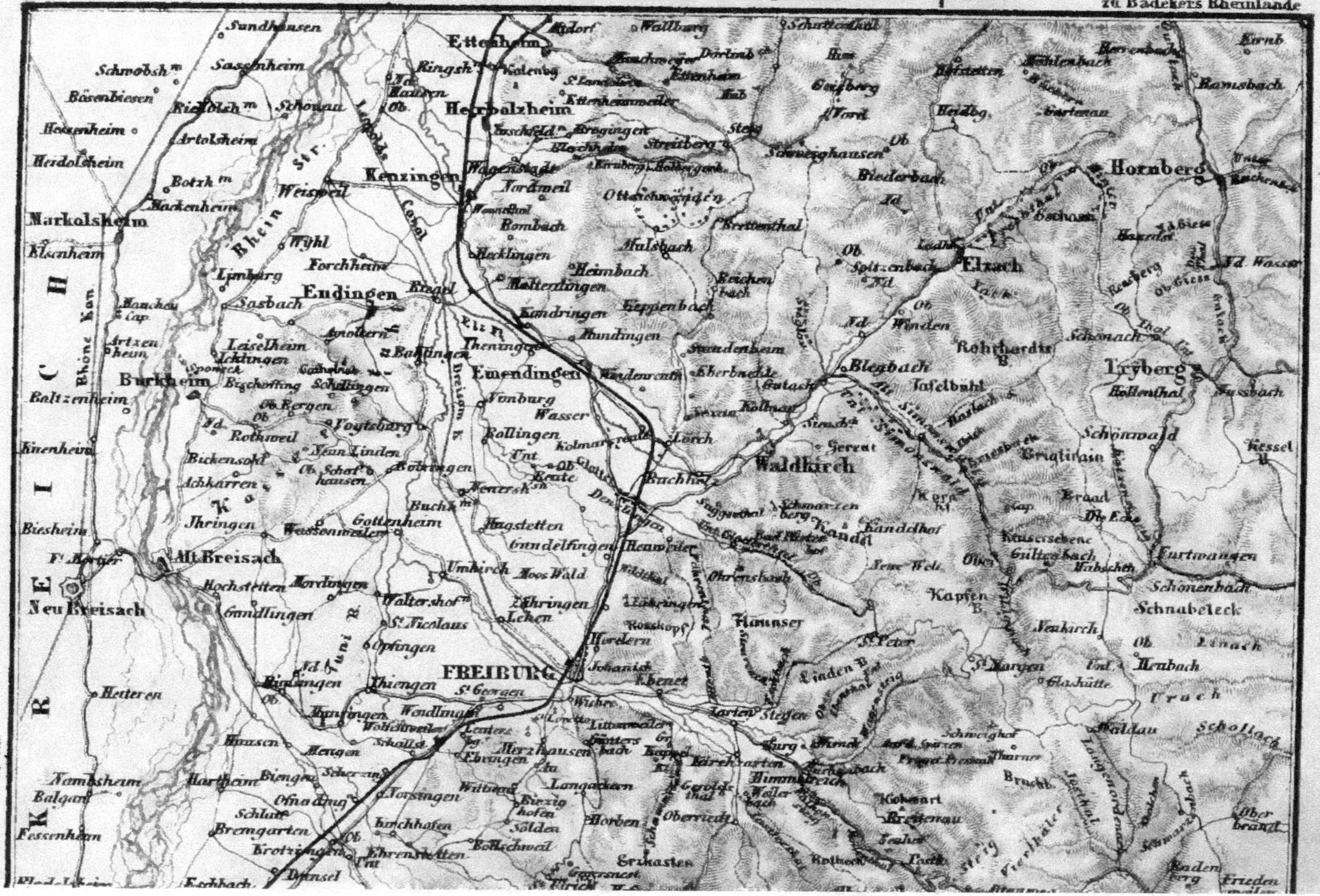

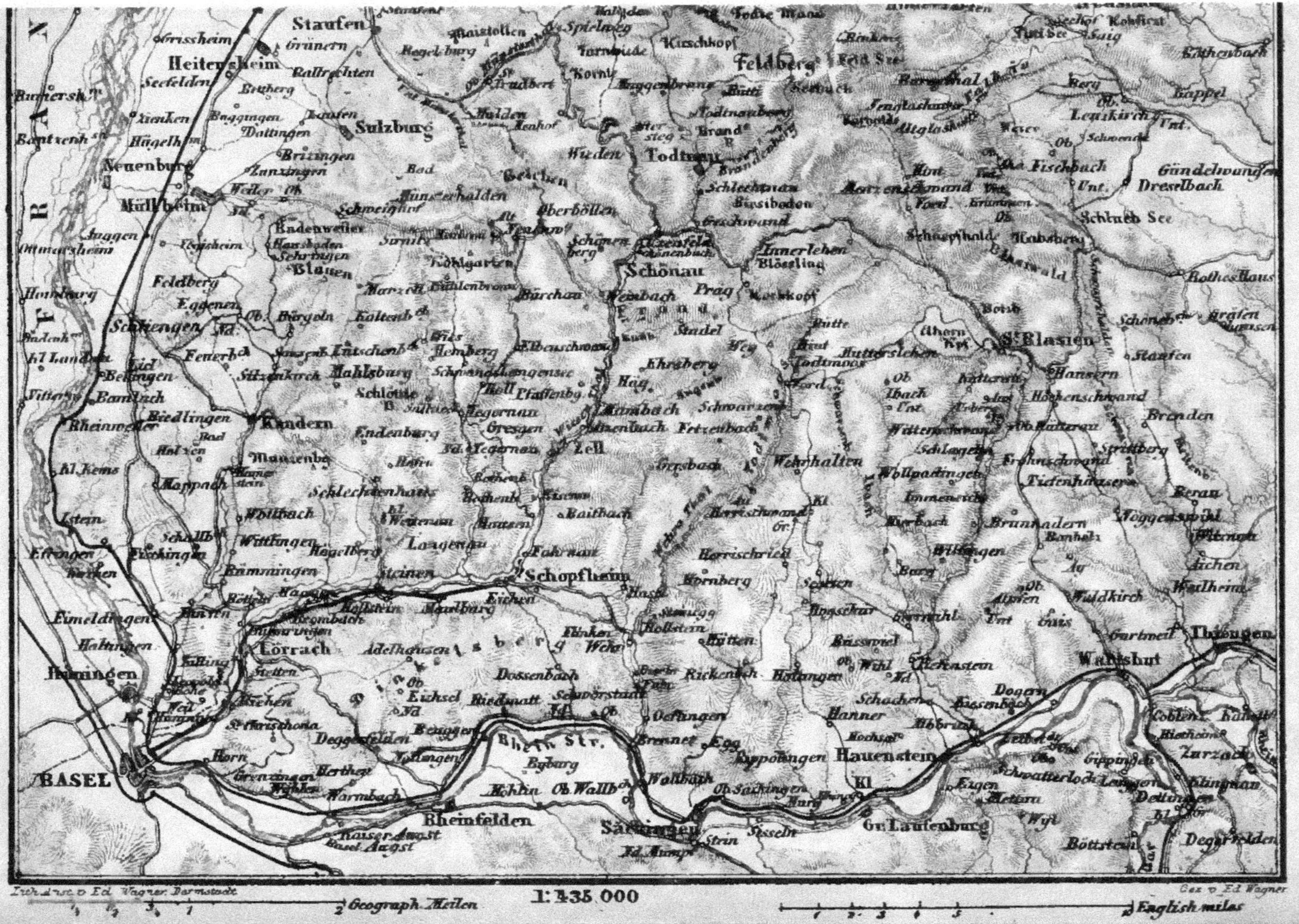
Staufen
Heitersheim
Sulzburg
Neuenburg
Müllheim
Feldberg
Todtnau
Schönau
Schopfheim
Kandern
Lörrach
St. Blasien
Waldshut
Thiengen
Hauenstein
Gr. Laufenburg
Säckingen
Rheinfelden
BASEL
Hüningen
Schliengen
Zell
Wehr
Rhein Str.
Lith. Anst. v. Ed. Wagner, Darmstadt
Geograph. Meilen
1: 435 000
Gez. v. Ed. Wagner
English miles

higher than the Sophienruhe; view similar, with wooded foreground.

A path across the bridge descends to the *Haus Baden*, a miners' tavern ($^3/_4$ M.), whence the pedestrian may either return to Badenweiler, or continue his walk to *Bürgeln*, which lies 5 M. to the S. By attending to the following directions, the road cannot be missed; but to prevent all possibility of mistake, a boy should be taken from Badenweiler (30 kr.) to the Sophienruhe, Alter Mann and Bürgeln. Donkey 1 fl. 20 kr.

Between the houses of Haus-Baden a narrow path leads in about 4 min. to the carriage-road, at the side of which are gypsum mines. Immediately after passing them, the turning to the r. must be taken; $^1/_2$ M. farther *Sehringen* is reached ($1^1/_2$ M. from Badenweiler), where the path joins the Badenweiler and Bürgeln road. The latter is little better than a cart-track, and leads chiefly through wood; $1^1/_2$ M. farther is a signpost indicating the direction of Bürgeln to the l.; $^1/_2$ M. beyond the post, the cart-road is crossed by the path which leads into a thick wood, and in 7 min. another signpost is reached, where however the direction must not be changed; 1 M. more brings the pedestrian to another signpost, 1 M. beyond which another is reached, indicating the way to the Blauen (6 M.), and to the r. at a sharp angle to Bürgeln ($^1/_2$ M.).

***Bürgeln** (2250), commonly called the *Bürgler Schloss* (*Inn*, moderate), was formerly a branch of the large and wealthy Benedictine foundation of St. Blasien (p. 262) in the Black Forest. The stag, the arms of St. Blasian, still serves as a weather-cock. It is most beautifully situated to the S., and almost at the foot of the Blauen, commanding a magnificent view, similar to that from the Blauen (see below), though less extensive. To the E. is seen the chain of mountains which bound the Wiesenthal (p. 260), S. E. the snow-clad Alps from the Scheerhorn to the Jungfrau (comp. p. 248), in front of them the Jura, and in the foreground well-wooded heights, on the most considerable of which Kandern (see below) is situated; a little farther back are Bâle, Hüningen with bridge of boats, Mühlhausen and the Rhine-Rhone canal, glimpses of the Rhine, and to the W. the long chain of the Vosges. The interior of the castle and church may be visited, but they contain few objects of interest.

Schliengen (p. 245), the nearest station, lies 6 M. to the W. of Bürgeln. Or the road may be taken to **Kandern** (1087 ft.) (*Blume; Ochs;* good beer at *Kümmich's*), $3^1/_2$ M. distant, and thence to Bâle 13 M.; or, as the road is uninteresting, by carriage from Kandern to Bâle (4 fl.).

The ascent of the ***Blauen** (3589 ft.), one of the five highest points of the Black Forest, at the N. base of which Badenweiler lies, is one of the easiest and most beautiful excursions from the latter place (donkey 1 fl. 20 kr.). The broad carriage-road through fir-woods cannot be missed, and the summit may easily be reached in 2 hrs. The Blauen is the nearest to the Rhine of all the peaks of the Black Forest, and the course of the river from Bâle to the Kaiserstuhl lies before the spectator. Four different mountain chains are visible to the naked eye, to the E. the Black Forest, to the W. the Vosges, to the S. the Jura, and in clear weather the snow-clad chain of the Alps in the following order: S.E. the broad back of the Glärnisch, the Tödi and the two-peaked Scheerhorn, beyond these the summit of the Titlis, farther S., one behind the other, are the Wetterhörner, Schreckhörner and the Finsteraarhorn, next the Eiger, Mönch, the Jungfrau, Blümlisalp, Altels, and finally to the W. the jagged Diablerets, Mont Blanc and the Dent du Midi. Schloss Bürgeln (p. 247) is 5 M. from the summit of the Blauen.

The excursion to the *Belchen* and *Münsterthal* requires an entire day. To the summit of the former is a walk of 4½ hrs., down to Neumühl 2 hrs., thence to stat. Krotzingen on foot in 3 hrs., or by carriage in 1¾ hr. Guide from Badenweiler to the Belchen not absolutely necessary, but desirable. Donkey 3 fl.

The view is still grander than that from the Blauen, as it comprises the beautiful Münsterthal, Wiesenthal, and other valleys which are not visible from the latter.

From Badenweiler to the Belchen by a good road in an E. direction; after 1½ M. to the r. in the wood; ¾ M. on the carriage-road in the valley to the village of *Schweighof;* then the broad road which ascends at first gently, and afterwards rapidly, through woods and rocky landscapes, leads to *Sirnitz* (4 M.), a forester's house (*Zum Auerhahn*) in a green dale, where refreshments may be procured. The same broad road must still be followed; it ascends in ½ hr. to the ridge from which the Belchen rises, then descends to the other side to the houses called *an der Halde* (1 M.), where the carriage-road must be left. Up to this point a guide is quite unnecessary, but the path now becomes more difficult to trace. By carefully attending to the following directions, however, the pedestrian may safely venture alone, if the weather be tolerably clear.

In 25 min. the wood is entered, and in 15 min. more a small open spot is reached; here at the boundary-stone the path is crossed by the road leading from the Münsterthal to *Neuenweg.* The narrow path now leads straight on, keeping the peak of the Belchen quite to the l., and ascends the narrow mountain ridge. In 10 min. more an open grass-plot on the N. slope of the ridge is reached. Here the pedestrian must turn to the l., and ascend by the fence in the direction of the two mountain peaks (Hochkelch). At the end of the enclosure it must be crossed, and the steep hill close past the two peaks ascended; in 20 min. more level ground is reached; in 10 min. the ridge which connects the Hochkelch with the Belchen is then arrived at, a boundary-stone is passed, and in 25 min. more the cross on the summit is attained.

The ***Belchen** (4356 ft.) commands a most extensive and magnificent view of the surrounding valleys, especially the picturesque animated Münsterthal to the N.W. and the Wiesenthal to the S. The distant view is the same as that from the Blauen, with the exception that the nearer part of the valley of the Rhine is concealed.

From the Belchen into the Münsterthal. The row of boundary-stones to the N. of the cross must be followed, and in 2 or 3 min. a good path is reached, which winds down over bilberry-clad slopes, and leads in 35 min. to the *Sennhütte in der Krinne* (3470 ft.), where refreshments may be procured. The Sennhütte must now be left about 100 paces to the r., and the stony road to the l. descends through wood into the valley, the bottom of which is reached in 50 min. Then through the valley, past some silver mines and stamping mill, worked by an English company, to *Neumühl* in 25 min., where at the **Krone* inn a one-horse carriage may be had to Krotzingen (9 M.) for 3 fl.

The **Münsterthal** is at the top narrow, but gradually widens towards the mouth. It is a well-populated valley, irrigated by the *Neumagen Bach*, but is not sufficiently attractive to induce the traveller to traverse it on foot. At the mouth of the valley, 6 M. from *Neumühl* and 3 M. from Krotzingen, lies the small and ancient town of **Staufen** (**Badischer Hof*), overtopped by the ruins of the Staufenburg, seat of a powerful race which became extinct in 1602. The vineyards which occupy the hill produce the "Burghalder" wine.

Between Staufen and stat. Krotzingen an omnibus runs several times a day. Conveyances to be had at the **Badischer Hof*, near the station.

63. The Black Forest *(Baden portion.)*

Pedestrian tour of ten days from Baden. 1st day. Ebersteinschloss (p. 215), Forbach, Schönmünzach (p. 251). — 2nd. Hornisgrinde, Mummelsee (p. 251), Allerheiligen. — 3rd. Oppenau, by carriage to Griesbach, Holzwälderhöhe, Rippoldsau, Schapbach (p. 255). — 4th. Wolfach, Hornberg, Tryberg (p. 256). — 5th. Furtwangen, Simonswald, Waldkirch (p. 257). — 6th. By carriage and railway to Freiburg. — 7th. (Carriage to entrance of) the Höllenthal, Feldberg (Albthal see p. 263), Todtnau (p. 260).— 8th. Wiesenthal to Schopfheim (p. 261). — 9th. Wehrathal (p. 262), thence by railway to Bâle (p. 264). — 10th. (Railway to) Müllheim, Badenweiler, Blauen (p. 245).

The following three routes have been so planned, that after a walk of 2—3 days the railway may always be reached. The pedestrian will find the following maps, published by *Herder* at Freiburg, of great service to him: 1. Baden and the Kniebisbäder. 2. Environs of Freiburg. 3. Southern valleys of the Black Forest. Mounted, 1 fl. 12 kr. each.

Of all the wooded districts of Germany, none offer such a succession of beautiful and varied landscapes as the Black Forest, especially the W. portion, belonging to Baden, the spurs of which decline precipitously towards the plain of the Rhine, whilst the E. slopes are more gradual. The lower heights are covered with fragrant fir and pine forest, and the populous and fertile valleys present a scene of luxurious vegetation, corn, wine and fruit being abundantly produced. The rocks consist of gneiss, granite and sandstone. The numerous mineral springs have given rise to many little watering-places, which offer tempting retreats to the weary traveller. Even in the more remote districts the inns are good (trout everywhere, but somewhat dear), and offer no mean additional attraction to this favoured locality.

A large proportion of the population is occupied with traffic in wood, which is conducted down the principal streams in the Forest to the Rhine, where the larger rafts are constructed, and afterwards navigated down to Holland. Watchmaking, a rapidly increasing branch of industry, engages a considerable number of persons. In this busy and prosperous district beggars are unknown.

a. **Murgthal, Hornisgrinde, Mummelsee.**

Comp. Map R. 52.

From Baden to Gernsbach and Allerheiligen.

Two days' walk: 1st. From Baden to *Gernsbach* (6 M.), thence to *Forbach* 10 M., from Forbach to *Schönmünzach* 7 M. — 2nd. From Schönmünzach to the summit of the *Hornisgrinde* 4½ hrs., down to the *Mummelsee* ½ hr., and to *Seebach* 1 hr., or to *Ottenhöfen*, and thence over the hill to Allerheiligen 1½ hr. — At Gernsbach, Forbach, and Schönmünzach conveyances may be procured: 2-horse carriages for 4 pers. from Gernsbach to Schönmünzach, inc. driver's fee, 6 fl. 45 kr. (from Forbach to Schönmünzach 4 fl.), from Schönmünzach to the Eckle (2 M. from the Hornisgrinde) 5 fl. 36 kr.; here the carriage-road ends. — Between Gernsbach and Schönmünzach an open diligence, accommodating 6 pers., runs every day in 4 hrs. (fare 1 fl.) to meet the coach between the latter place and Freudenstadt (fare 48 kr.)

The *Murg* takes its rise on the *Kniebis* (p. 253) from three springs which unite below Baiersbronn (p. 253). After a course of about 45 M. it empties itself into the Rhine below Rastadt. The inhabitants of its banks are almost exclusively engaged in the wood traffic. The timber, which is cut in winter, is carried down by the spring floods to the Rhine, and large crowds often assemble to witness the large masses being precipitated into the stream.

The Murgthal between Gernsbach and Schönmünzach presents a series of wild and beautiful landscapes. The sides of the valley are richly clothed with pines, firs and beeches, and the scene is often varied by green meadows, and cottages in the Swiss style interspersed among the woods. As far as Schönmünzach the rocks consist of granite, huge blocks of which lie scattered in the forest, and by the mountain brooks. Above Schönmünzach the formation is of gneiss, hence the rounded and smooth aspect of the slopes. Variegated sandstone occasionally makes its appearance. The valley here becomes broader, and thus loses much of its peculiar charm. It is seen to the best advantage in descending the stream.

From *Baden to Gernsbach* see p. 214. The road in the Murgthal gradually ascends at the foot of the hill on which the Ebersteinschloss is situated. The pedestrian descending the valley must take the footpath by the last house at *Obertsroth* to reach the castle.

At *Hilpertsau* the road crosses to the r. bank of the Murg, and leads through the villages of *Weissenbach*, *Langenbrand*, and *Gausbach*. That part of the valley which lies between Gernsbach and Forbach is the most animated as well as the most picturesque.

Forbach (**Krone*, conveyances; *Adler*) is the finest point in the whole valley; the church is picturesquely situated on an eminence.

The footpath from Baden to Forbach (12 M.) diverges to the r. from the carriage-road, 3/4 M. beyond *Oberbeuern* (p. 214), at the signpost; 3/4 M. farther is *Geisbach*, and 1 1/2 M. *Schmalbach*, where the path to the l. must be kept; 1 1/2 M. from Schmalbach, a broad pathway diverges from the road to the r., and leads for 1 M. along the E. slope of the mountain ridge, passing a meadow. At the end of the meadow the turning to the l. must be taken, 1/4 M. beyond which a cross-way is reached, where the path which ascends the hill in a straight direction must be kept; 1/4 M. more brings the pedestrian to the main road, which must be followed for 3/4 M., then at the signpost the turning to the l. must be taken to *Bermersbach* (1 1/4 M.). The path which ascends by the village well must now be taken, and 1 1/4 M. farther *Forbach* is reached.

Beyond Forbach the Murgthal becomes more deserted, but continues grand and beautiful, resembling some of the wildest Swiss valleys; at the bottom rushes the impetuous mountain stream over scattered fragments of rock, and on either side are dark overhanging pine-clad hills. Half way to Schönmünzach, the *Raumünzach* (on the r.) unites with the Murg.

Schönmünzach (*Glashütte; Waldhorn*) is the first village in the dominions of Württemberg, and consists of a considerable glass-manufactory and a group of houses. The brook of the same name here falls into the Murg. (Good bathing-place in the latter 1/4 M. above the post.)

The road to the Hornisgrinde and Mummelsee (12 M.) leads from this point along the Schönmünzach to *Zwiegabel* (3 M.), crosses the brook, and ascends to the r. along the *Langenbach*, past *Vorder-Langenbach* (1 1/2 M.) to *Hinter-Langenbach* (2 1/4 M.), where, at the small village inn (*Züfle*, tolerable wine), guides may be procured to tbe Hornisgrinde and Mummelsee.

Here the path becomes steeper, and leads to the *Eckle* (3 M.), a strip of wood on the ridge of the mountain, where a stone marks the boundary between Württemberg and Baden, and where a view of the distant Vosges is obtained. At this point are three different paths: that most to the r. enters the wood and constitutes the boundary line between the two dominions already mentioned; the 2nd, also inclining to the r., leads past the *Drei-Fürstenstein*, which bears the arms of Baden and Württemberg, to the Hornisgrinde (2 M.). The third path (to the *Mummelsee*), at first but little trodden, runs parallel with the road, and after a few paces joins a broad track, which, slightly ascending, skirts the hill-side; 10 min. from the Eckle, the broad stony path ascending to the r. must be taken, which in $^1/_4$ hr. leads to the extremity of the Mummelsee.

If the pedestrian follow the second of the above mentioned paths, it will conduct him to the ***Hornisgrinde** (3612 ft.), the highest point of which is marked by a massive square stone heap. The view is very extensive; to the E. is seen the Schwabian Alb, the Achalm at Reutlingen, Hohentwiel, and other peaks of the Höhgau; to the S. the heights of the Black Forest, the Feldberg, Belchen, Blauen, and beyond them even the Alps (comp. p. 248); to the S. W. the Kaiserstuhl (p. 243) and Vosges; to the W. the vast and populous plain of the Rhine, with its numerous villages and towns; almost exactly opposite is visible the spire of the cathedral of Strasburg, and on a mountain in the foreground the extensive ruins of the *Brigittenschloss* [usually ascended from Ottenhöfen (see below), fine view]; to the N. the mountains round Baden, the Mercuriusberg (p. 215), and even the Thurmberg (p. 206) at Durlach.

From the summit of the Hornisgrinde the path gradually descends in a S. W. direction, and soon becomes a more distinct tract, leading in $^1/_2$ hr. to the **Mummelsee,** a gloomy looking little lake, surrounded by fir-clad mountain walls, and, according to an old popular tradition, inhabited by water-sprites and goblins, whose supposed presence contributes more to the interest of the spot than the natural features of the scene. By the *Seebach*, the brook which flows out of the lake on the S. side, is a hut which serves as a resting-place and shelter in bad weather. About 10 yds. above the lake, at the N. W. corner, not far from the path from the Hornisgrinde, a spring of excellent water issues from the rock.

From the Mummelsee to **Seebach** (*Hirsch*, very unpretending) is a distance of about 3 M. From the latter place two paths lead to *Allerheiligen* (p. 254), one arduous and uninteresting over the mountains, and not to be ventured upon without a guide (36 kr.); the other and pleasanter leads through the valley to **Ottenhöfen** ($2^1/_4$ M.), and then follows the road described at p. 153.

It has already been said that the *Upper Murgthal* offers fewer attractions than the lower part of the valley, but the traveller who has already visited the Mummelsee and Allerheiligen should continue his way from Schönmünzach to

Reichenbach (7½ M.), formerly a monastery, where a pleasing retrospective view of the valley is obtained. Before reaching **Baiersbronn** the footpath descending to the r. into the valley may be taken, following the course of the stream through the picturesque and animated *Mittel-* and *Ober-Murythal*, with its numerous saw-mills and other signs of the industry of the inhabitants, to **Buhlbach** (* *Inn* near the glass-house, R. and B. 40 kr.), 7½ M. from Baiersbronn. The large glass-house yields annually upwards of half a million Champagne bottles. *Allerheiligen* is 6 M. to the W.; footpath over the *Gründe*.

The road from Buhlbach to the **Kniebis** ascends gradually through the wood the whole way. About 3 M. to the S. of Buhlbach the pedestrian reaches an open grass-plat where the road diverges to the r. at a right angle, but he must bear to the l. across the grass, and 5 min. will bring him to a broad stony track which leads to the Württemberg boundary-stone (¾ M.). Ten min. walk along the furrow marking the boundary line will now bring the traveller up the *Rossbühl* to the *Schwabenschanz* (3361 ft.), an intrenchment made at the close of the last century by an officer of Württemberg. The view from this point comprises the valley of the Rhine, Strasburg and the Swiss mountains.

Five minutes' walk S. from this point along the frontier line will bring the pedestrian to a large *Boundary stone*, bearing the date 1673, where, close to the E. side of the path, is the old *Schwedenschanze* (Swedish intrenchment). About 200 yds. to the E. of this point is the *Kniebis-Zufluchtshaus*, where wine may be procured. The path descending to the r. by the boundary-stone leads in 10 min. to the old high-road which traverses a succession of beautiful forest and mountain scenes to **Oppenau** (4½ M.) (p. 255). The entire distance from Schönmünzach to Buhlbach is about 15 M. (1-horse carriage in 3 hrs. for 3 fl. and from Buhlbach to Oppenau about 10 M.

b. Allerheiligen, Waterfalls of Büttenstein, Kniebisbäder, Waterfalls of Tryberg, Kinzigthal.

Comp. Map R. 52.

Pedestrian tour 3½ days. 1st. From *Achern* to *Griesbach* 24 M., or better by carriage. — 2nd. To *Hausach* 24 M. 3d. To *Tryberg* and back, and then to *Hasslach* 25½ M. 4th. To *Offenburg* 15 M. Should the traveller prefer it, he may accomplish this tour in 2 days by availing himself of the public and other conveyances. 1st day. From Achern to *Neuhaus* (1-horse carriage 2 fl. 42 kr., p. 216) in 1½ hr.; on foot over the mountain to *Allerheiligen* in ¾ hr., from the forest-house to the foot of the waterfalls in 20 min., then by carriage (1-horse 3½ fl.), to *Griesbach* in 2¼ hrs.; on foot over the Holzwälder Höhe to *Rippoldsau* in 2¼ hrs.; by carriage (4 fl.; omnibus, in the morning only, 1 fl.) to *Wolfach* in 2 hrs. 2nd day. By carriage to

Tryberg (visit to the waterfall on foot in 2 hrs.), and back to *Wolfach* (1-horse 5 fl.) in 5 hrs.; from Wolfach to *Offenburg* (1-horse 6 fl.; omnibus in the morning only 1 fl. 48 kr.) in 4 hrs.

Achern (p. 217) is the starting point for the above tour; if it be reached about the middle of the day, the *Turenne Monument* (p. 217), the *Erlenbad* and the *Lunatic Asylum* may be visited in the course of the afternoon.

The road to Allerheiligen leads through the *Cappeler Thal*, a pleasant, green dale (to the l. on the height, the *Brigittenschloss*, p. 252; in the valley, a Morocco leather factory), past the villages of *Cappel* (3 M.; *Ochs), *Ottenhöfen* (3 M.) (*Linde; *Pflug; beer at Birk's. — The "Edelfräulein's Grab," a picturesque waterfall, about 1 M. to the S.), then into the valley to the r. to *Neuhaus* (2 M.; Erbprinz). Here the path leaves the road. The former skirts the hillside to the r., leading straight past a solitary house (5 min.; ascent to the r. to be avoided) into the wood. At the top is a signpost where a short cut descends to the r. by numerous windings to (3/4 hr.) ***Allerheiligen** (2000 ft.). The first glance on issuing from the wood at the top is very striking. The grand ruins of the abbey, founded in 1196 by the Duchess Uta of Schauenburg, secularized in 1802, and partially destroyed by lightning in 1803, occupy almost the entire breadth of the wooded dale. In exploring them the traveller should use the utmost caution; a Prussian gentleman lost his life in Aug., 1862, by falling from the highest point. Good accommodation at *Mittenmaier's* (pension 2 fl.). One-horse carriage to Achern in 2 hrs. 3 1/2 fl., to Oppenau in 1 1/2 hr. 2 1/2 fl., to Griesbach in 2 1/2 hrs. 5 fl. to stat. Appenweier in 3 1/4 hrs. for 6 fl. The Schwedenschanze (p. 253) lies 6 M. to the S. E.; path through the wood with guide.

Immediately below the monastery is a rugged mountain-cleft, through which the *Grindenbach* is precipitated over masses of granite rock in 7 falls called the "Sieben Bütten" (Seven Tubs), or ***Büttenstein-Falls**, some of them 80 ft. in height, into the valley beneath. A well-kept path, cut in some places through the rock, or supported by means of ladders, descends by the falls to the (20 min.) bottom of the valley (1700 ft.). From the second "Rondel" or platform the double fall is seen to the best advantage.

At the signpost by the bridge beyond the falls the carriage-road from Allerheiligen is reached, and continues on the r. bank of the *Lierbach* (the name which the Grindenbach now assumes), high up on the slope of the hill. [Pedestrians coming from Oppenau must, after about one hour's walk, avoid descending to the r., but go straight on till the above-mentioned bridge (4 M. from Oppenau) is reached.] The road gradually descends to **Oppenau** (**Stahlbad; Post*), a small town about 5 M. from Allerheiligen, where "Kirschwasser" is manufactured in large quantities, and then enters the delightful valley of the impetuous *Rench*, on which the **Kniebis-Baths** (4½ M.) are situated. The first of these is a sulphur-bath at *Freyersbach*, a second is at *Petersthal* (¾ M.), and the last a chalybeate spring at *Griesbach*, about 2 M. farther, where casual visitors as well as patients may find good accommodation. A fourth bath at *Antogast* lies about 3 M. to the W.

About 1 M. beyond Griesbach, three paths diverge from the road to the r.; of these the traveller should select that farthest to the l., a good broad track provided with benches at intervals, which in ¼ hr. leads to a flight of steps on the l., ascending to an open space where a small waterfall is seen, and a fine view of the valley of Griesbach obtained.

A few yards farther on the path, two other paths diverge, but the same path (following the wires of the electric telegraph) must be kept straight up the hill. In 7 min. a signpost is reached, where the pedestrian must ascend to the l., and in 12 min. he will reach a bench whence a fine prospect is obtained of the W. slopes of the Black Forest, the valley of the Rhine, Strasburg, and in the background the Vosges. Another ¼ hr. leads to a signpost where the path ascends to the l.; 8 min. farther is another fine point of view, similar to the last, but still more extensive, comprising the chain of the Vosges with the Hoh-Königsburg (p. 232) to the S. After a straight ascent of 4 min. more the *Holzwälder Höhe* (3055 ft.), the highest point of the walk, is attained.

The path next descends through a fir-wood carpeted with bilberry plants, and then winds across an open space down to the road (¾ hr.) in the valley, by following which for 1 M. the traveller arrives at **Rippoldsau** (1886 ft.), the most frequented of the Kniebis baths, situated in a narrow and secluded valley. The principal constituent of the water is sulphate of soda. The large bath-establishment offers every comfort to the traveller (R. 48 kr., D. at 1 o'clock 1 fl. 12 kr.); below it is a small café with newspapers, where a band plays from 7 to 8 p.m. Omnibus (from June 15th to Sept. 15th) to Offenburg in 6½ hrs. (2 fl. 48 kr.); 1-horse carriage to Wolfach 4 fl.

The old Benedictine priory or "*Klösterle*," founded in the 12th cent., lies ¾ M. below the bath-house on the road, which traverses this picturesque valley (15 M. in length), following the course of the *Wolfach*. Farther on, a waterfall is seen on the roadside, and beyond it a precipitous group of rocks, with a summer-house. Six miles from Rippoldsau *Schapbach* (Armbruster) is reached, a long straggling village upwards of 6 M. in length, and remarkable for the quaint costume of the peasants and the curious construction of their cottages. (The ground-floor is a stable, the first-floor the dwelling-house, and above it a granary and hay-loft.) About 14 M. from Rippoldsau **Wolfach** (**Salm*, good Zeller wine) is reached; it possesses a Town-house formerly a castle of some importance, and is situated at the confluence of the *Wolfach* and the *Kinzig*.

Those whose time is limited may take the omnibus (1 fl. 48 kr.) at 6½ a.m., arriving at Offenburg before noon, but one day would be well spent in making an excursion to *Hornberg* and *Tryberg* (by carriage, 5—7 fl., in half a day). The pedestrian need not return the whole way to Wolfach, but on emerging from the valley at the Kinzig-bridge may at once proceed W. to Hausach and Hasslach.

The short distance (2 M.) between Wolfach and the Kinzig bridge just mentioned is remarkable for the picture of industry which it presents, as well as for its beauty; the road then enters the valley of the *Gutach*, which at this point falls into the Kinzig, and traverses a succession of rich pastures and orchards to **Gutach** (3 M.; *Krone; Löwe*), and **Hornberg** (3 M.; **Post*), an old place of some importance, and remarkable for the picturesque costume of the peasantry of the neighbourhood. The castle which contributes not a little to the beauty of the landscape, was taken by Marshal Villars in 1703, but soon afterwards recovered by the peasantry.

The most remarkable part of the whole excursion is the walk from Hornberg to Tryberg (7½ M.). The road, in many places hewn in the rock, winds through a series of the most picturesque and well wooded ravines till the *Tryberger Posthaus* is reached, where the valley widens. Here the road to the l. leads farther into the forest to *St. Georgen* and *Donaueschingen;* that to the r. to (¾ M.) the small town of **Tryberg** (**Löwe; Post*) situated 1850 ft. above the level of the sea, the central point of the Black Forest, and principal seat of the watch manufactories. (Furtwängler Brothers and Kellerer own the most considerable of these establishments.)

The grand object of interest for the traveller is the ****Waterfall** which is visible from a considerable distanee. The path to it ascends to the left by the *Löwe;* in 20 min. the highest bridge over the fall is attained; 280 yds. beyond this spot, from an open space on the l. bank, a fine view of the little town and the valley is obtained. The waterfall, the finest in W. Germany, is 542 ft. in height, and is divided into seven distinct parts by huge blocks of granite, over which the water is precipitated. The frame-work, like that of the Giessbach on the Lake of Brienz in Switzerland, is formed by tall dark-green pines. The finest near view of the falls is obtained from a mass of rock which forms the dam of the lowest fall; the general effect is best seen from a grass-grown projecting rock about 50 yds. from the bottom of the fall.

Those who have already visited the Kinzigthal will now proceed from Tryberg in a S. direction over the hill to **Furtwangen** (7 M.) (**Hôtel Fehrenbach*, good and moderate), another watch-manufacturing town with a school for teaching the art, whence a post-omnibus runs in 4 hrs. through **Simonswald** (*Krone*), and the cheerful little town of **Waldkirch** (**Post; Rebstock*), to the railway stat. *Denzlingen.* — Two-horse carriage from Tryberg to Simonswald (uninteresting road) 5 fl.; from the latter place through the valleys of Simonswald and the Elz very pretty. One-horse carriage from Tryberg to Hornberg 3, to Hausach or Wolfach 4½, and to St. Georgen 3½ fl.

We now return to **Hausach** (**Post*). Above the town stands an ancient round tower, the remains of the princely castle of the house of Fürstenberg, destroyed by the French in 1643.

Hasslach (**Kreuz*), 3½ M. distant from Hausach, is the principal town of the district. It formerly belonged to the principality of Fürstenberg, and was destroyed in 1704 by the French on their retreat after the battle of Höchstädt.

Steinach (*Sonne*), 2¼ M. farther, is an animated little town; from the village and post-station of **Bieberach** (*Krone; Sonne*), 3 M. farther, a road leads to *Lahr* (p. 237), 7½ M. distant, passing the ruins of the Castle of *Hohen-Geroldseck* (p. 237).

Near (6 M.) **Gengenbach** (*Adler; Salm; Badischer Hof*) the road crosses the *Kinzig*. The village was up to the peace of Luneville a free town of the empire, and owes its foundation to the handsome old *Benedictine Abbey*.

Beyond Gengenbach the valley of the Kinzig continues to widen. On a vine-clad hill at its mouth (3½ M.) rises the castle of ***Ortenberg**, a handsome modern edifice, founded on the ruins of the ancient castle destroyed by Marshal Crequi, which formerly commanded the entrance to the valley. It is now surrounded by tastefully laid out and well-kept grounds, the flowerbeds &c. being ornamented with stalactites. The prospect is fine, and embraces the entire chain of the Vosges. The castle vineyards, as well as those of the village of *Ortenberg* at the foot of the hill, yield a good wine.

Offenburg (p. 236) is 2¼ M. distant. Extensive tobacco manufactories on the road before entering the town.

c. Höllenthal, Feldberg, Wiesenthal, Wehrathal, Albthal.

Comp. Map R. 62.

Two days. From *Freiburg* to the *Himmelreich* by carriage in 1½ hr.; on foot through the *Höllenthal* to the *Stern Inn* (4½ M.), to the top of the *Feldberg* in 3¼ hrs., descent to *Todtnau* in 3 hrs., where pass the night. From Todtnau to *Lörrach* 8½ hrs. walk, or 4 hrs. drive, or to Bâle in 5 hrs. by carriage. To explore the *Wehrathal* would require a third day.

The broad and fertile valley of the *Dreisam*, bounded by lofty mountains, through which the road lies, is not sufficiently attractive to induce the traveller to traverse it on foot; it is therefore advisable to take a carriage as far as the *Himmelreich* (9 M.). The road passes the *Littenweiler Baths* (p. 243), on the l. bank of the stream, *Ebnet*, *Burg*, and *Kirchzarten* which lies to the r., and from which the upper part of the valley derives its name. Soon after passing it, the road enters a more mountainous district, the fertile tract at the commencement of which is called the *Himmelreich* (Kingdom of Heaven), on account of the contrast it presents to the deep and precipitous ravines of the *Hölle* (Hell) which lies beyond, and at the entrance to which is situated the ruined castle of *Falkenstein*.

The so-called ***Höllenpass** is ¾ M. in length, and resembles the Münsterthal in the Jura in its towering and overhanging rocks. The most beautiful and wildest point of the whole valley is at the **Hirschensprung*, an imposing and precipitous mass of rock, the clefts of which are overgrown with firs and underwood. The narrow road which winds through the pass, scarcely broader than required by the impetuous brook, was constructed by the Austrian government in 1770, when the Archduchess Marie Antoinette, the bride of the Dauphin, afterwards Louis XVI., passed through the ravine on her way to France. The same pass was also the scene of the celebrated retreat of Moreau in October, 1796, when pursued by the Archduke Charles.

At the end of the pass the picturesque *Chapel of St. Oswald* looks down into the valley from a projecting rock. The *Post-inn* is first reached, and 1 M. farther the **Stern* (R. 36—48, B. 24, A. 12 kr.; guide over the Feldberg to the chalet of Todtnau 1 fl. 12 kr., not absolutely necessary).

Here the road, which continues to wind up the hill, is quitted. The traveller crosses the brook to the r., and ascends by a broad and steep forest-track to the (40 min.) hamlet of *Albersbach*, situated in the midst of verdant meadows. In 5 min. more a cross is reached, where the path to the l. must be taken; in

10 min. to the r., in the hollow, to the saw-mill; in 10 min. more through the gate to the r.; in 3 min. the least trodden path to the l., leading to the *Guschpels Hof;* after $^1/_4$ hr. the stony track into the wood must be ascended. The two paths which separate at the pine-stump (12 min.), soon unite again, and lead in 5 min. to flat pasture land with a cross on the l. On entering the wood again the turning to the l. must be avoided; after 8 min. another turning to the l. must be avoided; in 5 min. more, to the r. again, along the grassy path by the wood in the direction of the white roof of the *Baldenweg Chalet.* In $^1/_2$ hr. 3 cottages, called *Auf dem Rinken*, are reached, at the last of which the narrow path ascends to the r. through meadows into the wood; in 25 min. more the above-mentioned chalet ("Viehhütte") is reached, where refreshments may be procured, and accommodation for the night if necessary. From this point to the Feldberg and Seebuck there are no regular paths, but, unless the weather be foggy, the services of a guide may be dispensed with.

The traveller now stands at the foot of the peak of the Feldberg, which may easily be attained in $^1/_2$ hr. Though the path can scarcely be distinguished, the pedestrian cannot well go wrong; he must continue to ascend round the E. and S.E. slopes of the mountain; he will then reach the ridge which connects the summit, or *Höchste*, with the *Seebuck*, which in a S.E. direction forms a continuation of the Feldberg table-land; a few min. more will bring him to the tower (*Friedrich-Louisen-Thurm*), the keys of which are kept in the *Todtnau Chalet* (see below). It occupies the summit of the **Feldberg** (4590 ft.), and is the highest point in the Black Forest, commanding a magnificent prospect. The distant view is similar to that from the Blauen (p. 247).

Another path to the Feldberg leads from the "Stern" to the r. to (15 min.) *Hinterzarten*, (30 min.) *Oberzarten*, (1 hr.) *Zipfelhof;* thence along the course of the *Seebach* to the (15 min.) *Feldsee* (see below); through forest, ascending to the (35 min.) *Lenzkirch Chalet* (refreshments in the Menzenschwand Chalet in the vicinity), whence, following the ridge of the mountain, the traveller reaches the *Höchste.*

Following the ridge which connects the *Höchste* with the **Seebuck** in a S.E. direction, a spot opposite to the Baldenweg chalet is reached in about 25 min., from which a beautiful *view, even more picturesque than that from the tower, is obtained. Far below, in a basin enclosed by precipitous pine-clad mountains, fed by several waterfalls, lies the *Feldsee,* a small black-looking lake, drained by the Seebach, a brook which traverses the romantic *Bärenthal* and precipitates itself,

6 M. below, into the *Titisee*, the W. extremity of which is visible from this point. Other distant valleys are also visible, and the background is formed by the Swabian chain of mountains, to the r. the basaltic summits of the Höhgau, the Hohentwiel, Hohenstoffeln, Hohenkrähen, &c. — The path down to the Feldsee, and through the Bärenthal to the Titisee well repays the traveller; it emerges at the lower (N.) end of the Titisee on the Freiburg and Schaffhausen road, about 5 M. to the E. of the *Stern Inn* (p. 258).

Half an hour's walk W. from the Seebuck, and at the same distance to the S. of the Feldberg lies the *Todtnau Chalet*, a small inn, where the keys of the tower on the Feldberg are kept (guide 30 kr.), and whence another beautiful prospect may be enjoyed, especially of the Wiesenthal; in the background are the snow-clad peaks of the Alps (p. 248).

From this point a broad and tolerably good path leads through the ravine (*Brandenburger Thal*), along the *Wiese* (in 2 hrs.) to **Todtnau** (1995 ft.) (**Ochs*, by the church, R. 30 kr., B. 24 kr.; *Rössle*), a clean and thriving little town, the highest in the valley of the Wiese. The principal arm of the brook rises below the Todtnau chalet, and emerges from its wild and romantic ravine immediately above the town, below which it is joined by the *Bergerbach.* At *Todtnauberg* (Stern), 3 M. to the N., the latter brook is precipitated over a rock, 200 ft. in height. The old arms of the town — a miner with hammer and pickaxe — prove that mining was the principal occupation of the inhabitants in very early times.

The ***Wiesenthal** from Todtnau to Lörrach, below which it opens into the plain of the Rhine, is about 27 M. in length. The greater part of it is narrow and well-wooded, the most picturesque part being that between Schönau and Zell. One-horse carriage to Schönau (in 1 hr.) 1½ fl., to Zell (in 2 hrs.) 3 fl., to Schopfheim (in 2¾ hrs.) 4½ fl., to Lörrach (in 4 hrs.) 7 fl. Diligence to Schopfheim in the morning, thence by railway to Bâle (see p. 264).

At **Geschwendt**, 1½ M. from Todtnau, a path to the l. diverges to *Präg, Todtmoos* and the ***Wehrathal.*

From the little town of **Schönau** (**Sonne*), 4½ M. from Geschwendt, with its extensive cotton-factory, the road leads through a romantic and well-wooded dale to **Zell** (*Löwe*), 7½ M. farther, another busy little town of weavers and cotton-spinners.

Where the ravine widens, half-way to Schopfheim, is situated the extensive grand-ducal iron-foundry of **Hausen,** the birth-place of the poet Hebel; the village itself, concealed by fruit-trees, lies on the r. bank of the Wiese. The inhabitants of the upper part of the valley are Rom. Cath., those below Hausen Protestant.

Schopfheim (**Pflug*), 4½ M. from Zell, is a clean little town of some importance, and carries on a considerable traffic with Bâle; railway by *Lörrach* to Bâle in 1 hr.; fares 66, 48, 33 kr. [The *Wehrathal* (p. 262) can be best visited from Schopfheim. One-horse carriage to Wehr, along the Wehrastrasse to Todtmoos-Au, back to Wehr, and thence to the railway stat. Brennet on the Rhine above Bâle, a drive of 5 hrs., for 6 fl.]

The Wiesenthal* widens considerably below Schopfheim; the stream is usefully employed in the irrigation of the land, as well as for the supply of numerous cotton and other mills situated on its banks.

Steinen (*Ochs*), the next village, is 3 M. from Schopfheim. Above the village of *Rötteln-Weiler* (**Inn*), about 4½ M. farther, rise the extensive ruins of *Schloss Rötteln*, one of the largest in the Duchy, commanding a fine view. It was formerly the residence of the Margraves of Hochberg, and afterwards of the Margraves of Baden; was taken by Bernhard of Weimar in 1638, and dismantled and blown up by the French in 1678.

Lörrach (**Hirsch*, R. 36, B. 24, D. 48 kr.), the most important place in the valley (7½ M. from Schopfheim and 6 M. from Bâle), is a modern manufacturing town, containing extensive shawl, cotton, cloth, and other factories. (One-horse carriage to Rötteln-Weiler 2½, to Kandern 4, to Zell 5, to the Wehrathal and stat. Brennet 7 fl.

The ***Tüllinger Höhe,** 2 M. to the S. of Lörrach, is a point well worth visiting, as it commands a magnificent view of the highlands of Baden, Alsace, Bâle, and the Swiss mountains. The foreground is formed by the broad and fertile plain, at the spectator's feet lie the villages of *Riehen* and *Weil* in the midst of orchards and vineyards. From the terrace behind the church the view is still more extended, and the garden of the *inn commands the finest prospect in a W. direction. It was after a contest near this spot, which terminated unfortunately for Germany, that the French general Villars was elevated to the dignity of marshal.

Below Lörrach the road enters the dominions of Bâle. The church of **St. Chrischona,** formerly a favorite resort of pilgrims, now a Prot. missionary establishment, situated on a wooded eminence above *Riehen*, commands a fine prospect similar to that from the Tüllinger Höhe. The road approaches Bâle through a succession of tasteful villas.

Travellers coming from the Feldberg, who are already acquainted with the Wiesenthal, may prefer to continue their excursion (on foot) as follows: From Todtnau to Geschwendt ($1\frac{1}{2}$ M.) in the Wiesenthal, then to the l. to **Präg** (3 M.) (*Hirsch*); thence over a steep bill to **Todtmoos** (2527 ft.) (**Adler*) in about 2 hrs.; from Todtmoos in the Wehrathal to (3 M.) *Todtmoos-Au* (*Inn*), and from here to (9 M.) **Wehr** (**Krone*, R. 36, B. 24 kr.), a village with Grand-ducal iron-foundry.

The ****Wehrastrasse**, a road made exclusively for the transport of timber, winds through the grandest rocky ravine, which commences $\frac{3}{4}$ M. beyond Todtmoos-Au, and terminates $1\frac{1}{4}$ M. before Wehr is reached, a length of about 7 M. It is enclosed on both sides by lofty wooded mountains, and is in many places so narrow that there is barely space for the road by the side of the impetuous *Wehra.* The variety of the foliage — the birch-trees, for example, contrasting with the sombre firs which clothe the precipitous walls — render this mountain-glen picturesque in the highest degree. In grandeur and wildness the rocks surpass even those of the *Hölle* (p. 258), and extend for a much greater distance, the latter being only $\frac{3}{4}$ M. in length. At the S. extremity of the valley the tower of *Bärenfels* is seen perched on tbe ridge of the mountain.

At the N.W. houses of Wehr a tract of meadow-land commences, in whicb ($1\frac{1}{2}$ M. from Wehr, and $\frac{1}{2}$ M. before reaching the village of **Hasel**) the **Erdmännleinhöhle,* a stalactite cavern, is situated. The schoolmaster, who lives next door to the *Pflug* inn at Hasel, keeps the key, and accompanies visitors to the cavern, which must be illuminated (fee 30 kr.). Like most other caverns, it contains its chapel, organ, dungeon, &c., formed by the stalactites. It is inferior in grandeur to tbose of the Harz mountains, but well deserves a visit. Travellers wishing to proceed from this point to Schopfheim need not return to Wehr, as a good road leads direct from Hasel to Schopfheim ($4\frac{1}{2}$ M.).

Beyond *Oeflingen*, 3 M. to the S. of Wehr, the road emerges from the valley of the Wehra at *Brennet*, a station on the Bâle and Waldshut Railway.

Another beautiful walk may be taken from the Feldberg by St. Blasien down the Albthal to the Bâle and Waldshut Railway. From the *Seebuck* (p. 259) the path leads to the *Lenzkirch Chalet* ($\frac{3}{4}$ M.), then at the back of tbe *Menzenschwand Chalet* (8 min.) to the r. to **Menzenschwand** ($3\frac{1}{2}$ M.), the birthplace of the eminent painters *Winterhalter*, at whose expense a handsome new inn has been erected, in which their niece officiates as hostess.

From this point a walk of 2 hrs. down the Albthal brings the pedestrian to **St. Blasien**, once celebrated for its wealthy and learned Benedictine abbey. The church, whose handsome dome is a conspicuous object in the distance, was built in 1786, after the model of the Pantheon at Rome. The buildings belonging to the Abbey were secularized in 1805, and have since served for industrial purposes, a portion having been converted into an inn.

Two miles farther is *Ober-Kutterau*, and 3 1/2 M. beyond it, *Immeneich* (small inn), where the new ***Albstrasse** commences. It leads through wild, rocky scenery, and penetrates the perpendicular mountain walls in 6 different places by means of tunnels; far below rushes the mountain stream. About 9 M. from Immeneich the road emerges at Albbruck, a station on the Bâle and Waldshut Railway (see below).

Another interesting excursion is from the *Seebuck*, passing the *Menzenschwand Chalet* and *Altglashütte*, to the picturesquely situated village of *Aha*, and thence in 1 1/2 hr. to the *Schluchsee*, a small lake abounding in fish, and the village (3200 ft.) of the same name, a delightful spot, noted for the salubrity of its atmosphere. Thence by the carriage-road to St. Blasien 7 1/2 M.

64. From Waldshut to Bâle.

By the Baden Railway in 1 1/2—2 1/2 hrs. Fares: 2 fl. 18, 1 fl. 33 kr., 1 fl. Finest views to the *left*.

Waldshut (*Rebstock*), on the lofty r. bank of the Rhine, is a station on the Baden railway to Schaffhausen and Constance. Below *Koblenz*, in the canton of Aargau, 1 1/2 M. to the S.E. of Waldshut, the *Aare* falls into the Rhine, and near it the Swiss-junction line crosses the Rhine.

The line only approaches the Rhine at intervals, as for example at *Dogern* and *Albbruck*, where the romantic Albstrasse (see above) emerges. After passing several smaller stations and traversing two lofty viaducts and one tunnel, the train arrives at the station of *Klein-Laufenburg*.

Laufenburg (*Post*), opposite to the station, on the l. bank of the Rhine, is in the canton of Aargau, picturesquely situated on a rock, below which is the Cataract of the Rhine. The salmon-fishery at this point is very productive. From the station at Klein-Laufenburg a view may be obtained of the rocks which here enclose the Rhine.

The line now runs along the bank of the Rhine which here rushes impetuously over its rocky bed, the l. (Swiss) bank being precipitous and wooded. **Säckingen** (*Bad* or *Löwe*) is a place of some importance, and contains an ancient church which in former times belonged to a powerful and extensive monastery.

At *Brennet* the Wehrstrasse emerges from its mountain ravine. The line next traverses the vineyards and gardens of *Beuggen*, form erly a lodge of the Teutonic order, now an asylum for children and training-school for teachers.

Rheinfelden (*Schiff; Krone*), on the l. bank of the Rhine in the canton of Aargau, was formerly strongly fortified and was one of the bulwarks of the holy Roman empire. After standing innumerable sieges it was at last dismantled by the French in 1744. Since 1801 it has belonged to Switzerland. Below the town another rapid of the Rhine forms a sort of whirlpool, termed the "*Höllenhaken.*"

Here the line leaves the Rhine and traverses the fruitful plain which lies between the spurs of the Black Forest and the river, passing the villages of *Warmbach* and *Grenzach* surrounded by vineyards, and terminating at *Klein-Basel.*

65. Bâle.

Hotels. *Three Kings (Pl. a) on the Rhine, R. 2, L. 1/2, B. 1 1/2, D. at 5 o'clock 4, A. 1 fr.; Schweizerhof at the Central Station, new; Stork (Pl. b), *Wild man (Pl. c) in both R. 1 1/2—2, B. 1, Table d'hôte at 1 o'cl. inc. W. 3, A. 3/4 fr.; Crown (Pl. d), *Kopf (Pl. e) both on the Rhine. — In *Klein-Basel* on the r. bank of the Rhine, *Bear (Pl. g), *Kreuz (Pl. h), starting point of the omnibus to the Wiesenthal (p. 260). Baseler Hof opp. to the Baden station, also a restaurant.

Cafés. *Café des Trois Rois, two houses above the hotel of the same name. *Café national near the bridge, beer good; Café Schildhof near the Elisabethenkirche, both restaurants. Sommer-Casino, not far from the Monument of St. Jacob; concert on Wed. from 6 to 9 p.m. Thomma's beergarden, near the Central Station.

Conveyances. Omnibus from the station to the town (50 lb. luggage free) 1/2 fr., from the Baden to the Swiss station 1 fr. Cabs in the market-place in front of the "Three Kings," and near the church of St. Clara in Klein-Basel &c.; charges for a 1/4 hr. 1—2 persons 80 cent., 3—4 pers. 1 fr. 20 c., by the hour 2—3 fr., to or from the station 1—4 pers. 1 1/2 fr., esch box 20 cent. extra. Two-horse carriages for 1/2 day 15 fr., for a whole day 25 fr.

Railway stations. Baden station in Klein-Basel 3/4 M. (straight) from the Rhine bridge (Swiss money not taken); duty payable on carved wood-work brought from Switzerland 10 kr. per lb. — The stations of the French and the Swiss lines are united at the Central Station at the Steinen-Thor. The Baden line is preferable to the French, the country is more beautiful, the carriages better and the fares more moderate. Paris time is 25 min. behind Bâle time.

Post and Telegraph Office (Pl. 15) in the Freien-Strssse.

Baths in the Rhine near the Münster, entrance from the Pfalz (p. 266). Warm baths at Sigmund's.

Newspapers in the Reading club by the Münster. Strangers must be introduced by a member, perhaps the landlord of their hotel.

English Church Service in the Three Kings Hotel.

Bâle or *Basel* (comp. *Baedeker's Switzerland*), the principal town of the canton Basel-Stadt (pop. 41,000; 9697 Rom. Cath.), is first mentioned in the year 374 under the name of *Basilēa,* and appears to have been founded by the Roman army when it fell back on the Rhine near the old *Colonia Augusta Rauracorum,* founded B.C. 27 by L. Munatius Plancus (now called *Basel Augst,* 5 M. from Bâle on the l. bank of the Rhine).

Nord
A
B
C
D
1
2
3
4
5
6
7
Kl: Basel
21 St. Clara (Kath. Kirche) C.3.
22 Klingenthal C.4.
23 St. Theodor E.2
24 Waisenhaus E.3.
Hôtels
g. Bär D.4.
h. Kreuz D.4.
i. Basler Hof C.1.
von Freiburg
nach Waldshut
Provisor.
Badischer Bahnhof
Bahnhof
Riehen Strasse
Hammer Strasse
Clara Matte
Riehen Thor
Klybeck Strasse
St. Bläsien Thor
Rebgasse
Rheingasse
N.
O.
W.
S.
R
H
E
I
Spital
Peters Platz
St. Peters Graben
St. Leonhard
Klingelberg
Hôtels
a Drei Könige C.5
b. Storch D.5
c. Wilde Mann E.5
d Krone D.5
e Kopf D.5
f Schwan C.5
Spahlen Thor
Mostac
300
1000

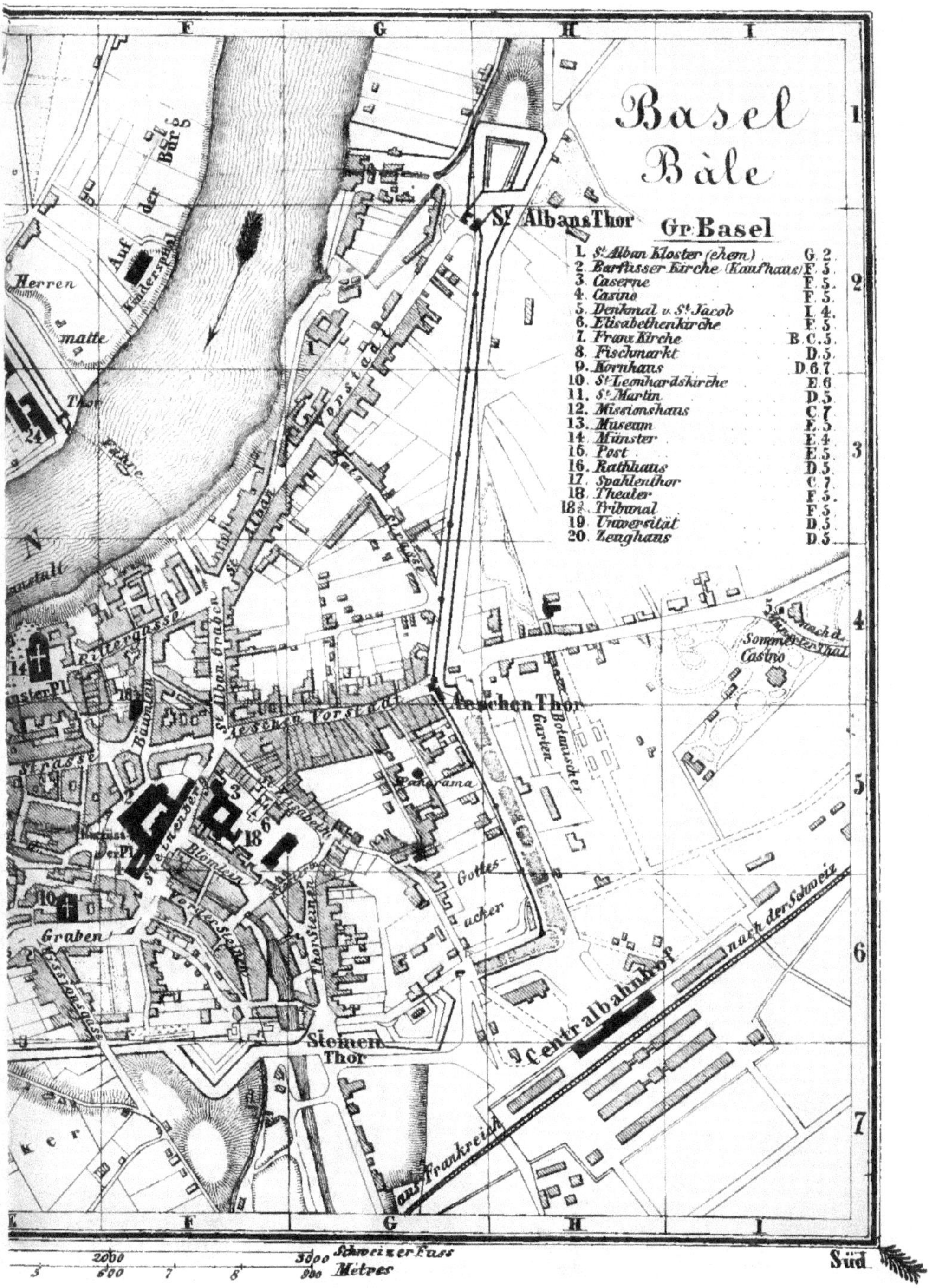
Basel
Bàle
Gr. Basel
1. St Alban Kloster (ehem) G. 2.
2. Barfüsser Kirche (Kaufhaus) F. 5.
3. Caserne F. 5.
4. Casino F. 5.
5. Denkmal v. St Jacob I. 4.
6. Elisabethenkirche F. 5.
7. Franz Kirche B. C. 5.
8. Fischmarkt D. 5.
9. Kornhaus D. 6. 7.
10. St Leonhardskirche E. 6.
11. St Martin D. 5.
12. Missionshaus C. 7.
13. Museum E. 5.
14. Münster E. 4.
15. Post E. 5.
16. Rathhaus D. 5.
17. Spahlenthor C. 7.
18. Theater F. 5.
18½. Tribunal F. 5.
19. Universität D. 5.
20. Zeughaus D. 5.
St Albans Thor
Aeschen Thor
Steinen Thor
Centralbahnhof
nach der Schweiz
aus Frankreich
Sommer Casino
Botanischer Garten
Gottes acker
Panorama
Rittergasse
St Alban Graben
Aeschen Vorstadt
Elisabethen
Steinenberg
Graben
Herren matte
Auf der Burg
Kinderspital
Thor
Fähre
Schweizer Fuss
Metres
Süd

The wealth of Bâle has become proverbial; for this the town is greatly indebted to its favourable position at the junction of the frontiers of Germany, France and Switzerland.

The town lies on the l. bank of the Rhine and is connected with *Klein-Basel* on the r. bank by a wooden bridge, 280 yds. in length.

The ***Münster** (Pl. 14), an imposing edifice, the two lofty towers of which are visible from a considerable distance, was formerly the Cathedral of the see of Bâle (the bishop's residence is now at Soleure). It was built by the Emperor Henry II. in 1010—1019, and was restored in 1185, after having been partially destroyed by fire. In 1356 the old building was all but levelled by an earthquake, but is now rebuilt in the Gothic style. Of the original structure the N. portal, or *St. Gallus* gate-way, still exists, and is adorned with statues of the evangelists, John the Baptist and other saints; over the church-door is a relief presenting the wise and foolish virgins; at the sides, in 6 niches, are the works of charity, and at the top Christ on the Judgment seat and the angels at the last day. The W. *front* under the towers, with the principal gateway and two side-entrances belong to the 14th cent.; on the front are represented the Virgin and Child, and under them the Emp. Henry, the founder and benefactor of the Church, with the Empress Helena; on the two side entrances are two knights, on the l. St. George and the Dragon, and on the r. St. Martin. The towers, which are 205 ft. in height, were not completed till 1500. In the year 1431 the convocation of the great *Council* in the Münster first began; it consisted of upwards of 500 clergymen, whose ostensible task was a "reformation of the Church in head and members," but after having disputed for years without any result, and having been excommunicated by Pope Eugene IV., the Convocation was at last dissolved in 1448. The Church is open to the public on Tues. and Frid. from 2 to 4 o'clock. The sacristan lives opposite to the principal entrance (fee ½ fr.); in summer he is generally to be found in the Church at the above hours.

The interior of the Münster was bereft of its most beautiful ornaments in the great iconoclasm of 1529, but was re-decorated in 1852—1856 with great skill, and is now one of the finest Protestant churches in existence. The beautiful rood-loft of 1381 now serves to support the organ, a very fine instrument, performances on which may be heard once or twice a week in summer from 6 to 7 p.m. (adm. 1 fr.). The pulpit is of 1424. The aisles and choir contain fine old monuments and tombstones built into the walls; in the N. nave the old episcopal chair; also reliefs of the 11th cent. (scenes from the lives of the martyrs); the font of 1465, and, on the pillar opposite to it, the tombstone of the learned Erasmus of Rotterdam (d. 1536) with a long Latin inscription. In the passage round the choir are the monuments of the empress Anna (d. 1281), consort of Rudolph of Habsburg and mother of Albrecht I., and of her youngest son Charles. The new stained-glass windows, representing Moses and David, Peter and Paul, and the four

Evangelists, are by artists of Zürich and St. Gall, and the newest, representing Christ as Judge of the world, is from the stained-glass Institution of Munich. The crypt, which belongs to the original edifice, contains relics of frescoes of the 13th cent., and 6 sarcophagi of members of the family of the Margraves of Baden-Durlach (1688—1709). A stair leads from the choir to the Council Hall, in which one of the five principal committees used to assemble. It is exactly in the state in which it was left 400 years ago. All that was considered worth preserving at the restoration of the church is kept here, such as antiquities of the middle ages, fragments of the nine frescoes of the celebrated Bâle *Death-dance*, painted in 1409 in remembrance of the plague, and erroneously attributed to Holbein. Here too may be seen the *Lällenkönig*, a large head formerly placed on the clock-tower of the Rhine bridge (taken down in 1839), which rolled its eyes and protruded its long tongue ("Lälli") at each stroke of the pendulum, erected in derision of the inhabitants of Klein-Basel in consequence of a dispute with them.

On the S. side of the Choir are extensive ***Cloisters**, built in the years 1362, 1400 and 1487, connecting the church with the Episcopal palace, and used as family burial-places. Among the monuments which they contain may be mentioned those of the reformers Œcolampadius (d. 1531) and Grynæus (d. 1541), and that of a Frau Forcart-Merian on one of the E. pillars, which possesses considerable artistic merit. These cloisters extend to the terrace behind the Münster, which overlooks the Rhine, rising 75 ft. immediately above it, and derives its name from an imperial **Pfalz**, or palace, to which it is said formerly to have belonged. It is planted with chestnuts and affords a pleasing prospect of the green river and the dark heights of the Black Forest. In its immediate vicinity are situated the swimming and bathing establishments, and near the most W. of the latter is the Reading Club (p. 264).

In the street, leading from the Münsterplatz in a N.W. direction to the bridge, is the ***Museum** (Pl. 13), open to the public on Sund. from 10 to 12, and Wed. from 2 to 4; on other days adm. 1 fr. It contains a picture-gallery and collections of natural and scientific curiosities belonging to the town.

The picture-gallery is principally remarkable for the paintings and drawings [1] which it contains of the younger Holbein (b. at Augsburg 1498, d. at London 1554). Ante-room. 1—11. Copies from *Hans Holbein*. — Collection of drawings. 1—86. by *Holbein the younger;* 132, 133, 134, by *Dürer*. 157. Drawings of the "Last Judgment" in the Ludwigskirche at Munich, by *Cornelius*. Room A. contains only pictures by Holbein: 6. 7. Schoolmaster's signboard of 1516; *15. Erasmus of Rotterdam; *25. The Passion in 8 sections, for which in 1641 the Elector Maximilian of Bavaria offered the sum of 30,000 fl. — Room B. contains old-German pictures: 71. The 11,000 Virgins, by *Grünewald;* 61. Miniature of Luther, by *Cranach*. — Room C. or Bâle-room: 113. Battle of St. Jacob, by *Hieron. Hess;* 127. Entrance into Bâle of the confederate ambassadors in 1501 to take the oaths of allegiance to the Confederation, by *Landerer;* 136. Schreckhorn and Wetterhorn, by *Calame*. — Room D.: 173. Lute-player, by *Teniers;* Sleep the Type of Death, by *Carracci;* Macbeth and the Witches, by *Koch;* Abraham visited by the Angels, by *Neher*. — Room E. Birmann's Collection: 267. The Nativity,

---

[1] Photographs from the originals, admirably executed and published by the directors of the Museum, are to be had of Mr. *Georg*, bookseller and dealer in works of art, near the Post-office.

by *An. Carracci;* *270. Madonna and Child, ascribed to *Gherardecia di Siena;* *281. Cardinal Fleury, by *Phil. de Champaigne;* 282. The Adoration, by *Mabuse;* *289. Portrait, ascribed to *Rembrandt;* 201. The Smoker, by *Teniers;* 311—324. Pictures by *Peter Birmann;* 325—330. Pictures by *Sam. Birmann* (d. 1847). — The Cabinet of Antiquities contains Roman and Greek antiquities, statuettes &c. principally found at Augst (p. 264) and Windisch; old ecclesiastical vessels, idols, Swiss coins, Etruscan vases, Mosaics, &c. — The Mexican Cabinet contains a number of interesting *Mexican curiosities, and among other objects of interest two mummies.

The **University Library** in the same building (adm. from 1 to 3) contains 70—80,000 volumes and 4000 MSS.; among the latter are transactions of the church council, "The praise of Folly" of Erasmus, with mariginal drawings by Holbein, writings of Luther, Melancthon, &c. The *University*, founded in 1459 by Pius II., is celebrated as the school of the great mathematicians *Bernouilli*, *Merian* and *Euler*. The hall contains upwards of 100 portraits of the learned men of Bâle, of the cosmographer *Sebastian Münster* (d. 1552), the reformers *Œcolampadius* and *Grynæus*, &c.

The **Town-Hall** (Pl. 16) in the Market-place was erected in 1508 in the so-called Burgundian style, and renewed in 1826. The façade is adorned with the town-arms (a black episcopal staff leaning on a fisherman's grappling-iron). The two *inscriptions* mark the height which the Rhine attained during inundations. In the court is erected a statue of *Munatius Plancus*, founder of Augst (p. 264), and according to some authorities of Bâle also.

The handsome **Spahlen-Thor** (*St. Paul*, Pl. 17), erected about the year 1400, deserves inspection; the other gates, bastions and ramparts are converted into public walks.

Among other **Architectural Curiosities** of the middle ages may be mentioned the *Fischmarkt-Fountain* (Pl. 8), erected in the 14th cent., the *Spahlen-Fountain*, with a bagpiper from a design by Albert Dürer, the Roman archway in the old *St. Alban's Monastery* (Pl. 1). The *Barfüsser-Church* (Pl. 2), dating from the beginning of the 13th cent., with its very lofty choir, now serves as a store-house.

The **Monument of St. Jacob** (Pl. 5), a Gothic obelisk, 10 min. walk S.E. from the Æschen gate on the high-road to the Münster-Thal, was erected in 1824 over the burial place of Swiss soldiers who fell in 1444 fighting for the liberties of their country. Large bodies of irregular troops had assembled in France under the Count Armagnac, with 30,000 of which the Dauphin marched against the Confederates at Bâle. The latter were stationed at the fortress of Farnsburg, about 15 M. S.E. from the town, and on the approach of the French 1300 men immediately attempted to force their passage to Bâle. After a desperate conflict they were all cut to pieces near the village of St. Jacob where the last and bloodiest struggle took place. The red wine (not of a very superior quality), yielded by the vineyards which now occupy the scene of the battle, is known by the name of "Swiss Blood."

The Mission-house (Pl. 12) educates missionaries for the promulgation of Christianity among the heathen. An excellent *Society for the promotion of the public welfare* has existed in Bâle, for 82 years, and has a very extensive sphere of operations. Under its auspices are clothing-clubs, Sunday-schools and classes for instruction in music, singing, swimming &c., popular libraries, saving-banks, loan and sick-funds &c. &c. There are also similar institutions in the neighbourhood, supported by contributions from Bâle, such as the Deaf and Dumb Asylum, Establishment for the Education of Protestant Sisters of Charity and Reformatory at *Riehen*, &c.

INDEX.

The pages printed in *Italics* refer to facts of minor importance.

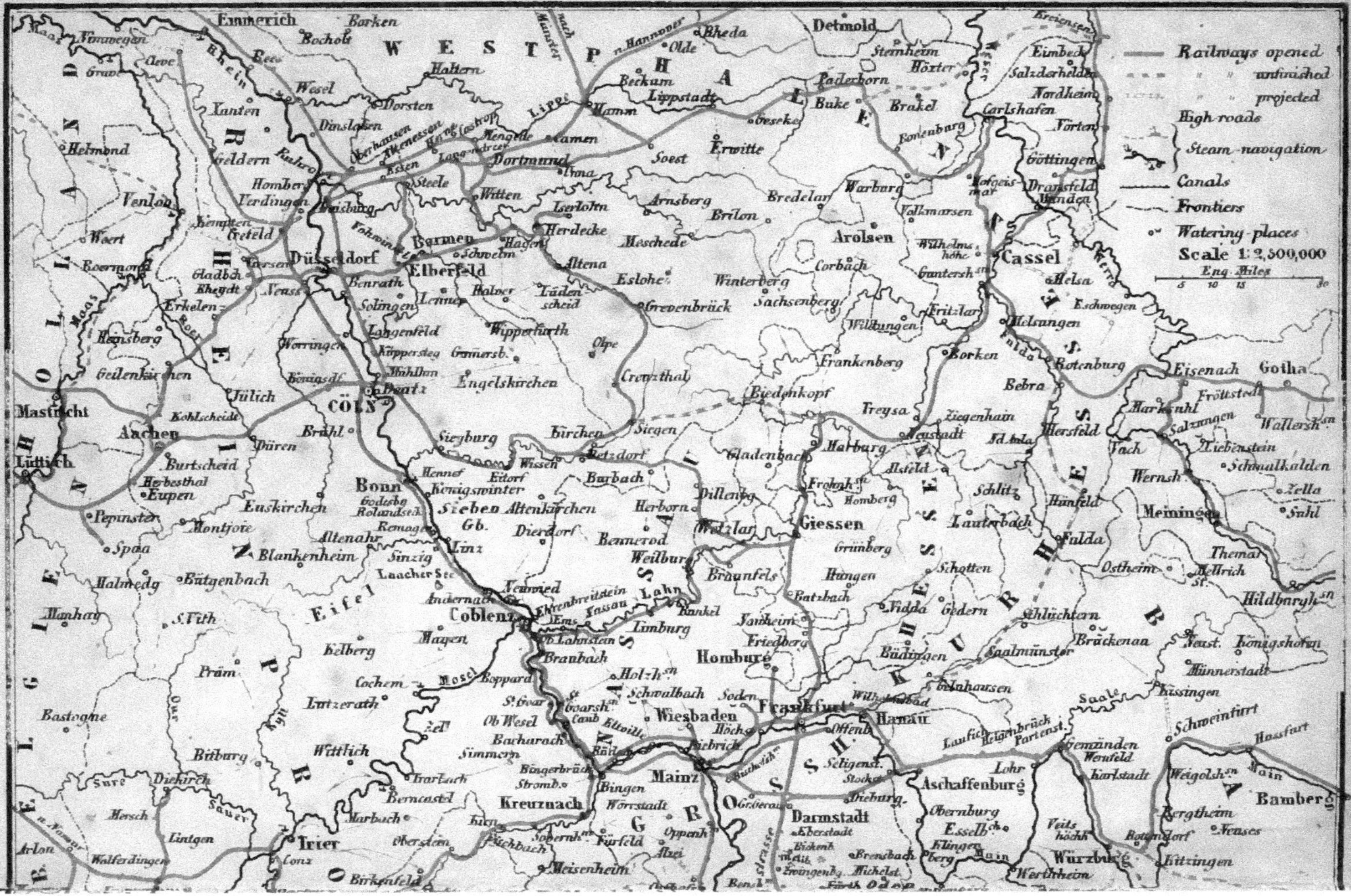
Railways opened
" " unfinished
" " projected
High roads
Steam navigation
Canals
Frontiers
Watering places
Scale 1:2,500,000
Eng. Miles
5 10 15 30
WESTPHALEN
RHEIN PROV.
HOLLAND
BELGIEN
NASSAU
KURHESSEN
GROSSH. HESSEN
BAYERN
Eifel
Emmerich
Detmold
Cassel
Göttingen
Düsseldorf
Elberfeld
Barmen
Cöln
Bonn
Coblenz
Aachen
Mastricht
Lüttich
Giessen
Frankfurt
Wiesbaden
Mainz
Darmstadt
Hanau
Aschaffenburg
Kreuznach
Trier
Fulda
Eisenach
Gotha
Bamberg
Würzburg
Arolsen
Homburg

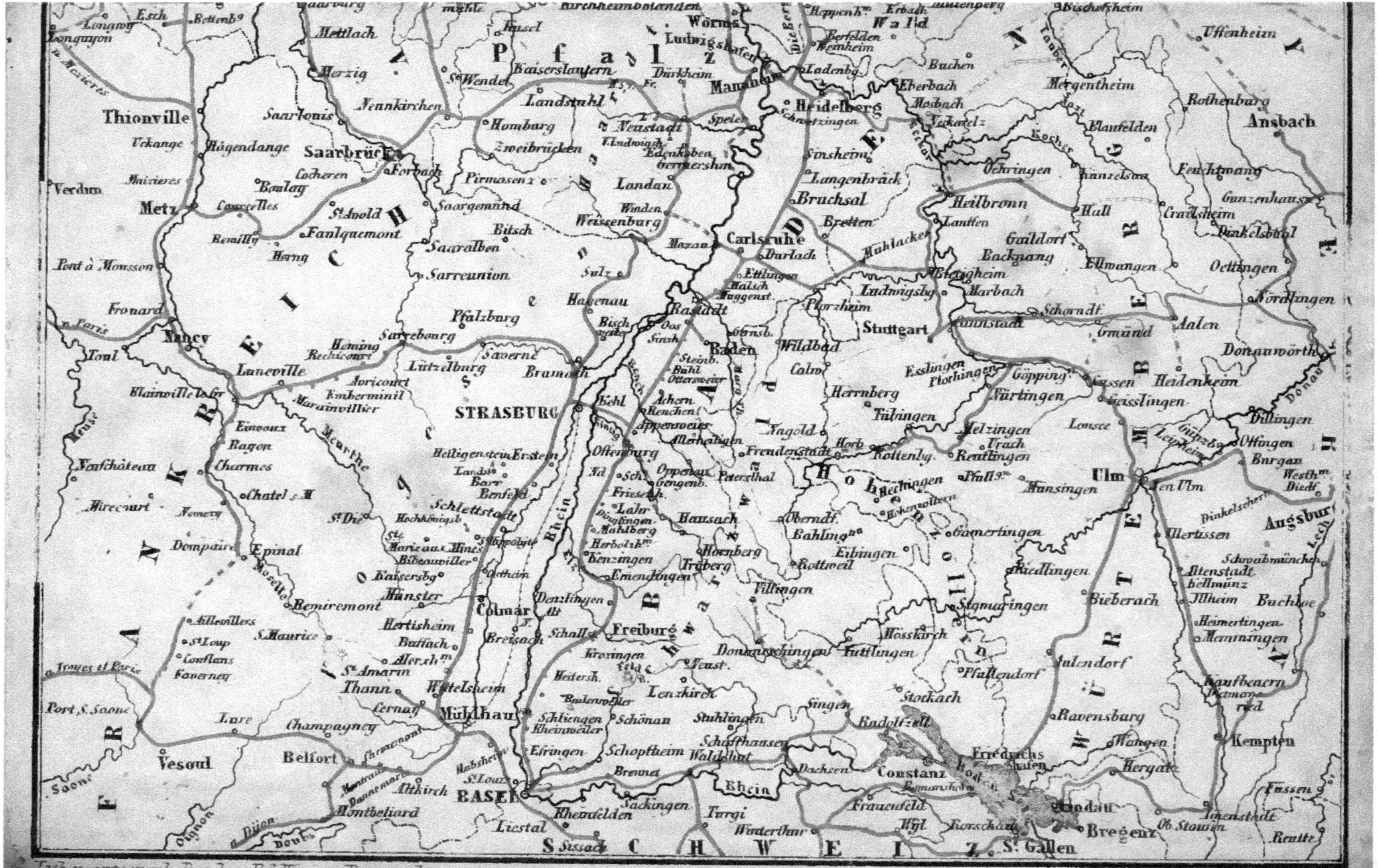

Lith. u. autograph. Druck v. Ed. Wagner Darmstadt.

gez. v. Ed. Wagner.

CPSIA information can be obtained
at www.ICGtesting.com
Printed in the USA
LVHW111702260322
714493LV00002B/245

9 783752 583939